The Matarese Circle

Robert Ludlum is the author of twenty-four novels and has been published in forty countries and thirty-two languages. The recognized master of the international thriller, his books include *The Chancellor Manuscript*, *The Apocalypse Watch* and *The Matarese Countdown.*

ROBERT LUDLUM

THE MATARESE CIRCLE

HarperCollins*Publishers*

HarperCollins*Publishers*
77–85 Fulham Palace Road,
Hammersmith, London W6 8JB

www.**fire**and**water**.com

This paperback edition 1995
15 17 18 16

Previously published in paperback by Grafton 1980
Reprinted nineteen times

First published in Great Britain by
Hart-Davis, MacGibbon Ltd 1979

Copyright © Robert Ludlum 1979

Robert Ludlum asserts the moral right to
be identified as the author of this work

This novel is entirely a work of fiction. The names,
characters and incidents portrayed in it are the work of the
author's imagination. Any resemblance to actual persons,
living or dead, events or localities is entirely coincidental.

ISBN 0 586 05029 9

Set in Times

Printed and bound in Great Britain by
Omnia Books Limited, Glasgow

For Jonathan,
with much love and deep respect

Book I

1

WE THREE KINGS OF ORIENT ARE,
BEARING GIFTS WE TRAVERSE AFAR . . .

The band of carollers huddled at the corner, stamping their feet and swinging their arms, their young voices penetrating the cold night air between the harsh sounds of automobile horns and police whistles and the metallic strains of Christmas music blaring from speakers above garishly lighted store fronts. The snowfall was dense, snarling traffic, causing the hordes of last-minute shoppers to shield their eyes and somehow manage to side-step suddenly lurching automobiles as well as mounds of slush and each other. Tyres spun on the wet streets; buses inched in maddening starts and stops, and the bells of uniformed Santas kept up their incessant if futile clanging.

FIELD AND FOUNTAIN,
MOOR AND MOW-AN-TEN . . .

A dark Cadillac sedan turned the corner and crept past the carollers. The lead singer, dressed in a costume that was somebody's idea of Dickens' Bob Cratchit, approached the right rear window, his gloved hand outstretched, his face contorted in song next to the glass.

FOLLOWING YA-HON-DER STAR . . .

The angry driver blew his horn and waved the begging caroller away, but the middle-aged passenger in the back seat reached into his overcoat pocket and pulled out several bills. He pressed a button; the rear window glided down and the grey-haired man thrust the money into the outstretched hand.

'God bless you, sir!' shouted the caroller. 'The Boys Club of East Fiftieth Street thanks you. Merry Christmas, sir!'

The words would have been more effective had there not been a stench of whisky emanating from the mouth that yelled them.

'Merry Christmas,' said the passenger, pressing the window button to shut off further communication.

There was a momentary break in the traffic. The Cadillac shot forward only to be forced to an abrupt, sliding stop thirty feet down the street. The driver gripped the steering wheel; it was a gesture that took the place of cursing out loud.

'Take it easy, Major,' said the grey-haired passenger, his tone of voice at once sympathetic and commanding. 'Getting upset won't solve anything; it won't get us where we're going any faster.'

'You're right, General,' answered the driver with a respect he did not feel. Normally, the respect was there, but not tonight, not on this particular trip. The general's self-indulgence aside, he had one hell of a nerve requesting his aide to be available for duty on Christmas Eve. For driving a rented, *civilian* car to New York so the general could play games. The major could think of a dozen acceptable reasons for being on duty tonight, but this was not one of them.

A whore house. Stripped of its verbal frills, that's what it was. The Chairman of the Joint Chiefs of Staff was going to a *whore house* on Christmas Eve! And because games were played, the general's most confidential aide had to be there to pick up the mess when the games were over. Pick it up, put it together, nurse it through the next morning at some obscure motel, and make goddamn sure no one found out what the games were or who the mess was. And by noon tomorrow the Chairman would resume his ramrod bearing, issue his orders, and the evening and the mess would be forgotten.

The major had made these trips many times during the past three years – since the day after the general had assumed his awesome position – but the trips always followed periods of intense activity at the Pentagon, or moments of national crisis, when the general had shown his professional mettle. But never on such a night as this. Never on Christmas Eve, for Christ's sake! If the general were anyone else but Anthony Blackburn, the major might have objected on the grounds that even a subordinate officer's family had certain holiday priorities.

But the major would never offer the slightest objection about anything where the general was concerned. 'Mad Anthony' Blackburn had carried a broken young lieutenant out of a North Vietnamese prison camp, away from torture and starvation, and brought him through the jungles back to UN lines. That was years ago; the lieutenant was a major now, the senior aide to the Chairman of the Joint Chiefs of Staff.

Military men often spoke bromidically of certain officers they'd follow to hell and back. Well, the major had been to hell and back with Mad Anthony Blackburn and he'd return to hell in a shot with a snap of the general's fingers.

They reached Park Avenue and turned north. The traffic was less snarled than the crosstown route, as befitted the better section of the city. Fifteen more blocks to go; the brownstone was on Seventy-first Street between Park and Lexington.

The senior aide to the Chairman of the Joint Chiefs of Staff would park the Cadillac in a prearranged space in front of the building and watch the general get out of the car and walk up the steps to the bolted entrance door.

11

He would not say anything, but a feeling of sadness would sweep over the major as he waited.

Until a slender woman – dressed in a dark silk gown with a diamond choker at her throat – re-opened the door in three and a half or four hours and flicked the front lights. It would be the major's signal to come up and collect his passenger.

'Hello, Tony.' The woman swept across the dimly lit hallway and kissed the general's cheek. 'How are you, darling?' she said, fingering her diamond choker as she leaned towards him.

'Tense,' replied Blackburn, slipping his arms out of his civilian overcoat, held by a uniformed maid. He looked at the girl; she was new and lovely.

The woman saw his glance. 'She's not ready for you, darling,' she commented, taking his arm. 'Perhaps in a month or two. Come along now, we'll see what we can do about that tension. We've got everything you need. The best hashish from Ankara, absinthe from the finest still in Marseilles, and precisely what the doctor ordered from our own special catalogue. Incidentally, how's your wife?'

'Tense,' said the general quietly. 'She sends you her best.'

'Do give her my love, darling.'

They walked through an archway into a large room with soft, multi-coloured lights that came from unseen sources; circles of blue and magenta and amber revolving slowly across the ceiling and the walls. The woman spoke again.

'There's a girl I want to have join you and your regular. Her background is simply tailor-made, darling. I couldn't believe it when I interviewed her; it's incredible. I just got her from Athens. You'll adore her.'

Anthony Blackburn lay naked on the king-sized bed, tiny spotlights shooting down from the mirrored ceiling of blue glass. Aromatic layers of hashish smoke were suspended in the still air of the dark room; three glasses of clear absinthe stood on the bedside table. The general's body was covered with streaks and circles of waterpaint, fingermarks everywhere, phallic arrows pointing to his groin, his testicles and erect penis coated in red, his breasts black, matching the matted hair of his chest, the nipples blue and joined by a straight fingerline of flesh-white. He moaned and whipped his head back and forth in sexual oblivion as his companions did their work.

The two naked women alternately massaged and spread the thick globules of paint on the writhing body. As one revolved her breasts about his moaning, moving face the other cupped his genitalia, groaning sensually with each stroke, uttering false, muted screams of climax as the general approached orgasm – halted by the professional who knew her business.

The auburn-haired girl by his face kept whispering breathless, incomprehensible phrases in Greek. She removed herself briefly to reach for a glass on the table; she held Blackburn's head and poured the thick liquid between his lips. She smiled at her companion, who winked back, Blackburn's red-coated organ in her hand.

Then the Greek girl slid off the bed, gesturing towards the bathroom door. Her associate nodded, extending her left hand up towards the general's head, inserting her fingers into his lips to cover for her companion's brief indisposition. The auburn-haired woman walked across the black carpet and went into the bathroom. The room resounded with the groans of the general's writhing euphoria.

Thirty seconds later, the Greek girl emerged, but she was no longer naked. She was dressed now in a dark tweed coat with a hood that covered her hair. She stood momentarily in the shadows, then stepped to the nearest window and gently pulled back the heavy drapes.

The sound of shattering glass filled the room and a rush of wind billowed the curtains. The figure of a broad-shouldered, stocky man loomed in the window; he had kicked in the panes, and now leaped through the frame, his head encased in a ski-mask, a gun in his hand.

The girl on the bed whipped around and screamed in terror as the killer levelled his weapon and pulled the trigger. The explosion was muted by a silencer; the girl slumped over the obscenely painted body of Anthony Blackburn. The man approached the bed; the general raised his head, trying to focus through the mists of narcotics, his eyes floating, guttural sounds coming from his throat. The killer fired again. And again, and again, the bullets entering Blackburn's neck and chest and groin, the eruptions of blood mingling with the glistening colours of the paint.

The man nodded to the girl from Athens; she rushed to the door, opened it and said in Greek, 'She'll be downstairs in the room with revolving lights. She's in a long red dress, with diamonds around her neck.'

The man nodded again and they rushed out into the corridor.

The major's thoughts were interrupted by the unexpected sounds that seemed to come from somewhere inside the brownstone. He listened, his breath suspended.

They were shrieks of some kind . . . yelling . . . *screams*. People were screaming!

He looked up at the house; the heavy door flew open as two figures ran outside and down the steps, a man and a woman. Then he saw it and a massive pain shot through his stomach: the man was shoving a gun into his belt.

Oh, my God!

The major thrust his hand under the seat for his Army automatic, pulled it out and leapt from the car. He raced up the steps and inside the hallway. Beyond, through the

14

arch, the screams mounted; people were running, several up the staircase, others down.

He ran into the large room with the insanely revolving coloured lights. On the floor he could see the figure of the slender woman with the diamonds around her neck. Her forehead was a mass of blood; she'd been shot.

Oh, Christ!

'*Where is he?*' he shouted.

'Upstairs!' came the scream from a girl huddled in the corner.

The major turned in panic and raced back to the ornate staircase, taking the steps three at a time, passing a telephone on a small table on the landing; its image stuck in his mind. He knew the room; it was always the same room. He turned in the narrow corridor, reached the door and lunged through it.

Oh, Jesus! It was beyond anything in his imagination, beyond any of the previous games, beyond any mess he had seen before. The naked Blackburn covered with blood and painted obscenities, the dead girl slumped over him, her face on his genitals. It was a sight from hell, if hell could be so terrible.

The major would never know where he found the self-control, but find it he did. He slammed the door shut and stood in the corridor, his automatic raised. He grabbed a woman who raced by towards the staircase, and shouted.

'Do as I say, or I'll kill you! There's a telephone over there. Dial the number I tell you! Say the words I tell you, the *exact words*!' He shoved the girl viciously towards the hallway phone.

The President of the United States walked grimly through the door into the Oval Office and over to his desk. Already there, and standing together, were the Secretary of State and the Director of the Central Intelligence Agency.

15

'I know the facts,' said the President harshly in his familiar drawl, 'and they turn my stomach. Now tell me what you're doing about them?'

The Director of the CIA stepped forward. 'New York Homicide is co-operating. We're fortunate in so far as the general's aide remained by the door and threatened to kill anyone who tried to get past him. Our people arrived, and were at the scene first. They cleaned up as best they could.'

'That's cosmetics, goddamn it!' said the President. 'I suppose they're necessary, but that's not what I'm interested in. What are your ideas? Was it one of those weird, kinky New York murders, or was it something else?'

'In my judgement,' answered the Director, 'it was something else. I said as much to Paul here last night. It was a thoroughly analysed, pre-arranged assassination. Brilliantly executed. Even to the killing of the establishment's owner, who was the only one who could shed any light.'

'Who's responsible?'

'I'd say KGB. The bullets fired were from a Russian Graz-Burya automatic, a favourite weapon of theirs.'

'I *must* object, Mr President,' said the Secretary of State. 'I can't subscribe to Jim's conclusion; that gun may be unusual, but it *can* be purchased in Europe. I was with the Ambassador for an hour this morning. He was as shaken as we were. He not only disclaimed any *possible* Russian involvement, but correctly pointed out that General Blackburn was far more acceptable to the Soviets than any who might immediately succeed him.'

'The KGB,' interrupted the Director, 'is often at odds with the Kremlin's diplomatic corps.'

'As the Company is with ours?' asked the Secretary.

'No more than your own Consular Operations, Paul,' replied the Director.

'Goddamn it!' said the President. 'I don't need that crap

from you two. Give me facts. You first, Jim. Since you're so sure of yourself, what have you come up with?'

'A great deal.' The Director opened the file folder in his hand, took out a sheet of paper and placed it in front of the President. 'We went back fifteen years and put everything we learned about last night into the computers. We cross-checked the concepts of method, location, egress, timing and teamwork. We matched it all with every known KGB assassination during the period. We've come up with three profiles. Three of the most elusive and successful killers in Soviet intelligence. In each case, of course, the man operates under normal covert procedures, but they're all assassins. We've listed them in order of expertise.'

The President studied the three names:

> *Taleniekov, Vasili*. Last reported post: South-west Soviet Sectors.
> *Krylovich, Nikolai*. Last reported post: Moscow, VKR.
> *Zhukovski, Georgi*. Last reported post: East Berlin, Embassy Attaché.

The Secretary of State was agitated; he could not remain silent. 'Mr President, this kind of speculation – based at best on the widest variables – can only lead to confrontation. It's not the time for it.'

'Now, wait a minute, Paul,' said the President. 'I asked for facts, and I don't give a damn whether the time's right or not right for a confrontation. The Chairman of the Joint Chiefs of Staff was killed. He may have been a sick son of a bitch in private life, but he was a hell of a good soldier. If it was a Soviet assassination, I want to know it.' The chief executive put the paper down on the desk, his eyes still on the Secretary. 'Besides,' he added, 'until more is known there won't be any confrontations. I'm certain Jim has kept this at the highest level of security.'

'Of course,' said the Director of the CIA.

There was a rapid knock on the Oval Office door. The

President's senior communications aide entered without waiting for a response.

'Sir, the Premier of Soviet Russia is on the Red telephone. We've confirmed the transmission.'

'Thank you,' said the President, reaching for a phone with very thick wires behind his chair. 'Mr Premier? This is the President.'

The Russian's words were spoken rapidly, briskly, and at the first pause, an interpreter translated. As was customary, the Soviet interpreter stopped and another voice – that of the interpreter's American counterpart – said simply, 'Correct, Mr President.'

The four-way conversation continued.

'Mr President,' said the Premier, 'I mourn the death – the murder – of General Anthony Blackburn. He was a fine soldier who loathed war, as you and I loathe war. He was respected here, his strength and perception of global problems a beneficial influence on our own military leaders. He will be sorely missed.'

'Thank you, Mr Premier. We, too, mourn his death. His murder. We are at a loss to explain it.'

'That is the reason for my call, Mr President. You must know beyond doubt that General Blackburn's death – his murder – would never be desired by the responsible leadership of the Soviet Socialist Republic. The contemplation of it would be an anathema. I trust I make myself clear, Mr President.'

'I think so, Mr Premier, and I thank you again. But if I may, are you alluding to the outside possibility of irresponsible leadership?'

'No more than those in your Senate who would bomb the Ukraine. Such idiots are dismissed, as they should be.'

'Then I'm not sure I grasp the subtlety of your phrasing, Mr Premier.'

'I shall be clearer. Your Central Intelligence Agency has produced three names it believes may be involved with the

18

death of General Blackburn. They are not, Mr President. You have my solemn word. They are *responsible* men, held in absolute control by their superiors. In point of fact, one man, Zhukovski, was hospitalized a week ago. Another, Krylovich, has been stationed at the Manchurian border for the past eleven months. And the respected Taleniekov is, to all intents and purposes, retired. He is currently in Moscow.'

The President paused and stared at the Director of the CIA. 'Thank you for the clarification, Mr Premier, and for the accuracy of your information. I realize it wasn't easy for you to make this call. Soviet intelligence is to be commended.'

'As is your own. There are fewer secrets these days; some say that is good. I weighed the values, and had to reach you. We were not involved, Mr President.'

'I believe you. I wonder who it was.'

'I'm troubled, Mr President. I think we should both know the answer to that.'

2

'Dimitri Yurievich!' roared the buxom woman good-naturedly as she approached the bed, a breakfast tray in her hand. 'It's the first morning of your holiday. The snow is on the ground, the sun is melting it, and before you shake the vodka from your head, the forests will be green again!'

The man buried his face in the pillow, then rolled over and opened his eyes, blinking at the sheer whiteness of the room. Outside the large windows of the *dacha*, the branches of the trees were sagging under the weight of their blinding white blankets.

Yurievich smiled at his wife, his fingers touching the hairs of his beard, grown more grey than brown. 'I think I burned myself last night,' he said.

'You would have!' laughed the woman. 'Fortunately, my peasant instincts were inherited by our son. He sees fire and doesn't waste time analysing the components, but puts it out!'

'I remember him leaping at me.'

'He certainly did.' Yurievich's wife put the tray on the bed, pushing her husband's legs away to make room for herself. She sat down and reached for his forehead. 'You're warm, but you'll survive, my Cossack.'

'Give me a cigarette.'

'Not before fruit juice. You're a very important man; the cupboards are filled with cans of fruit juice. Our lieutenant says they're probably there to put out the cigarettes that burn your beard.'

'The mentality of soldiers will never improve. We scientists understand that. The cans of juice are there to be mixed with vodka.' Dimitri Yurievich smiled again,

20

not a little forlornly. 'A cigarette, my love? I'll even let you light it.'

'You are impossible!' She picked up a pack of cigarettes from the bedside table, shook one out and put it between her husband's lips. 'Be careful not to breathe when I strike the match. We'd both explode, and I'll be buried in dishonour as the killer of the Soviet's most prominent nuclear physicist.'

'My work lives after me; let me be interred with smoke.' Yurievich inhaled as his wife held the match. 'Our son is faring well this morning?'

'He's fine. He was up early oiling the rifles. His guests will be here in an hour or so. The hunt begins around noon.'

'Oh, Lord, I forgot about that,' said Yurievich, pushing himself up on the pillow into a sitting position. 'Do I really have to go?'

'You and he are teamed together. Don't you remember telling everyone at dinner that father and son would bring home the prize game?'

Dimitri winced. 'It was my conscience speaking. All those years in the laboratories while he grew up somehow behind my back.'

His wife smiled. 'It will be good for you to get out in the cold air. Now finish your cigarette, eat your breakfast and get dressed.'

'You know something?' said Yurievich, taking his wife's hand. 'I'm just beginning to grasp it. This *is* a holiday. I can't remember our last one.'

'I'm not sure there ever was one. You work harder than any man I've known.'

Yurievich shrugged. 'It was good of the army to grant our son leave.'

'He requested it. He wanted to be with you.'

'That was good of him, too. I love him, but I hardly know him.'

21

'He's a fine officer, everyone says. You can be proud, my husband.'

'Oh I am, indeed, my wife. It's just that I don't know what to say to him. We have so little in common. The vodka made things easier last night.'

'You haven't seen each other in nearly two years.'

'I've had my work, everyone knows that.'

'You're a scientist.' His wife squeezed Dimitri's hand. 'But not today. Not for the next three weeks. No laboratories, no blackboards, no all-night sessions with eager young professors and students who want to tell everybody they've worked with the great Yurievich.' She took the cigarette from between his lips and crushed it out. 'Now, eat your breakfast and get dressed. A winter hunt will do you a world of good.'

'My dear woman,' protested Dimitri, laughing, 'it will probably be the death of me. I haven't fired a rifle in over twenty years!'

Lieutenant Nikolai Yurievich trudged through the deep snow towards the old building that was once the *dacha*'s stables. He turned and looked back at the huge three-storey main house. It glistened in the morning sunlight, a small alabaster palace set in an alabaster glen carved out of snow-laden forest. It was from another, far more graceful era that had disappeared, its like never to return again.

Moscow thought a great deal of his father. Everyone wanted to know about the great Yurievich, this brilliant, irascible man whose mere name frightened the leaders of the Western world. It was said that Dimitri Yurievich carried the formulae for a dozen nuclear tactical weapons in his head; that left alone in a munitions depot with an adjacent laboratory he could fashion a bomb that would destroy greater London, all of Washington and most of Peking.

That was the great Yurievich, a man immune from criticism or discipline, in spite of words and actions

22

which were at times intemperate. Not in terms of his devotion to the state; that was never in question. Dimitri Yurievich was the fifth child of impoverished peasants from Kourov. Without the state he would be behind a mule on some aristocrat's land. No, he was a Communist to his boots, but like all brilliant men he had no patience with bureaucracies. He had been outspoken about interference and he had never been taken to task for it.

Which was why so many wanted to know him. On the assumption, Nikolai suspected, that even knowing the great Yurievich would somehow transfer a touch of his immunity to them.

The lieutenant knew that was the case today and it was an uncomfortable feeling. The 'guests' who were now on their way to his father's *dacha* had practically invited themselves. One was the commander of Nikolai's battalion in Vilnius, the other a man Nikolai did not even know. A friend of the commander's from Moscow, someone the commander said could do a young lieutenant a good turn when it came to assignments. Nikolai did not care for such enticements; he was his own man first, his father's son second. He would make his own way; it was very important to him that he do so. But he could not refuse this particular commander, for if there was any man in the Soviet army who deserved a touch of 'immunity', it was Colonel Janek Drigorin.

Drigorin had spoken out against the corruption that was rife in the Select Officer Corps. The resort clubs on the Black Sea paid for with misappropriated funds, the stockhouses filled with contraband, the women brought in on military aircraft against all regulations.

He was cut off by Moscow, sent to Vilnius to rot in mediocrity. Whereas Nikolai Yurievich was a twenty-one-year-old lieutenant exercising major responsibility in a minor post, Drigorin was a major military talent relegated to oblivion in a minor command. If such a man wished to spend a day with his father, Nikolai could not protest. And, after all, the colonel was a delightful person; he wondered what the other man was like.

Nikolai reached the stables and opened the large door that led to the corridor of stalls. The hinges had been oiled; the old entrance swung back without a sound. He walked down past the immaculately kept enclosures that once had held the best of breeds and tried to imagine what that Russia had been like. He could almost hear the whinnies of fiery-eyed stallions, the impatient scuffing of hooves, the snorting of hunters eager to break out for the fields.

That Russia must have been something. If you weren't behind a mule.

He came to the end of the long corridor, where there was another wide door. He opened it and walked out into the snow again. In the distance, something caught his eye; it seemed out of place. *They* seemed out of place.

Veering from the corner of a grain bin towards the edge of the forest, there were tracks in the snow. Footprints, perhaps. Yet the two servants assigned by Moscow to the *dacha* had not left the main house. And the gamekeepers were in their barracks down the road.

On the other hand, thought Nikolai, the warmth of the morning sun could have melted the rims of any impressions in the snow; and the blinding light played tricks on the eyes. They were no doubt the tracks of some foraging animal. The lieutenant smiled to himself at the thought of an animal from the forest looking for grain here, at this cared-for relic that was the grand *dacha*'s stables. The animals had not changed, but Russia had.

Nikolai looked at his watch; it was time to go back to the house. The guests would be arriving shortly.

Everything was going so well, Nikolai could hardly believe it. There was nothing uncomfortable at all, thanks in large measure to his father and the man from Moscow. Colonel

Drigorin at first seemed ill-at-ease – the commander who had imposed himself on the well-known or well-connected subordinate – but Dimitri Yurievich would have none of it. He welcomed his son's superior as an anxious – if celebrated – father, interested only in furthering his son's position. Nikolai could not help but be amused; his father was so obvious. Vodka was delivered with the fruit juice and coffee, and Nikolai kept a sharp eye out for dangling cigarettes.

The surprise and delight was the colonel's friend from Moscow, a man named Brunov, a high-ranking party functionary in Military-Industrial Planning. Not only did Brunov and his father have mutual friends, it was soon apparent that they shared an irreverent attitude towards much of Moscow's bureaucracy – which encompassed, naturally, many of those mutual friends. The laughter was not long coming, each rebel trying to outdo the other with biting comments about this commissar-with-an-echo-chamber-for-a-head and that economist-who-could-not-keep-a-rouble-in-his-pocket.

'We are wicked, Brunov!' roared Nikolai's father, his eyes alive with laughter.

'Too true, Yurievich!' agreed the man from Moscow. 'It's a pity we're so accurate.'

'But be careful, we're with soldiers. They'll report us!'

'Then I shall withhold their payrolls and you'll design a back-firing bomb.'

Dimitri Yurievich's laughter subsided for a brief moment. 'I wish there were no need for the functioning kind.'

'And I that such large payrolls were not demanded.'

'Enough,' said Yurievich. 'The gamekeepers say the hunting here is superb. My son has promised to look out for me, and I promised to shoot the biggest game. Come now, whatever you lack we have here. Boots, furs . . . vodka.'

'Not while firing, Father.'

'By God, you *have* taught him something,' said Yurievich, smiling at the colonel. 'Incidentally, gentlemen, I won't hear of your leaving today. You'll stay the night, of course. Moscow is generous; there are roasts and fresh vegetables from Lenin-knows-where . . .'

'And flasks of vodka, I trust.'

'Not flasks, Brunov. *Casks!* I see it in your eyes. We'll both be on holiday. You'll stay.'

'I'll stay,' said the man from Moscow.

The gunshots rang through the forest, vibrating in the ears. Nor were they lost on the winter birds; screeches and the snapping of wings formed a rolling coda to the echoes. Nikolai could hear excited voices as well, but they were too far away to be understandable. He turned to his father.

'We should hear the whistle within sixty seconds if they hit something,' he said, his rifle angled down at the snow.

'It's an outrage!' replied Yurievich in mock anger. 'The gamekeepers swore to me – on the side, mind you – that all the game was in this section of the woods. Near the lake. There was *nothing* over there! It's why I insisted they go there.'

'You're an old scoundrel,' said the son, studying his father's weapon. 'Your safety's released. Why?'

'I thought I heard a rustle back there. I wanted to be ready.'

'With respect, my father, please put it back on. Wait until your sight matches the sound you hear before you release it.'

'With respect, my soldier, then there'd be too much to do at once.' Yurievich saw the concern in his son's eyes. 'On second thoughts, you're probably right. I'd fall and cause a detonation. That's something I know about.'

'Thank you,' said the lieutenant, suddenly turning. His

father was right; there was something rustling behind them. A crack of a limb, the snap of a branch. He released the safety on his weapon.

'What is it?' asked Dimitri Yurievich, excitement in his eyes.

'Sh,' whispered Nikolai, peering into the shaggy corridors of white surrounding them.

He saw nothing. He snapped the safety into its locked position.

'You heard it, too, then?' asked Dimitri. 'It wasn't just this pair of fifty-five-year-old ears.'

'The snow's heavy,' suggested the son. 'Branches break under its weight. That's what we heard.'

'Well, one thing we *didn't* hear,' said Yurievich, 'was a whistle. They didn't hit a damn thing!'

Three more distant gunshots rang out.

'They've seen *something*,' said the lieutenant. 'Perhaps now we'll hear their whistle . . .'

Suddenly they heard it. A sound. But it was not a whistle. It was, instead, a panicked, elongated scream, faint but distinct. Distinctly a terrible scream. It was followed by another, more hysterical, stretched out until the echoes enlarged it into waves of something horrible.

'My *God*, what *happened*?' Yurievich grabbed his son's arm.

'I don't . . .'

The reply was cut off by a third scream, searing and terrible. There were no words, only swallowed protests, shrieks of pain.

'Stay *here*!' yelled the lieutenant to his father. 'I'll go to them.'

'I'll follow,' said Yurievich. 'Go quickly, but be careful!'

Nikolai raced through the snow towards the source of the screams. They filled the woods now, less shrill, but more painful for the loss of power. The soldier used his rifle to crash his path through the heavy branches, bending, breaking, kicking up sprays of snow. His legs ached, the cold air swelled in his lungs, his sight was obscured by tears of fatigue.

He heard the roars first, and then he saw what he most feared, what no hunter ever wanted to see.

An enormous, wild black bear, his terrifying face a mass of blood, was wreaking his vengeance on those who'd caused his wounds, clawing, ripping, slashing at his enemy.

Nikolai raised his rifle and fired until there were no more shells in the chamber.

The giant bear fell. The soldier raced to the two men; he lost what breath he had as he looked at them.

The man from Moscow was dead, his throat torn, his bloodied head barely attached to his body. Drigorin was only just alive, and if he did not die in seconds, Nikolai knew he would reload his weapon and finish what the animal had not done. The colonel had no face; it was not there. In its place a sight that burned itself into the soldier's mind.

How? How could it have happened?

And then the lieutenant's eyes strayed to Drigorin's right arm and the shock was beyond anything he could imagine.

It was half severed from his elbow, the method of surgery clear: heavy calibre bullets.

The colonel's firing arm had been shot off!

Nikolai ran to Brunov's corpse; he reached down and rolled it over.

Brunov's arm was intact, but his left hand had been blown apart, only the gnarled, bloody outline of a palm left, the fingers strips of bone. His *left hand*. Nikolai Yurievich remembered the morning; the coffee and fruit juice and vodka and cigarettes.

The man from Moscow was left-handed.

Brunov and Drigorin had been rendered defenceless by someone with a gun, someone who knew what was in their path.

Nikolai stood up cautiously, the soldier in him primed, seeking an unseen enemy. And this was an enemy he wanted to find and kill with all his heart. His mind raced back to the footprints he had seen behind the stables. They were not those of a scavenging animal – though an animal's they were – they were the tracks of a killer so obscene there was nothing in the *Lubyanka* he did not deserve.

Who *was* it? Above all, *why*?

The lieutenant saw a flash of light. Sunlight off a weapon.

He made a move to his right, then abruptly spun to his left and lunged to the ground, rolling behind the trunk of an oak tree. He removed the empty magazine from his weapon, replacing it with a fresh one. He squinted his eyes up at the source of the light. It came from high in a pine tree.

A figure was straddling two limbs fifty feet above the ground, a rifle with a telescopic sight in his hands. The killer wore a white snow parka with a white fur hood, his face obscured behind wide black sunglasses.

Nikolai thought he would vomit in rage and revulsion. The man was smiling, and the lieutenant knew he was smiling down at him.

Furiously, he raised his rifle. An explosion of snow blinded him, accompanied by the loud report of a high-powered rifle. A second gunshot followed; the bullet thumped into the wood above his head. He pulled back into the protection of the trunk.

Another gunshot, this one in the near distance, not from the killer in the pine tree.

'Nikolai!'

His mind burst. There was nothing left but rage. The voice that screamed his name was his father's.

'Nikolai!'

Another shot. The soldier sprang up from the ground, firing his rifle into the tree and raced across the snow.

An icelike incision was made in his chest. He heard nothing and felt nothing until he knew his face was cold.

The Premier of Soviet Russia placed his hands on the long table beneath the window that looked out over the Kremlin. He leaned over and studied the photographs, the flesh of his large peasant face sagging with exhaustion, his eyes filled with anger and shock.

'Horrible,' he whispered. 'That men should die like this is horrible. At least, Yurievich was spared – not his life, but such an end as this.'

Across the room, seated around another table, were two men and a woman, their faces stern, watching the Premier. In front of each was a brown file folder, and it was apparent that each was anxious to proceed with the conference. But with the Premier one did not push nor intrude on his thoughts; his temper could be unleashed by such displays of impatience. The Premier was a man whose mind raced faster than anyone's in that room, but his deliberations were nevertheless slow, the complexities considered. He was a survivor in a world where only the most astute – and subtle – survived.

Fear was a weapon he used with extraordinary skill.

He stood up, pushing the photographs away in disgust, and strode back to the conference table.

'All nuclear stations are on alert, our submarines approaching firing positions,' he said. 'I want this information transmitted to all embassies. Use codes Washington has broken.'

One of the men at the table leaned forward. He was a diplomat, older than the Premier, and obviously an associate of long standing, an ally who could speak somewhat more freely than the other two. 'You risk a reaction I'm not sure is wise. We're not that certain. The American ambassador was profoundly shocked. I know him; he wasn't lying.'

'Then he wasn't informed,' said the second man curtly. 'Speaking for the VKR, we *are* certain. The bullets and shell casings were identified: seven-millimetre – grooved for implosion. Bore markings, unmistakable. They were fired from a Browning Magnum, Grade Four. What more do you need?'

'A great deal more than that. Such a weapon is not so difficult to obtain, and I doubt an American assassin would leave his business card!'

'He might if it was the weapon he was most familiar with. We've found a pattern.' The VKR man turned to the middle-aged woman, whose face was chiselled granite. 'Explain, if you will, Comrade Director.'

The woman opened her file folder and scanned the top page before speaking. She turned to the second page and addressed the Premier, her eyes avoiding the diplomat. 'As you know there were two assassins, presumably both male. One had to be a marksman of extreme skill and co-ordination, the other someone who undoubtedly possessed the same qualifications, but who was also an expert in electronic surveillance. There was evidence in the stables – bracket scrapings, suction imprints, footprints indicating unobstructed vantage points – that lead us to believe all conversations in the *dacha* were intercepted.'

'You describe CIA expertise, comrade,' interrupted the Premier.

'Or Consular Operations, sir,' replied the woman. 'It's important to bear that in mind.'

'Oh, yes,' agreed the Premier. 'The State Department's small band of "negotiators".'

'Why not the Chinese Tao-pans?' offered the diplomat earnestly. 'They're among the most effective killers on earth. The Chinese had more to fear from Yurievich than anyone else.'

'Physiognomy rules them out,' countered the man from VKR. 'If one was caught, even after cyanide, Peking knows it would be destroyed.'

'Get back to this pattern you've found,' interrupted the Premier.

The woman continued. 'We fed everything through KGB computers, concentrating on American intelligence personnel we know who have penetrated Russia, who speak the language fluently, and are known killers. We have arrived at four names. Here they are, Mr Premier. Three from the Central Intelligence Agency, one from the Department of State's Consular Operations.' She handed the page to the VKR man, who in turn rose and gave it to the Premier.

He looked at the names.

Scofield, Brandon Alan. State Department, Consular Operations. Known to have been responsible for assassinations in Prague, Athens, Paris, Munich. Suspected of having operated in Moscow itself. Involved in over twenty defections.

Randolph, David. Central Intelligence Agency. Cover is Import Traffic Manager, Dynamax Corporation, West Berlin Branch. All phases of sabotage. Known to have been instrumental in hydro-electrical explosions in Kazan and Tagil.

Saltzman, George Robert. Central Intelligence Agency. Operated as pouch courier and assassin in Vientiane under AID cover for six years. Oriental expert. Currently – since five weeks ago – in the Tashkent sector. Cover: Australian immigrant, sales manager: Perth Radar Corporation.

Bergstrom, Edward. Central Intelligence Agency . . .

'Mr Premier,' interrupted the man from VKR. 'My associate meant to explain that the names are in order of priority. In our opinion, the entrapment and execution of

Dimitri Yurievich bears all the earmarks of the first man on that list.'

'This is Scofield?'

'Yes, Mr Premier. He disappeared a month ago in Marseilles. He's done more damage, compromised more operations, than any agent the United States has fielded since the war.'

'Really?'

'Yes, sir.' The VKR man paused, then spoke hesitantly, as if he did not want to go on, but knew he must. 'His wife was killed ten years ago. In East Berlin. He's been a maniac ever since.'

'*East* Berlin?'

'It was a trap. KGB.'

The telephone rang on the Premier's desk; he crossed rapidly and picked it up.

It was the President of the United States. The interpreters were on the line; they went to work.

'We grieve the death – the terrible murder – of a very great scientist, Mr Premier. As well as the horror that befell his friends.'

'Your words are appreciated, Mr President, but as you know, those deaths and that horror were premeditated. I'm grateful for your sympathies, but I can't help but wonder if perhaps you are not somewhat relieved that the Soviet Union has lost its foremost nuclear physicist.'

'I am not, sir. His brilliance transcended our borders and differences. He was a man for all peoples.'

'Yet he chose to be a part of *one* people, did he not? I tell you frankly, my concern does not transcend our differences. Rather, it forces me to look to my flanks.'

'Then, if you'll forgive me, Mr Premier, you're looking for phantoms.'

'Perhaps we've found them, Mr President. We have evidence that is extremely disturbing to me. So much so that I have . . .'

33

'Forgive me once again,' interrupted the President of the United States. 'Your evidence has prompted my calling you, in spite of my natural reluctance to do so. The KGB has made a great error. Four errors, to be precise.'

'*Four* . . .'

'Yes, Mr Premier. Specifically the names Scofield, Randolph, Saltzman and Bergstrom. None was involved, Mr Premier.'

'You astonish me, Mr President.'

'No more than you astonished me the other week. There are fewer secrets these days, remember?'

'Words are inexpensive; the evidence is strong.'

'Then it's been so calculated. Let me clarify. Two of the three men from Central Intelligence are no longer in sanction. Randolph and Bergstrom are currently at their desks in Washington. Mr Saltzman was hospitalized in Tashkent; the diagnosis is cancer.' The President paused.

'That leaves one name, doesn't it?' said the Premier. 'Your man from the infamous Consular Operations. So bland in diplomatic circles, but infamous to us.'

'This is the most painful aspect of my clarification. It's inconceivable that Mr Scofield could have been involved. More so than any of the others, frankly. I tell you this because it no longer matters.'

'Words cost little . . .'

'Mr *Premier*, I must be explicit. For the past several years a covert, in-depth dossier has been maintained on Dr Yurievich, information added almost daily, certainly every month. In certain judgements, it was time to reach Dimitri Yurievich with viable options.'

'*What?*'

'Yes, Mr Premier. Defection. The two men who travelled to the *dacha* to make contact with Mr Yurievich did so in our interests. Their source-control was Scofield. It was his operation.'

The Premier of Soviet Russia stared across the room

at the pile of photographs on the table. He spoke softly.
'Thank you for your frankness.'
   'Look to other flanks.'
   'I shall.'
   'We both must.'

3

The late-afternoon sun was a fireball, its rays bouncing off
the waters of the canal in blinding oscillation. The crowds
walking west on Amsterdam's Kalverstraat squinted as
they hurried along the pavement, grateful for the February
sun and gusts of wind that came off the myriad waterways
that stemmed from the Amstel River. Too often February
brought the mists and rain, dampness everywhere; it was
not the case today and the citizens of the North Sea's most
vital port city seemed exhilarated by the clear, biting air
warmed from above.

One man, however, was not exhilarated. Neither was he
a citizen nor on the streets. His name was Brandon Alan
Scofield, attaché-at-large, Consular Operations, United
States Department of State. He stood at a window four
storeys above the canal and the Kalverstraat, peering
through binoculars down at the crowds, specifically at
the area of the pavement where a glass telephone booth
reflected the harsh flashes of sunlight. The light made him
squint, but there was no gratitude felt, no energy evident
on Scofield's pallid face, a face whose sharp features were
drawn and taut beneath a vaguely combed cover of light
brown hair, fringed at the edge with strands of grey.

He kept refocusing the binoculars, cursing the light
and the swift movements below. His eyes were tired,
the hollows beneath dark and stretched, the results of
too little sleep for too many reasons Scofield did not
care to think about. There was a job to do and he was
a professional; his concentration could not waver.

There were two other men in the room. A balding
technician sat at a table with a dismantled telephone,

wires connecting it to a tape machine, the receiver off the hook. Somewhere under the streets in a telephone complex, arrangements had been made; they were the only co-operation that would be given by the Amsterdam police, a debt called in by the attaché-at-large from the American State Department. The third person in the room was younger than the other two, in his early thirties and with no lack of energy on his face, no exhaustion in his eyes. If his features were taut, it was the tautness of enthralment; he was a young man eager for the kill. His weapon was a fast-film motion picture camera mounted on a tripod, a telescopic lens attached. He would have preferred a different weapon.

Down in the street, a figure appeared in the tinted circles of Scofield's binoculars. The figure hesitated by the telephone booth and in that brief moment was jostled by the crowds off to the side of the pavement, in front of the flashing glass, blocking the glare with his body, a target surrounded by a halo of sunlight. It would be more comfortable for everyone concerned if the target could be zeroed where he was standing now. A high-powered rifle calibrated for seventy yards could do it; the man in the window could squeeze the trigger. He had done so often before. But comfort was not the issue. A lesson had to be taught, another lesson learned, and such instruction depended on the confluence of vital factors. Those teaching and those being taught had to understand their respective roles. Otherwise an execution was meaningless.

The figure below was an elderly man, in his middle to late sixties. He was dressed in rumpled clothing, a thick overcoat pulled up around his neck to ward off the chill, a battered hat pulled down over his forehead. There was a stubble of a beard on his frightened face; he was a man-on-the-run and for the American watching him through the binoculars, there was nothing so terrible, or haunting as an old man-on-the-run. Except, perhaps, an old woman. He had seen both. Far more often than he cared to think about.

Scofield glanced at his watch. 'Go ahead,' he said to the technician at the table. Then he turned to the younger man who stood beside him. 'You ready?'

'Yes,' was the curt reply. 'I've got the son of a bitch centred. Washington was right; you proved it.'

'I'm not sure what I've proved yet. I wish I was. When he's in the booth, get his lips.'

'Right.'

The technician dialled the pre-arranged numbers and punched the buttons of the tape machine. He rose quickly from his chair and handed Scofield a semi-circular headset with a mouthpiece and single earphone. 'It's ringing,' he said.

'I know. He's staring through the glass. He's not sure he wants to hear it. That bothers me.'

'*Move*, you son of a bitch!' said the young man with the camera.

'He will,' said the older, light-haired Scofield, the binoculars and headset held firmly in his hands. 'He's frightened. Each half-second is a long time for him and I don't know why . . . There he goes; he's opening the door. Everybody quiet.' Scofield continued to stare through the binoculars, listened, and then spoke quietly into the mouthpiece. '*Dobri dyen, priyatyel* . . .'

The conversation, spoken entirely in Russian, lasted for eighteen seconds.

'*Da svidaniya*,' said Scofield, adding '*zaftra nochyu. Na mostye.*' He continued to hold the headset to his ear and watched the frightened man below. The target disappeared into the crowds; the camera's motor stopped, and the attaché-at-large put down the binoculars, handing the headset to the technician. 'Were you able to get it all?' he asked.

38

'Clear enough for a voice print,' said the balding operator, checking his dials.

'You?' Scofield turned to the young man by the camera.

'If I understood the language better, even I could read his lips.'

'Good. Others will; they'll understand it very well.' Scofield reached into his pocket, took out a small leather notebook, and began writing. 'I want you to take the tape and the film to the embassy. Get the film developed right away and have duplicates made of both. I want miniatures; here are the specifications.'

'Sorry, Bray,' said the technician, glancing at Scofield as he wound a coil of telephone wire. 'I'm not allowed within five blocks of the territory; you know that.'

'I'm talking to Harry,' replied Scofield, angling his head towards the younger man. He tore out the page from his notebook. 'When the reductions are made, have them inserted in a single watertight flatcase. I want it coated, good enough for a week in the water.'

'Bray,' said the young man, taking the page of paper. 'I picked up about every third word you said on the phone.'

'You're improving,' interrupted Scofield, walking back to the window and the binoculars. 'When you get to every other one, we'll recommend an upgrade.'

'That man wanted to meet tonight,' continued Harry. 'You turned him down.'

'That's right,' said Scofield, raising the binoculars to his eyes, focusing out the window.

'Our instructions were to take him as soon as we could. The cipher plain text was clear about that. No time lost.'

'Time's relative, isn't it? When the old man heard the telephone ring, every second was an agonizing minute for him. For us, an hour can be a day. In Washington, for Christ's sake, a day is normally measured by a calendar year.'

'That's no answer,' pressed Harry, looking at the note. 'We can get this stuff reduced and packed in forty-five minutes. We could make the contact tonight. Why don't we?'

'The weather's rotten,' said Scofield, the binoculars at his eyes.

'The weather's perfect. Not a cloud in the sky.'

'That's what I mean. It's rotten. A clear night means a lot of people strolling around the canals; in bad weather, they don't. Tomorrow's forecast is for rain.'

'That doesn't make sense. In ten seconds we block a bridge, he's over the side and dead in the water.'

'Tell that clown to shut up, Bray!' shouted the technician at the table.

'You heard the man,' said Scofield, focusing on the spires of the buildings outside. 'You just lost the upgrade. Your outrageous statement that we intend to commit bodily harm tarnishes our friends in the Company.'

The younger man grimaced. The rebuke was deserved. 'Sorry. It still doesn't make sense. The cipher was a priority alert; we should take him tonight.'

Scofield lowered the binoculars and looked at Harry. 'I'll tell you what *does* make sense,' he said quietly, with an edge to his voice. 'Somewhat more than those silly goddamned phrases someone found on the back of a cereal box. That man down there was terrified. He hasn't slept in days. He's strung out to the breaking point, and I want to know why.'

'There could be a dozen reasons,' countered the younger man. 'He's old. Inexperienced. Maybe he thinks we're on to him, that he's about to be caught. What difference does it make?'

'A man's life, that's all.'

'Come on, Bray, not from *you*. He's Soviet poison; a double agent.'

'I want to be sure.'

'And I want to get out of here,' broke in the technician, handing Scofield a reel of tape and picking up his machine. 'Tell the clown we never met.'

'Thanks, Mr No-name. I owe you.'

The CIA man left, nodding at Bray, avoiding any contact with his associate.

'There was no one here but us chickens, Harry,' said Scofield after the door was shut. 'You do understand that.'

'He's a nasty bastard . . .'

'Who could tap the White House toilets, if he hasn't already,' said Bray, tossing the reel of tape to the younger man. 'Get our unsolicited indictments over to the embassy. Take out the film and leave the camera here.'

Harry would not be put off; he caught the reel of tape, but made no move towards the camera. 'I'm in this, too. That cipher applied to me as well as you. I want to have answers in case I'm asked questions; in case something happens between tonight and tomorrow.'

'If Washington's right, nothing will happen. I told you. I want to be sure.'

'What more do you *need*? The target thinks he just made contact with KGB-Amsterdam! You engineered it. You proved it!'

Scofield studied the younger man for a moment, then turned away and walked back to the window. 'You know something, Harry? All the training you get, all the words you hear, all the experiences you go through, never take the place of the first rule.' Bray picked up the binoculars, brought them to his eyes, and focused on a faraway point above the skyline. 'Teach yourself to think like the enemy thinks. Not how you'd like him to think, but how he *really* thinks. It's not easy; you can kid yourself because that *is* easy.'

Exasperated, the younger man spoke angrily. 'For God's

sake, what's that got to do with anything? We've got our proof!'

'Do we? As you say, our defector's made contact with his own. He's a pigeon who's found his own particular route to Mother Russia. He's safe; he's out of the cold.'

'That's what he thinks, yes!'

'Then why isn't he a happy man?' asked Bray Scofield, angling the binoculars down at the canal.

The mist and the rain fulfilled Amsterdam's promise of winter. The night sky was an impenetrable blanket, the edges mottled by the shimmering lights of the city. There were no strollers on the bridge, no boats on the canal below; pockets of fog swirled overhead – evidence that the North Sea winds travelled south unencumbered. It was three o'clock in the morning. For some there would be no daybreak.

Scofield leaned against the iron railing at the west entrance of the ancient stone bridge. In his left hand was a small transistorized radio – not for verbal communication, only for receiving signals. His right hand was in his raincoat pocket, his extended fingers touching the barrel of a .22 calibre automatic, not much larger than a starter's pistol, with a report nowhere near as loud. At close range it was a very feasible weapon. It fired rapidly, with an accuracy sufficient for a distance measured in inches, and could barely be heard above the noises of the night. And usually not at all in a crowded street in daylight.

Two hundred yards away, Bray's young associate was concealed in a doorway on the Sarphatistraat. The target would pass him on the way to the bridge; there was no other route. When the old Russian did so, Harry would press a button on his transmitter: the signal. The execution was in progress; the victim was walking his last hundred yards – to the midpoint of the bridge, where his own personal hangman would greet him, insert a watertight packet in the victim's overcoat and carry out the appointed task.

In a day or so that packet would find its way to KGB-Amsterdam. A tape would be listened to, a film observed closely. And another lesson would be taught.

And, naturally, go unheeded, as all lessons went unheeded – as they always went unheeded. Therein lay the futility, thought Scofield. The never-ending futility that numbed the senses with each repetition.

What difference does it make? A perceptive question asked by an eager if not very perceptive young colleague.

None, Harry. None at all. Not any longer.

But on this particular night, the needles of doubt kept pricking Bray's conscience. Not his morality; long ago morality was replaced by the practical. If it worked, it was moral, if it did not, it wasn't practical, and *thus* was immoral. What bothered him tonight had its basis in that utilitarian philosophy. Was the execution practical? Was the lesson about to be taught the best lesson, the most feasible option? Was it worth the risks and the fallout that came with the death of an old man who'd spent his adult life in space engineering?

On the surface the answer would appear to be yes. Six years ago the Soviet engineer had defected in Paris during an international space exposition. He had sought and been granted asylum; he had been welcomed by the space fraternity in Houston, given a job, a house and protection. However, he was not considered an outstanding prize. The Russians had actually joked about his ideological deviation, implying that his talents might be more appreciated by the less demanding capitalistic laboratories than by theirs. He rapidly became a forgotten man.

Until eight months ago when it was discovered that Soviet tracking stations were gridding into American satellites with alarming frequency, reducing the value of photographic checks through sophisticated ground camouflage. It was as if the Russians knew in advance the great majority of orbital trajectories.

They did. And a trace was made; it led to the forgotten man in Houston. What followed was relatively simple. A technical conference that dealt exclusively with one forgotten man's small area of expertise was called in Amsterdam; he was flown over on government aircraft and the rest was up to a specialist in these matters. Brandon Scofield, attaché-at-large, Consular Operations.

Scofield had long since broken KGB-Amsterdam's codes and methods of contact. He put them in motion and was mildly surprised at the target's reaction; it was the basis of his profound concern now. The old man showed no relief at the summons. After six years of a balancing act, the target had every right to expect termination with honours, the gratitude of his government, and the last years of his life spent in comfort. Expect, hell! Bray had indicated as much in their ciphered conversations.

But the old Russian was not a happy man. And there were no overriding personal relationships evident in Houston. Scofield had requested the Four-Zero dossier on the target, a file so complete it detailed the projected hours of bowel movements. There was nothing in Houston; the man was a mole – apparently in both senses of the word. And that, too, bothered Bray. A mole in espionage did not assume the characteristics of the social equivalent.

Something was wrong. Yet the evidence was there, the proof of duplicity confirmed. The lesson had to be taught.

A short, sharp whine came from the transmitter in his hand. It was repeated three seconds later; Scofield acknowledged receipt with the press of a button. He put the radio in his pocket and waited.

Less than a minute passed; he saw the figure of the old man coming through the blanket of fog and rain, a

44

streetlight beyond creating an eerie silhouette. The target's gait was hesitant but somehow painfully determined, as if he were about to keep a rendezvous both desired and loathed. It did *not* make sense.

Bray glanced to his right. As he expected, there was no one in the street, no one anywhere to be seen in this deserted section of the city at three o'clock in the morning. He turned to his left and started up the ramp towards the midpoint of the bridge, the old Russian on the opposite side. He kept in the shadows; it was easy to do as the first three lights above the left railing had been shorted out.

The rain pounded the ancient cobblestones. Across the bridge proper, the old man stood facing the water below, his hands on the railing. Scofield stepped off the walkway and approached from behind, the sound of the downpour obscuring his footsteps. In his left raincoat pocket, his hand now gripped a round, flat case two inches in diameter and less than an inch thick. It was coated in waterproof plastic, the sides possessing a chemical that when immersed in liquid for thirty seconds became an instant adhesive; under such conditions it would remain where it was placed until cut free. In the case was the evidence: a reel of film and a reel of magnetic tape. Both could be studied by KGB-Amsterdam.

'*Plakhaya noch, stary priyatyel,*' said Bray to the Russian's back, while taking the automatic from his pocket.

The old man turned, startled. 'Why did you contact me?' he asked in Russian. 'Has anything happened? . . .' He saw the gun and stopped. Then he went on, an odd calm in his voice suddenly replacing the fear. 'I see it has, and I'm no longer of value. Go ahead, comrade. You'll do me an enormous favour.'

Scofield stared at the old man; at the penetrating eyes that were no longer frightened. He had seen that look before. Bray answered in English.

45

'You've spent an active six years. Unfortunately, you haven't done us any favours at all. You weren't as grateful as we thought you might be.'

The Russian nodded, 'American,' he said. 'I wondered. A hastily called conference in Amsterdam on problems as easily analysed in Houston. My being allowed out of the country, albeit covertly, and guarded – that protection something less than complete once here. But you had all the codes, you said all the right words. And your Russian is flawless, *priyatyel*.'

'That's my job. What was yours?'

'You know the answer. It's why you're here.'

'I want to know why.'

The old man smiled grimly. 'Oh, no. You'll get nothing but what you've learned. You see, I meant what I said. You'll do me a favour. You're my *listok*.'

'Solution to what?'

'Sorry.'

Bray raised the automatic; its small barrel glistened in the rain. The Russian looked at it and breathed deeply. The fear returned to his eyes, but he did not waver or say a word. Suddenly, deliberately, Scofield thrust the gun up beneath the old man's left eye, steel and flesh making contact. The Russian trembled but remained silent.

Bray felt sick.

What difference does it make?

None, Harry. Not at all. Not any longer.

A lesson had to be taught . . .

Scofield lowered the gun. 'Get out of here,' he said. 'What? . . .'

'You heard me. Get out of here. The KGB operates out of the diamond exchange on the Tolstraat. Its cover is a firm of Hasidim, *Diamant Bruusteen*. Beat it.'

'I don't understand,' said the Russian, barely audible. 'Is this another trick?'

'*Goddamn it!*' yelled Bray, trembling. 'Get out of here!'

Momentarily, the old man staggered, then grabbed the railing to steady himself. He backed away awkwardly, then started running through the rain.

'*Scofield!*' The shout came from Harry. He was at the west entrance of the bridge, directly in the path of the Russian. 'Scofield. For God's *sake!*'

'Let him go!' screamed Bray.

He was either too late or his words were lost in the pounding rain; he did not know which. He heard three muted, sharp reports and watched in disgust as the old man held his head and fell against the railing.

Harry was a professional. He supported the body, fired a last shot into the neck, and with an upward motion, edged the corpse over the railing into the canal below.

What difference does it make?

None at all. Not any longer.

Scofield turned away and walked towards the east side of the bridge. He put the automatic in his pocket; it seemed heavy.

He could hear racing footsteps drawing nearer through the rain. He was terribly tired and did not want to hear them. Any more than he wanted to hear Harry's abrasive voice.

'Bray, what the hell *happened* back there? He nearly got away!'

'But he didn't,' said Scofield, walking faster. 'You made sure of that.'

'You're damn right I did! For Christ's sake, what's *wrong* with you?' The younger man was on Bray's left; his eyes dropped to Scofield's hand. He could see the edge of the watertight case. '*Jesus!* You never planted it!'

'What?' Then Bray realized what Harry was talking about. He raised his head, looked at the small round receptacle, then threw it past the younger man over the railing.

'What are you *doing*?'

'Go to hell,' said Scofield quietly.

Harry stopped, Bray did not. In seconds, Harry caught up and grabbed the edge of Scofield's raincoat. 'Christ Almighty! You *let* him get away!'

'Take your hands off me.'

'*No*, damn it! You can't . . .'

It was as far as Harry got. Bray shot his right hand up, his fingers clasping the younger man's exposed thumb, and yanked it counterclockwise.

Harry screamed, his thumb was broken.

'Go to hell,' repeated Scofield. He continued walking off the bridge.

The safe-house was near the Rozengracht, the meeting to take place on the second floor. The sitting room was warmed by a fire, which also served to destroy any notes that might be taken. A State Department official had flown in from Washington; he wanted to question Scofield at the scene, as it were, in the event there were circumstances that only the scene could provide. It was important to understand what had happened, especially with someone like Brandon Scofield. He was the best there was, the coldest they had; he was an extraordinary asset to the American intelligence community, a veteran of twenty-two years of the most complicated 'negotiations' one could imagine. He had to be handled with care . . . at the source. Not ordered back on the strength of a departmental complaint filed by a subordinate. He was a specialist, and something had happened.

Bray understood this and the arrangements amused him. Harry was taken out of Amsterdam the next morning in such a way that there was no chance of Scofield's seeing him. Among the few at the embassy that had to be aware of the incident, Bray was treated as though no incident had taken place. He was told to take a few days off; a man was flying in from Washington to discuss a problem in Prague.

That's what the cipher said. Wasn't Prague an old hunting ground of his?

Cover, of course. And not a very good one. Scofield knew that his every move in Amsterdam was now being watched, probably by teams of Company men. And if he had walked to the diamond exchange on the Tolstraat, he undoubtedly would have been shot.

He was admitted into the safe-house by a nondescript maid of indeterminate age, a servant convinced that the old house belonged to the retired couple who lived there and paid her. He said he had an appointment with the owner and his attorney. The maid nodded and showed him up the stairs to the first-floor sitting room.

The old gentleman was there but not the man from State. When the maid closed the door, the owner spoke.

'I'll wait a few minutes and then go back up to my apartment. If you need anything, press the button on the telephone; it rings upstairs.'

'Thanks,' said Scofield, looking at the Dutchman, reminded of another old man on a bridge. 'My associate should be along shortly. We won't need anything.'

The man nodded and left. Bray wandered about the room, absently fingering the books on the shelves. It occurred to him that he wasn't even trying to read the titles; actually he didn't see them. And then it struck him that he didn't feel anything, neither cold nor heat, not even anger or resignation. He didn't feel *anything*. He was somewhere in a cloud of vapour, numbed, all senses dormant. He wondered what he would say to the man who had flown thirty-five hundred miles to see him.

He did not care.

He heard footsteps on the stairs beyond the door. The maid had obviously been dismissed by a man who knew his way in this house. The door opened and the man from State walked in.

Scofield knew him. He was from Planning and Development, a strategist for covert operations. He was around Bray's age, but thinner, a bit shorter, and given to old-school-tie exuberance which he did not feel but which he hoped concealed his ambition. It did not.

'Bray, how *are* you, old buddy?' he said in a half-shout, extending an exuberant hand for a more exuberant grip. 'My God, it must be damn near two years! Have I got a couple of stories to tell *you*!'

'Really?'

'*Have I!*' An exuberant statement, no question implied. 'I went up to Cambridge for my twentieth and naturally ran into friends of yours right and left. Well, old buddy, I got pissed and couldn't remember what lies I told *who* about you! Christ Almighty, I had you an import analyst in Malaya, a language expert in New Guinea, an under-secretary in Canberra. It was hysterical. I mean, I couldn't *remember* I was so pissed.'

'Why would anyone ask about me, Charlie?'

'Well, they knew we were both at State; we were friends, everybody knew that.'

'Cut it out. We were never friends. I suspect you dislike me almost as much as I dislike you. And I've never seen you drunk in your life.'

The man from State stood motionless; the exuberant smile slowly disappeared from his lips. 'You want to play it rough?'

'I want to play it as it is.'

'What happened?'

'Where? When? At Harvard?'

'You know what I'm talking about. The other night. What happened the other night?'

'You tell me. You set it in motion, you spun the first wheels.'

'We uncovered a dangerous security leak. A pattern of active espionage going back years that reduced the

50

effectiveness of space surveillance to the point where we now know it's been a mockery. We wanted it confirmed; you confirmed it. You knew what had to be done and you walked away.'

'I walked away,' agreed Scofield.

'And when confronted with the fact by an associate, you did bodily injury to him. To your *own man*!'

'I certainly did. If I were you I'd get rid of him. Transfer him to Chile; you can't fuck up a hell of a lot more down there.'

'*What?*'

'On the other hand, you won't do that. He's too much like you, Charlie. He'll never learn. Watch out. He'll take your job one day.'

'Are you drunk?'

'No, I'm sorry to say. I thought about it, but I've got a little acidity in my stomach. Of course, if I'd known they were sending you, I might have fought the good fight and tried. For old times' sake, naturally.'

'If you're not drunk, you're off your trolley.'

'The track veered; those wheels you spun couldn't take the curve.'

'Cut the horseshit!'

'What a dated phrase, Charlie. These days we say bullshit, although I prefer lizardshit . . .'

'That's enough! Your action – or should I say *in*action – compromised a vital aspect of counter-espionage.'

'Now, *you* cut the horseshit!' roared Bray, taking an ominous step towards the man from State. 'I've heard all I want to hear from you! I didn't compromise anything. *You* did! You and the rest of those bastards back there. You found an ersatz leak in your Goddamned sieve and so you had to plug it up with a corpse. Then you could go to the Forty Committee and tell *those* bastards how efficient you were!'

'What are you talking about?'

'The old man *was* a defector. He was reached, but he *was* a *defector*.'

'What do you mean "reached"?' asked the man from State defensively.

'I'm not sure; I wish I did. Somewhere in that Four-Zero dossier something was left out. Maybe a wife that never died, but was in hiding. Or grandchildren no one bothered to list. I don't know but it's there. Hostages, Charlie! That's why he did what he did. And I was his *listok*.'

'What's that mean?'

'For Christ's sake, learn the language. You're supposed to be an expert.'

'Don't pull that language crap on me, I *am* an expert. There's no evidence to support an extortion theory, no family reported or referred to by the target at any time. He was a dedicated agent for Soviet intelligence.'

'*Evidence?* Oh, come on, Charlie, even you know better than that. If he was good enough to pull off a defection, he was smart enough to bury what had to be buried. My guess is that the key was timing, and the timing blew up. His secret – or secrets – were found out. He was reached; it's all through his dossier. He lived abnormally, even for an abnormal existence.'

'We rejected that approach,' said the man from State emphatically. 'He was an eccentric.'

Scofield stopped and stared. 'You rejected? . . . An eccentric? Goddamn you, you *did* know. You could have *used* that, fed him anything you liked. But no, you wanted a quick solution so the men upstairs would see how good you were. You could have *used* him, not killed him! But you didn't know how, so you kept quiet and called out the hangmen.'

'That's preposterous. There's no way you could prove he'd been reached.'

'Prove it? I don't have to prove it, I know it.'

'How?'

'I saw it in his eyes, you son of a bitch.'

The man from State paused, then spoke softly. 'You're tired, Bray. You need a rest.'

'With a pension?' asked Scofield. 'Or with a casket?'

4

Taleniekov walked out of the restaurant into a cold blast of wind that disturbed the snow, swirling it up from the pavement with such force that it became a momentary haze, diffusing the light of the streetlamp above. It was going to be another freezing night. The weather report on Radio Moscow had the temperature dropping below minus eight Celsius.

Yet it had stopped snowing early that morning; the runways at Sheremetyevo Airport were cleared and that was all that concerned Vasili Taleniekov at the moment. Air France, Flight 85, had left for Paris ten minutes ago. Aboard that plane was a Jew who was scheduled to leave two hours later on Aeroflot for Athens.

He would not have left for Athens if he had shown up at the Aeroflot terminal. Instead, he would have been asked to step into a room. Greeting him would have been a team from the *Vodennaya Kontra Rozvedka*, and the absurdity would have begun.

It was stupid, thought Taleniekov, as he turned right, pulling the lapels of his overcoat up around his neck and the brim of his *addyel* lower on his head; it *was* freezing; it would soon snow again. Stupid in the sense that the VKR would have accomplished nothing but provide a wealth of embarrassment. It would have fooled no one, least of all those it was trying to impress.

A dissident recanting his dissidency! What comic literature did the young fanatics in the VKR read? Where were the older and wiser heads when fools came up with such schemes?

When Vasili had heard of the plan, he had laughed,

actually *laughed*. The objective was to mount a brief but strong campaign against Zionist accusations, to show people in the West that not all Jews thought alike in Soviet Russia.

The Jewish writer had become something of a minor cause in the American press – the New York press, to be specific. He had been among those who had spoken to a visiting senator in search of votes eight thousand miles away from a constituency. But race notwithstanding, he simply was not a good writer, and, in fact, something of an embarrassment to his co-religionists.

Not only was the writer the wrong choice for such an exercise, but for reasons intrinsic to another operation it was imperative that he be permitted to leave Russia. He was a blind trade-off for the senator in New York. The senator had been led to believe it was his acquaintanceship with an attaché at the consulate that had caused Soviet emigration to issue a visa; the senator would make capital out of the incident and a small hook would exist where one had not existed before. Enough hooks and an awkward relationship would suddenly exist between the senator and 'acquaintances' within the Soviet power structure; it could be useful. The Jew had to leave Moscow tonight. In three days the senator had scheduled a welcoming news conference at Kennedy Airport.

But the young aggressive thinkers at the VKR were adamant. The writer would be detained, brought to the *Lubyanka* – where the VKR had its headquarters replete with laboratories – and the process of transformation would commence. No one outside the VKR was to be told of the operation; success depended upon sudden disappearance, total secrecy. Chemicals would have been administered until the subject was ready for a different sort of news conference. One in which he revealed that Israeli terrorists had threatened him with reprisals against relatives in Tel Aviv if he did not follow their instructions and cry publicly to be able to leave Russia.

The scheme was preposterous and Vasili had said as much to his contact at the VKR, but was told confidentially that not even the extraordinary Taleniekov could interfere with Group Nine, *Vodennaya Kontra Rozvedka*. And what in the name of all the discredited Tzars was Group Nine?

It was the *new* Group Nine, his friend had explained. It was the successor to the infamous Section Nine, KGB, *Smert Shpionam*. That division of Soviet intelligence devoted exclusively to the breaking of men's minds and wills through extortion, torture and that most terrible of methods – killing loved ones in front of loved ones.

Killing was nothing strange to Vasili Taleniekov, but that kind of killing turned his stomach. The *threat* of such killing was often useful, but not the act itself. The State did not require it, and only sadists demanded it. If there was truly a successor to *Smert Shpionam*, then he would let it know with whom it had to contend within the larger sphere of KGB. Specifically, one 'extraordinary Taleniekov'. They would learn not to contradict a man who had spent twenty-five years roaming all of Europe in the cause of the State.

Twenty-five years. It had been a quarter of a century since a twenty-one-year-old student with a gift for languages had been taken out of his classes at the Leningrad University and sent to Moscow for three years of intensive training. It was training the likes of which the son of introspective Socialist teachers could barely believe. He had been plucked out of a quiet home where books and music and endless discussions of philosophy were the staple diet, and set down in a world of conspiracy and violence, where ciphers, codes and physical abuse were the main ingredients. Where all forms of surveillance and sabotage, espionage and the taking of life – not murder; murder was a term that had no application – were the subjects studied.

56

He might have failed had it not been for an incident that changed his life and gave him the motive to excel. It had been provided by animals . . . American animals.

He had been sent to East Berlin on a training exercise, an observer of undercover tactics at the height of the Cold War. He had formed a relationship with a young woman, a German girl who fervently believed in the cause of the Marxist state, and who had been recruited by the KGB. Her position was so minor her name was not even on a payroll; she was an unimportant organizer of demonstrations, paid with loose Reichsmarks from an expense drawer. She was quite simply a university student far more passionate in her beliefs than knowledgeable, a wild-eyed radical who considered herself a kind of Joan of Arc. But Vasili had loved her, loved her mad abandon, her impetuous grasping at life that was balanced by an ability to laugh.

They had lived together for several weeks and they were glorious weeks, filled with the excitement and anticipation of young love. And then one day she was sent across Checkpoint Kasimir. It was such an unimportant thing, a street-corner protest on the Kurfürstendamm. A child leading other children, mouthing words they barely understood, espousing commitments they were ill-prepared to accept. An unimportant ritual. Insignificant.

But not to the animals of the American Army of Occupation, G2 Branch, who set other animals upon her.

Her body was sent back in a hearse, her face bruised almost beyond recognition, the rest of her clawed to the point where the flesh was torn, the blood splotches of dried red dust. And the doctors had confirmed the worst. She had been repeatedly raped and sodomized, her pelvic area pounded by abuse.

Attached to the body – the note held in place by a nail driven into her arm – were the words: *Up your commie ass. Just like hers.*

Animals!

American animals who bought their way to victory without a shell having fallen on their soil, whose might was measured by unfettered industry that made enormous profits from the carnage of foreign lands, whose soldiers peddled cans of food to hungry children to gratify other appetites. All armies had animals, but the Americans were most offensive; they proclaimed such innocent right-eousness. Forever the proverb was right: beware the sanctimonious, beneath there is boiling dirt.

Taleniekov had returned to Moscow, the memory of the girl's obscene death burned into his mind. Whatever he had been, he became something else. According to many, he became the best there was, and by his own lights none could possibly wish to be better than he did. With all its faults – and there were many – the Marxist eventuality was the true democratic future. He had seen the enemy and he was filth. But that enemy had resources beyond imagination, wealth beyond belief; so it was necessary to be better than he was in things that could not be purchased. One had to learn to think as he did. Then out-think him. Vasili had understood this; he became the master of strategy and counter-strategy, the springer of unexpected traps, the deliverer of unanticipated shock – death in the morning sunlight on a crowded street corner.

Death in the Unter den Linden at five o'clock in the afternoon. At that hour when the traffic was at its maximum.

He had brought that about, too. He had avenged the murder of a laughing child-woman years later, when as the director of KGB operations, East Berlin, he had drawn the wife of an American killer across the checkpoint. She had been run down cleanly, professionally, with a minimum of conscious pain; it was a far more merciful death than that delivered by animals four years earlier.

He had nodded in appreciation at the news of that death, yet there was no joy. He knew what that man was going through, and deserved as it was, there was no elation. For Taleniekov also knew that man would not rest until he found his own vengeance.

He did. Three years later in Prague.

A brother.

Where was the hated Scofield these days? wondered Vasili. It was close to a quarter of a century for him, too. They each had served their causes well, that much could be said for both of them. But Scofield was more fortunate; things were less complicated in Washington, one's enemies within more defined. The despised Scofield did not have to put up with such amateurish maniacs as Group Nine, VKR. The American State Department had its share of madmen, but sterner controls were exercised, Vasili had to admit that. In a few years, if Scofield survived in Europe, he would retire to some remote place and grow chickens or oranges or drink himself into oblivion. He did not have to be concerned about surviving in Washington, just in Europe.

Taleniekov had to worry about surviving in Moscow.

Things . . . *things* had changed in a quarter of a century. And he had changed; tonight was an example, but not the first. He had covertly thwarted the objectives of a fellow intelligence unit. He would not have done so five years ago – perhaps even two years ago. He would have confronted the strategists of that unit, stating that he understood the necessity for their secrecy, but having learned of their plans, strenuously objected on professional grounds. He was an expert, and in his expert judgement, the operation was not only miscalculated but less vital than another with which it interfered.

He did not take such action these days. He had not done so during the past two years as director of the South-west Sectors. He had made his own decisions, caring little for the reactions of damn fools who knew far less than he did. Increasingly, those reactions caused minor furores back in Moscow, still he did what he believed was right. Ultimately, those minor furores became major grievances and he was recalled to the Kremlin and a desk where stratagems were remote, dealing with progressive abstractions such as shadowy hooks into an American politician.

Taleniekov had fallen, he knew that. It was only a question of time. How much time had he left? Would he be given a small *ferma* north of Grasnov and be told to grow his crops and keep his own council? Or would the maniacs interfere with that course of action too? Would they claim the 'extraordinary Taleniekov' was, indeed, too dangerous?

As he made his way along the street, Vasili felt so tired, so weary. Even the loathing he felt for the American killer who had murdered his brother was muted in the twilight of his feelings. He had so little feeling left.

The sudden snowstorm reached blizzard proportions, the winds gale force, causing eruptions of huge white sprays through the expanse of Red Square. Lenin's Tomb would be covered by morning. Taleniekov let the freezing particles massage his face as he trudged against the wind towards his flat. KGB had been considerate; his rooms were ten minutes from his office in Dzerzhinsky Square, three blocks away from the Kremlin. It was either consideration, or something less benevolent but infinitely more practical: his flat was ten minutes from the centres of crisis, three minutes in a fast automobile.

He walked into the entranceway of his building, stamping his feet as he pulled the heavy door shut, cutting off the harsh sound of the wind. As he always did, he checked his mail slot in the wall and, as always, there was nothing. It was a futile ritual that had become a meaningless habit for so many years, in so many mail slots, in so many different buildings.

The only personal mail he ever received was in foreign countries – under strange names – when he was in deep cover. And then the correspondence was in code and cipher, its meaning in no way related to the words on paper. Yet sometimes those words were very nice, often warm and friendly, and he would pretend for a few minutes that they were the real words, their meaning meant. But only for a few minutes; it did no good to pretend. Unless one was analysing an enemy.

He started up the narrow staircase, annoyed by the dim light of the low-wattage bulbs. He was quite sure the planners in Moscow's *Elektrichiskaya* did not live in such buildings.

Then he heard the creak. It was not the result of structural stress; it had nothing to do with the sub-freezing cold or the winds outside. It was the sound of a human being shifting his weight on a floorboard. His ears were the ears of a trained craftsman, distances judged quickly. The sound did not come from the landing above, but from higher up the staircase. His flat was on the next floor; someone was waiting for him to approach. Someone wanted him inside his rooms perhaps, egress awkward, a trap being set.

Vasili continued his climb, the rhythm of his footsteps unbroken. The years had trained him to keep such items as keys and cigarettes and coins in his left-hand pockets, freeing his right to reach quickly for a weapon, or to be used as a weapon itself. He came to the landing and turned; his door was only feet away, the upper staircase down the dimly lit corridor, around the bend of the railing.

There was the creak again, faint, barely heard, mixed with the sound of the distant wind outside. Whoever was on the staircase had moved back, and that told him two things: the intruder would wait until he was definitely inside the flat, and whoever it was was either careless or inexperienced or both. One did not move when this close to a quarry; the air was a conductor of motion.

In his left hand was his key; his right had unfastened the buttons of his overcoat and was now gripped around the handle of his automatic, strapped in an open holster across his chest. He inserted the key, opened the door, then yanked it shut, stepping back rapidly, silently into the shadows of the staircase. He stayed against the wall, his gun levelled in front of him over the railing.

The sound of footsteps preceded the rushing figure as it raced to the door. In the figure's left hand was an object; he could not see it now, it was hidden by the heavily clothed body. Nor were there seconds to wait. If the object was an explosive, it would be on a timer-release. The figure had raised his right hand to knock on the door.

'Press yourself into the door! Your *left hand in front* of you! Between your stomach and the wood! *Now!*'

'Please!' The figure spun half-way around; Taleniekov was on him, throwing him against the panel. He was a young man, a boy really, barely in his teens, thought Vasili. He was tall for his age, but his age was obvious from his face; it was callow, no trace of beard, the eyes wide and clear and frightened.

'Move back slowly,' said Taleniekov harshly. 'Raise your left hand. *Slowly.*'

The boy moved back, his left hand seen; it was clenched into a fist.

'I didn't do anything wrong, sir. I swear it!' The young man's whisper cracked in fear.

'Who are you?'

'Andrei Danilovich, sir. I live in the Cheryomushki.'

'You're a long way from home,' said Vasili, estimating that the housing development referred to by the boy was nearly forty-five minutes south of Red Square. 'The weather's terrible and someone your age could be picked up by the *militsianyer*.'

'I had to come here, sir,' answered the young man quickly. 'A man's been shot; he's hurt very badly. I think he's going to die. I am to give this to you.' The boy opened his left hand; in it was a brass emblem. An army insignia denoting the rank of general. Its design had not been used in over thirty years. 'The old man said to say the name Krupsky, Aleksie Krupsky. He made me say it several times so I wouldn't forget it. It's not the name he uses down at the Cheryomushki, but it's the one he said to give you. He said I must bring you to him. He's dying, sir!'

At the sound of the name, Taleniekov's mind raced back in time. Aleksie Krupsky! It was a name he had not heard in years, a name few people in Moscow wanted to hear. Krupsky was once the greatest teacher in the KGB, a man of infinite talent for killing and survival – as well he might be. He was the last of the notorious *istrebiteli*, that highly specialized group of *exterminators* that had been an élite outcrop of the old NKVD, its roots in the barely remembered OGPU.

But Aleksie Krupsky had disappeared – as so many had disappeared – at least a dozen years ago. There had been rumours linking him to the deaths of Beria and Zhukov, some even mentioning Stalin himself. Once in a fit of rage – or fear – Khrushchev had stood up in the Praesidium and called Krupsky and his associates a band of maniacal killers. That was not true; there was never any mania in the work of the *istrebiteli*, it was too methodical. Regardless, suddenly one day Aleksie Krupsky was no longer seen at the *Lubyanka*.

Yet there were other rumours. Those that spoke of documents prepared by Krupsky, hidden in some remote place, that were his guarantees to a personal old age. It was said these documents incriminated various leaders of the

Kremlin in scores of killings – reported, unreported and disguised. So it was presumed that Aleksie Krupsky was living out his life somewhere north of Grasnov, on a *ferma*, perhaps, growing crops and keeping his own council.

He had been the finest teacher Vasili ever had; without the old master's patient instructions, Taleniekov would have been killed years ago. 'Where is he?' asked Vasili.

'We brought him down to our flat. He kept pounding on the floor – our ceiling. We ran up and found him.'

'We?'

'My sister and I. He's a good old man. He's been good to my sister and me. Our parents are dead. And I think he will soon be dead, too. Please hurry, sir!'

The old man on the bed was not the Aleksie Krupsky Taleniekov remembered. The close-cropped hair and the clean-shaven face that once displayed such strength were no more. The skin was pale and stretched, wrinkled beneath the white beard, and the long white hair was a bird's nest of tiny thin strings – matted, separated, revealing splotches of greyish flesh that was Krupsky's gaunt skull. The man was dying and could barely speak. He lowered the covers briefly and lifted a blood-soaked cloth away from the perforated flesh of a bullet wound.

Virtually no time was spent on greetings; the respect and affection in each man's eyes were sufficient.

'I widened my pupils into the death-stare,' said Krupsky, smiling weakly. 'He thought I was dead. He had done his job and ran.'

'Who was it?'

'An assassin. Sent by the Corsicans.'

'The Corsicans? What are you talking about? What Corsicans?'

'The Matarese. They know I know . . . what they are doing, what they are about to do. I am the only one left who would recognize them, who would dare speak of them. I stopped the contacts once, but I had neither the courage – nor the ambition – to expose them.'

'I can't understand you.'

'I will try to explain.' Krupsky paused, gathering strength. 'A short while ago, a general named Blackburn was killed in America.'

'Yes, I know. The Chairman of the Joint Chiefs. We were not involved, Aleksie.'

'Are you aware that *you* were the one the Americans believed the most likely assassin?'

'No one told me. It's ridiculous.'

'No one tells you much any more, do they, my old student?'

'I don't fool myself, old friend. I've given. I don't know how much more I have to give. Grasnov is not far distant, perhaps.'

'If it is permitted,' interrupted Krupsky.

'I think it will be.'

'No matter . . . Last month, the scientist, Yurievich. He was murdered while on holiday up in a Provasoto *dacha*, along with Colonel Drigorin and the man, Brunov, from Industrial Planning.'

'I heard about it,' said Taleniekov. 'I gather it was horrible.'

'Did you read the report?'

'What report?'

'The one compiled by VKR . . .'

'Madmen and fools,' interjected Taleniekov softly.

'Not always,' corrected Krupsky. 'In this case they have specific facts, accurate as far as they go.'

'What are these supposedly accurate facts?'

Krupsky, breathing with difficulty, swallowed and continued. 'Shell casings, seven-millimetre, American. Bore markings from a Browning Magnum, Grade Four.'

'A brutal gun,' said Taleniekov, nodding. 'Very reliable.

And the last weapon that would be used by someone sent from Washington.'

'Also a fact that could be overlooked in the barrage of charges and counter-charges.' The old man paused, staring at his long-ago student. 'The gun used to kill General Blackburn was a Graz-Burya.'

Vasili raised his eyebrows. 'A prized weapon when obtainable.' He paused and added quietly, 'I favour mine.'

'Exactly. As the Magnum, Grade Four, is a favoured weapon of another.'

Taleniekov stiffened. 'Oh?'

'Yes, Vasili. VKR came up with several names it thinks could be responsible for Yurievich's death. The leading contender was a man you despise: "Beowulf Agate".'

Taleniekov spoke in a monotone. 'Brandon Scofield, Consular Operations. Code name, Prague – Beowulf Agate.'

'Yes.'

'Was he?'

'No.' The old man struggled to raise his head on the pillow. 'No more than you were involved with Blackburn's death. Don't you see? They know everything; even of operatives whose skills are proven but whose minds are tired. Who, perhaps, need a significant kill. Such men as you are diversions; there will be others. They shape events; they no longer serve them. They are testing the highest levels of power before they make their move.'

'Who? Who are *they*?'

'The Matarese. The Corsican fever . . .'

'What does that *mean*?'

'It spreads. It has changed, far more deadly in its new form.' The old *istrebitel* fell back on the pillow; talking was not easy for him.

'You must be clearer, Aleksie. I can see nothing. What is this Corsican fever, this . . . Matarese?'

Krupsky's eyes were wide, now staring at the ceiling;

he whispered. 'No one speaks; no one dares to speak. Our own Praesidium; England's Foreign Office, its MI6 board room; the French Société Diable d'État. And the Americans. Oh, never forget the Americans! The well-dressed men of the State Department, the cowards in CIA . . . No one speaks. We are all touched. We are stained by the Matarese.'

'*Stained?* How? What are you trying to say? What in heaven's name *is* the Matarese?'

The old man turned his head slowly; his lips trembled, his breathing was more difficult. 'Some say it goes back as far as Sarajevo. Others swear it claims Dollfuss, Bernadotte . . . even Trotsky on its list. We know about Stalin; we contracted for his death.'

'Stalin? It's true then what was said?'

'Oh, yes. Beria, too; we paid.' The *istrebitel*'s eyes seemed now to float out of focus. 'In 'forty-five . . . the world thought Roosevelt succumbed to a massive stroke.' Krupsky shook his head slowly, saliva at the corners of his mouth. 'There were financial interests who believed his policies with the Soviet Union were economically disastrous. They could not permit any further decisions on his part. They paid, and an injection was administered.'

Taleniekov was stunned. 'Are you telling me that Roosevelt was *killed*? By this *Matarese*?'

'Assassinated, Vasili Vasilievich Taleniekov. That is the word, and that is one of the truths no one will speak of. So many . . . for so many years. None dare talk of the contracts, the payments. The admissions would be catastrophic . . . for governments everywhere.'

'But *why*? Why was it used, this Matarese?'

'Because it was there. And available. And it removed the client from the scene.'

'It's preposterous! Assassins have been *caught*. There's been no such name ever mentioned!'

'You should know better than that, Vasili Vasilievich.

67

You've used the same technique yourself; no different from the Matarese.'

'What do you mean?'

'You both kill . . . and programme killers.' The old man acknowledged Taleniekov's nod. 'The Matarese was dormant for years. Then it came back, but it was not the same. Killings took place without clients, without payments. Senseless butchery without a pattern. Men of value kidnapped and slain; aircraft stolen or blown up in mid-air, governments paralysed – payments demanded or wholesale slaughter the result. The incidents have become more refined, more professional.'

'You're describing the work of terrorists, Aleksie. Terrorism has no central apparatus.'

Once again the old *istrebitel* struggled to raise his head. 'It does *now*. It has for the past several years. Baader-Meinhof, the Red Brigades, the Palestinians, the African maniacs – they all gravitate to the Matarese. It kills with impunity; it selects the subjects and leaves arrows that bring men and nations to the brink of disaster. It is throwing the two superpowers into chaos before it makes its boldest move. And that is to assume control of one or the other. Ultimately, both.'

'How can you be certain?'

'A man was caught, a blemish on his chest, a soldier of the Matarese. Chemicals were administered, everyone ordered from the room but my source. I had warned him.'

'*You?*'

'Hear me out. There is a timetable, but to speak of it would be to acknowledge the past; none dare do that! Moscow by assassination, Washington by purchase – murder if necessary. Two months, three at the outside; everything is in motion now. Action and reaction has been tested at the highest levels, unknown men positioned at the centres of power. Soon it will happen, and when it does, we are consumed. We are destroyed, subjects of the Matarese.'

'Where is this man?'

'Dead. The chemicals wore off; there was a cyanide pellet sewn into his skin. He tore his own flesh and reached it.'

'Assassinations? Purchase and murder? You must be more specific.'

Krupsky's breath came shorter as he fell back on the pillow. But strangely, his voice grew firmer. 'There is no time – I do not *have* the time. My source is the most reliable in Moscow – in all the Soviet.'

'Forgive me, dear Aleksie, you were the best, but you do not exist any more. Everyone knows that.'

'You must reach Beowulf Agate,' said the old *istrebitel*, as though Vasili had not spoken. 'You and he must find them. Stop them. Before one of us is taken, the other's destruction guaranteed. You and the man Scofield. You are the best now, and the best are needed.'

Taleniekov looked impassively at the dying Krupsky. 'That is something no one can ask me to do. If Beowulf Agate were in my vision, I would kill him. As he would kill me, if he were capable.'

'You are *insignificant*!' The old man's breath was exhausted; he had to breathe slowly, in desperation, to get the air back in his lungs. 'You have no time for yourselves, can't you understand that? They are in our clandestine services, in the most powerful circles of both governments. They used the two of you once; they will use you again, and *again*. They use only the best and they will kill only the best! You are their diversions, men and men like you!'

'Where is the proof?'

'In the pattern,' whispered Krupsky. 'I've studied it. I know it well.'

'What pattern?'

'The Graz-Burya shells in New York; the seven-milli-metre casings of a Browning Magnum in Provasoto. Within hours Moscow and Washington were at each other's throats. This is the way of the Matarese. It never kills without leaving evidence – often the killers themselves – but it is never the right evidence, never the true killers.'

'Men have been caught who pulled triggers, Aleksie.'

'For the wrong reasons, Vasili Vasilievich. Those reasons provided by the Matarese . . . Now, it takes us to the edge of chaos and overthrow.'

'But *why*?'

Krupsky turned his head, his eyes in focus, pleading. 'I don't *know*. The pattern is there but not the *reasons* for it. ⊤hat is what frightens me. One must go back to understand. The roots of the Matarese are in Corsica. The madman of Corsica; it started with him. The Corsican fever. Guillaume de Matarese. He was the high priest.'

'When?' asked Taleniekov. 'How long ago?'

'During the early years of the century. Before the first decade was over . . . Guillaume de Matarese and his council. The high priest and his ministers. They've come back. They must be stopped. You and the man, Scofield! Their last ploy was with you!'

'Who are they?' asked Vasili, disregarding the state-ment. 'Where are they?'

'No one knows.' The old man's voice was failing now. He was failing. 'The Corsican fever. It spreads.'

'Aleksie, *listen* to me,' said Taleniekov, disturbed by a possibility that could not be overlooked: the fantasies of a dying man could not be taken seriously. 'Who is this reliable source of yours? Who is the man so knowledgeable in Moscow – in all the Soviet? How did you get the information you've given me? About the killing of Blackburn, the VKR report on Yurievich? Above all, this unknown man who speaks of timetables?'

Through the personal haze of his approaching death,

Krupsky understood. A faint smile appeared on his thin, pale lips. 'Every few days,' he said, struggling to be heard, 'a driver comes to see me, perhaps take me for a ride in the countryside. Sometimes to meet quietly with another. It's the State's kindness to a pensioned old soldier whose name was appropriated. I am kept informed.'

'I don't understand, Aleksie.'

'The Premier of Soviet Russia is my son.'

Taleniekov felt a wave of cold rush through him. The revelation explained so much. The Premier had survived and won over so many others; he had emerged the victor as the barriers to power had been removed. One by one – selectively. Krupsky had to be taken seriously; the old *istrebitel* had possessed the information – the ammunition – to eliminate all who stood in the way of his son's march to premiership of Soviet Russia.

'Would he see me?'

'Never. At the first mention of the Matarese, he would have you shot. Try to understand, he would have no choice. But he knows I am right. He agrees, but will never acknowledge it; he cannot afford to. He simply wonders whether it is he or the American President who will be in the gunsight.'

'I understand.'

'Leave me now,' said the dying Krupsky. 'Do what you must do, Taleniekov. I have no more breath. Reach Beowulf Agate, find the Matarese. It must be stopped. The Corsican fever can spread no farther.'

'The Corsican fever? . . . In *Corsica*?'

'The answer may be there. Many, many years ago. I don't know.'

5

A coronary inefficiency had made it necessary for Robert
Winthrop to use a wheelchair, but in no way did it
impair the awareness of his mind, nor did he dwell on
the infirmity. He had spent his life in the service of his
government; there was never any lack of problems he
considered more important than himself.

Guests at his Georgetown home soon forgot the wheelchair. The slender figure with the graceful gestures and the
intensely interested face reminded them of the man he was:
an energetic aristocrat who had used his private fortune
to free himself from the marketplace and pursue a life of
public advocacy. Instead of an infirm elder statesman with
thinning grey hair and the still perfectly clipped moustache,
one thought of Yalta and Potsdam and an aggressive
younger man from the State Department forever leaning
over Roosevelt's chair or Truman's shoulder to clarify this
point or suggest that objection.

There were many in Washington – and in London and
Moscow as well – who thought the world would be a better
place had Robert Winthrop been made Secretary of State
by Eisenhower but the political winds had shifted and he
was not a feasible choice. And later, Winthrop could not
be considered; he had become involved in another area of
government that required his full concentration. He had
been quietly retained as Senior Consultant, Diplomatic
Relations, Department of State.

Twenty-six years ago Robert Winthrop had organized
a select division within State called Consular Operations.
And after sixteen years of commitment he had resigned –
some said because he was appalled at what his creation

72

had become, while others claimed he was only too aware of the necessary directions it had taken, but could not bring himself to make certain decisions. Nevertheless, during the ten years since his departure, he had been consistently sought out for advice and counsel. As he was tonight.

Consular Operations had a new director. A career intelligence officer named Daniel Congdon had been shifted from a ranking position at the National Security Agency to the clandestine chair at State. He had replaced Winthrop's successor and was finely attuned to the harsh decisions required by *Cons Op*. But he was new; he had questions. He also had a problem with a man named Scofield and was not sure how to handle it. He knew only that he wanted Brandon Alan Scofield terminated, removed from the State Department for good. His actions in Amsterdam could not be tolerated; they revealed a dangerous and unstable man. How much more dangerous would he be removed from the control of Consular Operations? It was a serious question; the attaché knew more about the State Department's clandestine networks than any other man alive. And since Scofield had initially been brought to Washington years ago by Ambassador Robert Winthrop, Congdon went to the source.

Winthrop had readily agreed to make himself available to Congdon but not in an impersonal office or an operations room. Over the years, the Ambassador had learned that men involved with clandestine operations instinctively reflected their surroundings. Short, cryptic sentences took the place of freer, rambling conversations wherein a great deal more could be revealed and learned. Therefore, he had invited the new director over for dinner.

The meal was finished, nothing of substance discussed. Congdon understood: the Ambassador was probing the surface before delving deeper. But now the moment had come.

'Let's go into the library, shall we?' said Winthrop, wheeling himself away from the table.

Once inside the book-lined room, the Ambassador wasted no time. 'So you want to talk about Brandon.'

'Very much so,' replied the new director of *Cons Op*.

'How do we thank such men for what they've done?' asked Winthrop. 'For what they've lost? The field extracts a terrible price.'

'They wouldn't be there if they didn't want to be,' said Congdon in polite counterpoint. 'If, for some reason, they didn't need it. But once having been out there and survived, there's another question. What do we do with them? They're walking explosives.'

'What are you trying to say?'

'I'm not sure, Mr Winthrop. I want to know more about him. Who is he? What is he? Where did he come from?'

'The child being the father of the man?'

'Something like that. I've read his file – a number of times, in fact – but I've yet to speak to anyone who really knows him.'

'I'm not sure you'll find such a person. Brandon . . .' The elder statesman paused briefly and smiled. 'Incidentally, he's called Bray, for reasons I've never understood. It's the last thing he does. Bray, I mean.'

'That's one of the things I have learned,' interrupted the director, returning Winthrop's smile as he sat down in a leather armchair. 'When he was a child he had a younger sister who couldn't say Brandon; she called him Bray. The name just stuck with him.'

'That must have been added to his file after I left. Indeed, I imagine a great deal has been added to that file. But as for his friends, or lack of them . . . he's simply a private person, quite a bit more so since his wife died.'

Congdon spoke quietly. 'She was killed, wasn't she?'

'Yes.'

'In fact, she was killed in East Berlin ten years ago next month. Isn't that right?'

'Yes.'

'And ten years ago next month you resigned the directorship of Consular Operations. The highly specialized unit you built.'

Winthrop turned, his eyes levelled at the new director. 'What I conceived and what finally emerged were two quite different entities. Consular Operations was designed as a humanitarian instrument, to facilitate the defection of thousands from a political system they found intolerable. As time went on – and circumstances seemed to warrant – the objectives were narrowed. The thousands became hundreds and, as other voices were heard, the hundreds were reduced to dozens. We were no longer interested in the scores of men and women who daily appealed to us, but instead listened to those select few whose talents and information were considered far more important than those of ordinary people. The unit concentrated on a handful of scientists and soldiers and intelligence specialists. As it does today. That's not what we began with.'

'But as you pointed our, sir,' said Congdon, 'the circumstances warranted the change.'

Winthrop nodded. 'Don't mistake me, I'm not naïve. I dealt with the Russians at Yalta, Potsdam, Casablanca. I witnessed their brutality in Hungary in 'fifty-six, and I saw the horrors of Czechoslovakia and Greece. I think I know what the Soviets are capable of as well as any strategist in covert services. And for years I permitted those more aggressive voices to speak with authority. I understood the necessity. Did you think I didn't?'

'Of course not. I simply meant . . .' Congdon hesitated.

'You simply made a connection between the murder of Scofield's wife and my resignation,' said the statesman kindly.

75

'Yes, sir, I did. I'm sorry, I didn't mean to pry. It's just that the circumstances . . .'

' "Warranted a change",' completed Winthrop. 'That's what happened, you know. I recruited Scofield; I'm sure that's in his file. I suspect that's why you're here tonight.'

'Then the connection . . . ?' Congdon's words trailed off.

'Accurate. I felt responsible.'

'But surely there were other incidents, other men . . . and women.'

'Not the same, Mr Congdon. Do you know why Scofield's wife was selected to be the target that afternoon in East Berlin?'

'I assume it was a trap meant for Scofield himself. Only she showed up and he didn't. It happens.'

'A trap meant for Scofield? In *East* Berlin?'

'He had contacts in the Soviet sector. He made frequent penetrations, set up his own calls. I imagine they wanted to catch him with contact sheets. Her body was searched, her purse taken. It's not unusual.'

'Your assumption being that he'd use his wife in the operation?' asked Winthrop.

Congdon nodded. 'Again, not unusual, sir.'

'Not unusual? I'm afraid in Scofield's case it was impossible. She was part of his cover at the embassy, but never remotely connected to his covert activities. No, Mr Congdon, you're wrong. The Russians knew they could never spring a trap on Bray Scofield in East Berlin. He was too good, too efficient . . . too elusive. So they tricked his wife into crossing the checkpoint and killed her for another purpose.'

'I beg your pardon?'

'An enraged man is a careless man. That's what the Soviets wanted to accomplish. But they, as you, misunderstood their subject. With his rage came a reaffirmation to sting the enemy in every way he could. If he was brutally professional before his wife's death, he was viciously so afterwards.'

'I'm still not sure I understand.'

'Try, Mr Congdon,' said Winthrop. 'Twenty-two years ago I ran across a government major at Harvard University. A young man with a talent for languages and a certain authority about him that indicated a bright future. He was recruited through my office, sent to the Maxwell School in Syracuse, then brought to Washington to become part of Consular Operations. It was a fine beginning for a possibly brilliant career in the State Department.' Winthrop paused, his eyes straying as if lost in a personal reverie. 'I never expected him to stay in *Cons Op*; strangely enough I thought of it as a springboard for him. To the diplomatic corps, to the ambassadorial level, perhaps. His gifts cried out to be used at international conference tables . . .

'But something happened,' continued the statesman, glancing absently back at the new director. 'As *Cons Op* was changing, so was Brandon Scofield. The more vital those highly specialized defections were considered, the more quickly the violence escalated. On both sides. Very early, Scofield requested commando training; he spent five months in Central America going through the most rigorous survival techniques – offensive and defensive. He mastered scores of codes and ciphers; he was as proficient as any cryptographer in NSA. Then he returned to Europe and became *the* expert.'

'He understood the requirements of his work,' said Congdon, impressed. 'Very commendable, I'd say.'

'Oh yes, very,' agreed Winthrop. 'Because, you see, it had happened; he'd reached his plateau. There was no turning back, no changing. He could never be accepted around a conference table; his presence would be rejected in the strongest diplomatic terms because his reputation was established. The bright young government major I'd recruited for the State Department was now a killer. No matter the justification, he was a professional killer.'

Congdon shifted his position in the chair. 'Many would say he was a soldier in the field, the battleground extensive, dangerous . . . never-ending. He had to survive, Mr Winthrop.'

'He had to and he did,' concurred the old gentleman. 'Scofield was able to change, to adapt to the new rules. But I wasn't. When his wife was killed, I knew I didn't belong. I saw what I had done: taken a gifted student for one purpose and seen that purpose warped. Just as the benign concept of Consular Operations had been warped – by circumstances that warranted those changes we spoke of. I had to face my own limitations. I couldn't continue any longer.'

'But you did ask to be kept informed of Scofield's activities for several years. That's in the file, sir. May I ask why?'

Winthrop frowned, as if wondering himself. 'I'm not sure. An understandable interest in him – even fascination, I suppose. Or punishment, perhaps; that's not out of the question. Sometimes the reports would stay in my safe for days before I read them. And, of course, after Prague I no longer wanted them sent to me. I'm sure that's in the file.'

'Yes, it is. By Prague, I assume you refer to the courier incident.'

'Yes,' answered Winthrop softly. ' "Incident" is such an impersonal word, isn't it? It fits the Scofield in that report. The professional killer, motivated by the need to survive – as a soldier survives, turned into a cold-blooded killer, motivated solely by vengeance. The change was complete.'

Again the new director of *Cons Op* shifted his position, crossing his legs uncomfortably. 'It was established that the courier in Prague was the brother of the KGB agent who ordered the death of Scofield's wife.'

'He was the brother, not the man who issued that order. He was a youngster, no more than a low-level messenger.'

'He might have become something else.'

'Then where does it end, Mr Congdon?'

'I can't answer that, Mr Winthrop. But I can understand Scofield's doing what he did. I'm not sure I wouldn't have done the same.'

'With no sense of righteousness,' said the ageing statesman, 'I'm not sure I would have. Nor am I convinced that young man in Cambridge twenty-two years ago would have done so. Am I getting through to you, as is so often asked these days?'

'Painfully, sir. But in my defence – and in defence of the current Scofield – we didn't create the world we operate in. I think that's a fair thing to say.'

'Painfully, fair, Mr Congdon. But you perpetuate it.' Winthrop wheeled his chair to his desk and reached for a box of cigars. He offered the box to the director, who shook his head. 'I don't like them, either, but ever since Jack Kennedy we're all expected to keep our supply of Havanas. Do you disapprove?'

'No. As I recall, the Canadian supplier was one of President Kennedy's more accurate sources of information about Cuba.'

'Have you been around that long?'

'I joined the National Security Agency when he was a senator . . . Did you know that Scofield has recently begun to drink steadily?'

'I know nothing about the current Scofield, as you called him.'

'His file indicates the use of alcohol, but no evidence of excess.'

'I would think not; it would interfere with his work.'

'It may be interfering now.'

'*May* be? It either is or it isn't. I don't think that's such a difficult thing to establish. If he's drinking a great deal, that's excess; it would have to interfere. I'm sorry to hear it, but I can't say I'm surprised.'

'Oh?' Congdon leaned forward in the chair. It was apparent that he thought he was about to be given the information he was seeking. 'When you knew him as well as you did, were there signs of potential instability?'

'None at all.'

'But you just said you weren't surprised.'

'I'm not. I wouldn't be surprised at any thinking man turning to alcohol after so many years of living so unnaturally. Scofield is – or was – a thinking man, and God knows he's lived unnaturally. If I'm surprised, it's only that it's taken so long to reach him, affect him. What got him through the nights?'

'Men condition themselves. As you put it, he adapted. Extremely successfully.'

'But still unnaturally,' maintained Winthrop. 'What are you going to do with him?'

'He's being recalled. I want him out of the field.'

'Good. Give him a desk and an attractive secretary and have him analyse theoretical problems. Isn't that the usual way?'

Congdon hesitated before replying. 'Mr Winthrop, I think I want him separated from the State Department.'

The creator of *Cons Op* arched his eyebrows. 'Really? Twenty-two years is insufficient for an adequate pension.'

'That's not a problem; generous settlements are made. It's common practice these days.'

'Then what does he do with his life? What is he? Forty-five . . . -six?'

'Forty-six.'

'Hardly ready for one of these, is he?' said the statesman, fingering the wheel of his chair. 'May I ask why you've come to that conclusion?'

'I don't want him around personnel involved with

covert activities. According to our latest information, he's displayed hostile reactions to basic policy. He could be a negative influence.'

Winthrop smiled. 'Someone must have pulled a beaut. Bray never did have much patience with fools.'

'I said *basic* policy, sir. Personalities are not the issue.'

'Personalities, Mr Congdon, unfortunately are *intrinsic* to basic policy. They form it. But that's probably beside the point . . . at this point. Why come to me? You've obviously made your decision. What can I add?'

'Your judgement. How will he take it? Can he be trusted? He knows more about our operations, our contacts, our tactics, than any man in Europe.'

Winthrop's eyes became suddenly cold. 'And what is your alternative, Mr Congdon?' he asked icily.

The new director flushed; he understood the implication. 'Surveillance. Controls. Telephone and mail intercepts. I'm being honest with you, sir.'

'Are you?' Winthrop now glared at the man in front of him. 'Or are you looking for a word from me – or a question – that you can use for another solution?'

'I don't know what you mean.'

'I think you do. I've heard how it's done, incidentally, and it appals me. Word is sent to Prague, or Berlin, or Marseilles that a man's no longer in sanction. He's finished, out. But he's restless, drinks a lot. Contacts' names might be revealed by this man, whole networks exposed. In essence, the word spreads: your lives are threatened. So it's agreed that another man, or perhaps two or three, get on planes from Prague or Berlin or Marseilles. They converge on Washington with but one objective: the silencing of that man who's finished. Everyone's more relaxed, and the American intelligence community – which has remained outside the *incident* – breathes easier. Yes, Mr Congdon, it appals me.'

The director of *Cons Op* remained motionless in the

chair. His reply was delivered in a quiet monotone. 'To the best of my knowledge, Mr Winthrop, that solution has been exaggerated far out of proportion to its practice. Again, I'll be completely honest with you. In fifteen years I've heard of its being exercised only twice, and in both . . . incidents . . . the agents out of sanction were beyond being salvaged. They had sold out to the Soviets; they *were* delivering names.'

'Is Scofield beyond salvage? That's the correct phrase, isn't it?'

'If you mean do I think he's sold out, of course not. It's the last thing he'd do. I really came here to learn more about him, I'm sincere about that. How is he going to react when I tell him he's terminated?'

Winthrop paused, his relief conveyed, then frowned again. 'I don't know because I don't know the current Scofield. It's drastic; what's he going to do? Isn't there a half-way measure?'

'If I thought there was one acceptable to us both, I'd leap at it.'

'If I were you I'd try to find one.'

'It can't be on the premises,' said Congdon firmly. 'I'm convinced of that.'

'Then may I suggest something?'

'Please do.'

'Send him as far away as you can. Some place where he'll find a peaceful oblivion. Suggest it yourself; he'll understand.'

'He will?'

'Yes. Bray doesn't fool himself, at least he never did. It was one of his finer gifts. He'll understand because I think *I* do. I think you've described a dying man.'

'There's no medical evidence to support that.'

'Oh, for God's sake!' said Robert Winthrop.

Scofield walked across the hotel room and turned off the television set. He had not seen an American news broadcast in several years – since he was last brought back for an inter-operations briefing – and he was not sure he wanted to see one again for the next several years. It wasn't that he thought all news should be delivered in the ponderous tones of a funeral, but the giggles and leers that accompanied descriptions of fire and rape struck him as odd. At any moment he ' expected the anchormen would throw spitballs at one another and dip the blond tresses of the vacuous arts' critic into a prop inkwell.

He looked at his watch; it was twenty past seven. He knew it because his watch read twenty past midnight; he was still on Amsterdam time. His appointment at the State Department was for eight o'clock.

P.M. That was standard for specialists of his rank, but what was not standard was the State Department itself. Attachés-at-large for Consular Operations invariably held strategy conferences in safe-houses, usually in the Maryland countryside, or perhaps in hotel suites in downtown Washington.

Never at the State Department. Not for specialists expected to return to the field. But then Bray knew he was not scheduled to return to the field. He had been brought back for only one purpose. Termination.

Twenty-two years and he was out. An infinitesimal speck of time into which was compressed everything he knew – everything he had learned, absorbed and taught. He kept waiting for his own reaction, but there was none. It was as though he were a spectator, watching the images of someone else on a white wall, the inevitable conclusion drawing near, but not drawing him into the events as they took place. He was only mildly curious. How would it be done?

The walls of Under-Secretary of State Daniel Congdon's office were white. There was a certain comfort in that, thought Scofield, as he half-listened to Congdon's droning narrative. He could see the images. Face after face, dozens of them, coming into focus and fading rapidly. Faces of people remembered and unremembered, staring, thinking, weeping, laughing, dying . . . death.

His wife. Five o'clock in the afternoon. Unter den Linden.

Men and women running, stopping. In sunlight, in shadows.

But where was he? He was not there.

He was a spectator.

Then suddenly he wasn't. He could not be sure he heard the words correctly. What had this coldly efficient under-secretary said? *Bern, Switzerland?*

'I beg your pardon?'

'The funds will be deposited in your name, proportionate allocations made annually.'

'In addition to whatever pension I'm entitled to?'

'Yes, Mr Scofield. And regarding that, your service record's been predated. You'll get the maximum.'

'That's very generous.' It *was*. Calculating rapidly, Bray estimated that his income would be over $50,000 a year.

'Merely practical. These funds are to take the place of any profits you might realize from the sale of books or articles based on your activities in Consular Operations.'

'I see,' said Bray slowly. 'There's been a lot of that recently, hasn't there? Marchetti, Agee, Snepp.'

'Exactly.'

Scofield could not help himself; the bastards *never* learned. 'Are you saying that if you'd banked funds for them they wouldn't have written what they did?'

'Motives vary, but we don't rule out the possibility.'

'Rule it out,' said Bray curtly. 'I know two of those men.'

'Are you rejecting the money?'

'Hell, no. I'll take it. When I decide to write a book, you'll be the first to know.'

'I wouldn't advise it, Mr Scofield. Such breaches of security are prohibited. You'd be prosecuted; years in prison inevitable.'

'And if you lost in the courts, there just *might follow* certain extralegal penalties. A shot in the head while driving in traffic, for example.'

'The laws are clear,' said the under-secretary. 'I can't imagine that.'

'I can. Look in my Four-Zero file. I trained with a man in Honduras. I killed him in Madrid. He was from Indianapolis and his name was . . .'

'I'm *not interested* in past activities,' interrupted Congdon harshly. 'I just want us to understand each other.'

'We do. You can relax. I'm not . . . breaching any security. I haven't the stomach for it. Also, I'm not that brave.'

'Look, Scofield,' said the under-secretary, leaning back in his chair, his expression pleasant. 'I know it sounds trite, but there comes a time for all of us to leave the more active areas of our work. I want to be honest with you.'

Bray smiled, a touch grimly. 'I'm always nervous when someone says that.'

'What?'

'That he wants to be honest with you. As if honesty was the last thing you should expect.'

'I *am* being honest.'

'So am I. If you're looking for an argument, you won't get it from me. I'll quietly fade away.'

'But we don't want you to do that,' said Congdon, leaning forward, his elbows on the desk.

'Oh?'

'Of course not. A man with your background is extraordinarily valuable to us. Crises will continue to arise; we'd like to be able to call upon your expertise.'

Scofield studied the man. 'But not in-territory.' A statement. 'Not in-strategy.'

'No. Not officially. Naturally, we'll want to know where you're living, what trips you make.'

'I'll bet you will,' said Bray softly. 'But for the record, I'm terminated.'

'Yes. However, we'd like it kept out of the record. A Four-Zero entry.'

Scofield did not move. He had the feeling that he was in the field, arranging a very sensitive exchange. 'Wait a minute, let me understand you. You want me officially terminated, but no one's supposed to know it. And although I'm officially finished, you want to maintain contact on a permanent basis.'

'Your knowledge is invaluable to us, you know that. And I think we're paying for it.'

'Why the Four-Zero then?'

'I'd have thought you'd appreciate it. Without official responsibilities you retain a certain status. You're still part of us.'

'I'd like to know why this way.'

'I'll be . . .' Congdon stopped, a slightly embarrassed smile on his face. 'We really *don't* want to lose you.'

'Then why terminate me?'

The smile left the under-secretary's face. 'I'll call it as I see it. You can confirm it with an old friend of yours if you like. Robert Winthrop. I told him the same thing.'

'Winthrop? He goes back a long time. What did you tell him?'

'That I don't want you around here. And I'm willing to pay out of budget and predate records to get you out. I listened to your words; you were taped by Charles Englehart in Amsterdam.'

Bray whistled softly. 'Old Crimson Charlie. I should have known it.'

'I thought you did. I thought you were sending us a

personal message. Nevertheless, we got it. We have a lot
to do here and your kind of obstinacy, your cynicism, isn't
needed.'

'Now, we're getting somewhere.'

'But everything else is true. We *do* need your expertise.
We have to be able to reach you any time. You have to be
able to reach *us*.'

Bray nodded. 'And the Four-Zero means that my
separation is top-secret. The field doesn't know I'm
terminated.'

'Precisely.'

'All right,' said Scofield, reaching into his pocket for
a cigarette. 'I think you're going to a lot of unnecessary
trouble to keep a string on me, but, as you said, you're
paying for it. A simple field directive could accomplish
the same thing: issue clearance until rescinded. Special
category.'

'Too many questions would be asked. It's easier this
way.'

'Really?' Bray lit the cigarette, his eyes amused. 'All
right.'

'Good.' Congdon shifted his weight in the chair. 'I'm
glad we understand each other. You've earned everything
we've given you and I'm sure you'll continue to earn
it . . . I was looking at your file this morning; you
enjoy the water. God knows your record's filled with
hundreds of contacts made in boats at night. Why not
try it in the daylight? You've got the money. Why not
go to someplace like the Caribbean and enjoy your life?
I envy you.'

Bray got up from his chair; the meeting was over.
'Thanks, I may do that. I like warm climates.' He extended
his hand; Congdon rose and took it. While they shook
hands, Scofield continued, 'You know that Four-Zero
business would make me nervous if you hadn't called me
in here.'

'What do you mean?' Their hands were clasped, but the movement stopped.

'Well, our own field personnel won't know I'm terminated, but the Soviets will. They won't bother me now. When someone like me is taken out-of-strategy, everything changes. Contacts, codes, ciphers, sterile locations; nothing remains the same. They know the rules; they'll leave me alone. Thanks very much.'

'I'm not sure I understand you,' said the under-secretary.

'Oh, come on, I said I'm grateful. We both know KGB-Washington keeps its cameras trained on this place twenty-four hours a day. No specialist who's to remain in sanction is *ever* brought here. As of an hour ago they know I'm out. Thanks again, Mr Congdon. It was considerate of you.'

The Under-Secretary of State, Consular Operations, watched as Scofield walked across the office and let himself out the door.

It was over. Everything. He would never have to hurry back to an antiseptic hotel room to see what covert message had arrived. No longer would it be necessary to arrange for three changes of vehicle to get from point *A* to point *B*. The lie to Congdon notwithstanding, the Soviets probably did know he had been terminated by now. If they didn't they would soon. After a few months of inactivity the KGB would accept the fact that he was no longer of value. The rules was constant; tactics and codes *were* altered. The Soviets would leave him alone; they would not kill him.

But the lie to Congdon had been necessary, if only to see the expression on his face. We'd like it kept out of the record. *Four-Zero entry!* The man was so transparent! He really believed he had created the climate for the execution of his own man, a man he considered dangerous.

That a supposedly active agent would be killed by the Soviets for the sake of a kill. Then – pointing to official separation – the Department of State would disclaim any responsibility.

The bastards *never* changed, but they knew so little. An execution for its own sake was pointless, the fallout often too hazardous. One killed for a purpose: to learn something by removing a vital link in a chain, or to stop something from happening. Or to teach a specific lesson. But always for a reason.

Except in instances like Prague, and even that could be considered a lesson. *A brother for a wife*.

But it was over. There were no strategies to create, no decisions to make that resulted in a defection or a turn-back, of someone living or not living. It was *over*.

Perhaps now even the hotel rooms would come to an end. And the stinking beds in rundown rooming houses in the worst sections of a hundred cities. He was so sick of them; he despised them all. With the exception of a single brief period – too brief, too *terribly brief* – he had not lived in a place he could call his own for twenty-two years.

But that terribly brief period, twenty-seven months in a lifetime, was enough to see him through the agonies of a thousand nightmares. The memories never left him; they would sustain him until the day he died.

It had been only a small flat in West Berlin, but it was the home of dreams and love and laughter he had never thought he'd be capable of knowing. His beautiful Karine, his adorable Karine. She of the wide, curious eyes and the laughter that came from deep inside her, and moments of quiet when she touched him. He was hers and she was his and . . .

Death in the Unter den Linden.

Oh, *God*! A telephone call and a password. Her husband needed her. *Desperately*. See a guard, cross the checkpoint. *Hurry!*

And a KGB pig had no doubt laughed. Until Prague. There was no laughter in that man after Prague.

Scofield could feel the sting in his eyes. The few sudden tears had made contact with the night wind. He brushed them aside with his glove and crossed the street.

On the other side was the lighted front of a travel agency, the posters in the window displaying idealized, unreal bodies soaking up the sun. The Washington amateur, Congdon, had a point; the Caribbean was a good idea. No self-respecting intelligence service sent agents to the islands in the Caribbean – for fear of winning. Another Cuba and the Kremlin might opt for a Section Eleven. Down in the islands, the Soviets would *know* he was out-of-strategy. He had wanted to spend some time in the Grenadines; why not now? In the morning he would . . .

The figure was reflected in the glass – tiny, obscure, in the background across the wide avenue, barely noticeable. In fact, Bray would *not* have noticed had the man not walked around the spill of a streetlamp. Whoever it was wanted the protection of the shadows in the street, whoever it was was following him. And he was good. There were no abrupt movements, no sudden jumping away from the light. The walk was casual, unobtrusive. He wondered if it was anyone he had trained.

Scofield appreciated professionalism; he would commend the man and wish him a lesser subject for surveillance next time. The State Department was not wasting a moment. Congdon wanted the reports to begin at once. Bray smiled; he would give the under-secretary his initial report. Not the one he wanted, but one he should have.

The amusement began, a short-lived pavane between professionals. Scofield walked away from the shop window, gathering speed until he reached the corner, where the circles of light from the four opposing streetlamps overlapped each other. He turned abruptly left, as if to head back to the other side of the street, then half-way through the intersection stopped. He paused in the middle of the traffic lane and looked up at the street sign – a man confused, not sure of where he was. Then he turned and walked rapidly back to the corner, his pace quickening until he was practically running when he reached the kerb. He continued down the pavement to the first unlighted shopfront, then he spun into the darkness of the doorway and waited.

Through the right-angled glass he had a clear view of the corner. The man following him would have to come into the overlapping circles of light now; they could not be avoided. A quarry was getting away! There was no time to look for shadows.

It happened. The overcoated figure came dashing across the avenue. His face came into the light.

His face came into the light.

Scofield froze. His eyes ached; blood rushed to his head. His whole body trembled, and what remained of his mind tried desperately to control the rage and the anguish that welled up and swept through him. The man at the corner was not from the State Department, the face under the light did not belong to anyone remotely connected to American intelligence.

It belonged to the KGB. To KGB-East Berlin.

It was a face on one of the half-dozen photographs he had studied – studied until he knew every blemish, every strand of hair – in Berlin ten years ago.

Death on the Unter den Linden. His beautiful Karine, his adorable Karine. Trapped by a team across the checkpoint, a unit set up by the filthiest killer in the Soviet. V. Taleniekov. Animal.

This was one of those men. That unit. One of Taleniekov's hangmen.

Here! In Washington! Within minutes of his termination at State!

So KGB had found out. And someone in Moscow had

decided to bring a stunning conclusion to the finish of Beowulf Agate. Only one man could think with such dramatic precision. V. Taleniekov. Animal.

As Bray stared through the glass, he knew what he was going to do, what he had to do. He would send a last message to Moscow; it would be a fitting capstone, a final gesture to mark the end of one life and the beginning of another – whatever it might be.

He would trap the killer from KGB. He would kill him.

Scofield stepped out of the doorway and ran down the sidewalk, racing in a zigzag pattern across the deserted street. He could hear running footsteps behind him.

6

Aeroflot's night flight from Moscow approached the Sea of Azov north-east of Crimea. It would arrive in Sevastopol by one o'clock in the morning, something over an hour. The aircraft was crowded, the passengers by and large jubilant, on winter holiday leaves from their offices and factories. A scattering of military personnel – soldiers and sailors – were less exuberant; for them the Black Sea was not a vacation, but a return to work at the naval and air bases. They'd had their leaves in Moscow.

In one of the rear seats sat a man with a dark leather violin case held firmly between his knees. His clothes were rumpled, undistinguished, somehow in conflict with the strong face and the sharp, clear eyes that seemed to belong above other apparel. His papers identified him as Pyotr Rydukov, musician. His flight pass explained curtly that he was on the way to join the Sevastopol Symphony Orchestra as a violinist.

Both items were false. The man was Vasili Taleniekov, master strategist, Soviet Intelligence.

Former master strategist. Former director of KGB operations – East Berlin, Warsaw, Prague, Riga and the South-west Sectors, which consisted of Sevastopol, the Bosphorus, the Sea of Marmara and the Dardanelles. It was this last post that dictated the papers that put him on board the Sevastopol plane. It was the beginning of his flight from Russia.

There were scores of escape routes out of the Soviet Union, and in his professional capacity he had exposed them as he had found them. Ruthlessly, more often than not killing the agents of the West who kept them open,

93

enticing malcontents to betray Russia with lies and promises of money. Always money. He had never wavered in his opposition to the liars and the proselytizers of greed; no escape route was too insignificant to warrant his attention.

Except one. A minor network-route through the Bosphorus and the Sea of Marmara into the Dardanelles. He had uncovered it several months ago, during his last weeks as director, KGB South-west Soviet Sectors. During the days when he found himself in continuous confrontation with hot-headed fools at the military bases and asinine edicts from Moscow itself.

At the time, he was not sure why he held back exposure; for a while he had convinced himself that by leaving it open and watching it closely, it could lead to a larger network. Yet in the back of his mind, he knew that was not true.

His time was coming; he was making too many enemies in too many places. There could be those who felt that a quiet retirement north of Grasnov was not for a man who held the secrets of the KGB in his head. Now he possessed another secret, more frightening than anything conceived of by Soviet intelligence. The Matarese. And that secret was driving him out of Russia.

It had happened so fast, thought Taleniekov, sipping the hot tea provided by the steward. *Everything* had happened so fast. The bedside – deathbed – talk with old Aleksie Krupsky and the astonishing things the dying man had said. Assassins sent forth to kill the élite of the nation – both nations. Pitting the Soviet and the United States against one another, until it controlled one or the other. A Premier and a President, one or both to be in a gunsight. Who were they? *What* were they, this fever that had begun in the first decades of the century in Corsica? The Corsican fever. The Matarese.

But it existed; it was functioning – alive and deadly. He knew that now. He had spoken its name, and for speaking it, a plan had been put in motion that called for his arrest; the sentence of execution would follow shortly.

Krupsky had told him that going to the Premier was out of the question so he had sought out four once-powerful leaders of the Kremlin, now generously retired, which meant that none dared touch them. With each he had spoken of the strange phenomenon called the Matarese, repeated the words whispered by the dying *istrebitel*.

One man obviously knew nothing; he was as stunned as Taleniekov had been. Two *said* nothing, but the acknowledgement was in their eyes, and in their frightened voices when they protested. Neither would be a party to the spreading of such insanity; each had ordered Vasili from his house.

The last man, a Georgian, was the oldest – older than the dead Krupsky – and in spite of an upright posture had little time left to enjoy a straight spine. He was ninety-six, his mind alert but given swiftly to an old man's fear. At the mention of the name Matarese, his thin, veined hands had trembled, then tiny muscular spasms seemed to spread across his ancient, withered face. His throat became suddenly dry; his voice cracked, his words barely audible.

It was a name from long ago in the past, the old Georgian had whispered, a name no one should hear. He had survived the early purges, survived the mad Stalin, the insidious Beria, but no one could survive the Matarese. In the name of all things sacred to Russia, the terrified man pleaded, walk *away* from the Matarese!

'We were fools, but we were not the only ones. Powerful men everywhere were seduced by the sweet convenience of having enemies and obstacles eliminated. The guarantee was absolute: the eliminations would never be traced to those who required them. Agreements were made through parties four and five times removed, dealing in fictitious purchases, unaware of what they were buying. Krupsky saw the danger; he knew. He warned us in 'forty-eight never to make contact again.'

'Why did he do that?' Vasili had asked. 'If the guarantee was proven true. I speak professionally.'

'Because the Matarese added a condition: the council of the Matarese demanded the right of approval. That's what I was told.'

'The prerogative of killers-for-hire, I'd think,' Taleniekov had interjected. 'Some targets simply aren't feasible.'

'Such approval was never sought in the past. Krupsky did not think it was based on feasibility.'

'On what, then?'

'Ultimate extortion.'

'How were the contacts made with this council?'

'I never knew. Neither did Aleksie.'

'*Someone* had to make them.'

'If they are alive, they will not speak. Krupsky was right about that.'

'He called it the Corsican fever. He said the answers might be in Corsica.'

'It's possible. It's where it began, with the maniac of Corsica. Guillaume de Matarese.'

'You still have influence with the party leaders, sir. Will you help me? Krupsky told me this Matarese must be . . .'

'*No!*' the old man had screamed, interrupting. 'Leave me in peace! I've said more than I should, admitted more than I had a right to. But only to warn you, to *stop* you! The Matarese can do no good for Russia! Turn your back on it!'

'You've misunderstood me. It is *I* who want to stop *it. Them.* This Matarese council. I gave my word to Aleksie that . . .'

'But you've had no words with *me!*' the withered, once-powerful leader had shouted, his voice childlike in its panic. 'I will deny you ever came here, deny anything you say! You are a stranger, and I do not know you!'

Vasili had left, disturbed, perplexed. He had returned to his flat expecting to spend the night analysing the enigma that was the Matarese, trying to decide what to do next.

As usual he had glanced at the mail slot in the wall; he had actually taken a step away before he realized there *was* something inside.

It was a note from his contact at the VKR, written in one of the eliptical codes they had arranged between them. The words were innocuous: an agreement to have a late dinner at 11.30 and signed with a girl's first name. The very blandness of the note concealed its meaning. There was a problem of magnitude; the use of *eleven* meant emergency. No time was to be lost making contact; his friend would be waiting for him at the usual place.

He had been there. At a *piva kafe* near the Lomonossov State University. It was a raucous drinking establishment in tune with the new student permissiveness. They had moved to the rear of the hall; his contact had wasted no seconds getting to the point.

'Make plans, Vasili, you're on their list. I don't understand it but that's the word.'

'Because of the Jew?'

'Yes, and it doesn't make sense! When that idiotic news conference was held in New York, we division men laughed. We called it "Taleniekov's surprise". Even a section chief from Group Nine said he admired what you did; that you taught a lesson to impetuous potato-heads. Then yesterday everything changed. What you did was no longer a joke, but rather a serious interference with basic policy.'

'Yesterday?' Vasili had asked his friend.

'Late afternoon. Past four o'clock. That bitch director marched through the offices like a gorilla in season. She smelled a gang rape and she loved it. She told each division man to be at her office at five o'clock. When we got there and listened, it was unbelievable. It was as if you were personally responsible for every setback we've sustained for the past two years. Those maniacs from Group Nine were there, but not the section chief.'

'How long have I got?'

'Three or four days at the outside. Incriminating evidence against you is being compiled. But silently, no one is to say anything.'

'Yesterday . . .'

'What happened, Vasili? This isn't a VKR operation. It's something else.'

It *was* something else and Taleniekov had recognized it instantly. The yesterday in question had been the day he had seen the two former Kremlin officials who had ordered him from their homes. The something else was the Matarese.

'One day I'll tell you, my friend,' Vasili had answered. 'Trust me.'

'Of course. You're the best we have. The best we've ever had.'

'Right now I need thirty-six, perhaps forty-eight hours. Do I have them?'

'I think so. They want your head, but they'll be careful. They'll document as much as they can.'

'I'm sure they will. One needs words to read over the corpse. Thank you. You'll hear from me.'

Vasili had not returned to his flat, but instead to his office. He had sat in the darkness for hours, arriving at his extraordinary decision. Hours before it would have been unthinkable, but not now. If the Matarese could corrupt the highest levels of the KGB, it could do the same in Washington. If the mere mentioning of its name called for the death of a master strategist of his rank – and there was no mistaking it: death was the objective – then the power it possessed was unthinkable. If, in truth, it was responsible for the murders of Blackburn and Yurievich, then Krupsky was right. There was a timetable. The Matarese were closing in, the Premier or President moving into the gunsight.

He had to reach a man he loathed. He had to reach Brandon Alan Scofield, American killer.

In the morning, Taleniekov had put several wheels in motion, one after the other. With his customary – if curtailed – freedom of decision, he let it be known quietly that he was travelling under cover to the Baltic Sea for a conference. He then scoured the rolls of the Musicians' Protective and found the name of a violinist who had retired five years ago to the Ural Mountains; he would do. Lastly, he had put the computers to work looking for a clue to the whereabouts of Brandon Scofield. The American had disappeared in Marseilles, but an incident had taken place in Amsterdam that bore the unmistakable mark of Scofield's expertise. Vasili had sent a cipher to an agent in Brussels, a man he could trust for he had saved his life on more than one occasion.

> Approach Scofield, white status. Amsterdam. Contact must be made. Imperative. Stay with him. Apprise situation South-west Sector codes.

Everything had happened so rapidly, and Taleniekov was grateful for the years that made it possible for him to arrive at swift decisions. Sevastopol was less than an hour away. In Sevastopol – and beyond – those years of hard experience would be put to the test.

He took a room at a small hotel on the boulevard Chersonesus and called a number at the KGB head-quarters that was not attached to a recorder; he had installed it himself.

VKR-Moscow had not as yet put out an alarm for him, that much could be ascertained from headquarters' warm greeting. An old friend had returned; it gave Vasili the latitude he needed.

'To be frank,' he said to the night duty officer, a former associate, 'we have our on-going problem with VKR. They've interfered again. You may get a teletype inquiry. You haven't heard from me, all right?'

'That's no problem as long as you don't show up here; you called on the right telephone. Are you staying in cover?'

'Yes. I won't burden you with my whereabouts. We're involved with a courier probe, convoys of trucks heading for Odessa, then south to the mountains. It's a CIA network.'

'That's easier than fishing boats through the Bosphorus. By the way, does Amsterdam fit into your blueprints?'

Taleniekov was startled. He had not expected so quick a reply from his man there. 'It could. What have you got?'

'It came in two hours ago; it took that long to break. Our cryptographer – the man you brought from Riga – recognized an old code of yours. We were going to send it on to Moscow with the morning's dispatches.'

'Don't do that,' said Vasili. 'Read it to me.'

'Wait a minute.' Papers were shuffled. 'Here it is. "Beowulf removed from orbit. Storm clouds Washington. On strength of imperative will pursue and deliver white contact. Cable instructions capitol depot." That's it.'

'It's enough,' said Taleniekov.

'Sounds impressive, Vasili. A white contact? You've struck a high-level defection, I gather. Good for you. Is it tied in with your probe?'

'I think so,' lied Taleniekov. 'But don't say anything. Keep VKR out.'

'With pleasure. You want us to cable for you?'

'No,' replied Vasili, 'I can do it. It's routine. I'll call you this evening. Say nine-thirty; that should be time enough. Tell my old friend from Riga I said hello. No one else, however. And thank you.'

'When your probe's over, let's have dinner. It's good to have you back in Sevastopol.'

'It's good to be back. We'll talk.' Taleniekov hung up, concentrating on the message from Amsterdam. Scofield had been recalled to Washington, but the circumstances were abnormal. Beowulf Agate had run into a severe State Department storm. That fact alone was enough to propel the agent from Brussels into a transatlantic pursuit, debts notwithstanding. A white status contact was a momentary truce; a truce generally meant that someone was about to do something drastic. And if there existed even the remote possibility that the legendary Scofield might defect, any risk was worth the candle. The man who brought in Beowulf Agate would have all of Soviet Intelligence at his feet.

But defection was not possible for Scofield . . . any more than it was for him. The enemy was the enemy; that would never change.

Vasili picked up the phone again. There was an all-night number in the Lazarev district of the waterfront used by Greek and Iranian businessmen to send out cables to their home offices. By saying the right words, priority would be given over the existing traffic; within several hours his cable would reach 'capitol depot'. It was a hotel on Nebraska Avenue in Washington, D.C.

He would meet Scofield on neutral ground, some place where neither could take advantage of the location. Within the departure gates of an airline where the security measures were the harshest – West Berlin or Tel Aviv, it did not matter; distance was inconsequential. But they had to meet, and Scofield had to be convinced of the necessity of that meeting. The cipher to Washington instructed the man from Brussels to convey the following to Beowulf Agate.

We have traded in blood very dear to both of us. In truth, I more than you but you could not know it. Now there is another who would hold us responsible for international slaughter on a scale to which neither of us can subscribe. I operate outside of authority and alone. We must exchange views – as loathsome as it may be to

101

both of us. Choose a neutral location, within an airport security compound. Suggest El Al, Tel Aviv or German domestic carrier, West Berlin. This courier will know how to reply.

My name is known to you.

It was nearly four o'clock in the morning before he closed his eyes. He had not slept in nearly three days, and when sleep came, it was deep and long. He had gone to bed before there was any evidence of the sun in the eastern sky; he awoke an hour after it had descended in the west. That was good. His mind and his body had needed the rest, and one travelled at night to the place he was going in Sevastopol.

There were three hours before the duty officer arrived at KGB; it was simpler not to involve anyone else at headquarters. The fewer who knew he was in the city, the better. Of course, the cryptographer knew, he had deduced the connection from the cipher out of Amsterdam, but the man would say nothing. Taleniekov had trained him, taken a bright young man from the austerity of Riga to the freer life in Sevastopol.

The time could be well spent, thought Vasili. He would eat, then make arrangements for passage in the hold of a Greek freighter that would cut straight across the sea, then follow the southern coast through the Bosphorus, and on to the Dardanelles. If any of the Greek or Iranian units in the pay of the CIA or SAVAK recognized him – and it was possible – he would be entirely professional. As the previous director of the KGB sector, he had not exposed the escape route for personal reasons. However, if a musician named Pyotr Rydukov did not make a telephone call to Sevastopol within two days after departure, exposure was guaranteed, KGB reprisals to follow. It would be a shame; other privileged men might wish to use the route later, their talents and information worth having.

Taleniekov put on the undistinguished, ill-fitting overcoat and his battered hat. A slouch and a pair of steel-rimmed spectacles were added. He checked his appearance in the mirror; it was satisfactory. He picked up the leather violin case; it completed his disguise, for no musician left his instrument in a strange hotel room. He went out the door, down the staircase – never an elevator – and out into the Sevastopol streets. He would walk to the waterfront; he knew where to go and what to say.

Fog rolled in from the sea, curling through the beams of the floodlights on the pier. There was activity everywhere as the hold of the freighter was loaded. Men shouted as giant cranes swung cables cradling enormous boxcars of merchandise over the side of the ship. The loading crews were Russian, supervised by Greeks. Soldiers and *militsianyeri* milled about, weapons slung casually over their shoulder, ineffectual patrols more interested in watching the machinery than in looking for irregularities.

If they wanted to know, mused Vasili as he approached the officer at the entrance gate, he could tell them. The irregularities were in the huge containers being lifted over the hull of the ship. Men and women packed in shredded cardboard, tubes from mouths to airspaces where necessary, instructions having been given to empty bladders and bowels several hours ago; there would be no relief until well past midnight when they were at sea.

The officer at the gate was a young lieutenant, bored with his work, irritation in his face. He scowled at the slouching, bespectacled old man before him.

'What do you want? The pier is off-limits unless you have a pass.' He pointed to the violin case. 'What's that?'

'My livelihood, Lieutenant. I'm with the Sevastopol Symphony.'

'I wasn't aware of any concerts scheduled for the docks.'

'Your name, please?' said Vasili casually.

'What?'

Taleniekov stood up to his full height, the slouch gradually but clearly disappearing. 'I asked you your name, Lieutenant.'

'What for?' The officer was somewhat less hostile. Vasili removed the spectacles and looked sternly into his bewildered eyes.

'For a commendation or a reprimand.'

'What are you talking about? Who are you?'

'KGB-Sevastopol. This is part of our waterfront inspection programme.'

The young lieutenant was politely hesitant; he was not a fool. 'I'm afraid I wasn't told, sir. I'll have to ask for your identification.'

'If you didn't, it would be the first reprimand,' said Taleniekov, reaching into his pocket for his KGB card. 'The second would come if you speak of my appearance here tonight. The name, please.'

The lieutenant told him, then added, 'Do you people suspect trouble down here?' He studied the plastic card and returned it.

'Trouble?' Taleniekov smiled, his eyes humorous and conspiratorial. 'The only trouble, Lieutenant, is that I'm being deprived of a warm dinner in the company of a lady. I think the new directors in Sevastopol feel compelled to earn their roubles. You men are doing a good job; they know that but don't care to admit it.'

Relieved, the young officer smiled back. 'Thank you, sir. We do our best in a monotonous job.'

'But don't say anything about my being here; they're serious about that. Two officers of the guard were reported last week.' Vasili smiled again. 'In the directors' secrecy lies their true security. Their jobs.'

The lieutenant grinned. 'I understand. Have you a weapon in that case?'

'No. Actually, it's a very good violin. I wish I could play it.'

Both men nodded knowingly. Taleniekov continued on to the pier, into the mêlée of machinery, dock workers and supervisors. He was looking for a specific supervisor, a Greek from Kaválla named Zaimis. Which was to say he was looking for a man whose heritage was Greek and whose mother's name was Zaimis, but whose citizenship was American.

Karras Zaimis was a CIA agent, formerly station chief in Salonika, now field expediter of the escape route. Vasili knew the agent's face from several photographs he had removed from the KGB files. He peered through the bodies and the fog and the floodlights; he could not spot the man.

Taleniekov threaded his way past rushing fork-lifts and crews of complaining labourers towards the huge cargo warehouse. Inside the enormous enclosure, the light was dim, the wire-meshed floodlights too high in the ceiling to do much good. Beams of flashlights crisscrossed the containers; men were checking numbers. Vasili wondered briefly how much talent was in those boxcars. How much information was being taken out of Russia. Actually, not a great deal of either, he reminded himself. This was a minor escape route; more comfortable accommodation was provided for serious talent and significant bearers of intelligence data.

His slouch controlling his walk and his spectacles awkwardly in place, he excused himself past a Greek supervisor arguing with a Russian foreman. He wandered towards the rear of the warehouse, past stacks of cartons and aisles blocked with freight dollies, studying the faces of those holding flashlights. He was becoming annoyed; he did not have the time to waste. Where was Zaimis? There had been *no* change of status; the freighter *was* the carrier, the agent *still* the conduit. He had read every report sent from Sevastopol; there had been no mention of the escape route whatsoever. Where *was* he?

Suddenly Taleniekov felt a shock of pain as the barrel of a gun was shoved viciously into his right kidney. Strong fingers gripped the loose cloth of his overcoat, crunching the flesh of his lower rib cage; he was propelled into a deserted aisle. Words were whispered harshly in English.

'I won't bother speaking Greek, or trying to get through to you in Russian. I'm told your English is as good as anyone's in Washington.'

'Conceivably better than most,' said Vasili through his teeth. 'Zaimis?'

'Never heard of him. We thought you were out of Sevastopol.'

'I am. Where is Zaimis? I must speak with Zaimis.'

The American disregarded the question. 'You've got balls, I'll say that for you. There's no one from KGB within ten blocks of here.'

'Are you sure about that?'

'Very. We've got a flock of night owls out there. They see in the dark. They saw you. A violin case, *Christ*!'

'Do they look to the water?'

'Seagulls do that.'

'You're very well organized, all you birds.'

'And you're less bright than everyone says. What did you think you were doing? A little personal reconnaissance?'

Vasili felt the grip lessen on his ribs, then heard the muted sound of an object pulled out of rubber. A vial of serum. A *needle*. 'Don't!' he said firmly. 'Don't do that! Why do you think I'm here alone? I want to get out.'

'That's just where you're going. My guess would be an interrogation hospital somewhere in Virginia for about three years.'

'*No*. You don't understand. I have to make contact with someone. But not *that* way.'

106

'Tell it to the nice doctors. They'll listen to everything you say.'

'There's no time!' There *was* no time. Taleniekov could feel the man's weight shift; in seconds a needle would puncture his clothes and enter his flesh. It could not happen this way! He could not deal with Scofield officially!

None dare talk. The admissions would be catastrophic . . . for governments everywhere. The Matarese.

If he could be destroyed in Moscow, the Americans would not think twice about silencing him.

Vasili raised his right shoulder – a gesture of pain from the gun barrel in his kidney. The gun was abruptly pressed farther into his back – a reaction to the gesture. In that split instant, the pressure point of the hand holding the gun was on the heel of the palm, not the index finger; but only for the briefest of instants. Taleniekov's movement was timed for it.

He spun to his left, his arm arching up, crashing down over the American's elbow, vicing it into his hip until the forearm cracked. He jabbed the fingers of his right hand into the man's throat, bruising the windpipe. The gun fell to the floor, its clatter obscured by the din of the warehouse. Vasili picked it up and shoved the CIA agent against a boxcar container. In his pain, the American held the hypodermic needle limply in his left hand; it, too, dropped to the floor. His eyes were glazed, but not beyond cognizance.

'Now, you *listen* to me,' said Taleniekov, his face against Zaimis' face. 'I've known about "Operation Dardanelles" for nearly seven months. You deal in mediocre traffic; you're not significant. But that's not the reason I didn't blow you apart. I thought one day you might be of use to me. That time has come. You can accept it or not.'

'Taleniekov defect?' said Zaimis, holding his throat. 'No way. You're Soviet poison. A double entry, but no defector.'

107

'You're right. I do not defect. And if that unthinkable option ever entered my mind, I'd contact the British, or the French before you. I said I wanted to get out of Russia, not betray it.'

'You're lying,' said the American, his hand slipping down to the lapel of his heavy cloth jacket. 'You can go to anywhere you want.'

'Not at the moment, I'm afraid. There are complications.'

'What did you do, turn capitalist? Make off with a couple of pouches?'

'Come on, Zaimis. Which of us doesn't have his small box of resources? Often legitimate; funnelled monies can be delayed. Where's yours? I doubt Athens, and Rome is too unstable. I'd guess Berlin or London. Mine's quite ordinary: certificates of deposit, Chase Manhattan, New York City.'

The CIA man's expression remained passive, his thumb curled beneath his jacket's lapel. 'So you got caught,' he said absently.

'We're wasting time!' Vasili barked. 'Get me to the Dardanelles. I'll make my own way from there. If you don't, if a telephone call is not received here in Sevastopol when expected, your operation is finished. You'll be . . .'

Zaimis' hand shot up towards his mouth; Taleniekov grabbed the agent's fingers and twisted them violently outward. Stuck to the American's thumb was a small tablet.

'You damn *fool*! What do you think you're doing?'

Zaimis winced, the pain excruciating. 'I'd rather go this way than in the *Lubyanka*.'

'You *ass*! If anyone goes to the *Lubyanka*, it will be *me*! Because there are maniacs just like you sitting at their desks in Moscow. And *fools* – just like you – who would prefer a tablet rather than listen to the truth! You want to die, I'll accommodate you. But first get me to the Dardanelles!'

The agent, breathing with difficulty, stared at Taleniekov. Vasili released his hand, removing the tablet from Zaimis' thumb.

'You're for real, aren't you?' Zaimis said.

'I'm for real. Will you help me?'

'I haven't got anything to lose,' said the agent. 'You'll be on our carrier.'

'Don't forget. Word must get back here from the Dardanelles. If it doesn't, you're finished.'

Zaimis paused, then nodded. 'Check. We trade off.'

'We trade off,' agreed Taleniekov. 'Now, can you get me to a telephone?'

The cinderblock cubicle in the warehouse had two phones – installed by Russians and no doubt electronically monitored by SAVAK and the CIA for intercepts, thought Vasili. They would be sterile; he could talk. The American agent picked up his when Taleniekov finished dialling. The instant the call was answered, Vasili spoke.

'Is this you, my old comrade?'

It was and it was not. It was not the section chief he had spoken with earlier; instead, it was the cryptographer Taleniekov had trained years ago in Riga and brought to Sevastopol. The man's voice was low, anxious.

'Our mutual friend was called to the code room; it was arranged. I said I'd wait for your call. I have to see you right away. Where are you?'

Zaimis reached over, his bruised fingers gripping the mouthpiece of Vasili's phone. Taleniekov shook his head; in spite of the fact that he trusted the cryptographer, he had no intention of answering the question.

'That's of no consequence. Did the cable come from "depot"?'

'A great deal more than that, old friend.'

'But it *came*?' pressed Vasili.

'Yes. But it's not in any cipher I've ever heard of.

Nothing you and I ever used before. Neither during our years in Riga nor here.'

'Read it to me.'

'There's something else,' insisted the code man, his tone now intense. 'They're after you *openly*. I recycled the teletype to Moscow for in-house confirmation and burnt the original. It will be back in less than two hours. I can't *believe* it. I *won't* believe it!'

'Calm down. What was it?'

'There's an alert out for you from the Baltic to the Manchurian borders.'

'VKR?' asked Vasili, alarmed but controlled; he had expected Group Nine to act swiftly but not quite this swiftly.

'*Not* just VKR. *KGB* – and every intelligence station we *have*! As well as all military units. *Everywhere*. This isn't *you* they speak of, it couldn't be. I will not believe it!'

'What do they say?'

'That you've betrayed the State. You're to be taken, but there's to be no *detention*, no interrogation *at all*. You're to be . . . executed . . . without delay.'

'I see,' said Taleniekov. And he did see; he expected it. It was not the VKR. It was powerful men who'd heard he had spoken a name that no one should hear. *Matarese*. 'I've betrayed no one. Believe that.'

'I do. I know you.'

'Read me the cable from "depot".'

'Very well. Have you a pencil? It makes no sense.'

Vasili reached into his pocket for his pen; there was paper on the table. 'Go ahead.'

The man spoke slowly, clearly. 'As follows: "Invitation Kasimir. Schrankenwarten five goals" . . .' The crypto-grapher stopped: Taleniekov could hear voices in the distance over the line. 'I can't go on. People are coming,' he said.

'I *must* have the rest of that cable!'

110

'Thirty minutes. *Amar Magazin*. I'll be there.' The line went down.

Vasili slammed his fist on the table, then replaced the phone as Zaimis did the same. 'I *must have it*,' he repeated in English.

'What's the Amar Magazin – the Lobster Shop?' asked the CIA man.

'A fish restaurant on Kerenski Street, about seven blocks from headquarters. No one who knows Sevastopol goes there; the food is terrible. But it fits what he was trying to tell me.'

'What's that?'

'Whenever the cryptographer wanted me to screen certain incoming material before others saw it, he would suggest we meet at the *Amar*.'

'He didn't just come to your office and talk?'

Taleniekov glanced over at the American. 'You know better than that, Karras Zaimis. You people perfected electronic surveillance. We merely stole it.'

The agent looked hard at Vasili. 'They want you very dead, don't they?'

'It's a gargantuan error.'

'It always is,' said Zaimis, frowning. 'You trust him?'

'You heard him. When do you sail?'

'Eleven-thirty. Two hours. Roughly the same time that confirmation's due back from Moscow.'

'I'll be here.'

'I know you will,' said the agent. 'Because I'm going with you.'

'You *what*?'

'I've got protection out there in the city. Of course, I'll want my gun back. *And* yours. We'll see how much you want to get through the Bosphorus.'

'Why should you do this?'

'I have an idea you may reconsider that unthinkable option of yours. I want to bring you in.'

111

Vasili shook his head slowly. 'Nothing ever changes. It will not happen. I can still expose you and you don't know how. And by exposing you, I blow apart your Black Sea network. It would take years to re-establish. Time is always the issue, isn't it?'

'We'll see. You want to get to the Dardanelles?'

'Of course.'

'Give me the gun,' said the American.

The restaurant was filled, the waiters' aprons as dirty as the sawdust on the floor. Taleniekov sat alone by the right rear wall, Zaimis two tables away in the company of a Greek merchant seaman whose face was creased with loathing for his surroundings. Vasili sipped iced vodka which helped disguise the taste of the fifth-rate caviar.

The cryptographer came through the door, spotted Taleniekov, and weaved his way awkwardly between waiters and patrons to the table. His eyes behind the thick lenses of his glasses conveyed at once joy and fear and a hundred unspoken questions.

'It's all so incredible,' he said, sitting down. 'What have they *done* to you?'

'It's what they're doing to themselves,' replied Vasili. 'They don't want to listen, they don't want to hear what has to be said, what has to be stopped. It's all I can tell you.'

'But to call for your *execution*. It's inconceivable!'

'Don't worry, old friend. I'll be back – and, as they say – rehabilitated with honours.' Taleniekov smiled and touched the man's arm. 'Never forget. There are good and decent men in Moscow, more committed to their country than to their own fears and ambitions. They'll always be there, and those are the men that I will reach. They'll welcome me and thank me for what I've done. Believe that . . . Now, we're dealing in minutes. Where is the cable?'

The cryptographer opened his hand. The paper was neatly folded, creased into his palm. 'I wanted to be able to throw it away, if I had to. I know the words.' He handed the cipher to Vasili.

A dread came over Taleniekov as he read the message from Washington.

Invitation Kasimir. Schrankenwarten five goals, Unter den Linden. Przseclvac zero. Prague. Repeat text. Zero. Repeat again at will. Zero.

Beowulf Agate

When he had finished reading, the former master strategist of KGB whispered, 'Nothing ever changes.'

'What is it?' asked the cryptographer. 'I didn't understand it. It's no code we've ever used.'

'There's no way that you could understand,' answered Vasili, anger and sadness in his voice. 'It's a combination of two codes. Ours and theirs. Ours from the days in East Berlin, theirs from Prague. This cable was not sent by the man from Brussels. It was sent by a killer who won't stop killing.'

It happened so fast there were only seconds to react, and the Greek seaman moved first. His weathered face had been turned towards the incoming customers. He spat out the words.

'Watch it! The goats are filthy!'

Taleniekov looked up; the cryptographer spun in his chair. Twenty feet away, in an aisle peopled by waiters, were two men who had not come in for a meal; their expressions were set, their eyes darting about the room. They were scanning the tables but not for friends.

'Oh, my *God*!' whispered the cryptographer turning back to Vasili. 'They found the phone and tapped it. I was afraid of that.'

'Followed you, yes,' said Taleniekov, glancing over at

Zaimis, who was half out of his chair, the *idiot*. 'They know we're friends; you're being watched. But they didn't find the phone. If they were certain that I was here, they'd break in with a dozen soldiers. They're district VKR. I know them. Calmly now, take off your hat and slide out of your chair. Head towards the back hallway, to the men's room. There's a rear exit, remember?'

'Yes, yes, I remember,' spluttered the man nervously. He got up, his shoulders hunched, and started for the narrow corridor several tables away.

But he was an academic, not a field man, and Vasili cursed himself for trying to instruct him. One of the two VKR men spotted him and came forward, pushing aside the waiters in the aisle.

Then he saw Taleniekov and his hand whipped into the open space of his jacket towards an unseen weapon. As he did so, the Greek seaman lurched up from his chair, weaving unsteadily, waving his arms like a man with too much vodka in him. He slammed against the VKR man, who tried to push him away. The Greek feigned drunken indignation and pushed back with such force that the Russian went sprawling over a table, sending dishes and food crashing to the floor.

Vasili sprang up and raced past his old friend from Riga, pulling him towards the narrow hallway; then he saw the American. Zaimis was on his feet, his gun in his hand. *Idiot*.

'Put that *away*!' shouted Taleniekov. 'Don't expose . . .'

It was too late. A gunshot exploded through the sounds of chaos, escalating it instantly into pandemonium. The CIA man brought both his hands to his chest as he fell, the shirt beneath his jacket suddenly drenched with blood.

Vasili grabbed the cryptographer by the shoulder, yanking him through the narrow archway. There was a second gunshot; the code man arched spastically, his

114

legs together, an eruption of flesh at his throat. He had been shot through the back of the neck.

Taleniekov lunged to the floor of the hallway, stunned at what followed. He heard a third gunshot, a shrill scream after it, penetrating the cacophony of screams surrounding it. And then the Greek seaman crashed through the archway, an automatic in his hand.

'Is there a way out back here?' he roared in broken English. 'We have to run. The first goat got away. Others will come!'

Taleniekov scrambled to his feet and gestured for the Greek to follow him. Together they raced through a door into a kitchen filled with the terrified cooks and waiters, and out into an alley. They turned left and ran through a maze of dark connecting pavements between the old buildings until they reached the back streets of Sevastopol.

They kept running for over a mile. Vasili knew every inch of the city, but it was the Greek who kept shouting the turns they must make. As they entered a dimly lit side street, the seaman grabbed Taleniekov's arm; the man was out of breath.

'We can rest here for a minute,' he said, gasping for air. 'They won't find us.'

'It's not a place we think of first in a search,' agreed Vasili, looking at the row of neat apartment buildings.

'Always hide out in a well-kept neighbourhood,' said the seaman. 'The residents veer away from controversy; they'd inform on you in a minute. Everybody knows it so they don't look in such places.'

'You say we can stay "for a minute",' said Taleniekov. 'I'm not sure where we'll go after that. I need time to think.'

'You rule out the ship then?' asked the Greek, nodding, still breathless. 'I thought so.'

'Yes. Zaimis had papers on him. Worse, he had my

gun. The VKR will be swarming over the piers within the hour.'

The Greek studied Vasili in the dim light. 'So the great Taleniekov flees Russia. He can remain only as a corpse.'

'Not from Russia, only from frightened men. But I do have to leave – for a while. I've got to figure out how.'

'There is a way,' said the merchant seaman simply. 'We'll head over the north-west coast, then south into the mountains. You'll be in Greece in three days.'

'How?'

'There's a convoy of trucks that goes first to Odessa . . .'

Taleniekov sat on the hard bench in the back of the truck, the early light of dawn seeping through the billowing canvas flaps that covered the sides. In a while, he and the others would have to crawl beneath the floorboards, remaining motionless and silent on a concealed ledge between the axles, while they passed through the next checkpoint. But for an hour or so they could stretch and breathe air that did not reek of burned oil and grease.

He reached into his pocket and took out the cipher from Washington, the cable that had already cost three lives.

Invitation Kasimir. Schrankenwarten five goals, Unter den Linden. Przseclvac zero. Prague. Repeat text. Zero. Repeat again at will. Zero.

Beowulf Agate

Two codes. One meaning.

With his pen, Vasili wrote out that meaning beneath the cipher. *Come and take me, as you took someone else across a checkpoint at five o'clock on the Unter den Linden. I've broken and killed your courier, as another courier was killed in Prague. Repeat: Come to me. I'll kill you.*

Scofield

Beyond the American killer's brutal decision, the most electrifying aspect of Scofield's cable was the fact that he was no longer in the service of his country. He had been separated from the intelligence community. And considering what he had done and the pathological forces that drove him to do it, the separation was undoubtedly savage. For no government professional would murder a courier in the circumstances of this extraordinary Soviet contact. And if Scofield was nothing else, he was a professional.

The storm clouds over Washington had been catastrophic for Beowulf Agate. They had destroyed him.

As the storm over Moscow had destroyed a master strategist named Taleniekov.

It was strange, bordering on the macabre. Two enemies who loathed each other had been chosen by the Matarese as the first of its lethal decoys – plays and diversions, as old Krupsky had called them. Yet only one of those enemies knew it; the other did not. He was concerned solely with ripping scars open, letting the blood between them flow again.

Vasili put the paper back into his pocket, and breathed deeply. The coming days would be filled with move and counter-move, two experts stalking each other until the inevitable confrontation.

My name is Taleniekov. We will kill each other or we will talk.

7

Under-Secretary of State Daniel Congdon shot up from the chair, the telephone in his hand. Since his early days at NSA he had learned that one way of controlling an outburst was to physically move during a moment of crisis. And control was the key to everything in his profession; at least, the appearance of it. He listened as this particular crisis was defined by an angry Secretary of State.

Goddamn it, *he* was controlled.

'I've just met privately with the Soviet ambassador and we both agree the incident must not be made public. The important thing now is to bring Scofield in.'

'Are you *certain* it was Scofield, sir? I can't believe it!'

'Let's say that until he denies it with irrefutable proof that he was a thousand miles away during the past forty-eight hours we must assume it *had* to be Scofield. No one else in clandestine operations would have committed such an act. It's unthinkable.'

Unthinkable? *Incredible*. The body of a dead Russian delivered through the gates of the Soviet Embassy in the back seat of a Yellow Cab at 8.30 in the morning at the height of Washington's rush-hour traffic. And a driver who knew absolutely nothing except that he had picked up *two* drunks, not one – although one was in worse shape than the other. What the hell had happened to the other guy? The one who sounded like a Russkie and wore a hat and dark glasses and said the sunlight was too bright after a whole night of *Wodka*. Where was he? And was the fellow in the back seat all right? He looked like a mess.

'Who was the man, Mr Secretary?'

'He was a Soviet intelligence officer stationed in Brussels. The ambassador was frank; the KGB had no knowledge he was in Washington.'

'A possible defection?'

'There's no evidence whatsoever to support that.'

'Then what ties him to Scofield? Beyond the method of dispatch and delivery.'

The Secretary of State paused, then replied carefully. 'You must understand, Mr Congdon, the ambassador and I have a unique relationship that goes back several decades. We are often more candid with each other than diplomatic. Always with the understanding that neither speaks for the record.'

'I understand, sir,' said Congdon, realizing that the answer about to be given could never be referred to officially.

'The intelligence officer in question was a member of a KGB unit in East Berlin roughly ten years ago. I assume in the light of your recent decisions that you're familiar with Scofield's file.'

'His wife?' Congdon sat down. 'The man was one of those who killed Scofield's *wife*?'

'The ambassador made no reference to Scofield's wife; he merely mentioned the fact that the dead man had been part of a relatively autonomous section of the KGB in East Berlin ten years ago.'

'That section was controlled by a strategist named Taleniekov. He gave the orders.'

'Yes,' said the Secretary of State. 'We discussed Mr Taleniekov and the subsequent incident several years later in Prague at some length. We looked for the connection you've just considered. It may exist.'

'How is that, sir?'

'Vasili Taleniekov disappeared two days ago.'

'*Disappeared?*'

'Yes, Mr Congdon. Think about it. Taleniekov learned

that he was to be officially retired, mounted a simple but effective cover, and disappeared.'

'Scofield's been terminated . . .' Congdon spoke softly, as much to himself as into the telephone.

'Exactly,' agreed the Secretary of State. 'The parallel is our immediate concern. Two retired specialists now bent on doing what they could not do – or pursue – officially. Kill each other. They have contacts everywhere, men who are loyal to them for any number of reasons. Their personal vendetta could create untold problems for both governments during these precious months of conciliation. This cannot happen.'

The director of *Cons Op* frowned; there was something wrong in the Secretary's conclusions. 'I spoke with Scofield myself three nights ago. He didn't appear consumed with anger or revenge or anything like that. He was a tired field agent who'd lived . . . abnormally . . . for a long time. For years. He told me he just wanted to fade away, and I believed him. I discussed Scofield with Robert Winthrop, by the way, and he felt the same way about him. He said . . .'

'Winthrop knows *nothing*,' interrupted the Secretary of State with unexpected harshness. 'Robert Winthrop is a brilliant man, but he's never understood the meaning of confrontation except in its most rarefied forms. Bear in mind, Mr Congdon, Scofield killed that intelligence officer from Brussels.'

'Perhaps there were circumstances we're not aware of.'

'Really?' Again the Secretary of State paused, and when he spoke, the meaning behind his words was unmistakable. 'If there *are* such circumstances, I submit we have a far more potentially dangerous situation than any personal feud might engineer. Scofield and Taleniekov know more about the field operations of both intelligence services than any two men alive. They must not be permitted to make contact. Either as enemies intent on killing one another, or for those circumstances we know nothing about. Do I make myself clear, Mr Congdon? As director of Consular Operations, it is your responsibility. How you *execute* that responsibility is no concern of mine. You may have a man beyond salvage. That's for you to decide.'

Daniel Congdon remained motionless as he heard the click on the other end of the line. In all his years of service he had never received such an ill-disguised if oblique order. The language could be debated, not the command. He replaced the phone in its cradle and reached for another on the left side of his desk. He pressed a button and dialled three digits.

'Internal Security,' said the male voice answering.

'This is Under-Secretary Congdon. Pick up Brandon Scofield. You have the information. Bring him in at once.'

'One minute, sir,' replied the man politely. 'I think a level-two surveillance entry on Scofield came in a couple of days ago. Let me check the computer. All the data's there.'

'A couple of days ago?'

'Yes, sir. It's on the screen now. Scofield checked out of his hotel at approximately eleven P.M. on the sixteenth.'

'The sixteenth? Today's the nineteenth.'

'Yes, sir. There was no time lapse as far as the entry was concerned. The management informed us within the hour.'

'Where is he?'

'He left two forwarding addresses, but no dates. A sister's residence in Minneapolis and a hotel in Charlotte Amalie, St Thomas, US Virgin Islands.'

'Have they been verified?'

'As to accuracy, yes, sir. A sister does live in Minneapolis and the hotel in St Thomas is holding a pre-paid reservation for Scofield effective the seventeenth. The money was wired from Washington.'

'Then he's there.'

'Not as of noon today, sir. A routine call was made; he hasn't arrived.'

'What about the sister?' interrupted Congdon.

'Again a routine call. She confirmed the fact that Scofield called her and said he'd stop by, but he didn't say when. She added that it wasn't unusual; it was normal for him to be casual about visits. She expected him sometime during the week.'

The director of *Cons Op* felt the urge to get up again, but he suppressed it. 'Are you telling me you don't really know where he is?'

'Well, Mr Congdon, an S-level-two operates on reports received, not continuous visual contact. We'll shift to level-one right away. Minneapolis won't be any problem; the Virgin Islands could be, though.'

'Why?'

'We have no reliable sources there, sir. Nobody does.'

Daniel Congdon got up from his chair. 'Let me try to understand you. You say Scofield's on level-two surveillance, yet my instructions were clear; his whereabouts were to be known at all times. Why *wasn't* a level-one put on him? Why wasn't continuous visual contact maintained?'

The man from Internal Security answered haltingly. 'That wouldn't be my decision, sir, but I think I can understand it. If a level-one was put on Scofield, he'd spot it and . . . well, sheer perversity would make him mislead us.'

'What the hell do you think he's just *done*? Find him! Report your progress hourly to this office!' Congdon sat down angrily, replacing the phone with such force that it jarred the bell. He stared at the instrument, picked it up, and dialled again.

'Overseas Communications, Miss Andros,' said the woman's voice.

'Miss Andros, this is Under-Secretary Congdon. Please send a cipher specialist to my office immediately. Classification code *A* maximum security and priority.'

'An emergency, sir?'

'Yes, Miss Andros, an emergency. The cable will be sent in thirty minutes. Clear all traffic to Amsterdam, Marseilles . . . and Prague.'

Scofield heard the footsteps in the hallway and got out of the chair. He walked to the door and peered through the tiny round disc in the centre. The figure of a man passed by; he did not stop at the door across the way, the entrance to the suite of rooms used by Taleniekov's courier. Bray went back to the chair and sat down. He leaned his head against the rim, staring at the ceiling.

It had been three days since the race in the streets, three nights since he'd taken the messenger from Taleniekov – messenger three nights ago, killer on the Unter den Linden ten years before. It had been a strange night, an odd race, a finish that might have been otherwise.

The man could have lived; the decision to kill him had gradually lost its urgency for Bray, as so much had lost urgency, so few convictions were left. The courier had brought it upon himself. The Soviet had gone into panic and pulled out a four-inch, razor-sharp blade from the recesses of the hotel chair and attacked. His death was due to Scofield's reaction; it was not the premeditated murder planned in the street.

Nothing ever changed much. The KGB courier had been used by Taleniekov. The man was convinced that Beowulf Agate was coming over, and the Russian who brought him in would be given the brassiest medal in Moscow along with all the perks that went with it.

'You've been tricked,' Bray had told the courier while studying the cable in the hotel suite on Nebraska Avenue.

'Impossible!' the Soviet had yelled. 'This is Taleniekov!'

'It certainly is. And he chooses a man from the Unter den Linden to make contact, a man whose face he knows I'll never forget. The odds were that I'd lose control and kill you. In *Washington*. I'm exposed, vulnerable . . . And you've been taken.'

'*You're wrong!* It's a white contact!'

'So was East Berlin, you son of a bitch!'

'What are you going to do?'

'Earn some of my severance pay. You're coming in.'

'No!'

'Yes.'

The man had lunged at Scofield.

Three days had passed since that moment of violence, three mornings since Scofield had deposited the package at the embassy and sent the cipher to Sevastopol. Still no one had come to the door across the hall; and that was not normal. The suite was leased by a brokerage house in Bern, Switzerland, to be available for its 'executives'. Standard procedure for international businessmen, and also a transparent cover for a Soviet drop.

Bray had forced the issue. The cipher and the courier's dead body *had* to provoke *someone* into checking the suite of rooms. Yet no one had; it did not make sense.

Unless part of Taleniekov's cable was true: he was acting alone. If that were the case, there was only one explanation: the Soviet killer had been terminated, and before retiring to an isolated life somewhere in the vicinity of Grasnov, he had decided to settle an outstanding debt.

He had sworn to do so after Prague; the message had been clear: *You're mine, Beowulf Agate. Someday, somewhere. I'll see you take your last breath.*

A brother for a wife. The husband for the brother. It was vengeance rooted in loathing and that loathing never left. There'd be no peace for either of them until the end came for one. It was better to know that now, thought Bray, rather than find out on a crowded street or a deserted stretch of beach, with a knife in the side or a bullet in the head, fired from a dune of wild grass.

The courier's death was an accident, Taleniekov's would not be. There *would* be no peace until they met, and then death would come – one way or the other. It was a question now of drawing the Russian out; he had made the first move. He was the stalker, the role established.

The strategy was classic: tracks clearly defined for the stalker to follow, and at the chosen moment – least expected – the tracks would not be there, the stalker bewildered, exposed – the trap sprung.

Like Bray, Taleniekov could travel anywhere he wished, with or without official sanction. Over the years, both had learned too many methods; a plethora of false papers was out there for purchase, hundreds of men everywhere ready to provide concealment or transportation, cover or weapons – any and all. There were only two basic requirements: identities and money.

Neither he nor Taleniekov lacked either. Both came with the profession, the identities quite naturally, the money less so – more often than not the result of having been hung up by bureaucratic delays in the forwarding of payments demanded. Every specialist worth his rank had his own personal sources of funds. Payments exaggerated, monies diverted and deposited in stable territories. The objective was neither theft nor wealth, merely survival. A man in the field had to be burned only once or twice to learn the necessity of economic back-ups.

Bray had accounts under various names in Paris, Munich, London, Geneva and Lisbon. One avoided Rome and the Communist bloc; the Italian Treasury was madness, and banking in the Eastern satellites too corrupt.

Scofield rarely thought about the monies that were his for the spending; in the back of his mind he supposed he would give them back one day. Had the predatory Congdon not flirted with his own temptations and made the official termination so complicated, Bray might have walked in the next morning and handed him the bankbooks.

Not now. The Under-Secretary's actions ruled it out. One did not hand over several hundred thousand dollars to a man who tried – however timorously – to orchestrate one's elimination while remaining outside the act itself. It was a very professional concept. Scofield recalled that years ago it had been brought to its zenith by the killers of the Matarese. But they were assassins for hire; there'd been no one like them in centuries, since the days of Hasan ibn as-Sabbāh. There would be no one like them ever again, and someone like Daniel Congdon was a pale joke in comparison.

Congdon. Scofield laughed and reached into his pocket for his cigarettes. The new director of Consular Operations was not a fool and only a fool would underestimate him, but he had the upper-Washington mentality so prevalent in the management of clandestine services. He did not really understand what being in the field did to a man; he might mouth the phrases – twisted psychological terms reeking of depression and self-pity – but he did not see the simple line of action and reaction. Few did, or wanted to, because to recognize it meant admitting knowledge of abnormality in a subordinate whose function the department – or the Company – could do without. Quite simply, pathological behaviour was a perfectly normal way of life for a field man, and no particular emphasis was given to it. The man in the field accepted the fact that he was a criminal before any crimes had been committed. Therefore, at the first hint of activity he took measures to protect himself before anything happened; it was second nature.

Bray had done just that. While the messenger from Taleniekov had been seated across the room in the hotel on Nebraska Avenue, Scofield had made several calls. The first was to his sister in Minneapolis: he was flying out to the Mid-west in a couple of hours and would see her in a day or so. The second was to a friend in Maryland who was a deep-sea fisherman with a roomful of stuffed victims and trophies on the walls: where was a good, small place in the Caribbean that would take him on short notice? The friend had a friend in Charlotte Amalie; he owned a hotel and always kept two or three rooms open for just such emergencies. The fisherman from Maryland would call him for Bray.

So, for all intents and purposes, as of the night of the sixteenth, he was en route to the Mid-west . . . or the Caribbean. Both over fifteen hundred miles from Washington – where he remained unobserved, never leaving the hotel room across the hall from the Soviet drop.

How often had he hammered the lesson into younger, less experienced field agents? Too many times to count. A man standing motionless in a crowd was difficult to spot, and a man who gave the appearance of running, but still remained motionless even more so.

So simple.

But Taleniekov was not simple and every hour escalated the complexity. All possible explanations had to be examined. The most obvious was that the Russian had activated a dormant drop known to him and his messenger; instructions could be sent quietly to Bern, the suite of rooms leased by cable. It would take weeks before the information was filtered back to Moscow – one drop among thousands everywhere.

If so – and it was perhaps the only explanation – Taleniekov was not merely acting alone, he was acting in conflict with KGB interests. His vendetta superseded his allegiance to his government, if the term had meaning any longer; it had little for Scofield. It was the only explanation. Otherwise the suite of rooms across the hall would be swarming with Soviets. They might wait twenty-four or thirty-six hours to check out FBI observation, but no more than that; there were too many ways to elude the bureau's surveillance.

Bray had the gut instinct that he was right, an instinct developed over the years to the point where he trusted it implicitly. Now he had to put himself into Taleniekov's place, think like Vasili Taleniekov would think. It was his protection against a knife in the side or a bullet from a high-powered rifle. It was the way to bring it all to an end, and not have to go through each day wondering what the shadows held. Or the crowds.

The KGB man had no choice; it was his move and it had to be in Washington. One started with the physical connection, and it was the dormant drop across the hall. In a matter of days – perhaps hours now – Taleniekov would fly into Dulles Airport and the hunt would begin.

But the Russian was no idiot; he would not walk into a trap. Instead, another would come, someone who knew nothing, who had been paid to be an unknowing decoy. An unsuspecting passenger whose friendship was carefully cultivated on a transatlantic flight; or one of dozens of blind contacts Taleniekov had used in Washington. Men and women who had no idea that the European they did well-paid favours for was a strategist for KGB. Among them would be the decoy, or decoys, and the birds. Decoys knew nothing; they were bait. Birds watched, sending out alarms when the bait was being taken. Birds and decoys; they would be Taleniekov's weapons.

Someone would come to the hotel on Nebraska Avenue. Whoever it was would have no instructions beyond getting into those rooms; no telephone number, no name that meant anything. And nearby, the birds would be gliding around, watching, waiting for the quarry to go after the bait.

When the quarry was spotted the birds must reach the hunter. Which meant that the hunter was also nearby.

This would be Taleniekov's strategy, for no other was

available; it was also the strategy that Scofield would use. Three or four – five people at the outside – readily available for such employment. Simply mounted: phone calls placed at the airport, a meeting at a downtown restaurant. An inexpensive exercise considering the personal value of the quarry.

Sounds came from beyond the door. Voices. Bray got out of the chair and walked quickly to the tiny glass circle in the panel.

Across the hall a well-dressed woman was talking with the bell captain who carried her overnight bag. Not a suitcase, not luggage from a transatlantic flight, but a small overnight case. The decoy had arrived, the birds not far away. Taleniekov had landed; it had started.

The woman and the bell captain disappeared into the suite of rooms.

Scofield walked to the telephone. It was the moment to begin the counter-exercise. He needed time; two or three days were not out of the question. The waiting game had begun.

He called the deep-sea fisherman on the Maryland shore, making sure to dial direct. He capped the mouth-piece with his right hand, filtering his voice through his barely separated fingers. The greeting was swift, the caller in a hurry. 'I'm in the Keys and can't reach that damned hotel in Charlotte Amalie. Call it for me, will you? Tell them I'm on a charter out of Tavernier and will be there in a couple of days.'

'Sure, Bray. On a real vacation, aren't you?'

'More than you know. And thanks.'

The next call needed no such artifice. It was to a Frenchwoman he had lived with briefly in Paris several years ago. She had been one of the most effective under-cover personnel at Interpol until her cover was blown; she worked now for a CIA proprietary company based in Washington. There was no sexual attraction between

129

them any longer but they were friends. No questions were asked when obscure requests were made.

He gave her the name of the hotel on Nebraska Avenue. 'Call in fifteen minutes and ring suite two-eleven. A woman will answer. Ask for me.'

'Will she be furious, darling?'

'She won't know who I am. But someone else will.'

Taleniekov leaned against the brick of the dark alleyway across from the hotel. For several moments he let his body sag and rolled his neck back and forth, trying to ease the tension, reduce the exhaustion. He had been travelling for nearly three days, flying for over eighteen hours, driving into cities and villages, finding those men who would provide him with false documents that would get him through three immigration stations. From Salonika to Athens, Athens to London, London to New York. Finally a late-afternoon shuttle-flight to Washington after visits to three banks in lower Manhattan.

He had made it; his people in place. An expensive whore he'd brought from New York and three others from Washington, two men and an older woman. All but one were well-spoken *nichevo*, what the Americans called *hustlers*. Each had performed services in the past for the generous 'businessman' from The Hague, who had a proclivity for checking up on his associates and a penchant for confidence, both of which he paid for in large sums.

They were primed for their evening's employment. The whore was in the suite of rooms that was the Bern–Washington depot; within minutes Scofield would know it. But Beowulf Agate was no amateur; he would receive the news – from a desk clerk or switchboard operator – and send another to question the girl.

Whoever it was would be seen by one or all of Taleniekov's birds. The two men and the older woman. He had provided each with a miniaturized walkie-talkie no larger than a hand-held recorder; he had purchased four at the Mitsubi complex on Fifth Avenue. They could reach him instantly, unobtrusively. Except for the whore. No risk could be taken that such a device would be found on her. She was expendable.

One of the two men sat in a booth in the dimly lit cocktail lounge with small candle lanterns on each table. Beside him was an open attaché case, papers pulled out and placed under candlelight, a salesman summarizing the events of a business trip. The other man was in the dining room, the table set for two, the reservation made by a highly-placed aide at the White House. The host was delayed: several apologetic calls were received by the maître d'hôtel. The guest would be treated as befitted one receiving such apologies from 1600 Pennsylvania Avenue. Above any suspicion whatsoever.

But it was the older woman Taleniekov counted on most; she was paid well above the others and with good reason. She was not a *nichevo*, no hustler at all. She was a killer.

His unexpected weapon. A gracious, articulate woman of distinction who had no compunction about firing a weapon into a target across the room, or plunging a knife into the stomach of a dinner companion. Who could, at a moment's notice, change her appearance from the dignified to the harridan – and all shades in between. Vasili had paid her thousands over the past half-dozen years, several times having flown her to Europe for chores that suited her extraordinary talents. She had not failed him; she would not fail him tonight. He had reached her soon after landing at Kennedy Airport; she had had a full day to prepare for the evening. It was sufficient.

Taleniekov pushed himself away from the brick wall, shaking his fingers, breathing deeply, forcing thoughts of sleep from his mind. He had covered his flanks; now he could only wait. *If* Scofield wanted to keep the appointment – in the American's judgement, fatal to one of them. And why wouldn't he? It was better to get it over with than be obsessed with every patch of darkness or each crowded street in sunlight, wondering who might be concealed . . . taking aim, unsheathing a knife. No, it was far more desirable to conclude the hunt; that would be Beowulf Agate's opinion. And yet, how *wrong* he was! If there was only some way to reach him, *tell* him! There was the *Matarese*! There were people to see, to appeal to, to convince! Together they could do it; there were decent men in Moscow *and* Washington, men who would *not* be afraid.

But there was no way to reach Brandon Scofield on neutral ground, for no ground would be neutral to Beowulf Agate. At the first sight of his enemy, the American would instantly use every weapon he had mustered to blow that enemy away. Vasili understood, for if he were Scofield, he would do the same. So it was a question of waiting, circling, knowing that each thought the other was the quarry which would expose himself first; each manoeuvring to cause his adversary to make that mistake.

The terrible irony was that the only significant mistake would come about if Scofield won. Taleniekov could not let that happen. Wherever Scofield was, he had to be taken, immobilized, *forced to listen*.

Which was why the waiting was so important now. And the master strategist of East Berlin and Riga and Sevastopol was an expert in patience.

'The waiting paid off, Mr Congdon,' said the excited voice over the phone. 'Scofield's on a charter out of Tavernier in the Florida Keys. We estimate he'll arrive in the Virgin Islands the day after tomorrow.'

'What's the source of your information?' asked the Director of Consular Operations apprehensively, clearing the sleep from his throat, squinting at the clock on his bedside table. It was 3.00 in the morning.

'The hotel in Charlotte Amalie.'

'What's the source of *their* information?'

'They received an overseas call asking that the reservation be held. That he'd be there in two days.'

'Who made the call? Where did it come from?'

There was a pause on the other end of the State Department line. 'We assume Scofield. From the Keys.'

'Don't assume. Find out.'

'We're confirming everything, of course. Our man in Key West is on his way to Tavernier now. He'll check out all the charter logs.'

'Check out that phone call. Let me know.' Congdon hung up and raised himself on the pillow. He looked over at his wife on the twin bed next to him. She had pulled the sheet over her head. The years had taught her to sleep through the all-night calls. He thought about the one he had just received. It was too simple, too believable. Scofield was covering himself in the haze of casual, spur-of-the-moment travelling; an exhausted man getting away for a while. But there was the contradiction: Scofield was not a man ever exhausted to the point of being casual about anything. He deliberately obscured his movements . . . which meant he *had* killed the intelligence officer from Brussels.

KGB. Brussels. Taleniekov.

East Berlin.

Taleniekov and the man from Brussels had worked together in East Berlin. In a 'relatively autonomous section of KGB' – which meant East Berlin . . . and beyond.

In Washington? Had that 'relatively autonomous' unit from East Berlin sent men to Washington? It was not unreasonable. The word 'autonomous' had two meanings. Not only was it designed to absolve superiors from certain acts of their subordinates but it signified freedom of movement. A CIA agent in Lisbon might track a man to Athens. Why not? He was familiar with an operation. Conversely, a KGB agent in London would follow an espionage suspect to New York. Given general clearance, it was in his line of duty. Taleniekov had operated in Washington; there was speculation that he had made a dozen trips or more to the United States within the past decade.

Taleniekov and the man from Brussels; *that* was the connection they had to examine. Congdon sat forward and reached for the telephone, then stopped. Timing was everything now. The cables had been received in Amsterdam, Marseilles and Prague nearly twelve hours ago. According to reliable informants, they had stunned the recipients. Covert sources in all three cities had reacted to the news of Scofield's 'unsalvageable' behaviour with some panic. Names could be revealed, men and women tortured, killed, whole networks exposed; no time was to be lost eliminating Beowulf Agate. Word had been relayed by early evening that two men had already been chosen. In Prague and Marseilles; they were in the air now, on their way to Washington, no delays anticipated regarding passports or immigration procedures. A third would be leaving Amsterdam before morning; it was morning now in Amsterdam.

By noon, an execution team totally dissociated from the United States government would be in Washington. Each man had the same telephone number to call, an untraceable phone in the Baltimore ghetto. Whatever information had been gathered on Scofield would be relayed by the person at that number. And only one man could give that information to Baltimore. The man responsible: the director of Consular Operations. No one else in the United States government had the number.

Could one final connection be made? wondered Congdon. There was so little time and it would take extraordinary co-operation. Could that co-operation be requested, even approached? Nothing like it had ever happened. But it *could* be made, a location might be uncovered, a dual execution guaranteed.

He had been about to call the Secretary of State to suggest a very unusual, early-morning meeting with the Soviet ambassador. But too much time would be consumed with diplomatic complications, neither side wishing to acknowledge the objective of violence. There was a better way; it was dangerous but infinitely more direct.

Congdon got out of bed quietly, went downstairs and entered the small study that was his office at home. He went to his desk which was bolted into the floor, the lower right-hand drawers concealing a safe with a combination lock. He turned on the lamp, opened the panel and twisted the dial. The lock clicked; the steel plate sprang open. He reached inside and took out an index card with a telephone number written on it.

The number was one he never thought he would call. The area code was 902 – Nova Scotia – and it never went unanswered; it was the number for a computer complex, the central clearing house for all Soviet intelligence operations in North America. By calling it, he exposed information that should not be revealed; the complex in Nova Scotia was not supposedly known by US intelligence, but time and the extraordinary circumstances overrode security. There was a man in Nova Scotia who would understand; he would not be concerned about appearances. He had called for too many sentences of death. He was the highest-ranking KGB officer outside Russia.

Congdon reached for the telephone.

'Cabot Strait Exporters,' said the male voice in Nova Scotia. 'Night dispatcher.'

'This is Daniel Congdon, Under-Secretary of State, Consular Operations, United States Government. I request that you put a trace on this call to verify that I'm telephoning from a private residence in Herndon Falls, Virginia. While you're doing that, please activate electronic scanners for evidence of taps on the line. You won't find any. I'll wait as long as you wish, but I must speak with Voltage One, *Vol't Odin*, I think you call him.'

His words were greeted by silence from Nova Scotia. It did not take much imagination to visualize a stunned operator pushing emergency buttons. Finally, the voice replied.

'There seems to be interference. Please repeat your message.'

Congdon did so.

Again, silence. Then. 'If you'll hold on, the supervisor will speak with you. However, we think you've reached the wrong party here in Cape Breton.'

'You're not in Cape Breton. You're in Saint Peter's Bay, Prince Edward Island.'

'Hold on, please.'

The wait took nearly three minutes. Congdon sat down; it was working.

Voltage One got on the line. 'Please wait for a moment or two,' said the Russian. There followed the hollow sound of a connection still intact but suspended; electronic devices were in operation. The Soviet returned. 'This call, indeed, originates from a residential telephone in the town of Herndon Falls, Virginia. The scanners pick up no evidence of interference but, of course, that could be meaningless.'

'I don't know what other proof to give you . . .'

'You mistake me, Mr Under-Secretary. The fact that you possess this number is not in itself earthshaking; the fact that you have the audacity to use it and ask for me by my code name, perhaps is. I have the proof I need. What is this business between us?'

Congdon told him in as few words as possible. 'You

136

want Taleniekov. We want Scofield. The contact ground is Washington. I'm convinced of it. The key to the location is your man from Brussels.'

'If I recall, his body was delivered to the embassy several days ago.'

'Yes.'

'You've connected it with Scofield?'

'Your own ambassador did. He pointed out that the man was part of a KGB section in East Berlin in 1968. Taleniekov's unit. There was an incident involving Scofield's wife.'

'I see,' said the Russian. 'So Beowulf Agate still kills for revenge.'

'That's a bit much, isn't it? May I remind you that it would appear Taleniekov is coming after Scofield, not the other way around.'

'Be specific, Mr Under-Secretary. Since we agree in principle, what do you want from us?'

'It's in your computers, or in a file somewhere. It probably goes back a number of years, but it's there; it would be in ours. We believe that at one time or another the man from Brussels and Taleniekov operated in Washington. We need to know the address of the hole. It's the only connection we have between Scofield and Taleniekov. We think that's where they'll meet.'

'I see,' repeated the Soviet. 'And presuming there is such an address, or addresses, what would be the position of your government?'

Congdon was prepared for the question.

'No position at all,' he replied in a monotone. 'The information will be relayed to others, men very much concerned about Beowulf Agate's recent behaviour. Outside of myself, no one in my government will be involved.'

'A ciphered cable, identical in substance, was sent to three counter-revolutionary cells in Europe. To Prague, Marseilles and Amsterdam. Such cells can provide killers.'

'I commend you on your interception,' said the Director of *Cons Op*.

'You do the same with us every day. No compliments are called for.'

'You made no move to interfere?'

'Of course not, Mr Under-Secretary. Would you?'

'No.'

'It's eleven o'clock in Moscow. I'll call you back within the hour.'

Congdon hung up and leaned back in the chair. He desperately wanted a drink, but would not give in to the need. For the first time in a long career he was dealing directly with faceless enemies in Moscow. There could be no hint of irresponsibility; he was alone and in that solitary contact with his protection. He closed his eyes and pictured blank walls of white concrete in his mind's eye.

Twenty-two minutes later the phone rang. He sprang forward and picked it up.

'There is a small, exclusive hotel on Nebraska Avenue . . .'

8

Scofield let the cold water run in the basin, leaned against the sink, and looked into the mirror. His eyes were bloodshot from lack of sleep, the stubble of his beard pronounced. He had not shaved in nearly three days, the periods of rest were cumulatively not much more than three hours. It was shortly past four in the morning and no time to consider sleeping or shaving.

Across the hall, Taleniekov's well-dressed decoy was getting no more sleep than he was; the telephone calls were coming every fifteen minutes now.

> *Mr Brandon Scofield, please.*
> *I don't know any Scofield! Stop calling me! Who are you?*
> *A friend of Mr Scofield's. It's urgent that I speak with him.*
> *He's not here! I don't know him. Stop it! You're driving me crazy. I'll tell the hotel not to ring this phone any more!*
> *I wouldn't do that, if I were you. Your friend would not approve. You wouldn't be paid.*
> *Stop it!*

Bray's former lover from Paris was doing her job well. She had asked only one question when he had made the request that she keep up the calls.

'Are you in trouble, darling?'

'Yes.'

'Then I'll do as you ask. Tell me what you can, so I'll know what to say.'

'Don't talk over twenty seconds. I don't know who controls the switchboard.'

'You *are* in trouble.'

Within an hour, or less, the woman across the hall would go into panic and flee the hotel. Whatever she had been promised was not worth the macabre phone calls, the escalating sense of danger. The decoy would be removed; the hunter stymied.

Taleniekov would then be forced to send in his birds and the process would start over again. Only the phone calls would come less frequently, perhaps every hour, just when sleep was settling in. Eventually, the birds would fly away, there being limits as to how long they could stay in the air. The hunter's resources were extensive, but not *that* extensive. He was operating in foreign territory; how many decoys and birds were available to him? He could not go on indefinitely calling blind contacts, setting up hastily summoned meetings, issuing instructions and money.

No, he could not do that. Frustration and exhaustion would converge and the hunter would be alone, at the end of his resources. Finally, he would show himself. He had no choice; he could not leave the drop unattended. It was the only trap he had, the only connection between himself and the quarry.

Sooner or later Taleniekov would walk down the hotel corridor and stop at the door of suite 211. When he did, it would be the last sight he'd see.

The Soviet killer was good, but he was going to lose his life to the man he called Beowulf Agate, thought Scofield. He turned off the faucet and plunged his face into the cold water.

He pulled up his head; there were sounds of movement in the corridor. He walked to the tiny circular peephole. Across the way, a matronly-looking hotel maid was unlocking the door. Draped over her right forearm were several towels and sheets. A maid at four o'clock in the morning? Bray silently acknowledged Taleniekov's imagination; he had hired an all-night maid to be his late-night eyes inside. It was an able move, but flawed. Such an individual was too limited, too easily removed; she could be called away by the front desk. A guest had had an accident, a burning cigarette, an overturned pitcher of water. Too limited. And with a greater flaw.

In the morning she would go off duty. And when she did, she would be summoned by a guest across the hall.

Scofield was about to go back to his cold basin when he heard the commotion; he looked once more through the glass circle.

The well-dressed woman had walked out of the room, her overnight case in her hand. The maid stood in the door passively as the decoy's words were heard plainly.

'Tell him to go to hell!' shouted the woman. 'He's a fucking nut, dear. This whole goddamn place is filled with nuts!'

The maid watched in silence as the woman walked rapidly down the corridor. Then she closed the door, remaining inside.

The matronly-looking maid had been paid well; she would be paid better in the morning by a guest across the hall. The negotiations would begin quickly the second she stepped out of the suite. Who was the man paying her? Where was he?

The string was drawing tighter, everything was patience now. And staying awake.

Taleniekov walked the streets, aware that his legs were close to buckling, struggling to stay alert and avoid colliding with the crowds on the sidewalk. He played mental games to keep his concentration alive, counting footsteps and cracks in the pavement and blocks between telephone booths. The radios could not be used any longer; the citizen-bands were filled with babble. He cursed the fact that there had not been time to purchase more sophisticated equipment. But he never thought it could possibly go on so *long*! Madness!

It was twenty minutes past eleven in the morning, the city of Washington vibrating, people rushing, automobiles and buses clogging the streets . . . and still the insane telephone calls kept coming to the suite at the Hotel on Nebraska Avenue.

Brandon Scofield, please. It's urgent that I speak with him . . .

Insanity!

What was Scofield *doing*? Where *was* he? Where were his intermediaries?

Only the old woman remained in the hotel. The whore had revolted, the two men long since exhausted, their presence merely embarrassing, accomplishing nothing. The woman stayed in the suite, getting what rest she could between the maddening telephone calls, relaying every word spoken by the caller. A female with a pronounced 'foreign' accent, probably French, never staying on the line more than ten or twelve seconds, unable to be drawn out and very abrupt. She was either a professional, or being instructed by a professional; there could be no tracing the number or the location of the calls.

Vasili approached the phone booth fifty yards north of the hotel's entrance on the opposite side of the street. It was the fourth call he had made from this particular booth, and he had memorized the graffiti and the odd numbers scratched on the grey metal of the edge. He walked in, pulled the glass door shut, and inserted a coin; the tone hummed in his ear and he reached for the dial.

Prague!

His eyes were playing tricks on him! Across Nebraska Avenue a man got out of a taxi and stood on the pavement looking down the street towards the hotel. He knew that *man*!

At least, he knew the face. And it *was* Prague!

The man had a history of violence, both political and non-political. His police record was filled with assaults,

142

theft and unproven homicides, his years in prison nearer ten than five. He had worked against the state more for profit than for ideology; he had been well paid by the Americans. His firing arm was good, his knife better.

That he was in Washington and less than fifty yards from this particular hotel could only mean he had a connection with Scofield. Yet there was no sense in the connection! Beowulf Agate had scores of men and women he could call upon for help in dozens of cities, but he would not call on someone from Europe *now*, and he certainly would not call on *this* man; the streak of sadism was conceivably unmanageable. Why was he here? Who had summoned him?

Who *sent* him? And were there others?

But it was the *why* that burned into Taleniekov's brain. It was profoundly disturbing. Beyond the fact that the Bern–Washington depot had been revealed – undoubtedly, unwittingly by Scofield himself – someone knowing it had reached Prague for a walking gun known to have performed extensively for the Americans.

Why? Who was the target?

Beowulf Agate?

Oh, God! There *was* a method; it had been used before by Washington . . . and strangely enough there was a vague similarity to the ways of the Matarese. *Storm clouds over Washington* . . . Scofield had run into a storm so severe that he had not only been terminated, but conceivably his execution had been ordered.

Vasili had to be sure; the man from Prague might himself be a ploy, a brilliant ploy, designed to trap a Russian, not kill an American.

His hand was still suspended in front of the dial. He pressed down on the coin return lever and thought for a moment, wondering if he could take the risk. Then he saw the man across the street check his watch and turn towards the entrance of a coffee shop; he was going to

143

meet someone. There *were* others, and Vasili knew that he could not afford *not* to take the risk. He had to find out; there was no way to know how much time was left. It might only be minutes.

There was a *pradavyet* at the embassy, a diplomatic assistant whose left foot had been blown off during a counter-insurgency operation in Riga a number of years ago. He was a KGB veteran and he and Taleniekov had once been friends. It perhaps was not the moment to test that former friendship, but Vasili had no choice. He knew the number of the embassy; it had not changed in years. He reinserted the coin and dialled.

'It's been a long time since that terrible night in Riga, old friend,' said Taleniekov after having been connected to the *pradavyet*'s office. He added quickly, 'I heard that our former cryptographer was killed in Sevastopol. A tragedy.'

'That would depend on the circumstances,' was the swift, professional reply. The layers of memory had been peeled away rapidly, calmly, voice and words associated; not a beat had been lost. 'Those circumstances have not been clarified. Would you remain on the line, please. I have another call.'

Vasili stared at the telephone. If the wait was over thirty seconds, he'd have his answer; the former friendship would not survive. There were ways for even the Soviets to trace a call in the national capital of the United States. He turned his wrist and kept his eyes on the thin, jumping hand of his watch. *Twenty-eight, twenty-nine, thirty, thirty-one . . . thirty-two.* He reached up to break the connection when he heard the voice.

'*Taleniekov?* It *is* you?'

Vasili recognized the echoing sound of an activated jamming device placed over the mouthpiece of a telephone. It operated on the principle of electronic spillage; any intercepts would be clogged with static. 'Yes, old friend. I nearly hung up on you.'

'Riga was not that long ago. What *happened*? The stories we get are crazy.'

'I'm no traitor.'

'No one over here thinks you are. We assume you stepped on some large Muscovite feet. But can you return?'

'Someday, yes.'

'I can't believe the charges. Yet you're *here*!'

'Because I must be. For Russia's sake, for all our sakes. *Trust* me. I need information quickly. If anyone at the embassy has it, you would.'

'What is it?'

'I've just seen a man from Prague, someone the Americans used for his more violent talents. We kept an extensive file on him; I assume we still keep it. Do you know anything . . .'

'Beowulf Agate,' interrupted the diplomat quietly. 'It's Scofield, isn't it? That's what drives you still.'

'Tell me what you know!'

'Leave it alone, Taleniekov. Leave *him* alone. Leave him to his own people; he's finished.'

'My God, I'm *right*,' said Vasili, his eyes on the coffee shop across Nebraska Avenue.

'I don't know what you think you're right about, but I know three cables were intercepted. To Prague, Marseilles and Amsterdam.'

'They've sent a team,' broke in Taleniekov.

'Stay away. You have your revenge, the sweetest imaginable. After a lifetime, he's taken by his own.'

'It can't happen! There are things you *don't know*.'

'It can happen regardless of what I know. We can't stop it.'

Suddenly, Vasili's attention was drawn to a pedestrian about to cross the intersection not ten yards from the telephone booth. There was something about the man, the set expression of his face, the eyes that darted from

145

side to side behind the lightly tinted glasses – bewildered, perhaps, but not lost, studying his surroundings. And the man's clothes, loose-fitting, inexpensive tweeds, thick and made to last . . . they were French. The glasses were *French*, the man's face itself *Gallic*. He looked across the street towards the marquee of the hotel, and hastened his step.

Marseilles had arrived.

'Come in to us.' The diplomat was speaking. 'Whatever happened cannot be irreparable in light of your extraordinary contributions.' The former comrade from Riga was being persuasive. Too persuasive. It was not in character between professionals. 'The fact that you came in voluntarily will be in your favour. Heaven knows, you'll have our support. We'll ascribe your flight to a temporary aberration, a highly emotional state. After all, Scofield killed your brother.'

'I killed his wife.'

'A wife is not blood. These things are understandable. Do the right thing. Come in, Taleniekov.'

The excessive persuasion was now illogical. One did not voluntarily turn oneself in until the evidence of exoneration was more concrete. Not with an order for summary execution on one's head. Perhaps, after all, the former friendship could not stand the strain. 'You'll protect me?' he asked the *pradavyet*.

'Of course.'

A lie. No such protection could be promised. Something *was* wrong.

Across the street, the man wearing tinted glasses approached the coffee shop. He slowed his pace, then stopped and went up to the window as if studying a menu affixed to the glass. He reached into his pocket, took out a cigarette and lit it. From inside, barely seen in the sunlight, there was a flicker of a match. The Frenchman went inside. Prague and Marseilles had made contact.

'Thank you for your advice,' said Vasili into the phone. 'I'll think it over and call you back.'

'It would be best if you didn't delay,' answered the diplomat, urgency replacing sympathetic persuasion. 'Your situation would not be improved by any involvement with Scofield. You should not be seen down there.'

Seen down there? Taleniekov reacted to the words as though a gun had been fired in front of his face. In his old friend's knowledge was the betrayal! Seen down *where?* His colleague from Riga knew! The hotel on Nebraska Avenue. Scofield had not exposed the Bern depot – unwittingly or otherwise. *KGB had!* Soviet intelligence was a participant in Beowulf Agate's execution. *Why?*

The Matarese? There was no time to think, only act . . . The hotel! Scofield was not sitting alone by a phone in some out-of-the-way place, waiting to hear from intermediaries. He was in the *hotel.* No one would have to leave the premises to report to Beowulf Agate, no bird could be followed to the target. The target had executed a brilliant manoeuvre; he was in the direct range of fire, but unseen, observing but unobservable.

'You really *must* listen to me, Vasili.' The *praduvyet's* words came faster now; he obviously sensed indecision. If his former colleague from Riga had to be killed, it could be done any number of ways within the embassy. That was infinitely preferable to a comrade's corpse being found in an American hotel, somehow tied to the murder of an American intelligence officer by foreign agents. Which meant the KGB had revealed the location of the depot to the Americans, but had not known the precise schedule of the execution at the time.

They knew it now. Someone in the State Department had told them, the message clear. His countrymen had to stay away from the hotel – as did the Americans. None could be involved. Vasili had to buy minutes, for minutes might be all he had left. Diversion.

'I'm listening.' Taleniekov's voice was choked with sincerity, an exhausted man coming to his senses. 'You're right. I've nothing to gain now, only everything to lose. I put myself in your hands. If I can find a taxi in this insane traffic, I'll be at the embassy in thirty minutes. Watch for me. I need you.'

Vasili broke the connection, and inserted another coin. He dialled the hotel's number; no second could be wasted.

'He's *here*?' said the old woman incredulously, in response to Taleniekov's statement.

'My guess would be nearby. It would explain the timing, the phone calls, his knowing when someone was in the suite. He could hear sounds through the walls, open a door when he heard someone in the corridor. Are you still in your uniform?'

'Yes. I'm too tired to take it off.'

'Check the surrounding rooms.'

'Good heavens, do you know what you're asking? What if he . . .'

'I know what I'm paying; there's more if you do it. Do it! There's not a moment to be lost! I'll call you back in five minutes.'

'How will I *know* him?'

'He won't let you into the room.'

Bray sat shirtless between the open window and the door and let the cold air send shivers through his body. He had brought the temperature of the room down to fifty degrees, the chill was necessary to keep him awake. A cold tired man was far more alert than a warm one.

There was the tiny, blunt sound of metal slapping against metal, then the twisting of a knob. Outside in the hallway a door was being opened. Scofield got up from the chair, crossed to the window and closed it. He then walked quickly to another window, his minute lookout on a narrow world that soon would be the site of his reverse trap. It *had* to be soon; he was not sure how much longer he could go on.

Across the way, the pleasant-looking elderly maid had come out of the suite, towels and sheets still draped over her arm. From the expression on her face, she was perplexed but resigned. Undoubtedly, from her point of view, an unheard-of sum of money had been offered by a foreigner who only wished her to remain in a grand suite of rooms and stay awake to receive a series of very strange telephone calls.

And someone else had stayed awake to make those calls. Someone Bray owed a great deal to; he would repay her one day. But right now he concentrated on Taleniekov's bird. She was leaving; she was not capable of staying in the air any longer.

She had abandoned the drop. It was only a question of time now and very little time at that. The hunter would be forced to examine his trap. And be caught in it.

Scofield walked over to his open suitcase on the luggage rack and took out a fresh shirt. Starched, not soft; a crisp, starched shirt was like a cold room, a benign irritant; it kept one alert.

He put it on, and crossed to the bedside table where he had placed his gun, a Browning Magnum, Grade Four, with a custom-made silencer drilled to his specifications.

Bray spun around at an unexpected sound. There was a knocking, a hesitant tapping at his door. Why? He had paid for total isolation. The front desk had made it clear to those few employees who might have reason to enter room 213 that the sign on the knob was to be respected.

Do Not Disturb.

Yet someone was now disregarding that order, by-passing a guest's request that had been reinforced with several hundred dollars. Whoever it was was either deaf or illiterate or . . .

It was the maid. Taleniekov's bird, still in the air.

Scofield peered through the tiny circle of glass that magnified the aged features of the face only inches away. The tired eyes, encased in wrinkled flesh swollen by lack of sleep, looked to the left, then to the right, then dropped to the lower part of the door. The old woman had to be aware of the *Do Not Disturb* sign, but it had no meaning for her. Beyond the contradictory behaviour, there was something odd about the face . . . but Bray had no time to study it further. In these new circumstances, the negotiations had to begin quickly. He shoved the gun into his shirt, the stiff cloth keeping the bulge to a minimum.

'Yes?' he asked.

'Maid service, sir,' was the reply, spoken in an indeterminate brogue, more guttural than definable. 'The management has asked that all rooms be checked for supplies, sir.'

It was a poor lie, the bird too flawed to think of a better one.

'Come in,' said Scofield, reaching for the latch.

'There's no answer in suite two-eleven,' said the switchboard operator, annoyed by the persistence of the caller.

'Try it *again*,' replied Taleniekov, his eyes on the entrance of the coffee shop across the street. 'They may have stepped out for a moment, but they'll be right back. I *know* it. Keep ringing, I'll stay on the line.'

'As you wish, sir,' snapped the operator.

Madness! Nine minutes had passed since the old woman had begun the search, nine minutes to check four doors in the hallway. Even assuming all the rooms were occupied, and a maid had to give explanations to the occupants, nine minutes was far longer than she needed. A fourth conversation would be brief and blunt. *Go away. I am not to be disturbed.* Unless . . .

A match flared in the sunlight, its reflection sharp in the dark glass of the coffee shop window. Vasili blinked and stared; from one of the unseen tables inside there was a corresponding signal, extinguished quickly.

Amsterdam had arrived; the execution team was complete. Taleniekov studied the figure walking towards the small restaurant. He was tall and dressed in a black overcoat, a grey silk muffler around his throat. His hat, too, was grey, and obscured his profile, the features unable to be seen clearly.

The ringing on the telephone was now abrasive. Long sudden bursts resulting from a furious operator punching a switchboard button. There was no answer and Vasili began to think the unthinkable: Beowulf Agate had intercepted his bait. If so, the American was in greater danger than he could imagine. Three men had flown in from Europe to be his executioners, and – no less lethal – a gentle-appearing old woman whom he might try to compromise would kill him the instant she felt cornered. He would never know where the shot came from, nor that she even had a weapon.

'I'm sorry, sir!' said the operator angrily. 'There's still no pick-up in suite two-eleven. I suggest you call again.' She did not wait for a reply; the switchboard line was disconnected.

The *switchboard*? *The operator*?

It was a desperate tactic, one he would never condone except as a last-extremity measure; the risk of exposure was too great. But it *was* the last extremity and if there were alternatives he was too exhausted to think of them. Again, he knew only that he had to act, each decision an instinctive reflex, the shaping of those instincts trusted. He reached into his pocket for his money and removed five one-hundred-dollar bills. Then he took out his passport case, and extracted a letter he had written on an English-language typewriter five days ago in Moscow. The letterhead was that of a brokerage house in Bern, Switzerland; it identified the bearer as one of the firm's partners. One never knew . . .

He walked out of the telephone booth and entered the flow of pedestrians until he was directly opposite the entrance of the hotel. He waited for a break in the traffic, then walked rapidly across Nebraska Avenue.

Two minutes later a solicitous day manager introduced a Monsieur Blanchard to the operator of the hotel switchboard. This same manager – as impressed with Monsieur Blanchard's credentials as he was with the two hundred dollars the Swiss financier had casually insisted he take for his troubles – dutifully provided a relief operator while the woman talked alone with the generous Monsieur Blanchard.

'I ask you to forgive a worried man's rudeness over the telephone,' said Taleniekov, as he pressed three one-hundred-dollar bills into her nervous hand. 'The ways of international finance can be appalling in these times. It is a bloodless war, a constant struggle to prevent unscrupulous men from taking advantage of honest brokers and legitimate institutions. My company has just such a problem. There's someone in this hotel . . .'

A minute later, Vasili was reading a master list of telephone charges, recorded by a mindless computer. He concentrated on the calls made from the second floor; there were two corridors, suites 211 and 212 opposite three double rooms in the west wing, four single rooms on the other side. He studied all charges billed to telephones 211 through 215. Names would mean nothing; local calls were not identified by number; long distance charges were the only items that might provide information. Beowulf Agate had to build a cover and it would not be in Washington. He had killed a man in Washington.

The hotel was, as Taleniekov knew, an expensive one. This was further confirmed by the range of calls made by guests who thought nothing of picking up a telephone

152

and calling London as easily as a nearby restaurant. He scanned the sheets, concentrating on the *O.O.T.* areas listed.

```
212 . . . London, UK chgs: $26.50
214 . . . Des Moines, Ia. chgs: $4.75
214 . . . Cedar Rapids, Ia. chgs: $6.20
213 . . . Minneapolis, Minn. chgs: $7.10
215 . . . New Orleans, La. chgs: $11.55
214 . . . Denver, Colo. chgs: $6.75
213 . . . Easton, Md. chgs: $8.05
215 . . . Athens, Ga. chgs: $3.15
212 . . . Munich, Germ. chgs: $41.10
213 . . . Easton, Md. chgs: $4.30
212 . . . Stockholm, Swed. chgs: $38.25
```

Where was the pattern? Suite 212 had made frequent calls to Europe, but that was too obvious, too dangerous. Scofield would not place such traceable calls. Room 214 was centred in the Mid-west, Room 215 in the South. There *was* something but he could not pinpoint it. *Something* that triggered a memory.

Then he saw it and the memory was activated, clarified. The one room without a pattern. Room 213. Two calls to Easton, Maryland, one to Minneapolis, Minnesota. Vasili could see the words in the dossier as if he were reading them. Brandon Scofield had a sister in Minneapolis, Minnesota.

Taleniekov memorized both numbers in case it was necessary to use them, if there was *time* to use them, to confirm them. He turned to the operator. 'I don't know what to say. You've been most helpful but I don't think there's anything here that will help.'

The switchboard operator had entered into the minor conspiracy, and was enjoying her prominence with the impressive Swiss. 'If you'll note, Monsieur Blanchard, suite two-twelve placed a number of overseas calls.'

'Yes, I see that. Unfortunately, no one in those cities

would have anything to do with the present crisis. Strange, though. Room two-thirteen telephoned Easton, Maryland and Minneapolis. An odd coincidence, but I have friends in both places. However, nothing relevant . . .' Vasili let his words drift off, inviting comment.

'Just between the two of us, Monsieur Blanchard, I don't think the gentleman in room two-thirteen is all there, if you know what I mean.'

'Oh?'

The woman explained. The DND on 213 was a standing order; no one was to disturb the man's privacy. Even room service was instructed to leave the tray tables in the hallway, and maid service was to be suspended until specifically requested. To the best of the operator's knowledge, there had been no such request in three days. Who could live like that?

'Of course, we get people like him all the time. Men who reserve a room so they can stay drunk for hours on end, or get away from their wives or meet other women. But three days without maid service, I think is *sick*.'

'It's hardly fastidious.'

'You see it more and more,' said the woman confidentially. 'Especially in the government, everyone's so harried. But when you think our taxes are *paying* for it – I don't mean *yours*, Monsieur . . .'

'He's in the government?' interrupted Taleniekov.

'Oh, we think so. The night manager wasn't supposed to say anything to *anybody*, but we've been here for years, if you know what I mean.'

'Old friends, of course. What happened?'

'Well, a man came by last evening – actually it was this morning, around five A.M. – and showed the manager a photograph.'

'A picture of the man in two-thirteen?'

The operator glanced around briefly; the door of the office was open, but she could not be overheard. 'Yes.

Apparently he's *really* sick. An alcoholic or something, a psychiatric case. No one's to say anything; they don't want to alarm him. A doctor will be coming for him some time today.'

'Some time today? And, of course, the man who showed the photograph identified himself as someone from the government, didn't he? I mean, that's how you learned the guest upstairs was *in* the government?'

'When you've spent as many years in Washington as we have, Monsieur Blanchard, you don't have to ask for identification. It's all over their faces.'

'Yes, I imagine it is. Thank you very much. You've been a great help.'

Vasili left the room quickly and rushed out into the lobby. He had his confirmation. He had found Beowulf Agate.

But others had found him, too. Scofield's executioners were only a few hundred feet away, preparing to close in on the condemned man.

To break into the American's room to warn him would be to invite an exchange of gunfire; one or both would die. To reach him on the telephone would provoke only disbelief; where was the credibility in such an alarm delivered by an enemy one loathed about a *new* enemy one did not know existed.

There had to be a way and it had to be found quickly. If there were only time to send another with something on his person that would explain the truth to Scofield. Something Beowulf Agate would accept . . .

There was no time. Vasili saw the man in the black overcoat walk through the entrance of the hotel.

9

Scofield knew the instant the maid walked through the door what disturbed him about the elderly face. It was the eyes. There was an intelligence behind them beyond that of a plain-spoken domestic who spent her nights cleaning up the soil of pampered hotel guests. She was frightened – or perhaps merely curious – but whichever, neither was born of a blunt mind.

An actress, perhaps?

'Forgive my disturbin' you, sir,' said the woman, noticing his unshaven face and the cold room and heading for the open bathroom door. 'I'll not be a minute.'

An actress. The brogue was an affectation, no roots in Ireland or the Highlands. Too, the walk was light; she did not have the leg muscles of an old woman used to the drudgery of carrying linens and bending over beds. And the hands were white and soft, not those of someone used to abrasive cleansers.

Bray found himself pitying her even while faulting Taleniekov's choice again. A maid would have been better – the fears were different.

'You've a fresh supply of towels, sir,' said the old woman, coming out of the bathroom and heading for the door. 'I'll be on my way. Sorry for disturbin' you.'

Scofield stopped her with a small gesture. An authentic maid changing towels in a hotel would not have noticed.

'Sir?' asked the woman, her eyes alert.

'Tell me, what part of Ireland do you come from? I can't place the dialect. County Wicklow, I think.'

'Yes, sir.'

'The south country?'

'Yes, sir; very good, sir,' she said rapidly, her left hand on the doorknob.

'Would you mind leaving me an extra towel? Just put it on the bed.'

'Oh?' The old woman turned, the perplexed expression again on her face. 'Yes, sir, of course.' She started towards the bed.

Bray went to the door and pushed the bolt into place. He spoke as he did so, but gently; there was nothing to be gained by alarming Taleniekov's frightened bird. 'I'd like to talk to you. You see, I watched you last night, at four o'clock this morning to be precise . . .'

A rush of air, the scratching of fabric. Sounds he was familiar with. *Behind him in the room.*

He spun, but not in time. He heard the muted spit and felt a razorlike cut across the skin of his neck. An eruption of blood spread over his left shoulder. He lunged to his right; a second shot followed, the bullet embedding itself in the wall above him. He swung his arm in a violent arc, sending a lamp off a table towards the *impossible* sight six feet away, in the centre of the room.

The old woman had dropped the towels and in her hand was a gun. Gone was her soft, gentle bewilderment, in its place the calm, determined face of an experienced killer. *He should have known!*

He dived to the floor, his fingers gripping the base of the table; he spun again to his right, then twisted to his left, lifting the table by its leg like a small battering ram. He rose, crashing forward; two more shots were fired, splintering the wood inches above his head.

He rammed the woman, hammering her back into the wall with such force that a stream of saliva accompanied the expulsion of breath from the snarling lips.

'*Bastard!*' The scream was swallowed as the gun clattered to the floor. Scofield dropped the table, slamming it down on her feet as he reached for the weapon.

He held it, stood up and grabbed the bent-over woman by the hair, yanking her away from the wall. The red wig beneath the ruffled maid's cap came off in his hand, throwing him off balance. From somewhere beneath the uniform, the grey-haired killer had pulled a knife – a thin stiletto. Bray had seen such weapons before; they were as deadly as any gun, the blades coated with succinylcholine. Paralysis began in seconds, death seconds later. A scrape or a superficial puncture was all the attacker needed to inflict.

She was on him, the thin knife plunging straight forward, the most difficult thrust to parry, used by the most experienced. He leaped backwards, crashing the gun down on the woman's forearm. She withdrew it quickly in pain, but no suspension of purpose.

'Don't *do* it!' he shouted, levelling the gun directly at her head. 'Four shots were fired; two shells left! I'll kill you!'

The old woman stopped and lowered the knife. She stood motionless, speechless, breathing heavily, staring at him in a kind of ethereal disbelief. It occurred to Scofield that she had never been in this position before; she had always won.

Taleniekov's bird was a vicious hawk in the guise of a small, grey dove. That protective coloration was her irresistible insurance. It had never failed her.

'Who are you? KGB?' asked Bray, reaching for the towel on the bed, holding it against the wound on his neck.

'What?' she whispered, her eyes barely in focus.

'You work for Taleniekov. Where is he?'

'I'm paid by a man who uses many names,' she replied, the lethal knife still held limply in her hand. Her fury was gone, replaced by fear and exhaustion. 'I don't know who he is. I don't know where he is.'

'He knew where to find you. You're something. Where did you learn? When?'

'When?' she repeated in her bloodless whisper. 'When you were a child. Where? Out of Belsen and Dachau . . . to other camps, other fronts. All of us.'

'*Christ* . . .' uttered Scofield softly. *All of us*. They were legion. Girls taken from the camps, sent to the war fronts, to barracks everywhere, to airfields. Surviving as whores, dishonoured by their own, unwanted, ostracized. They became the scavengers of Europe. Taleniekov *did* know where to find his flocks.

'Why do you work for him? He's no better than those who sent you to the camps.'

'I have to. He'll kill me. Now you say you will.'

'Thirty seconds ago, I would have. You didn't give me a choice; you can now. I'll take care of you. You stay in contact with this man. How?'

'He calls. In the suite across the hall.'

'How often?'

'Every ten or fifteen minutes. He'll call again soon.'

'Let's go,' said Bray cautiously. 'Move to your right and drop the knife on the bed.'

'Then you'll *shoot*,' whispered the old woman.

'If I was going to, I'd do it now,' said Scofield. He *needed* her, needed her confidence. 'There'd be no reason to wait, would there? Let's get over to that phone. Whatever he was paying, I'll double.'

'I don't think I can walk. I think you broke my foot.'

'I'll help you.' Bray lowered the towel and took a step towards her. He held out his hand. 'Take my arm.'

The old woman placed her left foot in front of her painfully. Then suddenly, like an enraged old lioness, she lunged forward, her face again contorted, her eyes wild.

The blade came rushing towards Scofield's stomach.

Taleniekov followed the man from Amsterdam into the elevator. There was one other couple in the car. Young, rich, pampered Americans; fashionably dressed lovers or newly-weds, aware only of themselves and their hungers. They had been drinking, the stale odour of wine hanging about them.

The Hollander in the black overcoat removed his grey Homburg, as Vasili, his face briefly turned away, stood next to him against the panelled wall of the small enclosure. The doors closed. The girl laughed softly; her companion pressed the button for the fifth floor. The man from Amsterdam stepped forward and touched number two.

As he moved back, he glanced to his left, his eyes making contact with Taleniekov's. The man froze, the shock total, the recognition absolute. And in that shock, that recognition, Vasili saw another truth: the execution trap was meant for him as well. The team had a priority, and it was Beowulf Agate, but if a KGB agent known as Taleniekov appeared on the scene he was to be taken out as ruthlessly as Scofield.

The man from Amsterdam swung his hat in front of his chest, plunging his right hand into his pocket. Vasili rushed him, pinning him against the wall, his left hand gripping the wrist in the pocket, slipping down, separating hand from weapon, groping for the thumb, twisting it back until the bone cracked and the man bleated. He sank to his knees.

The girl screamed. Taleniekov spoke in a loud voice. He addressed the couple.

'You will not be harmed. I repeat, you will not be harmed if you do as I say. Make no noise, and take us to your room.'

The Hollander lurched to the right; Vasili slammed his knee into the man's face, vicing the head against the wall. He took his gun from his pocket and held it up, pointing at the ceiling.

'I will not use this. I *will not* use this unless you disobey. You're no part of our dispute and I don't want you harmed. But you must do as I say.'

'*Jesus!* Jesus *Christ* . . . !' The young man's lips trembled.

'Take out your key,' ordered Taleniekov almost amiably. 'When the doors open walk casually in front of us to your room. You will be perfectly safe if you do as I say. If you don't, if you cry out, or try to raise an alarm, I shall have to shoot. I won't kill you; instead, I'll fire into your spines. You'll be paralysed for life.'

'Oh, *Christ, please* . . . !' The young man's trembling spread throughout his head, neck and shoulders.

'*Please*, mister! We'll do whatever you say!' The girl at least was lucid; she took the key from her lover's pocket.

'Get up!' said Vasili to the man from Amsterdam. He reached into the killer's overcoat pocket and removed the Hollander's weapon.

The elevator doors opened. The couple walked out stiffly, passing an elderly man reading a newspaper, and turned right down the corridor. Taleniekov, his Graz-Burya concealed at his side, gripped the cloth of Amsterdam's overcoat, propelling him forward.

'One sound, Dutchman,' he whispered. 'And you'll not make another. I'll blow your back away; you won't have time to scream.'

Inside the double room, Vasili shoved the Hollander into a chair, held his gun on him, and issued orders once again to the frightened couple. 'Get inside that clothes closet. *Quickly!*'

Tears were streaming down the young man's pampered face; the girl pushed him into their dark, temporary cell. Taleniekov propped a chair underneath the knob and kicked it until it was wedged firmly between the metal and the rug. He turned to the Hollander.

'You have exactly five seconds to explain how it's to be done,' he said, raising the automatic diagonally across the executioner's face.

'You'll have to be clearer,' came the professional reply.

'By all means,' Vasili slashed the barrel of the Graz-Burya downward, ripping the flesh of the assassin's face. Blood spread; the man raised his hands. Taleniekov bent over the chair and cracked both wrists in rapid succession. 'Don't touch! We've just begun. Drink it! Soon you'll have no lips. Then no teeth, no chin, no cheekbones! Finally, I'll take your eyes. Have you ever seen a man like that? The face is a terrible source of pain, puncturing the eyes unendurable.' Vasili struck again, now arching upwards, catching the man's nostrils in the swing.

'No . . . *No!* I followed *orders!*'

'Where have I heard that before?' Taleniekov raised the weapon; again the hands were raised and again they were repulsed with blows. 'What *are* those orders, Dutchman? There are three of you and the five seconds have passed! We must be serious now.' He tapped the barrel of the Graz-Burya harshly over the Hollander's left eye, then the right. 'No more time!' He pulled the weapon back, then shoved it knifelike into Amsterdam's throat.

'*Stop!*' screamed the man, his air cut off, the word garbled. 'I'll tell you . . . He betrays us, he takes money for our names. He's sold out to our enemies!'

'No judgements. The *orders!*'

'He's never seen me. I'm to draw him out.'

'*How?*'

'*You.* I've come to warn him. You're on your way.'

'He'd reject you. Kill you! A transparent device. How did you know the room?'

'We have a photograph.'

'*Of him.* Not of me.'

'Both of you, actually. But I show him only his. The night manager identified him.'

'Who gave you this photograph?'

'Friends from Prague, operating in Washington, with ties to the Soviet. Former friends of Beowulf Agate who know what he's done.'

Taleniekov stared at the man from Amsterdam. He was telling the truth, because the explanation was based on partial truth. Scofield would look for flaws, but he would not reject Amsterdam's words; he could not afford that luxury. He would take the Dutchman as hostage, and then position himself. Waiting, watching, unseen. Vasili pressed the barrel of the Graz-Burya into the Hollander's right eye.

'Marseilles and Prague. Where are they? Where will they be?'

'Other than the main elevators there are only two exits from the floors. The staircase and the service lift. One will be stationed in each.'

'Which are where?'

'Prague on the staircase, Marseilles on the service lift.'

'What's the schedule? By minutes.'

'It's floating. I approach the door at ten past twelve.'

Taleniekov glanced at the ersatz antique clock on the hotel room desk. It was eleven minutes past twelve. 'They're in position now.'

'I don't know. I can't see my watch, the blood's in my eyes.'

'What's the termination? If you lie, I'll know it. You'll die in a way you've never dreamed of. Describe it!'

'Zero-lock is five minutes past the half hour. If Beowulf has not appeared in either location, the room is to be stormed. Frankly, I don't trust Prague. I think he'd throw Marseilles and myself in first to take the initial fire. He's a maniac.'

Vasili stood up. 'Your judgement exceeds your talents.'

'I've told you everything! Don't strike me again. For God's sake, let me wipe my eyes. I can't *see*.'

'Wipe them. I want you to see clearly. Get up!' The Hollander rose, his hands covering his face, brushing away the rivulets of blood, the Graz-Burya jammed into his neck.

Taleniekov stood motionless for a moment, looking at the telephone across the room. He was about to speak with an enemy he had hated for a decade, about to hear his voice.

He would try to save that enemy's life.

Scofield spun away as the lethal blade sliced into his shirt, blunted by the steel of his gun concealed under the starched cloth only minutes ago. The old woman was insane, suicidal! He would have to kill her and he did not *want* to kill her!

The *gun*.

He said four shells had been fired, two were left. *She* knew differently!

She was coming at him again, the knife criss-crossing in slashing diagonals; anything in its path would have to be touched, scraped – under normal circumstances a meaningless scratch, but not with this blade. He aimed the gun at her head and squeezed the trigger; there was nothing but the click of the firing pin.

He lashed his right foot, catching her between her breast and her armpit, staggering her for an instant, but only an instant. She was wild, clutching the knife as if it were her passport to life; if she touched him, she was free. She crouched, swinging her left arm in front of her, covering the blade that worked furiously in her right. He jumped back, looking for something, *anything* he could use to parry her lunges.

Why had she delayed before? Why had she suddenly stopped and spoken with him, telling him *things* that would make him think? Then he knew. The old hawk was not only vicious, but wise; she knew when she had to restore dissipated strength, knew she could do it only by engaging her enemy, lulling him, waiting for the unguarded instant . . . one *touch* of the coated blade.

She lunged again, the knife arcing up from the floor

towards his legs. He kicked; she whipped the blade back, then slashed laterally, missing the kneecap by centimetres. As her arm swung left with the slash, he caught her shoulder with his right foot and hammered her backwards.

She fell; he grabbed the nearest upright object – a floor lamp with a heavy brass base – hurling it down at her as he kicked again at the hand that held the stiletto.

Her wrist was bent; the point of the blade pierced the fabric of her maid's uniform, entering the flesh above her left breast.

What followed was a sight he did not care to remember. The old woman's eyes grew wide and thyroid, her lips stretched into a macabre, horrible grin that was no smile. She began to writhe on the floor, her body convulsed and trembling. She rolled into a foetal position, pulling her thin legs into her stomach, the agony complete. Prolonged, muffled screams came from her throat as she rolled again, clawing the rug; mucus disgorged from her convoluted mouth, a swollen tongue blocking passage.

Suddenly there was a horrible gasp and a final expulsion of breath. Her body jerked off the floor spastically; it became rigid. Her eyes were open wide, staring at nothing, her lips parted in death. The process had taken less than sixty seconds.

Bray leaned over and lifted the hand, separating the bony fingers. He removed the knife, stood up and walked to the bureau where there was a book of matches. He struck one and held it under the blade. There was an eruption of flame, spitting so high that it singed his hair, the heat so intense it burned his face. He dropped the stiletto, stamping the fire out under his foot.

The phone rang.

'This is Taleniekov,' said the Russian into the silence of the telephone. It had been picked up but there was no voice on the line. 'I submit that your position is not lessened by acknowledging our contact.'

'Acknowledged,' was the one-word reply.

'You reject my cable, my white flag, and were I you, I would do the same. But you're wrong and I would be wrong! I swore I'd kill you, Beowulf Agate, and perhaps one day I will, but not now and not *this* way. I am no schoolboy who proclaims victory before going on to the rugby field. It's not a logical way of doing things in our business. I think that's a reasonable statement.'

'You read my cipher,' was the answer, delivered in a monotone. 'You killed my wife. Come and get me. I'm ready for you.'

'*Stop it!* We both killed. You took a *brother* . . . and before that, an innocent young girl who knew only slogans! No threat to the animals who raped her and killed her!'

'What?'

'There's no time! There are men who want to kill you, but I'm not one of them! I've caught one, however; he's with me now . . .'

'You sent another,' interrupted Scofield. 'She's dead. The knife went into her, not me. The cut didn't have to be very deep.'

'You had to have provoked her; it *was not* planned! But we waste seconds and you don't have them. Listen to the man I put on the phone. He's from Amsterdam. His face is damaged and he can't see very well, but he can speak.' Vasili pressed the telephone against the Hollander's bloody lips and shoved the Graz-Burya into his neck. 'Tell him, Dutchman!'

'Cables were sent . . .' The injured man whispered, choking on fear and blood. 'Amsterdam, Marseilles, Prague. Beowulf Agate was beyond salvage. We could all be killed if he lived. The cables made the usual statements: they were alerts, urging us to take precautions, but we knew what they meant. Don't take precautions, take out

166

the problem, eliminate Beowulf ourselves . . . None of this is new to you, Herr Scofield. You have given such orders; you know they must be carried out.'

Taleniekov yanked the phone away while keeping the barrel of his weapon pressed against Amsterdam's neck. 'You heard it. The trap you set for me is being used to ambush *you*. By your own people.'

Silence. Beowulf Agate said nothing. Vasili's patience was running out. 'Don't you *understand*? They've exchanged information, it's the only way they could have found the depot – what you call a "drop". Moscow *provided* it, can't you *see* that? Each of us is being used as the reason to execute the other, to kill us *both*. My people are more direct than yours. The order for my death has been sent to every Soviet station, civilian and military. Your State Department does it somewhat differently, the analysts take no responsibility for such unconstitutional decisions. They simply send warnings to those who care little for abstractions, but deeply for their lives.'

Silence. Taleniekov exploded.

'What more do you *want*? Amsterdam was to draw you out; you would have had no choice. You would have tried to position yourself in one of two exits: the service area or the staircase. At this moment, Marseilles is by the service elevator, Prague on the staircase. The man from Prague is one you know well, Beowulf. You've employed his gun and his knife on many occasions. He's waiting for you. In less than fifteen minutes, if you do not appear in either place, they will take you in your room. What more *do* you want?'

Scofield answered at last. 'I want to know why you're telling me this.'

'Re-read my cipher to you! This isn't the first time you and I have been used. An incredible thing is happening and it goes beyond you and me. A few men know about it. In Washington *and* Moscow. But they say nothing; no one can say anything. The admissions are catastrophic.'

'What admissions?'

'The hiring of assassins. On both sides. It goes back years, *decades*.'

'How does it concern me? I don't care about you.'

'Dimitri Yurievich.'

'What about him?'

'They said you killed him.'

'You're lying, Taleniekov. I thought you'd be better at it. Yurievich was leaning, he was a probable. The civilian killed was my contact, under *my* source-control. It was a KGB operation. Better a dead physicist than a defected one. I repeat, come and get me.'

'You're *wrong*! . . . Later! There's no time to argue. You want proof? Then listen! I trust your ear is more skilled than your mind!' The Russian quickly shoved the Graz-Burya into his belt and held the mouthpiece up in the air. With his left hand he gripped the throat of the man from Amsterdam, his thumb centring on the rings of trachea cartilage. He pressed; his hand was a vice, his fingers talons crushing fibre and bone as the vice closed. The Hollander twisted violently, his arms and hands thrashing, trying to break Vasili's grip, the effort useless. His cry of pain was an unbroken scream that diminished into a wail of agony. The man from Amsterdam fell to the floor unconscious. Taleniekov spoke again into the telephone. 'Is there human bait alive who would permit what I've just done?'

'Was he given an alternative?'

'You're a *fool*, Scofield! Get yourself killed!' Vasili shook his head in desperation; it was a reaction to his own loss of control. '*No* . . . No, you mustn't. You can't understand, and I must try to grasp that, so you must try to understand me. I loathe everything you are, everything you stand for. But right now, we can do what few others can do. Make men listen, make them speak out. If for no other reason than they fear us, fear what we know. The fear is on *both* sides . . .'

'I don't know what you're talking about,' interrupted Scofield. 'You're mounting a nice KGB strategy; they'll probably give you a large *dacha* in Grasnov, but no sale. I repeat, come and get me.'

'*Enough!*' shouted Taleniekov, looking at the clock on the desk. 'You have eleven minutes! You know where your final proof is. You can find it in a service lift or on the staircase. Unless you care to learn it as you die in your room. If you create a disturbance, you'll draw a crowd. That's more to their liking, but I don't have to tell you that; you may recognize Prague, you won't Marseilles. You can't call the police, or risk the chance that the management will, we both know that. Go find your proof, Scofield! See if this enemy is lying. You'll get as far as your first turn in the corridor! If you live – which is unlikely – I'm on the fifth floor. Room five-zero-five. I've done what I can!' Vasili slammed down the phone, the gesture equal parts artifice and anger. Anything to jar the American, anything to make him think.

Taleniekov needed every second now. He had told Beowulf Agate that he had done what he could, but it was not true. He knelt down and tore off the black overcoat from Amsterdam's unconscious body.

Bray replaced the phone, his mind was working. If he'd only had sleep, or if he had not gone through the totally unexpected violence of the old woman's attack, or if Taleniekov had not told him so much of the truth, things would be clearer. But it had all happened and, as he had done so often in the past, he had to shift into a state of blind acceptance and think in terms of immediate purpose.

It was not the first time he had been the target of factions distinct from each other. One got used to it when dealing with opposing partisans from the same broad-based camps, although killing was rarely the objective. What was unusual was the timing, the converging of separate assaults. Yet it was so understandable, so *clear*.

Under-Secretary of State Daniel Congdon had really done it! The seemingly bloodless desk-man had found the courage of his own convictions. More specifically, he had found Taleniekov and Taleniekov's moves towards Beowulf Agate. What better reasoning existed for breaking the rules and eliminating a terminated specialist he considered dangerous? What better motive for reaching the Soviets, who could only favour the dispatch of both men?

So clear. So well orchestrated he or Taleniekov might have conceived the strategy. Denials and astonishment would go hand in hand, statesmen in Washington and Moscow decrying the violence of *former* intelligence officers – from another era. An era when personal animosities often superseded national interests. *Christ*, he could hear the pronouncement, couched in sanctimonious platitudes made by men like Congdon who concealed filthy decisions under respectable titles.

The infuriating thing was that the reality supported the platitudes, the words were validated by Taleniekov's hunt for revenge. *I swore I'd kill you, Beowulf Agate, and perhaps one day I will.*

That day was today, the *perhaps* without meaning for the Russian. Taleniekov wanted Beowulf Agate for himself; he would brook no interference from killers recruited and programmed by desk-men in Washington and Moscow. *I will see you take your last breath* . . . Those were Taleniekov's words six years ago; he meant them then and he meant them now.

Certainly he would save his enemy from the guns of Marseilles and Prague. His enemy was worthy of a better gun, *his* gun. And no ploy was too unreasonable, no words too extreme, to bring his enemy into that gunsight.

He was tired of it all, thought Scofield, taking his hand away from the phone. Tired of the tension of move and counter-move. In the final analysis, who cared? The crisis was that of a non-event. Who gave a goddamn for two ageing *specialists*, dedicated to the proposition that each's counterpart should die?

Bray closed his eyes, pressing his lids together, aware that there was moisture in his sockets. Tears of fatigue, mind and body spent; it was no time to acknowledge exhaustion. Because he *cared*. If he had to die – and it was always an around-the-corner possibility – he was not going to be taken by guns from Marseilles, Prague *or* Moscow. He was better than that; he had always *been* better.

According to Taleniekov he had eleven minutes; two had passed since the Russian had made the statement. The trap was his room and if the man from Prague was the one Taleniekov had described, the attack would be made quickly, with a minimum of risk. Gas-filled pellets would precede any use of weapons, the fumes immobilizing anyone in the room. It was a tactic favoured by the killer from Prague; he took few gambles.

The immediate objective, therefore, was to get out of the trap. Walking in the corridor was not feasible, perhaps not even opening the door. Since it was Amsterdam's function to draw him out, and he had not been drawn, Prague and Marseilles would close in. If there was no one in the hallway – as the absence of sound indicated – they had nothing to lose. Their schedule would not be postponed, but it could be accelerated.

No one in the hallway . . . *someone* in the hallway. People milling around, excited, creating a diversion. Most of the time a crowd was to the killers' advantage, not the target's, especially if the target was identifiable and one or more of the killers were not. On the other hand, a target who knew precisely when and where the attack was to be made, could use a crowd to cover his run from ground-zero. An escape based on confusion and a change of appearance. The change did not have to be much, just enough to cause indecision; indiscriminate gunfire during an execution had to be avoided.

Eight minutes. Or less. Everything was preparation. He would have his essential belongings, for when he began running, he'd have to keep running; how long and how far there was no way to tell, nor could he think about that now. He had to get out of the trap and elude three men who wanted him dead, one more dangerous than the other two for he was not sent by Washington or Moscow. He had come himself.

Bray crossed rapidly to the dead woman on the floor, dragged her to the bathroom, rolled the corpse inside, and closed the door. He picked up the heavy-based lamp and smashed it down on the knob; the lock was jammed, the door could be opened only by breaking it down.

His clothes could be left behind. There were no laundry marks or overt evidence connecting them immediately to Brandon Scofield; fingerprints would do that, but lifting and processing them would take time. He would be far away by then – if he got out of the hotel alive. His attaché case was something else; it contained too many tools of his profession. He closed it, spun the combination lock, and threw it on the bed. He put on his jacket and went back to the telephone. He picked it up and dialled the operator.

'This is room two-thirteen,' he said in a whisper, effortlessly made to sound weak. 'I don't want to alarm you, but I know the symptoms. I've had a stroke. I need help . . .'

He let the phone crash against the table and drop to the floor.

10

Taleniekov put on the black overcoat and reached down for the grey scarf, still draped around Amsterdam's neck. He yanked it off, wound it around his throat and picked up the grey hat which had fallen beside the chair. It was too large; he creased the crown so it covered his head less awkwardly, and started for the door, passing the closet. He spoke firmly to the couple within.

'Remain where you are and make no sound! I shall be outside in the corridor. If I hear noise, I'll come back and you'll be the worse for it.'

In the hall, he ran towards the main elevators, and then beyond them, to the plain dark elevator at the end of the corridor. Against the wall was a tray table used by room service. He removed his Graz-Burya from his belt, shoved it in his overcoat pocket and pushed the button with his left hand. The red light went on above the door; the elevator was on the second floor. Marseilles was in position, waiting for Beowulf Agate.

The light went off and seconds later the number *three* shone brightly, then number *four*. Vasili turned around, his back to the sliding panel.

The door opened, but there were no words of recognition, no surprise expressed at the sight of the black overcoat or the grey hat. Taleniekov spun around, his finger on the trigger of his gun.

There was no one inside the elevator. He stepped in and pressed the button for the second floor.

'*Sir? Sir?* My God, it's the crazy one in two-thirteen!' The excited voice of the operator floated up piercingly from the telephone on the rug. 'Send up a couple of boys! See what they can do! I'll call an ambulance. He's had an attack or something . . .'

The words were cut off; the chaos had begun.

Scofield stood by the door, unlatched it and waited. No more than forty seconds passed when he heard the racing footsteps and the shouts in the corridor. The door burst open; the bell captain ran in, followed by a younger, larger man, a bellboy.

'Thank Christ it wasn't locked! *Where* . . . ?'

Bray kicked the door shut, revealing himself to the two men. In his hand was his automatic. 'No one's going to get hurt,' he said calmly. 'Just do exactly as I tell you. You,' Bray ordered the younger man, 'take off your jacket and your cap. And you,' he continued, speaking to the bell captain, 'get on the phone and tell the operator to send up the manager. You're scared; you don't want to touch anything, there may have been trouble up here. You think I'm dead.'

The older man stuttered, his eyes riveted on the gun, then ran to the phone. The performance was convincing, he was frightened out of his wits. He delivered the message almost verbatim.

Bray took the maroon and gold-striped jacket held out for him by the large subordinate. He removed his coat and put it on, bunching his own under his arm. 'The *cap*,' demanded Scofield. It was given.

The bell captain finished, his eyes staring wildly at Bray, his last plea screamed: 'For Christ's sake, *hurry*! Get someone up here!'

Scofield gestured with his weapon. 'Stand by the door next to me,' he said to the frantic man, then addressed the younger. 'There's a closet over there beyond the bed. Get inside. *Now!*'

The large, dense bellboy hesitated, looked at Bray's face, and retreated quickly into the closet. Scofield, his weapon pointed at the bell captain, took the necessary steps towards the closet and kicked the door shut. He spoke while picking up the heavy-based lamp by its stem. 'Get over to your right! Do you understand? Answer me!'

'Yeah,' was the muffled reply from inside.

'Knock on the door!'

The tap came from the extreme left, the young man's right. Bray crashed the base of the lamp down on the knob; it broke off. Then he raised his gun, its silencer attached, and fired one shot into the right side of the door. 'That was a bullet!' he said. 'No matter what you hear, keep your mouth shut or there'll be another. I'm right outside this door!'

'Oh, my *God* . . . !'

The man would stay silent through an earthquake. Scofield went back to the bell captain, picking up the attaché case on the way. 'Where's the staircase?'

'Down the hall to the elevators, turn right. It's at the end of the corridor.'

'The service elevator?'

'Same thing, the other way, the other end. Turn left at . . .'

'Listen to me,' interrupted Bray, 'and remember what I tell you. In a few seconds we'll hear the manager and probably others coming down the hall. When I open the door, you step outside and shout – and I mean scream your fucking head off – then start running down the corridor with me.'

'*Christ!* What am I supposed to say?'

'That you want to get out of here,' answered Bray. 'Say it any way you like. I don't think it'll be difficult for you.'

'Where are we *going*? I got a wife and four kids!'

'That's nice. Why don't you go home?'

'*What?*'

'What's the quickest way to the lobby?'

'Christ, *I* don't know!'

'Elevators can take a long time.'

'The staircase? The *staircase*!' The panicked bell captain found triumph in his deduction.

'Use the staircase,' said Scofield, his ear at the door.

The voices were muffled, but intense. He could hear the words *police* and *ambulance*, and then *emergency*. There were three or four people.

Bray yanked the door back and pushed the bell captain out into the corridor. '*Now*,' he said.

Taleniekov turned away as the service elevator opened on the second floor. Again the black overcoat and the distinctive grey hat evoked no sounds of recognition, and again he spun, his hand gripping the Graz-Burya in his pocket. Marseilles was nowhere in sight. There were tray tables of half-eaten food and the odour of coffee – remnants of late breakfasts piling up outside the elevator door – but no Marseilles.

A pair of hinged metal doors opened into the second-floor corridor, round windows in the centre of each panel. Vasili approached and peered through the right circle.

There he was. The figure in the heavy tweed suit was edging his way along the wall towards the corner of the intersecting hallway that led to room 213. Taleniekov looked at his watch; it was 12.31. Four minutes until the attack; a lifetime if Scofield kept his head about him. A diversion was needed; fire was the surest. A telephone call, a flaming pillow case stuffed with cloth and paper thrown into the hallway. He wondered if Beowulf Agate had thought of it.

Scofield had thought of *something*. Down the hall the light above one of the two main elevators went on; the door opened, and three men rushed out talking frantically. One was the manager, now close to panic; another man carried a black bag: a doctor. The third was burly, his face

176

set, the hair close-cropped . . . the hotel's private police officer.

They raced past the startled Marseilles – who turned abruptly away – and proceeded down the long corridor that led to Scofield's room. The Frenchman reached into his pocket and took out a gun.

At the other end of the hallway, below a red *Exit* sign, a heavy door with a crash bar was pulled back. The figure of Prague stepped out, nodding at Marseilles. In his right hand was a long-barrelled, heavy-calibre automatic, in his left what looked like . . . it was . . . a *grenade*. The thumb was curved, pressing on the lever; the firing pin was out!

And if he had one grenade he had more than one. Prague was an arsenal. He would take whoever was in the area, as long as he took Beowulf Agate. A grenade hurled into a dead-end corridor, a swift race into the carnage before the smoke had cleared to put bullets into the heads of those surviving, making sure Scofield was the first. No matter what the American had thought of, he was cornered. There was no way out through the gauntlet.

Unless Prague could be stopped where he was, the grenade exploding beneath him. Vasili pulled the Graz-Burya from his pocket and pushed the swinging door in front of him.

He was about to shout when he heard the scream . . . screams from a man in panic.

'*Get out of here!* For Christ's sake, I've got to get *out of here*!'

What followed was madness. Two men in hotel uniforms came running out of the corridor, one turning right, crashing into Prague, who propelled him away, beating him with the barrel of his gun. Prague shouted at Marseilles, ordering him down the corridor.

Marseilles was no fool – any more than Amsterdam was; he saw the grenade in Prague's hand. The two men screamed at each other.

The elevator door closed.

It *closed*. The light went *off*. It had been on *Hold*!

Beowulf Agate had made his escape.

Taleniekov spun back behind the metal doors; in the confusion he had not been spotted. But Prague and Marseilles had seen the elevator; it obviously prodded the immediate recollection of a second man in a dark red jacket, running straight ahead, without panic, knowing what he was doing . . . and *carrying something under his left arm*. Like Vasili, the two executioners watched the lighted numbers above the elevator door, expecting, as Taleniekov expected, the letter *L* to light up, signifying the lobby. It did not.

The light reached *three*. It stopped.

What was Scofield *doing*? He could be running in the streets in seconds, finding safety in the crowds, heading for any of a hundred sanctuaries. He was staying at the killing ground! Again, *madness*!

Then Vasili understood. Beowulf Agate was coming after *him*.

He looked through the circular service window. Prague was talking wildly. Marseilles nodded, holding his finger on the left elevator button, as Prague ran back towards the staircase and disappeared beyond the door.

Taleniekov had to know what had been said. It could save seconds – if he could learn in seconds. He put the Graz-Burya in his pocket, burst through the swinging door, the grey silk scarf bunched high around his neck, the grey hat firmly down on his head, his face obscured. He shouted.

'*Qu'est-ce que vous avez trouvé, par hasard?*'

In Marseilles' excitement, the swiftness and the deception had their effect. The black overcoat, the grey blur of silk and fur and the French spoken with a Dutchman's guttural inflections; they were enough to confuse the image of a man he had met only once, briefly in a coffee shop. He was stunned; he ran towards Taleniekov, shouting in his native tongue, the words so rushed they were barely clear.

'What are you doing *here*? All hell has broken loose! Men are yelling in Beowulf's room; they break down doors! He got *away*. Prague has . . .'

Marseilles stopped. He saw the face in front of him and his stunned expression turned into one of shock. Vasili's hand shot out, gripping the weapon in the Frenchman's hand, twisting it with such force that Marseilles screamed aloud. The gun was pried out of his fingers. Taleniekov slammed the man against the wall, hammering his knee into the Frenchman's groin, his left hand tearing at Marseilles' right ear.

'Prague has *what*? You have one second to tell me!' He crashed his knee up into the Frenchman's testicles. '*Now!*'

'We work our way to the roof . . .' Marseilles choked the answer, spitting it out between clenched teeth, his hand sprung back in pain. 'Floor by floor . . . to the roof.'

'Why?' My God! thought Vasili. They knew about the *roof*. There was a metal air duct connecting the hotel to the adjacent building. Did they know? He rammed his knee again and repeated.

'*Why?*'

'Prague believes Scofield thinks you have men in the streets . . . at the hotel doors. He'll wait until the police come . . . the confusion. He did something in the room! In the name of God, *stop*!'

Vasili smashed the handle of the Frenchman's gun into Marseilles' skull behind his left temple. The assassin collapsed, as the wound spat blood. Taleniekov propelled the unconscious, falling body along the wall, letting it drop, so that it fell across the intersecting corridor. Whoever came out of room 213 would be greeted by another unexpected sight. The panic would mount, precious minutes obtained.

The elevator on the left had responded to the Frenchman's call. Vasili raced inside and pressed the button for the third floor. The doors closed, as far down the hallway two excited men ran out of room 213. One was the hotel manager; he saw the fallen Frenchman in the centre of a blood-soaked carpet. He screamed.

Scofield took off the jacket and the cap, bunching them in a corner, and put on his coat. The elevator stopped at the third floor; he tensed at the sight of a portly maid who walked in carrying towels over her arm. She nodded; he stared at her. The doors closed and they proceeded to the fourth, where the maid got off. Bray reached over quickly and again pressed the button for the sixth floor; there were none above it.

If it were possible, one part of the insanity was going to be over with. He was not going to run away only to start running again, wondering where the next trap would be sprung. Taleniekov was in the hotel and that was all he had to know.

Room five-zero-five. Taleniekov had given the number over the phone; he had said he would be waiting. Bray tried to think back, tried to recall a cipher or a code that matched the digits, but there were none he could remember, and he doubted the KGB man would pinpoint his location.

Five – Zero – Five.

Five – *Death* – Five?

I'm waiting for you on the fifth floor. One of us will die.

Was it as simple as that? Was Taleniekov reduced to a challenge? Was his ego so inflamed or his exhaustion so complete, that there was nothing left but spelling out the duelling ground?

For Christ's sake, let's get it over with! I'm coming, Taleniekov! You may be good, but you're no match for the man you call Beowulf Agate!

180

Ego. So necessary. So tiring.

The elevator reached the sixth floor. Bray held his breath as two well-dressed men entered. They were talking business, last year's figures being the bothersome topic. Both glanced briefly, disapprovingly, at him; he understood. The beard, his bloodshot eyes. He clutched his attaché case and avoided their looks. The door started to close and Bray stepped forward, his hand inside his jacket.

'Sorry,' he muttered. 'My floor.'

There was no one in the long corridor directly ahead, four storeys above 211 and 213. Far down on the right were two doors with circular windows. The service elevator. One panel had just swung shut; it still trembled. Scofield pulled his automatic partially out of his belt, then held it in place when he heard the rattle of dishes beyond the swinging doors. A service tray was being taken away; a man concealing himself with intent to kill did not make noise.

Down on the left, towards the staircase, a cleaning woman had finished a room. She pulled the door shut and wearily began to roll her cart towards the next.

Five-zero-five.

Five-death-five.

If there was a meeting ground, he was above it, on the high ground. But it was a high ground from which he could not see and time was running out. He thought briefly of approaching the cleaning woman, using her as a point somehow, but his appearance ruled it out. His appearance ruled out a great many things; shaving had been a luxury he could not afford, relieving himself precious moments given up, away from the sounds of the trap. The little things became so ominous, so all-important during the waiting games. And he was so tired.

Using the service elevator had to be ruled out; it was an enclosure too easily immobilized, isolated. The staircase was not much better, but he had an advantage; except for a roof – if there was an exit for the roof – it did not go higher. The sight-lines favoured the one above. Birds of prey swooped, they rarely attacked from below.

Sharks did, however.

Diversion. Any kind of diversion. Sharks were known to lunge up at inanimate objects, floating debris.

Bray walked rapidly towards the heavy door to the staircase, stopping briefly at the cleaning woman's cart. He removed four glass ashtrays, stuffing them into his pockets, and wedged the attaché case between his arm and chest.

As quietly as he could, he pressed on the crash bar; the heavy steel door opened. He started down the steps, staying close to the wall, listening to the sound of his enemy.

It was there. Several storeys below he could hear rapid footsteps slapping against the concrete stairs. They stopped and Scofield stood motionless. What followed confused him. There was a slicing sound, a series of quick movements – abrasive, metallic. What was it?

He looked back up the steps at the metal door he had just walked through, and he knew. The staircase was essentially a fire exit; the crash bars opened from the inside, not from the staircase, thus inhibiting thieves. The person below was using a thin sheet of metal, or plastic, stabbing the crack around the lock, pulling up and down to catch the rounded latch and open the door. The method was universal; most fire exits could be manipulated this way, if they were functional. They would be functional in this hotel.

The abrasive slicing stopped; the door had been opened.

Silence.

The door slammed shut. Scofield moved to the edge of the steps and looked below; he saw nothing but angled railings, squared at the corners, descending into darkness. Silently, he lowered one foot at a time and reached the next landing. He was on the fifth floor.

Five-zero-five. A meaningless number, a meaningless verbal complication.

Taleniekov's strategy was clear now. And logical. Bray would have used it himself. Once the chaos had begun, the Russian waited in the lobby, watching the elevators for a sign of his enemy, and when he did not appear, the assumption had to be that Beowulf was cut off, roving, probing for a way out.

Only after Taleniekov was certain that his enemy was not running into the streets, could he begin the final hunt from the staircase, lurching into the hallways, his weapon levelled for his moving target.

But the Russian could not start the kill from the top, he had to begin from the staircase in the lobby. He was forced to give up the high ground, as deadly a disadvantage on the staircase as it was in the hill country. Scofield put down his attaché case and took out two of the glass ashtrays from his pocket. The waiting was about over; it would happen any second now.

The door below crashed open. Bray hurled the first ashtray down between the railings; the smashing of glass echoed throughout the descending walls of concrete and steel.

Footsteps lurching. The thud of a heavy body lunging, making contact with a wall. Scofield sprang towards the open space; he threw down the second ashtray. The glass shattered directly beneath; the figure below darted past the edge of the railing. Bray fired his gun; his enemy screamed: twisting in the air, hurling himself out of the sight-line.

Scofield took three steps down, pressing himself against the wall. He saw a thrashing leg and fired again. There was the singing sound of a bullet ricocheting off steel, embedding itself in cement. He had missed; he had wounded the Russian, but not lamed him.

There was suddenly another sound. Sirens. Distant. Outside. Drawing closer. And shouting, muted by the heavy exit doors; orders were being screamed in corridors and hallways.

Options were being cut off, the chance of escape diminishing with each new sound. It had to end now. There was nothing left but a final exchange. A hundred lessons from the past were summarized in one: *draw fire first, make the gun expose itself which means exposing part of you. A superficial wound means nothing if it saves your life.*

The seconds ticked off; there was no alternative.

Bray took out the two remaining ashtrays from his pocket and hurled them over the open space above the railing. He stepped down, and at the first sound of shattering glass, swung out his left arm and shoulder, jabbing the air, arcing in a half-circle, part of him in the Russian's direct line of fire. But not his weapon; it was ready for his own attack.

Two deafening explosions filled the vertical tunnel . . .

The gun was blown out of his hand! Out of his *right hand*! He watched helplessly as the weapon sprang out of his fingers, specks of blood spreading over his palm, the high-pitched ring of still-ricocheting bullet bouncing from steel to steel.

He had been disarmed by a misplaced shot. Killed by an echo. The Browning automatic clattered down the staircase. He dived for it, yet even as he did so he knew it was too late. The killer below came into view, struggling to his feet, the large barrel of his gun rising, directed at Scofield's head.

It was not Taleniekov, not the face in a thousand photographs, the face he had hated for a decade! It was the man from Prague, a man he had used so often in the cause of free-thinking people. That man was going to kill him now.

Two thoughts came rapidly, one upon the other. Final summations, as it were. His death would come quickly; he was grateful for that. And, at the last, he had deprived Taleniekov of his trophy.

'We all do our jobs,' said the man from Prague, his three fingers tightening on the handle of the gun. 'You taught me that, Beowulf.'

'You'll never get out of here.'

'You forget your own lessons. "Drop your weapons, leave with the crowds." I'll get out. But you won't. If you did, too many would die.'

'*Padazdit!*' The voice thundered from above, no crash of a door preceding it, the man who roared having intruded swiftly, silently. The executioner from Prague spun to his left, ducking, swinging his powerful gun up the stairs at Vasili Taleniekov.

The Russian fired one shot, drilling a hole in Prague's forehead. The Czech fell across Scofield as Bray lunged for his gun, grabbing it off the step, rolling furiously down around the bend in the staircase. He fired wildly up at the KGB man; he would not permit Taleniekov to save him from Prague only to preserve his trophy.

I'll see you take your last breath . . .

Not here! Not now! Not while I can move!

And then he could not move. The impact came and Scofield only knew that his head seemed to have split wide open. His eyes were filled with blinding streaks of jagged white light, somehow mingling with sounds of chaos. Sirens, screams, voices yelling from distant chasms far below.

In his rolling dive to get out of Taleniekov's line of fire, he had crashed his skull into the sharp steel edge of the corner railing post. A misplaced bullet, an echo, an inanimate shaft of structural steel. They would lead to his death.

The image was blurred but unmistakable. The figure of the powerfully built Russian came running down the staircase. Bray tried to raise the gun still in his hand; he could not. It was being crushed under a heavy boot; the weapon was being prised out of his hand.

185

'Do it,' whispered Scofield. 'For Christ's sake, do it now! You've won by an accident. It's the only way you could.'

'I've won *nothing*! I want no such victory. Come! Move! The police are here; they'll be swarming up the staircase any moment.'

Bray could feel the strong arms lifting him up, pulling his arm around a thick neck, a shoulder shoved into his side for support. 'What the hell are you *doing*?' He was not sure the words were his; he could not think through the pain.

'You're hurt. The wound in your neck has opened; it's not bad. But your head is cut, I don't know how severely.'

'What?'

'There is a way out. This was my depot for two years. I know every inch of the building. Come! *Help* me. Move your legs! The *roof*.'

'My case . . .'

'I've got it.'

They were in a large, pitch-black metal enclosure, steady blasts of cold air causing the corrugated sides to rattle, the near-freezing temperature producing audible vibrations. They crawled along the ribbed floor in darkness.

'This is the main air duct,' explained Taleniekov, his voice low, aware of the magnified echo. 'The unit serves the hotel and the adjacent office building. Both are comparatively small structures, owned by the same company.'

Scofield had begun to find his mind again, the sheer movement forcing him to send impulses to his arms and legs. The Russian had torn a silk scarf apart, wrapping one half around Bray's head, the other around his throat. The bleeding had not stopped, but it was contained. He had found part of his mind, but there was still no clarity in what was happening.

'You saved my life. I want to know *why*!'

'Keep your voice down!' whispered the KGB man. 'And keep moving.'

'I want an answer!'

'I gave it to you.'

'You weren't convincing.'

'You and I, we live only with lies. We see nothing else.'

'From you I expect nothing else.'

'In a few minutes you can make your determination. I give you that.'

'What do you mean?'

'We'll reach the end of the duct; there is a transom ten or twelve feet from the floor. In a rooftop storage area. Once down I can get us out on the street, but every second counts. Should there be people in the vicinity of the transom, they must be frightened away. Gunshots will do it; fire above their heads.'

'*What?*'

'Yes. I'll give you your gun back.'

'You killed my wife.'

'You killed my brother. Before that your Army of Occupation returned the corpse of a young girl – a child – I loved very much. What came back was not pleasant.'

'I don't know anything about that.'

'Now you do. Make your determination.'

The metal-webbed transom was perhaps four feet wide. Below was a huge, dimly lit room that served as a miniature warehouse filled with crates and boxes of supplies. There was no one in sight. Taleniekov handed Scofield the automatic, and began forcing the metal screen from its brackets with his shoulder. It sprung loose and fell crashing to the cement floor. The Russian waited several moments for a response to the noise; there was none.

He turned his body around and, legs first, began sliding

out of the duct. His shoulders and head passed over the rim, his fingers gripping the edge; he was finding his balance, prepared for the drop to the floor.

The strange sound came faintly at first, then louder. *Step . . . scrape. Step . . . scrape. Step . . . scrape. Step.* Taleniekov froze, his body suspended between transom and floor.

'Good morning, Comrade,' said the voice softly in Russian. 'My walk has improved since Riga, no? They gave me a new foot.'

Bray pulled back into the shadows of the duct. Below, beside a large crate was a man with a cane. A cripple whose right leg was no leg at all, but instead a limb of stiff, straight wood beneath the trousers. The man continued as he took a gun from his pocket.

'I knew you too well, old friend. You were a great teacher. You gave me an hour to study your depot. There were several means of escape, but this is the one you would choose. I'm sorry, my teacher. We cannot afford you any longer.' He raised his gun.

Scofield fired.

They raced into the alley across the street from the hotel on Nebraska Avenue. Both leaned against the brick wall, breathing heavily, their eyes on the activity beyond. Three patrol cars, their lights revolving on their roofs, blocked the entrance of the hotel, hemming in an ambulance. Two stretchers were carried out, the bodies underneath covered with canvas; another emerged, Taleniekov could see the bloodied head of Prague. Uniformed police held back curious pedestrians, as their superiors rushed back and forth, barking into hand-held radios, issuing orders to unseen recipients.

A net was being formed around the hotel, all exits covered, all windows observed, weapons drawn against the unexpected.

'When you feel strong enough,' said Taleniekov, speaking between swallows of air, 'we'll slip into the crowds and walk several blocks away where it will be safer to find a taxi. However, I'll be honest with you. I don't know where to go.'

'I do,' said Scofield, pushing himself away from the wall. 'We'd better get going while there's confusion out there. Pretty soon they'll start an area search. They'll look for anyone wounded; there was a lot of gunfire.'

'One moment.' The Russian faced Bray. 'Three days ago I was on a truck in the hills outside Sevastopol. I knew then what I would say to you if we met. I say it now. We will either kill each other, Beowulf Agate, or we will talk.'

Scofield stared at Taleniekov. 'We may do both,' he said. 'Let's go.'

11

The cabin was in the backwoods of Maryland, on the banks of the Patuxent River, fields on three sides, water below. It was isolated, no other houses within a mile in any direction, accessible only by a primitive dirt road over which no taxi would venture. None was asked to do so.

Instead, Bray telephoned a man at the Iranian embassy, an unregistered SAVAK agent into hard drugs and exchange students whose exposure would be embarrassing to a benevolent Shah. A rented car was left for them in a metered parking lot on K Street, the keys under the floor mat.

The cabin belonged to a professor of political science at Georgetown, a closet homosexual Scofield had befriended years ago when he had torn up a fragment of a dossier that had nothing to do with the man's ability to evaluate classified data for the State Department. Bray had used the cabin a number of times during his recalls to Washington, always when he wished to be beyond reach of the desk-men, usually with a woman. A phone call to the professor was all that it took; no questions were asked, the location of the house key was given. This afternoon it was nailed beneath the second shingle from the right on the front roof. Bray got it by using a ladder propped against a near-by tree.

Inside, the decor was properly rustic; heavy beams and spartan furniture relieved by a profusion of quilted cushions, white walls and red-checked curtains. Flanking the stone fireplace were floor-to-ceiling bookcases, filled to capacity, the varied bindings lending additional colour and warmth.

'He is an educated man,' said Taleniekov, his eyes scanning the titles.

'Very,' replied Bray, lighting a gas-fed Franklin stove. 'There are matches on the mantel, the kindling stacked and ready to light.'

'How convenient,' said the KGB man, taking a wooden match from a small glass on the mantel, kneeling down and striking it.

'It's part of the rent. Whoever uses the cabin cleans the fireplace and stacks it.'

'Part of the rent? What are the other arrangements?'

'There's only one. Say nothing. About the place or the owner.'

'Again, convenient.' Taleniekov pulled his hand back as the fire leaped up from the dry wood.

'Very,' repeated Scofield, adjusting the heater, satisfied it was functioning. He stood up and faced the Russian. 'I don't want to discuss anything until I've had some sleep. You may not agree, but that's the way it's going to be.'

'I have no objection. I'm not sure I'm capable of being lucid right now, and I must be when we talk. If it's possible, I've had less sleep than you.'

'Two hours ago we could have killed each other,' said Bray, standing motionless. 'Neither of us did.'

'Quite the reverse,' agreed the KGB man, returning Scofield's gaze. 'We prevented others from doing it.'

'Which cancels any obligation between us.'

'No such obligations exist, of course. However, I submit you may find a larger one when we talk.'

'You could be right, but I doubt it. You may have to live with Moscow, but I don't have to live with what happened here in Washington today. I can do something about it. Maybe that's the difference between us.'

'For both our sakes – for all our sakes – I fervently hope you're right.'

'I am. I'm also going to get some sleep.' Scofield pointed

to a couch against the wall. 'That pulls out into a bed; there are blankets in the closet over there. I'll use the bedroom.' He started for the door, then stopped and turned to the Russian. 'Incidentally, the door will be locked, and I'm a very light sleeper.'

'A condition that afflicts us both, I'm sure,' said Taleniekov. 'You have nothing to fear from me.'

'I never did,' Bray said.

Scofield heard faint, sharp crackling sounds and spun under the sheets, his hand gripping the Browning automatic by his knees. He raised it between the covers as his feet shot out over the side of the bed; he was prepared to crouch and fire.

There was no one in the room. Moonlight streamed through the north window, shafts of colourless white light separated by the thick panes into single streaks of suspended, eerie illumination. For a moment he was not sure where he was, so complete had been his exhaustion, so deep his sleep. He knew by the time his feet touched the floor; his enemy was in the next room. A very strange enemy who had saved his life, and whose life he had saved minutes later.

Bray looked at the luminous dial of his watch. It was quarter past four in the morning. He had slept nearly thirteen hours, the heavy weight of his arms and legs, the adhesive moisture in his eyes, and the dryness of his throat evidence of having moved very little during that time. He sat for a while on the side of the bed, breathing the cold air deeply, putting the gun down and shaking his hands, slapping his fingers together. He looked over at the locked door of the bedroom.

Taleniekov was up and had started a fire, the sharp crackling was now the unmistakable sound of burning wood. Scofield decided to put off seeing the Russian for a few more minutes. His face itched, the growth of his beard so uncomfortable it had caused the beginning of a rash on his neck. There was always shaving equipment in the bathroom; he would afford himself the luxury of a shave and change the bandages he had placed on his neck and skull fourteen hours ago. It would postpone for a bit longer his talk with the former – defected? – KGB man. Whatever it concerned, Bray wanted no part of it, yet the unexpected events and decisions of the past twenty-four hours told him he was already involved. The bullet graze on his neck stung, the pain in his head a numbing throb.

It was 4.37 when he unlocked the door and opened it. Taleniekov was standing in front of the fire, sipping from a cup in his hand.

'I apologize if the fire awakened you,' the Russian said. 'Or the sound of the front door – if you heard it.'

'The heater went out,' said Scofield, looking down at the flameless gas Franklin that was the cabin's source of heat.

'I think the propane tank is empty.'

'Is that why you went outside?'

'No, I went outside to relieve myself; there's no toilet here.'

'I forgot.'

'Did you hear me leave? Or return?'

'Is that coffee?'

'Yes,' answered Taleniekov. 'A bad habit I picked up from the West. Your tea has no character. The pot's on the burner.' The KGB man gestured beyond a room divider where stove, sink and refrigerator were lined up against the wall. 'I'm surprised you did not smell the aroma of freshly made coffee.'

'I thought I did,' lied Scofield, crossing to the stove and the pot. 'But it was weak.'

'And now we've both made our childish points.'

'Childishly,' added Bray, pouring coffee. 'You keep saying you have something to tell me. Go ahead.'

'First, I shall ask you a question. Have you ever heard of an organization called the Matarese?'

Scofield paused, remembering; he nodded. 'Political killers for hire, run by a council in Corsica. It started well over a half-century ago and died out in the late 'forties, after the war. What about it?'

'It never died out. It went farther underground – became dormant, if you like – but it returned in a far more dangerous form. It's been operating since the early 'sixties. It operates now. It has infiltrated the most sensitive and powerful areas of both our governments. Its objective is the control over both our countries. The Matarese was responsible for the murders of General Blackburn here and Dimitri Yurievich in my country.'

Bray sipped his coffee, studying the Russian's face over the rim of the cup. 'How do you know that? Why do you believe it?'

'An old man who saw more in his lifetime than you and I combined made the identification. He was not wrong; he was one of the few who admitted – or will ever admit – having dealt with the Matarese.'

'*Saw? Was?* Past tenses.'

'He died. He called for me while he was dying; he wanted me to know. He had access to information neither you nor I would be given under any circumstances.'

'Who was he?'

'Aleksie Krupsky. The name is meaningless, I realize, so I'll explain.'

'Meaningless?' interrupted Scofield, crossing to an armchair in front of the fire, and sitting down. 'Not entirely: Krupsky, the white cat of *Krivoi Rog. Istrebitel.* The last of the exterminators from Section Nine, KGB. The original Nine, of course.'

'You do your school work well, but then, as they say, you're a Harvard man.'

'That kind of school work can be helpful. Krupsky was

banished twenty years ago. He became a non-person. If he were alive, I figured he was vegetating in Grasnov, not a consultant being fed information by people in the Kremlin. I don't believe your story.'

'Believe it now,' said Taleniekov, sitting down opposite Bray. 'Because it was not "people" in the Kremlin, just one man. His son. For thirty years one of the highest-ranking survivors of the Politburo. For the past six, Premier of Soviet Russia.'

Scofield put his cup down on the floor and again studied the KGB man's face. It was the face of a practised liar, a professional liar, but not a liar by nature. He was not lying now. 'Krupsky's son the Premier? That's . . . a shock.'

'As it was to me, but not so shocking when you think about it. Guided at every turn, protected by his father's extensive collection of . . . shall we say memorabilia. Hypothetically, it could have happened here. Suppose your late John Edgar Hoover had a politically ambitious son. Who could have stood in his way? Hoover's secret files would have paved any road, even the floors leading to the Oval Office. The landscape is different, but the trees are the same genus. They haven't varied much since the senators gave Rome to Caligula.'

'What did Krupsky tell you?'

'The past first. There were things I could not believe, until I spoke of them to several retired leaders of the Politburo. One frightened old man confirmed them, the others caused a plan to be mounted that called for my execution.'

'Your . . . ?'

'Yes. Vasili Vasilievich Taleniekov, master strategist, KGB. An irascible man who may have seen his best years, but whose knowledge could be called upon for several decades perhaps – from a farm in Grasnov. We are a practical people; that would have been the practical solution. In spite of the minor doubts we all have, I

195

believed that; I knew it was my future. But not after I mentioned the Matarese. Abruptly, everything changed. I, who have served my country well, was suddenly the enemy.'

'What specifically did Krupsky say? What – in your judgement – was confirmed?'

Taleniekov recounted the dying *istrebitel*'s words, admissions that traced scores of assassinations to the Matarese, including Stalin, Beria and Roosevelt. How the Corsican organization had been used by all the major governments, both within their borders and outside of them. None was exempt from the stain. Soviet Russia, England, France, Germany, Italy . . . the United States; the leaders of each, at one time or another, had made contracts with the Matarese.

'That's all been speculated upon before,' said Bray. 'Quietly, I grant you, but nothing concrete ever came out of the investigations.'

· 'Because no one of substance ever dared testify. In Krupsky's words, the revelations would be catastrophic for governments everywhere. Now, there are new tactics being employed, all for the purpose of creating instability in the power centres.'

'What are they?'

'Acts of terrorism. Bombings, kidnappings, the hijacking of aircraft; ultimatums issued by bands of fanatics, wholesale slaughter promised if they are not met. They grow in numbers every month and the vast majority are funded by the Matarese.'

'How?'

'I can only surmise. The Matarese council studies the objectives of the parties involved, sends in the experts, and provides covert financing. Fanatics do not labour over the sources of funds, only their availability. I submit that you and I have used such men and women more often than we can count.'

'For distinctly accountable purposes,' said Bray, picking up his cup from the floor. 'What about Blackburn and Yurievich? What did the Matarese accomplish by killing them?'

'Krupsky believed it was to test the leaders, to see if their own men could control each government's reactions. I'm not so sure now. I think perhaps there was something else. Frankly, because of what you've told me.'

'What's that?'

'Yurievich. You said he was your operation. Is that true?'

Bray frowned. 'True, but not that simple. Yurievich was grey; he wasn't going to defect in any normal sense. He was a scientist, convinced both sides had gone too far. He didn't trust the maniacs. It was a probe; we weren't sure where we were going.'

'Are you aware that General Blackburn, who was nearly destroyed by the war in Korea, did what no Chairman of the Joint Chiefs has ever done in your history? He met secretly with your potential enemies. In Sweden, in the city of Skellefteå on the Gulf of Bothnia, travelling under cover as a tourist. It was our judgement that he would go to any lengths to avoid the repetition of pointless slaughter. He abhorred conventional warfare, and he did not believe nuclear weapons would ever be used.' The Russian stopped and leaned forward. 'Two men who believed deeply, passionately, in the rejection of human sacrifice, who sought accommodation – both killed by the Matarese. So perhaps testing was only a part of the exercise. There could well have been another: to eliminate powerful men who believed in stability.'

At first Scofield did not reply; the information about Blackburn was astonishing. 'In the testing then, they pointed at me with Yurievich . . .'

'And at me with Blackburn,' completed Taleniekov.

'A Browning Magnum, Grade Four, was used to kill Yurievich; a Graz-Burya for Blackburn.'

'And both of us set up for execution.'

'Exactly,' said the Soviet. 'Because above all men in either country's intelligence service, we cannot be permitted to live. That will never change because we cannot change. Krupsky was right: we are diversions; we will be used and killed. We are too dangerous.'

'Why do they think so?'

'They've studied us. They know we could no more accept the Matarese than we do the maniacs within our own branches. We are dead men, Scofield.'

'Speak for yourself!' Bray was suddenly angry. 'I'm out, terminated, *finished*! I don't give a Goddamn what happens out there! Don't you make judgements about me!'

'They've already been made. By others.'

'Because *you* say so?' Scofield got up, putting the coffee down, his hand not far from the Browning in his belt.

'Because I *believed* the man who told me. It's why I'm *here*, why I *saved* your life and did not take it myself.'

'I have to wonder about that, don't I?'

'What?'

'Everything timed, even to your knowing where Prague was on the staircase.'

'I killed a man who had you under his gun!'

'*Prague?* A minor sacrifice. I'm a terminated encyclopaedia. I have no proof my government reached Moscow, only possible conclusions based on what *you* told me. Maybe I'm missing the obvious, maybe the great Taleniekov is eating a little temporary crow to bring in Beowulf Agate.'

'*Damn* you, Scofield!' roared the KGB man, springing up from the chair. 'I should have let you die! Hear me clearly. What you suggest is unthinkable and the KGB knows it. My feelings run too deep. I'd never bring you in. I'd kill you first.'

Bray stared at the Russian, the honesty of Taleniekov's

statement so clear. 'I believe you,' said Scofield, nodding, his anger diminishing in weariness. 'But it doesn't change anything. I don't care. I really don't give a Goddamn . . . I'm not even sure I want to kill you any more. I just want to be left alone.' Bray turned away. 'Take the keys to the car and get out of here. Consider yourself . . . alive.'

'Thank you for your generosity, Beowulf, but I'm afraid it's too late.'

'What?' Scofield turned back to the Soviet.

'I did not finish. A man was caught, chemicals administered. There is a timetable, two months, three at the outside. The words were: "Moscow by assassination; Washington by purchase – murder, if necessary." When it happens, neither you nor I will survive. They'll track us to the ends of the earth.'

'Wait a minute,' said Bray, furious. 'Are you telling me that your people *have* a man!'

'Had,' interrupted Taleniekov. 'Cyanide was implanted under his skin; he reached it.'

'But he was *heard*. He was taped, recorded. His words were there!'

'Heard. Not taped, not recorded. And only by one man – who was warned by his father not to permit anyone else to listen.'

'The *Premier*?'

'Yes.'

'Then he knows!'

'Yes, he knows. And all he can do is try to protect himself – nothing particularly new in his position – but he can't speak of it. For to speak of it, as Krupsky said, is to acknowledge the past. This is the age of conspiracy, Scofield. Who cares to bring up past contracts? In my country there are a number of unexplained corpses; you're not so different over here. The Kennedys, Martin Luther King; perhaps most stunning, Franklin Roosevelt. We could all be at each other's throats – more precisely on the nuclear buttons – if our combined pasts were revealed. What would you do, if you were the Premier?'

'Protect myself,' said Bray softly. 'Oh, my God . . .'

'Now do you see?'

'I don't want to. I *really* don't *want* to. I'm out!'

'I submit that you cannot be. Nor I. The proof was yesterday on Nebraska Avenue. We're marked; they want us. They convinced others to have us killed – for the wrong reasons – but they were behind the strategy. Can you doubt it?'

'I wish I could. The manipulators are always easiest to manipulate, con-men the biggest suckers. Jesus!' Scofield walked to the stove to pour himself more coffee. Suddenly, he was struck by something not said, unclear. 'I don't understand. From what little's known about the Matarese, it started as a cult and evolved into a business. It accepted contracts – or *supposedly* accepted contracts – on the basis of feasibility and price. It killed for money; it was never interested in power, *per se*. Why is it interested now?'

'I don't know,' said the KGB man. 'Neither did Krupsky. He was dying and not very lucid, but he said the answer might be in Corsica.'

'Corsica? Why?'

'It's where it all began.'

'Not where it *is*. *If* it is. The word was that the Matarese moved out of Corsica in the mid-'thirties. Contracts were negotiated as far away as London, New York . . . even Berlin. Centres of international traffic.'

'Then perhaps clues to an answer is more appropriate. The council of the Matarese was formed in Corsica, only one name ever revealed. Guillaume de Matarese. Who were the others? Where did they go? Who are they *now*?'

'There's a quicker way of finding out than going to Corsica. If the Matarese is even a whisper in Washington, there's one person who can track it down. He's the one

I was going to call anyway. I wanted my life straightened out.'

'Who is he?'

'Robert Winthrop,' said Bray.

'The creator of Consular Operations.' The Russian nodded. 'A good man who had no stomach for what he built.'

'The *Cons Op* you're referring to isn't the one he began. He's still the only man I've heard of who can call up the White House and see the President in twenty minutes. Very little goes on that he doesn't know about. Or can't find out about.' Scofield glanced over at the fire, remembering. 'It's strange. In a way he's responsible for everything I am, and he doesn't approve of me. But I think he'll listen.'

The nearest telephone booth was three miles down the highway beyond the dirt road to the cabin. It was ten past eight when Bray stepped in, shielding his eyes from the glare of the morning sun, and pulled the glass door shut. He had found Winthrop's private number in his attaché case; he had not called it in years. He dialled, hoping it was still the same.

It was. The cultivated voice on the line brought back many memories. Possibilities missed, many others taken.

'Scofield! Where *are* you?'

'I'm afraid I can't tell you that. Please try to understand.'

'I understand you're in a great deal of trouble, and nothing will be served by running *away*. Congdon called. The man killed in the hotel was shot with a Russian gun . . .'

'I know. The Russian who killed him saved my life. That man was *sent* by Congdon, so were the other two. They were my execution team. From Prague, Marseilles and Amsterdam.'

201

'Oh, my *God* . . .' The elder statesman was silent for a moment and Bray did not interrupt that silence. 'Do you know what you're saying?' asked Winthrop.

'Yes, sir. You know me well enough to know I *wouldn't* say it unless I were sure. I'm not mistaken. I spoke to the man from Prague before he died.'

'He *confirmed* it?'

'In oblique words, yes. But then, that's how those cables are sent; the words are always oblique.'

Again there was a moment of silence before the old man spoke. 'I can't believe it, Bray. For a reason you couldn't know. Congdon came to see me a week ago. He was concerned how you'd take retirement. He had the usual worries: a highly knowledgeable agent terminated against his will with too much time on his hands, perhaps too much to drink. He's a cold fellow, that Congdon, and I'm afraid he angered me. After all you've been through to have so little trust . . . I rather sardonically mentioned what you've just described – not that I ever dreamed he would consider such a thing, just that I was appalled at his attitude. So I *can't* believe it. Don't you see? He'd know I'd recognize it. He wouldn't take that risk.'

'Then someone gave him the order, sir. That's what we have to talk about. Those three men knew where to find me, and there was only one way they could've learned. It was a KGB drop and they were *Cons Op* personnel. Moscow gave it to Congdon; he relayed it.'

'Congdon reached the *Soviets*? That's not plausible. Even if he tried, why would they co-operate? Why would they reveal a drop?'

'Their own man was part of the negotiation; they wanted him killed. He was trying to contact me. We'd exchanged cables.'

'Taleniekov?'

It was Scofield's moment to pause. He answered quietly. 'Yes, sir.'

'A *white* contact?'

'Yes. I misread it, but that's what it was. I'm convinced now.'

'*You* . . . and Taleniekov? *Extraordinary* . . .'

'The circumstances are extraordinary. Do you remember an organization from the 'forties that went by the name of the Matarese . . . ?'

They agreed to meet at nine o'clock that evening, a mile north of the Missouri Avenue exit of Rock Creek Park on the eastern side. There was an indented stretch of pavement off the road where automobiles could park and strollers could enter the various paths that overlooked a scenic ravine. Winthrop intended to cancel the day's appointments and concentrate on learning whatever there was to learn about Bray's astonishing – if fragmentary – information.

'He'll convene the Forty Committee, if he has to,' said Scofield to Taleniekov on the way back to the cabin.

'Can he do that?' asked the Russian.

'The President can,' answered Bray.

The two men talked little during the day, the strain of proximity uncomfortable for each. Taleniekov read from the extensive bookshelves, glancing at Scofield now and then, the look in his eyes a mixture of remembered fury and curiosity.

Bray felt the glances; he refused to acknowledge them. He listened to the radio for news reports about the carnage at the hotel on Nebraska Avenue, and the death of a Russian attaché in the adjacent building. They were played down, de-emphasized, no mention made of the dead embassy official. It was suggested that the hotel killings were foreign in origin – that much was allowed – and no doubt criminally orientated, probably related to upper levels of the narcotics trade. The suppressants had been applied; the Department of State had moved swiftly, with sure-footed censorship.

And with each progressively fading report Scofield felt progressively trapped. He was becoming intrinsic to something he wanted no part of; his new life was not around the corner any longer. He began to wonder where it was, or if it would be. He was being inexorably drawn into an enigma called the Matarese.

At four o'clock he went for a walk in the fields and along the banks of the Patuxent. As he left the cabin, he made sure the Russian saw him slip the Browning automatic into his holster. The KGB man did see; he placed his Graz-Burya on the table next to the chair.

At five o'clock, Taleniekov made an observation. 'I think we should position ourselves a good hour before the appointment.'

'I trust Winthrop,' replied Bray curtly.

'With good reason, I'm sure. But can you trust those he'll be contacting?'

'He won't tell anyone he's meeting us. He wants to talk to you at length. He'll have questions. Names, past positions, military ranks.'

'I'll try to provide answers where they are relative to the Matarese. I will not be compromised in other areas.'

'Bully for you.'

'Nevertheless, I still think . . .'

'We'll leave in fifteen minutes,' interrupted Scofield. 'There's a diner on the way; we'll eat separately.'

At 7.35, Bray drove the rented car into the south end of the parking area on the border of Rock Creek Park. He and the KGB man made four penetrations into the woods, sweeping in arcs off the paths, checking the trees and the rocks and the ravine below for signs of intruders. The night was bitterly cold; there were no strollers, no one anywhere. They met at a pre-arranged spot on the edge of the small gorge. Taleniekov spoke first.

'I saw nothing; the area is secure.'

Scofield looked at his watch in the darkness. 'It's nearly eight-thirty. I'll wait by the car; you stay up here at this end. I'll meet with him first and then signal you.'

'How? It's several hundred yards.'

'I'll strike a match.'

'Very appropriate.'

'What?'

'Nothing. It's unimportant.'

At two minutes to nine, Winthrop's limousine came out of the Rock Creek exit, drove into the parking area, and stopped within twenty feet of the rented car. The sight of the chauffeur disturbed Bray, but only momentarily. Scofield recognized the huge man instantly; he had been with Robert Winthrop for over two decades. Rumours about a chequered Marine Corps career cut short by several courts martial followed the chauffeur, but Winthrop never discussed him other than to call him 'my friend Stanley'. No one ever pressed.

Bray walked out of the shadows towards the limousine. Stanley opened the door and was on the pavement in one motion, his right hand in his pocket, in his left a flashlight. He turned it on. Scofield shut his eyes. It went off in seconds.

'Hello, Stanley,' said Bray.

'It's been a long time, Mr Scofield,' replied the chauffeur. 'Nice to see you.'

'Thanks. Good to see you.'

'The ambassador's waiting,' continued the driver, reaching down and snapping the lock release. 'The door's open now.'

'Fine. By the way, in a couple of minutes I'm going to get out of the car and strike a match. It's the signal for a man to come and join us. He's up at the other end; he'll walk out of one of the paths.'

'I gotcha. The ambassador said there'd be two of you. OK.'

'What I'm trying to say is, if you still smoke those thin cigars of yours, wait till I get out before you light up. I'd like a few moments alone with Mr Winthrop.'

'You've got a hell of a memory,' said Stanley, tapping his jacket pocket with the flashlight. 'I was about to have one.'

Bray got into the back seat of the car and faced the man who was responsible for his life. Winthrop had grown old, so old, but in the dim light his eyes were still electric, still filled with concern. They shook hands, the elder statesman prolonging the grip.

'I've thought about you often,' he said softly, his eyes searching Scofield's, then noting the bandages and wincing. 'I have mixed feelings, but I don't think I have to tell you that.'

'No, sir, you don't.'

'So many things changed, didn't they, Bray? The ideals, the opportunities to do so much for so many. We were crusaders, really. At the beginning.' The old man released Scofield's hand and smiled. 'Do you remember? You came up with a processing plan that was to be cross-collateralized with lend-lease. Debts in occupied territories for multiple immigration. A brilliant concept in economic diplomacy, I've always said that. Human lives for monies that were never going to be repaid anyway.'

'It would have been rejected.'

'Probably, but in the arena of world opinion it would have pushed the Soviets to the wall. I recall your words. You said "if we're supposed to be a capitalistic government, don't walk away from it. Use it, define it. American citizens paid for half the Russian Army. Stress the psychological obligation. Get something, get *people*." Those were your words.'

'That was a graduate student expounding on naïve theoretical geopolitics.'

'There's often a great deal of truth in such naïveté. You know, I can still see that graduate student. I wonder about him . . .'

'There's no time now, sir,' interrupted Scofield. 'Taleniekov's waiting. Incidentally, we checked the area; it's clear.'

The old man's eyes blinked. 'Did you think it would be otherwise?'

'I was worried about a tap on your phone.'

'No need for that,' said Winthrop. 'Such devices have to be listed somewhere, recorded somewhere. I wouldn't care to be the person who did such a thing. Too many private conversations take place on my telephone. It's my best protection.'

'Did you learn anything?'

'About the Matarese? No . . . and *yes*. No, in the sense that even the most rarefied intelligence data contained no mention of it whatsoever, hasn't for the past forty-three years. The President assured me of this and I trust him. He was appalled; he leapt at the possibility and put men on the alert. He was furious, and frightened, I think.'

'What's the "yes"?'

The old man chose his words carefully. 'It's obscure but it's there. Before I decided to call the President, I reached five men who for years – decades – have been involved in the most sensitive areas of intelligence and diplomacy. Of the five, three remembered the Matarese and were shocked. They offered to do whatever they could to help, the spectre of the Matarese's return was quite terrifying to them . . . Yet the other two – men, who if anything, are far more knowledgeable than their colleagues – claimed *never* to have heard of it. Their reactions made no sense; they *had* to have heard of it. Just as I had – my information minimal but certainly not forgotten. When I said as much, when I pressed them, both behaved rather strangely, and considering our past associations, not without insult. Each treated me as though I were some kind of aged patrician, given to senile fantasies. Really, it was astonishing.'

'Who were they?'

'Again, odd . . .'

A flash of light in the distance; Scofield's eyes were drawn to it. And another . . . and *another*. Matches were being struck in rapid succession.

Taleniekov.

The KGB man was cupping matches and lighting one after another furiously. It was a warning. Taleniekov was warning him that something had happened – *was happening*. Suddenly the distant flame was constant, but broken by a hand held in front of the flame – in rapid sequences, more light, less light. Basic Morse. Dots and dashes.

Three dots repeated twice. *S.* A long spill, repeated once. A single dash. *T.*

S. T.

'What's the matter?' asked Winthrop.

'Just a second,' replied Scofield.

Three dots, broken, then followed by a dash. The letters *S* and *T* were being repeated. *S. T.*

Surveillance. Terminal.

The flame moved to the left, towards the road bordering the woods of the parking area, and was extinguished. The Soviet agent was repositioning himself. Bray turned back to the old man.

'How certain are you about your telephone?'

'Very. It's never been tapped. I have ways of knowing.'

'They may not be extensive enough.' Scofield touched the window button; the glass rolled down and he called to the chauffeur standing in front of the limousine. 'Stan, come here!' The driver did so. 'When you drove through the park, did you check to see if anyone followed you?'

'Sure did, and no way. I keep an eye on the rear view mirror. I always do, especially when we're meeting someone at night . . . Did you see the light up there? Was it your man?'

'Yes. He was telling me someone else was here.'

'Impossible,' said Winthrop emphatically. 'If there is, it's no concern of ours. This is, after all, a public park.'

'I don't want to alarm you, sir, but Taleniekov's experienced. There are no headlights, no cars in the road. Whoever's out there doesn't want us to know it, and it's not a night for a casual walk. I'm afraid it does concern us.' Bray opened the door. 'Stan, I'm going to grab my briefcase from my car. When I get back, drive out of here. Stop briefly at the north end of the lot by the road . . .'

'What about the Russian?' asked Winthrop.

'That's why we're stopping. He'll know enough to jump in. He'd better.'

'*Wait* a minute,' said Stanley, no deference in his voice. 'If there's any trouble, I'm not stopping for anyone. I've only got one job. To get *him* out of here. Not you or anybody else.'

'We don't have time to argue. Start the engine.' Bray ran to the rented car, the keys in his hand. He unlocked the door, removed his attaché case from the front seat, and started back towards the limousine.

He never reached it. A beam of powerful light pierced through the darkness, aimed at Robert Winthrop's huge automobile. Stanley was behind the wheel, gunning the motor, prepared to bolt out of the area. Whoever held the light was not going to allow that to happen. He wanted that car . . . and whoever was in that car.

The limousine's wheels spun, screeching on the pavement, as the huge car surged forward. A staccato spray of gunfire erupted; windows shattered, bullets crunched into metal. The limousine wove back and forth in abrupt half-circles, seemingly out of control.

Two loud reports came from the woods beyond; the searchlight exploded, a scream of pain followed. Winthrop's car straightened out briefly, then lurched into a sharp left turn. Caught in the headlights were two men, weapons drawn, a third on the ground.

Bray's gun was in his hand; he dropped to the pavement and fired. One of the two men fell as the limousine completed the turn and roared out of the parking lot into the south-bound road.

Scofield rolled to his right; two shots were fired, the bullets singing off the pavement where he had been seconds ago. Bray got to his feet and ran in the darkness towards the railing that fronted the ravine.

He lunged over the top rail, his attaché case slamming into the wood post, the sound distinct. The next gun-shot was expected; it came as he hugged the earth and the rocks.

Lights. Headlights! Two beams shooting overhead, accompanied by the sound of a racing car. The smashing of glass came hard upon tyres screeching to a sudden stop. A shout – unclear, hysterical . . . cut off by a loud explosion – preceded silence.

The engine had stalled, the headlights still on, revealing curls of smoke and two immobile bodies on the ground, a third on his knees, looking around in panic. The man heard something; he spun and raised his gun.

A weapon was fired from the woods. It was final; the would-be killer fell.

'*Scofield!*' Taleniekov shouted.

'Over here!' Bray lunged up over the railing and ran towards the source of the Russian's voice. Taleniekov walked out of the woods; he was no more than ten feet from the stalled automobile. Both men approached the car warily; the driver's window had been shattered, blown apart by a single shot from the KGB man's automatic. The head beyond the fragmented glass was bloodied but recognizable. The right hand was wrapped in a tight bandage – still wrapped from an injured thumb broken on a bridge in Amsterdam at three o'clock in the morning by an angry, tired older man.

It was the aggressive young agent, Harry, who had killed so needlessly in the rain that night.

'Good *God*!' said Scofield.

'You know him?' asked Taleniekov, a curious note in his voice.

'His name was Harry. He worked for me in Amsterdam.'

The Russian was silent for a moment, then spoke. 'He was *with* you in Amsterdam, but he did not work for you, and his name was not "Harry". That young man is a Soviet intelligence officer, trained since the age of nine at the American Compound in Novograd. He was a VKR agent.'

Bray studied Taleniekov's face, then looked back through the shattered window at Harry. 'Congratulations. Things fall into place more clearly now.'

'They don't for me, I'm afraid,' said the KGB man. 'Believe me when I tell you that it is most unlikely that any order out of Moscow would include a direct attack on Robert Winthrop. We're not fools. He's above reprisals – a voice and a skill to be preserved, not struck down. And certainly not for such – personnel – as you and me.'

'What do you mean?'

'This was an execution team, as surely as those men at the hotel. You and I were not to be isolated, not to be taken separately. The kill was inclusive. Winthrop was to be executed as well, and for all we know he may have been. I submit that the order did not come from Moscow.'

'It didn't come from the State Department. I'm damn sure of that.'

'Agreed. Neither Washington nor Moscow, but a source capable of issuing orders in the name of one, or the other, or both.'

'The Matarese?' said Scofield.

The Russian nodded. 'The Matarese.'

Bray held his breath, trying to think, to absorb it all. 'If Winthrop's still alive, he'll be caged, tapped, held under a microscope. I won't be able to get near him. They'd kill me on sight.'

'Again, I agree. Are there others you trust that can be reached?'

'It's crazy,' said Scofield, shivering in the cold – and at the thought that now struck him. 'There should be, but I don't know who they are. Whoever I went to would have to turn me over, the laws are clear about that. Police warrants aside, there's a little matter of national security. The case against me will be built quickly, legally. Suspected of treason, internal espionage, delivering information to the enemy. No one will touch me.'

'Surely there are people who will *listen* to you.'

'Listen to what? What do I tell them? What have I got? *You?* You'd be thrown into a maximum security hospital before you could say your name. The words of a dying *istrebitel*? A Communist killer? Where's the verification, even the logic? Goddamn it, we're cut off. All we've got are shadows!'

Taleniekov took a step forward, his conviction in his voice. 'Perhaps old Krupsky was right; perhaps the answer is in Corsica, after all.'

'Oh, Christ . . .'

'Hear me out. You say we have only shadows. If so, if we *had* more, traced even a few names, constructed a fabric of probability – built our own case if you will. Then could you go to someone, force him to listen to you?'

'From a distance,' answered Bray slowly. 'Only from a distance. Beyond reach.'

'Naturally.'

'The case would have to be more than probable, it'd have to get goddamned conclusive.'

'I, too, could move men in Moscow if I had such proof. It was my hope that over here an inquiry might be made with less evidence. You're notorious for your never-ending Senate inquiries. I merely assumed it could be done, that you could bring it about.'

'Not now. Not me.'

'Corsica, then?'

'I don't know. I'd have to think about it. There's still Winthrop.'

'You said yourself you could not reach him. If you tried to get near him, they'd kill you.'

'People have tried before. I'll protect myself. I've got to find out what happened. He saw it for himself; if he's alive and I can talk to him, he'll know what to do.'

'And if he's *not* alive, or you cannot reach him?'

Scofield looked at the dead men on the pavement. 'Maybe the only thing that's left. Corsica.'

The KGB man shook his head. 'I look at odds more thoroughly than you, Beowulf. I won't wait. I won't risk that "hospital" you speak of. I'll go to Corsica now.'

'If you do, start on the south-east coast, north of Porto Vecchio.'

'Why?'

'It's where it all began. It's Matarese country.'

Taleniekov nodded. 'Again, the school work. Thank you. Perhaps we'll meet in Corsica.'

'Can you get out of the country?' asked Bray.

'Getting in, getting out . . . easily managed. These are not obstacles. What about yourself? If you decide to join me.'

'I can buy my way to London, to Paris. I've got accounts there. If I do, count on three days, four at the outside. There are small inns up in the hills. I'll find you . . .'

Scofield stopped. Both men turned swiftly at the sound of an approaching automobile. A sedan swung casually off the road into the parking area. In the front seat was a couple, the man's arm draped over the woman's shoulder. The headlights shone directly on the immobile bodies on the pavement, the spill illuminating the shattered window of the stalled car and the bloody head inside.

The driver whipped his arm off the woman's shoulder, pushing her down on the seat, and gripped the steering wheel with both hands. He spun it violently to the right and sped back into the road, the roar of the motor echoing throughout the woods and the open space.

'They'll reach the police,' said Bray. 'Let's get out of here.'

'I submit it would be best not to use that car,' replied the KGB man.

'Why not?'

'Winthrop's chauffeur. You may trust him. I'm not sure I do.'

'That's crazy! He was damn near killed!'

Taleniekov gestured at the dead men on the pavement. 'These were marksmen, Russian or American, it makes no difference, they were experts – the Matarese would employ no less. The windshield of that limousine was at least five feet wide, the driver behind it an easy target for a novice. Why wasn't he shot? Why wasn't that car stopped? We look for traps, Beowulf. We were led into one and we didn't see it. Perhaps even by Winthrop himself.'

Bray felt sick; he had no answer. 'We'll separate. It's better for both of us.'

'Corsica, perhaps?'

'Maybe. You'll know if I get there. Three, four days at the outside. If I go.'

'Very well.'

'Taleniekov?'

'Yes?'

'Thanks for using the matches.'

'Under the circumstances, I believe you would have done the same for me.'

'Under the circumstances . . . yes, I would.'

'Has it struck you? We did not kill each other, Beowulf Agate. We talked.'

'We talked.'

A lone siren was carried on the cold night wind. Others would be heard soon; patrol cars would converge on the killing ground. Both men turned away from each other and ran, Scofield down the dark patch into the woods beyond the rented car, Taleniekov towards the railing that fronted the ravine in Rock Creek Park.

Book II

12

The thick-beamed fishing boat ploughed through the chopping swells like a heavy awkward animal dimly aware that the waters were unfriendly. Waves slapped against the bow and the sides, sending cascading sprays over the gunwhales, the tails of salt whipped by the early-morning winds into the faces of men handling the nets.

One man, however, was not involved with the drudgery of the catch. He pulled at no rope and manipulated no hook, nor did he join in the cursing and laughter that were by-products of making a living from the sea. Instead, he sat alone on the deck, a thermos of coffee in one hand, a cupped cigarette in the other. It was understood that should French or Italian patrol boats approach, he would become a fisherman, but if none did he was to be left by himself. No one objected to this strange man without a name, for each member of the crew was 10,000 lire richer for his presence. The boat had picked him up on a pier in San Vincenzo. The vessel's schedule had called for a dawn departure from the Italian coast, but the stranger had suggested that if the coast of Corsica were seen by dawn, captain and crew would have a far better catch for their labours. Rank had its privileges; the captain received 15,000 lire. They had sailed out of San Vincenzo before midnight.

Scofield twisted the top back on to the thermos and threw his cigarette over the side. He stood up and stretched, peering through the mists at the coastline. They had made good time. According to the captain they would be in sight of Solenzara within minutes; and within an hour they would drop off their esteemed passenger between Sainte Lucie and Porto Vecchio. No problems were anticipated; there were scores of deserted inlets on the rocky shoreline for a temporarily disabled fishing boat.

Bray yanked on the cord looped around the handle of his attaché case and strapped to his wrist; it was firm – and wet. The string-burn on his wrist was irritated by the salt water, but it would heal quickly, actually aided by the salt. The precaution might seem unwarranted, but the appearance of it was as valuable as the attachment. One could doze, and *Corsos* were known to be quick to relieve travellers of valuables – especially travellers who journeyed without identification, but with money.

'*Signore!*' The captain approached, his wide smile revealing an absence of eye teeth. '*Ecco*. Solenzara! *Trenta minuti. Nord di* Porto Vecchio!'

'*Grazie.*'

'*Prego!*'

In a half hour he'd be on land, in Corsica, in the hills where the Matarese was born. That it had been born was not disputed, that it had provided assassins-for-hire until the mid-'thirties was accepted as a firm probability. But so very little was known about it that no one really knew how much of its story was myth and how much based in reality. The legend was both encouraged and scorned at the same time; it was basically an enigma because no one understood its origins. Only that a madman named Guillaume de Matarese had summoned a council – from where was never recorded – and gave birth to a band of assassins, based, some said, on the killer-society of Hasan ibn as-Sabbāh in the eleventh century.

Yet this smacked of cult-orientation, thus feeding the myth and diminishing the reality. No court testimony was ever given, no assassin ever caught who could be traced to an organization called the Matarese; if there were confessions, none was ever made public. Still the rumours persisted. Stories were circulated in high places;

articles appeared in responsible newspapers, only to be denied editorial substance in later editions. Several independent studies were begun; if any was completed, no one knew about it. And through it all, governments made no comment. Ever. They were silent.

And for a young intelligence officer studying the history of assassination years ago, it was this silence that lent a certain credibility to the Matarese.

Just as another silence, suddenly imposed three days ago, convinced him that the rendezvous in Corsica was no proposal made in the heat of violence, but the only thing that *was* left. The Matarese remained an enigma, but it was no myth. It was a reality. A powerful man had gone to other powerful men and spoken in alarm; it was not to be tolerated.

Robert Winthrop had disappeared.

Bray had run from Rock Creek Park three nights before and made his way to a motel on the outskirts of Fredericksburg. For six hours he had travelled up and down the highway calling Winthrop from a series of telephone booths, never the same one twice, hitching rides on the pretext of a disabled car to put distance between them. He had talked to Winthrop's wife, alarming her he was sure, but saying nothing of substance, only that he had to speak with the ambassador. Until it was dawn, and there was no answer on the phone, just interminable rings spaced farther and farther apart – or so it seemed – and no one at all on the line.

There had been nowhere to turn, no one to go to; the networks were spreading out for him. If they found him, his termination would be complete; he understood that. If he were permitted to live, it would be within the four walls of a cell, or worse, as a vegetable. But he did not think he would be permitted to live. Taleniekov had been right; they were both marked.

If there was an answer, it was four thousand miles away

221

in the Mediterranean. In his attaché case were a dozen false passports, five bank books under assumed names, and a list of men and women who could find him all manner of transportation. He had left Fredericksburg at dawn two days ago, had stopped at banks in London and Paris, and late last night had reached a fishing pier in San Vincenzo.

And now he was within minutes of setting foot on Corsica. The long stretches of immobility in the air and over the water had given him time to think, or at least the time to organize his thoughts. He had to start with the incontrovertible; there were two established facts.

Guillaume de Matarese had existed and there'd been a group of men who had called themselves the Council of the Matarese, dedicated to the insane theories of its sponsor. The world moved forward by constant, violent changes of power. Shock and sudden death were intrinsic to the evolution of history. Someone had to provide the means. Governments everywhere would pay for political murder. Assassination – carried out under the most controlled methods, untraceable to those contracting for it – could become a global resource with riches and influence beyond imagination. This was the theory of Guillaume de Matarese.

Among the international intelligence community, a minority maintained that the Matarese had been responsible for scores of political killings from the second decade of the century through the mid-'thirties, from Sarajevo to Mexico City, from Tokyo to Berlin and points in between. In their view, the collapse of the Matarese was attributed to the explosion of World War II, with its growth of covert services where such murders were legitimized, or the council's absorption by the Sicilian Mafia, now entrenched everywhere, but centralized in the United States.

But this positive judgement was decidedly a minority

viewpoint. The vast majority of professionals agreed with Interpol, Britain's MI6, and the American Central Intelligence Agency, who claimed that the power of the Matarese was exaggerated. It undoubtedly had killed a number of minor political figures in the maze of passionately ineffective French and Italian politics, but there was no hard evidence of anything beyond this. It was essentially a collection of paranoiacs led by a wealthy eccentric who was as misinformed about philosophy as he was about governments accepting his outrageous contracts. If it were anything else, these professionals claimed further, why had not *they* ever been contacted?

Because, Bray had believed years ago, as he believed now, *you were – we were – the last people on earth the Matarese wanted to do business with. From the beginning we were the competition – in one form or another*.

'*Quindici minuti!*' bellowed the captain from the open wheelhouse. '*Andare entro costa!*'

'*Grazie.*'

'*Prego!*'

The Matarese. *Was* it possible? A group of men selecting and controlling global assassinations, providing structure to terrorism, spawning chaos everywhere?

For Bray the answer was now yes. The words of a dying *istrebitel*, the sentence of death imposed by the Soviets on Vasili Taleniekov, his own execution team recruited from Marseilles, Amsterdam and Prague . . . all were a prelude to the disappearance of Robert Winthrop. All were tied to this modern Council of the Matarese. It was the unseen, unknown mover.

Who were they, these hidden men who had the resources to reach into the highest places of governments as readily as they financed wild-eyed terrorists and selected celebrated men for murder? The larger question was why. *Why?* For what purpose or purposes did they exist?

The *who* was the riddle that had to be unravelled first

. . . and whoever they were, there had to be a connection between them and those fanatics initially summoned by Guillaume de Matarese; where else could they have come from, how else could they have known? Those early men had come to the hills of Porto Vecchio; they had names. The past was the only point of departure he had.

There'd been another, he reflected, but the flare of a match in the woods of Rock Creek Park had erased it. Robert Winthrop had been about to name two powerful men in Washington who had vehemently denied any knowledge of the Matarese. In their denials was their complicity; they *had* to have heard of the Matarese – one way or the other. But Winthrop had not said those names; the violence had intervened. Now he would never say them.

Names past could lead to names present; in this case, they had to. Men left their works, their imprints on their times . . . their money. All could be traced and led somewhere. If there were keys to unlock the vaults that held the answers to the Matarese, they would be found in the hills of Porto Vecchio. He had to find them . . . as his enemy, Vasili Taleniekov had to find them. Neither would survive unless they did. There'd be no farm in Grasnov for the Russian, no new life for Beowulf Agate, until they found the answers and delivered them to those elusive men of conscience Taleniekov had spoken of three nights ago in Washington.

'*Attualmente!*' roared the captain, spinning the wheel. '*Lo accesso roccio!*' He turned, grinning at his passenger through the wind-blown spray. '*Cinque minuti, signore! La terra di Corsica!*'

'*Grazie.*'

'*Prego.*'

Corsica.

Taleniekov raced up the rocky hill in the moonlight, ducking into the patches of tall grass to obscure his movements, but not the path he was breaking. He did not want those following him to give up the hunt, merely to be slowed down, separated if possible; if he could trap one, that would be ideal.

Old Krupsky had been right about Corsica, Scofield accurate about hills north of Porto Vecchio. There were secrets here; it had taken him less than two days to learn that. Men now chased him through the hills in the darkness to prevent him from learning anything further.

Four nights ago Corsica had been a wildly speculative source, an alternative to capture, Porto Vecchio merely a town on the south-east coast of the island, the hills beyond unknown.

The hills were still unknown; the people who lived in them were distant, strange and uncommunicative, their Oltramontanan dialect difficult to understand, but the speculation had been removed. The mere mention of the Matarese was enough to cloud eyes that were hostile to begin with; pressing for even the most innocuous information was enough to end conversations barely begun. It was as if the name itself were part of a tribal rite of which no one spoke outside the enclaves in the hills, and never in the presence of strangers. Vasili had begun to understand within hours after he had entered the rock-dotted countryside; it had been dramatically confirmed the first night.

Four days ago he would not have believed it; now he knew it was so. The Matarese was more than legend, more than a mystic symbol to primitive hill people; it was a form of religion. It *had* to be; men were prepared to die to keep its secret.

Four days and the world had changed for him. He was no longer dealing with knowledgeable men, sophisticated equipment at their disposal. There were no computer tapes whirling inside glass panels at the touch of a button, no green letters rat-tat-tatting across black screens, delivering immediate information necessary for the next decision. He was probing the past among people of the past.

Which was why he wanted so desperately to trap one of the men following him up the hill in the darkness. He judged there were three of them; the crest of the hill was long and wide and dense with ragged trees and jagged rocks. They would have to separate in order to cover the various descents that led to further hills and the flatlands that preceded the mountain forests. If he could take one man and have several hours to work on his mind and body, he could learn a great deal. He had no compunction about doing so. The night before a wooden bed had been blown apart in the darkness as a Corsican stood silhouetted in the door frame, a Lupo shotgun in his hand. Taleniekov was presumed to have been in that bed . . . Just one man – *that* man – thought Vasili, suppressing his anger, as he ran into a small cluster of wild fir trees just beneath the crown of the hill. He could rest for a few moments.

Far below he could see the weak beams of flashlights. *One, two . . . three.* Three men and they *were* separating. The one on the extreme left was covering his area; it would take that man ten minutes of climbing to reach the cluster of wild fir. Taleniekov hoped it was the man with the Lupo. He leaned against a tree, breathing heavily, and let his body go limp.

It had happened so fast, the excursion into this primitive world. Yet there was a symmetry of a kind. He had begun running at night along the wooded banks of a ravine in Washington's Rock Creek Park and here he was in an isolated, tree-lined sanctuary high in the hills of Corsica. At night. The journey had been swift; he had known precisely what to do and when to do it.

Two days ago he had been in Rome's Leonardo da Vinci Airport, where he had negotiated for a private flight to Bonifacio, due west, on the southern tip of Corsica. He had reached Bonifacio by seven in the evening and a taxi had driven him north along the coast to Porto Vecchio and up to an inn in the hill country. He had sat down to a heavy Corsican meal, engaging the curious owner in off-hand conversation.

'I am a scholar of sorts,' he had said. 'I seek information about a *padrone* of many years ago. A Guillaume de Matarese.'

'I do not understand,' the innkeeper had replied. 'You say a scholar of sorts. It would seem to me that one either is or is not, *signore*. Are you with some great university?'

'A private foundation, actually.' Taleniekov had answered slowly, even hesitantly, thus opening a door with obvious reluctance. 'But universities have access to our studies.'

'*Una fondazione?*'

'*Una organizzazione accademica*. My section deals with little-known history in Sardinia and Corsica during the late nineteenth and early twentieth centuries. Apparently there was this *padrone* . . . Guillaume de Matarese . . . who controlled much of the land in these hills north of Porto Vecchio.'

'He owned most of it, *signore*. He was good to the people who lived on his lands. If that is control it is *benevolo*, no?'

'Naturally. And we would like to grant him a place in Corsica's history. I'm not sure I know where to begin.'

'Perhaps . . .' The innkeeper had leaned back in the chair, his eyes levelled, his voice strangely non-committal. 'The ruins of the Villa Matarese. It is a clear night, *signore*. They are quite beautiful in the moonlight. I could find someone to take you. Unless, of course, you are too exhausted from your journey.'

'Not at all. It was a quick flight. From Milan.'

He had been taken farther up into the hills, to the skeletal remains of a once-sprawling estate, the remnants of the great house itself covering nearly an acre of land. Jagged walls and broken chimneys were the only structures still standing. On the ground, the brick borders of an enormous circular drive could be discerned beneath the overgrowth as it swung in front of flat tiered relics that once had been marble steps. On both sides of the great house, stone paths sliced through the tall grass, dotted by broken trellises; remembrances of lushly cultivated gardens long since destroyed.

The entire ruins stood eerily on the hill in silhouette, heightened by the backwash of moonlight. Guillaume de Matarese had built a monument to himself and the power of the edifice had lost nothing in its destruction by time and the elements. Instead, the skeleton had a force of its own, giving rise to images that perhaps could not be fulfilled when whole. Villa Matarese had a mystic quality about it and that mysticism had been intrinsic to the dramatic lesson that had followed.

Vasili had heard the voices behind him, the young boy who'd escorted him was nowhere to be seen. There had been two men and those opening words of dubious greeting had been the beginning of an interrogation that had lasted over an hour. It would have been a simple matter to subdue both Corsicans and reverse the proceedings, but Taleniekov knew he could learn more through passive resistance; unschooled interrogators imparted more than they dragged forth when they dealt with trained subjects. He had stayed with his story of the *organizzazione accademica*; at the end, he had been advised bluntly.

'Go back where you came from, *signore*. There is no knowledge here that would serve you; we know nothing. Disease swept through these mountains years ago; none is left who might help you.'

'There must be older people in the hills. Perhaps if I wandered about and made a few inquiries.'

'We are older people, *signore*, and we cannot answer your inquiries. Go back. We are ignorant men in these parts, shepherds by trade and ownership. We are not comfortable when strangers intrude on our simple ways. Go back.'

'I shall take your advice under consideration . . .'

'Do not take such trouble, *signore*. Just leave us,' had been the reply.

In the morning, Vasili had walked back up into the hills, to the Villa Matarese and beyond, stopping at numerous thatched farmhouses, asking his questions, noting the dark Corsican eyes that had glared before the non-answers had been delivered, aware that he was being followed.

He had been told nothing, of course, but in the progressively hardened reactions to his presence he had learned something of consequence. Men were not only following him, they had been preceding him, alerting families in the hills that a stranger was coming. He was to be treated indifferently, no traveller to be brought in front of a fire or given tea; he was to be sent away, told nothing.

That night – last night, thought Taleniekov, as he watched the weaving beam of the flashlight on the left slowly ascend the hill – the innkeeper had approached his table.

'I am afraid, *signore*, that I cannot permit you to stay here any longer. I have rented the room.'

Vasili had glanced up, no hesitation now in his speech. 'A pity. I need only an armchair or a cot, if you could spare one. I shall be leaving first thing in the morning. I've found what I came for.'

'And what is that, *signore*?'

'You'll know soon enough, my friend. Others will come after me, with the proper equipment and land records. There'll be a very thorough, very scholarly investigation. What happened here is fascinating. I speak academically, of course.'

'Of course . . . Perhaps one more night.'

Six hours later a man had burst into his room and fired two shots from the thick barrels of a deadly sawed-off shotgun called the Lupo – the 'wolf'. Taleniekov had been waiting; he had watched from behind a partially open closet door as the wooden bed exploded, the firm stuffing beneath the covers blown into the dark wall.

The sound had been shattering, an explosion echoing throughout the small country inn, yet no one had come running to see what had happened. Instead, the man with the Lupo had stood in the door frame and had spoken quietly in Oltramontanan, as if uttering an oath.

'*Perro nostro circulo*,' he had said; then he had raced away.

It had meant nothing, yet Vasili knew then that it meant everything. Words delivered as an incantation after taking a life . . . *For our circle*.

Taleniekov had gathered his things together and fled from the inn. He had made his way towards the single dirt road that led up from Porto Vecchio and had positioned himself in the underbrush twenty feet from the edge. Several hundred yards below, he had seen the glow of a cigarette. The road was being guarded; he had waited. He had to.

If Scofield was coming he would use that road; it had been the dawn of the fourth day. The American had said that if Corsica was all that was left, he'd be there in three or four days.

By three in the afternoon there had been no sign of him, and an hour later Vasili knew he could wait no longer. Men had sped *down* the road towards the burgeoning port resort. Their mission had been clear: the intruder had eluded the roadblock. Find him, kill him.

Search parties had begun fanning through the woods; two Corsicans slashing the overgrowth with mountain machetes had come within thirty feet of him; soon the patrols would become more concentrated, the search more thorough. He could not wait for Scofield; there was no guarantee that Beowulf Agate had even escaped from the net being spread for him in his own country, much less was on his way to Corsica.

Vasili had spent the hours until sundown creating his own assaults on those who would trap him. Like a swamp fox, his trail appeared one moment heading in *this* direction, his appearance sighted over *there*; broken branches and trampled reeds were proof that he was cornered in a stretch of marshland that fronted on unclimbable rock wall, and as men closed in, his figure could be seen racing through a field a mile to the west. He was a yellowjack on the wind, visually stinging in a dozen different places at once.

When darkness had come, Taleniekov began the strategy that led him to where he was at the moment, hidden in a cluster of fir trees below the crown of a high hill, waiting for a man carrying a flashlight to approach. The plan was simple, carried out in three stages, each phase logically evolved from the previous. First came the diversion, drawing off the largest number of the attack pack as possible; then the exposure to the few left behind, pulling them farther away from the many; finally the separation of those few and the trapping of one. The third phase was about to be concluded as the fires raged a mile and a half below to the east.

He had made his way through the woods, descending in the direction of Porto Vecchio, travelling on the right side of the dirt road. He had gathered together dried branches and leaves, breaking several Graz-Burya shells, sprinkling the powder inside the pile of debris. He had ignited his pyre in the forest, waited until it had erupted and he had heard the shouts of the converging Corsicans. He had raced northward, across the road, into a denser, drier section of the wooded hill and repeated the action, lighting a larger pile of dried foliage next to a dead chestnut tree. It had spread like a fire-bomb, the flames leaping upward through the tree, promising to leap again, laterally into the surrounding forest. He had run once more to the north and had set his last and largest fire, choosing a beech tree long since destroyed by insects. Within a half hour the hills were blazing in three distinct areas, the hunters racing from one to another, containment and the search vying for priority.

He had crossed diagonally back to the south-west, climbing through the woods to the road that fronted the inn. He had emerged within sight of the window through which he had escaped the night before. He had walked out on the road, seeing several men with rifles – one weapon short-barrelled and thick: a Lupo – standing, talking anxiously among themselves. The rearguard, confused by the chaos below, unsure whether they should remain where they were, as instructed by superiors, or go to the aid of their island brothers.

The irony of coincidence had not been lost on Vasili as he had struck the match. The striking of a match had started it all so many days ago on Washington's Nebraska Avenue; it was the sign of a trap. It signified another in the hills of Corsica.

'*Ecco!*'

'*Leggiero!*'

'*E l'uomo lui! L'uomo!*'

The chase had begun; it was now coming to an end. The man with the flashlight was within a stone's throw from him; he would climb up into the cluster of wild fir before the next thirty seconds elapsed. Below, on the slope of the hill, the flashlight in the centre was several hundred yards to the south, its beam criss-crossing the ground in front of the Corsican holding it. Far down to the right, the third flashlight, which only seconds before had been sweeping frantically back and forth in semi-circles, was now oddly stationary, its beam angled down to a single spot. The position of the light and its abrupt immobility bothered Taleniekov, but there was no time to evaluate either fact.

The approaching Corsican had reached the first tree in Vasili's natural sanctuary.

The man swung the beam of light into the cluster of trunks and hanging limbs. Taleniekov had broken a number of branches, stripping more than a few so that any light would catch the white wood. The Corsican stepped forward, following the trail; Vasili stepped to his left, concealed by a tree. The hunter passed within eighteen inches, his rifle at the ready. Taleniekov watched the Corsican's feet in the wash of light; when the left foot moved forward a beat would be lost for a right-handed marksman, the brief imbalance impossible to recover.

The foot left the ground and Vasili lunged, lashing his arm around the man's neck, his fingers surging in for the trigger enclosure, ripping the rifle out of the Corsican's hand. The beam of the flashlight shot up into the trees. Taleniekov crashed his right knee into his victim's kidney, dragging him backward, down on to the ground. He scissored the man's waist with his legs, forcing the Corsican's neck into a painful arch, the man's ear next to his lips.

'You and I will spend the next hour together,' he whispered in Italian. 'When the time's up, you'll have told me what I want to know, or you won't speak again. I'll use your own knife. Your face will be so disfigured no one will recognize you. Now get up slowly. If you raise your voice, you're dead!'

Gradually, Vasili released the pressure on the man's waist and neck. Both men started to rise, Taleniekov's fingers gripped around the man's throat.

There was a sudden *crack* from above, the sound echoing throughout the trees. A foot had stepped on a fallen branch. Vasili spun around, peering up into the dense foliage. What he saw caused him to lose his breath.

A man was silhouetted between two trees, the silhouette

233

familiar, last seen in the door frame of a country inn. And as that last time, the thick barrels of a Lupo were levelled straight ahead. But now they were levelled at him.

In the rush of thought, Taleniekov understood that not all professionals were trained in Moscow and Washington. The frenetically waving beam of light at the base of the hill, suddenly still, motionless. A flashlight strapped to a sapling or a resilient limb, pulled back and set in motion to give the illusion of movement, its owner racing in darkness up a familiar incline.

'You were very clever last night, *signore*,' said the man with the Lupo. 'But there is nowhere to hide here.'

'The *Matarese*!' screamed Vasili at the top of his lungs. '*Perro nostro circulo!*' he roared. He lunged to his left. The double-barrelled explosion of the Lupo filled the hills.

13

Scofield jumped over the side of the skiff and waded through the waves toward the shoreline. There was no beach, only boulders joined together, forming a three-dimensional wall of jagged stone. He reached a promontory of flat, slippery rock and braced himself against the waters, balancing the attaché case in his left hand, his canvas duffelbag in his right.

He rolled on to the sandy, vine-covered ground until the surface was level enough to stand. Then he ran into the tangled brush that concealed him from any wandering patrols above on the broken cliffs. The captain had warned him that the police were inconsistent; some could be bought, others not.

He knelt down, took a penknife from his pocket, and cut the webbed strap off his wrist, freeing the case. Then he opened the duffelbag and took out dry corduroy trousers, a pair of ankle boots, a dark sweater, a cap and a coarse woollen jacket, all bought in Paris, all labels torn off. They were sufficiently rough in appearances to be accepted as native garb.

He changed, rolled up the wet clothes and stuffed them into the duffelbag along with the attaché case, then started the long, winding climb to the road above. He had been to Corsica twice before – Porto Vecchio once – both trips basically concerned with an obnoxious, constantly sweating owner of fishing boats in Bastia who operated out of Murato and was on State's payroll as one more 'observer' of Soviet Ligurian Sea operations. The brief sojourn south to Porto Vecchio had been in connection with the feasibility of covertly financing resort projects in the Tyrrhenian; he never knew what happened. While in Porto Vecchio he had rented a car and driven up into the hills. He had seen the ruins of Villa Matarese in the broiling afternoon sun and had stopped for a glass of beer at a roadside *taverna*, but the excursion had faded quickly from his mind. It never occurred to him that he would ever return. The legend of the Matarese was no more alive than the ruins of the villa. Not then.

He reached the road and pulled the cap down, the cloth covering the bruise on his upper forehead where he had collided with an iron post in a stairwell. A staircase where his life might have ended but for an enemy who had saved it.

Taleniekov. Had he reached Corsica? Was he somewhere in the hills of Porto Vecchio? It would not take long to find out. A stranger asking questions about a legend would be easily tracked down. On the other hand, the Russian would be cautious; if it had occurred to them to go back to the source of the legend, it might well occur to others to do the same.

Bray looked at his watch; it was nearly eleven-thirty. He took out a map, estimating his position as two and a half miles south of Sainte Lucie; the most direct line to the hills – to the Matarese hills, he reflected – was due west. But there was something to find before he entered those hills. A base of operations. A place where he could conceal his things with the reasonable expectation that they would be there when he came back. That ruled out any normal stop a traveller might make. He could not master the Oltramontanan dialect in a few hours; he'd be marked as a stranger and strangers were marks. He would have to make camp in the woods, near water if possible, and preferably within walking distance of a store or inn where he could get food.

He had to assume he would be in Porto Vecchio for several days. No other assumption was feasible; anything could happen once he found Taleniekov – *if* he found him – but for the moment the necessities had to be considered before any plan was formulated. All the little things.

There was a path – too narrow for any car to travel, a shepherd's route perhaps – that veered off the road into a gently rising series of fields; it headed west. He shifted the canvas duffelbag to his left hand and entered it, pushing aside low-hanging branches until he was in the tall grass.

By 12.45 he had walked no more than five or six miles inland, but he had purposely travelled in a zig-zag pattern that afforded him the widest views of the area. He found what he was looking for, a section of forest that rose abruptly above a stream, thick branches of Corsican pine sweeping down to the ground on the banks. A man and his belongings would be safe behind those walls of green. A mile or so to the south-west there was a road that led farther up into the hills. From what he could remember he was fairly certain this was the road he had taken to the ruins of Villa Matarese; there had been only one. Again, if memory served, he recalled driving past a number of isolated farmhouses on the way to the ruins on the hill and the inn where he had stopped for native beer during that hot afternoon. Only the inn came first, near that road on the hill, where a narrower road swung off it. To the *right* on the way up, on the *left* returning to Porto Vecchio. Bray checked his map again; it showed the hill road, and the branch to the right. He knew where he was.

He waded across the stream, and climbed the opposite bank to the cascading pines. He crawled underneath, opened his duffelbag and took out a small shovel, amused that two packets of toilet paper fell out with the instrument. The little things, he thought, as he started to dig into the soft earth.

It was nearly four o'clock. He had set up his camp beneath the screen of green branches, his duffelbag buried, the bandage on his neck changed, his face and hands washed in the stream. Too, he had rested, staring up at the filtered sunlight strained through the webbing of pine needles. His mind wandered, an indulgence he tried to reject but could not. Sleep would not come; thoughts did.

He was under a tree on the banks of a stream in Corsica, a journey that had begun on a bridge at night in Amsterdam. And now he could never go back unless he and Taleniekov found what they were looking for in the hills of Porto Vecchio.

It would not be so difficult to disappear. He had arranged many such disappearances in the past with less money and less expertise than he had now. There were so many places – the Melanesians, the Fijis, New Zealand, across to Tasmania, the vast expanses of Australia, Malaysia, or any of a dozen Sunda islands – he had sent men to such places, stayed cautiously in touch with a few over the years. Lives had been rebuilt, past histories beyond the reach of present associates, new friends, new occupations, even families.

He could do the same, thought Bray. Maybe he would; he had the papers and the money. He could pay his way to Polynesia or the Cook Islands, buy a boat for charter, probably make a decent living. It could be a good life, an anonymous existence, an end to the deadly games.

Then he saw the face of Robert Winthrop, the electric eyes searching his, and heard the anxiety in the old man's voice as he spoke of the Matarese.

He heard something else, too. Less distant, immediate, above in the sky. Birds were swooping down in frantic circles, their screeches echoing harshly, angrily over the fields and throughout the woods. Intruders had disturbed their fiefdom. He could hear men running, hear their shouts.

Had he been *spotted*? He rose quickly to his knees, taking his Browning from his jacket pocket, and peered through a spray of pine needles.

238

Below, a hundred yards to the left, two men had hacked their way with machetes down the overgrown bank to the edge of the stream. They stood for a moment, pistols in their belts, glancing swiftly in every direction, as if unsure of their next moves. Slowly Bray let out his breath; they were not after him; he had not been seen. Instead, the two men had been hunting – an animal that had attacked their goats, perhaps, or a wild dog. Not him. Not a stranger wandering in the hills.

Then he heard the words and knew he was only partially right. The shout did not come from either Corsican holding a machete; it came from over the bank of the stream, from the field beyond.

'*Il uomo. Eccolo! Il campo!*'

It was no animal being pursued, but a man. A man was running from other men, and to judge from the fury of his pursuers, that man was running for his life. Taleniekov? Was it Taleniekov? And if it was, why? Had the Russian learned something so quickly? Something that the Corsicans in Porto Vecchio would kill for?

Scofield watched as the two men below took the guns from their belts and ran up the bank out of sight into the bordering field. He crawled back to the trunk of the tree and tried to gather his thoughts. Instinct convinced him that *Il uomo, eccolo!* was Taleniekov. If so, there were several options. He could head for the road and walk up into the hills, an Italian crewman with a fishing boat in for repairs and time on his hands; he could stay where he was until nightfall, then thread his way under cover of darkness, hoping to get near enough to hear men's conversations; or he could leave now and follow the hunt.

The last was the least attractive – but likely to be the most productive. He chose it.

It was 5.35 when Bray first saw him, running along the crest of a hill, shots fired at his weaving, racing figure in the glare of the setting sun. Taleniekov, as expected, was doing the unexpected. He was not trying to escape; rather he was using the chase to sow confusion and through that confusion learn something. The tactic was sound; the best way to uncover vital information was to make the enemy protect it.

But what had he so far learned that would justify the risk? How long would he – or could he – keep up the pace and the concentration to elude his enemy? . . . The answers were as clear as the questions: isolate, trap and break. Within the territory.

Scofield studied the terrain as best he could from his prone position in the field. The early-evening breezes made his task easier; the grass bent with each gentle sweep of wind, his view clearer for it. He tried to analyse the choices open to Taleniekov, where best to intercept him. The KGB man was running due north; another mile or so and he would reach the base of the mountains where he would stop. Nothing could be achieved by going up into them. He would double back, heading south-west to avoid being hemmed in by the roads. And somewhere he would create a diversion, one significant enough to escalate the confusion into a moment of chaos, the trap to follow shortly.

Intercepting Taleniekov might have to wait until that moment, thought Bray, but he preferred that it did not; there would be too much activity compressed into a short period of time. Mistakes were made that way. It would be better to reach the Russian beforehand. That way, they could develop the strategy together. Crouching, Scofield made his way south-west through the tall grass.

The sun fell behind the distant mountains; the shadows lengthened until they became long shafts of ink, spilling over the hills, enveloping whole fields that moments ago had been drenched in orange sunlight. Darkness came and still there was no sign, no sound of Taleniekov. Bray moved swiftly within the logical perimeters of the Russian's logical area of movement, his eyes adjusting to the darkness, his ears picking up every noise foreign to the fields and the woods. *Still* no Taleniekov.

Had the KGB man taken the risk of using either dirt road for faster mobility? If he had, it was foolhardy, unless he had conceived of a tactic better employed in the lower hills. The entire countryside was now alive with search parties ranging in size from two to six men, all armed, knives, guns and mountain machetes hanging from their clothing, their flashlight beams criss-crossing each other like intersecting lasers. Scofield raced farther west to higher ground, the myriad beams of light his protection against the roving, angry Corsicans; he knew when to stop, when to run.

He ran, cutting between two teams of converging men, halting abruptly at the sight of a whining animal, its fur thick, its eyes wide and staring. He was about to use his knife when he realized it was a shepherd's dog, its nostrils uninterested in human scent. The realization did not prevent him from losing his breath; he stroked the dog, reassuring it, then ducked beneath a flashlight beam that shot out of the woods, and scrambled farther up the sloping field.

He reached a boulder half buried in the ground and threw himself behind it. He got up slowly, his hands on the rock, prepared to spring away and run again. He looked over the top, down at the scene below, the flashlight beams breaking up the darkness, defining the whereabouts of the search parties. He was able to make out the crude wooden structure that was the inn he had stopped at years ago. In front of it was the primitive dirt road he had crossed several hours before to reach the higher ground. A hundred yards to the right of the inn was the wider, winding road that descended out of the hills down into Porto Vecchio.

The Corsicans were spread over the fields. Here and

there Bray could hear the barking of dogs amid angry human shouts and the slashing of machetes. It was an eerie sight, no figures seen, just beams of light, shooting in all directions; invisible puppets dancing on illuminated strings in the darkness.

Suddenly, there was another light, yellow not white. *Fire*. An abrupt explosion of flames in the distance, to the right of the road that led to Porto Vecchio.

Taleniekov's diversion. It had its effect.

Men ran, shouting, the beams of light converging on the road, racing towards the spreading fire. Scofield held his place, wondering – clinically, professionally – how the KGB man would use his diversion. What would he do next? What method would he use to spring his trap on one man?

The beginning of the answer came three minutes later. A second, larger eruption of flames surged skyward about a quarter of a mile to the *left* of the road to Porto Vecchio. A single diversion was now two, dividing the Corsicans, confusing the search; fire was lethal in the hills.

He could see the puppets now, their strings of light fusing with the glow of the spreading flames.

Another fire appeared, this one massive, an entire tree bursting into a ball of yellowish white as though detonated by napalm. It was three hundred or four hundred yards *farther* left, a third diversion greater than the previous two. Chaos spread as rapidly as the flames, both in danger of leaping out of control. Taleniekov was covering all his bases; if a trap was not feasible he could escape in the confusion.

But if the Russian's mind was working as his might, thought Bray, the trap would be sprung in moments. He crawled around the boulder and started down the expanse of descending field, keeping his shoulders close to the ground, propelling himself as an animal, hands and feet working in concert.

There was a sudden flash far below on the road. It lasted no more than a second, a tiny eruption of light. A match had been struck. It appeared senseless until Bray saw a flashlight beam shoot out from the right, followed instantly by two others. The three beams converged in the direction of the briefly held match; seconds later they separated at the base of the hill that bordered the road below.

Scofield knew what the tactic was now. Four nights ago a match had been struck in Rock Creek Park to expose a trap; it was struck now to execute one. By the same man. Taleniekov had succeeded in throwing the Corsicans' search into chaotic paralysis; he was now drawing off the few left behind. The final chase had started; the Russian would take one of those men.

Bray took the automatic from the holster strapped beneath his jacket and reached into his pocket for his silencer. Snapping it into place, he unlatched the safety and began running diagonally to his left, below the crest of the hill. Somewhere within those acres of grassland and forest the trap would be sprung. It was a question of finding out precisely where, if possible immobilizing one of the pursuers, thus favouring the odds for the trap's success. Better still, taking one of the Corsicans; two sources of information were better than one.

He ran in spurts, staying close to the ground, his eyes on the three flashlight beams below. Each was covering a section of the hill, and in the spills he could see weapons clearly; at the first sign of the hunted, shots would be fired . . .

Scofield stopped. Something was wrong; it was the beam of light on the right, the one perhaps two hundred yards directly beneath him. It was waving back and forth too rapidly, without focus. And there was no reflection – not even a dull reflection – of light bouncing off metal – even dull metal. There was no weapon.

There was no hand holding that flashlight! It had been

243

secured firmly to a thick branch or a limb; a feint, a false placement given false motion to cover another movement. Bray lay on the ground, concealed by the grass and the darkness, watching, listening for signs of a man running.

It happened so fast, so unexpectedly, that Scofield nearly fired his gun in instinctive defence. The figure of a large Corsican was suddenly beside him, above him, the crunch of a racing foot not eighteen inches from his head. He rolled to his left, out of the running man's path.

He inhaled deeply, trying to throw off the shock and the fear, then rose cautiously and followed as best he could the trail of the racing Corsican. The man was heading directly north along the hill, below the ridge, as Bray had intended doing, relying on beams of light and sound – or the sudden absence of both – to find Taleniekov. The Corsican was familiar with the terrain. Scofield quickened his pace, passing the centre beam of light still far below, and by passing it knowing that Taleniekov had fixed on the third man. The flashlight – barely seen – on the extreme north side of the hill.

Bray hurried faster; instinct told him to keep the Corsican in his sight. But the man was nowhere to be seen, no silhouette on the skyline, no sounds of running feet. All was silent, too silent. Scofield dropped to the ground and joined that silence, peering about in the darkness, his finger around the trigger of his automatic. It would happen any second. But how? *Where?*

About a hundred and fifty yards ahead, diagonally down to the right, the third beam of light appeared to go off and on in a series of short, irregular flashes. No . . . It was not being turned off and on rapidly; the light was being *blocked. Trees.* Whoever held the flashlight was walking into a cluster of trees growing on the side of the hill.

Suddenly, the beam of light shot upward, dancing briefly in the higher regions of the thinning trunks, then plummeted down, the glow stationary, dulled by the foliage on the ground. That was it! The trap had been sprung, but Taleniekov did not know a Corsican was waiting for a sign of that trap.

Bray got to his feet and ran as fast as he could, his boots making harsh contact with the profusion of rocks on the hillside. He had only seconds, there was so much ground to cover, and too much darkness; he could not tell where the trees began. If there was only an outline to fire at, the sound of a voice . . . *Voice*. He was about to shout, to warn the Russian, when he heard a voice. The words were in that strange Italian spoken by the southern Corsicans; the sound floated up in the night breezes.

Thirty feet below him! He saw the man standing between two trees, his body outlined in the spill of the muted, immobile beam of light that glowed up from the ground; the Corsican held a shotgun in his hands. Scofield pivoted to his right and sprang towards the armed man, his automatic levelled.

'The *Matarese!*' The name was screamed by Taleniekov, as was the enigmatic phrase that followed. '*Perro nostro circulo!*'

Bray fired into the back of the Corsican, the three rapid spits overwhelmed by an explosion from the shotgun. The man fell forward. Scofield dug his feet into the body, crouching, expecting an attack. What he saw prohibited it; the Corsican trapped by Taleniekov had been blown apart by his would-be rescuer.

'*Taleniekov?*'

'You! Is it *you*, Scofield?'

'Put that light out!' cried Bray. The Russian lunged for the flashlight on the ground, snapping it off. 'There's a man on the hill; he's not moving. He's waiting to be called.'

'If he comes, we must kill him. If we don't call, he'll go for help. He'll bring others back with him.'

'I'm not sure his friends can spare the time,' replied Scofield, watching the beam of light in the darkness.

'You've got them pretty well tied up . . . There he goes! He's running down the hill.'

'Come!' said the Russian, getting up, approaching Bray. 'I know a dozen places to hide. I've got a great deal to tell you.'

'You must have.'

'I do. It's here!'

'What is?'

'I'm not sure . . . the answer, perhaps. Part of it anyway. You've seen for yourself. They're hunting me; they'd kill me on sight. I've intruded . . .'

'*Ferma!*' The sudden command was shouted from beyond Scofield on the hill. Bray spun on the ground; the Russian raised his gun. '*Basta!*' The second command was accompanied by the snarling of an animal, a dog straining on a leash. 'I have a two-barrelled rifle in my hands, *signori*,' continued the voice . . . the unmistakable voice of a woman, speaking now in English. 'As the one fired moments ago, it is a Lupo, and I know how to use it better than the man at your feet. But I do not wish to. Hold your guns to your sides, *signori*. Do not drop them; you may need them.'

'Who are you?' asked Scofield, squinting his eyes at the woman above. From what he could barely see in the night light, she was dressed in trousers and a field jacket. The dog snarled again.

'I look for the scholar.'

'The *what*?'

'I am he,' said Taleniekov. 'From the *organizzazione accademica*. This man is my associate.'

'What the hell are you . . . ?' Bray looked over at the KGB man.

'*Basta!*' said the Russian quietly. 'Why do you look for me, yet do not kill me?'

'Word goes everywhere. You ask questions about the *padrone* of *padroni*.'

246

'I do. Guillaume de Matarese. No one wants to give me answers.'

'One does,' replied the woman. 'An old woman in the mountains. She wants to speak with the *erudito*, the scholar. She has things to tell him.'

'But you know what's happened here,' said Taleniekov, probing. 'Men are hunting me; they would kill me. You're willing to risk your own life to bring me – bring us – to her?'

'Yes. It is a long journey, and a hard one. Five or six hours up into the mountains.'

'Please answer me. Why are you taking this risk?'

'She is my grandmother. Everyone in the hills despises her; she cannot live down here. But I love her.'

'Who is she?'

'She is called the whore of Villa Matarese.'

14

They travelled swiftly through the hills to the base of the mountains and up into winding trails cut out of the mountain forests. The dog had sniffed both men as the woman had placed her hand on each's shoulder; it was set free and preceded them along the overgrown paths, sure in its knowledge of the way, awaiting them at every turn.

Scofield thought it was the same dog he had come across so suddenly, so frighteningly, in the fields. He said as much to the woman.

'*Probabilmente, signore*. We were there for many hours. I was looking for you and I let him roam, but he was always near in case I needed him.'

'Would he have attacked me?'

'Only if you raised your hand to him. Or to me.'

It was past midnight when they reached a flat stretch of grassland that fronted what appeared to be a series of imposing, wooded hills. The low-flying clouds had thinned out; moonlight washed over the field, highlighting the peaks in the distance, lending grandeur to this section of the mountain range. Bray could see that Taleniekov's shirt beneath the open jacket was as drenched with sweat as his own; and the night was cool.

'We can rest for a while now, *signori*,' said the woman, pointing to a dark area several hundred feet ahead, in the direction the dog had raced. 'Over there is a cave of stone in the hill. It is not very deep, but it is shelter.'

'Your dog knows it,' added the KGB man.

'He expects me to build a fire,' laughed the girl. 'When it is raining, he takes sticks in his mouth and brings them inside to me. He is fond of the fire.'

The cave was dug out of dark rock, no more than ten feet deep, but at least six in height. They entered.

'Shall I light a fire?' Taleniekov asked, stroking the dog.

'If you wish. Ucello will like you for it. I am too tired.'

'*Uccello?*' asked Scofield. ' "Bird"?'

'He flies over the ground, *signore*.'

'You speak English very well,' said Bray, as the Russian piled sticks together within a circle of stones obviously used for previous fires. 'Where did you learn?'

'I went to the convent school in Vescovato. Those of us who wished to enter the government programmes studied French and English.'

Taleniekov struck a match beneath the kindling; the fire caught instantly, the flames crackling the wood, throwing warmth and light through the cave. 'You're very good at that sort of thing,' said Scofield to the KGB man.

'Thank you. It's a minor talent.'

'It wasn't minor a few hours ago.' Bray turned back to the woman, who had removed her cap and was shaking free her long dark hair. For an instant he stopped breathing and stared at her. Was it the hair? Or the wide, clear brown eyes that were the colour of a deer's eyes, or the high cheekbones or the chiselled nose above the generous lips that seemed so ready to laugh? Was it any of these things, or was he simply tired and grateful for the sight of an attractive, capable woman? He did not know; he knew only that this Corsican girl of the hills reminded him of Katrine, his wife whose death had been ordered by the man three feet away from him in that Corsican cave. He suppressed his thoughts and breathed again. 'And did you,' he asked, 'enter the government programmes?'

'As far as they would take me.'

'Where was that?'

'To the *scuola media* in Bonifacio. The rest I managed with the help of others. Monies supplied by the *fondos*.'

'I don't understand.'

'I am a graduate of the University of Bologna, *signore*. I am a *Comunista*. I say it proudly.'

'Bravo . . .' said Taleniekov softly.

'One day we shall set things right throughout all Italy,' continued the girl, her eyes bright. 'We shall end the chaos, the Christian stupidity.'

'I'm sure you will,' agreed the Russian.

'But never as Moscow's puppets, that we will never be. We are *independents*. We do not listen to vicious bears who would devour us and create a worldwide fascist state. Never!'

'Bravo,' said Bray.

The conversation trailed off, the young woman reluctant to answer further questions about herself. She told them her name was Antonia, but beyond that said little. When Taleniekov asked why she, a political activist from Bologna, had returned to this isolated region of Corsica, she replied only that it was to be with her grandmother for a while.

'Tell us about her,' said Scofield.

'She will tell you what she wants you to know,' said the girl, getting up. 'I have told you what she instructed me to say.'

' "The whore of Villa Matarese," ' repeated Bray.

'Yes. They are not words I would choose. Or ever use. Come, we have another two hours to walk.'

They reached a flat crown of a mountain and looked down a gentle slope to a valley below. It was no more than a hundred and fifty yards from mountain crest to valley floor, perhaps a mile across the basin. The moon had grown progressively brighter; they could see a small farmhouse in the centre of the pasture, a barn at the end of a short roadway. They could hear the sound of rushing water; a stream flowed out of the mountain near where they stood, tumbling down the slope between a row of rocks, passing within fifty feet of the small house.

'It's very beautiful,' said Taleniekov.

'It is the only world she has known for over half a century,' replied Antonia.

'Were you brought up here?' asked Scofield. 'Was this your home?'

'No,' said the girl, without elaborating. 'Come, we will see her. She has been waiting.'

'At this hour of the night?' Taleniekov was surprised.

'There is no day or night for my grandmother. She said to bring you to her as soon as we arrived. We have arrived.'

There *was* no day or night for the old woman sitting in the chair by the wood-burning stove, not in the accepted sense of sunlight and darkness. She was blind, her eyes two vacant orbs of pastel blue, staring at sounds and at the images of remembered memories. Her features were sharp and angular beneath the covering of wrinkled flesh; the face had once been that of an extraordinarily beautiful woman.

Her voice was soft, with a hollow whispering quality that forced the listener to watch her thin white lips. If there was no essential brilliance about her, neither was there hesitancy nor indecision. She spoke rapidly, a simple mind secure in its own knowledge. She had things to say and death was in her house, a reality that seemed to quicken her thoughts and perceptions. She spoke in Italian, but it was an idiom from an earlier era.

She began by asking both Taleniekov and Scofield to answer – each in his own words – why he was so interested

251

in Guillaume de Matarese. Vasili replied first, repeating his story of an academic foundation in Milan, his department concentrating on Corsican history. He kept it simple, thus allowing Scofield to elaborate in any way he wished. It was standard procedure when two or more intelligence officers were detained and questioned together. Neither had to be primed for the exercise; the fluid lie was second nature to them both.

Bray listened to the Russian and corroborated the basic information, adding details on dates and finances he believed pertinent to Guillaume de Matarese. When he finished, he felt not only confident about his response, but superior to the KGB man; he had done his 'school work' better than Taleniekov.

Yet the old woman just sat there, nodding her head in silence, brushing away a lock of white hair that had fallen to the side of her gaunt face. Finally, she spoke.

'You're both lying. The second gentleman is less convincing. He tries to impress me with facts any child in the hills of Porto Vecchio might learn.'

'Perhaps in Porto Vecchio,' protested Scofield gently, 'but not necessarily in Milan.'

'Yes. I see what you mean. But then neither of you is from Milan.'

'Quite true,' interrupted Vasili. 'We merely work in Milan. I myself was born in Poland . . . northern Poland. I'm sure you detect my imperfect speech.'

'I detect nothing of the sort. Only your lies. However, don't be concerned, it doesn't matter.'

Taleniekov and Scofield looked at each other, then over at Antonia, who sat curled up in exhaustion on a pillow in front of the window.

'What doesn't matter?' Bray asked. 'We *are* concerned. We want you to speak freely.'

'I will,' said the blind woman. 'For your lies are not those of self-seeking men. Dangerous men, perhaps, but

252

not men moved by profit. You do not look for the *padrone* for your own personal gain.'

Scofield could not help himself; he leaned forward. 'How do you know?'

The old woman's vacant yet powerful pale blue eyes held his; it was hard to accept the fact that she could not see. 'It is in your voices,' she said. 'You are afraid.'

'Have we reason to be?' asked Taleniekov.

'That would depend on what you believe, wouldn't it?'

'We believe a terrible thing has happened,' said Bray. 'But we know very little. That's as honestly as I can put it.'

'What *do* you know, *signori*?'

Again Scofield and Taleniekov exchanged glances; the Russian nodded first. Bray realized that Antonia was watching them closely. He spoke as obviously to her as to the old woman. 'Before we answer you, I think it would be better if your granddaughter left us alone.'

'No!' said the girl so harshly that Uccello snapped up his head.

'Listen to me,' continued Scofield. 'It's one thing to bring us here, two strangers your grandmother wanted to meet. It's something else again to be involved with us. My . . . associate . . . and I have experience in these matters. It's for your own good.'

'Leave us, Antonia.' The blind woman turned in the chair. 'I have nothing to fear from these men and you must be tired. Take Uccello with you; rest in the barn.'

'All right,' said the girl, getting up, 'but Uccello will remain here.' Suddenly, from beneath the pillow, she took out the Lupo and levelled it in front of her. 'You both have guns. Throw them on the floor. I don't think you would leave here without them.'

'That's ridiculous!' cried Bray, as the dog got to its feet growling.

'Do as the lady says,' snapped Taleniekov, shoving his Graz-Burya across the floor.

Scofield took out his Browning, checked the safety and threw the weapon on the rug in front of Antonia. She bent down and picked up both automatics, the Lupo held firmly in her hand. 'When you've finished, open the door and call out to me. I will summon Uccello. If he does not come, you won't see your guns again. Except looking down the barrels.' She let herself out quickly; the dog emitted a growl and returned to the floor.

'My granddaughter is high-spirited,' said the old woman, settling back in her chair. 'The blood of Guillaume, though several times removed, is still apparent.'

'She's *his* granddaughter?' asked Taleniekov.

'His great-grandchild, born to my daughter's child quite late in *her* life. But that first daughter was the result of the *padrone* bedding his young whore.'

' "The whore of Villa Matarese," ' said Bray. 'You told her to tell us that was what you were called.'

The old woman smiled, brushing aside a lock of white hair. For an instant she was in that other world, and vanity had not deserted her. 'Many years ago. We will go back to those days, but before we do, your answers, please. What *do* you know? What brings you here?'

'My associate will speak first,' said Taleniekov. 'He is more learned in these matters than I am, although I came to him with what I believed to be startling new information.'

'Your name, please,' interrupted the blind woman. 'Your true name and where you come from.'

The Russian glanced at the American; in the look between them was the understanding that no purpose would be served by further lies. On the contrary, that purpose might be thwarted by them. This simple but strangely eloquent old woman had listened to the voices of liars for the better part of a century – in darkness; she was not to be fooled.

'My name is Vasili Vasilivich Taleniekov. Formerly external affairs strategist, KGB, Soviet Intelligence.'

'And you?' The woman shifted her blind eyes to Scofield.

'Brandon Scofield. Retired intelligence officer, Euro-Mediterranean Sectors, Consular Operations, United States Department of State.'

'I see.' The old courtesan brought her thin hands and delicate fingers up to her face, a gesture of quiet reflection. 'I am not a learned woman, and live an isolated life, but I am not without news of the outside world. I often listen to my radio for hours at a time. The broadcasts from Rome come in quite clearly, as do those from Genoa, and frequently Nice. I pretend no knowledge, for I have none, but your coming to Corsica together would appear strange.'

'It is, *madame*,' said Taleniekov.

'Very,' agreed Scofield.

'It signifies the gravity of the situation.'

'Then let your associate begin, *signore*.'

Bray sat forward in the chair, his arms on his knees, his eyes on the blind eyes in front of him. 'At some point between the years 1911 and 1913, Guillaume de Matarese summoned a group of men to his estate in Porto Vecchio. Who they were and where they came from has never been established. But they gave themselves a name . . .'

'The date was 4 April 1911,' interrupted the old woman. 'They did not give themselves a name, the *padrone* chose it. They were to be known as the Council of the Matarese . . . Go on, please.'

'You were *there*?'

'Please continue.'

The moment was unsettling; they were talking about an event that had been the object of speculation for decades, with no records of dates or identities, no witnesses. Now – delivered in a brief few seconds – they were told the correct year, the exact month, the precise day.

'*Signore . . . ?*'

'Sorry. During the next thirty years or so, this Matarese and his "council" were the subject of controversy . . .' Scofield told the story rapidly, without embellishment, keeping his words in the simplest Italian he knew so there'd be no misunderstanding. He admitted that the majority of experts who had studied the Matarese legend had concluded it was more myth than reality.

'What do *you* believe, *signore*? That is what I asked you at the start.'

'I'm not sure what I believe, but I know a very great man disappeared four days ago. I think he was killed because he spoke to other powerful men about the Matarese.'

'I see.' The old woman nodded. 'Four days ago. Yet I thought you said thirty years . . . from that first meeting in 1911. What happened then, *signore*? There are many years to be accounted for.'

'According to what we know – or what we think we know – after Matarese died the council continued to operate out of Corsica for a number of years, then moved away, negotiating contracts in Berlin, London, Paris, New York and God knows where else. Its activities began to fade at the start of the Second World War. After the war it disappeared; nothing was heard from it again.'

A trace of a smile was on the old woman's lips. 'So from nowhere it comes back, is that what you are saying?'

'Yes. My associate can tell you why we believe it.' Bray looked at Taleniekov.

'Within recent weeks,' said the Russian, 'two men of peace from both our countries were brutally assassinated, each government led to believe the other was responsible. Confrontation was avoided by a swift exchange between our leaders, but they were dangerous moments. A dear friend sent for me; he was dying and there were things he

256

wanted me to know. He had very little time and his mind wandered, but what he told me compelled me to seek out others for help, for guidance.'

'What did he tell you?'

'That the Council of the Matarese was very much with us. That, in fact, it never disappeared but instead went underground, where it continued to grow silently and spread its influence. That it was responsible for hundreds of acts of terrorism and scores of assassinations during recent years for which the world condemned others. Among them the two men I just mentioned. But the Matarese no longer killed for money; instead, it killed for its own purposes.'

'Which were?' asked the old woman in that strange, echoing voice.

'He did not know. He knew only that the Matarese was a spreading disease that had to be stamped out, but he could not tell me how, or whom to go to. No one who ever had dealings with the council will speak of it.'

'He offered you nothing, then?'

'The last thing he said to me before I left him was that the answer might be in Corsica. Naturally, I was not convinced of that until subsequent events left no alternative. For either me or my associate, agent Scofield.'

'I understand your associate's reason: a great man disappeared four days ago because he spoke of the Matarese. What was yours, *signore*?'

'I, too, spoke of the Matarese. To those men from whom I sought guidance, and I was a man of credentials in my country. The order was put out for my execution.'

The old woman was silent and, again, there was that slight smile on her wrinkled lips. 'The *padrone* returns,' she whispered.

'I think you must explain that,' said Taleniekov. 'We've been frank with you.'

'Did your dear friend die?' she asked instead, her blind eyes questioning.

'The next day. He was given a soldier's funeral and he was entitled to it. He lived a life of violence without fear. Yet at the end, the Matarese frightened him profoundly.'

'The *padrone* frightened him,' said the old woman.

'My friend did not know Guillaume de Matarese.'

'He knew his disciples. It was enough; they were him. He was their Christ, and as Christ, he died for them.'

'The *padrone* was their god?' asked Bray.

'And their prophet, *signore*. They believed him.'

'Believed what?'

'That they would inherit the earth. That was his vengeance.'

15

The old woman's vacant eyes stared at the wall as she spoke in her half whisper.

He found me in the convent at Bonifacio and negotiated a favourable price with the Mother Superior. 'Render unto Caesar,' he said, and she complied for she agreed that I was not given to God. I was frivolous and did not take to my lessons and looked at myself in dark windows for they showed me my face and my body. I was to be given to man, and the padrone *was the man of all men.*

I was ten and seven years of age and a world beyond my imagination was revealed to me. Carriages with silver wheels and golden horses with flowing manes took me above the great cliffs and into the villages and the fine shops where I could purchase whatever struck me. There was nothing I could not have, and I wanted everything, for I came from a poor shepherd's family – a God-fearing father and mother who praised Christ when I was taken into the convent and never saw me again.

And always at my side was the padrone. *He was the lion and I was his cherished cub. He would take me around the countryside, to all the great houses and introduce me as his* protetta, *laughing when he used the word. Everyone understood and joined in the laughter. His wife had died, you see, and he had passed his seventieth year. He wanted people to know – his two sons above all, I think – that he had the body and the strength of youth, that he could lie with a young woman and satisfy her as few men could.*

Tutors were hired to teach me the graces of his court: music and proper speech, even history and mathematics, as well as the French language which was the fashion of

*the time for ladies of bearing. It was a wondrous life. We
sailed often across the sea, on to Rome, then would train
north to Switzerland and across into France and to Paris.
The* padrone *made these trips every five or six months. His
business holdings were in those places, you see. His two sons
were his directors, reporting to him everything they did.*

*For three years I was the happiest girl in the world for
the world was given me by the* padrone. *And then that
world fell apart. In a single week it came crashing down
and Guillaume de Matarese went mad.*

*Men travelled from Zurich and Paris, from as far away
as the great exchange in London, to tell him. It was a time
of great banking investments and speculation. They said that
during the four months that had passed, his sons had done
terrible things, made unwise decisions, and most terrible of
all had entered into dishonest agreements, committing vast
sums of money to dishonourable men who operated outside
the laws of banking and the courts. The governments of
France and England had seized the companies and stopped
all trade, all access to funds. Except for the accounts he held
in Genoa and Rome, Guillaume de Matarese had nothing.*

*He summoned his two sons by wireless, ordering them
home to Porto Vecchio to give him an accounting of what
they had done. The news that came back to him, however,
was like a thunderbolt striking him down in a great storm;
he was never the same again.*

*Word was sent through the authorities in Paris and
London that both the sons were dead, one by his own
hand, the other killed – it was said – by a man he had
ruined. There was nothing left for the* padrone; *his world
had crumbled around him. He locked himself in his library
for days on end, never coming out, taking trays of food
behind the closed door, speaking to no one. He did not lie
with me for he had no interest in matters of the flesh. He was
destroying himself, dying by his own hand as surely as if he
had taken a knife to his stomach.*

Then one day a man came from Paris and insisted on breaking into the padrone's *privacy. He was a journalist who had studied the fall of the Matarese companies, and he brought with him an incredible story. If the* padrone *was driving himself into madness before he heard it, afterwards he was beyond hope.*

The destruction of his world was deliberately brought about by bankers working with their governments. His two sons had been tricked into signing illegal documents, and blackmailed – held up to ruin – over matters of the flesh. Finally, they had been murdered, the false stories of their deaths acceptable, for the 'official' evidence of their terrible crimes was complete.

It was beyond reason. Why had these things been done to the great padrone? *His companies stolen from him and destroyed; his sons killed. Who would want such things to be done?*

The man from Paris gave part of the answer. 'One mad Corsican was enough for Europe for five hundred years,' was the phrase he had heard. The padrone *understood. In England, Edward was dead but he had brought about the French and English treaties of finance, opening the way for the great companies to come together, fortunes made in India and Africa and the Suez. The* padrone, *however, was Corsican. Beyond making profit from them, he had no use for the French, less so for the English. He not only refused to join the companies and the banks but he opposed them at every turn, instructing his sons to outmanoeuvre their competitors. The Matarese fortune blocked powerful men from carrying out their designs.*

For the padrone *it was all a great game. For the French and English companies, his playing was a great crime to be answered with greater crimes. The companies and their banks controlled their governments. Courts of law and the police, politicians and statesmen, even kings and presidents – all were lackeys and servants to the men who possessed vast sums of money. It would never change. This was the beginning of his final madness. He would find a way to destroy the corruptors and the corrupted. He would throw governments everywhere into chaos, for it was the political leaders who were the betrayers of trust. Without the co-operation of government officials his sons would be alive, his world as it was. And with governments in chaos, the companies and the banks would lose their protectors.*

'They look for a mad Corsican!' he screamed. 'They will not find him, yet he will be there.'

We made a last trip to Rome – not as before, in finery and in carriages with silver wheels, but as a humble man and woman staying in cheap lodgings in the Via Due Macelli. The padrone *spent days prowling the* Borsa Valori, *reading the histories of the great families who had come to ruin.*

We returned to Corsica. He composed five letters to five men known to be alive in five countries, inviting them to journey in secrecy to Porto Vecchio on matters of the utmost urgency, matters pertaining to their own personal histories.

He was the once-great Guillaume de Matarese. None refused.

The preparations were magnificent, Villa Matarese made more beautiful than it had ever been. The gardens were sculptured and bursting with colour, the lawns greener than a brown cat's eyes, the great house and the stables washed in white, the horses curried until they glistened. It was a fairyland again, the padrone *running everywhere at once, checking all things, demanding perfection. His great vitality had returned, but it was not the vitality we had known before. There was a cruelty in him now. 'Make them remember, my child,' he roared at me in the bedroom. 'Make them remember what once was theirs!'*

For he came back to my bed, but his spirit was not the same. There was only brute strength in the performance of his manhood; there was no joy.

If all of us – in the house and the stables and in the fields

262

– knew then what we soon would learn, we would have killed him in the forest. I, who had been given everything by the great padrone, *who worshipped him as both father and lover, would have plunged in the knife myself.*

The great day came, the ships sailed in at dawn from Lido di Ostia, and the carriages were sent down to Porto Vecchio to bring up the honoured guests to Villa Matarese. It was a glorious day, music in the gardens, enormous tables heaped with delicacies, and much wine. The finest wines from all Europe, stored for decades in the padrone's *cellars.*

The honoured guests were given their own suites, each with a balcony and a magnificent view, and – not the least – each guest was provided with his own young whore for an afternoon's pleasure. Like the wines they were the finest, not of Europe, but of southern Corsica. Five of the most beautiful virgins to be found in the hills.

Night came and the grandest banquet ever seen at Villa Matarese was held in the great hall. When it was over, the servants placed bottles of brandy in front of the guests and were told to remain in the kitchens. The musicians were ordered to take their instruments into the gardens and continue playing. We girls were asked to go to the upper house to await our masters.

We were flushed with wine, the girls and I, but there was a difference between myself and them. I was the protetta *of Guillaume de Matarese and I knew a great event was taking place. He was my* padrone, *my lover, and I wished to be a part of it. In addition to which I'd spent three years with tutors, and although hardly a learned woman, I was given to better things than the giddy talk of ignorant girls from the hills.*

I crept away from the others and concealed myself behind a railing on the balcony above the great hall. I watched and listened for hours, it seems, understanding very little then of what my padrone *was saying, only that he was most persuasive, his voice at times barely* heard, at others shouting as though he were possessed by the fever.

He spoke of generations past when men ruled empires given them by God and by their own endeavours. How they ruled them with iron might because they were able to protect themselves from those who would steal their kingdoms and the fruits of their labours. However, those days were gone and the great families, the great empire builders – such as those in that room – were now being stripped by thieves and corrupt governments that harboured thieves. They – those in that room – had to look to other methods to regain what was rightfully theirs.

They had to kill – cautiously, judiciously, with skill and daring – and divide the thieves and their corrupt protectors. They were never to kill themselves, for they were the decision-makers, the men who selected victims – wherever possible victims chosen by others among the corrupted. Those in that room were to be known as the Council of the Matarese, and word was to go forth in the circles of power that there was a group of unknown, silent men who understood the necessity of sudden change and violence, who were unafraid to provide the means, and who would guarantee beyond living doubt that those performing the acts could never be traced to those purchasing them.

He went on to speak of things I could not understand: of killers trained by great pharaohs and Arabian princes centuries ago. How men could be trained to do terrible things beyond their wills, even beyond their knowledge. How others needed only the proper encouragement for they sought the assassin's martyrdom. These were to be the methods of the Matarese, but in the beginning there would be disbelief in the circles of power, so examples had to be made.

During the next few years selected men were to be assassinated. They would be chosen carefully, killed in ways that would breed mistrust, pitting political faction

*against political faction, corrupt government against cor-
rupt government. There would be chaos and bloodshed and
the message would be clear: the Matarese existed.*

The padrone *distributed to each guest pages on which he
had written down his thoughts. These writings were to be
the council's source of strength and direction, but they were
never to be shown to eyes other than their own. These pages
were the Last Will and Testament of Guillaume de Matarese
. . . and those in that room were his inheritors.*

*Inheritors? asked the guests. They were compassionate,
but direct. In spite of the villa's beauty and the servants and
the musicians and the feast they had enjoyed, they knew he
had been ruined – as each of them had been ruined. Who
among them had anything left but his wine cellars and his
lands and rents from tenants to keep but a semblance of his
former life intact? A grand banquet once in a great while,
but little else.*

The padrone *did not answer them at first. Instead, he
demanded to know from each guest whether that man
accepted the things he had said, if that man was prepared
to become a* consigliere *of the Matarese.*

*They replied yes, each more vehement than the last,
pledging himself to the* padrone's *goals, for great evil had
been done to each of them and they wanted revenge. It was
apparent that Guillaume de Matarese appeared to each at
that moment a saint.*

*Each, except one, a deeply religious Spaniard who spoke
of the word of God and of His commandments. He accused
the* padrone *of madness, called him an abomination in the
eyes of God.*

'Am I an abomination in your eyes, sir?' asked the padrone.

'You are, sir,' replied the man.

*Whereupon the first of the most terrible things happened.
The* padrone *took a pistol from his belt, aimed it at the man,
and fired. The guests sprang up from their chairs and stared
in silence at the dead Spaniard.*

265

'He could not be permitted to leave this room alive,' said the padrone.

As if nothing had happened, the guests returned to their chairs, all eyes on this mightiest of men who could kill with such deliberateness, perhaps afraid for their own lives, it was difficult to tell. The padrone went on.

'All in this room are my inheritors,' he said. 'For you are the Council of the Matarese and you and yours will do what I can no longer do. I am too old and death is near – nearer than you believe. You will carry out what I tell you, you will divide the corruptors and the corrupted, you will spread chaos and, through the strength of your achievements, you will inherit far more than I leave you. You will inherit the earth. You will have your own again.'

'What do you – can you – leave us?' asked a guest.

'A fortune in Genoa and a fortune in Rome. The accounts have been transferred in the manner described in a document, one copy of which has been placed in each of your rooms. Therein also will you find the conditions under which you will receive the monies. These accounts were never known to exist; they will provide millions for you to begin your work.'

The guests were stunned until one had a question.

'"Your" work? Is it not "our" work?'

'It will always be ours, but I shall not be here. For I leave you something more precious than all the gold in the Transvaal. The complete secrecy of your identities. I speak to each of you. Your presence here this day will never be revealed to anyone on earth. No name, no description, no likeness of your face, no pattern of your speech can ever be traced to you. Neither will it ever be forced from the senile wanderings of an old man's mind.'

Several of the guests protested – mildly to be sure – but with reason. There were many people at Villa Matarese that day. The servants, the grooms, the musicians, the girls . . .

The padrone held up his hand. It was as steady as his eyes

were glaring. 'I will show you the way. You must never step back from violence. You must accept it as surely as the air you breathe, for it is necessary to life. Necessary to your lives, to the work you must do.'

He dropped his hand and the peaceful, elegant world of Villa Matarese erupted in gunfire and screams of death everywhere. It came first from the kitchen. Deafening blasts of shotguns, glass shattering, metal crashing, servants slain as they tried to escape through the doors into the great hall, their faces and chests covered with blood. Then from the gardens; the music abruptly stopped, replaced by supplications to God, all answered by the thunder of the guns. And then – most horribly – the high-pitched screams of terror from the upper house where the young ignorant girls from the hills were being slaughtered. Children who only hours ago had been virgins, defiled by men they had never seen before on the orders of Guillaume de Matarese, now butchered by new commands.

I pressed myself back into the wall in the darkness of the balcony, not knowing what to do, trembling, frightened beyond any fear I could imagine. And then the gunfire stopped, the silence that followed more terrible than the screams, for it was the evidence of death.

Suddenly I could hear running – three or four men, I could not tell – but I knew they were the killers. They were rushing down staircases and through doors, and I thought, Oh, God in heaven, they are looking for me. But they were not. They were racing to a place where all would gather together; it seemed to be the north veranda, I could not be sure, all was happening so fast. Below in the great hall, the four guests were in shock, frozen to their chairs, the padrone *holding them in their places by the strength of his glaring eyes.*

There came what I thought would be the final sounds of gunfire until my own death. Three shots – only three – between terrible screams. And then I understood. The killers had themselves been killed by a lone man given those orders.

The silence came back. Death was everywhere – in the shadows and dancing on the walls in the flickering candlelight of the great hall. The padrone *spoke to his guests.*

'It is over,' he said. 'Or nearly over. All but you at this table are dead save one man you will never see again. It is he who will drive you in a shrouded carriage to Bonifacio where you may mingle with the night revellers and take the crowded morning steamer to Naples. You have fifteen minutes to gather your things and meet on the front steps. There are none to carry your luggage, I'm afraid.'

A guest found his voice, or part of it. 'And you, padrone?' *he whispered.*

'At the last, I give you my life as your final lesson. Remember me! I am the way. Go forth and become my disciples! Rip out the corruptors and the corrupted!' He was raving mad, his shouts echoing throughout the great house of death. 'Entrare!' *he roared.*

A small child, a shepherd boy from the hills, walked through the large doors of the north veranda. He held a pistol in his two hands; it was heavy and he was slight. He approached the master.

The padrone *raised his eyes to the heavens, his voice to God. 'Do as you were told!' he shouted. 'For an innocent child shall light your path!'*

The shepherd boy raised the heavy pistol and fired it into the head of Guillaume de Matarese.

The old woman had finished, her unblinking eyes filled with tears.

'I must rest,' she said.

Taleniekov, rigid in his chair, spoke softly. 'We have questions, *madame*. Surely you know that.'

'Later,' said Scofield.

16

Light broke over the surrounding mountains as pockets of mist floated up from the fields outside the farmhouse. Taleniekov found tea, and with the old woman's permission, boiled water on the wood-burning stove.

Scofield sipped from his cup, watching the rippling stream from the window. It was time to talk again; there were too many discrepancies between what the blind woman had told them and the facts as they were assumed to be. But there was a primary question: why had she told them at all? The answer to that might make clear whether any part of her narrative should be believed.

Bray turned from the window and looked at the old woman in the chair by the stove. Taleniekov had given her tea and she drank it delicately, as though remembering those lessons in the social graces given a girl of 'ten and seven years of age' decades ago. The Russian was kneeling by the dog, stroking its fur again, reminding it they were friends. He glanced up, as Scofield walked towards the old woman.

'We've told you our names, *signora*,' said Bray, speaking in Italian. 'What is yours?'

'Sophia Pastorine. If one goes back to look, I'm sure it can be found in the records of the convent at Bonifacio. That is why you ask, is it not? To be able to check?'

'Yes,' answered Scofield. 'If we think it's necessary, and have the opportunity.'

'You will find my name. The *padrone* may even be listed as my benefactor, to whom I was ward – as an intended bride for one of his sons, perhaps. I never knew.'

'Then we must believe you,' said Taleniekov, getting

269

to his feet and crossing to the chair in front of Sophia Pastorine. 'You would not be so foolish as to direct us to such a source if it were not true. Records that have been meddled with are easily detected these days.'

The old woman smiled, a smile with its roots in sadness. 'I have no understanding of such matters, but I can understand if you have doubts.' She put down her cup of tea on the ledge of the stove. 'There are none in my memories. I have spoken the truth.'

'Then my first question is as important as any we may ask you,' said Bray, sitting down. 'Why did you tell us this story?'

'Because it had to be told and no one else could do so. Only I survived.'

'There was a man,' interrupted Scofield. 'And a shepherd boy.'

'They were not in the great hall to hear what I heard.'

'Have you told it before?' asked Taleniekov.

'Never,' replied the blind woman.

'Why not?'

'Who was I to tell it to? I have few visitors, and those that come are from down in the hills, bringing me the few supplies I need. To tell them would be to bring them death, for surely they would tell others.'

'Then the story *is* known,' pressed the KGB man.

'Not what I've told you.'

'But there's a secret down there! They tried to send me away, and when I would not go they tried to kill me.'

'My granddaughter did not tell me that.' She seemed truly surprised.

'I don't think she had time to,' said Bray.

The old woman did not seem to be listening, her focus still on the Russian. 'What did you say to the people in the hills?'

'I asked questions.'

'You must have done more than that.'

270

Taleniekov frowned, remembering. 'I tried to provoke the innkeeper. I told him I would bring back others, scholars with historical records to study further the question of Guillaume de Matarese.'

The woman nodded. 'When you leave here, do not go back the way you came. Nor can you take my child's granddaughter with you. You must promise me that. If they find you, they will not let you live.'

'We know that,' said Bray. 'We want to know why.'

'All the lands of Guillaume de Matarese were willed to the people of the hills. The tenants became the heirs of a thousand fields and pastures, streams and forests. It was so recorded in the courts of Bonifacio and great celebrations were held everywhere. But there was a price, and there were other courts that would take away the lands if that price were known.' The blind Sophia stopped, as if weighing another price, one of betrayal, perhaps.

'*Please*. Signora Pastorine,' said Taleniekov, leaning forward in the chair.

'Yes,' she answered quietly. 'It must be told . . .'

Everything was to be done quickly for fear of unwanted intruders happening upon the great house of Villa Matarese and the death that was everywhere. The guests gathered their papers and fled to their rooms. I remained in the shadows of the balcony, my body filled with pain, the silent vomit of fear all around me. How long I stayed there, I could not tell, but soon I heard the running feet of the guests racing down the staircase to their appointed meeting place. Then there was the sound of carriage wheels and the neighing of horses; minutes later the carriage sped away, hooves clattering on the hard stone along with the rapid cracking of a whip, all fading away quickly.

I started to crawl towards the balcony door, not able to think, my eyes filled with bolts of lightning, my head trembling so I could barely find my way. I pressed my hands on the wall, wishing there were brackets I could hold on to, when I heard a shout and threw myself to the floor again. It was a terrible shout for it came from a child, and yet it was cold and demanding.

'Attualmente! E presto detto!'

The shepherd boy was screaming at someone from the north veranda. If all was senseless up to that moment, the child's shouts intensified the madness beyond any understanding. For he was a child . . . and a killer.

Somehow I rose to my feet and ran through the door to the top of the staircase. I was about to run down, wanting only to get away, into the air and the fields and the protection of darkness, when I heard other shouts and saw the figures of running men through the windows. They were carrying torches, and in seconds crashed through the doors.

I could not run down for I would be seen, so I ran above to the upper house, my panic such that I no longer knew what I was doing. Only running . . . running. And, as if guided by an unseen hand that wanted me to live, I burst into the sewing room and saw the dead. There they were, sprawled everywhere in blood, mouths stretched in such terror that I could still hear their screams.

The screams I heard were not real, but the shouts of men on the staircase were; it was the end for me. There was nothing left, I was to be caught. I would be killed . . .

And then, as surely as an unseen hand had led me to that room, it forced me to do a most terrible thing – I joined the dead.

I put my hands in the blood of my sisters, and rubbed it over my face and clothes, I fell on top of my sisters and waited.

The men came into the sewing room, some crossing themselves, others whispering prayers, but none deterred from the work they had to do. The next hours were a nightmare only the devil could conceive of.

The bodies of my sisters and I were carried down the staircase and hurled through the doors, beyond the marble steps into the drive. Wagons had been brought from the stables, and by now many were filled with bodies. Again, my sisters and I were thrown into the back of a cart, crowded with dead, like so much refuse.

The stench of waste and blood was so overpowering I had to sink my teeth into my own flesh to keep from screaming. Through the corpses above me and over the railings, I could hear men shouting orders. Nothing could be stolen from the Villa Matarese; anyone found doing so would join the bodies inside. For there were to be many bodies left inside, charred flesh and bones to be found at a later time.

The wagons began to move, smoothly at first, then we reached the fields, and the horses were whipped unmercifully. The wagons raced through the grass and over the rocks at immense speeds, as if every second was a second our living guards wished to leave behind in hell. There was death below me, death above me, and I prayed to Almighty God to take me also. But I could not cry out, for although I wanted to die, I was afraid of the pain of dying. The unseen hand held me by the throat. But mercy was granted me. I fell into unconsciousness: how long I do not know, but I think it was a very long time.

I awakened; the wagons had come to a stop and I peered through the bodies and the slats in the side. There was moonlight and we were far up in the wooded hills, but not in the mountains. Nothing was familiar to me. We were far, far away from Villa Matarese, but where I could not tell you then and cannot tell you now.

The last of the nightmare began. Our bodies were pulled off the wagons and thrown into a common grave, each corpse held by two men so that they could hurl it into the deepest part. I fell in pain, my teeth sinking into my fingers to keep my mind from crossing into madness. I opened my eyes and the vomit came again at what I saw. All around me dead faces, limp arms, gaping mouths. Stabbed, bleeding carcasses that only hours ago had been human beings.

The grave was enormous, wide and deep – and strangely, it seemed to me in my silent hysteria, shaped in the form of a circle.

Beyond the edge I could hear the voices of our grave-diggers. Some were weeping, while others cried out to Christ for mercy. Several were demanding that the blessed sacraments be given to the dead, that for the sake of all their souls, a priest be brought to the place of death and intercede with God. But other men said no, they were not the killers, merely those chosen to put the slain to rest. God would understand.

'Basta!' they said. It could not be done. It was the price they paid for the good of generations yet to be born. The hills were theirs; the fields and streams and forests belonged to them! There was no turning back now. They had made their pact with the padrone, *and he had made it clear to the elders: only the government's knowledge of a* conspirazione *could take the lands away from them. The* padrone *was the most learned of men, he knew the courts and the laws; his ignorant tenants did not. They were to do exactly as he had instructed the elders or the high courts would take the lands from them.*

There could be no priests from Porto Vecchio or Sainte Lucie or anywhere else. No chance taken that word would go out of the hills. Those who had other thoughts could join the dead; their secret was never to leave the hills. The lands were theirs!

It was enough. The men fell silent, picked up their shovels, and began throwing dirt over the bodies. I thought then that surely I would die, my mouth and nostrils smothered under the earth. Yet I think all of us trapped with death find ways to elude its touch, ways we could never dream of before we are caught. It happened for me.

As each layer of earth filled the circular grave and was trampled upon, I moved my hand in the darkness, clawing the dirt above me so that I could breathe. At the very end

I had nothing but the smallest passage of air but it was enough; there was space around my head, enough for God's air to invade. The unseen hand had guided mine and I lived.

It was hours later, I believe, when I began to burrow my way to the surface, a . . . blind . . . unknowing animal seeking life. When my hand reached through to nothing but cold moist air, I wept without control, and a part of my brain went into panic, frightened that my weeping would be heard.

God was merciful; everyone had left. I crawled out of the earth, and I walked out of that forest of death into a field and saw the early sunlight rising over the mountains. I was alive, but there was no life for me. I could not go back to the hills for surely I would be killed, yet to go elsewhere, to arrive at some strange place and simply be, was not possible for a young woman in this island country. There was no one I could turn to, having spent three years a willing captive of my padrone. *Yet I could not simply die in that field with God's sunlight spreading over the sky. It told me to live, you see.*

I tried to think what I might do, where I might go. Beyond the hills, on the ocean coasts, were other great houses that belonged to other padroni, *friends of Guillaume. I wondered what would happen were I to appear at one of them and plead for shelter and mercy. Then I saw the error of such thinking. Those men were not my* padrone; *they were men with wives and families, and I was the whore of Villa Matarese. While Guillaume was alive, my presence was to be tolerated, even enjoyed, for the great man would have it no other way. But with him dead, I was dead.*

Then I remembered. There was a man who tended the stables of an estate in Nonza. He had been kind to me during those times we visited and I rode his employer's mounts. He had smiled often and guided me as to my proper deportment in the saddle, for he saw that I was not born to the hunt.

275

Indeed, I admitted it and we had laughed together. And each time I had seen the look in his eyes. I was used to glances of desire, but his eyes held more than that. There was gentleness and understanding, perhaps even respect – not for what I was, but for what I did not pretend to be.

I looked at the early sun and knew that Nonza was on my left, probably beyond the mountains. I set out for those stables and that man.

He became my husband, and although I bore the child of Guillaume de Matarese, he accepted her as his own, giving us both love and protection through the days of his life. Those years and our lives during those years are no concern of yours, they do not pertain to the padrone. It is enough to say that no harm came to us. For years we lived far north in Vescovato, away from the danger of the hill people, never daring to mention their secret. The dead could not be brought back, you see, and the killer and his killer son – the man and the shepherd boy – had fled Corsica.

I have told you the truth, all of it. If you still have doubts, I cannot put them to rest.

Again she had finished.

Taleniekov got up and walked slowly to the stove and the pot of tea. '*Peru nostro circolo,*' he said, looking at Scofield. 'Almost seventy years have passed and still they would kill for their grave.'

'*Perdon?*' The old woman did not understand English, so the KGB man repeated his statement in Italian. Sophia nodded. 'The secret goes from father to son. These are the two generations that have been born since the land was theirs. It is not so long. They are still afraid.'

'There aren't any laws that could take it from them,' said Bray. 'I doubt there ever were. Men might have been sent to prison for withholding information about the massacre; but in those days, who would prosecute? They buried the dead, that was their conspiracy.'

276

'There was a greater conspiracy. They did not permit the blessed sacraments.'

'That's another court. I don't know anything about it.' Scofield glanced at the Russian, then brought his eyes back to the blind eyes in front of him. 'Why did you come back?'

'I was able to. And I was old when we found this valley.'

'That's not an answer.'

'The people of the hills believe a lie. They think the *padrone* spared me, sent me away before the guns began. To others I am a source of fear and hatred. It is whispered that I was spared by God to be a remembrance of their sin, yet blinded by God so as never to reveal their grave in the forests. I am the blind whore of Villa Matarese, permitted to live because they are afraid to take the life of God's reminder.'

Taleniekov spoke from the other side of the stove. 'But you said a while ago that they would not hesitate to kill you if you told the story. Perhaps if they were even aware that you *knew* it. Yet now you tell it to us, and imply that you want us to bring it out of Corsica. Why?'

'Did not a man in your own country call for you and tell you things he wanted you to know?' The Russian began to reply; Sophia Pastorine interrupted. 'Yes, *signore*. As with that man, the end of my life draws near; with each breath I know it. Death, it seems, invites those of us who know some part of the Matarese to speak of it. I'm not sure I can tell you why, but for me, there was a sign. My granddaughter travelled down to the hills and came back with news of a scholar seeking information about the *padrone*. You were my sign. I sent her back to find you.'

'Does she know?' asked Bray. 'Have you ever told her? She could have brought the story out.'

'Never! She is known in the hills, but she is not *of* the hills! She would be hunted down wherever she went. She would be killed. I asked for your word, *signori*, and you must give it to me. You must have nothing further to do with her!'

'You have it,' agreed Taleniekov. 'She's not in this room because of us.'

'What did you hope to accomplish by speaking to my associate?' asked Bray.

'What his friend hoped for, I think. To make men look beneath the waves, to the dark waters below. It is there that the power to move the sea is found.'

'The Council of the Matarese,' said the KGB man, staring at the blind eyes.

'Yes . . . I told you. I listen to the broadcasts from Rome and Milan and Nice. It is happening everywhere. The prophecies of Guillaume de Matarese are coming true. It does not take an educated person to see that. For years I listened to the broadcasts and wondered. Could it be so? Was it possible they survive still? Then one night many days ago I heard the words and it was as though time had no meaning. I was suddenly back in the shadows of the balcony in the great hall, the gunfire and the screams of horror echoing in my ears. I was *there*, with my eyes before God took them from me, watching the terrible scene below. And I was remembering what the *padrone* had said moments before: "You and *yours* will do what I can no longer do."' The old woman stopped, her blind eyes swimming, then began again, her sentences rushed in fear.

'It *was* true! They *had* survived – not the council as it was then, but as it is today. "You and yours." The *yours* had survived! Led by the one man whose voice was crueller than the wind.' Sophia Pastorine abruptly stopped again, her frail, delicate hands grasping for the wooden arm of her chair. She stood up and with her left hand reached for her cane by the edge of the stove.

'The list. You must have it, *signori*! I took it out of a

blood-soaked gown almost seventy years ago after crawling out of the grave in the mountains. It had stayed next to my body through the terror. I had carried it with me so I would not forget their names and their titles, to make my *padrone* proud of me.' The old woman tapped the cane in front of her as she walked across the room to a primitive shelf on the wall. Her right hand felt the edge, her fingers hesitantly dancing among the various jars until she found the one she wanted. She removed the clay top, reached inside, and pulled out a scrap of soiled paper, yellow with age. She turned. 'It is yours. Names from the past. This is the list of honoured guests who journeyed in secrecy to Villa Matarese on the fourth of April, in the year nineteen hundred and eleven. If by giving it to you I do a terrible thing, may God have mercy on my soul.'

Scofield and Taleniekov were on their feet. 'You haven't,' said Bray. 'You've done the right thing.'

'The only thing,' added Vasili. He touched her hand. 'May I?' She released the faded scrap of paper; the Russian studied. 'It's the key,' he said to Scofield. 'It's also quite beyond anything we might have expected.'

'Why?' asked Bray.

'Two of these names will startle you. To say the least, they are prominent. Here.' Taleniekov crossed to Scofield, holding the paper delicately between two fingers so as not to damage it further. Bray took it in the palm of his hand.

'I don't believe it,' said Scofield, reading the names. 'I'd like to get this analysed to make sure it wasn't written five days ago.'

'It wasn't,' said the KGB man.

'I know. And that scares the hell out of me.'

'*Perdoni?*' Sophia Pastorine stood by the shelf. Bray answered her in Italian.

'We recognize two of these names. They are well-known men . . .'

'But they are not the men!' broke in the old woman,

stabbing her cane on the floor. 'None of them! They are only the inheritors! They are controlled by *another*. He is the man!'

'What are you talking about? Who?'

The dog growled. Neither Scofield nor Taleniekov paid any attention; an angry voice had been raised. The animal got on its feet, now snarling, the two men – their concentration on Sophia – still ignoring it. But the old woman did not. She held up her hand, a gesture for silence. She spoke, her anger replaced by alarm.

'Open the door. Call out for my granddaughter. *Quickly!*'

'What is it?' asked the Russian.

'Men are coming. They're passing through the thickets, Uccello hears them.'

Bray walked rapidly to the door. 'How far away are they?'

'On the other side of the ridge, nearly here. Hurry!'

Scofield opened the door and called out. 'You! Antonia, come here. Quickly!'

The dog's snarls were now emitted through bared teeth. Its head thrust forward, its legs stretched and taut, prepared to defend or attack. Leaving the door open, Bray crossed to a counter and picked up a lettuce leaf. He tore it in half and placed the yellow scrap of paper between the two sections, and folded them together. 'I'll put this in my pocket,' he said to the KGB man.

'I've memorized the names and the countries,' replied Taleniekov. 'But then, I'm sure you have, too.'

The girl ran through the door, breathless, her field jacket only partially buttoned, the Lupo in her hand, the bulges of the automatics in her side pockets. 'What's the matter?'

Scofield turned from the counter. 'Your . . . grandmother said men were coming. The dog heard them.'

'On the other side of the hill,' interrupted the old woman. 'Nine hundred paces perhaps, no more.'

'Why would they *do* that?' asked the girl. 'Why would they come?'

'Did they see you, my child? Did they see Uccello?'

'They must have. But I said nothing. I did not interfere with them. They had no reason to think . . .'

'But they saw you the day before,' said Sophia Pastorine, interrupting again.

'Yes. I bought the things you wanted.'

'Then why would you come back?' The old woman spoke rhetorically. 'That is what they tried to understand, and they did. They are men of the hills; they look down at the grass and the dirt and see that three people travelled over the ground, not one. You must leave. All of you!'

'I will not do that, grandmother!' cried Antonia. 'They won't harm us. I'll say I may have been followed, but I know nothing.'

The old woman stared straight ahead. 'You have what you came for, *signori*. Take it. Take her. Leave!'

Bray turned to the girl. 'We owe her that,' he said. He grabbed the shotgun out of her hands. She tried to fight back but Taleniekov pinned her arms and removed the Browning and the Graz-Burya automatics from her pockets. 'You saw what happened down there,' continued Scofield. 'Do as she says.'

The dog raced to the open door and barked viciously. Far in the distance, voices were carried on the morning breezes; men were shouting to others behind them.

'Go!' said Sophia Pastorine.

'Come on.' Bray propelled Antonia in front of him. 'We'll be back after they've left. We haven't finished.'

'A moment, *signori*!' shouted the blind woman. 'I think we have finished. The names you possess may be helpful to you, but they are only the inheritors. Look for the one whose voice is crueller than the wind. I heard it! Find him. The shepherd boy. It is he!'

17

They ran along the edge of the pasture on the border of the woods and climbed to the top of the ridge.

The shadows of the eastern slope kept them from being seen. There had been only a few seconds when they might have been spotted; they were prepared for that but it did not happen. The men on the opposite ridge were distracted by a barking dog, deciding whether or not to use their rifles on it. They did not, for the dog was retrieved by a whistle before such a decision could be made. Uccello was beside Antonia now in the grass, his breath coming as rapidly as hers.

There were four men on the opposite ridge – as there were four names on the scrap of yellow paper in his pocket, thought Scofield. He wished finding them, trapping *them*, were as easy as trapping and picking off the four men who now descended into the valley. But the four men on the list were just the beginning.

There was a shepherd boy to find. 'A voice crueller than the wind' . . . a *child's* voice recognized decades later as one and the same . . . coming over the air waves from the throat of what had to be a very, very old man.

I heard the words and it was as though time had no meaning . . .

What were those *words*? Who was that *man*? The true descendant of Guillaume de Matarese . . . an old man who uttered a phrase that peeled away seventy years from the memory of a blind woman in the mountains of Corsica. In what *language*? It had to be French or Italian; she understood no other.

They had to speak with her again; they had to understand far more. They had *not* finished with Sophia Pastorine.

Bray watched as the four Corsicans approached the farmhouse, two covering the sides, two walking up to the door, all with weapons drawn. The men by the door paused for an instant; then the one on the left raised his boot and rammed it into the wood, crashing the door inward.

Silence.

Two shouts were heard, questions asked harshly. The men outside ran around opposite corners of the farmhouse and went inside. There was more shouting . . . and the unmistakable sound of flesh striking flesh.

Antonia started to get up, fury on her face. Taleniekov pulled her down by the shoulder of her field jacket. The muscles in her throat were pronounced; she was about to scream – Scofield had no choice. He clamped his hand over her mouth, forcing his fingers into her cheeks; the scream was reduced to a series of coughs.

'Be quiet!' whispered Bray. 'If they hear you, they'll use her to get you down there!'

'It would be far worse for her,' said Vasili, 'and for you. You would hear her pain, and they would take you.'

Antonia's eyes blinked; she nodded. Scofield relieved his grip, but did not release it. She whispered through his hand. 'They hit her! A blind woman and they hit her!'

'They're frightened,' said Taleniekov. 'More than you can imagine. Without their land, they have nothing.'

The girl's fingers gripped Bray's wrist. 'What do you mean?'

'Not now!' commanded Scofield. 'There's something wrong. They're staying in there too long.'

'They've found something, perhaps,' agreed the KGB man.

'Or she's telling them something, Oh, *Christ*, she can't!'

'What are you thinking?' asked Taleniekov.

'She said we'd finished. We *haven't*. But she's going to

make sure of it! They'll see our footprints on the floor; we walked over wet ground; she can't deny we were there. With her hearing, she knows which way we went. She'll send them in another direction.'

'That's fine,' said the Russian.

'Goddamn it, they'll *kill* her!'

Taleniekov snapped his head back towards the farmhouse below. 'You're right,' he said. 'If they believe her – and they will – they can't let her live. She's the source; she'll tell them that, too, if only to convince them. Her life for the shepherd boy. So we can find the shepherd boy!'

'But we don't *know* enough! Come on, let's go!' Scofield got to his feet, yanking the automatic from his belt. The dog snarled; the girl rose and Taleniekov pushed her down to the ground again.

They were not in time. Three gunshots followed one upon the other.

Antonia screamed; Bray lunged, holding her, cradling her. '*Please*, please!' he whispered. He saw the Russian pull a knife from somewhere inside his coat. 'No! It's all right!'

Taleniekov palmed the knife and knelt down, his eyes on the farmhouse below. 'They're running outside. You were right; they're heading for the south slope.'

'*Kill them!*' The girl's words were muffled by Scofield's hand.

'To what purpose now?' said the KGB man. 'She did what she wished to do, what she felt she had to do.'

The dog would not follow them; commands from Antonia had no effect. It raced down into the farmhouse and would not come out; its whimpering carried up to the ridge.

'Goodbye, Uccello,' said the girl, sobbing. 'I will come back for you. Before *God*, I will come back!'

They walked out of the mountains, circling north-west beyond the hills of Porto Vecchio, then south to Sainte

Lucie, following the stream until they reached the massive pine under which Bray had buried his attaché case and duffelbag. They travelled cautiously, using the woods as much as possible, separating and walking in sequence across open stretches so no one would see them together.

Scofield pulled the shovel from beneath a pile of branches, dug up his belongings, and they started out again, retracing the stream north towards Sainte Lucie. Conversation was kept to a minimum; they wasted no time putting distance between themselves and the hills.

The long silences and brief separations served a practical purpose, thought Bray, watching the girl as she pressed forward, bewildered, following their commands without thinking, tears intermittently appearing in her eyes. The constant movement occupied her view; she had to come to some sort of acceptance of her 'grandmother's' death. No words from relative strangers could help her; she needed the loneliness of her own thoughts. Scofield suspected that in spite of her handling of the Lupo, Antonia was not a child of violence. She was no child to begin with; in the daylight he could see that she would not see thirty again, but beyond that, she came from a world of radical academics, not revolution. He doubted she would know what to do at the barricades.

'We must stop *running*!' she cried suddenly. 'You may do what you like, but I am returning to Porto Vecchio. I'll see them *hanged*!'

'There's a great deal you don't know,' said Taleniekov.

'She was killed! That is all I *have* to know!'

'It's not that simple,' said Bray. 'The truth is she killed herself.'

'*They* killed her!'

'She forced them to.' Scofield took her hand, gripping it firmly. 'Try to understand me. We can't let you go back; your grandmother knew that. What happened during the past forty-eight hours has got to fade away just as fast as possible. There'll be a certain amount of panic up in those hills; they'll send men trying to find us, but in several weeks when nothing happens, they'll cool off. They'll live with their own fears but they'll be quiet. It's the only thing they can do. Your grandmother understood that. She counted on it.'

'But *why*?'

'Because we have other things to do,' said the Russian. 'She understood that, too. It's why she sent you back to find us.'

'What are these things?' asked Antonia, then answered for herself. 'She said you had names. She spoke of a shepherd boy.'

'But you must speak of neither,' ordered Taleniekov. 'Not if you wish her death to mean anything. We cannot let you interfere.'

Scofield caught the sound in the KGB man's voice and for an instant found himself reaching for his gun. In that split second, the memory of Berlin ten years ago was prodded to the surface. Taleniekov had already made a decision: if the Russian had the slightest doubt, he would kill this girl.

'She won't interfere,' said Bray, without knowing why he gave such a guarantee, but delivering it firmly. 'Let's go. We'll make one stop; I'll see a man in Murato. Then if we can reach Bastia, I can get us out.'

'To *where, signore*? You cannot order me . . .'

'Be quiet,' said Bray. 'Don't press your luck.'

'No, don't,' added the KGB man, glancing at Scofield. 'We must talk. As before, we should travel separately, divide our work, set up schedules and points of contact. We have much to discuss.'

'By my guess, there are ninety miles between here and Bastia. There'll be plenty of time to talk.' Scofield reached down for his attaché case; the girl snapped her hand out of his, angrily moving away; the Russian leaned over for the duffelbag.

'I suggest we talk alone,' he said to Bray. 'She's not an asset, Beowulf.'

'You disappoint me.' Scofield took the duffelbag from the KGB man. 'Hasn't anyone ever taught you to convert a liability into an asset?'

Antonia had lived in Vescovato, on the Golo River, twenty-odd miles south of Bastia. Her immediate contribution was to get them there without being seen. It was important that she make decisions, if only to take her mind off the fact that she was following orders she disagreed with. She did so rapidly, choosing primitive back roads and mountain trails she knew as a child and as a girl growing up in the province.

'The nuns brought us here for a picnic,' she said, looking down at a dammed-up stream. 'We built fires and ate sausage, and took turns going into the woods to smoke cigarettes.'

They went on.

'This hill has a fine wind in the morning,' she said. 'My father made marvellous kites and we would fly them here on Sundays. After Mass, of course.'

'We?' asked Bray. 'Do you have brothers and sisters?'

'One of each. They're older than I am and still live in Vescovato. They have families and I do not see them often; there's not much to talk about between us.'

'They didn't go to the upper schools then?' said Taleniekov.

'They thought such pursuits were foolish. They're good people but prefer a simple life. If we need help, they will offer it.'

'It would be better not to seek it,' said the Russian. 'Or them.'

'They are my family, *signore*. Why should I avoid them?'

'Because it may be necessary.'

'That's no answer. You kept me from Porto Vecchio and the justice that should be done; you can't give me orders any longer.'

The KGB man looked at Scofield, his intent in his eyes. Bray expected the Russian to draw his weapon. He wondered briefly what his own reaction would be; he could not tell. But the moment passed, and Scofield understood something he had not fully understood before. Vasili Taleniekov did not wish to kill, but the professional in him was in strong conflict with the man. The Russian was pleading with him. He wanted to know how to convert a liability into an asset. Scofield wished he knew.

'Take it easy,' said Bray. 'Nobody wants to tell you what to do except where your own safety's concerned. We said that before and it's ten times more valid now.'

'I think it is something else. You wish me to stay silent. *Silent* over the killing of a blind, old woman!'

'Your safety depends on it, we told you that. She understood.'

'She's dead!'

'But you want to live,' insisted Scofield calmly. 'If the hill people find you, you won't. And if it's known that you've talked to others, they'll be in danger, too. Can't you see that?'

'Then what am I to *do*?'

'Just what we're doing. Disappear. Get out of Corsica.' The girl started to object; Bray cut her off. 'And *trust us*. You *must* trust us. Your grandmother did. She did so we could live and find some people who are involved in terrible things that go beyond Corsica.'

'You are not talking to a child. What do you mean, "terrible things"?'

Bray glanced at Taleniekov, accepting his disapproval, but by nodding, overriding it. 'There are men – we don't know how many – whose lives are committed to killing other men, who spread mistrust and suspicion by choosing victims and financing murder. There's no pattern except violence, *political* violence, pitting faction against faction, government against government . . . people against people.' Scofield paused, seeing the concentration in Antonia's face. 'You said you were a political activist, a Communist. Fine. Good. So's my associate here; he was trained in Moscow. I'm an American, trained in Washington. We're enemies; we've fought each other a long time. The details aren't important, but the fact that we're working together now is. The men we're trying to find are much more dangerous than any difference between us, between our governments. Because these men can escalate those differences into something nobody wants; they can blow up the globe.'

'Thank you for telling me,' said Antonia pensively. Then she frowned. 'But how could she know of such things?'

'She was there when it all began,' answered Bray simply. 'Nearly seventy years ago at Villa Matarese.'

The words emerged slowly as Antonia whispered. ' "The whore of Villa Matarese" . . . The *padrone*, Guillaume?'

'He was as powerful as any man in England or France, an obstacle to the cartels and the combines. He stood in their way and won too often, so they destroyed him. They used their governments to bring about his collapse; they killed his sons. He went crazy . . . but in his madness – and with the resources he had left – he put in motion a long-range plan to get revenge. He called together other men who'd been destroyed the same way he had; they became the Council of the Matarese. For years their speciality was assassination; years later they were presumed to have died. Now they've come back, more deadly than they ever were.' Scofield paused; he had told her enough. 'That's as plainly as I can explain it and I hope you understand. You want the men who killed your grandmother to pay for it. I'd like to think that one day

289

they will, but I've also got to tell you that they don't much matter.'

Antonia was silent for a few moments, her intelligent brown eyes riveted on Bray. 'You're quite clear, Signore Scofield. If they don't matter, then I don't matter, either. Is that what you're saying?'

'I guess I am.'

'And my socialist comrade,' she added, glancing at Taleniekov, 'would as soon remove my insignificant presence as not.'

'I look at an objective,' answered Vasili, 'and I do my best to analyse the problems inherent in reaching it.'

'Yes, of course.'

'Then do I turn around and walk into the woods, expecting the gunshot that will end my life?'

'That's your decision,' said Taleniekov.

'I have a choice then? You would take my word that I'll say nothing?'

'No,' replied the KGB man. 'I would not.'

Bray studied Taleniekov's face, his right hand inches from the Browning automatic in his belt. The Russian was leading up to something, testing the girl as he did so.

'Then what is the choice?' continued Antonia. 'To let one or the other of your governments put me away, until you have found the men you seek?'

'I'm afraid that's not possible,' said Taleniekov. 'We're acting outside our governments; we do not have their approval. To put it frankly, they seek us as intensely as we seek the men we spoke of.'

The girl reacted to the Russian's startling information as though struck. 'You're hunted by your own people?' she asked.

Taleniekov nodded.

'I see. I understand clearly now. You will not accept my word and you cannot imprison me. Therefore I am a threat to you – far more than I imagined. So I have *no* choice, do I?'

'You may have,' replied the KGB man. 'My associate mentioned it.'

'What was that?'

'Trust us. Help us get to Bastia and trust us. Something may come of it.' Taleniekov turned to Scofield and spoke one word. 'Conduit.'

'We'll see,' said Bray, removing his hand from his belt. They were thinking along the same lines.

The State Department contact in Murato was not happy; he did not want the complication he was faced with. As an owner of fishing boats in Bastia he wrote reports on Soviet naval manoeuvres for the Americans. Washington paid him well and Washington had cabled *alerts* to stations everywhere that Brandon Alan Scofield, former specialist in Consular Operations, was to be considered a defector. Under such a classification the rules were clear: take into custody, if possible, but if custody was out of the question, employ all feasible measures for dispatch.

Silvio Montefiori wondered briefly if such a course of action was worth a try. But he was a practical man and in spite of the temptation he rejected the idea. Scofield had the proverbial knife to Montefiori's mouth, yet there was some honey on the blade. If Silvio refused the American's request, his activities would be exposed to the *Soviets*. Yet if Silvio acceded to Scofield's wishes, the defector promised him ten thousand dollars. And ten thousand dollars – even with the poor rate of exchange – was probably more than any bonus he might receive for Scofield's death.

Also, he would be alive to spend the money.

Montefiori reached the warehouse, opened the door and walked through the dark, deserted cavern until he stood next to the rear wall, as instructed. He could not see the American – there was too little light – but he knew Scofield was there. It was a matter of waiting while birds circled and signals were somehow relayed.

He took a thin, crooked cigar from his handkerchief pocket, fumbled through his trousers for a box of matches, extracted one and struck it. As he held the flame to the tip of the cigar, he was annoyed to see that his hand trembled.

'You're sweating, Montefiori.' The voice came from the shadows on the left. 'The match shows up the sweat all over your face. The last time I saw you, you were sweating. I was in charge of the pouch then, and asked you certain questions.'

'Brandon!' exclaimed Silvio, his greeting effusive, if nervous. 'My dear good friend! How fine it is to see you again . . . if I could see you.'

The tall American walked out of the shadows into the dim light. Montefiori expected to see a gun in his hand, but, of course, it was not there. Scofield never did the expected.

'How are you, Silvio?' said the defector.

'Well, my dear good friend!' Montefiori knew better than to reach for a handshake. 'Everything's arranged. I take a great risk, pay my crew ten times their wages, but nothing is too much for a friend I admire so. You and the *provocateur* need only to go to the end of Pier Seven in Bastia at one o'clock this morning. My best trawler will get you to Livorno by daybreak.'

'Is that its usual run?'

'Naturally not. The usual port is Piombino. I pay for the extra fuel gladly, with no thought of my loss.'

'That's generous of you.'

'And why not? You have always been fair with me.'

'And why not? You've always delivered.' Scofield reached into his pocket and took out a roll of bills. 'But I'm afraid there'll be some changes. To begin with, I need two boats; one is to sail out of Bastia to the south, the other north, both staying within a thousand yards of the coastline. Each will be met by a speedboat which will be scuttled. I'll board one, the Russian the other, I'll give you the signals. Once on board, he and I will both head for open water, where the two courses will be charted, the destinations known only to the captains and ourselves.'

'So many complications, my friend! They are not necessary, you have my word!'

'And I'll treasure it, Silvio, but while it's locked in my heart, do as I say.'

'Naturally!' said Montefiori, swallowing. 'But you must realize how this will add to my costs.'

'Then they should be covered, shouldn't they?'

'It gladdens me you understand.'

'Oh, I do, Silvio.' The American peeled off a number of very large bills. 'For starters, I want you to know that your activities on behalf of Washington will never be revealed by me; that in itself is a considerable payment, if you place any value on your life. And I want you to have this. It's five thousand dollars.' Scofield held out the money.

'My dearest fellow, you said *ten* thousand! It was on your *word* that I prepared my very expensive arrangements!' Perspiration oozed from Montefiori's pores. Not only was his relationship with the Department of State in untenable jeopardy, but this pig of a traitor was about to steal him blind!

'I haven't finished, Silvio. You're much too anxious. I know I said ten thousand and you'll have it. That leaves five thousand due you, without figuring in your additional expenses. Is that right?'

'Quite right,' said the Corsican. 'The expenses are murderous.'

'So much is these days,' agreed Bray. 'Let's say . . . fifteen per cent above the original price, is that satisfactory?'

'With others I might argue, but never with you.'

'Then we'll settle for an additional fifteen hundred,

OK? That leaves a total of six thousand, five hundred coming to you.'

'That is a troublesome phrase. It implies a future delivery and my expenses are current. They cannot be put off.'

'Come on, old friend. Certainly someone of your reputation can be trusted for a few days.'

'A few days, Brandon? Again, so vague. A "few days" and you could be in Singapore. Or Moscow. Can you be more specific?'

'Sure. The money will be in one of your trawlers, I haven't decided which yet. It'll be under the forward bulkhead, to the right of the centre strut, and hidden in a hollow piece of stained wood attached to the ribbing. You'll find it easily.'

'Mother of God, so will others!'

'Why? No one will be looking unless you make an announcement.'

'It's far too risky! There's not a crewman on board who would hesitate to kill his mother in front of his priest for such an amount! Really, my dear friend, come to your senses!'

'Not to worry, Silvio. Meet your boats in the harbour. If you don't find the wood, look for a man with his hand blown off; he'll have the money.'

'It will be trapped?' asked Montefiori incredulously, the sweat drenching his shirt collar.

'A set-screw on the side; you've done it before. Just remove it and the charge is deactivated.'

'I'll hire my brother . . .' Silvio was depressed; the American was not a nice person. It was as if Scofield had been reading his thoughts. With the money on board, it would be counter-productive to have either boat sunk; the State Department might not pay in full. And by the time both were back in Bastia, the despicable Scofield could be sailing down the Volga. Or the Nile. 'You won't reconsider, my dear good friend?'

'I'm afraid I can't. And I won't tell anybody how much Washington thinks of you, either. Don't fret, Silvio, the money will be there. You see, we may be in touch again. Very soon.'

'Do not hurry, Brandon. And please, say nothing further. I do not care to know anything. Such burdens! What are the signals for tonight?'

'Simple. Two flashes of light, repeated several times, or until the trawlers stop.'

'Two flashes, repeated . . . Distressed speedboats seeking help. I cannot be responsible for accidents at sea. *Ciao*, my old *friend*.' Montefiori blotted his neck with his handkerchief, turned in the dim light of the warehouse, and started across the concrete floor.

'Silvio?'

Montefiori stopped.

'Yes?'

'Change your shirt.'

They had watched her closely for nearly two days now, both men silently acknowledging that a judgement had to be made. She would either be their conduit or she would have to die. There was no middle ground, no security prison or isolated compound to which she could be sent. She would be their conduit or an act of sheer, cold necessity would take place.

They needed someone to relay messages between them. They could not communicate directly; it was too dangerous. There had to be a third party, stationed in one spot, under cover, familiar with whatever basic codes they mounted – above all secretive and accurate. Was Antonia capable of being that person? And if she was, would she accept the risks that went with the job? So they studied her as if thrown into a crash-analysis of an impending exchange between enemies on neutral ground.

She was quick and had surface courage, qualities they

had seen in the hills. She was also alert, conscious of danger. Yet she remained an enigma; her core eluded them. She was defensive, guarded, quiet for long periods, her eyes darting in all directions at once as though she expected a whip to crack across her back, or a hand to grab her throat from the shadows behind. But there were no whips, no shadows in the sunlight.

Antonia was a very strange woman and it occurred to both professionals that she was hiding something. Whatever it was – if it was – she was not about to reveal it. The moments of rest provided nothing; she kept to herself – intensely to herself – and refused to be drawn out.

But she did what they had asked her to do. She got them to Bastia without incident, even to the point of knowing where to flag down a broken-down bus that carried labourers from the outskirts into the port city. Taleniekov sat with Antonia in the front while Scofield remained at the rear, watching the other passengers.

They emerged on the crowded streets, Bray still behind them, still watching, still alert for a break in the pattern of surrounding indifference. A face suddenly rigid, a pair of eyes zeroing in on the erect, middle-aged man walking with the dark-haired woman thirty paces ahead. There was only indifference.

He had told the girl to head for a bar on the waterfront, a rundown hole where no one dared intrude on a fellow drinker. Even most *Corsi* avoided the place; it served the dregs of the piers.

Once inside, they separated again, Taleniekov joining Bray at a table in the corner, Antonia ten feet away at another table, the chair next to her angled against the edge, reserved. It did nothing to inhibit the drunken advances of the customers. These, too, were part of her testing; it was important to know how she handled herself.

'What do you think?' asked Taleniekov.

296

'I'm not sure,' said Scofield. 'She's elusive. I can't find her.'

'Perhaps you're looking too hard. She's been through an emotional upheaval, you can't expect her to act with even the semblance of normalcy. I think she can do the job. We'd know soon enough if she can't; we can protect ourselves with prearranged cipher. And quite frankly, who else do we turn to? Is there a man at any station anywhere you could trust? Or I could trust? Even what you call drones outside the stations; who would not be curious? Who could resist the pressures of Washington or Moscow?'

'It's the emotional upheaval that bothers me,' Bray said. 'I think it happened long before we found her. She said she was down in Porto Vecchio to get away for a while. Get away from what?'

'There could be a dozen explanations. Unemployment is rampant throughout Italy. She could be without work. Or an unfaithful lover, an affair gone sour. Such things are not relevant to what we would be asking her to do.'

'Those aren't the things I saw. Besides, why should we trust her, and even if we took the chance, why would she accept?'

'She was there when that old woman was killed,' said the Russian. 'It may be enough.'

Scofield nodded. 'It's a start, but only if she's convinced there's a specific connection between what we're doing and what she saw.'

'We made that clear. She heard the old woman's words; she repeated them.'

'While she was still confused, still in shock. She's got to be convinced.'

'Then convince her.'

'Me?'

'She trusts you more than she does her "socialist comrade", that's obvious.'

Scofield lifted his glass. 'Were you going to kill her?'

'No. That decision would have had to come from you. It still does. I was uncomfortable seeing your hand so close to your belt.'

'So was I.' Bray put down the glass and glanced over at the girl. Berlin was never far away – Taleniekov understood that – but Scofield's mind and his eyes were not playing tricks with his memories now; he was not in a cave on the side of a hill watching a woman toss her hair free in the light of a fire. There was no similarity between his wife and Antonia any longer. He could kill her if he had to. 'She'll go with me, then,' he said to the Russian. 'I'll know in forty-eight hours. Our first communication will be direct; the next two through her in prearranged code so we can check the accuracy . . . If we want her and she says she'll do it.'

'And if we do not, or she does not?'

'That'll be my decision, won't it.' Bray made a statement; he did not ask a question. Then he took out the leaf of lettuce from his jacket pocket and opened it. The yellowed scrap of paper was intact, the names blurred but legible. Without looking down, Taleniekov repeated them.

' "Count Alberto Scozzi, Rome. Sir John Waverly, London. Prince Andrei Voroshin, St Petersburg" – the name Russia is added, and, of course, the city is now Leningrad. "Señor Manuel Ortiz Ortega, Madrid. Josus" – which is presumed to be Joshua – "Appleton, State of Massachusetts, America." The Spaniard was killed by the *padrone* at Villa Matarese, so he was never part of the council. The remaining four have long since died, but two of their descendants are very prominent, very available. David Waverly and Joshua Appleton the fourth. Britain's Foreign Secretary and the senator from Massachusetts. I say we go for immediate confrontation.'

'I don't,' said Bray, looking down at the paper and the childlike writing of the letters. 'Because we do know who they are, and we don't know anything about the others.

Who are their descendants? Where are they? If there're more surprises, let's try to find them first. The Matarese isn't restricted to two men, and these two in particular may have nothing to do with it.'

'Why do you say that?'

'Everything I know about both of them would seem to deny anything like the Matarese. Waverly had what they call in England a "good war"; a young commando, highly decorated. Then a hell of a record in the Foreign Office. He's always been a tactical compromiser, not an inciter; it doesn't fit . . . Appleton's a Boston Brahmin who bolted the class lines and became a liberal reformer for three terms in the Senate. Protector of the working man as well as the intellectual community. He's a shining knight on a solid, political horse that most of America thinks will take him to the White House next year.'

'What better residence for a *consigliere* of the Matarese?'

'It's too jarring, too pat. I think he's genuine.'

'The art of conviction – in both instances, perhaps. But you're right; they won't vanish. So we start in Leningrad and Rome, trace what we can.'

' "You and *yours* will do what I can no longer do . . ." Those were the words Matarese used seventy years ago. I wonder if it's that simple.'

'Meaning the "yours" could be selected, not born?' asked Taleniekov. 'Not direct descendants?'

'Yes.'

'It's possible, but these were all once-powerful families. The Waverlys and the Appletons still are. There are certain traditions in such families, the blood is always uppermost. Start with the families. They were to inherit the earth; those were his words, too. The old woman said it was his vengeance.'

Scofield nodded. 'I know. She also said they were only the survivors, that they were controlled by another . . . that we should look for someone else.'

299

' "With a voice crueller than the wind,"' interrupted the Russian. ' "It is he," she said.'

'The shepherd boy,' added Bray, staring at the scrap of yellow paper. 'After all these years, who is he? What is he?'

'Start with the families,' repeated Taleniekov. 'If he's to be found, it is through them.'

'Can you get back into Russia? To Leningrad?'

'Easily. Through Helsinki. It will be a strange return for me. I spent three years at the university in Leningrad. It's where they found me.'

'I don't think anyone'll throw you a welcome-home party.' Scofield folded the scrap of yellow paper into the leaf of lettuce and put it in his pocket. He took out a small notebook. 'When you're in Helsinki, stay at the Tavastian Hotel until you hear from me. I'll tell you who to see there. Give me a name.'

'Rydukov, Pyotr,' replied the KGB man without hesitating.

'Who's that?'

'A violinist in the Sevastopol Symphony Orchestra. I'll have his papers somewhat altered.'

'I hope no one asks you to play.'

'Severe arthritis has caused indisposition.'

'Let's work out our codes,' said Bray, glancing at Antonia, who was smoking a cigarette and talking to a young Bastian soldier standing next to her. She was handling herself well; she laughed politely but coolly, putting a gentle distance between herself and the impertinent young man. In truth, there was more than a hint of elegance in her behaviour, out of place in the waterfront café, but welcome to the eyes. His eyes, reflected Scofield, without thinking further.

'What do you think will happen?' asked Taleniekov, watching Bray.

'I'll know in forty-eight hours,' Scofield said.

18

The trawler approached the Italian coastline. The winter
seas had been turbulent, the cross-currents angry and the
boat slow; it had taken them nearly seventeen hours to
make the trip from Bastia. It would be dark soon, and
a small lifeboat would be lowered over the side to take
Scofield and Antonia ashore.

Besides getting them to Italy where the hunt for the
family of Count Alberto Scozzi would begin, the tediously
slow journey served another purpose for Bray. He had the
time and the seclusion to try to learn more about Antonia
Gravet – for that unexpectedly was her last name, her
father having been a French artillery sergeant stationed
in Corsica during the Second World War.

'So you see,' she had told him, the curve of a smile on
her lips, 'my French lessons were very inexpensive. It was
only necessary to anger *papa*, who was never comfortable
with my mother's Cismontan Italian.'

Except for those moments when her mind wandered
back to Porto Vecchio, a change had come over her. She
began to laugh, her brown eyes matching the laughter,
bright, infectious, at times nearly manic, as if the act of
laughing itself were a release she needed. It was almost
impossible for Scofield to realize that the girl sitting next to
him, dressed in khaki trousers and a torn field jacket, was
the same woman who had been so sullen and unresponsive.
Or who had shouted orders in the hills and handled the
Lupo so effectively. They had several minutes left before
going into the lifeboat, so he asked her about it. The Lupo,
not the sudden laughter.

'I went through a phase; we all do, I think. A time when

301

drastic social change seems only possible through violent activism. Those maniacs from the *Brigate Rosse* knew how to play upon our dramatics.'

'The Brigades? You were with the *Red Brigades*? Good God!'

She nodded. 'I spent several weeks at a *Brigatisti* camp in Medicina, learning how to fire weapons, and scale walls and hide contraband – none of which I did particularly well, incidentally – until one morning when a young student, a boy, really, was killed in what the leaders called a "training accident". A *training accident*, such a *military* sound, but they were not soldiers. Only brutes and bullies, let loose with knives and guns. He died in my arms, the blood flowing from his wound . . . his eyes so frightened and bewildered. I hardly knew him but when he died, I couldn't stand it. Guns and knives and clubs were not the way; that night I left and returned to Bologna.

'So what you saw in Porto Vecchio did not settle that question, have we settled ours?'

'What question?'

'Where I'm going. You and the Russian said I was to trust you, do as you were doing, leave Corsica and say nothing. Well, *signore*, we've left Corsica and I've trusted you. I didn't run away.'

'Why didn't you?'

Antonia paused briefly. 'Fear, and you know it. You're not normal men. You speak courteously, but you move too quickly for courteous men. The two don't go together. I think underneath you are what the crazy people in the *Brigate Rosse* would like to be. You frighten me.'

'That stopped you?'

'The Russian wanted to kill me. He watched me closely; he would have shot me the instant he thought I was running.'

'Actually, he didn't want to kill you and he wouldn't have. He was just sending a message.'

'I don't understand.'

'You don't have to, you were perfectly safe.'

'Am I safe now? Will you take my word that I will say nothing and let me go?'

'Where to?'

'Bologna. I can always get work there.'

'Doing what?'

'Nothing very impressive. I'm hired as a researcher at the university. I look up boring statistics for the *professori* who write their boring books and articles.'

'A researcher?' Bray smiled to himself. 'You must be very accurate.'

'What is it to be accurate? Facts are facts. Will you let me go back to Bologna?'

'Your work isn't steady then?'

'It is work I *like*,' replied Antonia. 'I work when I wish to, leaving me time for other things.'

'You're actually a self-employed freelancer with your own business,' said Scofield, enjoying himself. 'That's the essence of capitalism, isn't it?'

'And you're maddening! You ask questions but you don't answer mine!'

'Sorry. Occupational hazard. What was your question?'

'Will you let me go? Will you accept my word; will you trust me? Or must I wait for that moment when you cannot be watching and run?'

'I wouldn't do that, if I were you,' replied Bray courteously. 'Look, you're an honest person. I don't meet many. A minute ago you said you didn't run away before because you were afraid to, not because you trusted us. That's being honest. You brought us up to Bastia. Be honest with me now. Knowing what you know – seeing what you saw in Porto Vecchio – how good is your word?'

At midships, the lifeboat was being hoisted over the railing by four crewmen; Antonia watched it as she spoke. 'You're being unfair. You know what I saw, and you know what you told me. When I think about it, I want to cry out and . . .' She did not finish; instead she turned back to him, her voice weary. 'How good is my word? I don't know. So what's left for me? Will it be you and not the Russian who fires the bullet?'

'I may offer you a job.'

'I don't want work from you.'

'We'll see,' said Bray.

'*Signore, presto, presto! La scialuppa!*'

The lifeboat was in the water. Scofield reached for the duffelbag at his side and got to his feet. He held out his hand for Antonia Gravet. 'Come on. I've had easier people to deal with.'

The statement was true. He could kill this woman if he had to. Still, he would try not to have to.

Where was the new life for Beowulf Agate now?

God, he hated this one.

Bray hired a taxi in Fiumicino, the driver at first reluctant to accept a fare to Rome, changing his mind instantly at the sight of the money in Scofield's hand. They stopped for a quick meal and still reached the inner city before eight o'clock. The streets were crowded, the shops doing a brisk evening's business.

'Pull up in that parking space,' said Bray to the driver. They were in front of a clothing store. 'Wait here,' he added, including Antonia in the command. 'I'll guess your size.' He opened the door.

'What are you doing?' asked the girl.

'A transition,' replied Scofield in English. 'You can't walk into a decent shop dressed like that.'

Five minutes later he returned carrying a box containing denim slacks, a white blouse and a woollen sweater. 'Put these on,' he said.

'You're mad!'

'Modesty becomes you, but we're in a hurry. The

stores'll close in an hour. I've got things to wear; you don't.' He turned to the driver, whose eyes were riveted on the rear view mirror. 'You understand English better than I thought,' he said in Italian. 'Drive around. I'll tell you where to go.' He opened his duffelbag and pulled out a tweed jacket.

Antonia changed in the back seat of the taxi, glancing frequently at Scofield. As she slipped the khakis off and the denims on, her long legs caught the light of the streets. Bray looked out the window, conscious of being affected by what he saw in the corner of his eye. He had not had a woman in a very long time; he would not have this one. It was entirely possible that he might have to kill her.

She pulled the sweater over her blouse; the loose-fitting wool did not conceal the swell of her breasts and Scofield made it a point to focus his eyes on hers. 'That's better. Phase one complete.'

'You're very generous, but these would not have been my choice.'

'You can throw them away in an hour. If anyone asks you, you're off a charter boat in Ladispoli.' He addressed the driver again. 'Go to the Via de Condotti. I'll pay you there; we won't need you any longer.'

The shop on the Via de Condotti was expensive, catering to the idle and the rich, and it was obvious that Antonia Gravet had never been in one like it. Obvious to Bray; he doubted to anyone else. For she had innate taste – born, not cultivated. She might have been bursting at the sight of the wealth of garments displayed, but she was the essence of control. It was the elegance Bray had seen in the filthy waterfront café in Bastia.

'Do you like it?' she asked, coming out of a fitting room in a subdued, dark silk dress, a wide-brimmed white hat and a pair of high-heeled white shoes.

'Very nice,' said Scofield, meaning it, and her, and everything he saw.

'I feel like a traitor to all the things I've believed for so long,' she added, whispering. 'These prices could feed ten families for a month! Let's go somewhere else.'

'We don't have time. Take them and get some kind of coat and anything else you need.'

'You *are* mad.'

'I'm in a hurry.'

From a booth on the Via Sistina, he called a *pensione* in the Piazza Navona where he stayed frequently when in Rome. The landlord and his wife knew nothing at all about Scofield – they were not curious about any of their transient tenants – except that Bray tipped generously whenever they accommodated him. The owner was happy to do so tonight.

The Piazza Navona was crowded; it was always crowded, thus making it an ideal location for a man in his profession. The Bernini statues and fountains were magnets for citizens and tourists alike, the profusion of outdoor cafés places of assignation, planned and spontaneous; Scofield's had always been planned. A table in a crowded square was a good vantage point for spotting surveillance. It was not necessary to be concerned about such things now.

Now it was only necessary to get some sleep, let the mind clear itself. Tomorrow a decision would have to be made. The life or the death of the woman at his side whom he guided through Navona to an old stone building and the door of the *pensione*.

The ceiling of their room was high, the windows enormous, opening on to the square three storeys below. Bray pushed the overstuffed sofa against the door and pointed to the bed across the room.

'Neither of us slept very much on that damned boat. Get some rest.'

Antonia opened one of the boxes from the shop in the

Via de Condotti and took out the fine silk dress. 'Why did you buy me these expensive clothes?'

'Tomorrow we're going to a couple of places where you'll need them.'

'Why are we going to these places? They must surely be extravagant.'

'Not really. There are some people I have to see, and I want you with me.'

'I wanted to thank you. I've never had such beautiful clothes.'

'You're welcome.' Bray went over to the bed and removed the spread; he returned to the sofa. 'Why did you leave Bologna and go to Corsica?'

'More questions,' she said quietly.

'I'm just curious, that's all.'

'I told you. I wanted to get away for a while. Is that not a good enough reason?'

'It's not much of an explanation.'

'It's the one I prefer to give.' She studied the dress in her hands.

Scofield slapped the spread over the sofa. 'Why Corsica?'

'You saw that valley. It is remote, peaceful. A good place to think.'

'It's certainly remote; that makes it a good place to hide out. Were you hiding from someone – or something?'

'Why do you say things like that?'

'I have to know. Were you hiding?'

'Not from anything you would understand.'

'Try me.'

'*Stop* it!' Antonia held the dress out for him. 'Take your clothes. Take anything you want from me, I can't stop you! But leave me *alone*.'

Bray approached her. For the first time, he saw fear in her eyes. 'I think you'd better tell me. All that talk about Bologna . . . it was a lie. You wouldn't go back there even if you could. Why?'

307

She stared at him for a moment, her brown eyes glistening. When she began, she turned away, and walked to the window overlooking the Piazza Navona. 'You might as well know, it doesn't matter any longer . . . You're wrong. I can go back; they expect me back. And if I do not return, one day they will come looking for me.'

'Who?'

'The leaders of the Red Brigades. I told you on the boat how I had run away from the camp in Medicina. That was over a year ago and for over a year I have lived a lie far greater than the one I told you. They found me, and I was put on trial in the Red Court – they call it the Red Court of Revolutionary Justice. Sentences of death are not mere phrases, they are very real executions, as the world knows now.

'I had not been indoctrinated, yet knew the location of the camp and had witnessed the death of the boy. Most damaging, I had run away. I couldn't be trusted. Of course, I didn't matter compared to the objectives of the revolution; they said I had proved myself less than insignificant. A traitor.

'I saw what was coming, so I pleaded for my life. I claimed that I had been the student's lover, and that my reaction – although perhaps not admirable – was understandable. I stressed that I had said nothing to *anyone* let alone the police. I was as committed as any in that court to the revolution – more so than most, for I came from a truly poor family.

'In my own way, I was persuasive, but there was something else working for me. To understand you must know how such groups are organized. There is always a cadre of strong men, and one or two among these who vie for leadership, like male wolves in a pack – snarling, dominating, choosing their various mates at will, for that is part of the domination. A man such as this wanted me among the women. He was probably the most vicious of the pack; the others were frightened of him – and so was I.

'But he could save my life, and I made my choice. I lived with him for over a year, hating every day, despising the nights he took me, loathing myself as much as I loathed him.

'Still, I could do nothing. I lived in fear; in such a terrible fear that my slightest move would be mistaken, and my head blown away . . . their favourite method of execution.' Antonia turned from the window. 'You asked me why I did not run from you and the Russian. Perhaps you understand better now; the conditions of my survival were not new to me. To run away meant death; to run away from you means death now. I was a captive in Bologna, I became a captive in Porto Vecchio . . . and I am a captive now in Rome.' She paused then spoke again. 'I am tired of you all. I can't stand it much longer. The moment will come and I will run . . . and you will shoot.' She held out the dress again. 'Take your clothes, Signore Scofield. I am faster in a pair of trousers.'

Bray did not move, nor did he object by gesture or voice. He almost smiled, but he could not do that, either. 'I'm glad to hear that your sense of fatalism doesn't include intentional suicide. I mean, you *do* expect to give us a "run".'

'You may count on it.' She dropped the dress on the floor.

'I won't kill you, Antonia.'

She laughed quietly, derisively. 'Oh, yes, you will. You and the Russian are the worst kind. In Bologna, they kill with fire in their eyes, and mouthing slogans. You kill without anger . . . you need no inner urging.'

I once did. You get over it. There's no compulsion, only necessity. Please don't talk about these things. The way you've lived is your stay of execution; that's all you need to know.

'I won't argue with you. I didn't say I couldn't – or wouldn't – I simply said I won't. I'm trying to tell you, you don't have to run.'

The girl frowned. 'Why?'

'Because I need you.' Scofield knelt down and picked up the dress. He took her hand gently and gave it back to her. 'All I've got to do is convince you that you need me.'

'To save my life?'

'To give it back to you, at any rate. In what form, I'm not sure, but better than before. Without the fear, eventually.'

' "Eventually" is a long time. Why should I believe you?'

'I don't think you have a choice. I can't give you any other answer until I know more, but let's start with the fact that the *Brigatisti* aren't confined to Bologna. You said if you didn't go back, they'd come looking for you. Their . . . packs . . . roam all over Italy. How long can you keep hiding until they find you – if they want to find you badly enough?'

'I could have for years in Corsica. In Porto Vecchio. They would *never* find me.'

'That's not possible now, and even if it were, is that the kind of existence you want? To spend your life as a recluse in those goddamn hills? Those men who killed that old woman are no different from the Brigades. One wants to keep its world – and its filthy little secret – and it will kill to do it. The other wants to change the world – with terror – and it kills every day to do *that*. Believe me, they're connected to each other. That's the connection Taleniekov and I are looking for. We'd better find it before the maniacs blow us all up. Your grandmother said it: it's happening *everywhere*. Stop hiding. Help us. Help *me*.'

'There's no way I can help you.'

'You don't know what I'm going to ask.'

'Yes, I do. You want me to go back!'

'Later, perhaps. Not now.'

'I won't! They're pigs. He's the pig of the world!'

'Then remove him from the world. Remove *them*. Don't let them grow, don't let them make you a prisoner – whether you're in Corsica or here or anywhere else. Don't you understand? They *will* find you if they think you're a threat to them. Do you want to go back that way? To an execution?'

Antonia broke away, stopped by the overstuffed sofa Bray had placed in front of the door. 'How will they find me? Will you help them?'

'No,' said Scofield, remaining motionless. 'I won't have to.'

'There are a hundred places I can go . . .'

'And there are a thousand ways they have of tracing you.'

'That's a lie!' She turned and faced him. 'They have no such methods.'

'I think they do. Groups like the Brigades everywhere are being fed information, financed, given access to sophisticated equipment, and most of the time they don't know how or why. They're all pawns and that's the irony, but they'll find you.'

'Pawns for what?'

'The Matarese.'

'*Madness!*'

'I wish it were but I'm afraid it isn't. Too much has happened to be coincidence any longer. Men who believed in peace have been killed; a statesman respected by both sides went to others and spoke of it. He disappeared. It's in Washington, Moscow . . . in Italy and Corsica and God knows where. It's *there*, but we can't *see* it. I only know we've got to find it, and that old woman in the hills gave us the first concrete information to go on. She gave up what was left of her life to give it to us. She was blind but she saw it . . . because she was there when it began.'

311

'Words!'

'Facts. Names.'

A sound. Not part of the hum from the square below, but beyond the door blocked by the sofa. All sounds were part of a pattern, or distinctly their own; this was its own. A footstep, a shifting of weight, a scratch of leather against stone. Bray brought his index finger to his lips, then gestured for Antonia to move to the left end of the sofa while he walked quickly to the right. She was bewildered; she had heard nothing. He motioned for her to help him lift the sofa away from the door. Smoothly, silently.

It was done.

Scofield waved her back into the corner, took out his Browning and resumed a normal conversational tone as he inched his way to the door, his face turned away from it.

'It's not too crowded in the restaurants. Let's go down to *Tre Scalini* for some food. God knows I could use . . .'

He pulled the door open; there was no one in the hallway. Yet he had not been mistaken; he knew what he had heard; the years had taught him not to *make* mistakes about such things. And the years had also taught him when to be furious with himself over his own carelessness. Since Fiumicino he had been very careless, disregarding the probability of surveillance. Rome was a low-priority station; since the heavy traffic four years ago, CIA, *Cons Op* and KGB activity had been held to a minimum. It had been over eleven months since he had been in the city, and the scanner sheets then had shown no agents of status in operation there. If anything Rome had lessened in intelligence potential during the past year; who could be around?

Someone was and he had been spotted. Someone moments ago had been close to the door, listening, trying to confirm a sighting. The sudden break in conversation had served to warn whoever it was, but he was there, somewhere in the shadows of the squared-off hallway or on the staircase.

Goddamn it, thought Bray angrily as he walked silently around the landing, had he forgotten that alerts had been sent to every station in the world by now? He was a *fugitive* and he had been careless. Where had he been picked up? In the Via de Condotti? Crossing the Navona?

He heard a rush of air, and even as he heard it, his instinct told him he was too late to react. He stiffened his body as he spun to his right, lunging downward to lessen the impact of the blow.

A door behind him had suddenly been yanked open and a figure that was only a blur above his back rushed out, an arm held high, but only for an instant. It came crashing down, the sickening bolt of pain spreading from the base of his skull throughout his chest, surging downward into his kneecaps where it settled, bringing on the wind of collapse and darkness.

He blinked his eyes, tears of blunt hurt filling them, disorienting him, but somehow providing a measure of relief. How many minutes had he been lying on the hallway floor? He could not tell, yet he sensed it was not long; his mouth was not filled with the dried spit which accompanied any lengthy period of breathing in pain. He rose slowly and looked at his watch, focusing on the dial in the dim light.

He had been out for roughly fifteen minutes; had he not twisted the instant before impact, the elapsed time would have been closer to an hour.

Why was he *there*? Alone? Where was his captor? It did not make sense! He had been taken, then left by himself. What was his capture *for*?

He heard a muted cry, quickly cut off, and turned towards the source, bewildered. Then the bewilderment left him. *He* was not the target; he never had been. It was *she*. Antonia. *She* was the one who had been spotted, not him.

Scofield got to his feet, braced himself against the railing

313

and peered down at the floor around him. His Browning was gone, naturally, and he had no other weapon. But he had something else. Consciousness. His assailant would not expect that – the man had known precisely where to hammer the butt of his gun; in his mind his victim would be unconscious far longer than the few minutes involved. Drawing that man out was not a significant problem.

Bray walked noiselessly to the door of the single room and put his ear to the wood. The moans were more pronounced now. Sharp cries of pain, abruptly stilled. A strong hand clasped over a mouth, fingers pressed into flesh, choking off all but throated protests. And there were words, spoken harshly in Italian.

'*Whore! Pig!* It was to be *Marseilles*! Nine hundred thousand *lire*! Two or three weeks at most! We sent our people; you were not *there*. *He* was not there. No courier of drugs had ever heard of you! *Liar! Whore!* Where were you? What have you *done*!? *Traitor!*'

A scream was suddenly formed, more suddenly cut off, the guttural cry that followed searing in its torment. What in the name of God was *happening*? Scofield slammed his hand against the door, shouting as though only half-conscious, incoherent, his words slurred and barely comprehensible.

'Stop it! *Stop* it! What *is* this? I can't . . . can't . . . *Wait!* I'll run downstairs! There are police in the square. I'll bring the *police*!'

He pounded his feet on the stone floor as if running, his shouts trailing off until there was silence. He pressed his back into the wall and waited, listening to the commotion within. He heard cracks of slapping, gasps of pain as punches were delivered and hysterical cries aborted.

There was a sudden loud thud. A body – her body – was slammed into the door, and then the door was pulled open, Antonia propelled through it with such force she sprawled forward falling to her knees. What Bray saw

314

of her caused him to suppress all reaction. There was no emotion, only movement . . . and the inevitable: he would inflict punishment.

The man rushed through the door, weapon first. Scofield shot out his right hand, catching the gun, pivoting as he did so, his left foot arcing up viciously into the attacker's groin. The man grimaced in shock and sudden agony; the gun fell to the floor, metal clattering against stone. Bray grabbed the man's throat, smashing his head into the wall, and twisting him by the neck into the open door frame. He held the Italian upright, and hammered his fist into the man's lower rib cage; he could hear the bone crack. He plunged his knee into the small of the man's back and with both hands acting as a battering ram, sent him plummeting through the door into the double room. The Italian collapsed over the obstructing sofa and fell senseless to the floor beyond it. Scofield turned and ran to Antonia.

Reaction was allowed now; he felt sick. Her face was bruised, spidery veins of red had spread from the swellings caused by repeated blows to the head. The corner of her left eye was so battered the skin had broken; a two-pronged rivulet of blood flowed down her cheek. The loose-fitting sweater had been removed by force, the white blouse torn to shreds, nothing left but ragged patches of fabric. Beneath, her brassiere had been pulled from its hasps, yanked off her breasts, hanging from a single shoulder strap.

It was the flesh of this exposed part of her body that made him swallow in revulsion. There were cigarette burns, ugly little circles of charred skin, progressing from her pelvic area across the flat of her stomach over the swell of her right breast to the small red nipple.

The man who had done this to her was no interrogator seeking information; that rôle was secondary. He was a sadist, indulging his sickness as brutally and as

315

rapidly as possible. And Bray had not finished with that man.

Antonia moaned, shaking her head back and forth, pleading not to be hurt again. He picked her up and carried her back into the room, kicking the door shut, edging his way around the sofa, past the unconscious man on the floor, to the bed. He placed her gently down, sat beside her and drew her to him.

'It's all right. It's over, he can't touch you any more.' He felt her tears against his face, and then was aware that she had put her arms around him. She was suddenly holding him fiercely, her body trembling, the cries from her throat more than pleas for release from immediate pain. She was begging to be set free from a torment that had been deep within her for a very long time. But it was not the time now to probe; the extent of her wounds had to be examined and treated.

There was a doctor on the Viale Regina, and a man on the floor to be dealt with. Getting Antonia to the doctor might be difficult unless he could calm her down; disposing of the sadist on the floor would be simple. It might even accomplish something.

He would call the police from a booth somewhere in the city and direct them to the *pensione*. They would find a man and his weapon and a crude sign over his unconscious body.

Brigatisti.

19

The doctor closed the door of the examining room and spoke in English. He had been schooled in London and recruited by British intelligence. Scofield had found him during an operation involving *Cons Op* and MI6. The man was safe. He thought all clandestine services were slightly mad, but since the British had paid for his last two years in medical school, he accepted his part of the bargain. He was simply on-call to treat unbalanced people in a very foolish business. Bray liked him.

'She's sedated and my wife is with her. She'll come out of it in a few minutes and you can go.'

'How is she?'

'In pain, but it won't last. I've treated the burns with an ointment that acts as a local anaesthetic for the skin areas. I've given her a jar.' The doctor lit a cigarette; he had not finished. 'An ice pack or two should be applied to the facial contusions; the swellings will go down overnight. The cuts are minor, no stitches required.'

'Then she's all right,' said Scofield, relieved.

'No, she's not, Bray.' The doctor exhaled smoke. 'Oh, medically she's sound and with a little makeup and dark glasses she'll no doubt be up and about by noon tomorrow. But she is not all right!'

'What do you mean?'

'How well do you know her?'

'Barely. I found her several days ago, it doesn't matter where . . .'

'I'm not interested,' interrupted the doctor. 'I never am. I just want you to know that tonight was not the first time

317

this has happened to her. There is evidence of previous beatings, some quite severe.'

'Good Lord . . .' Scofield thought immediately of the cries of anguish he had heard less than an hour ago. 'What kind of evidence?'

'Scars from multiple lacerations and burns. All small and precisely placed to cause maximum pain.'

'Recent?'

'Within the last year or so, I'd say. Some of the tissue is still soft, relatively new.'

'Any ideas?'

'Yes. During severe trauma, people speak of things.' The doctor stopped, inhaling on his cigarette. 'I don't have to tell you that; you count on it.'

'Go on,' said Bray.

'I think she was systematically, psychologically broken. She kept repeating catchwords. Allegiances to this and that; loyalty beyond death and torture of self and comrades. That sort of garbage.'

'The *Brigatisti* were busy little pricks,' Bray said.

'What?'

'Forget it.'

'Forgotten. She has a mass of confusion in that *lovely head* of hers.'

'Not as much as you think. She got away.'

'Intact and functioning?' asked the doctor.

'Mostly.'

'Then she's remarkable.'

'More to the point, she's exactly what I need,' said Scofield.

'Is that, too, a required response?' The medical man's ire was apparent. 'You people never cease to amaze me – in a disappointing way. That woman's scars aren't only on her skin, Bray. She's been brutalized.'

'She's alive. I'd like to be there when she comes out of sedation. May I?'

'So you can catch her while her mind is only *half* alive, extract your *own* responses?' The doctor paused again. 'I'm sorry, it's not my business.'

'I'd like her to be your business if she needs help. If you don't mind.'

The doctor studied him. 'My services are limited to medicine, you know that.'

'I understand. She has no one else, she's not from Rome. Can she come to you . . . if any of those scars get torn away?'

The Italian nodded. 'Tell her to come and see me if she needs medical attention. Or a friend.'

'Thank you very much. And thanks for something else. You've fitted several pieces into a puzzle I couldn't figure out. I'll go in now, if it's all right.'

'Go ahead. Send my wife out here.'

Scofield touched Antonia's cheek. She lay still on the bed, but at the touch rolled her head to the side, her lips parted, a moan of protest escaping her throat. Things *were* clearer now, the puzzle that was Antonia Gravet coming more into focus. For it was the focus that had been lacking; he had not been able to see through the opaque glass wall she had erected between herself and the outside world. The commanding woman in the hills who displayed courage without essential strength; yet who could face a man she believed wanted her dead and tell him to fire away. And the childlike woman on the trawler drenched by the sea, given to sudden moments of infectious laughter. The laughter had confused him. But it was her way of grasping for small periods of relief and normality. The boat was her temporary sanctuary; she would not be hurt while at sea, and so she had made the most of it. An abused child – or a prisoner – allowed an hour of fresh air and sunshine. Take the moments and find joy in them. If only to forget. For those brief moments.

A scarred mind worked that way. Scofield had seen too many scarred minds not to recognize the syndrome once he understood the scars. The doctor had used the phrase 'a mass of confusion' in her lovely head. What could anyone expect? Antonia Gravet had spent her own eternity in a maze of pain. That she had survived above a vegetable was not only remarkable . . . it was the sign of a professional.

Strange, thought Bray, but that conclusion was the highest compliment he could pay. In a way, it made him sick.

She opened her eyes, blinking in fear, her lips trembling. Then she seemed to recognize him; the fear receded and the trembling stopped. He touched her cheek again and her eyes reflected the comfort she felt at the touch.

'*Grazie*,' she whispered. 'Thank you, thank you, thank you . . .'

He bent over her. 'I know most of it,' he said quietly. 'The doctor told me what they did to you. Now tell me the rest. What happened in Marseilles?'

Tears welled up in her eyes and the trembling began again. 'No! No, you must not ask me!'

'*Please*. I have to know. They can't touch you; they'll never touch you again.'

'You saw what they *do*! Oh, God, the *pain* . . .'

'It's over.' He brushed away the tears with his fingers. 'Listen to me. I understand now. I said stupid things to you because I didn't know. Of course you wanted to get away, stay away, isolate yourself – resign from the human race, for Christ's sake – I *understand* that. But don't you see? You *can't*. Help us stop them, help *me* stop them. They've put you through so much . . . make them pay for it, Antonia. Goddamn it, get *angry*. I look at you and I'm angry as hell!'

He was not sure what it was; perhaps the fact that he cared, for he did, and he did not try to conceal that care. It was in his eyes, in his words; he knew it. Whatever it was, the tears stopped, her brown eyes glistened, as they

320

had glistened on the trawler. Anger and purpose were surfacing. She told the rest of her story.

'I was to be the drug whore,' she said. 'The woman who travelled with the courier, keeping her eyes open and her body available at all times. I was to sleep with men – or women, it made no difference – performing whatever services they wished.' Antonia winced, the memories sickening to her. 'The drug whore is valuable to the courier. She can do things he cannot do, being bribe and decoy and unsuspected watchdog. I was . . . trained. I let them think I had no resistance left. My courier was chosen, a foul-mouthed animal who could not wait to have me, for everyone knew he would, and I had been the favourite of the strongest; it gave him status. I was sick to my stomach at what was before me, but I counted the hours, knowing that each one brought me closer to what I had dreamed of for months. My filthy courier and I were taken to La Spezia where we were smuggled aboard a freighter, our destination Marseilles and the contact who would set up the drug runs.

'The courier could not wait, and I was ready for him. We were put into a storage room below deck. The ship was not scheduled to sail for over an hour, so I said to the pig that perhaps we should wait and not risk being intruded upon. But he would not and I knew he would not; if he had I would have provoked him, displaying one breast at a time, groping his soiled trousers if I had to. For each minute was precious to me. I knew I could not go out to sea; once at sea what remained of my life was over. I had made a promise to myself. I would leap into the water at night and drown in peace rather than face Marseilles where the horror would begin again. But I did not have to . . .'

Antonia stopped, the pain of the memory choking her. Bray took her hand and held it in his. 'Go on,' he said. She had to say it. It was the final moment she had to somehow face and exorcize; he felt it as surely as if it were his own.

'The pig pulled off my coat and tore the blouse from my chest. It did not matter that I was willing to remove them, he had to show his bull strength; he had to rape, for he was taking – not being given. He ripped the skirt off my waist until I stood naked before him. Like a maniac, he removed his own clothes and placed himself under the light, I suppose so that I might stand in awe of his nakedness.

'He grabbed me by the hair and forced me to my knees . . . to his waist . . . and I was sick beyond sickness. But I knew the time was coming, and so I shut my eyes and played my part and thought about the beautiful hills in Porto Vecchio, where my grandmother lived . . . where I would live for the rest of my life.

'It happened. The courier threw himself upon me, grunting like an animal, his sweat pouring over me, his stench filling my nostrils.

'I moved us both closer to the coil of rope, shouting in frenzied whispers the things my rapist wanted to hear, as I inched my hand towards the middle of the coil. My moment had come. I had carried a knife – a plain dinner knife I had sharpened on stone – and had shoved it into the coil of rope. I touched the handle and thought again about the beautiful hills in Porto Vecchio.

'And as that scum lay naked on top of me, I raised the knife behind him and plunged it into his back. He screamed and tried to raise himself, but the wound was too deep. I pulled it out and brought it down again, and again, and again . . . and, *O mother of Christ*, again and *again*! I could not *stop killing*!'

She had said it, and now she cried uncontrollably, Scofield held her, stroking her hair, saying nothing for there was nothing he could say that would ease the pain. Finally, the terrible control she forced upon herself returned.

'It had to be done. You understand that, don't you?' Bray said.

She nodded, 'Yes.'

'He didn't deserve to live, that's clear to you, isn't it?'

'Yes.'

'That's the first step, Antonia. You've got to accept it. We're not in a court of law where lawyers can argue philosophies. For us, it's cut and dried. It's a war and you kill because if you don't, someone will kill you.'

She breathed deeply, her eyes roaming over his face, her hand still in his. 'You are an odd man. You say the right words, but I have the feeling you don't like saying them.'

I don't. I do not like what I am. I did not choose my life, it fell down upon me. I am in a tunnel deep in the earth and I cannot get out. The right words are a comfort. And most of the time I need them for my sanity.

Bray squeezed her hand. 'What happened after . . . ?'

'After I killed the courier?'

'After you killed the animal who raped you – who would have killed you.'

'*Grazie ancora,*' said Antonia. 'I dressed in his clothes, rolled up the trousers, pushing my hair into the cap, and filling out the large jacket with what was left of my blouse and skirt. I made my way up to the deck. The sky was dark, but there was light on the pier. Dock workers were walking up and down the gangplank carrying boxes like an army of ants. It was simple. I got in line and walked off the ship.'

'Very good,' said Scofield, meaning it.

'It was not difficult. Except when I first put my foot on the ground.'

'Why? What happened?'

'I wanted to scream. I wanted to shout and laugh and run off the pier yelling to everyone that I was free. *Free!* The rest was very easy. The courier had been given money; it was in his trousers' pocket. It was more than enough to get

323

me to Genoa, where I bought clothes and a ticket on the plane to Corsica. I was in Bastia by noon the next day.'

'And from there to Porto Vecchio?'

'Yes. Free!'

'Not exactly. God knows the prison was different, but you were still a prisoner. Those hills were your cell.'

Antonia looked away. 'I would have been happy there for the rest of my life. Since I was a child I loved the valley and the mountains.'

'Keep the memories,' said Bray. 'Don't try to go back.'

She turned her head towards him. 'You said one day I could! Those men must pay for what they did! You, yourself, agreed to that!'

'I said I hoped they would. Maybe they will, but let others do the work, not you. Someone would blow your head off if you set foot in those hills.' Scofield released her hand and brushed away the strands of dark hair that had fallen over her cheek when she turned so abruptly to him. Something disturbed him; he was not sure what it was. Something was missing, a quantum jump had been made, a step omitted. 'I know it's not fair to ask you to talk about it, but I'm confused. These drug runs . . . how are they mounted? You say a courier is chosen, a woman assigned to travel with him, both to meet a contact at some given location?'

'Yes. A specific article of clothing is worn by the woman and the contact approaches her first. He pays for an hour of her time and they go off together, the courier following. If anything happens, anything like police interception, the courier claims he is the girl's *mezzano* . . . pimp.'

'So the contact and the courier rendezvous through the woman. Is the narcotics delivery made then?'

'I don't think so. Remember, I never actually made a run, but I believe the contact only sets up the distribution schedules. Where the drugs are to be taken and who is to receive them. After that, he sends the courier to a source, again using the whore as his protection.'

'So if there are any arrests, the . . . whore . . . takes the fall?'

'Yes. Drug authorities do not pay much attention to such women; they're let out quickly.'

'But the source is now known, the schedules in hand and the courier protected . . .' What *was* it? Bray stared at the wall, trying to sort out the facts, trying to spot the omission that bothered him so. Was it in the pattern?

'Most of the risks are reduced to the minimum,' said Antonia. 'Even the delivery runs are made in such a way that the merchandise can be abandoned at a moment's notice. At least, that's what I gathered from the other girls.'

' "Most of the risks" . . .' repeated Scofield, ' "reduced to a minimum"?'

'Not all, of course, but a great many. It is very well organized. Each step has what is called a *covata evasione*. A way to escape.'

'Organized? Escape . . . ?' *Organized!* That was *it*. Minimum risks, maximum returns! It *was* the pattern, the *entire* pattern. It went back to the beginning . . . to the concept *itself*. 'Antonia, tell me, where did the contacts come from? How did they reach the Brigades in the first place?'

'The Brigades make a great deal of money from narcotics. The drug market is its main source of income.'

'But how did it start? When?'

'A few years ago, when the Brigades began to expand.'

'It didn't just *happen*. *How* did it happen?'

'I can only tell you what I heard. A man came to the leaders – several were in jail. He told them to find him when they got out on the streets again. He could lead them to large sources of money that could be made without the heavy risks involved in robbery and kidnapping.'

'In other words,' said Scofield, thinking rapidly as he

spoke, 'he offered to finance them in a major way with minor effort. Teams of two people going out for three or four weeks – and returning with something like nine hundred thousand lire. Seventy thousand dollars for a month's work. Minimum risk, maximum return. Very few personnel involved.'

'Yes. In the beginning, the contacts came from him, that man. They in turn led to others. As you say, it does not take many people and they bring in large amounts of money.'

'So the Brigades can concentrate on their true calling,' completed Bray sardonically. 'The disruption of the social order. In a single word, terrorism.' He got up from the bed. 'That man who came to see the leaders in jail. Did he stay in touch with them?'

She frowned. 'Again, I can only tell you what I heard. He was never seen after the second meeting.'

'I'll bet he wasn't. Every negotiation always five times removed from the source . . . A geometric progression, no single line to retrace. That's how they do it.'

'Who?'

'The Matarese.'

Antonia stared at him. 'Why do you say that?'

'Because it's the only explanation. Serious dealers in narcotics wouldn't *touch* maniacs like the Brigades. It's a controlled situation, a charade mounted to finance terrorism, so the Matarese can continue to finance the guns and the killing. In Italy it's the Red Brigades; in Germany, Baader-Meinhof; in Lebanon, the PLO; in my country, the Minutemen and the Weathermen, the Ku-Klux-Klan and the JDL and all the goddamn fools who blew up banks and laboratories and embassies. Each financed differently, secretly. All pawns for the Matarese – maniacal pawns, and that's the scary thing. The longer they're fed the bigger they grow, and the bigger they grow the more damage they do.' He reached for her hand, aware that he had done so only after they had touched. 'What the hell is it all about?'

'You are convinced, aren't you? That it's happening.'

'Now more than ever. You just showed me how one small part of the whole is manipulated. I knew – or thought I knew – it was *being* manipulated but I didn't know how. Now I do and it doesn't take much imagination to think of variations. It's a guerilla war with a thousand battlegrounds, none of them defined.'

Antonia lifted his hand, as though reassuring herself it was there, freely given; and then her dark brown eyes shifted to his, suddenly questioning. 'You talk as if it were new to you, this war. Surely that's not so. You're an intelligence agent . . .'

'I was,' corrected Bray. 'Not any more.'

'That doesn't change what you know. You said to me only a moment ago that certain things must be accepted, that courts and *avvocati* had no place, that one killed in order not to be killed oneself. Is this war so different now?'

'More than I can explain,' answered Scofield, glancing up at the white wall. 'We were professionals and there were rules – most of them our own, most harsh, but there *were* rules and we abided by them. We knew what we were doing, nothing was pointless. I guess you could say we knew when to stop.' He turned back to her. 'These are wild animals, let loose in the streets. They have no rules. They don't know when to stop, and those who are financing them never want them to learn. Don't fool yourself; they're capable of paralysing governments . . .'

Bray caught himself, his voice trailing off. He heard his own words and they astonished him. *He had said it.* In a single phrase he had said it! It was there all the time and neither he nor Taleniekov had seen it. They had approached it, circled it, used words that came close to defining it, but they had never clearly faced it.

. . . they're capable of paralysing governments . . .

When paralysis spreads, control is lost, all functions

stop. A vacuum is created for a force *not* paralysed to move into the host and assume control.

You will inherit the earth. You will have your own again. Other words, spoken by a madman seventy years ago. Yet those words were not political; they were, in fact, *a-political*. Nor did they apply to given borders, no single nation rising to ascendancy. Instead, they were directed to a council, a group of men bound together by a common bond.

But those men were dead; who were they now? And what bound them together? *Now. Today.*

'What is it?' asked Antonia, seeing the strained expression on his face.

'There is a timetable,' said Bray, his voice barely above a whisper. 'It's being orchestrated. The terrorism escalates every month, as if on schedule. Blackburn, Yurievich . . . they *were* tests, probes for reaction at the highest level. Winthrop raised alarms in those circles; he had to be silenced. It all fits.'

'And you're talking to yourself. You hold my hand, but you're talking to yourself.'

Scofield looked at her, struck by another thought. He had heard two remarkable stories from two remarkable women, both tales rooted in violence as both women were tied to the violent world of Guillaume de Matarese. The dying *istrebitel* had said in Moscow that the answer might lie in Corsica. The answer did not, but the first clues to that answer did. Without Sophia Pastorine and Antonia Gravet, mistress and descendant, there was nothing; each in her own way had provided startling revelations. The enigma that was the Matarese remained still an enigma, but it was no longer inexplicable. It had form; it had purpose. Men bound together by some common cause, whose objective was to paralyse governments and assume control . . . *to inherit the earth.*

Therein lay the possibility of catastrophe: that same

earth could be blown up in the process of inheriting it.

'I'm talking to myself,' agreed Bray, 'because I've changed my mind. I said I wanted you to help me, but you've gone through enough. There are others; I'll find them.'

'I see.' Antonia pressed her elbows into the bed, raising herself. 'Just like that, I'm no longer needed?'

'No.'

'Why was I considered at all?'

Scofield paused before replying; he wondered how she would accept the truth. 'You were right before: it *was* one or the other. Enlisting you or killing you.'

Antonia winced. 'But that is no longer true. It's not necessary to kill me?'

'No. It'd be pointless. You won't say anything. You weren't lying, I know what you've lived through. You don't want to go back; you were going to kill yourself rather than land in Marseilles. I believe you would have.'

'Then what's to become of me?'

'I found you in hiding, I'll send you back in hiding. I'll give you money, and in the morning get you papers and a flight out of Rome to some place very far away. I'll write a couple of letters; you'll give them to the people I tell you to. You'll be fine.' Bray stopped for a moment. He could not help himself; he touched her swollen cheek and brushed aside a strand of hair. 'You may even find another valley in a mountain, Antonia. As beautiful as the one you left, but with a difference. You won't be a prisoner there. No one from this life will ever bother you again.'

'Including you, Brandon Scofield?'

'Yes.'

'Then I think you had better kill me.'

'What?'

'I will *not* leave! You cannot force me to, you cannot send me away because it is convenient . . . or *worse*, because you pity me!' Antonia's dark Corsican eyes glistened again. 'What *right* have you? Where were you when the terrible things were done? To *me*, not to *you*. Don't make such decisions for me! Kill me first!'

'I don't want to kill you – I don't *have* to. You wanted to be free, Antonia. I'm offering you that freedom. Take it. Don't be a damn fool.'

'*You're* the fool! I can help you in ways no one else could!'

'How? The courier's whore?'

'If need be, *yes*! Why not?'

'For Christ's sake, *why*?'

The girl was rigid; her answer was spoken quietly. 'Because of things you said . . .'

'I know,' interrupted Scofield. 'I told you to get angry.'

'There is something else. You said that all around the world, people who believe in causes – many not wisely, many with anger and defiance – are being manipulated by others, encouraged to violence and murder. Well, I've seen something of causes. Not all are unwise, and not all believers are animals. There are those of us who want to change this unfair world, and it is our right to try! And no one had the right to turn us into whores and killers. You call these manipulators the Matarese. I say they are richer, more powerful, but no better than the Brigades, who kill children and make liars and murderers out of people like me! I *will* help you. I will *not* be sent away!'

Bray studied her battered but still lovely face. 'You're all alike,' he said. 'You can't stop making speeches.'

Antonia smiled; it was a wry smile, engaging yet shy. 'Most of the time, they're all we have.' The smile disappeared, replaced by a sadness Scofield was not sure he understood. 'There's another thing.'

'What's that?'

'You. I've watched you. You are a man with so much sorrow. It's as clear on your face as the marks on my

330

body. But I can remember when I was happy. Can you?'

'The question's not relevant.'

'It is to me.'

'Why?'

'I could say you saved my life and that would be enough, but that life wasn't worth much. You have given me something else: reason to leave the hills. I never thought anyone could ever do that for me. You offered me freedom just now but you're too late. I already have it, you gave it to me. I am breathing again. So you're important to me. I would like you to remember when you were happy.'

'Is this the courier's . . . woman speaking?'

'She is not a whore. She never was.'

'I'm sorry.'

'Don't be. It is permitted. And if that is the gift you want, take it. I would like to think there are others.'

Bray suddenly ached. The ingenuousness of her offer moved him, pained him. She was hurt and he had hurt her again and he knew why. He was afraid; he preferred whores; he did not want to go to bed with anyone he cared about – it was better not to remember a face or recall a voice. It was far better to remain deep within the earth; he had been there so long. And now this woman wanted to pull him out and he was afraid.

'You learn the things I teach you, that'll be gift enough.'

'Then you'll let me stay?'

'You just said there wasn't anything I could do about it.'

'I meant that.'

'I know you did. If I thought otherwise I'd be on the telephone to one of the best counterfeiters in Rome.'

'Why *are* we in Rome? Will you tell me now?'

Bray did not answer for a moment; then he nodded. 'Why not? To find what's left of a family named Scozzi.'

'Is it one of the names my grandmother gave you?'

331

'The first. They were from Rome.'

'They're still from Rome,' said Antonia, as if commenting on the weather. 'At least a branch of the family, and not far outside Rome.'

Amazed, Scofield looked at her. 'How do you know?'

'The Red Brigades. They kidnapped a nephew of the Scozzi-Paravicinis from an estate near Tivoli. His index finger was cut off and sent to the family along with the ransom demand.'

Scofield remembered the newspaper stories; the young man had been released, but Bray did not recall the name Scozzi, only Paravicini. However, he recalled something else: no ransom had ever been paid. The negotiations had been intense, a young life in balance. But there'd been a breakdown, a defection, the nephew released by a frightened kidnapper, several *Brigatisti* subsequently killed, led into an ambush by the defector.

Had the Red Brigades been taught a lesson by one of their unseen sponsors?

'Were you involved?' he asked. 'In *any* way?'

'No. I was at the camp in Medicina.'

'Did you overhear anything?'

'A great deal. The talk was mainly about traitors and how to kill them in brutal ways to make examples of them. The leaders always talked like that. With the Scozzi-Paravicini kidnapping it was very important to them. The traitor had been bribed by the Fascists.'

'What do you mean by "Fascists"?'

'A banker who represented the Scozzis years ago. The Paravicini interests authorized payment.'

'How did he reach him?'

'With a large sum of money there are ways. Nobody really knows.'

Bray got up from the bed. 'I won't ask you how you're feeling, but are you up to getting out of here?'

'Of course,' she replied, wincing as she swung her long

332

legs over the side of the bed. The pain struck her; a sharp intake of breath followed. She remained still for a moment; Scofield held her shoulders.

Again he could not help himself; he touched her face. 'The forty-eight hours are over,' he said softly. 'I'll cable Taleniekov in Helsinki.'

'What does that mean?'

'It means you're alive and well and living in Rome. Come on, I'll help you dress.'

She brought her fingers up to his hand. 'If you had suggested that yesterday I am not sure what I'd have said.'

'What do you say now?'

'Help me.'

20

There was an expensive restaurant on the Via Frascati owned by the three Crispi brothers, the oldest of whom ran the establishment with the perceptions of an accomplished thief and the eyes of a hungry jackal, both masked by a cherubic face, and a sweeping ebullience. Most who inhabited the velvet lairs of Rome's *dolce vita* adored Crispi, for he was always understanding and discreet, the discretion more valuable than the sympathy. Messages left with him were passed between men and their mistresses, wives and their lovers, the makers and the made. He was a rock in the sea of frivolity, and the frivolous children of all ages loved him.

Scofield used him. Five years ago when NATO's problems had reached into Italy, Bray had put his clamp on Crispi. The restaurateur had been a willing drone.

Crispi was one of the men Bray had wanted to see before Antonia had told him about the Scozzi-Paravicinis; now it was imperative. If anyone in Rome could shed light on an aristocratic family like the Scozzi-Paravicinis, it was the effusive crown prince of foolishness that was Crispi. They would have lunch at the restaurant on the Via Frascati.

An early lunch for Rome, considered Scofield, putting down his coffee and looking at his watch. It was barely noon, the sun outside the window warming the sitting room of the hotel suite, the sounds of traffic floating up from the Via Veneto below. The doctor had called the Excelsior and made the arrangements shortly past midnight, explaining confidentially to the manager that a wealthy patient was in sudden need of quarters – confidentially. Bray and Antonia had been met at the delivery entrance and taken up the service elevator to a suite on the eighth floor.

He had ordered a bottle of brandy and poured three successive glasses for Antonia. The cumulative effects of the alcohol, the medication, the pain and the tension had brought about the state he knew was best: sleep. He had carried her into the bedroom, undressed her and put her to bed, covering her, touching her face, resisting the ache that would have placed him beside her.

On his way back to the couch in the sitting room he had remembered the clothes from the Via de Condotti, he had stuffed them in his duffelbag before leaving the *pensione*. The white hat was the worse for the packing, but the silk dress was less wrinkled than he had thought it would be. He had hung them up before sleeping himself.

He had got up at ten, gone down to the shops in the lobby to buy a flesh-coloured makeup base that would cover Antonia's bruises and a pair of Gucci sunglasses that looked remarkably like the eyes of a grasshopper. He had left them along with the clothes on the chair next to the bed.

She had found them an hour ago, the dress the first thing she had seen when she had opened her eyes.

'You are my personal *fanciulla*!' she had called out to him. 'I am a princess in a fairy tale and my hand-maidens wait upon me! What will my socialist comrades think?'

'That you know something they don't know,' Bray had replied. 'They'd hang Marx in effigy to change places with you. Have some coffee and then get dressed. We're having lunch with a disciple of the Medicis. You'll love his politics.'

She was dressing now, humming fragments of an unfamiliar tune that sounded like a Corsican sea shanty. She had found part of her mind again and a semblance of freedom; he hoped she could keep both. There were no guarantees. The hunt would accelerate at the restaurant in the Via Frascati and she was part of it now.

The humming stopped, replaced by the sound of high-heeled shoes crossing a marble floor. She stood in the door and the ache returned to Scofield's chest. The sight of her moved him and he felt oddly helpless. Stranger still, for a moment he wanted only to hear her speak, listen to her voice, as if hearing it would somehow confirm her immediate presence. Yet she did not speak. She stood there, so lovely, so vulnerable, a grown-up child seeking approval, resentful that she felt the need to seek it. The silk dress was tinged with deep red, complementing her skin, bronzed by the Corsican sun; the large wide hat was angled, framing half her face in white, the other half bordered by her long dark brown hair. The strains of France and Italy had merged in Antonia Gravet; the results were striking.

'You look fine,' said Bray, getting up from the chair.

'Does the makeup cover the marks on my face?'

'I forgot about them so I guess it does.' In the ache he *had* forgotten. 'How are you feeling?'

'I'm not sure. I think the brandy did as much damage as the *Brigatisti*.'

'There's a remedy. A few glasses of wine.'

'I think not, thank you.'

'Whatever you say. I'll get your coat; it's in the closet.' He started across the room, then stopped, seeing her wince. 'You're not all right, are you? It hurts.'

'No, please, really, I'm fine. The salve your doctor friend gave me is very good, very soothing. He's a nice man.'

'I want you to go back and see him any time you need help,' he said. 'Whenever anything bothers you.'

'You sound as though you won't be with me,' she replied. 'I thought we settled that. I accepted your offer of employment, remember?'

Bray smiled. 'It'd be hard to forget, but we haven't defined the job. We'll be together for a while in Rome, then depending on what we find, I'll be moving on. Your job will be to stay here and relay messages between Taleniekov and me.'

'I am to be a *telegraph* service?' asked Antonia. 'What kind of job is that?'

'A vital one. I'll explain as we go along. Come on, I'll get your coat.' He saw her close her eyes again. Pain had jolted her. 'Antonia, listen to me. When you hurt, don't try to hide it, that doesn't help anybody. How bad is it?'

'Not so bad. It will pass, I know. I've been through this before.'

'Do you want to go back to the doctor?'

'No. But thank you for your concern.'

The care was still there, but Scofield resisted it. 'My only concern is that a person can't function well when he's hurt. Mistakes are made when he's in pain. You won't be allowed any mistakes.'

'I may have that glass of wine after all.'

'Please do,' he said.

They stood in the foyer of the restaurant, Bray aware of the glances Antonia attracted. Beyond the delicate lattice work that was the entrance to the dining room, the oldest Crispi was all teeth and obsequiousness. When he saw Bray he was obviously startled; for a split second his eyes became clouded, serious, then he recovered and approached them.

'*Benvenuto, amico mio!*' he cried, the crown prince of frivolity.

'It's been over a year,' said Scofield, returning the firm grip. 'I'm here on business for only a day or so, and wanted my friend to try your *fettucine*.'

These were the words that meant Bray wished to speak

337

privately with Crispi at the table when the opportunity arose.

'They are the best in Rome, *signorina*!' Crispi snapped his fingers for an inferior brother to show the couple to their table. 'I shall hear you say it yourself momentarily. But first, have some wine, in case the sauce is not perfect!' He winked broadly, giving Scofield's hand an additional clasp to signify he understood. Crispi never came to Bray's table unless summoned.

A waiter brought them a chilled bottle of Pouilly Fumé, compliments of the *fratelli*, but it was not until the *fettucine* had come and gone that Crispi came to the table. He sat in the third chair; introductions and the small talk that accompanied them were brief.

'Antonia's working with me,' Scofield explained, 'but she's never to be mentioned. To anyone, do you understand?'

'Of course.'

'And neither am I. If anyone from the embassy – or anywhere else – asks about me, you haven't seen me. Is that clear?'

'Clear, but unusual.'

'In fact, no one's to know I'm here. Or *was* here.'

'Even your own people?'

'Especially my own people. My orders supersede embassy interests. That's as plainly as I can put it.'

Crispi arched his brows, nodding slowly. 'Defectors?'

'That'll do.'

Crispi's eyes became serious. 'Very well, I have not seen you, Brandon. Then why are you here? Will you be sending people to me?'

'Only Antonia. Whenever she needs help getting cables off to me . . . and to someone else.'

'Why should she need my help to send cables?'

'I want them re-routed, different points of origin. Can you do it?'

'If the idiot *Communisti* do not strike the telephone service again, it is no problem. I call a cousin in Firenzi, he sends one; an exporter in Athens or Tunis or Tel Aviv, they do the same. Everybody does what Crispi wants and no one asks a single question. But you know that.'

'What about your own phones? Are they clean?'

The prince of foolishness laughed. 'With what is known to be said on my telephone, there is not an official in Rome who could permit such impertinence.'

Scofield remembered Robert Winthrop in Washington. 'Someone else said that to me not so long ago. He was wrong.'

'No doubt he was,' agreed Crispi, his eyes amused. 'Forgive me, Brandon, but you people deal merely in matters of state. We on the Via Frascati deal in matters of the heart. Ours take precedence where confidentiality is concerned. They always have.'

Bray returned the Italian's smile. 'You know, you may be right.' He lifted the glass of wine to his lips. 'Let me throw a name at you. Scozzi-Paravicini.' He drank.

Crispi nodded reflectively. 'Blood seeks money, and money seeks blood. What else is there to say?'

'Say it plainly.'

'The Scozzis are one of the noblest families in Rome. The venerable *contessa* to this day is chauffeured in her restored Bugatti up the Veneto, her children pretenders to thrones long since abandoned. Unfortunately, all they had were their pretensions, not a thousand lire between them. The Paravicinis had money, a great deal of money, but not a drop of decent blood in their veins. It was a marriage made in the heavenly courts of mutual convenience.'

'Whose marriage?'

'The *contessa*'s daughter to Signor Bernardo Paravicini. It was a long time ago, the dowry a number of millions and gainful employment for her son, the count. He assumed his father's title.'

339

'What's his name?'

'Guillamo. Count Guillamo Scozzi.'

'Where does he live?'

'Wherever his interests – financial and otherwise – take him. He has an estate near his sister's in Tivoli, but I don't think he's there very often. Why do you ask? Is he connected with defectors? It's hardly likely.'

'He may not be aware of it. It could be he's being used by people who work for him.'

'Even more unlikely. Beneath his charming personality, there's the mind of a Borgia. Take my word for it.'

'How do you know that?'

'I know *him*,' said Crispi, smiling. 'He and I are not so different.'

Bray leaned forward. 'I want to meet him. Not as Scofield, of course. As someone else. Can you arrange it?'

'Perhaps. If he's in Italy, and I think he is. I read somewhere that his wife is a patron of the *Festa Villa d'Este*, being held tomorrow night. It is a charity affair for the gardens. He would not miss it; as they say, everyone in Rome will be there.'

'Your Rome, I trust,' interrupted Scofield. 'Not mine.'

He watched her across the hotel room as she lifted the skirt out of the box and folded it on her lap as though checking for imperfections. He understood that the pleasure he derived from buying her things was out of place. Clothes were a necessity; it was as simple as that, but his knowing it did not erase the warmth that spread through him watching her.

The prisoner was free, the decisions restored, and although she had commented about the exorbitant prices at the Excelsior she had not refused to let him buy clothes for her at the shops. It had been a game. She would look over at Bray; if he nodded, she would frown, feigning disapproval – invariably glancing at the price tag – then slowly re-evaluate, ultimately acknowledging his taste.

His wife used to do that in West Berlin. In West Berlin it had been one of *their* games. His Katrine was always worried about money. They were going to have children one day, money was important, and the government was not a generous corporation. No Grade Twelve foreign service officer was about to open a Swiss bank account.

Of course, by then Scofield had. In Bern. And in Paris and London and, naturally, Berlin. He had not told her; his true professional life had never touched her. Until it touched her with finality. Had things been different, he might have given her one of those accounts. After he had transferred out of Consular Operations into a civilized branch of the State Department.

Goddamn it! He was *going* to! It had only been a matter of *weeks*!

'You are so far away.'

'What?' Bray brought the glass to his lips; it was a reflex gesture for he had finished the drink. It occurred to him that he was drinking too much.

'You're looking at me, but I don't think you see me.'

'I certainly do. I miss the hat. I liked the white hat.'

She smiled. 'You don't wear a hat inside. The waiter who brought us dinner would have thought me silly.'

'You wore it at Crispi's place. That waiter didn't.'

'A restaurant is different.'

'Both inside.' He got up and walked to the small table where the whisky was next to an ice bucket. He poured himself a drink.

'Thank you again for these.' Antonia glanced at the boxes and shopping bags beside the chair. 'It is like Christmas Eve, I don't know which to open next.' She laughed. 'But there was never a Christmas in Corsica like this! *Papa* would scowl for a month at the sight of such things. Yes, I *do* thank you.'

'No need to.' Scofield remained by the table, adding more whisky to his glass. 'They're equipment. Like an office typewriter or an adding machine or file cabinets. They go with the job.'

'I see.' She replaced the skirt and the blouse into the box. 'But you don't,' she said.

'I beg your pardon?'

'*Niente*. Does the whisky help you relax?'

'You could say that. Would you like one?'

'No, thank you. I'm more relaxed than I have been in a very long time. It would be wasted.'

'To each according to his needs. Or wants,' said Scofield, lowering himself into the chair. 'You can go to bed, if you like. Tomorrow's going to be a long day.'

'Does my company bother you?'

'No, of course not.'

'But you prefer to be alone.'

'I hadn't thought about it.'

She used to say that. In West Berlin, when there were problems and I would sit by myself trying to think as others might think. She would be talking and I would not hear her. She used to get angry – not angry, hurt – and say, 'You'd rather be alone, wouldn't you?' And I would, but I could not explain. Perhaps if I had explained . . . Perhaps an explanation would have served as a warning.

'If something's troubling you, why not talk about it?'

Oh, God, her words! In West Berlin.

'Stop trying to be *somebody else*!' He heard the statement shouted in his own voice. It was the whisky, the goddamn *whisky*! 'I'm sorry, I didn't mean that,' he added quickly, putting the glass down. 'I'm tired and I've had too much to drink. I didn't mean it.'

'Of course you did,' said Antonia, getting up. 'I think I understand now. But you should understand also. I am not somebody else. I have had to pretend to be someone who was not me and that is the surest way to know who you are. I am myself, and you helped me – find that person again.' She turned and walked rapidly into the bedroom, closing the door behind her.

'Toni, I'm *sorry* . . .' Bray stood up, furious with himself. In an outburst, he had revealed far more than he cared to. He hated the loss of control.

There was a knock on the door, the hallway door; Scofield spun around. Instinctively felt the holster strapped to his chest under his jacket. He went to the side of the door and spoke.

'*Si? Chic'é?*'

'*Uno messaggio, Signor Pastorine. Da vostro amico, Crispi. Di Via Frascati.*'

Bray put his hand inside his jacket, checked the chain on the door and opened it. In the hallway stood the waiter from Crispi's who had served their table. He held up an envelope and handed it to Scofield through the open space. Crispi had taken no risks; his own man was the messenger.

'*Grazie. Uno momento,*' said Bray, reaching into his pocket for a lira note.

'*Prego,*' replied the waiter, accepting the tip.

Scofield closed the door, and tore open the envelope. Two gold-embossed tickets were attached to a note. He removed them and read Crispi's message, the handwriting as well as the language florid.

Word has reached Count Scozzi from the undersigned that an American named Pastor will introduce himself at Villa d'Este. The Count understands that this Pastor has extensive connections in the OPEC countries, acting frequently as a purchasing agent for oil-soaked sheiks. These are endeavours such men never discuss, so just smile and learn where the Arabian Gulf is located. The Count understands too that Pastor is merely on holiday

343

and seeks pleasant diversions. All things considered, the Count may offer them.

I kiss the hand of the *bella signorina*.

Ciao,

Crispi

Bray smiled. Crispi was right; no one who performed middleman services for the sheiks ever discussed those services. Profiles were kept excessively low because the stakes were excessively high. One simply did not talk about them – as he would not at Villa d'Este. Instead, he would talk of other things with Count Guillamo Scozzi.

He heard the latch turn on the bedroom door. There was a moment of hesitation before Antonia opened it. When she did, Bray realized why. She stood in the door frame in a black slip he had bought her downstairs. She had removed her brassiere, her breasts swelling against the sheer silk, her long legs outlined below in opaque darkness. She was barefoot, the bronzed skin of her calves and ankles in perfect concert with her arms and face. Her lovely face, striking yet gentle, with the dark eyes that held his without wavering, without judgement.

'You must have loved her very much,' she said quietly.

'I did. It was a long time ago.'

'Not long enough, apparently. You called me Toni. Was that her name?'

'No.'

'I'm glad. I would not wish to be mistaken for someone else.'

'You made that clear. It won't happen again.'

Antonia was silent, remaining motionless in the doorway, her eyes still without judgement. When she spoke, it was a question. 'Why do you refuse yourself?'

'I'm not an animal in the hold of a freighter.'

'We both know that. I've seen you look at me, then look away as though it were not permitted. You're tense, but you seek no release.'

344

'If I want that kind of . . . release . . . I know where to find it.'

'I offer it to you.'

'The offer will be taken under consideration.'

'*Stop it!*' cried Antonia, stepping forward. 'You want a whore? Then think of me as a courier's *whore!*'

'I can't do that.'

'Then do not look at me the way you do! A part of you with me, another far away, what do you want?'

Please don't do this. Leave me where I was, deep in the earth, comfort in the darkness. Don't touch me, for if you do, you die. Can't you understand that? Men will call you across a barrier and they will kill you. Leave me with whores, professionals – as I am a professional. We know the rules. You don't.

She stood in front of him; he had not seen her come to him, she was simply there. He looked down at her, her face tilted up to his, her eyes close, her tears near, her lips parted.

Her whole body was trembling; she was gripped by fear, the scars had been torn away; he had ripped them because she had seen the ache in his eyes.

SHE could not erase HIS pain. What made her think he could erase hers?

And then, as if she were reading his thoughts, she whispered again.

'If you loved her so much, love me a little. It may help.'

She reached up to him, her hands cupping his face, her lips inches from his, the trembling no less for the nearness. He put his arms around her; their lips touched and the ache was released. He was drawn into a wind; he felt his own tears well up in his eyes and roll down his cheeks, mingling with hers. He let his hands fall down her back, caressing her, pulling her to him, holding her, *holding* her. Please, *closer*, the moisture of her mouth arousing him, replacing the ache of pain with the ache of wanting her

345

beside him. He swept his hand around to her breast; she pulled her own hand down and pressed it over his, pushing herself against him, revolving her body up to the rhythm that infused them both.

She pulled her mouth away. 'Take me to bed. In the name of God, *take me*. And love me. Please, love me a little.'

'I tried to warn you,' he said, 'I tried to warn us both.'

He was coming out of the earth and there was sunlight above. Yet in the distance there was the darkness still. And fear; he felt it sharply. But for the moment, he chose to remain in the sunlight – if only for a while. With her.

21

The magnificence of the Villa d'Este was not lost in the chill of the evening. The floodlights had been turned on and the banks of fountains illuminated – thousands of cascading streams caught in the light as they arced in serrated ranks down the steep inclines. In the centres of the vast pools, the gushers surged up into the night, the umbrella sprays sparkling in the floodlights like diadems. And at each formation of rock constructed into a waterfall, screens of rushing silver fell in front of ancient statuary; saints and centaurs were drenched in splendour.

The gardens were officially closed to the public; only Rome's most beautiful people were invited to the *Festa Villa d'Este*. The purpose was ostensibly to raise funds for its maintenance, augmenting the dwindling government subsidies; but Scofield had the distinct impression that there was a secondary, no less desirable motive: to provide an evening when Villa d'Este could be enjoyed by its true inheritors, unencumbered by the tourist world. Crispi was right. Everyone in Rome was there.

Not his Rome, thought Bray, feeling the velvet lapels of his tuxedo. Their Rome.

The huge rooms of the villa itself had been transformed into palace courtyards, complete with banquet tables and gilded chairs lining the walls – resting spots for the courtiers and courtesans at play. Russian sable and mink, chinchilla and golden fox, draped shoulders dressed by Givenchy and Pucci; webs of diamonds and strings of pearls fell from elongated throats, and all too often from too many chins. Slender *cavalieri*, dashing in their scarlet cummerbunds and greying temples, co-existed with squat, bald men who had cigars, and more power than their appearances might signify. Music was provided by no fewer than four orchestras, ranging in size from six to twenty instruments, playing everything from the stately strains of Monteverdi to the frenzied beat of the disco. Villa d'Este belonged to the *belli Romani*.

Of all the beautiful people, one of the most striking was Antonia – Toni. (It was Toni now by dual decree arrived at in the comfort of the bed.) No jewels adorned her neck or wrists; somehow they would have been impediments to the smooth, bronzed skin set off by the simple gown of white and gold. The facial swellings had receded, as the doctor said they would. She wore no sunglasses now, her wide brown eyes reflecting the light. She was as lovely as any part of her surroundings, lovelier than most of her would-be equals, for her beauty was understated, and grew with each second of observation in the beholder's eyes.

For convenience, Toni was introduced quite simply as the rather mysterious Mr Pastor's friend from Lake Como. Certain parts of the lake were known to be retreats for the expensive children of the Mediterranean. Crispi had done his job well; he had provided just enough information to intrigue a number of guests. Those who might wish to learn the most about the quiet Mr Pastor were told the least, while others too engrossed with themselves to care about Pastor were told more, so they could relate what they had learned as gossip, which was their major industry.

Those men whose concerns were more directly – even exclusively – financial, were prone to take his elbow and inquire softly about the projected status of the dollar or the stability of investments in London, San Francisco and Buenos Aires. With such inquisitors, Scofield inclined his head briefly at some suggestions and shook it with a single motion at others. Eyebrows were raised – unobtrusively. Information had been imparted, although Bray had no idea what it was.

348

After one such encounter with a particularly insistent questioner he took Toni's arm and they walked through a massive archway into the next crowded 'courtyard'. Accepting two glasses of champagne from a waiter's tray, Bray handed one to Toni and looked around over the crystal rim as he drank.

Without having seen him before Scofield knew he had just found Count Guillamo Scozzi. The Italian was in a corner chatting with two long-legged young women, his eyes roaming from their attentive stares, glancing about the room with feigned casualness. He was a tall, slender man, a *cavaliero* complete with tails and greying hair that spread streaks from his temples throughout his perfectly groomed head. In his lapel were tiny colourful ribbons, around his waist a thin gold sash, bordered in dark red and knotted off-centre. If any missed the significance of the ribbons, they could not overlook the mark of distinction inherent in the sash; Scozzi wore his escutcheons prominently. In his late fifties the count was the embodiment of the *bello Romano*; no *Siciliano* had ever crept into the bed of his ancestors and *per Dio* the world had better know it.

'How will you find him?' asked Antonia, sipping the wine.

'I think I just have.'

'Him? Over there?' she asked. Bray nodded. 'You're right, I've seen his picture in the newspapers. He's a favourite subject of the *paparazzi*. Are you going to introduce yourself?'

'I don't think I'll have to. Unless I'm mistaken, he's looking for me.' Scofield gestured towards a buffet table. 'Let's walk over to the end table, by the pastries. He'll see us.'

'But how would he know you?'

'Crispi. Our benevolent intermediary may not have bothered to describe me, but he sure as hell wouldn't overlook describing you. Not with someone like Scozzi.'

349

'But I had those huge sunglasses on.'

'You're very funny,' said Bray.

It took less than a minute before they heard a mellifluous voice behind them at the buffet table.

'Signore Pastor, I believe.'

They turned. 'I beg your pardon? Have we met?' Scofield asked.

'We are about to, I think,' said the count, extending his hand. 'Scozzi. Guillamo Scozzi. It is a pleasure to make your acquaintance.' The title was emphasized by its absence.

'Oh, of *course*. Count Scozzi. I told that delightful fellow Crispi I'd look you up. We arrived here less than an hour ago and it's been a little hectic. I would have recognized you, naturally, but I'm surprised you knew me.'

Scozzi laughed, displaying teeth so white and so perfectly formed they could not possibly have come with the original machine. 'Crispi is, indeed, delightful, but I'm afraid a bit of a rascal. He was rapturous over *la bella signorina*.' The count inclined his head to Antonia. 'I see her, I find you. As always, Crispi's taste is impeccable.'

'Excuse me.' Scofield touched Toni's forearm. 'Count Scozzi, my friend, Antonia . . . from Lake Como.' The first name and the lake said it all; the count took her hand and raised it to his lips.

'An adorable creature. Rome must see more of you.'

'You're too kind, Excellency,' said Antonia, as if born to attend the *Festa Villa d'Este*.

'Truthfully, Mr Pastor,' continued Scozzi, 'I've been told that many of my more bothersome friends have been annoying you with questions. I apologize for them.'

'No need to. I'm afraid Crispi's descriptions included more mundane matters.' Bray smiled with disarming humility. 'When people learn what I do, they ask questions. I'm used to it.'

'You're very understanding.'

'It's not hard to be. I just wish I were as knowledgeable as so many think I am. Usually I simply try to implement decisions taken before I got there.'

'But in those decisions,' said the count, 'there is knowledge, is there not?'

'I hope so. Otherwise an awful lot of money's being thrown away.'

'Blown away with the desert winds, as it were,' clarified Scozzi. 'Why do I think we actually *have* met before, Mr Pastor?'

The sudden question had been considered by Scofield; it was always a possibility and he was prepared for it. 'If we had I think I'd remember; but it might have been the American embassy. Those parties were never as grand as this, but just as crowded.'

'Then you are a fixture on Embassy Row?'

'Hardly a fixture, but sometimes a last-minute guest.' Bray smiled, self-deprecatingly. 'It seems there are times when my countrymen are as interested in asking me questions as your friends here in Tivoli.'

Scozzi chuckled. 'Information is often the road to heroic national stature, Mr Pastor. You are a reluctant hero.'

'Not really. I have to make a living, that's all.'

'I would not care to negotiate with you,' said Scozzi. 'I detect the mind of an experienced bargainer.'

'That's too bad,' replied Scofield, altering the tone of his voice just enough to signal to the Italian's inner antenna. 'I thought we might talk for a bit.'

'Oh?' The count glanced at Antonia. 'But we bore the *bella signorina*.'

'Not at all,' said Toni pleasantly. 'I've learned more about my friend during the last several minutes than for the past week. But I *am* famished . . .'

'Say no more,' interrupted Scozzi, as if her hunger were a matter of corporate survival. He raised his hand. In a second a young, dark-haired man dressed in tails appeared beside him. 'My aide will see to your needs, *signorina*. His name is Paolo and, incidentally, he is a charming dancer. I believe my wife taught him.'

Paolo bowed, avoiding the count's eyes, and offered his arm to Antonia. She accepted it, stepping forward, her face turned to Scozzi and Bray.

'*Ciao*,' she said, her eyes wishing Scofield good hunting.

'You are to be envied, Mr Pastor,' remarked Count Guillamo Scozzi, watching the receding figure in white. 'She *is* adorable. You bought her in Como?'

Bray glanced at the Italian. Scozzi meant exactly what he said. 'To be honest with you, I'm not even sure she's ever been there,' he answered, knowing the double lie was mandatory; the count could make inquiries too easily. 'Actually, a friend in Ar-Riyād gave me a number to call at the lake. She joined me in Nice. From where I've never asked.'

'Would you consider, however, asking her about her calendar? Tell her from me the sooner the better. She may reach me through the Paravicini offices in Torino.'

'Turin?'

'Our plants in the north. Agnelli's Fiat gets far more attention, but I can assure you, Scozzi-Paravicini runs Turin – as well as a great deal of Europe.'

'I never realized that.'

'You didn't? I thought it was perhaps the basis for your wishing to . . . "talk for a bit", I believe you said.'

Scofield drank the last of his champagne, speaking as he took the glass from his lips. 'Do you think we might go outside for a minute or two? I have a confidential message for you from a client on – let's say, the Arabian Gulf. It's why I'm here tonight.'

Scozzi's eyes clouded. 'A message for me? Naturally, as most of Rome and Torino, I've met casually with a number of gentlemen from the area, but none I can recall by name. But, of course, we'll take a stroll. You intrigue me.' The count started forward, but Bray stopped him with a gesture.

'I'd rather we weren't seen going out together. Tell me where you'll be and I'll show up in twenty minutes.'

'How extraordinary! Very well.' The Italian paused. 'Ippolito's Fountain, do you know it?'

'I'll find it.'

'It's quite a distance. There shouldn't be anyone around.'

'That's fine. Twenty minutes.' Scofield nodded. Both turned and walked away, through the crowds, in opposite directions.

There were no floodlights at the fountain, nor sounds of disturbance as a man crawled around the rocks and walked silently through the foliage. Bray was taking no chances that Scozzi had stationed aides in the vicinity. If he had, Scofield would have sent a message to the Italian, naming a second, immediate rendezvous.

They were alone – or would be in a matter of minutes. The count was strolling down the path towards the fountain. Bray doubled back through a weed-filled garden, emerging on the path fifty feet behind Scozzi. He cleared his throat the moment Scozzi reached the waist-high wall of the fountain's pool. The count turned; there was just enough light from the terraces above for each to see the other. Scofield was bothered by the darkness. Scozzi could have chosen any number of places more convenient, less filled with shadows. Bray did not like shadows.

'Was it necessary to come down this far?' he asked. 'I wanted to see you alone, but I hadn't figured on walking half-way back to Rome.'

'Nor had I, Mr Pastor, until you made the statement that you did not care to have us seen leaving together. It brought to my mind the obvious. It is, perhaps, not to my advantage to be seen talking in private with you. You are a broker for the sheiks.'

'Why should that bother you?'

'Why did you wish to leave separately?' Scozzi had a quick mind, bearing out Crispi's allusion to a Borgia mentality.

'A matter of being *too* obvious, I'd say. But if someone wandered down here and saw us, that would also be too obvious. There's a middle ground, a casual encounter in the gardens, for example.'

'You have the encounter and no one will see us,' said the count, fingering his thin gold sash in the shadows. 'There is only one entrance to the fountain of Ippolito; it is forty metres behind us. I have an aide standing there. Guillamo Scozzi has been known to stroll with a companion of his choice down – if you will – a primrose path. At such times he does not care to be disturbed.'

'Does my doing what I do call for those precautions?'

The count raised his head. 'Remember, Mr Pastor. Scozzi-Paravicini deals throughout all Europe and both Americas. We look constantly for new markets, but we do not look for Arab capital. It is highly suspect; barriers are being erected everywhere to prevent its excessive infusion. We would not care to be so scrutinized. Jewish interests in Paris and New York alone could cost us dearly.'

'What I have to say to you has nothing to do with Scozzi-Paravicini,' said Scofield. 'It concerns the Scozzi part, not the Paravicini.'

'You allude to a sensitive area, Mr Pastor. Please be specific.'

'You are the son of Count Alberto Scozzi, aren't you?'

'It is well known. As are my contributions to the growth of Paravicini Industries. The significance of the corporate conversion to the name of *Scozzi-Paravicini* is, I trust, not lost on you.'

'It isn't, but even if it were, it doesn't matter. I'm only a go-between, supposedly the first of several contacts, each

354

farther removed from the other. As far as I'm concerned, I ran into you casually at a charity affair in Tivoli. We never had this talk.'

'Your message must, indeed, be dramatic. Who sends it?'

It was Bray's turn to raise his hand. 'Please. As we understand the rules, identities are never specific at the first conference. Only a geographical area and a political equation that involves hypothetical antagonists.'

Scozzi's eyes narrowed; the lids fell in concentration. 'Go on,' he said.

'You're a count, so I'll bend the rules a bit. Let's say there's a prince living in a sizable country, a sheikdom, really, on the Gulf. His uncle, the king, is from another era; he's old and senile but his word is law, just as it was when he led a Bedouin tribe in the desert. He's squandering millions with bad investments, depleting the sheikdom's resources, taking too much out of the ground too quickly. This hypothetical prince would like him removed. For everyone's good. He appeals to the council through the son of Alberto Scozzi, named for the Corsican *padrone*, Guillaume . . . That's the message. Now I'd like to speak for myself.'

'Who *are* you?' interrupted the Italian, his eyes now wide. 'Who sent you?'

'Let me finish,' said Bray quickly. He had to get past the initial jolt, jump to a second plateau. 'As an observer of this . . . hypothetical equation, I can tell you it's reached a crisis. There isn't a day to lose. The prince needs an answer and, frankly, if I bring it to him, I'll be a much richer man for it. You, of course, can name the council's price. And I can tell you that . . . fifty million, American, is not out of the question.'

'Fifty *million*.'

It worked; the second plateau was reached. Even for a man like Guillamo Scozzi, the amount was staggering.

His arrogant lips were parted in amazement. It was the moment to complicate, to stun again.

'The sum is conditional, of course. It's a maximum figure that presumes an immediate answer, eliminating subsequent contacts, and delivery of the package within seven days. It won't be easy. The old man is guarded day and night by *fida'is* – they're a collection of mad dogs who . . .' Scofield paused. 'But then, I don't have to tell you about anything related to Hasan ibn as-Sabbāh, do I? From what I gather the Corsican drew on him pretty extensively. At any rate, the prince suggests a programmed suicide . . .'

'*Enough!*' whispered Scozzi. 'Who *are* you, Pastor? Is the name intended to mean something to me? Pastor? *Priest?* Are you a high priest sent to *test* me?' The Italian's voice rose stridently. 'You talk of things buried in the past. How *dare you?*'

'I'm talking about fifty million American dollars. And don't tell me – or my client – about things buried. His father was buried with his throat slit from chin to collar bone by a maniac sent by the council. Check your records, if you keep them; you'll find it. My client wants his own back again and he's willing to pay roughly fifty times what his father's brother paid.' Bray stopped for a moment and shook his head in disapproval and sudden frustration. 'This is crazy! I told him for less than half the amount I could buy him a legitimate revolution, sanctioned by the United Nations. But he wants it *this* way. With you. And I think I know why. He said something to me; I don't know if it's part of his message but I'll deliver it anyway. He said, "The way of the Matarese is the only way. They'll see my faith." He wants to join you.'

Guillamo Scozzi recoiled; his legs were pressed against the wall of the fountain, his arms rigidly at his side. 'What right have you to say these things to me? You are insane, a madman! I don't know what you're talking about.'

'Really? Then we've got the wrong man. We'll find the right one; I'll find him. We were given the words; we know the response.'

'What words?'

'*Perro nostro* . . .' Scofield let his voice trail off, his eyes riveted on Scozzi's lips in the dim light.

Involuntarily, the lips parted. The Italian was about to utter the third word, complete the phrase that had lived for seventy years in the remote hills of Porto Vecchio. Guillamo Scozzi was about to say . . . *circulo*.

He did not. Instead, he whispered again, shock replaced by a concern so deeply felt he could barely be heard. 'My *God*! You cannot . . . you *must* not! Where have you *come* from? What have you been *told*?'

'Just enough to know I've found the right man. One of them, at any rate. Do we deal?'

'Do not presume, Mr Pastor! Or whatever your name is.' There was fury now in the Italian's voice.

'Pastor'll do. All right, I've got my answer. You pass. I'll tell my client.' Bray turned.

'*Fermato!*'

'*Perchè? Che causa?*' Scofield spoke over his shoulder without moving.

'Your Italian is very quick, very fluent.'

'So are several other languages. It helps when you travel a lot. I travel a lot. What do you want?'

'You will stay here until I say you may leave.'

'Really?' said Scofield, turning to face Scozzi again. 'What's the point? I've got my answer.'

'You'll do as I tell you. I have only to raise my voice and an aide will be beside you, blocking any departure you may consider.'

Bray tried to understand. This powerful *consigliere* could deny everything – he had, after all, said nothing – and have a strange American followed. Or he could call for help; or he might simply walk away himself and send

armed men to find him. He could do any of these things –
he *was* part of the Matarese; the admission was in his eyes
– but he chose to do none of them.

Then Scofield thought he did understand. Guillamo
Scozzi, the quick-thinking industrial pirate with the Borgia
mentality, was not sure what he should do. He was caught
in a dilemma that had suddenly overwhelmed him. It had
all happened too fast, he was not prepared to make a
decision. So he made none.

Which meant that there was someone else – someone
near-by, accessible – who *could*.

Someone at Villa d'Este that night.

'Does this mean that you're reconsidering?' asked Bray.

'It means *nothing*!'

'Then why should I stay? I don't think you should give
orders to me; I'm not one of your Praetorians. We don't
deal; it's as simple as that.'

'It is *not* that simple!' Scozzi's voice rose again, fear
more pronounced than anger now.

'I say it is, and I say the hell with it,' said Scofield,
turning again. It was important that the Italian summon
his unseen guard. Very important.

Scozzi did so. '*Veni! Presto!*'

Bray heard racing feet on the dark path; in seconds a
broad-shouldered, stocky man in evening clothes came
running out of the shadows.

'*Esitare! Vicino!*'

The guard did not hesitate. He pulled out a short-
barrelled revolver, levelling it at Bray. Scozzi spoke, as if
imposing a control on himself, explaining the unnecessary.

'These are troubled times, Signore Pastor. All of us
travel with these Praetorians you just mentioned. Terrorists are everywhere.'

The moment was irresistible. It was the instant to
insert the final, verbal blade. 'That's something you
people should know about. Terrorists, I mean. Like

358

the Brigades. Do the orders come from the shepherd boy?'

It was as though Scozzi had been struck by an unseen hammer. His upper body convulsed, fending off the blow, feeling its impact, trying to recover but not sure it was possible. In the dim light, Scofield could see perspiration forming at the Italian's hairline, matting the perfectly groomed grey temples. His eyes were the eyes of a terrified animal.

'*Rimanere*,' he whispered to the guard, then rushed away up the dark path.

Scofield turned to the man, looking afraid and speaking in Italian. 'I don't know what this is all about any more than *you* do! I offered your boss a lot of money from someone and he goes crazy. Christ, I'm just a salesman!' The guard said nothing, but Bray's obvious fear relieved him. 'Do you mind if I have a cigarette? Guns scare the hell out of me.'

'Go ahead,' said the broad-shouldered man.

It was the last thing he would say for several hours. Scofield reached into his pocket with his left hand, his right at his side – in shadow, under the guard's elbow. As he pulled out a pack of cigarettes, he shot his right hand up, clasping his fingers around the short barrel of the guard's revolver, twisting hand and weapon violently in a counter-clockwise motion. Dropping the cigarettes, he gripped the man's throat with his left hand, choking off all sound, propelling the guard off the path, over the bordering rocks into the dense foliage beyond. As the man fell, Bray ripped the gun away from the twisted wrist, and brought the handle down sharply on the man's skull. The guard went limp; Scofield pulled him farther into the weeds.

No second could be wasted. Guillamo Scozzi had raced away seeking counsel; it was the only explanation. Somewhere quiet, on a terrace or in a room, the *consigliere* was bringing his shocking information to another. Or others.

Bray ran up the path, keeping in the shadows as much as possible, slowing down to a rapid walk as he emerged on the plateau of terraces that fronted the final incline of steps into the villa itself. Somewhere just above, *somewhere* was the panicked Scozzi. To whom was he running? Who could make the decision this powerful, frightened man was incapable of making?

Scofield took the steps rapidly, the guard's revolver in his trouser pocket, his Browning strapped to his chest beneath his tuxedo. He walked through the French doors into a crowded room; it was the 'courtyard' devoted anachronistically to the crashing sounds of the disco beat. Revolving mirrored globes of coloured lights hung from the ceiling, spinning crazily as dancers weaved and jolted their bodies, their faces set in rigid expressions, lost in the beat and grass and alcohol.

This was the nearest room to the most direct set of steps from the terrace closest to the path from Ippolito's Fountain. In Scozzi's state of mind it *had* to be the one he entered first; there were two entrances. Which had he taken?

There was a break in the movement on the dance floor, and Bray had his answer. There was a heavy door in the wall behind a long buffet table. Two men were rushing towards it; they had been summoned; an alarm had been raised.

Scofield made his way to the door, excusing himself around the rim of frenzied bodies, and slowly pushed it open, his hand on the Browning under his jacket. Beyond was a narrow winding staircase of thick reddish stone; he could hear footsteps above.

There were other sounds as well. Men were shouting, two voices raised in counterpoint, one stronger, calmer, the other on the verge of hysteria. The latter voice was Count Guillamo Scozzi's.

Bray started up the steps, pressing his back against the

wall, the Browning held at his side. Around the first curve was a door, but the voices did not come from within it; they were farther up, beyond a second door, diagonally above on a second landing. Scozzi was screaming now. Scofield was close enough to hear the words clearly.

'He spoke of the *Brigades*, and – oh, my *God*! – of the *shepherd*! Of the *Corsican*! He *knows*! Mother of Christ, he *knows*!'

'*Silence!* He probes, he does not know. We were told he might do so; the old man telephoned about him, and he had certain facts. More than we'd assumed, and that is troublesome, I grant you.'

'*Troublesome?* It's *chaos*! A word, a hint, a breath, and I could be *ruined*! Everywhere!'

'You?' said the stronger voice contemptuously. 'You are nothing, Guillamo! You are only what we tell you you are. Remember that . . . You walked away, of course. You gave him no inkling that there was a shred of credence to what he said.'

There was a pause. 'I called my guard, told the American to remain where he was. He is under the gun, still by the fountain.'

'You *what*!? You left him with a *guard*? An *American*? Are you *mad*? That is impossible. He is no such thing!'

'He's American, of course he is! His English is American – *completely* American. He uses the name Pastor, I told you that!'

Another pause, this one ominous, the tension electric. 'You were always the weakest link, Guillamo; we know that. But now you've caved in too far. You've left an open question where there can be *none*! That man is Vasili Taleniekov! He changes languages as a chameleon alters its colours, and he will kill a guard with no more effort than stepping on a maggot. We cannot afford you, Guillamo. There can be no link at all. None whatsoever.'

Silence . . . brief, cut short by a gunshot and a guttural explosion of breath. Guillamo Scozzi was dead.

'Leave him!' commanded the unknown *consigliere* of the Matarese. 'He'll be found in the morning, his car at the bottom of the gorge of Hadrian. Go find this "Pastor", this elusive Taleniekov! He won't be taken alive, don't try. Find him. Kill him . . . And the girl in white. She, also. Kill them both.'

Scofield lunged down the narrow staircase, around the curve. The last words he heard from beyond the door above, however, were so strange, so arresting, he nearly stopped, tempted to fire at the emerging killers and go back up to face the unknown man, who spoke them.

'. . . *Scozzi!* Mother of Christ! Reach Turin. Tell them to cable the eagles, the cat. The burials must be absolute . . .'

There was no time to think, he had to reach Antonia; he had to get them out of Villa d'Este. He pulled back the door and rushed out into the pounding madness that was the disco scene. Suddenly, he was aware of the row of chairs lined up against the wall; most were empty, some draped with discarded capes and furs and stoles.

If he could eliminate one pursuer the advantage would be manifold. One man sending out an alarm would be far less effective than two. And there was something else: A trapped man convinced he was about to lose his life would more than likely reveal an identity to save it. He turned to the wall, his hands on the rim of a chair, a *cavaliero* with too much wine in him.

The heavy door burst open and the first of the two killers raced out, his companion close behind him, but still behind him. The first man headed for the French doors and the steps to the terrace below; the second started around the edge of the dance floor towards the far archway.

Scofield leaped forward, twisting his body in a series of contortions as though he were a lone dancer gone wild with the percussive sounds of the rock music; he was not the only picture of drunkenness; there were more than a few on the crowded dance floor. He reached the second man and threw his arm over a shoulder, clamping his hand on the holster beneath the jacket, immobilizing the weapon inside it by gripping the handle through the cloth, forcing the barrel into the man's chest. The Italian struggled; it was useless and in seconds he knew it. Bray surged his right hand along the edge of the man's waist and dug his fingers into the base of the rib cage, yanking back with such force that the man screamed.

The scream went unnoticed for there were screams everywhere, and deafening music and revolving lights that blinded one moment, leaving residues of white the next. Scofield pulled the man back to the row of chairs against the wall and spun him around, forcing him down into the one at the end nearest the heavy door. He plunged his fingers into the Italian's throat, his left hand now under the jacket, his fingers inching towards the trigger, the barrel still jammed into the man's flesh. He put his lips next to the killer's ear.

'The man upstairs! Who *is he*? Tell me, or your own gun will blow your lungs out! The shot won't even be heard in here! Who *is* he?'

'*No!*' The man tried to arch out of the chair; Bray sunk his kneecap into the rising groin, his fingers choking the windpipe. He pressed both; pain without release or relief.

'I warn you and it's final! *Who is he?*'

Saliva poured out of the man's mouth, his eyes two circles of red webs, his chest heaving in surrender. He abandoned his cause, and he expelled the name in a strained whisper.

'*Paravicini.*'

Bray viced a last clamp on the killer's windpipe; the air to the lungs and the head was suspended for slightly more than two seconds; the man fell limp. Scofield angled him down over the adjacent chair, one more *bello Romano* drunk.

He turned and threaded his way through the narrow path between the row of chairs and the jagged line of fever-pitched dancers. The first man had gone outside; Bray could roam freely for a minute or two; but no longer. He pressed his way through the crowd in the entranceway and walked into a less frenzied gathering in the next room.

He saw her in the corner, the dark-haired Paolo standing next to her, two other *cavalieri* in front, all vying for her attention. Paolo, however, seemed less insistent; he knew future possessions when he saw them, where his count was concerned. The first thought that came to Bray's mind was that Toni's dress had to be covered.

. . . the girl in white. She, also, kill them both . . .

He walked rapidly up to the foursome, knowing precisely what he would do. A diversion was needed, the more hysterical the better. He touched Paolo's arm, his eyes on Antonia, his look telling her to stay quiet.

'You *are* Paolo, aren't you?' he asked the dark-haired man in Italian.

'Yes, sir.'

'Count Guillamo wants to see you right away. It's some kind of emergency, I think.'

'Of course! Where is he, sir?'

'Go through the arch over there and turn right, past a row of chairs, to a door. There's a staircase . . .' The young Italian rushed away. Bray excused Toni and himself from the remaining two men. He held her arm and propelled her towards the arch that led into the disco.

'What's happening?' she asked.

'We're leaving,' he answered. 'Inside here, there are some coats and things on chairs. Grab the darkest and the largest one you can find. Quickly, we haven't much time.'

She found a long black cape, as Bray stood between

her and the jolting contortionists on the dance floor. She bunched it under her arm and they elbowed their way to the French doors and the steps outside.

'Here, put it on,' ordered Scofield, draping it over her shoulders. 'Let's go,' he said, starting down the steps. 'We'll cut through the terraces to the right and back inside through the hall to the parking . . .'

Screams erupted from inside. Men were shouting, women shrieking, and within seconds figures in various stages of drunkenness surged out of doors, colliding with each other. There was a sudden chaos inside and the panicked words were clear.

Omicidio!

Terroristi!

Fuggine!

The body of Count Guillamo Scozzi had been found.

Bray and Antonia raced down to the first level of terraces and began running by the wall filled with ornate boxes of plants. At the end of the enclosure there was a narrow opening into the next. Scofield held her hand and pulled her through.

'*Fermata!* You stay!'

The shout came from above; the first man, who had rushed out of the door only minutes before, stood on the stone steps, a weapon in his hand. Bray slammed his shoulder into Antonia, sending her crashing into the wall. He dived to his right on the concrete, rolled to his left, and yanked the Browning from his holster. The man's shots exploded the ancient stone above Scofield; Bray aimed from his back, his shoulders off the pavement, his right hand steadied by his left. He fired twice; the killer fell forward, tumbling down the steps.

The gunshots accelerated the chaos; screams of terror filled the elegant terraces of the Villa d'Este as the panicked crowds of revellers raced everywhere. Bray reached Antonia; she was crouching by the wall.

'Are you all right?'

'I'm alive.'

'Come on!'

They found a break in the wall where a trough carried a rushing stream of water to a pool below. They stepped through and ran down the side of the man-made rivulet to the first path, an alleyway, bordered on both sides by what appeared to be hundreds of stone statues spewing arcs of water in unison. The floodlights filtered through the trees; the scene was eerily peaceful, juxtaposed to but not affected by the stampeding chaos from the terraces above.

'Straight through!' said Scofield. 'At the end there's a waterfall and another staircase. It'll get us back up there.'

They started running through the tunnel of foliage, mist from the arcs of water joining the sweat on their faces.

'*Dannazione!*' Antonia fell, the long black cape torn from her shoulders by a branch of a sapling. Bray stopped and pulled her up.

'*Eccola!*'

'*La donna!*'

The shouts came from behind them; gunshots followed. Two men came racing through the water-filled alleyway; they were targets, silhouetted by the light from the fountain beyond. Scofield fired three rounds. One man fell, holding his thigh; the second grabbed his shoulder, his gun flying out of his hand as he dived for the protection of the nearest statue.

Bray and Antonia reached the staircase at the end of the path. An entrance of the villa. They ran up, taking the steps two at a time, until they joined the panicked crowds rushing out through the enclosed courtyard into the huge parking lot.

Chauffeurs were everywhere, standing by elegant automobiles, protecting them, waiting for sight of their employers – and as with all chauffeurs in Italy in these times, their guns were drawn, levelled; protection was everything. They had been schooled; they were prepared.

One, however, was not prepared enough. Bray approached him. 'Is this Count Scozzi's car?' he asked breathlessly.

'No, it is not, *signore*! Stand back!'

'Sorry.' Scofield took a step away from the man, sufficient to allay his fears, then lunged forward, hammering the barrel of his automatic into the side of the chauffeur's skull. The man collapsed. 'Get in!' he yelled to Antonia. 'Lock the doors and stay on the floor until we're out of here.'

It took them nearly a quarter of an hour before they reached the highway out of Tivoli. They sped down the road for six miles, then took an offshoot to the right that was devoid of traffic. Bray pulled over to the side of the road, stopped, and for several moments let his head fall back against the seat and closed his eyes. The pounding lessened; he sat up, reached into his pocket for his cigarettes, and offered one to Antonia.

'Normally, I do not,' she said. 'But right now I will. What happened?'

He lighted both their cigarettes and told her, ending with the murder of Guillamo Scozzi, the enigmatic words that he had heard on the staircase, and the identity of the man who spoke them. Paravicini. The specifics were clear, the conclusions less so. He could only speculate.

'They thought I was Taleniekov; they'd been warned about him. But they knew nothing about *me*, my name was never mentioned. It doesn't make sense, Scozzi described an American. They should have known.'

'Why?'

'Because Washington and Moscow both knew Taleniekov was coming after me. They tried to trap us; they failed, and so they had to presume we made contact . . .' Or did they? wondered Scofield. The only one who actually

knew he and the Russian had made contact was Robert
Winthrop, and if he was alive, his silence could be counted
upon. The rest of the intelligence community had only
circumstantial carnage to go on; no one had actually seen
them together. Still, the presumption had to be made,
unless . . . 'They think I'm dead,' he said out loud, staring
through the cigarette smoke to the windshield. 'It's the
only explanation. Someone told them I was dead. That's
what "impossible" meant.'

'Why would anyone do that?'

'I wish I knew. If it were purely an intelligence
manoeuvre, it could be for a reason as basic as buying
time, throwing the opposition off, your own trap to
follow. But this isn't that kind of thing, it couldn't be.
The Matarese has lines into Soviet and US operations – I
don't doubt it for a minute – but not the other way round.
I don't understand.'

'Could whoever it was think you *are* dead?'

Bray looked at her, his mind racing. 'I don't see how. Or
why. It's a damn good idea but I didn't think of it. To pull
off a burial without a corpse takes a lot of doing.'

Burial . . . The burials must be absolute.

Reach Turin . . . Tell them to cable the eagles, the cat.

Turin. Paravicini.

'Have you thought of something?' asked Antonia.

'Something else,' he replied. 'This Paravicini. He runs
the Scozzi-Paravicini companies in Turin?'

'He did once. And in Rome and Milan, New York and
Paris, as well. All over. He married the Scozzi daughter
and as time went on her brother, the count, assumed
more and more control. The count's the one who ran the
companies. At least, that's what the newspapers said.'

'It's what Paravicini wanted them to say. It wasn't true.
Scozzi was a well-put-together figurehead.'

'Then he wasn't part of the Matarese?'

'Oh, he was part of it all right, in some ways the most

368

important part. Unless I'm wrong, he brought it with him. He and his mother, the *contessa*, presented it to Paravicini along with his blue-blooded new wife. But now we come to the real question. Why would a man like Paravicini even listen? Men like Paravicini need, above all things . . . political stability. They pour fortunes into governments that have it and candidates who promise it – because they lose fortunes when it isn't there. They look for strong authoritarian regimes, capable of stamping out a Red Brigade or a Baader-Meinhof no matter how indiscriminate the process, or how much legitimate dissent goes down with them.'

'That government does not exist in Italy,' interrupted Antonia.

'And in not many other places, either. That's what doesn't make sense. The Paravicinis of this world thrive on law and order. They have nothing to gain by, or nothing to substitute *for*, its breakdown. Yet the Matarese is against all that. It wants to *paralyse* governments; it feeds the terrorists, funnels money to them, spreads the paralysis as quickly as possible.' Scofield drew on his cigarette. The clearer some things became, the more obscure did others.

'You're contradicting yourself, Bray.' Antonia touched his arm; it had become a perfectly natural gesture during the past twenty-four hours. 'You say Paravicini *is* the Matarese. Or part of it.'

'He is. That's what's missing. The reason.'

'Where do you look for it?'

'Not here any longer. I'll ask the doctor to pick up our things at the Excelsior. We're getting out.'

'We?'

Scofield took her hand. 'Tonight changed a lot of things. *La bella signorina* can't stay in Rome now.'

'Then I can go with *you*.'

'As far as Paris,' said Bray hesitantly, the hesitation not born of doubt, only of how to arrange the avenues of communication in Paris. There were others. 'You'll stay there. I'll work out the procedures and get you a place to stay.'

'Where will you go?'

'London. We know about Paravicini now; he's the Scozzi factor. London's next.'

'Why there?'

'Paravicini said Turin was to cable "the eagles, the cat". With what your grandmother told us in Corsica, that code isn't hard to figure out. One eagle is my country, the other Taleniekov's.'

'It doesn't follow,' disagreed Antonia. 'Russia is the bear.'

'Not in this case. The Russian bear is Bolshevik, the Russian eagle, Czarist. The third guest at Villa Matarese in April nineteen eleven was a man named Voroshin. Prince Andrei Voroshin. From St Petersburg. That's Leningrad now. Taleniekov's on his way there.'

'And the "cat"?'

'The British lion. The second guest, Sir John Waverly. A descendant, David Waverly, is England's Foreign Secretary.'

'A very high position.'

'Too high, too visible. It doesn't make sense for him to be involved, either. Any more than the man in Washington, a senator who will probably be President next year. And because it doesn't make sense, it scares the hell out of me.' Scofield released her hand, and reached for the ignition. 'We're getting closer. Whatever there is to be found under the two eagles and the cat may be harder to dig out, but it's there. Paravicini made that clear. He said the "burials" had to be "absolute". He meant that all the connections had to be re-examined, put farther out of reach.'

'You'll be in a great deal of danger.' She touched his arm again.

'Nowhere near as much as Taleniekov. As far as the

Matarese is concerned, I'm dead, remember? He's not. Which is why we're going to send our first cable. To Helsinki. We've got to warn him.'

'About what?'

'That anyone prowling around Leningrad looking for information about an illustrious old St Petersburg family named Voroshin will probably get his head blown off.' Bray started the car. 'It's wild,' he said. 'We're going after the inheritors – or we think we are – because we've got their names. But there's someone else, and I don't think any of them means much without him.'

'Who is that?'

'A shepherd boy. He's the one we've really got to find, and I don't have the vaguest idea of how to do it.'

22

Taleniekov walked to the middle of the block on Helsinki's Itä Kaivopuisto, noting the lights of the American embassy down the street. The sight of the building was appropriate; he had been thinking of Beowulf Agate off and on for most of the day.

It had taken him most of the day to absorb the news in Scofield's cable. The words themselves were innocuous, a salesman's report to an executive of a home office regarding Italian imports of Finnish crystal, but the new information was startling and complex. Scofield had made extraordinary progress in a very short time.

He had found the first connection; it *was* a Scozzi – the first name on the guest list of Guillaume de Matarese – and the man was dead, killed by those who controlled him. Therefore, the American's assumption in Corsica that the members of the Matarese council were not born but selected, proved accurate. The Matarese had been taken over, a mixture of descendants and usurpers, it was consistent with the dying words of Aleksie Krupsky in Moscow.

The Matarese was dormant for years. No one could make contact. Then it came back, but it was not the same. Killings . . . without clients, senseless butchery without a pattern . . . governments paralysed.

This was, indeed, a new Matarese and infinitely more deadly than a cult of fanatics dedicated to paid political assassination.

And Beowulf had added a warning to his cable. The Matarese now assumed that the guest list had been found; the stalking of the Voroshin family in Leningrad was infinitely more complicated than it might have been only days ago.

Men were waiting in Leningrad for someone to ask questions about the Voroshins. But not the men – or man – he would reach, thought Taleniekov, stamping his feet against the cold, looking for a sign of the automobile that was to meet him and drive him east along the coast past Hamina towards the Soviet border.

Scofield was on his way to Paris with the girl, the American to continue on to England after setting up procedures in Paris. The Corsican woman had passed whatever tests Beowulf Agate had created; she would live and be their conduit. But, as Vasili was beginning to learn, Scofield rarely operated on a simple line; there was a third party: the manager of the Tavastian Hotel in Helsinki.

Once in Leningrad, Taleniekov was to cable the manager with whatever particulars he could put into ciphers, and the man, in turn, would wait for direct telephone calls from Paris and relate the codes received from Leningrad. It was then up to the woman to reach Scofield in England. Vasili knew that monitoring cable traffic was a particular talent of the KGB; the only sure way to eliminate it was to use KGB equipment. Somehow, he would find a way to do that.

An automobile pulled up to the kerb, the headlights dimming once, the driver wearing a red muffler, one end draped over a dark leather jacket. Taleniekov crossed the pavement and got in the front seat beside the driver. He was on his way back to Russia.

The town of Vainikkala was on the north-west shore of the lake; across the water was the Soviet Union, the south-east banks patrolled by teams of soldiers and dogs plagued more often than not by *ennui* than by threats of penetration or escape. During the interminable winter months prolonged exposure to the freezing winds was simply too dangerous, and in summer the interminable flow of tourist visas in and out of Tallinn and Riga, to say nothing of Leningrad itself, made those cities the easiest routes. As a result the north-west garrisons along the Finnish border were staffed by the least motivated military personnel, often a collection of misfits and drunks commanded by men being punished for errors of judgement. Checkpoint Vainikkala was a logical place to cross into Russia; even the dogs were third-rate.

The Finns, however, were not; nor had they ever lost their hatred of the Soviet invaders who had lunged into their country in '39. As they had been masters of the lakes and the forests then, repulsing whole divisions with brilliantly executed traps, so they were masters forty years later at avoiding others. It was not until Taleniekov had been escorted across an inlet of ice and brought up beyond the patrols above the snow-clogged banks that he realized Checkpoint Vainikkala had become an escape route of considerable magnitude. It was no longer minor.

'If ever,' said the Finn who had taken him on his last leg of the journey, 'any of you men from Washington wants to get beyond these Bolshevik bastards, remember us. Because we do not forget.'

The irony was not lost on Vasili Vasilievich Taleniekov, former master strategist for the KGB. 'You should be careful with such offers,' he replied. 'How do you know I'm not a Soviet plant?'

The Finn smiled. 'We traced you to the Tavastian and made our own inquiries. You were sent by the best there is. He has used us in a dozen different Baltic operations. Give the quiet one our regards.' The man extended his hand. 'Arrangements have been made to drive you south through Vyborg into Zelenogorsk,' continued the escort.

'*What?*' Taleniekov had made no such request; he had made it clear that once inside the Soviet Union, he preferred to be on his own. 'I didn't ask you to do that. I didn't pay for it.'

The Finn smiled condescendingly. 'We thought it best; it will be quicker for you. Walk two kilometres down this road. You'll find a car parked by the snowbank. Ask the man inside for the time, saying your car has broken down – but speak Russian; they say you can do so passably well. If the man answers, then begins winding his watch, that's your ride.'

'I really don't think this is necessary,' objected Vasili. 'I expected to make my own arrangements – for both our sakes.'

'Whatever you might arrange, this is better; it will be daybreak soon and the roads are watched. You have nothing to worry about. The man you're meeting has been on Washington's payroll for a long time.' The Finn smiled again. 'He is second-in-command, KGB-Vyborg.'

Taleniekov returned the smile. Whatever annoyance he had felt evaporated. In one sentence his escort had provided the answers to several problems. If stealing from a thief was the safest form of larceny, a 'defector' compromising a traitor was even safer.

'You're a remarkable people,' he said to the Finn. 'I'm sure we'll do business again.'

'Why not? Geography keeps us occupied. We have scores to settle.'

Taleniekov had to ask. 'Still? After so many years?'

'It never ends. You are fortunate, my friend, you don't live with a wild, unpredictable bear in your backyard. Try it some time, it's depressing. Haven't you heard? We drink too much.'

Vasili saw the car in the distance, a black shadow among other shadows surrounded by the snow on the road. It was dawn; in an hour the sun would throw its yellow shafts across the arctic mists and the mists would disappear. As a child, he had been warmed by that sun.

He was home. It had been so many years, but there was no sense of return, no joy at the prospect of seeing familiar sights, perhaps a familiar face . . . grown so much older, as he had grown older.

There was no elation at all, only purpose. Too much had happened; he was cold and the winter sun would bring no warmth on this trip. There was only a family named Voroshin. He approached the car, staying as far to the right as possible, in the blind spot, his Graz-Burya in his gloved right hand. He stepped through the shoulder of snow, keeping his body low, until he was parallel with the front window. He raised his head and looked at the man inside.

The glow of a cigarette partially illuminated the vaguely familiar face. Taleniekov had seen it before, in a dossier photograph, or perhaps during a brief interview in Riga too insignificant to be remembered. He even remembered the man's name, and that name triggered his memory of the facts.

Maletkin. Pyotr Maletkin. From Grodno, just east of the Polish border. He was in his early fifties – the face confirmed that – considered a sound if uninspired professional, someone who did his work quietly, by rote-efficiency, but with little else. Through seniority he had risen in the KGB, but his lack of initiative had delegated him to a post in Vyborg.

The Americans had made a perceptive choice in his recruitment. Here was a man doomed to insignificance by his own insignificance, yet privy to ciphers and schedules because of accumulated rank. A second-in-command at Vyborg knew the end of a rather inglorious road had been reached. Resentments could be played upon; promises of a richer life were powerful inducements. He could always be shot crossing the ice on a final trip to Vainikkala. No one would miss him, a minor success for the Americans, a minor embarrassment to the KGB. But all that was changed now. Pyotr Maletkin was about to become a very important person. He himself would know it the instant Vasili walked up to the window, for if the traitor's face was vaguely familiar to Taleniekov, the 'defector's' would be completely known to Maletkin. Every KGB station in the world was after Vasili Vasilievich Taleniekov.

Sheltered by the bank of snow he crept back some twenty metres behind the automobile, then walked out on the road. Maletkin was either deep in thought or half asleep; he gave no indication that he saw anyone, no turn of the head, no crushing out of the cigarette. It was not until Vasili was within ten feet of the window that the traitor jerked his shoulders around, his face turned to the glass. Taleniekov angled his head away as if checking the road behind him as he walked; he did not want his face seen until the window was rolled down: it would interfere with what he had in mind. He stood directly by the door, his head hidden above the roof.

He heard the cranking of the handle, felt the brief swell of heat from inside the car. As he expected, the beam of a flashlight shot out from the seat; he bent over and showed his face, the Graz-Burya shoved through the open window.

'Good morning, Comrade Maletkin. It is Maletkin, isn't it?'

'My *God*! You!'

With his left hand, Taleniekov reached in and held the flashlight, turning it slowly away, no urgency in the act. 'Don't upset yourself,' he said. 'We have something in common now, haven't we? Why don't you give me the keys?'

'What . . . *what?*' Maletkin was paralysed; he could not speak.

'Let me have the keys, please,' continued Vasili. 'I'll

give them back to you as soon as I'm inside. You're nervous, comrade, and nervous people do nervous things. I don't want you driving away without me. The keys, please.'

The ominous barrel of the Graz-Burya was inches from Maletkin's face, his eyes shifting alternately, rapidly, between the gun and Taleniekov; he fumbled for the ignition switch and removed the keys. 'Here,' he whispered.

'Thank you, comrade. And we are comrades, you know that, don't you? There'd be no point in either of us trying to take advantage of the other's predicament. We'd both lose.'

Taleniekov walked around the front of the car, stepped through the snowbank, and climbed in the front seat beside the morose traitor.

'Come now, Colonel Maletkin – it is colonel by now, isn't it? – there's no reason for this hostility. I want to hear all the news.'

'I'm a temporary colonel; the rank has not been made permanent.'

'A shame. We never did appreciate you, did we? Well, we were certainly mistaken. Look what you've accomplished right under our noses. You must tell me how you did it. In Leningrad.'

'*Leningrad?*'

'An hour's ride from Zelenogorsk. It's not so much, and I'm sure Vyborg's second-in-command can come up with a reasonable explanation for the trip. I'll help you. I'm very good at that sort of thing.'

Maletkin swallowed, his eyes apprehensively on Vasili. 'I am to be back in Vyborg tomorrow morning. To hold a briefing with the patrols.'

'Delegate it, Colonel! Everyone loves to have responsibility delegated to them. It shows they're appreciated.'

'It was delegated to me,' said Maletkin.

'See what I mean? By the way, where are *your* bank

accounts? Norway? Sweden? New York? Certainly not in Finland; that would be foolish.'

'In the city of Atlanta. A bank owned by Arabs.'

'Good thinking.' Taleniekov handed him the keys. 'Shall we get started, comrade?'

'This is *crazy*,' said Maletkin. 'We are dead men.'

'Not for a while. We have business in Leningrad.'

It was noon when they drove over the Kirov Bridge, past the summer gardens wrapped in burlap, and south to the enormous boulevard that was the Nevsky Prospekt. Taleniekov fell silent as he looked out the window at the monuments of grandeur that were Leningrad. The blood of millions had been sacrificed to turn the freezing mud and marshland of the Neva River into Peter's window-on-Europe.

They reached the end of the Prospekt under the gleaming spire of the Admiralty Building and turned into the Quay. There along the banks of the river stood the Winter Palace; its effect on Vasili was the same as it had always been. It made him think about the Russia that once had been and ended here when the cruiser *Aurora* steamed up the Neva and fired its cannons into the seat of the false provisional government of Kerensky, signifying the emergence of the new Soviet. The True Russia.

There was no time for such reflections, nor was this the Leningrad he would roam for the next several days – although, ironically, it was *this* Leningrad, *that* Russia, that brought him here. Prince Andrei Voroshin had been part of both.

'Drive over the Anichkov Bridge and turn left,' he said. 'Head into the old housing development district. I'll tell you where to stop.'

'What's down there?' asked Maletkin, his apprehension growing with each block, each bridge they crossed, as they travelled into the heart of the city.

379

'I'm surprised you don't know; you should. A string of illegal boarding houses, and equally illegal cheap hotels that seem to have a collectively revisionist attitude regarding official papers.'

'In *Leningrad*?'

'You *don't* know, do you?' said Taleniekov. 'And no one ever told you. You *were* overlooked, comrade. When I was stationed in Riga, those of us who were area leaders frequently came up here and used the district for conferences we wished to keep secret, the ones that concerned our own people throughout the sector. It's where I first heard your name, I believe.'

'*Me? I* was brought up?'

'Don't worry, I threw them off and protected you. You and the other man in Vyborg.'

'*Vyborg?*' Maletkin lost his grip on the wheel; the car swerved, narrowly avoiding an oncoming truck.

'Control yourself!' Vasili shouted. 'An accident would send us both to the black rooms of *Lubyanka!*'

'But Vyborg!' repeated the astonished traitor. 'KGB-Vyborg? Do you know what you're *saying*?'

'Precisely,' repeated Taleniekov. 'Two informers from the same source, neither aware of the other. It's the most accurate way to verify information. But if one does learn about the other . . . well, he has the best of both worlds, wouldn't you say? In your case, the advantages would be incalculable.'

'Who *is* he!?'

'Later, my friend, later. You co-operate fully with everything I ask and you'll have his name when I leave.'

'Agreed,' said Maletkin, his composure returning.

Taleniekov leaned back in the seat as they progressed down the traffic-laden Sadovaya into the crowded streets of the old housing district, the *dom-vashen*. The patina of clean pavements and sand-blasted buildings concealed the mounting tensions rampant within the area. Two and three families living in a single flat, four and five people sleeping in a room; it would all explode one day.

Vasili glanced at the traitor beside him; he despised the man. Maletkin thought he was going to be given an advantage undreamed-of only minutes before: the name of a high-ranking KGB intelligence officer from his own station, a traitor like himself, who could be manipulated unmercifully. He would do almost anything to get that name. It would be given to him – in three words, no other identification necessary. And, of course, it would be false. Pyotr Maletkin would not be shot by the Americans crossing the ice to Vainikkala, but instead in a barracks courtyard in Vyborg. So much for the politics of the insignificant man, thought Vasili, as he recognized the building he was looking for down the street.

'Stop at the next corner, comrade,' he said. 'Wait for me. If the person I want to see isn't there, I'll be right back. If he's home, I'll be an hour or so.' Maletkin pulled to the right behind a cluster of bicycles chained to a post on the kerb. 'Do remember,' Taleniekov continued, 'that you have two alternatives. You can race away to KGB headquarters – it's on the Ligovsky Prospekt, incidentally – and turn me in; that will lead to a chain of revelations which will result in your execution. Or you can wait for me, do as I ask you to do, and you will have bought yourself the identity of someone who can bring you present and future rewards. You'll have your hook in a very important man.'

'Then I don't really have a choice, do I?' said Maletkin. 'I'll be here.' The traitor grinned; he perspired on his chin and his teeth were yellow.

Taleniekov approached the stone steps of the building; it was a three-storey structure with twenty to thirty flats, many crowded, but not hers. Lodzia Kronescha had her own apartment; that decision had been made by the KGB five years ago.

With the exception of a brief weekend conference

fourteen months ago in Moscow, he had not seen her since Riga. During the conference they had spent one night together – the first night – but had decided not to meet subsequently, for professional reasons. The 'brilliant Taleniekov' had been showing signs of strain, his oddly intemperate behaviour annoying too many people – and too many people had been talking about it, whispering about it. Him. It was best they sever all associations outside the conference rooms. For in spite of total clearance, she was still being watched. He was not the sort of man she should be seen with; he had told her that, insisted upon it.

Five years ago Lodzia Kronescha had been in trouble; some said it was serious enough to remove her from her post in Leningrad. Others disagreed, claiming her lapses of judgement were due to a temporary siege of depression brought on by family problems. Besides, she was extremely effective in her work; whom would they get to replace her during those times of crisis? Lodzia was a highly qualified mathematician, a doctoral graduate from Moscow University, and trained in the Lenin Institute. She was among the most knowledgeable computer programmers in the field.

So she was kept on and given the proper warnings regarding her responsibility to the state – which had made her education possible. She was relegated to night operations, Computer Division, KGB-Leningrad, Ligovsky Prospekt. That was five years ago; she would remain there for at least another two.

Lodzia's 'crimes' might have been dismissed as professional errors – a series of minor mathematical variations – had it not been for a disturbing occurrence thirteen hundred miles away in Vienna. Her brother had been a senior air defence officer and he had committed suicide, the reasons for the act unexplained. Nevertheless, the air defence plans for the entire south-west German border had been altered. And Lodzia Kronescha had been called in for questioning.

Taleniekov had been present, intrigued by the quiet, academic woman brought in under the KGB lamps. He had been fascinated by her slow, thoughtful responses that were as convincing as they were lacking in panic. She had readily admitted that she adored her brother and was distressed to the point of a breakdown over his death and the manner of it. No, she had known of nothing irregular about his life; yes, he had been a devoted member of the party; no, she had not kept his correspondence – it had never occurred to her to do so.

Taleniekov had kept silent, knowing what he knew by instinct and a thousand encounters with concealed truth. She had been lying. From the beginning. But her lies were not rooted in treason, or even for her own survival. It was something else. When the daily KGB surveillance was called off, he had flown frequently to Leningrad from near-by Riga to institute his own.

Vasili's trailing of Lodzia had revealed what he then knew he would find. Extremely artful contacts in the parks of the Petrodvorets with an American agent out of Helsinki. The meetings were not sought, they had been forced upon her.

He had followed her to her flat one evening and had confronted her with his evidence. Instinct had told him to hold back official action. There was far less than treason in her activities.

'What I have done is *insignificant*!' she had cried, tears of exhaustion filling her eyes. 'It is *nothing* compared to what they want! But if they have proof of my doing *something*, they will not do what they threaten to do!'

The Americans had shown her photographs, dozens of them, mostly of her brother, but also of other high-ranking Soviet officials in the Vienna sectors. They depicted the grossest obscenities, extremes of sexual behaviour – male with female, and male with male – all taken while the subjects were drunk, all showing a Vienna of excessive debauchery in which responsible Soviet figures were willingly corrupted by any who cared to corrupt them.

The threat was simple: these photographs would be spread across the world. Her brother – as well as those superior to him in rank and stature – would be held up to universal ridicule. As would the Soviet Union.

'What did you hope to gain by doing what you did?' he had asked.

'Wear them out!' she had replied. 'They will keep me on a string, never knowing what I will do, can do . . . have *done*. Every now and then they get word of computer errors. They are minor, but it is enough. They will not carry out their threats.'

'There is a better way,' he had suggested. 'I think you should leave it to me. There's a man in Washington who spent his fire in South-east Asia, a general named Blackburn. Mad Anthony Blackburn.'

Vasili had returned to Riga and sent out word through his network in London. Washington got the information within hours: whatever exploitation American intelligence cared to make out of Vienna would be matched by equally devastating exposure – and photographs – of one of the most respected men in the American military establishment.

No one from Helsinki ever bothered Lodzia Kronescha again. And she and Taleniekov had become lovers.

As Vasili climbed the dark staircase to the second floor, memories came back to him. Theirs had been an affair of mutual need, without any feverish emotional attachment. They had been two insular people, dedicated to their professions almost to the exclusion of everything else; they had both required the release of mind and body. Neither had demanded more than that release from the other, and when he had been transferred to Sevastopol, their goodbyes were the painless parting of good friends who liked each other a great deal but who felt no dependence, grateful in fact for its absence. He wondered what she would say when she saw him, what she would feel . . . what he would feel.

He looked at his watch: ten minutes to one. If her schedule had not been altered, she would have been relieved from duty at eight in the morning, arrived home by nine, read the papers for a half hour and fallen asleep. Then a thought struck him. Suppose she had a lover, as he had been her lover? If so, he would not put her in danger; he would leave quickly before any identification was made. But he hoped it was not the case; he needed Lodzia. The man he had to reach in Leningrad could not be approached directly; she could help him – if she would.

He knocked on her door. Within seconds he heard the footsteps beyond, the sharp cracks of leather heels against hard wood. Oddly, she had not been in bed. The door opened half-way and Lodzia Kronescha stood there fully clothed – strangely clothed – in a bright-coloured cotton dress, a *summer* dress, her light brown hair falling over her shoulders, her sharp, aquiline face set in a rigid expression, her hazel-green eyes staring at him – *staring* at him – as if his sudden appearance after so long were not so much unexpected as an intrusion.

'How nice of you to drop by, old friend,' she said without a trace of an inflection.

She was telling him something. There was someone inside with her. Someone waiting for him.

'It's good to see you again, old friend,' said Taleniekov, nodding in acknowledgement, studying the crack between the door. He could see the cloth of a jacket, the brown fabric of a pair of trousers. There was only one man, she was telling him that, too. He pulled out his Graz-Burya, holding up his left hand, three fingers extended, gesturing to his left. On the third nod of his head, she was to dive to her right; her eyes told him she understood. 'It's been many months,' he continued casually. 'I was in the district, so I thought I would . . .'

He gave the third nod; she lunged to her right. Vasili crushed his shoulder into the door – into the left panel so the arc would be clean, the impact total – then battered it again, crushing the figure behind it into the wall.

He plunged inside, pivoting to the right, his shoulder smashing the door again. He ripped a gun out of the man's hand, peeling the body away from the wall, hammering his knee into the exposed neck, propelling his would-be assailant off his feet into a near-by armchair where he collapsed on the floor.

'You *understood*,' cried Lodzia, crowding against the wall. 'I was so worried that you wouldn't!'

Taleniekov shut the door. 'It's not yet one o'clock,' he said, reaching for her hand. 'I thought you'd be asleep.'

'I was hoping you'd realize that.'

'Also it's freezing outside, hardly the season for a summer dress.'

'I knew you'd notice that. Most men don't, but you would.'

He held her shoulders, speaking rapidly. 'I've brought you terrible trouble. I'm sorry. I'll leave immediately. Tear your clothes, say you tried to stop me. I'll break into a flat upstairs and . . .'

'Vasili, *listen* to me! That man's not one of us. He's not KGB.'

Taleniekov turned towards the man on the floor. He was regaining consciousness slowly, trying to rise and orient himself at the same time. 'Are you sure?'

'Very. To begin with he's an Englishman, his Russian shouts with it. When he mentioned your name I pretended to be shocked, angry that our people would think me capable of harbouring a fugitive . . . I said I wanted to telephone my superior. He refused to let me. He said,

"We have all we want from you." Those were his exact words.'

Vasili looked at her. 'Would you have called your superior?'

'I'm not sure,' replied Lodzia, her hazel-green eyes steady on his. 'I suppose it would have depended on what he said. It's very difficult for me to believe you're what they say you are.'

'I'm not. On the other hand, you must protect yourself.'

'I was hoping it wouldn't come to that.'

'Thank you . . . old friend.' Taleniekov turned back to the man on the floor and started towards him.

He saw it. He was too late!

Vasili lunged, diving at the figure by the chair, his hands ripping at the man's mouth, pulling it apart, his knee hammering the stomach, jamming it up into the rib cage, trying to induce vomit.

The acrid odour of almonds. Potassium cyanide. A massive dose. Oblivion in seconds, death in minutes.

The cold blue English eyes beneath him were wide and clear with satisfaction. The Matarese had escaped.

23

'We have to go over it *again*,' insisted Taleniekov, looking up from the naked corpse. They had stripped the body; Lodzia was sitting in a chair checking the articles of clothing meticulously for the second time. 'Everything he said.'

'I've left out nothing. He wasn't that talkative.'

'You're a mathematician; we must fill in the missing numbers. The sums are clear.'

'Sums?'

'Yes, sums,' repeated Vasili, turning the corpse over. 'He wanted me, but was willing to kill himself if the trap failed. That warrants two conclusions: first, he could not risk being taken alive because of what he knew. And second, he expected no assistance. If I thought otherwise, you and I would not be here now.'

'But why did he think you would come here to begin with?'

'Not would,' corrected Taleniekov. '*Might*. I'm sure it's in a file somewhere in Moscow that you and I saw a lot of each other. And the men who want me have access to those files, I know that. But they'll cover only the people here in Leningrad they think I *might* contact. They won't bother with the sector leaders or the Ligovsky staff. If any of them got wind of me they'd send out alarms heard in Siberia; those who want me would step in then. No, they'll only concern themselves with people they can't trust to turn me in. You're one of them.'

'Are there others? Here in Leningrad?'

'Three or four, perhaps. A Jew at the university, a good friend I'd drink and argue with all night; he'll be watched.

Another at the *Zhdanov*, a political theorist who teaches Marx but is more at home with Adam Smith. One or two others, I suppose. I never really worried about whom I was seen with.'

'You didn't have to.'

'I know. My post had its advantages; there were a dozen explanations for any single thing that I did, any person I saw.' He paused. 'How extensive *is* their coverage?'

'I don't understand.'

'There's one man I do want to reach. They'd have to go back a great many years to find him, but they may have.' Vasili paused again, his finger on the base of the spine of the naked body beneath him. He looked up at the strong yet curiously gentle face of the woman he had known so well. 'What were the words again? "We have all we want from you."'

'Yes. At which point he grabbed the telephone away from my hand.'

'He was convinced you were going to call Leningrad?'

'I was convincing. Had he told me to go ahead, I might have changed tactics, I don't know. Remember, I knew he was English. I didn't think he would let me call. But he did not deny being KGB.'

'And later, when you put on the dress. He didn't object?'

'On the contrary. It convinced him you were actually coming here, that I was co-operating.'

'What were his words, then? The precise words. You said he smiled and said something about women-being-all-alike; you don't recall what else.'

'It was trivial.'

'Nothing is. Try to remember. Something about "whiling away the hours", that's what you mentioned.'

'Yes. The language was ours but the phrase was very English, I remember that. He said he'd "while away the hours pleasantly" . . . more so than others. That there were . . . "no such sights on the Quay". I told you, he insisted I change clothes in front of him.'

'The "Quay". The Hermitage. Malachite Hall. There's a woman there,' said Taleniekov, frowning. 'They were thorough. One more missing number.'

'My lover was unfaithful?'

'Frequently, but not with her. She was an unreconstructed Czarist put in charge of the architectural tours and perfectly delightful. She's also closer to seventy than sixty, although neither seems so far away to me now. I took her to tea quite often.'

'That's touching.'

'I enjoyed her company. She was a fine instructor in things I knew little about. Why would anyone have put her on a list in a file?'

'Speaking for Leningrad,' said Lodzia, amused, 'if we saw our competition from Riga meeting with such a person, we'd insert it.'

'It's probably as stupid as that. What else did he say?'

'Nothing memorable. While I was in my underthings, he made a foolish remark to the effect that mathematicians had the advantage over academics and librarians. We studied figures . . .'

Taleniekov got to his feet. 'That's it!' he said. 'The missing number. They've found him.'

'What are you talking about?'

'Our Englishman either couldn't resist the bad pun, or he was probing. The Quay – the Hermitage Museum. The academics – my drinking companions at the *Zhdanov*. The reference to a librarian – the Saltykov-Shchedrin Library. The man I want to reach is there.'

'Who is he?'

Vasili hesitated. 'An old man who years ago befriended a young university student and opened his eyes to things he knew nothing about.'

'Who was he? Who is he?'

Taleniekov approached her, minor excitement returning with his memories. 'I was a very confused young man,' he said. 'How was it possible for over three-quarters of the world to reject the teachings of the revolution? I could not accept the fact that so many millions were unenlightened. But that's what the textbooks said, what our professors told us. But *why*? I had to understand how our enemies thought the way they did.'

'And this man was able to tell you?'

'He *showed* me. He let me find out for myself. I was sufficiently fluent in English and French then, reasonably so in Spanish. He opened the doors, literally *opened* the steel doors, of the forbidden books – thousands of volumes Moscow disapproved of – and left me free with them. I spent weeks, months poring over them, trying to understand. It was there that the . . . "great Taleniekov" . . . learned the most valuable lesson of all: how to see things as the enemy sees them, how to be able to *think* like him. That is the keystone of every success I've ever had. My old friend made it possible.'

'And you must reach him now?'

'Yes. He's lived all his life here in Leningrad. When he was born it was St Petersburg; when a young man, Petrograd. He's seen it all happen and he's survived. If anyone can help me, he can.'

'What are you looking for? I think I have a right to know.'

'Of course you do, but it's a name you must forget. At least, never mention it. I need information about a family named Voroshin.'

'A family? From Leningrad?'

'Yes.'

Lodzia shook her head in exasperation. 'Sometimes I think the great Taleniekov is a great fool! I can run the name through our computers!'

'The minute you did, you'd be marked – for all purposes,

dead. That man on the floor has accomplices everywhere.'
He turned and walked back to the body, kneeling down
to continue his examination of the corpse. 'Besides, you'd
find nothing; it's too many years ago, too many changes
of regimes and emphases. If any entry, or entries, had
ever been made, I doubt they'd be there now. The
irony is that if there was something in the data banks,
it would probably mean the Voroshin family is no longer
involved.'

'Involved with *what*, Vasili?'

He did not answer immediately, for he had turned the
nude body over and saw it. A small discoloration of the
skin on the lower mid-section of the chest, around the area
of the heart, barely seen through the matted hair. It was
tiny, no more than half an inch in diameter – and it *was* a
diameter, for the bluish-purple mark was a circle. At first
glance it appeared to be a birthmark, a perfectly natural
phenomenon, in no way superimposed on the flesh. But it
was not natural; it was placed there by a very experienced
needle. Old Krupsky had said the words as he lay dying:
*A man was caught, a blemish on his chest, a soldier of the
Matarese*.

'With this.' Taleniekov separated the black hair on the
dead man's chest so the jagged circle could be seen clearly.
'Come here.'

Lodzia got up, walked to the corpse, and knelt down.
'What? The birthmark?'

'*Perro nostro circulo*,' he said quietly. 'It wasn't there
when our Englishman was born. It had to be earned.'

'I don't understand.'

'You will. I'm going to tell you everything I know. I
wasn't sure that I wanted to, but I don't think there's a
choice now. They might easily kill me. If they do, there's
someone you must reach. I'll tell you how. Describe this
mark, fourth rib, border of the cage, near the heart. It was
not meant to be found.'

Lodzia was silent as she looked at the bluish mark on the flesh, and finally at Taleniekov. 'Who is "they"?'

'They go by the name of the Matarese . . .'

He told her. Everything. When he was finished, Lodzia did not speak for a long time, nor did he intrude on her thoughts. For she had heard shocking things, not the least of which was the incredible alliance between Vasili Vasilievich Taleniekov and a man known throughout the KGB world as Beowulf Agate. She sat up and walked to the window overlooking the dreary street in Leningrad's *dom-vashen*. She spoke, her face to the glass.

'I imagine you've asked this question of yourself a thousand times; I ask it again. Was it necessary to contact Scofield?'

'Yes,' he said simply.

'Moscow *wouldn't* listen to you?'

'Moscow ordered my execution. Washington ordered his.'

'Yes, but you say that neither Moscow nor Washington knows about this Matarese. The trap set for you and Beowulf was based on keeping you apart. I can understand that.'

'*Official* Washington and *official* Moscow are blind to the Matarese. Otherwise, someone would have stepped forward on our behalf; we would have been summoned to present what we know – what I brought Scofield. Instead, we're branded traitors, ordered to be shot on sight, no provisions made to give us a hearing. The Matarese orchestrated it using the clandestine apparatuses of both countries.'

'Then this Matarese *is* in Moscow, in Washington?'

'Absolutely. In, but not of. Capable of manipulating, but unseen.'

'Not unseen, Vasili,' objected Lodzia. 'The men you spoke to in Moscow . . .'

'Panicked *old* men,' interrupted Taleniekov. 'Dying war

393

horses put out to pasture, frightened by actions taken, contracts made, decades ago. Impotent.'

'Then the man Scofield approached. The statesman, Winthrop. What of him?'

'Undoubtedly dead by now.'

Lodzia walked away from the window and stood in front of him. 'Then where do you go? You're cornered, stopped.'

Vasili shook his head. 'On the contrary, we're making progress. The first name on the list, Scozzi, was accurate. Now, we have our dead Englishman here. No papers, no proof of who he is or where he came from, but with a mark more telling than a wallet filled with false documents. He was part of their army, which means there's another soldier here in Leningrad watching an old man who's curator of literary archives at the Saltykov-Shchedrin Library. I want him almost as much as I want to reach my old friend; I want to break him, get answers. The Matarese are in Leningrad to protect the Voroshins, to conceal the truth. We're getting closer to that truth.'

'But suppose you *find* it. Whom can you take it to? You cannot protect yourselves because you don't know who they are.'

'We know who they are not, and that's enough. The Premier and the President to begin with.'

'You won't get near them.'

'We will if we have our proof. Beowulf was right about that; we need incontrovertible proof. Will you help us? Help *me*?'

Lodzia Kronescha looked into his eyes, her own softening. She reached up with both her hands and cupped his face. 'Vasili Vasilievich. My life had become so uncomplicated, and now you return.'

'I didn't know where else to go. I couldn't approach that old man directly. I testified on his behalf at a security hearing in nineteen fifty-four. I'm terribly sorry, Lodzia.'

'Don't be. I've missed you. And, of course, I'll help you. Were it not for you, I might be teaching primary classes in our Tashkent sectors.'

He touched her face, returning her gesture, staring into her hazel-green eyes. 'That must not be the reason for your help.'

'It isn't. What you've told me frightens me.'

Under no condition was the traitor Maletkin to be aware of Lodzia. The Vyborg officer had remained in the automobile at the corner, but when more than an hour had passed Taleniekov could see him pacing nervously on the pavement below.

'He's not sure whether it's this building or the one next door,' said Vasili, stepping back from the window. 'The cellars still connect, don't they?'

'They did when I was last there.'

'I'll go down and come out on the street several doors away. I'll meet him and tell him the man I'm with wants another half hour. That should give us enough time. Finish dressing the Englishman, will you?'

Lodzia was right, nothing had changed in the old buildings. All had merely grown older and dirtier and in greater disrepair. Each cellar connected with the one next door, the filthy, damp underground alleyway extending along most of the block. Taleniekov emerged on the street four buildings away from Lodzia's flat. He walked up to the unsuspecting Maletkin, startling him.

'I thought you went in there!' said the traitor from Vyborg, nodding his head at the staircase on his left.

'There?'

'Yes, I was sure of it.'

'You're still too excited, comrade, it interferes with your observation. I don't know anyone in that building. I came down to tell you that the man I'm meeting with needs more time. I suggest you wait in the car; it's not only extremely cold, but you'll draw less attention to yourself.'

'You won't be any longer than that, will you?' asked Maletkin anxiously.

'Are you going somewhere? Without me?'

'No, no, of course not. I have to go to the toilet.'

'Discipline your bladder,' said Taleniekov, hurrying away.

Twenty minutes later he and Lodzia had worked out the details of his contact with the curator of archives at the Saltykov-Shchedrin Library on the Maiorov Prospekt. She would telephone the scholar at his office, speaking the truth without naming names. It was vital that a growing sense of fear be engendered – for everyone's sake. A student from many years ago, an exceptional student of languages and books as well as a friend – a man who had risen high in government office and who had testified for the old gentleman in 1954 – wanted to meet with him privately. That student, this friend, could not be seen in public; he was in trouble and needed help.

There was to be no doubt as to the identity of that student, nor of the danger in which he found himself. The old man had to be jolted, frightened, concern for a once-dear young friend brought to the surface. He had to communicate his alarms to any who might be watching him closely – the arrangements for the meeting just complicated enough to confuse an old man's mind. For in the scholar's confusion and fear would be found tentative movements, bewildered starts and stops, first in one direction, then in another, sudden turns and abrupt reversals, decisions made and instantly rejected. In these circumstances, whoever followed the old man would be revealed; for whatever moves the scholar made, the one following would have to make. They would not be natural.

Lodzia would instruct the old man to leave the enormous library complex by the south-west exit at ten minutes to six that evening; the streets would be dark and no snow was expected. He would be told to walk a number of blocks one way, then another. If no contact was made, he was to return to the library, and wait; if it were at all possible, his friend from long ago would try to get there. However, there were no guarantees.

Placed in this situation of stress, the numbers alone would serve to confuse the scholar, for Lodzia was to abruptly terminate the telephone call without repeating them. Vasili would take care of the rest, a traitor named Maletkin serving as an unknowing accomplice.

'What will you do after you see the old man?' asked Lodzia.

'That depends on what he tells me, or what I can learn from the man who follows him.'

'Where will you stay? Will I see you?'

Vasili stood up. 'It could be dangerous for you if I come back here.'

'I'm willing to risk that.'

'I'm not willing to let you. Besides, you work until morning.'

'I can go in early and get off at midnight. Things are much more relaxed than when you were last in Leningrad. We trade hours frequently, and I am completely rehabilitated.'

'Someone will ask you why.'

'I'll tell them the truth. An old friend has arrived from Moscow.'

'I don't think that's such a good idea.'

'A party secretary from the Praesidium with a wife and several children. He wishes to remain anonymous.'

'As I said, a splendid idea.' Taleniekov smiled. 'I'll be careful and go through the cellars.'

'What will you do with him?' Lodzia nodded at the dead Englishman.

'Leave him in the farthest cellar I can find. Do you have a bottle of vodka?'

397

'Are you thirsty?'

'He is. One more unknown suicide in paradise. We don't publicize them. I'll need a razor blade.'

Pyotr Maletkin stood next to Vasili in the shadows of an archway across from the south-west entrance to the Saltykov-Shchedrin Library. The floodlights in the rear courtyard of the complex shone down in wide circles from the high walls, giving the illusion of an enormous prison compound. But the arches that led to the street beyond were placed symmetrically every hundred feet in the wall; the prisoners could come and go at will. It was a busy evening at the library; streams of prisoners came and went.

'You say this old man is one of us?' asked Maletkin.

'Get your pronouns straight, comrade. The old fellow's KGB, the man following him – about to make contact – is one of *us*. We've got to reach him before he's trapped. The scholar is one of the most effective weapons Moscow's developed for counter-intelligence. His name is known to no more than five people in KGB; to be aware of him marks a person as an American informer. For God's sake, don't ever mention him.'

'I've never heard of him,' interrupted Maletkin. 'But the Americans think he's *theirs*?'

'Yes. He's a plant. He reports everything directly to Moscow on a private line.'

'Incredible,' muttered the traitor. 'An old man. Ingenious.'

'My former associates are not fools,' said Taleniekov, checking his watch. 'Neither are your present ones. Forget you've ever heard of Comrade Mikovsky.'

'That's his name?'

'Even I would rather not repeat it . . . There he is.'

An old man bundled up in an overcoat and a black fur hat walked out of the entrance, vapour from his breath

398

meeting the cold air. He stood for a moment on the steps, looking around as if trying to decide which archway to take into the street. His short beard was white, what could be seen of his face was filled with wrinkles and tired, pale flesh. He started down the marble stairs cautiously, holding on to the railing. He reached the concrete courtyard and walked towards the nearest arch on his right.

Taleniekov studied the stream of people that came out through the glass doors after the old curator. They seemed to be in groups of twos and threes; he looked for a single man whose eyes strayed to the courtyard below. None did and Vasili was disturbed. Had he been wrong? It did not seem likely, yet there was no single man Taleniekov could pick out of the crowds whose focus was on Mikovsky, now half-way across the courtyard. When the scholar reached the street, there was no point in waiting any longer; he *had* been wrong. The Matarese had not found his friend.

A woman. He was *not* wrong. It was a *woman*. A lone woman broke away from the crowd and hurried down the steps, her eyes on the old man. How plausible, thought Vasili. A single woman remaining for hours alone in a library would draw far less attention than a man. Among its élite soldiers, the Matarese trained women.

He was not sure why it surprised him – some of the best agents in the Soviet KGB and the American Consular Operations were women, but their duties rarely included violence. *That's* what startled him now. The woman following old Mikovsky was trailing the curator only to find *him*. Violence was intrinsic to that assignment.

'That woman,' he said to Maletkin. 'The one in the brown overcoat and the visored cap. She's the informer. We've got to stop her from making contact.'

'A *woman*?'

'She is capable of a variety of things which you are not, comrade. Come along now, we must be careful. She won't approach him right away; she'll wait for the most

399

opportune moment and so must we. We've got to separate her, take her when she's far enough away from him so he can't identify her if there's any noise.'

'Noise?' interrupted the perplexed Maletkin. 'Why would she make any noise?'

'Women are unpredictable, it's common knowledge. Let's go.'

The next eighteen minutes were as disorganized and as painful to watch as Taleniekov had anticipated. Painful in that a concerned old man grew progressively bewildered as the moments passed, his agitation turning into panic when there was no sign of his young friend. He crossed the bitterly cold streets, automobiles and omnibuses blowing their horns as his walk was too slow, his legs unsteady. He kept checking his watch, the light too dim for his eyes; he was jostled by rushing pedestrians whenever he stopped. And he stopped incessantly, breath and strength diminishing. Twice he started for an omnibus shelter in the block beyond where he stood, momentarily convinced that he had made the wrong count of the streets; at the intersection where the Kirov Theatre stood, there were three shelters and his confusion mounted. He visited all three, more and more bewildered.

The strategy had the expected effect on the woman following Mikovsky. She interpreted the old man's actions as those of a subject aware that he might be under surveillance, a subject unschooled in methods of evasion but also old and frightened and capable of creating an uncontrollable situation. So the woman in the brown overcoat and visored cap kept her distance, staying in shadows, going from darkened shopfronts to dimly-lit alleyways, propelled into agitation herself by the unpredictability of her subject.

The old scholar started on his return pattern to the library. Vasili and Maletkin watched from a vantage point seventy-five metres away. Taleniekov studied the route directly across the wide avenue; there were two alleyways, both of which would be used by the woman as Mikovsky passed her on the way back.

'Come along,' ordered Vasili, grabbing Maletkin's arm, pushing him forward. 'We'll get behind him in the crowd on the other side. She'll turn away as he goes by, and when he passes that second alleyway, she'll use it.'

'Why are you so sure?'

'Because she used it before; it's the natural thing to do. I'd use it. *We* will use it now.'

'How?'

'I'll tell you when we're in position.'

The moment was drawing near and Taleniekov could feel the drumlike beat in his chest. He had orchestrated the events of the past sixteen minutes, the next few would determine whether the orchestration had merit. He knew two indisputable facts: one, the woman would recognize him instantly; she would have been provided with photographs and a detailed physical description. Two, should the violence go against her, she would take her own life as quickly and as efficiently as the Englishman had done in Lodzia's flat.

Timing and shock were the only tools at his immediate disposal. He would provide the first, the traitor from Vyborg the second.

They crossed the square with a group of pedestrians and walked into the crowds in front of the Kirov Theatre.

Vasili glanced over his shoulder and saw Mikovsky weave his way awkwardly through the line forming for tickets, breathing with difficulty.

'Listen to me and do exactly as I say,' said Taleniekov, holding Maletkin's arm. 'Repeat the words I say to you . . .'

They entered the flow of pedestrians walking up the pavement, remaining behind a quartet of soldiers, their bulky overcoats serving as a wall.

Vasili could see beyond at will. The scholar up ahead approached the first alleyway; the woman briefly disappeared into it, then re-emerged as he passed.

Moments now. Only moments.

The second alleyway. Mikovsky was in front of it, the woman within.

'*Now!*' he ordered, rushing with Maletkin towards the entrance.

He heard the words Maletkin shouted so they would be unmistakable above the noise of the streets.

'Comrade, wait. Stop! *Circulo! Nostro circulo!*'

Silence. The shock was almost total.

'Who *are* you?' The question was asked in a cold, tense female voice.

'Stop everything! I have news from the shepherd!'

'What?'

The shock was now complete.

Taleniekov spun around the corner of the alley, rushing towards the woman, his hands two springs uncoiling as he lunged.

He grabbed her arms, his fingers sliding instantly down to her wrists, immobilizing her hands, one of which was in her overcoat pocket, gripped around a gun. She recoiled, spinning to her left, her weight dead, pulling him forward, then sprang to her right, her left foot lashing up into him, close to her body like an enraged cat's claw repelling another animal.

He countered, attacking directly, lifting her off her feet, crashing her twisting, writhing body into the alleyway wall, pummelling her with his shoulder, crushing her into the brick.

It happened so fast he was only vaguely aware of what she was doing until he felt her teeth sinking into the flesh of his neck. She had thrust her face into his – a move so unexpected he could only twist away in pain. Her mouth was wide, her red lips parted grotesquely.

The bite was vicious, her jaws two clamps vicing into the side of his neck. He could feel blood drenching his collar; she *would not let go!* The pain was excruciating; the harder he battered her into the wall, the deeper her teeth went into his flesh. He *could not stand it*. He released her arms, his hands clawing at her face, pulling her from him.

The explosion was loud, distinct, yet muffled by the heavy cloth of her overcoat, the echo carried on the wind throughout the alley; she fell away from him, limp against the stone.

He looked at her face; her eyes were wide and dead; she sank slowly to the pavement. She had done precisely what she had been programmed to do: she had appraised the odds – two men against herself – and fired the weapon in her pocket, blowing away her chest.

'She's *dead!* My God, she *killed* herself!' screamed Maletkin. 'The *shot*, people will have heard it! We've got to run! The police!'

Several curious passersby stood motionless at the alley's entrance, peering in.

'Be quiet!' commanded Taleniekov. 'If anyone comes in use your KGB card. This is official business, no one's permitted here. I want thirty seconds.'

Vasili pulled a handkerchief from his pocket and pressed it against his neck, reducing the flow of blood. He knelt over the body of the dead woman. With his right hand he ripped the coat away, exposing a blouse stained everywhere with red. He tore the drenched fabric away from the skin; the hole below her left breast was massive, tissue and intestines clogging the opening. He probed the flesh around the wound; the light was too dim. He took out his cigarette lighter.

He snapped it, stretching the bloody skin beneath the breast, holding the light inches above it; the flame danced in the wind.

'For God's sake, *hurry*!' Maletkin stood several feet away, his voice a panicked whisper. 'What are you doing?'

Taleniekov did not reply. Instead, he moved his fingers around the flesh, wiping away the blood to see more clearly.

He found it. In the crease beneath the left breast, angled towards the centre of the chest. A jagged circle of blue surrounded by white skin streaked with red. A blemish that was no blemish at all, but the mark of an incredible army.

The Matarese circle.

24

They walked rapidly out of the far end of the alley, melting into the crowds heading north. Maletkin was trembling, his face ashen. Vasili's right hand gripped the traitor's elbow, controlling the panic that might easily cause Maletkin to burst into a run, riveting attention on both of them. Taleniekov needed the man from Vyborg; a cable had to be sent that eluded KGB interception and Maletkin could send it. He realized that he had very little time to work out the cipher for Scofield. It would take old Mikovsky another ten minutes before he reached his office, but soon after that Vasili knew he should be there. A frightened old man could say the wrong things too.

Taleniekov held the handkerchief against the wound on his neck. The bleeding had ebbed to a trickle in the cold, it would stop sufficiently for a bandage soon; it occurred to Vasili that he should purchase a high-necked sweater to conceal it.

'Slow down!' he ordered, yanking Maletkin's elbow. 'There's a café up ahead. We'll go inside for a few minutes, get a drink.'

'I could *use* one,' whispered Maletkin, his eyes glazed. 'My God, she *killed* herself! Who *was* she?'

'Someone who made a mistake. Don't you make another.'

The café was crowded; they shared a table with two middle-aged women, who objected to the intrusion and morosely kept to themselves; it was a splendid arrangement.

'Go up to the manager by the door,' said Taleniekov. 'Tell him your friend had too much to drink and cut himself. Ask for a bandage and some adhesive.' Maletkin started to object; Vasili reached for his forearm. 'Just do it. It's nothing unusual in a place like this.'

The traitor got up and made his way to the man at the door. Taleniekov refolded the handkerchief, pressing the cleaner side against the torn skin, and dug into his pocket for a pencil. He moved the coarse paper napkin in front of him and began selecting the cipher for Beowulf Agate.

His mind closed out all noise, and he concentrated on an alphabet and progression of numbers. Even as Maletkin returned with a cotton bandage and a small roll of tape, Vasili wrote, crossing out errors as rapidly as he made them. Their drinks arrived; the traitor had ordered three apiece. Taleniekov kept writing.

Eight minutes later he was finished. He tore the napkin in two and copied the wording clearly in large unmistakable letters. He handed it to Maletkin. 'I want this cable sent to Helsinki, to the name and hotel listed on top. I want it routed on a white line, commercial traffic, not subject to duplicate interception.'

The traitor's eyes grew wide. 'How do you expect *me* to do that?'

'The same way you get information to our friends in Washington. You know the unmonitored schedules; we all protect ourselves from ourselves. It's one of our more finely-honed talents.'

'That's through Stockholm. We by-pass Helsinki!' Maletkin flushed; his state of agitation and the rapid infusion of alcohol had made him careless. He had not meant to reveal the Swedish connection. It wasn't done, even among fellow defectors.

Nor could Vasili use Stockholm. The cable would then be under American scrutiny, the manager of the Tavastian Hotel in Helsinki undoubtedly questioned by CIA personnel. There was another way.

'How often do you come down here to the Ligovsky headquarters for sector conferences?'

The traitor pursed his lips in embarrassment. 'Not often. Perhaps three or four times during the past year.'

'You're going over there now,' said Taleniekov.

'I'm *what*? You've lost your head!'

'You'll lose yours if you don't. Don't worry, Colonel. Rank still has its privileges and its effect. You are sending an urgent cable to a Vyborg man in Helsinki. White line, non-duplicated traffic. However, you must bring me a verifying copy.'

'Suppose they *check* with Vyborg?'

'Who on duty up there now would interfere with the second-in-command?'

Maletkin frowned nervously. 'There will be questions later.'

Vasili smiled, the promise of untold riches in his voice. 'Take my word for it, Colonel. When you return to Vyborg there won't be anything you cannot have . . . or command.'

The traitor grinned, the sweat on his chin glistening. 'Where do I bring the verifying copy? Where will we meet? When?'

Taleniekov held the bandage in place over the wound on his neck and unrolled a strip of tape, the end in his teeth. 'Tear it,' he said to Maletkin. It was done and Vasili applied it, ripping off another strip as he spoke. 'Stay the night at the Yevropeiskaya Hotel on Brodsky Street. I'll contact you there.'

'They'll demand identification.'

'By all means, give it to them. A colonel of the KGB will no doubt get a better room. A better woman, too, if you go down to the lounge.'

'Both cost money.'

'My treat,' Taleniekov said.

* * *

It was the dinner hour. The huge reading rooms of the Saltykov-Shchedrin Library with their tapestried walls and the enormously high ceilings were nowhere near as crowded as usual. A scattering of students sat at the long tables, a few groups of tourists strolled about studying the tapestries and the oil paintings, speaking in hushed whispers, awed by the grandeur that was the Shchedrin.

As Vasili walked through the marble hallways towards the complex of offices in the west wing, he remembered the months he had spent in these rooms – that room – awakening his mind to a world he had known so little about. He had not exaggerated to Lodzia; it was here, through the enlightened courage of one man, that he had learned more about the enemy than in all the training he had later received in Moscow and Novograd.

The Saltykov-Shchedrin was his finest school, the man he was about to see after so many years his most accomplished teacher. He wondered whether the school or the teacher could help him now. If the Voroshin family was bound to the new Matarese there would be no revealing information in the intelligence data banks, of that he was certain. But was it here? Somewhere in the thousands of volumes that detailed the events of the revolution, of families and vast estates banished and carved up, all documented by historians of the time because they knew the time would never be seen again, the explosive beginnings of a new world. It had happened here in Leningrad – St Petersburg – and Prince Andrei Voroshin was a part of the cataclysm. The revolutionary archives at Saltykov-Shchedrin were the most extensive in all Russia; if there was a repository for any information about the Voroshins, it would be here. But being here was one thing, finding it something else again. Would his old teacher know where to look?

He turned left into the corridor lined with glass-panelled office doors, all dark except one at the end of the hallway.

There was a dim light on inside, intermittently blocked by the silhouette of a figure passing back and forth in front of a desk lamp. It was Mikovsky's office, the same room he had occupied for over a quarter of a century, the slow-moving figure beyond the rippled glass unmistakably that of the scholar.

He walked up to the door and knocked softly; the dark figure loomed almost instantly behind the glass.

The door opened and Yanov Mikovsky stood there, his wrinkled face still flushed from the cold outside, his eyes beyond the thick lenses of his spectacles wide, questioning and afraid. He gestured for Vasili to come in quickly, shutting the door the instant Taleniekov was inside.

'Vasili Vasilievich!' The old man's voice was part whisper, part cry. He held out his arms, embracing his younger friend. 'I never thought I'd see you again.' He stepped back, his hands still on Taleniekov's overcoat, peering up at him, his wrinkled mouth tentatively forming words that did not emerge. The events of the past half hour were more than he could accept. Halting sounds emerged, but no meaning.

'Don't upset yourself,' said Vasili as reassuringly as he could. 'Everything's fine.'

'But *why*? Why this secrecy? This running from place to place? Can it be called for? Of all men in the Soviet . . . *you*. The years you were in Riga you never came to see me, but I heard from others how respected you were, how you were in charge of so many things.'

'It was better that we did not meet during those days. I told you that over the telephone.'

'I never understood.'

'They were merely precautions that seemed reasonable at the time.' They had been more than reasonable, thought Taleniekov. He had learned that the scholar was drinking heavily, depressed over the death of his wife. If the head of KGB-Riga had been seen with the old man, people might have looked for other things. And found them.

'No matter, now,' said Mikovsky. 'It was a difficult period for me, as I'm sure you were told. There are times when some men should be left to themselves, even by old friends. But this is now! What's *happened* to you?'

'It's a long story; I'll tell you everything I can. I must, for I need your help.' Taleniekov glanced beyond the scholar; there was a kettle of water on the coils of an electric plate on the right side of the desk. Vasili could not be sure but he thought it was the same kettle, the same electric burner he remembered from so many years ago. 'Your tea was always the best in Leningrad. Will you make some for us?'

The better part of a half hour passed as Taleniekov spoke, the old scholar sitting in his chair, listening in silence. When Vasili first mentioned the name, Prince Andrei Voroshin, he made no comment. But he did when his student had finished.

'The Voroshin estates were confiscated by the new revolutionary government. The family's wealth had been vastly reduced by the Romanovs and their industrial partners. Nicholas and his brother, Michael, loathed the Voroshins, claiming they were the thieves of all northern Russia and the sea routes. And, of course, the prince was marked by the Bolsheviks for execution. His only hope was Kerenski, who was too indecisive or corrupt to cut off the illustrious families so completely. That hope vanished with the collapse of the Winter Palace.'

'What happened to Voroshin?'

'He was sentenced to death. I'm not positive, but I think his name was announced on the execution lists. Those who escaped were generally heard from during the succeeding years; I would have remembered had Voroshin been among them.'

'Why would you? There were hundreds here in Leningrad alone. Why the Voroshins?'

'They were not easily forgotten for many reasons. It was not often that the czars of Russia called their own kind thieves and pirates and sought to destroy them. The Voroshin family was notorious. The prince's father and grandfather dealt in the Chinese and African slave trades, from the Indian Ocean to the American South; they manipulated the Imperial banks, forcing merchant fleets and companies into bankruptcies and absorbing them. It is said that when Nicholas secretly ordered Prince Andrei Voroshin from the palace court, he proclaimed: "Should our Russia fall prey to maniacs, it will be because of men like you. You drive them to our throats." That was a number of years before the revolution.'

'You say "secretly ordered" him. Why secretly?'

'It was not a time to expose dissent among the aristocrats. Their enemies would have used it to justify the cries of national crisis. The revolution was in foment decades before the event. Nicholas understood; he knew it was happening.'

'Did Voroshin have sons?'

'I don't know, but I would presume so – one way or the other. He had many mistresses.'

'What about the family itself?'

'Again I have no specific knowledge, but I assume they perished. As you're aware the tribunals were usually lenient where women and children were concerned. Thousands were allowed to flee; only the most frantic wanted that blood on their hands. But I don't believe the Voroshins were allowed to. Actually, I'm quite sure of it, but I don't know specifically.'

'I need specific knowledge.'

'I understand that, and in my judgement you have it. At least enough to refute any theory involving Voroshin and this incredible Matarese society.'

'Why do you say that?'

'Because had the prince escaped, it would not have been

to his advantage to keep silent. The Whites in exile were organizing everywhere. Those with legitimate titles were welcomed with open arms and excessive remuneration by the great companies and the international banks; it was good business. It was not in Voroshin's nature to reject such largesse and notoriety. No, Vasili. He was killed.'

Taleniekov listened to the scholar's words, looking for an inconsistency. He got up from the chair and went to the pot of tea; he filled his cup and stared absently at the brown liquid. 'Unless he was offered something of greater value to keep silent, to remain anonymous.'

'This Matarese?' asked Mikovsky.

'Yes.' Vasili looked down at the scholar. 'Money had been made available. In Rome and in Genoa. It was their initial funding.'

'But it was earmarked for just that, wasn't it?' Mikovsky leaned forward. 'From what you've told me, it was to be used for the hiring of assassins, spreading the gospel of vengeance according to this Guillaume de Matarese, is that not so?'

'That's what the old woman implied,' agreed Taleniekov.

'Then it was not to be spent recouping individual fortunes or financing new ones. You see, that's what I can't accept where Voroshin is concerned. If he had escaped he would not have turned his back on the opportunities offered him. Not to join an organization bent on political vengeance; he was far too pragmatic a man.'

Vasili had started back to his chair; he stopped and turned, the cup suspended, motionless in his hand. 'What did you just say?'

'That Voroshin was too pragmatic to reject . . .'

'No,' interrupted Taleniekov. 'Before that. The money was not to be used recouping fortunes or . . . ?'

'Financing new ones. You see, Vasili, large sums of capital *were* made available to the exiles.'

Taleniekov held up his hand. '"Financing new ones,"'

he repeated. 'There are many ways to spread a gospel. Beggars and lunatics do it in the streets, priests from pulpits, politicians from rostrums. But how can you spread a gospel that cannot stand scrutiny? How do you *pay* for it?' Vasili put the cup down on the small table next to his chair. 'You do both anonymously, using the complicated methods and procedures of an existing structure. One in which whole areas operate as separate entities, distinct from one another yet held together by a common identity. Where enormous sums of capital are transferred daily.' Taleniekov walked back to the desk and leaned over, his hands on the edge. 'You make the necessary *purchase*! You buy the seat of decision! The structure is yours for the using!'

The scholar studied Vasili's face, observing the words. 'If I follow you – and I believe I do – the money left by Matarese was to be divided, and used to buy participation in giant, established enterprises.'

'Exactly. I'm looking in the wrong *place* – sorry, the *right* place, but the wrong *country*. Voroshin *did* escape. He got out of Russia probably a long time before he had to because the Romanovs crippled him, stripped him, watched his every financial move. He was hamstrung here . . . and later the sort of investments Guillaume de Matarese envisioned were prohibited in the Soviet. Don't you see, he had no reason to stay in Russia. His decision was made long *before* the revolution; it's why you never heard of him in exile. He became someone *else*.'

'You're wrong, Vasili. His name was among those sentenced to death. I remember seeing it myself.'

'But you're not sure you saw it later, in the announcements of those actually executed.'

'There were so many.'

'That's my point.'

'There were his communications with the Kerensky provisional government; they're a matter of record.'

413

'Easily dispatched and recorded.' Taleniekov pushed himself away from the desk, his every instinct telling him he was near the truth. 'What better way for a man like Voroshin to lose his identity but in the chaos of a revolution? The mobs out of control; the discipline did not come for weeks, and it was a miracle it came then. Absolute chaos. How easily it could be done.'

'You're oversimplifying,' said Mikovsky. 'Although there was a period of rampage, teams of observers travelled throughout the cities and countryside writing down everything they saw and heard. Not only facts but impressions, opinions, interpretations of what they witnessed. The academicians insisted upon it, for it was a moment in history that would never be repeated and they wanted no instant lost, none unaccounted for. Everything was written down, no matter how harsh the observation. *That* was a form of discipline, Vasili.'

Taleniekov nodded, holding the scholar's eyes with his own. 'Why do you think I'm here?'

The old man sat forward. 'The archives of the revolution?'

'I must see them.'

'An easy request to make but most difficult to grant. The authority must come from Moscow.'

'How is it relayed?'

'Through the Ministry of Cultural Affairs. A man is sent over from the Leningrad office with the key to the rooms below. There is no key here.'

Vasili's eyes strayed to the mounds of papers on Mikovsky's desk. 'Is that man an archivist? A scholar such as yourself?'

'No. He is merely a man with a key.'

'How often are the authorizations granted?'

Mikovsky frowned. 'Not very frequently. Perhaps twice a month.'

'When was the last time?'

'About three weeks ago. An historian from the *Zhdanov* doing research.'

'Where did he do his reading?'

'In the archive rooms. Nothing is permitted to be taken from them.'

Taleniekov held up his hand. 'Something was. It was sent to you. For everyone's sake it should be returned to the archives immediately. Your telephone call to the Leningrad office should be rather excited.'

The man arrived in twenty-one minutes, his face burnt from the cold.

'The night duty officer said it was urgent, sir,' said the young man breathlessly, opening his briefcase and removing the key, so intricately ridged it would take a precision-tooled instrument to duplicate it.

'Also highly irregular and without question a criminal offence,' replied Mikovsky, getting up from his chair.

'But no harm done now that you're here.' The scholar walked around the desk, a large envelope in his hand. 'Shall we go below?'

'Is that the material?' asked the man with the key.

'Yes.' The scholar lowered the envelope.

'*What* material?' Taleniekov's voice was sharp, the question an accusation.

The man was caught. He dropped the key and reached for his belt. Vasili lunged, grabbing the young man's hand, pulling it downward, throwing his shoulder into the man's chest, hurling him to the floor. 'You said the wrong thing!' shouted Vasili. 'No duty officer tells a messenger the particulars of an emergency. *Perro nostro circulo!* There'll be no pills this time! No guns. I've got you, *soldier*! And by your Corsican christ, you'll tell me what I want to know!'

'*Bei unserem Ring! Unsere Gottheit!*' whispered the young man, his mouth stretched, his lips bulging, his tongue . . . his *tongue*. His *teeth*. The bite came, the jaw clamped, the results irreversible.

Taleniekov watched in furious astonishment as the capsule's liquid entered the throat, paralysing the muscles. In seconds it happened; an expulsion of air, a final breath.

'Call the ministry!' he said to the shocked Mikovsky. 'Tell the night duty officer that it will take several hours to re-insert the material.'

'I don't *understand. Anything!*'

'They tapped the ministry's phone. This one intercepted the man with the key. He would have left it and fled after he had killed us both.' Vasili ripped the dead man's overcoat apart and then the shirt beneath.

It was there. The blemish that was no blemish, the jagged blue circle of the Matarese.

The old scholar reached for the two ledgers on the top shelf of the metal racks and handed them to Taleniekov. They were the seventeenth and eighteenth volumes they had each gone through, searching for the name Voroshin.

'It would be far easier if we were in Moscow,' said Mikovsky, descending the ladder cautiously, heading for the long table. 'All this material has been transcribed and indexed. One volume would tell us exactly where to look.'

'There'll be something; there *has* to be.' Taleniekov handed one book to the scholar and opened the other record for himself. He began to scan the handwritten entries of ink, cautiously turning the brittle pages, yellowed with age.

Twelve minutes later Yanov Mikovsky spoke. 'It's here.'

'What?'

'The crimes of Prince Andrei Voroshin.'

'His execution?'

'Not yet. His life, and the lives and criminal acts of his father and grandfather.'

'Let me see.'

It was all there, meticulously if superficially recorded by a steady, precise hand. The fathers Voroshin were described as enemies-of-the-masses, replete with the crimes of wanton murder of serfs and tenants, and the more rarefied manipulations of the Imperial banks, causing thousands to be unemployed, casting thousands more into the ranks of the starving. The prince had been sent to southern Europe for his higher education, a grand tour that lasted five years, solidifying his pursuance of imperialistic dominance and the suppression of the people.

'*Where?*' Taleniekov spoke out loud.

'Referring to what?' asked the scholar, reading the same page.

'Where was he *sent*?'

Mikovsky turned the page. 'Krefeld. The University of Krefeld. Here it is.'

'That bastard spoke *German. Bei unserem Ring! Unsere Gottheit!* It's in Germany!'

'What is?'

'Voroshin's new identity. It's *here*. Read further.'

They read. The prince had spent three years at Krefeld, two in graduate studies at Düsseldorf, returning frequently in his adult years when he developed close personal ties with such German industrialists as Gustav von Bohlen-Halbach, Friedrich Schotte and Wilhelm Habernicht.

'Essen,' said Vasili. 'Düsseldorf led to Essen. It was territory Voroshin knew, a language he spoke. The timing was perfect; war in Europe, revolution in Russia, the world in chaos. The armaments companies in Essen, that's what he became a part of.'

'*Krupp?*'

'Or Verachten. Krupp's competitor.'

'You think he bought himself into one of them?'

'Through a rear door and a new identity. German industrial expansion then was as chaotic as the Kaiser's war, management personnel raided and shifted about like small armies. The circumstances were ideal for Voroshin.'

'Here is the execution,' interrupted Mikovsky, who had turned the pages. 'The description starts here at the top. Your theory loses credence, I'm afraid.'

Taleniekov leaned over, scanning the words. The entry detailed the deaths of Prince Andrei Voroshin, his wife, two sons and their wives, and one daughter, on the afternoon of 21 October 1917, at his estate in Tsarskoye Selo on the banks of the Slovyanka River. It described in bloody particulars the final minutes of fighting, the Voroshins trapped in the great house with their servants, repelling the attacking mob, firing weapons from the windows, hurling cans of flaming petrol from the sloping roofs – at the end, releasing their servants and, in a pact of death, using their own gunpowder to blow up themselves and the great house in a final conflagration. Nothing was left but the burning skeleton of a czarist estate, the remains of the Voroshins consumed in the flames.

Images came back to Vasili, memories from the hills at night high above Porto Vecchio. The ruins of Villa Matarese. There, too, was a final conflagration.

'I must disagree,' he said softly to Mikovsky. 'This was no execution at all.'

'The tribunals' courts may have been absent,' countered the scholar, 'but I daresay the results were the same.'

'There were no results, no evidence, no proof of death. There were only charred ruins. This entry is false.'

'Vasili Vasilievich! These are the *archives*, every document was scrutinized and approved by the academicians! At the *time*.'

'One was bought. I grant you a great estate was burned to the ground, but that is the limit of existing proof.' Taleniekov turned several pages back. 'Look. This report is very descriptive. Figures with guns at windows, men on

418

roofs, servants streaming out, explosions starting in the kitchens, everything seemingly accounted for.'

'Agreed,' said Mikovsky, impressed with the minute details he read.

'Wrong. There's something missing. In every entry of this nature that we've seen – the storming of palaces and estates, the stopping of trains, the demonstrations – there are always such phrases as "the advance column was led by Comrade So-and-So, the retreat under fire from the czarist guards commanded by provisional Captain Such-and-Such, the execution carried out under the authority of Comrade Blank. As you said before, these entries are all bulging with identities, everything recorded for future confirmation. Well, read this again.' Vasili flipped the pages back and forth. 'The detail *is* extraordinary, even to the temperature of the day and the colour of the afternoon sky and the fur overcoats worn by the men on the roof. But there's not one identity. Only the Voroshins are mentioned by name, no one else.'

The scholar put his fingers on a yellowed page, his old eyes racing down the lines, his lips parted in astonishment. 'You're right. The excessive detail obscures the absence of specific information.'

'It always does,' said Taleniekov. 'The execution of the family Voroshin was a hoax. It never happened.'

25

'That young man of yours was quite impossible,' said Mikovsky into the telephone, words and tone harshly critical of the night duty officer at the Ministry of Cultural Affairs. 'I made it quite clear – as I assume *you* made it clear – that he was to remain in the archives until the material was returned. *Now*, what do I find? The man gone and the key shoved under my door! Really, it's most irregular. I suggest you send someone over to pick it up.'

The old scholar hung up quickly, terminating any chance for the duty officer to speak further. He glanced up at Taleniekov, his eyes filled with relief, but looking for approval.

'That performance would have merited you a certificate from Stanislavsky.' Vasili smiled, as he continued to wipe his hands with paper towels taken from the near-by washroom. 'We're covered – *you're* covered. Just remember, a body without papers will be found behind the furnaces. If you're questioned, you know nothing, you've never seen him before, your only reaction is one of shock and astonishment.'

'But Cultural Affairs, surely *they'll* know him!'

'Surely they won't. He wasn't the man sent over with the key. The ministry will have its own problem, quite a serious one. It will have the key back in its possession, but it will have lost a messenger. If that phone is still tapped, the one listening will assume his man was successful. We've bought time.'

'For what?'

'I've got to get to Essen.'

'Essen. On an assumption, Vasili? On speculation?'

'It's more than speculation. Two of the names mentioned in the Voroshin report were significant. Schotte and Bohlen-Halbach. Friedrich Schotte was convicted by the German courts soon after the First World War for transferring sums of money out of the country; he was killed in prison the night he arrived. It was a highly publicized murder, the killers found. I think he made a mistake and the Matarese called for his silence. Gustav Bohlen-Halbach married the sole survivor of the Krupp family and assumed control of the Krupp Works. If these were Voroshin's friends more than half a century ago, they could have been extraordinarily helpful to him. It all fits.'

Mikovsky shook his head. 'You're looking for sixty-year-old ghosts.'

'Only in the hope that they will lead to present substances. God knows they exist. Do you need further proof?'

'No. It's their existence that frightens me for you. An Englishman waits for you at someone's flat, a woman follows me, a young man arrives here with keys to the archives he steals from another . . . all from this Matarese. It seems they have you trapped.'

'From their point of view, they do. They've studied my files and sent out their soldiers to cover my every conceivable course of action, the assumption being that if one fails another will not.'

The scholar removed his spectacles, his watery eyes staring up at Taleniekov. 'Where do they find such . . . soldiers, as you call them? Where are to be found these motivated men and women who give up their lives so readily?'

'The answer to that may be more frightening than either of us can imagine. Its roots go back centuries, to an Islamic prince named Hasan ibn as-Sabbāh. He formed cadres of political killers to keep him in power. They were called *fida'is*.'

Mikovsky dropped his glasses on the desk; the sound was sharp. 'The *fida'is*? The assassins? I'm familiar with what you're talking about, but the concept is preposterous. The *fida'is* – the assassins of Sabbāh – were based on the prohibitions of a stoic religion. They were Faustian; they exchanged their souls, their minds, their bodies for the pleasures of a Valhalla while on this earth. Such incentives are not credible in these times.'

'In these times?' asked Vasili. 'These *are* the times. The larger house, the fattened bank account, or the use of a *dacha* for a longer period of time, supplied more luxuriously than one's comrades; a greater fleet of aircraft or a more powerful battleship; the ear of a superior or an invitation to an event others cannot attend. These are very much the times, Yanov. The world you and I live in – personally, professionally, even vicariously – is a global society bursting with greed, nine out of ten inhabitants a Faust. I think it was something Karl Marx never understood.'

'A deliberate transitional omission, my friend. He understood fully; there were other issues to be attacked first.'

Taleniekov smiled. 'That sounds dangerously like an apology.'

'Would you prefer words to the effect that the governing of a nation is too important to be left to the people?'

'A monarchist statement. Hardly applicable. It could have been made by the Czar.'

'But it wasn't. It was made by America's Thomas Jefferson. Again, exercising a transitional omission. Both countries, you see, had just gone through their revolutions; each was a new, emerging nation. Words and decisions had to be practical.'

'Your erudition does not change my judgement. I've seen too much, used too much.'

'I don't want to change anything, least of all your talents of observation. I would like only for you to keep things in perspective, my old pupil. Perhaps we're all in a state of transition.'

'To what?'

Mikovsky lifted his spectacles off the desk and put them on carefully. 'To heaven or hell, Vasili. I haven't the vaguest idea which. My only consolation is that I will not be here to find out. How will you get to Essen?'

'Back through Helsinki.'

'Will it be difficult?'

'No. There is a man from Vyborg who'll help.'

'When will you leave?'

'In the morning.'

'You're welcome to stay the night with me.'

'No, it could be dangerous for you.'

The scholar raised his head in surprise. 'But I thought you said that my performance on the phone removed such concerns.'

'I believe it. I don't think anything will be said for days. Eventually, of course, the police will be called; but by then the incident – as far as you're concerned – has faded into an unpleasant lapse in procedures.'

'I understand that, so where is the immediate problem?'

'That I'm wrong. In which case I will have killed us both.'

Mikovsky smiled. 'There's a certain finality in that.'

'I had to do what I did. There was no one else. I'm sorry.'

'Don't be, my old pupil. And you are older, you know. In some ways older than me.' The scholar rose from his chair and walked unsteadily around the desk. 'You must go then, and I will not see you again. Embrace me, Vasili Vasilievich. Heaven or hell, which will it be? I think you know. It is the latter and you have reached it.'

'I got there a long time ago,' said Taleniekov, holding the gentle old man he would never see again.

*   *   *

'Colonel Maletkin?' asked Vasili, knowing that the hesitant voice on the other end of the line belonged indeed to the traitor from Vyborg.

'Where are you?'

'At a telephone in the street, not far away. Do you have something for me?'

'Yes.'

'Good. And I have something for you.'

'Also good,' Maletkin said. 'When?'

'Now. Walk out the front entrance of the hotel and turn right. Keep walking, I'll catch up with you.'

There was a moment of silence. 'It's almost midnight.'

'I'm glad your watch is accurate. It must be expensive. It is one of those Swiss chronometers so popular with the Americans?'

'There's a woman here.'

'Tell her to wait. *Order* her, Colonel. You're an officer of the KGB.'

Seven minutes later Maletkin emerged ferret-like on the pavement in front of the entrance, looking smaller than life and glancing in several directions at once without seemingly turning his head. Although it was cold and dark, Vasili could almost see the sweat on the traitor's chin; in a day or so there would be no chin. It would be blown off in a courtyard in Vyborg.

Maletkin began walking north. There were not many pedestrians on Brodsky Street, a few couples linked arm in arm, the inevitable trio of young soldiers looking for warmth somewhere, anywhere, before returning to the sterility of their barracks.

Taleniekov waited, watched the scene in the street, looking for someone who did not belong.

There was no one. The traitor had not considered double-cross nor had any soldier of the Matarese picked him up. Vasili left the shadows of the doorway and hastened up the block; in sixty seconds he was directly across from Maletkin. He began whistling *Yankee Doodle Dandy*.

'There's your cable!' said the traitor, spitting out the words in the darkness of a recessed shopfront. 'This is the only duplicate. Now tell me. Who is the informer in Vyborg?'

'The *other* informer, don't you mean?' Taleniekov spoke as he snapped his cigarette lighter and looked at the copy of the coded message to Helsinki. It was accurate. 'You'll have the name in a matter of hours.'

'I want it *now*! For all I know someone's already checked with Vyborg. I want my protection; you guaranteed it! I'm leaving here first thing in the morning.'

'*We're* leaving,' interrupted Vasili. 'Before morning, actually.'

'No!'

'Yes. It's a two-hour drive; you'll make that briefing after all.'

'I don't want anything more to *do* with you. Your photograph's on every KGB bulletin board; there were *two* of them down at the Ligovsky headquarters! I found myself perspiring.'

'I wouldn't have thought it! But, you see, you must drive me back to the lake and put me in contact with the Finns. My business here in Leningrad is finished.'

'Why *me*? I've done enough!'

'Because if you don't, I will not be able to remember a name you should know in Vyborg.' Taleniekov patted the traitor's cheek; Maletkin flinched. 'Go back to your woman, comrade, and perform well. But finish with her before too long. I want you checked out of the hotel by three-thirty.'

'Three-thirty?'

'Yes. Drive your car to the Anichkov Bridge; be there no later than four o'clock. Make two trips over the bridge and back. I'll meet you on one side or the other.'

'The *militsianyeri*. They stop suspicious vehicles, and a car travelling back and forth over the Anichkov at four in the morning is not a normal sight.'

'Exactly. If there are *militsianyeri* around, I want to know it.'

'Suppose they stop me?'

'Must I keep reminding you that you are a colonel of the KGB? You're on official business. Very official and very secret.' Vasili started to leave, then turned back. 'It just struck me,' he said. 'It may have occurred to you to borrow a weapon and shoot me down at an opportune moment. On the one hand, you could take credit for bringing me in, and on the other, you could swear you tried to prevent my being killed at great risk to yourself. As long as you were willing to forgo the name of the man in Vyborg, such a strategy would appear to be sound. Very little risk, rewards from both camps. But you should know that every step I take in your presence here in Leningrad is being watched by another now.'

Maletkin's immobile head did not prevent his eyes from sweeping about in an 180-degree arc. He spoke with mounting intensity. 'I *swear* to you such a thing never occurred to me!'

You really are a damn fool, thought Taleniekov. 'Four o'clock then, comrade.'

The row of old buildings in the *dom-vashen* was a decaying black wall of stone mottled by an irregular pattern of dim lights in the windows. The night sounds were a muted cacophony that belonged to the district: voices raised in abrasive arguments alongside laughter that too often was too hysterical, too drunk.

Vasili approached the staircase of the building four doors down the block from Lodzia's flat. He had glanced up at her windows; her lights were on. She was home.

He climbed the steps slowly, as a tired man might,

returning to an uninviting home after putting in unwanted, unpaid-for overtime behind a never-ending conveyor belt in the cause of some new economic plan no one understood. He opened the glass door and went inside the small vestibule.

Instantly, he straightened up, the brief performance over; there was no hesitation now. He opened the inner door, walked to the basement staircase, and descended into the dark, filthy environs of the connecting cellars. He passed the door behind which he had placed the dead Englishman, vodka poured down the throat, wrists slashed with a razor. He pulled out his lighter, ignited it and pushed the door back.

The Englishman was gone. Not only was he gone but there were no signs of blood; everything had been scrubbed clean.

Taleniekov's body went rigid, his thoughts suspended in shock. *Something terrible had happened. He had been wrong.*

So wrong!

Yet he had been so *sure*. The soldiers of the Matarese were expendable, but the last thing they would do would be to return to a scene of violence. The possibilities of a trap were too great; the Matarese would not, *could* not, take that risk!

But they had, the target worth the gamble. What had he *done*?

Lodzia!

He left the door ajar and started walking rapidly, through the connecting cellars, his Graz-Burya in his hand, his steps silent, his eyes and ears primed.

He reached Lodzia's building and started up the steps to the ground-level foyer. He pulled the door back slowly and listened; there was a burst of laughter from the staircase above. A high-pitched female voice, joined seconds later by the laughter of a man.

427

Vasili put the Graz-Burya in his pocket and stepped inside around the railing, and walked quickly, unsteadily up the steps after the couple. They approached the second-floor landing, diagonally across from Lodzia's door. Taleniekov spoke, a foolish grin on his face.

'Would you young people do a middle-aged lover a favour? I'm afraid I had that one vodka too many.'

The couple turned, smiling as one.

'What's the problem, friend?' the young man asked.

'My friend is the problem,' said Taleniekov, gesturing at Lodzia's door. 'I was to meet her after the performance at the Kirov. I'm afraid I was delayed by an old army comrade. I think she's angry as hell. Please knock for me; if she hears my voice she probably won't let me in.' Vasili grinned again, his thoughts in opposition to his smile. The possible sacrifice of the young and the attractive grew more painful as one got older.

'It's the least we can do for a soldier,' said the girl, laughing brightly. 'Go on, husband-mine, do your bit for the military.'

'Why not?' The young man shrugged and walked to Lodzia's door. Taleniekov crossed beyond it, his back to the wall, his right hand again in his pocket. The youthful husband knocked.

There was no sound from within. He glanced over at Vasili, who nodded, indicating another try. The young man knocked again, now louder, more insistent, and again there was only silence from inside.

'Perhaps she's still waiting for you at the Kirov,' said the girl.

'Then again,' added the young man, smiling, 'perhaps she found your old army comrade and they're both avoiding you.'

Taleniekov tried to smile back but could not. He knew only too well what he might find behind the door. 'I'll wait here,' he said. 'Thank you very much.'

The husband seemed to realize he had been facetious at the wrong moment. 'I'm sorry,' he mumbled, taking his wife's arm.

'Good luck,' said the girl, awkwardly. They both walked rapidly up the staircase.

Vasili waited until he heard the sound of a door closing two storeys above. He took his automatic from his pocket and reached for the knob in front of him, afraid to find out that it was not locked.

It was not and his fear mounted. He pushed the door open, stepped inside and closed it. What he saw sent a pain through his chest; he knew a greater pain would follow shortly. The room was a shambles, chairs, tables and lamps overturned; books and cushions were strewn on the floor, articles of clothing lying in scattered disarray. The scene was created to depict a violent struggle, but it was false, overdone, as such constructed scenes were usually overdone. There had been no struggle, but there had been something else. There had been an interrogation based in torture.

The bedroom door was open; he walked towards it, knowing the greater pain would come in seconds, sharp bolts of anguish. He went inside and looked at her. She was on the bed, her clothes torn from her body, the positioning of her legs indicating rape, the act, if it was done, done only for the purposes of an autopsy, undoubtedly performed after she had died. Her face was battered, lips and eyes swollen, teeth broken. Streaks of blood had flowed down her cheeks leaving abstract patterns of deep red on her light skin.

Taleniekov turned away, a terrible passivity sweeping over him. He had felt it many times before; he wanted only to kill. He would kill.

And then he was touched, so deeply that his eyes filled suddenly with tears and he could not breathe. Lodzia Kronescha had not broken; she had not revealed to the animal who had operated on her that her lover from the days of Riga was due after midnight. She had done more than keep the secret, far more. She had sent the animal off in another direction. What she must have *gone* through!

He had not loved in more than half a lifetime; he loved now and it was too late.

Too late? Oh, God!

. . . where is the problem?

. . . that I'm wrong. In which case I will have killed us both.

Yanov Mikovsky.

If a follow-up soldier had been sent by the Matarese to Lodzia Kronescha, another surely would have been sent to seek out the scholar.

Vasili raced into the sitting room, to the telephone that had carefully not been disturbed. It did not matter whether or not the line was tapped; he would learn what he had to learn in seconds, be away seconds later before anyone intercepting him could send men to the *dom-vashen*.

He dialled Mikovsky's number. The phone was picked up immediately . . . too quickly for an old man.

'Yes?' The voice was muffled, unclear.

'Dr Mikovsky, please.'

'Yes?' repeated the male voice. It was not the scholar's.

'I'm an associate of Comrade Mikovsky and it's urgent that I speak with him. I know he wasn't feeling well earlier; does he need medical attention? We'll send it right away, of course.'

'No.' The man spoke too swiftly. 'Who is calling, please?'

Taleniekov forced a casual laugh. 'It's only his office neighbour, Comrade Rydukov. Tell him I've found the book he was looking for . . . no, let me tell him myself.'

Silence.

'Yes?' It was Mikovsky; they had let him get on the line.

'Are you all right? Are those men friends?'

'*Run, Vasili! Get away! They are* . . .'

A deafening explosion burst over the line. Taleniekov held the telephone in his hand, staring at it. He stood for a moment, allowing sharp bolts of pain to sear through his chest. He loved two people in Leningrad and he had killed them both.

No, that was not true. The Matarese had killed them. And now he would kill in return. Kill . . . and kill . . . and *kill*.

He went into a telephone booth on the Nevsky Prospekt and dialled the Yevropeiskaya Hotel. There would be no small talk, no teasing indulgences that kept a puppet dancing on a string; there was no time to waste on insignificant men. He had to get across Lake Vainikkala, into Helsinki, reach the Corsican woman in Paris and send the word to Scofield. He was on his way to Essen, for the secret of the Voroshins was there and animals were loose, killing to prevent that secret from being revealed. He wanted them now . . . so badly . . . these élite soldiers of the Matarese. They were all dead men in his hands.

'Yes, yes what is it?' were the rushed, breathless words of the traitor from Vyborg.

'Get out of there at once,' commanded Taleniekov. 'Drive to the Moskva Station. I'll meet you at the kerb in front of the first entrance.'

'*Now?* It is barely two o'clock! You said . . .'

'Forget what I said, do as I *say*. Did you make the arrangements with the Finns?'

'A simple telephone call.'

'Did you *make* it?'

'It can be done in a minute.'

'Do it. Be at the Moskva in fifteen.'

The drive north was made in near-total silence, broken only by Maletkin's intermittent whining over the events of the past twenty-four hours. He was a man dealing in things so far beyond his depth that even his treachery had a rancid, shallow quality about it.

They drove through Vyborg, past Selzneva, towards the border. Vasili recognized the snow-bordered road he had walked down from the edge of the frozen lake; soon they would reach the fork in the road where he had first observed the traitor beside him. It had been dawn then; soon it would be dawn again. And so much had happened, so much learned. So tragically.

He was exhausted. He had had no sleep, and he needed it badly. He knew better than to try to function while his mind resisted thought; he would get to Helsinki and sleep for as long as his body and his faculties would permit, then make his arrangements. To Essen.

But there was a final arrangement to be made now, before he left his beloved Russia, *for* his Russia.

'In less than a minute we'll reach the rendezvous at the lake,' Maletkin said. 'You'll be met by a Finn along the path to the water's edge. Everything's arranged. Now, *comrade*, I've carried out my end of the bargain, you deliver yours. Who is the other informer at Vyborg?'

'You don't need his name. You just need his rank. He's the only man in your sector who can give you orders, your sole superior. First in command at Vyborg.'

'*What?* He's a tyrant, a fanatic!'

'What better cover? Drop in to see him . . . privately. You'll know what to say.'

'Yes,' agreed Maletkin, his eyes on fire, slowing the car down as they approached a break in the snowbank. 'Yes, I think I will know what to say . . . Here's the path.'

'And here is your gun,' said Taleniekov, handing the traitor his weapon, minus its firing pin.

'Oh? Yes, thank you,' replied Maletkin, not listening, his thoughts on power unimagined only seconds ago.

Vasili got out of the car. 'Goodbye,' he said, closing the door.

As he rounded the back of the automobile towards the path, he heard the sound of Maletkin's window being rolled down.

'It's *incredible*,' said the traitor, sheer gratitude in his voice. '*Thank* you.'

'You're welcome.'

The window was rolled up. The roar of the engine joined the screaming whine of the tyres as they spun on the snow. The car sped forward; Maletkin would waste no time getting back to Vyborg.

To his execution.

Taleniekov entered the path that would take him to an escort, to Helsinki, to Essen. He began whistling softly; the tune was *Yankee Doodle Dandy*.

26

The gentle-looking man in the rumpled clothes and the high-necked cotton sweater clamped a violin case between his knees and thanked the Finnair stewardess for the container of tea. If anyone on board was inclined to guess the musician's age, he'd probably say somewhere between fifty-five and sixty, possibly a little older. Those sitting farther away would start at sixty-plus and add that he was probably older than that.

Yet with the exception of streaks of white brushed into his hair he had used no cosmetics. Taleniekov had learned years ago that the muscles of the face and body conveyed age and infirmity far better than powders and liquid plastics.

The trick was to set the muscles in the desired position of abnormal stress, then go about one's business as normally as possible, overcoming the discomfort by fighting it, as older people fight the strain of age and cripples do the best they can with their deformities.

Essen. He had been to the 'black jewel of the Ruhr' twice, neither trip recorded for they were sensitive assignments involving industrial espionage – operations Moscow did not care to have noted anywhere. Therefore, the Matarese had no information that could help it in Essen. No contacts to keep under surveillance, no friends to seek out and trap, nothing. No Yanov Mikovsky, no . . . Lodzia Kronescha.

Essen. Where could he begin? The scholar had been right: he was looking for a sixty-year-old ghost, a hidden absorption of one man and his family into a vast industrial complex during a period of world chaos. Legal documents going back more than half a century would be out of reach – if they had ever existed in the first place. And even if they had, and were available, they would be so obscured that it could take weeks to trace money and identities – in the tracing his own exposure guaranteed.

Too, the court records in Essen had to be among the most gargantuan and complicated anywhere. The practice of law in Essen the most lucrative of all professions. Where was the man who could make his way through such a maze? Where was the time to do it?

There *was* a man, a patent attorney, who would no doubt throw up his hands at the thought of trying to find the name of a single Russian entering Essen fifty years ago. But he *was* a lawyer; he was a place to start. If he was alive, and if he was willing to talk with a long-ago embarrassment. Vasili had not thought of the man in years. Heinrich Kassel had been a thirty-five-year-old junior partner in a firm that did legal work for many of Essen's prominent companies. The KGB dossier on him had depicted a man often at odds with his superiors, a man who championed extremely liberal causes – some so objectionable to his employers they had threatened to fire him. But he was too good; no superior cared to be responsible for his dismissal.

The conspiratorial asses in Moscow had decreed in their wisdom that Kassel was prime material for patent design espionage. In their better wisdom, the asses had sent their most persuasive negotiator, one Vasili Taleniekov, to enlist the attorney for a better world.

It took Vasili less than an hour over a trumped-up dinner to realize how absurd the assignment was. The realization came when Heinrich Kassel leaned back in his chair and exclaimed.

'Are you out of your *mind*? I do what I do to keep you bastards out!'

There had been nothing for it. The persuasive negotiator and the misguided attorney had got drunk, ending the evening at dawn, watching the sun come up over the gardens in Gruga Park. They had made a drunken pact: the lawyer would not report Moscow's attempt to the Bonn government – in so far as Moscow had conceived of it so badly – if Taleniekov would guarantee that the KGB dossier was substantially altered – in so far as such erroneous evaluations would do the attorney no good where a full partnership was concerned if they ever leaked out. The lawyer had kept silent, and Vasili had returned to Moscow, amending the German's file with the judgement that the 'radical' attorney was probably a *provocateur* in the pay of the Americans. Kassel might help him, at least tell him where he could start.

If he was able to reach Heinrich Kassel. So many things might have happened to prevent it. Disease, death, relocation, accidents of living and livelihood; it had been twelve years since the abortive assignment in Essen.

There was something else he had to do in Essen, he mused. He had no gun; he would have to purchase one. The West German airport security was such these days that he could not chance the dismantling of his Graz-Burya and packing it in his carry-on travel bag.

There was so much to do, so little time. But a pattern was coming into focus. It was obscure, elusive, contra-dictory . . . but it was there. The Corsican fever was spreading, the infectors using massive sums of money and ingenious financing methods to create pockets of chaos everywhere, recruiting an army of élite soldiers who would give up their lives instantly to protect the cause. But again, *what* cause? To what purpose? What were the violent philosophical descendants of Guillaume de Matarese trying to achieve? Assassination, terrorism, indiscriminate bombings and riots, kidnapping and murder . . . all the things that men of wealth had to detest, for in the breakdown of order was their undoing. This was the giant contradiction. *Why?*

He felt the plane dip, the pilot was starting his descent into Essen.

Essen. Prince Andrei Voroshin. Who had he become?

'I don't believe it!' exclaimed Heinrich Kassel over the telephone, his voice conveying the same good-natured incredulity Taleniekov remembered from twelve years ago. 'Every time I pass the gardens in the Gruga, I pause for a moment and laugh. My wife thinks it must be the memory of an old girl-friend.'

'I trust you cleared that up.'

'Oh, yes. I tell her it was where I nearly became an international spy and she's *convinced* it's an old girl-friend.'

'Meet me at the Gruga, please. It's urgent and has nothing to do with my former business.'

'Are you sure? It would not do for one of Essen's more prominent attorneys to have a Russian connection. These are odd times. Rumours abound that the Baader-Meinhof are financed by Moscow, that our neighbours to the far north are up to some nasty old tricks.'

Taleniekov paused for a moment, wincing at the coincidence. 'You have the word of an old conspirator. I'm unemployed.'

'Really? How interesting. Gruga Park then. It's almost noon. Shall we say one o'clock? Same place in the gardens, although there'll be no flowers this time of year.'

The ice on the pond glistened in the sunlight, the shrubbery curled for the cold of winter, yet briefly alive in the noonday's warmth from the sky. Vasili sat on the bench; it was fifteen minutes past one and he felt the stirrings of concern. Without thinking, he touched the bulge in his right-hand pocket that was the small automatic he had purchased in Kopstadt Square, then took his hand away when he saw the hatless figure walking rapidly up the garden path.

Kassel had grown portly and nearly bald. In his large

overcoat with the black fur lapels he was the image of a successful burgomaster, his obviously expensive attire at odds with Taleniekov's memory of the fiery young lawyer who had wanted to *keep you bastards out*! As he drew nearer, Taleniekov saw that the face was cherubic – a great deal of *Schlag* had gone down that throat, but the eyes were alive, still humorous . . . and sharp.

'I'm so sorry, my dear fellow,' said the German as Taleniekov got up and accepted the outstretched hand. 'A last-minute problem with an American contract.'

'That has a certain symmetry to it,' replied Vasili. 'When I returned to Moscow twelve years ago, I wrote in your file that I thought you were on Washington's payroll.'

'How perceptive. Actually, I'm paid out of New York, Detroit and Los Angeles, but why quibble over cities?'

'You look well, Heinrich. Quite prosperous. What happened to that very vocal champion of the underdog?'

'They made him an overdog.' The lawyer chuckled. 'It would never have happened if you people controlled the *Bundestag*. I'm an unprincipled capitalist who assuages his guilt with sizeable contributions to charity. My Reichsmarks do far more than my vocal cords ever did.'

'A reasonable statement.'

'I'm a reasonable man. And what appears somewhat unreasonable to me now is why you would look me up. Not that I don't enjoy your company, for I do. But why now? You say you're not employed in your former profession; what could I possibly have that you'd be interested in?'

'Advice.'

'You have legal problems in *Essen*? Don't tell me a dedicated Communist has private investments in the Ruhr?'

'Only of time, and I have very little of that. I'm trying to trace a man, a family from Leningrad who came to Germany – to Essen, I'm convinced – between sixty and seventy years ago. I'm also convinced they entered illegally, and secretly bought into Ruhr industry.'

Kassel frowned. 'My dear fellow, you're mad. I'm trying to tick off the decades – I was never very good at figures – but if I'm not mistaken, you're referring to the period between 1910 and 1920. Is that correct?'

'Yes. They were turbulent times.'

'You don't say. There was merely the great war to the south, the bloodiest revolution in history in the north, mass confusion in the eastern Slavic states, the Atlantic ports in chaos, and the ocean a graveyard. In essence, all Europe was – if I may be permitted – in flames and Essen itself experiencing an industrial expansion unseen before or since, including the Hitler years. Everything, naturally, was secret, fortunes made every day. Into this insanity comes one White Russian selling his jewels – as hundreds did – to buy himself a piece of the pie in any of a dozen companies, and you expect me to *find* him?'

'I thought that might be your reaction.'

'What other could I possibly have?' Kassel laughed again. 'What is the name of this man?'

'For your own good, I'd rather not tell you.'

'Then how can I help you?'

'By telling me where you would look first if you were me.'

'In Russia.'

'I did. The revolutionary archives. In Leningrad.'

'You found nothing?'

'On the contrary. I found a detailed description of a mass family suicide so patently at odds with reality that it had to be false.'

'How was this suicide described? Not the particulars, just in general.'

'The family's estate was stormed by the mobs; they fought all day, but in the end used the remaining explosives and blew themselves up with the main house.'

'One family holding off a rioting mob of Bolsheviks for an entire day? Hardly likely.'

'Precisely. Yet the account was as detailed as a von Clausewitz exercise, even to the climate and the brightness of the sky. Every inch of the vast estate was described, but apart from the name of the family itself, not one other identity was entered. There were no witnesses listed to confirm the event.'

The attorney frowned again. 'Why did you just say that "every inch of the vast estate was described"?'

'It was.'

'But why?'

'To lend credibility to the false account, I assume. A profusion of detail.'

'Too profuse, perhaps. Tell me, were the actions of this family on that day described in your usual enemies-of-the-people vitriol?'

Taleniekov thought back. 'No, they weren't, actually. They could almost be termed individual acts of courage.' Then he remembered specifically. 'They released their servants before they took their own lives . . . they *released* them. That *wasn't* a normal thing.'

'And the inclusion of such a generous act in a revolutionary's account would not really be all that acceptable, would it?'

'What are you driving at?'

'That account may have been written by the man himself, or a literate member of the family, and then passed on through corrupt channels to the archives.'

'Entirely possible, but I still don't understand your point.'

'The odds are long, I grant you, but bear with me. Over the years I've learned that when a client is asked to outline a deposition, he always shows himself in the best light; that's understandable. But he also invariably includes trivial particulars about things that mean a great deal to him. They slip out unconsciously: a lovely wife or a beautiful child, a profitable business or a . . . beautiful home. "Every inch of the vast estate." That was this family's passion, wasn't it? Land. Property.'

'Yes.' Vasili recalled Mikovsky's descriptions of the Voroshin estates. How the patriarchs were absolute rulers over the land, even to holding their own courts of law. 'You could say they were excessively addicted to property.'

'Might they have brought this addiction to Germany?'

'They might have. Why?'

The attorney's eyes turned cold. 'Before I answer that, I must ask the old conspirator a very serious question. Is this search a Soviet reprisal of some sort? You say you're unemployed, that you're not working at your former occupation, but what proof do I have?'

Taleniekov breathed deeply, levelling his eyes with the German's. 'I could say the word of a KGB strategist who altered an enemy's file twelve years ago, but I'll go farther than that. If you have connections with Bonn intelligence and can inquire discreetly, ask them about me. Moscow has sentenced me to death.'

The coldness thawed in Kassel's eyes. 'You wouldn't say such a thing if it weren't true. An attorney who deals every day with international business could check too easily. But you were a dedicated Communist.'

'I still am.'

'Then surely an enormous mistake has been made.'

'A manipulated mistake,' said Vasili.

'So this is not a Moscow operation, not in the Soviet interest?'

'No. It's in the interests of both sides, all sides, and that is all I'll say. Now, I've answered your serious question very seriously. Answer mine. What was your point regarding this family's preoccupation with the land?'

The lawyer pursed his thick lips, squinted at Taleniekov, then sighed as he spoke. 'Tell me the name. I may be able to help you.'

'How?'

'The Records of Property that are filed in the State House. There were rumours that several of the great estates in Rellinghausen and Stadtwald – those on the northern shores of Lake Baldeney – were bought by Russians decades ago.'

'They would not have bought in their own name, I'm certain of that.'

'Probably not. I said the odds were long, but the covert acquisition of property is not unlike depositions. Things slip out. Possession of land is very close to a man's view of himself; in some cultures he is the land.'

'Why can't I look for myself? If the records are available, tell me where to find them.'

'It wouldn't do you any good. Only certified attorneys are permitted to search the titles. Tell me the name.'

'It could be dangerous for anyone who looks,' said Taleniekov quietly.

'Oh, *come* now.' Kassel laughed, his eyes amused again. 'A seventy-year-old purchase of land.'

'I believe there's a direct connection between that purchase and the extreme acts of violence that are occurring everywhere today.'

'Extreme acts of . . .' The lawyer trailed off the phrase, his expression solemn. 'An hour ago I mentioned Baader-Meinhof on the phone. Your silence was quite loud. Are you suggesting . . . ?'

'I'd rather not suggest anything,' interrupted Vasili. 'You're a prominent man, a resourceful man. Give me a letter of certification and get me into the Records of Property.'

The German shook his head. 'No, I won't do that. You wouldn't know what to look for. But you may accompany me.'

'You'd do this yourself? Why?'

'I despise extremists who deal in violence. I remember too vividly the screams and diatribes of the Third Reich.

442

I shall, indeed, look for myself, and if we get lucky you can tell me what you wish.' Kassel lightened his voice, but sadness was there. 'Besides, anyone sentenced to death by Moscow cannot be all bad. Now, tell me the name.'

Taleniekov stared at the attorney, seeing another sentence of death. 'Voroshin,' he said.

The uniformed clerk in the Essen Hall of Records, *Eigentum Abteilung*, treated the prominent Heinrich Kassel with extreme deference. Herr Kassel's firm was one of the most important in the city. He made it plain that the receptionist behind the desk would be delighted to make copies of anything Herr Kassel wished to have duplicated.

The steel filing cabinets in the enormous room that housed the Records of Property were like grey robots stacked one on top of the other, circling the room, staring down at the open cubicles where the certified lawyers did their research.

'Everything is recorded by date,' said Kassel. 'Year, month, day. Be as specific as you can. What was the earliest Voroshin might have reasonably bought property in the Essen districts?'

'Allowing for the slow methods of travel at the time, say late May or early June of 1911. But I told you, he wouldn't have bought under his own name.'

'We won't be looking for his name, or even an assumed name. Not to begin with.'

'Why not an assumed name? Why couldn't he arrive and buy what was available under another name if he had the funds?'

'Because of the times, and they haven't changed that much. A man does not simply enter a community with his family and proceed to assume ownership of a large estate without arousing curiosity. This Voroshin, as you've described him, would hardly have wanted that. He would establish a false identity very slowly, very carefully.'

'Then what do we look for?'

'A purchase made by attorneys for owners *in absentia* or by a trust legation from a bank for an estate investment; or by officers of a company or a limited partnership for acquisition purposes. There are any number of ways to set up concealed ownership, but eventually the calendar runs out; the owners want to move in. It's always the pattern, whether you talk about a sweet shop or a conglomerate or a large estate. All the legal manoeuvres are no match for human nature.' Kassel paused, looking at the grey cabinets. 'Come. We'll start with the month of May 1911. If there's anything here it may not be that difficult to find. There were no more than thirty or forty such estates in the whole of the Ruhr, perhaps ten to fifteen in the Rellinghausen-Stadtwald districts.'

Taleniekov felt the same anticipation he had experienced with Yanov Mikovsky in the archives in Leningrad. The same feeling of peeling away layers of time, looking for a clue in documents recorded with precision decades ago. But now he was awed by the seeming irrelevancies that Heinrich Kassel spotted and extracted from the thick pages of legales. The attorney was like a child in that sweet shop he had referred to; a young expert whose eyes roamed over the jellybeans and the acid drops, picking out the flawed items for sale.

'Here. Learn something, my international spy. This tract of land in Bredeney, thirty-seven acres in the Baldeney valley – ideal for someone like Voroshin. It was purchased by the Staatsbank of Duisburg for the minors of a family in Remscheid.'

'What's the name?'

'It's irrelevant. A device. We find out who moved in a year or so after, *that's* the name we want.'

'You think it may be Voroshin. Under his new identity?'

'Don't jump. There are others like this.' Kassel laughed. 'I had no idea my predecessors were so full of legal caprice;

it's positively shocking. Look,' he said, pulling out another sheaf of papers, his eyes automatically riveted on an indented clause on the first page. 'Here's another. A cousin of the Krupps is transferring ownership of property in Rellinghausen to a woman in Düsseldorf in gratitude for her many years of service. Really!'

'It's possible, isn't it?'

'Of course not; the family would never permit it. A relative found a way to make a handsome profit by selling to someone who did not want his peers – or his creditors – to know he had the money. Someone who controlled the woman in Düsseldorf, if she ever existed. The Krupps probably congratulated their cousin.'

And so it went: 1911, 1912, 1913, 1914 . . . 1915.

20 August 1915.

The name was there. It meant nothing to Heinrich Kassel, but it did to Taleniekov. It brought to mind another document two thousand miles away in the archives in Leningrad. The crimes of the family Voroshin, the intimate associates of Prince Andrei.

Friedrich Schotte.

'Wait a minute!' Vasili placed his hand over the pages. 'Where's this?'

'Stadtwald. There's nothing irregular here. As a matter of fact, it's absolutely legal; very clean.'

'Perhaps too legal, too clean. Just as the Voroshin massacre was too profuse with detail.'

'What in God's name are you talking about?'

'What do you know of this Friedrich Schotte?'

The attorney grimaced in thought, trying to recall irrelevant history; this was not what he was looking for. 'He worked for the Krupps, I think, in a very high position. It would have had to be for him to buy this. He got in trouble after the First World War. I don't remember the circumstances – a prison sentence or something – but I can't see how it's relevant.'

'I can,' said Taleniekov. 'He was convicted of manipulating money out of Germany. He was killed on the first night of that prison sentence in 1919. Was the estate sold then?'

'I would think so. It would appear by the map survey to be a rather expensive property for a prison widow to maintain.'

'How can we find out?'

'Look through the year 1919. We'll get there . . .'

'Let's get there now. *Please*.'

Kassel sighed. He got up and headed for the cabinets, returning a minute later with a bulging folder. 'When a brief is interrupted continuity is lost,' he muttered.

'Whatever we lose can be restored; we may gain time.'

It took nearly thirty minutes before Kassel extracted a file within a file and placed it on the table. 'I'm afraid we have just wasted half an hour.'

'Why?'

'The estate was purchased by the Verachten family on 12 November 1919.'

'The Verachten Works? Krupps' competitor?'

'Not then. More so now, perhaps. The Verachtens came to Essen from Munich soon after the turn of the century, sometime around nineteen six, or seven. It's common knowledge, the Verachtens were Munichers and they couldn't be more respectable. You have a *V*, but no Voroshin.'

Vasili's mind raced back over the information already known. Guillaume de Matarese had summoned the heads of once-powerful families, stripped – nearly but not entirely – of their past riches and influences. According to old Mikovsky, the Romanovs had waged a long battle against the Voroshins, labelling them the thieves of Russia, provokers of revolution . . . It was clear! The *padrone* from the hills of Porto Vecchio had summoned a man – and by extension, his family – *already* in the *process* of a covert

446

emigration, taking with them everything they could out of Russia!

'The imperial *V*, that's what we found,' said Taleniekov. 'My God, what a strategy! Even to the prolonged use of truckloads of gold and silver sent out of Leningrad with the imperial *V*!' Vasili picked up the pages in front of the attorney. 'You said it yourself, Heinrich. Voroshin would build a false identity very slowly, very carefully. That's exactly what he did; he simply began five or six years before I thought he had. I'm sure if such records were kept or memories could be activated, we'd find that Herr Verachten came first to Essen alone, until he was established. A man of wealth, testing new waters for investments and a future, bringing with him a carefully constructed history from faraway Munich, money flowing through the Austrian banks. So simple, and the times were so right!'

Suddenly Kassel frowned. 'His wife,' said the lawyer quietly.

'What about his wife?'

'She was not a Municher. She was Hungarian, from a wealthy family in Dèbrecen, it was said. Her German was never very good.'

'Translated, she was from Leningrad and a poor linguist. What was Verachten's full name?'

'Ansel Verachten,' said the attorney, his eyes now on Taleniekov. '*Ansel*.'

'*Andrei*.' Vasili let the pages fall. 'It's incredible how the ego strives to be sublime, isn't it? Meet Prince Andrei Voroshin.'

27

They strolled across the Gildenplatz, the Kaffee Hag building blazing with light, the Bosch insignia subdued but prominent below the enormous clock. It was eight in the evening now, the sky dark, the air cold. It was not a good night for walking, but Taleniekov and Kassel had spent nearly six hours in the Records of Property; the wind that blew across the square was refreshing.

'Nothing should shock a German from the Ruhr,' said the lawyer, shaking his head. 'After all, we are the Zürich of the north. But this is incredible. And I know only a *part* of the story. You won't reconsider and tell me the rest?'

'One day I may.'

'That's too cryptic. Say what you mean.'

'If I'm alive.' Vasili looked at Kassel. 'Tell me everything you can about the Verachtens.'

'There isn't that much. The wife died in the mid-'thirties, I think. One son and a daughter-in-law were killed in a bombing raid during the war, I remember that. The bodies weren't found for several days, buried under the rubble as so many were. Ansel lived to a ripe old age, somehow avoiding the war-crimes penalties that caught the Krupps. He died in style, heart seizure while on horseback some time in the 'fifties.'

'Who's left?'

'Walther Verachten, his wife and their daughter; she never married, but it didn't prevent her from enjoying connubial pleasures.'

'What do you mean?'

'She cut a bold figure, as they say, and when she was younger, had one to match her reputation. The Americans have a term that fits: she was – in some ways, still is – a "man-eater".' The attorney paused. 'Strange how things turn out. It's Odile who really runs the companies now. Walther and his wife are in their late seventies and are rarely seen in public these days.'

'Where do they live?'

'They're still in Stadtwald, but not at the original estate, of course. As we saw, it was one of those sold to post-war developers; it's why I didn't recognize it. They have a house farther out in the countryside now.'

'What about the daughter, this Odile?'

'*That*,' replied Kassel, chuckling, 'depends on the lady's whims. She keeps a penthouse on the Werden Strasse, and through those portals pass many a business adversary who wakes up the next morning too exhausted to best her at the conference table. When she's not in the city I understand she maintains a cottage in her parents' grounds.'

'She sounds like quite a woman.'

'In the forty-five-plus sweepstakes, few outclass her on the track.' Kassel paused again, again not finished. 'She has a flaw, however, and I'm told it's maddening. Although she runs Verachten firmly, when things aren't going well and swift decisions are called for, she often announces that she must confer with her father, thus postponing actions sometimes for days. At heart she's a woman, forced by circumstances to wear a man's hat, but the power still resides with old Walther.'

'Do you know him?'

'We're acquaintances, that's all.'

'What do you think of him?'

'Not much, never did. He always struck me as a rather pretentious autocrat without a great deal of talent.'

'The Verachten Works thrive, however,' said Vasili.

'I know, I know. That's what I'm told whenever I voice that opinion. My weak rejoinder is that it might do so much better without him; and it *is* weak. If Verachten did any better, it would own Europe. So, I assume it's a personal dislike on my part and I'm wrong.'

Not necessarily, thought Taleniekov. *The Matarese make strange and effective arrangements. They need only the apparatus.*

'I want to meet him,' said Vasili. 'Alone. Have you ever been to his house?'

'Once, several years ago,' replied Kassel. 'The Verachten lawyers called us in on a patent problem. Odile was out of the country. I needed a Verachten signature on the affidavit of complaint – couldn't proceed without it, as a matter of fact – and so I called old Walther and drove out to get it. The dam broke when Odile got back to Essen. She shouted at me over the telephone: "My father should not have been disturbed! You will never serve Verachten again!" Oh, she was impossible. I told her as courteously as I could that we never would have served her in the first place had *I* received the initial request.'

Taleniekov watched the attorney's face as he spoke: the German was genuinely angry. 'Why did you say that?'

'Because it's true. I don't like the company – companies. There is a meanness over there.' Kassel laughed at himself. 'My feeling's probably a hangover from that radical young lawyer you tried to recruit twelve years ago.'

It is the perceptive instinct of a decent man, thought Vasili. You sense the Matarese, yet you know nothing.

'I have a last request to make of you, my old friendly enemy,' said Taleniekov. 'Two, actually. The first is not to say anything to anyone about our meeting today, or what we found. The second is to describe the location of the Verachten house and whatever you can remember about it.'

The corner of the brick wall loomed into view in the glare of the headlights. Vasili pressed down on the accelerator of the rented Mercedes, his eyes glancing at the odometer, judging the distance between the start of the wall and the iron gate. Three-tenths of a mile, nearly 1,800 feet. The tall gate was closed; it was electronically operated, electronically protected.

He came to the end of the wall; this length was somewhat shorter than its counterpart on the other side of the gate. Beyond there was only the extension of the forest, in the middle of which had been built the Verachten compound. He depressed the pedal and looked for an opening off the road, somewhere he could conceal the Mercedes.

He found it between two trees, the shrubs dampened down by previous snows. He angled the coupé into the natural cave of greenery, plunging in as far off the road as possible. He turned off the engine, got out and retraced the car's path, pulling up the bushes until he reached the road fifteen feet away. He stood on the shoulder and examined the camouflage; in the darkness, it was sufficient. He started back towards the Verachten wall.

If he could get over it without setting off any alarms, he knew he could reach the house. There was no way to scan a forest electronically; wires and cells were too easily tripped by animals and birds. It was the wall itself that had to be negotiated. He reached it and studied the brick in the flame of his cigarette lighter. There were no devices of any sort. It was an ordinary brick wall, its very ordinariness misleading, and Vasili knew it. There was a tall oak on his right, limbs curling up above the top of the wall, but not extending over it.

He leaped, his hands clawing the bark, his knees vicing the trunk; he scaled up to the first limb, swinging his leg over it, pulling himself up into a sitting position, his back against the tree. He leaned forward and downward, his hands balancing his body on the limb until he was prone, and studied the top of the wall in the dim light. He found what he knew had to be there.

Grooved into the flat surface of the concrete was a

451

criss-crossing network of wire-coated plastic tubing through which air and current flowed. The electricity was of sufficient voltage to inhibit animals from gnawing at the plastic, and the air pressure was calibrated to set off alarms the instant a given amount of weight fell over the tube. The alarms were undoubtedly received in a scanning room in the compound, where instruments selected the point of penetration. Taleniekov knew the system was practically fail-safe; if one strand was shorted out, there were five or six others to back it up, and the pressure of a knife across the wire coating would be enough to set off the alarm.

But practically fail-safe was not totally fail-safe. Fire. Melting the plastic and releasing the air without the pressure of a blade. The only alarm set off in this was that of malfunction; the trace would begin where the system originated, which had to be much nearer the house.

He estimated the distance between the edge of the tree limb and the top of the wall. If he could loop his leg as close to the end as possible, swing underneath and brace himself with one hand against the ridge of the wall, his free hand could hold his lighter against the successive tubes of plastic.

He pulled out his cigarette lighter – his American lighter, he reflected with a certain chagrin – and pushed the tiny butane lever to its maximum. He tested it; the flame shot out and held steady; he lowered it slightly, for the light was too bright. He took a deep breath, firmed the muscles of his right leg and dropped to his left, the left hand making contact with the edge of the wall as he arced downward. He steadied himself and began breathing slowly, orienting his vision to the upside-down view. The blood raced to his head; he revolved his neck briefly to lessen the pressure, then snapped on the lighter, holding the flame against the first tube.

There was a crackling of electricity, then an expulsion of air as the tube turned black and melted. He reached the

452

second in the immediate series; this one exploded like a small, wet firecracker, the sound no more than a low-gauge air gun. The third grew into a thin outsized bubble. A *bubble*. Pressure! Weight! He pushed the flame into it and it burst; he held his breath, waiting for the sound of an alarm. It did not come; he had punctured the tube in time, before the heat and the expansion had reached the weight tolerance. It taught him something: hold the flame closer at first contact. He did so with the following two strands, each bursting on touch. There was a final tube.

Suddenly the flame receded, sinking back into its invisible source. He was out of fuel. He closed his eyes for a moment in frustration, and sheer anger. His leg ached furiously; the blood in his head made him dizzy. Then he thought of the obvious, annoyed with himself that he had not considered it immediately. The one remaining tube might well prevent a full malfunction-alarm; he was far better off leaving it intact. There were at least fifteen free inches on the surface of the concrete, more than enough to place a foot on and plunge over the wall to the other side.

He struggled back up to the limb and rested for a while, letting his head clear. Then slowly, carefully, he lowered his left foot to the wall, setting it securely on top of the burnt-out tubes. With equal caution he raised his leg over the limb, sliding down until the limb was in the small of his back. He took a deep breath, tensed his muscles and leaped forward, pressing his left foot into the stone, propelling himself over the wall. He fell to the ground, rolling to break his fall. He was inside the Verachten compound.

He got to his knees, listening for any sounds of an alert. There were none, so he rose to his feet and started threading his way through the dense woods towards what he presumed to be the central area of the property. The fact that he was half-walking, half-crawling in the right direction was confirmed in less than a minute. He could see the lights of the main house filtered through the trees, the beginning of a large expanse of lawn clearer with each step.

The glow of a cigarette! He dropped to the ground. Directly ahead, perhaps fifty feet away, stood a man at the edge of the lawn. Instantly, Taleniekov was aware of the forest breezes; he listened for the sounds of an animal.

Nothing. There were no dogs. Walther Verachten had confidence in his electronic gates and sophisticated alarm system; he needed only human patrols to make the darkness of his compound secure.

Vasili inched forward, his eyes on the guard ahead. The man was in uniform, visored hat and a heavy winter jacket pinched at the waist by a thick belt that held a holster gun. The guard checked his watch and stripped his cigarette, shaking the tobacco to the grass; he had been in the military, for it was a military custom. He walked several paces to his left, stretched, yawned, proceeded another twenty feet, then strolled aimlessly back towards where he had been standing. That short stretch of ground was his post, other guards were no doubt stationed every several hundred feet, ringing the main house like Caesar's Praetorian Guard. But these were neither Caesar's times nor Caesar's dangers; the duty was boring, relieved by openly smoked cigarettes and yawns and aimless wandering. The guard would not be a problem.

But getting across the stretch of lawn to the shadows of the drive on the right side of the house might well be. He would have to walk briefly in the glare of the floodlights that shot down from the roof.

A hatless man in a dark sweater and trousers doing such a thing would be ordered to stop, shot at if he did not. But a guard dressed in a visored cap and a heavy jacket with a holster at his side would not cause so much concern. And if reprimanded, that guard could always return to his post; it was important to bear that in mind.

Taleniekov crawled through the underbrush, elbows and knees working on the hard ground, pausing with every snap of a branch, blending what noise he made into the sounds of the night forest. He was within five feet, a spray of juniper between himself and the guard. The bored man reached into his jacket pocket and took out his pack of cigarettes. It was not the moment for the striking of a match; the juniper was too thin and a man bent his head in the cold to light a cigarette.

It was the moment to move. *Now.*

Vasili sprang up, his left hand clutching the guard's throat, his left heel dug into the earth to provide backward leverage. In one motion, he pulled the man off his feet, arcing him down into the juniper bush, crashing the guard's skull into the ground, his fingers clawing the windpipe, tightening around it. The shock of the assault combined with the blow to the head and the choking of air rendered the man unconscious. There was a time when Taleniekov would have finished the job, killing the guard because it was the most practical thing to do; that time was past. This was no soldier of the Matarese; there was no point in his death. He removed the man's jacket and visored hat, put them on quickly and buckled the holster around his waist. He dragged the guard farther into the woods, angled the head into the dirt, removed his own small weapon and smashed the handle down above the man's right ear. He would remain unconscious for hours; if the time was not sufficient, nothing was.

Vasili crept back to the edge of the lawn, stood up, breathed deeply and started across the grass. He had watched the guard walk – a slight casual swagger, the neck settled, the head angled back, and he imitated the memory. With each step he expected a loud rebuke or an order or an inquiry; if any were shouted he would shrug and return to the man's post. None came.

He reached the drive and the shadows. Fifty yards down

the pavement there was a light streaming out of an open door and the figure of a woman opening a garbage can, two paper bags at her feet. Vasili walked faster, his decision made. He approached the woman; she was in the white uniform of a maid.

'Excuse me, the captain ordered me to bring a message to Herr Verachten.'

'Who the hell are you?' asked the stocky woman.

'I'm new. Here, let me help you.' Taleniekov picked up the bags.

'You *are* new. It's Helga this, Helga that. What do they care? What's the message? I'll take it to him.'

'I wish I could give it to you. I've never met the old man and I don't want to, but that's what I was told to do.'

'They're all farts down there. *Kommandos!* A bunch of beer-soaked ruffians, I say. But you're better-looking than most of them.'

'Herr Verachten, please? I was told to hurry.'

'Everything's hurry this and hurry that. It's ten o'clock. The old fool's wife is in her rooms and he's in his chapel, of course.'

'Where . . . ?'

'Oh, all right. Come on in, I'll show you . . . You *are* better-looking, more polite, too. Stay that way.'

Helga led him through a corridor that ended at a door opening into a large entrance hall. Here the walls were covered with numerous Renaissance oil paintings, the colours vivid and dramatic under pinpoint spotlights. They extended up a wide circular staircase, the steps of Italian marble. Branching off the hall were several larger rooms, and the brief glimpses Taleniekov had of them confirmed Heinrich Kassel's description of a house filled with priceless antiques. But the glimpses were brief; the maid turned the corner beyond the staircase and they approached a thick mahogany door filled with ornate biblical carvings. She opened it and they descended steps carpeted in scarlet until they reached some kind of ante-room, the floor marble like the staircase in the great hall, the walls here covered with tapestries depicting early Christian scenes. An ancient church pew was on the left, the bas-relief examples of an art long forgotten; it was a place of meditation, for the tapestry facing it was of the Stations of the Cross. At the end of the small room was an arched door, beyond it obviously Walther Verachten's chapel.

'You can interrupt, if you want to,' said Helga without enthusiasm. 'The head *Kommando* will be blamed for it, not you. But I'd wait a few minutes; the priest will be finished with his claptrap by then.'

'A *priest*?' The word slipped out of Vasili's throat; the presence of such a man was the farthest thing in his mind. A *consigliere* of the Matarese with a priest?

'His fart-filled holiness, that's what I say.' Helga turned and started back. 'Do as you wish,' she said, shrugging. 'I don't tell anybody what to do.'

Taleniekov waited for the heavy mahogany door above to open and close. Then he walked quietly to the door of the chapel, his ear against the wood, trying to pick up meaning from the sing-song chant he could hear from within.

Russian. The language being chanted was Russian!

He was not sure why he was so startled. After all, the congregation inside consisted of the sole surviving son of Prince Andrei Voroshin. It was the service itself that was so astonishing.

Vasili placed his hand on the knob, turned it silently and opened the door several inches. Two things struck him instantly: the sweet-sour odour of incense and the shimmering flames of outsized candles, which caused him to blink his eyes, adjusting to the chiaroscuro effect of bright fires against the moving black shadows on the grey concrete walls. Recessed in those walls everywhere were

457

icons of the Russian Orthodox Church, those nearest the altar raising their saintly arms, reaching for the cross of gold in the centre.

In front of the cross was the priest, dressed in his cassock of white silk, trimmed with silver and gold. He had his eyes closed, his hands folded across his chest, and out of his barely moving mouth came words of a chant fashioned over a thousand years ago.

Then Taleniekov saw Walther Verachten – an old man with thinning white hair, strands of which fell over the back of a long, gaunt neck. He was prostrate on the three marble steps of the altar, at the feet of the high priest; his arms stretched out in supplication, his forehead pressed against the marble in absolute submission. The priest raised his voice, signifying the finish of the Orthodox *Kyrie Eleison*. The Litany of Forgiveness commenced; priestly statement followed by sinner's response, a choral exercise in self-indulgence and self-delusion. Vasili thought of the pain inflicted, demanded by the Matarese, and was revolted. He opened the door, stepped inside.

The priest opened his eyes, startled, his hands surging down from his chest in indignation. Verachten spun on the steps, his skeletal body trembling. Awkwardly, painfully, he struggled to his knees.

'How dare you interfere!' he shouted in German. 'Who gave you permission to come in here?'

'An historian from Petrograd, Voroshin,' said Taleniekov in Russian. 'That's as good an answer as any, isn't it?'

Verachten fell back on the steps, gripping the edge of the stone with his hands. Steadying himself, he brought them up to his face, covering his eyes as if they had been clawed or burned. The priest dropped to his knees, grabbing the old man by the shoulders, embracing him. The cleric turned to Vasili, his voice harsh.

'Who *are* you? What *right* have you?'

'Don't talk to me of rights, *priest*! You turn my stomach. Parasite!'

The priest held his place, cradling the white-haired Verachten. 'I was summoned years ago and I came. Like my predecessors in this house, I ask for nothing and I receive nothing.'

The old man lowered his hands from his face, struggling to compose himself, nodding his trembling head; the priest released him. 'So you've come at last,' he said. 'They always said you would. Vengeance is the Lord's, but then you people do not accept that, do you? You've taken God from the people and given so little in return. I have no quarrel with you on this earth. Take my life, Bolshevik. Carry out your orders, but let this good priest go. He's no Voroshin.'

'You *are*, however.'

'It is my burden.' Verachten's voice grew firmer. 'And our secret. I've borne both well, as God has given me the vision to do so.'

'One talks of rights, the other of God!' spat out Taleniekov. 'Hypocrites!' And then he shouted, '*Perro nostro circulo!*'

The old man blinked, no reaction in them whatsoever. 'I beg your pardon?'

'You heard me! *Perro nostro circulo!*'

'I hear you, but I don't understand you.'

'Corsica! Porto Vecchio! *Guillaume de Matarese!*'

Verachten looked up at the priest. 'Am I senile, my father? What's he talking about?'

'Explain yourself,' said the priest curtly. 'Who are you? What do you want? What's the meaning of these words?'

'*He* knows!'

'I know *what*?' Verachten leaned forward. 'We Voroshins have blood on our souls, I accept that. But I cannot accept what I don't know.'

459

'The *shepherd* boy,' said Taleniekov with quiet condemnation. 'With a voice crueller than the wind. Do you need more than that? The shepherd boy!'

'The Lord is my shepherd . . .'

'Stop it, you sanctimonious *liar*!'

The priest stood up. '*You* stop it, whoever you are! This good and decent man has lived his life in atonement for sins that were never *his*! Since a child he wanted to be a man of God, but it was not permitted. Instead, he has become a man *with* God. Yes, *with God*.'

'He is a Matarese!'

'I don't know what that is, but I know what *he* is. Millions dispensed every year to the starving, to the deprived. And he asks in return only our presence to see him through his devotions. It is all he has *ever* asked.'

'You're a *fool*! Those funds are Matarese funds! They buy death!'

'They buy *hope*. You're the liar now!'

The door of the chapel burst open. Vasili spun around. A man in a dark business suit stood inside the frame, legs apart, arms outstretched, a gun in his right hand, steadied by his left. 'Don't move!' The language was German.

Through the door came two women. One was tall and slender, dressed in an ankle-length velvet blue gown, a fur stole around her shoulders, her face very white, very angular, very beautiful. The woman at her side was short, in a cloth overcoat, her face puffy, her narrow eyes bewildered, yet filled with opportunity as she stared at Taleniekov. He had seen her only hours ago; a guard had said she would be accommodating should Heinrich Kassel need duplicates.

'That's the man,' said the receptionist who had sat behind the desk at the Records of Property.

'Thank you,' replied Odile Verachten. 'You may go now, the chauffeur will drive you back into the city.'

'Thank *you*, ma'am. Thank you *very* much.'

'You're most welcome. The chauffeur's in the hallway. Good night.'

'Good night, ma'am.' The woman left.

'*Odile!*' cried her father, struggling to his feet. 'This man came in . . .'

'I'm *sorry*, father,' interrupted the daughter. 'Putting off unpleasantries only compounds them; it's something you never understood. I'm sure this . . . man . . . said things you shouldn't have heard.'

With those few words, Odile Verachten nodded at her escort. He shifted the weapon to his left and fired. The explosion was deafening; the old man fell. The killer raised his gun and fired again; the priest spun, the top of his head blown away.

Silence.

'That was one of the most brutal acts I've ever witnessed,' said Taleniekov, the final decision of his life being made. He would kill . . . *somehow*.

'From Vasili Vasilievich Taleniekov, that's quite a statement,' said the Verachten woman, taking a step forward. 'Did you really believe that this ineffectual old man – this would-be priest – could be a part of *us*?'

'My error was in the man, not in the name. Voroshin is Matarese.'

'Correction, Verachten. We are not merely born, we are chosen.' Odile gestured at her dead father. 'He never was. When his brother was killed during the war, Ansel chose me!' She glared at him. 'We wondered what you had learned in Leningrad.'

'Would you really like to know?'

'A name,' answered the woman. 'A name from a chaotic period in recent history. Voroshin. But it hardly matters that you know. There is nothing you could say, no accusation you could make, that the Verachtens could not deny.'

'You don't *know* that.'

'We know enough, don't we?' said Odile, glancing at the man with the gun.

'We know enough,' repeated the killer. 'I missed you in Leningrad. But I did not miss the woman, Kronescha, did I? If you know what I mean.'

'*You!*' Taleniekov started forward; the man clicked the gun's hammer back with his thumb.

Vasili held his place, body and mind aching. He *would* kill; to do so control had to be found. And shock. *Lodzia my Lodzia! Help me.*

He stared at Odile Verachten, and spoke the words softly, slowly, giving each equal emphasis. '*Perro . . . nostro . . . circulo.*'

The smile faded from her lips, her white skin grew paler. 'Again from the past. From a primitive people who don't know what they're saying. We should have known you might learn it.'

'You believe that? You think they don't know what they're saying?'

'Yes.'

It was now, or it was not, thought Taleniekov. He took a deliberate step towards the woman. The killer's gun inched out, only feet away, aimed directly at his skull. 'Then why do they talk of the shepherd boy?'

He took another step; the killer breathed abruptly, audibly through his nostrils – prelude to fire – the trigger was being squeezed.

'Stop!' screamed the Verachten woman.

The explosion came as Vasili dropped to a crouch. Odile Verachten had thrust her arm out in a sudden command to prevent the gunshot, and in that instant, Taleniekov sprang, eye and mind and body on a single object. The gun, the *barrel* of the gun.

He reached it, his fingers gripping the warm steel, hand and wrist twisting counter-clockwise, pulling downward to inflict the greatest pain. He threw his right hand – fingers curled and rigid – into the man's stomach, tearing at the muscles, feeling the protrusion of the rib cage. He yanked up with all his strength; the killer screamed, and fell.

Vasili spun and lunged at the Verachten woman. In the brief moment of violence, she had hesitated; now she reacted with precision, her hand underneath her fur stole pulling out a gun. Taleniekov tore at that hand, that gun, throwing Odile to the chapel floor, his knee hammering into her chest. The handle of her own gun pressed across her throat.

'There'll be no mistake this time!' he said. 'No capsules in the mouth.'

'You'll be killed!' she whispered hoarsely.

'Probably,' agreed Vasili. 'But you'll go with me, and you don't want that. I was wrong. You're not one of your soldiers; the chosen don't take their own lives.'

'I'm the only one who can save yours.' She choked under the pressure of the steel, but went on. 'The *shepherd* . . . Where? *How?*'

'You want information. Good! So do I.' Taleniekov removed the gun from her throat, clamping his left hand where it had been, the fingers of his right hand entering her mouth, depressing the tongue, digging through the soft tissue downward. She coughed again, only mucus and spit rolling down her chin; there were no lethal pills in her mouth. He had been right; the chosen did not commit suicide. He then spread the stole and ran his hand over her body, pulling her off the floor, and reaching around her back, pushing her down again and plunging his hand between her legs, ankles to pelvis, feeling for the hard metal of a gun or a knife. There was nothing. 'Get up!' he ordered.

She rose only partially, her knees pulled up under her, holding her neck. '*You must tell* me!' she whispered. 'You know you can't get out. Don't be a fool, Russian! Save your life! What do you know of the shepherd?' Odile Verachten screamed.

'What am I offered to tell you?'

'What do you *want*?'

'What does the *Matarese* want!?'

The woman paused. 'Order.'

'Through *chaos*?'

'Yes! The shepherd? In the name of God, tell me!'

'I'll tell you when we're out of the compound.'

'No! *Now*.'

'Do you think I'd trade that off?' He pulled her to her feet. 'We're leaving now. Your friend here will wake up before too long; he'll know what to do, it's part of his job. If it wasn't I'd kill him. But you and I will be far away when he kills himself.'

'No!'

'Then you'll die,' said Taleniekov simply. 'I got in, I'll get out.'

'I gave orders! No one's to leave!'

'Who's leaving? A uniformed guard returns to his post. Those aren't Matarese out there. They're exactly what they're supposed to be: former *Kommandos* hired to protect a wealthy executive.' Vasili jammed the gun into her throat. 'Your choice? It doesn't matter to me.'

She flinched; he grabbed the back of her neck, pulling it into the barrel. She nodded. 'We will talk in my father's car,' she whispered. 'We're both civilized people. You have information I need, and I have a revelation for you. You have nowhere to turn but to us now. It could be far worse for you.'

He sat next to her in the front seat of Walther Verachten's limousine. He had taken off the uniform and was now no more than another stud in Odile Verachten's stable. She was behind the wheel, his arm around her shoulders, his automatic again jammed into her, out of sight. As the guard at the gatehouse nodded and turned to press the release button, he leaned into her; one uncalled for move, one gesture, and she was dead. She knew it; none came.

She sped through the open gate, turning the wheel to the left. He grabbed it, his foot reaching across hers to the brake, and spun the wheel to the right. The car skidded into a half spin; he steadied it and slammed his foot over hers on the accelerator.

'What are you *doing*?' she cried.

'Avoiding any prearranged rendezvous.'

It was in her eyes; another car had been waiting on the road to Essen. For the third time, Odile Verachten was genuinely frightened.

They sped down the country road; several hundred yards ahead he could see a fork clearly in the headlights. He waited; instinctively she bore to the right. The fork was reached, the turn began; he moved his hand swiftly to the rim of the wheel and pushed it up, sending them into the left road.

'You'll *kill* us!' screamed the Verachten woman.

'Then both of us will go,' said Taleniekov. The surrounding woods diminished; there were open spaces ahead. 'That field on the right. Pull over.'

'*What?*'

He raised the gun and put it against her temple. 'Stop the car,' he repeated.

They got out. Vasili took the keys from the ignition and put them in his pocket. He pushed her forward, into the grass, and they walked towards the middle of the field. In the distance was a farmhouse, beyond it a barn. There were no lights; the farmers of Stadtwald were asleep. But the winter moon was brighter now than it was in the Gildenplatz.

'What are you going to do?' asked Odile.

'Find out if you have the courage you demand of your soldiers.'

'Taleniekov, *listen* to me! No matter what you do to me, you won't change anything. We're too far along. The world needs us too desperately!'

'This world needs killers?'

'To *save* it from killers! You talk of the shepherd. *He* knows. Can you *doubt* it? Join us. Come with us.'

'Perhaps I will. But I have to know where you're going.'

'Do we trade?'

'Again, perhaps.'

'Where did you hear of the shepherd?'

Vasili shook his head. 'Sorry, you first. Who are the Matarese? *What* are they? What are they doing?'

'Your first answer,' said Odile, parting her stole, her hands on the neckline of her gown. She ripped it downward, the white buttons breaking from the threads, exposing her breasts. 'It's one we know you've found,' she added.

In the moonlight Taleniekov saw it. Larger than he had seen before, a jagged circle that was part of the breast, part of the body. The mark of the Matarese. 'The grave in the hills of Corsica,' he said quietly. '*Perro nostro circulo.*'

'It can be *yours*,' said Odile, reaching out to him. 'How many lovers have lain across these breasts and admired my very distinctive birthmark. You are the *best*, Taleniekov. *Join* the best! Let me bring you over!'

'A little while ago, you said I had no choice. That you would reveal something to me, force me to turn to you. What is it?'

Odile pulled the top of her gown together. 'The American is dead. You are alone.'

'*What?*'

'Scofield was killed.'

'*Where?*'

'In Washington . . .'

The sound of a powerful engine interrupted her words.

Headlights pierced the darkness of the road that wound out of the woods from the south; a car came into view. Then suddenly, as if suspended in a black void, it stopped on the shoulder behind the limousine. Before the headlights could be extinguished, three men could be seen leaping out, the driver following. All were armed; two carried rifles. All were predators.

'They've found me!' cried Odile Verachten. 'Your answer, Taleniekov! You really have no choice, you see that, don't you? Give me the gun. An order from me can change your life. Without it, you're dead.'

Stunned, Vasili looked behind him; the fields stretched into pastures, the pastures into darkness. Escape was not a problem – perhaps not even the right decision. Scofield *dead*? In *Washington*? He had been on his way to England; what had sent him prematurely to Washington? But Odile Verachten was not lying; he would bank his life on it! She had spoken the truth as she knew the truth – just as her offer was made in truth. The Matarese would make good use of one Vasili Taleniekov.

Was it the *way*? The *only* way?

'Your *answer*!' Odile stood motionless, her hand outstretched.

'Before I give it, tell me. When was Scofield killed? How?'

'He was shot two weeks ago in a place called Rock Creek Park.'

A *lie*. A *calculated* lie! She had been lied to! Someone *within* the Matarese was trying to *betray* the Matarese. They had an ally deep within the council! He had to reach that man. Vasili spun the automatic in his hand, offering it to Odile. 'There's nowhere else to turn. I'm with you. Give your order.'

She turned from him and shouted. 'You men! Put up your guns! Hold your fire!'

A single flashlight beam shot out and Taleniekov saw

what she did not see – and knew instantly what she did not know. The light was held by one man to free the other three; and although he was in the spill, the beam was not directed at him. It was directed at *her*. He dived to his left into the grass. A fusillade of bullets erupted from the rifles across the field.

Another order had been given. Odile Verachten screamed. She was blown off her feet, her body caved forward, then arched backward in mid-air under the force of the shells.

Other gunshots followed, digging up the earth to the right of Taleniekov as he lurched, scrambling through the grass away from the target ground. The shouts grew louder as the men attacked, converging on the site on which only seconds ago a living member of the Matarese council had stood – issuing an order that was not hers to give.

Vasili reached the relative safety of the woods. He rose and started running into the darkness, knowing that soon he would stop, and turn, and kill a man on his way back to the limousine. In other darkness.

But now he kept running.

The ageing musician sat in the last row of the plane, a shabby violin case between his knees. Absently, he thanked the stewardess for the cup of hot tea; his thoughts consumed him.

He would be in Paris in an hour, meet with the Corsican girl, and set up direct communications with Scofield. It was imperative they work in concert now; things were happening too rapidly. He had to join Beowulf Agate in England.

Two of the names on the guest list of Guillaume de Matarese seventy years ago were accounted for.

Scozzi. Dead.

Voroshin-Verachten. Dead.

Sacrificed.

The direct descendants were expendable, which meant

they were not the true inheritors of the Corsican *padrone*. They had been merely messengers, bearing gifts for others far more powerful, far more capable of spreading the Corsican fever.

This world needs killers?

To save it from killers! Odile Verachten.

Enigma.

David Waverly, Foreign Secretary, Great Britain.

Joshua Appleton IV, Senator, United States Congress.

Were they, too, expendable messengers? Or were they something else? Did each carry the mark of the jagged blue circle on his chest? Had Scozzi? And if either did, or Scozzi had, was that unnatural blemish the mark of mystical distinction Odile Verachten had thought it was, or was it, too, something else? A symbol of expendability, perhaps. For it occurred to Vasili that wherever that mark appeared, death was a partner.

Scofield was searching in England now. The same Beowulf Agate that someone within the Matarese had reported killed in Rock Creek Park. Who was that someone, and why had the false report gone out? It was as though that person – or persons – wanted Scofield spared, beyond reach of the Matarese killers. But why?

You talk of the shepherd. He knows! Can you doubt it?

The shepherd. A shepherd boy.

Enigma.

Taleniekov put the tea down on the tray in front of him, his elbow jarred by his seat companion. The businessman from Essen had fallen asleep, his arm protruding over the divider. Vasili was about to remove it when his eyes fell on the folded newspaper spread out on the German's lap.

The photograph stared up at him and he stopped breathing, sharp bolts of pain returning to his chest – as they had in Leningrad.

The smiling, gentle face was that of Heinrich Kassel.

The bold print above the photograph screamed the information.

Taleniekov reached over and picked up the paper, the pain accelerating as he read:

> *Heinrich Kassel, one of Essen's most prominent attorneys, was found murdered in his car outside his residence last evening. The authorities have called the killing bizarre and brutal. Kassel was found garrotted, with multiple head injuries and lacerations of the face and body. An odd aspect of the killing was the tearing of the victim's upper clothing, exposing the chest area on which was painted a circle of dark blue. The paint was still wet when the body was discovered shortly past midnight . . .*

Perro nostro circulo.

Vasili closed his eyes. He had pronounced Kassel's sentence of death with the name *Voroshin*.

It had been carried out.

Book III

Book II

28

'*Scofield?*' The grey-faced man was astonished, the name uttered in shock.

Bray broke into a run through the crowds in the London Underground, towards the Charing Cross exit. It had happened; it was bound to happen sooner or later. No brim of a hat could conceal a face if trained eyes saw that face, and no unusual clothing dissuaded the professional once the face had been marked.

He had just been marked; the man making the identification – and without question now racing to a phone – was a veteran agent for the Central Intelligence Agency stationed at the American embassy on Grosvenor Square. Scofield knew him slightly; one or two lunches at The Guinea; two or three conferences, inevitably held prior to Consular Operations invading areas the Company considered possessively sacrosanct. Nothing close, only cold; the man was a fighter for CIA prerogatives and Beowulf Agate had transgressed too frequently.

Goddamn it! Within minutes the US network in London would be put on alert, within hours every available man, woman and paid informer would spread throughout the city looking for him. It was conceivable that even the British would be called in, but it was not likely. Those in Washington who wanted Brandon Alan Scofield wanted him dead, not questioned, and this was not the English style. No, the British would be avoided.

Bray counted on it. There was a man he had helped several years ago, in circumstances that had little to do with their allied professions, that had made it possible for the Englishman to remain in British Intelligence. Not only remain but advance to a position of considerable responsibility.

Roger Symonds had dropped £2,000 of MI6 funds at the tables of Les Ambassadeurs. Bray had replaced the sum from one of his accounts. He had never asked for repayment, but he would ask now.

The money had never been repaid – not by default, only because Scofield had not crossed Symonds' path. In their work, one did not leave a forwarding address.

A form of repayment would be asked for now. That it would be offered, Scofield did not question, but whether it could be delivered was something else again. Yet it would be neither if Roger Symonds learned that he was on Washington's terminal list. Debts aside, the Englishman took his work seriously; there'd be no Fuchs or Philby on his conscience. Much less a former killer from Consular Operations conceivably turned paid assassin.

Bray wanted Symonds to arrange a private, isolated meeting between himself and England's Foreign Secretary, David Waverly. The meeting, however, had to be negotiated without Scofield's name being used – the British agent would balk at that, refuse entirely if he learned of Washington's hunt for him. Scofield knew he had to come up with a credible motive; he had not thought of one yet.

He ran out of Charing Cross station and walked into the flow of pedestrians heading across the Strand. At Trafalgar Square, he crossed the wide intersection, joining the early-evening crowds. He looked at his watch. It was 6.15, 7.15 in Paris. In thirty minutes he was to start calling Toni at her flat in the rue du Bac; there was a telephone centre a few blocks away at Haymarket. He would make his way there by a roundabout route, stopping at one of the garishly lighted shops to buy a new hat and jacket. The CIA man would give a precise description of his clothing; changing it was imperative.

He was wearing the same windbreaker he had worn in

474

Corsica, the same visored fishing cap. He left them in a curtained dressing room at a branch of Dunn's, buying a dark tweed jacket and an Irish walking hat, the soft brim falling around his head, a circle of narrow fabric throwing the shadows downward across his face. He walked again, more rapidly now, and cut through the winding back streets into Haymarket.

He chose a telephone box, went inside and closed the glass door, wishing it were solid. It was ten minutes to seven. Antonia would be waiting by the phone. They always allowed a variable of half an hour for cross-Channel telephone traffic; if he did not reach her by 8.15, Paris time, she could expect his next call between 11.45 and 12.15. The one condition Toni had insisted upon was for them to talk to each other every day. Bray had not objected; he had come out of the earth and found something very precious to him, something he had thought he had lost permanently. He could love again; the excitement of anticipation had come back. The sound of a voice stirred him, the touch of a hand was meaningful. He had found Antonia Gravet at the most inopportune time of his life, yet finding her gave a significance to his life he had not felt for a number of years. He wanted to live and grow old with her, it was as simple as that. And remarkable. He had never thought about growing old before; it was time he did.

If the Matarese allowed it.

The *Matarese*. An international power without a profile, its leaders faceless men trying to achieve *what*?

Chaos? *Why?*

Chaos. Scofield was suddenly struck by the root meaning of the word. The state of formless matter, of clashing bodies in space, before the creation. Before order was imposed on the universe.

He dialled the code. Antonia answered quickly.

'Vasili's here,' she said. 'This afternoon. He's hurt.'

475

'How badly?'

'His neck. He should have stitches.'

There was a brief hollow sound as the phone was being passed. Or taken.

'He should have sleep,' said Taleniekov in English. 'But I have things to tell you first, several warnings.'

'What about Voroshin?'

'He kept the V for practical if foolish purposes. He became Essen's Verachten. Ansel Verachten.'

'The *Verachten* Works?'

'Yes.'

'Good Christ!'

'His son believed that.'

'What?'

'It's irrelevant; there's too much to tell you. His grand-daughter was the chosen one. She's dead, killed on Matarese orders.'

'As Scozzi was,' interrupted Scofield.

'Exactly,' agreed the Soviet. 'They were vessels; they carried the plans but were commandeered by others. It will be interesting to see what happens to the Verachten companies. They have no leadership now. We must watch and note who assumes control.'

'We've reached the same conclusion then,' said Bray. 'The Matarese work through large corporations.'

'It would appear so, but to what end I haven't the faintest idea. It's extremely contradictory.'

'Chaos . . .' Scofield spoke the word softly.

'I beg your pardon.'

'Nothing. You said you wanted to warn me.'

'Yes. They've studied our files under microscopes. It seems they know every drone we've ever used, every past friend, every contact, every . . . teacher and lover. Be careful.'

'They can't know what was never entered; they can't cover everyone.'

'Don't bank on that. You received my cable about the body marks?'

'It's crazy! Squads of killers identifying themselves? I'm not sure I believe it.'

'Believe it,' said Taleniekov firmly. 'But there's something I wasn't able to explain. They're suicidal; they won't be taken. Which leads me to believe they're not as extensive in numbers as the leaders would like us to think. They're some kind of élite soldiers sent out to the troubled areas, not to be confused with hired guns employed by second and third parties.'

Bray paused, remembering. 'You know what you're describing, don't you?'

'All too well,' replied the Russian. 'Hasan ibn as-Sabbāh. The *fida'is*.'

'Cadres of assassins . . . till death us do part from our pleasures. How is it modernized?'

'I have a theory; it may be worthless. We'll discuss it when I see you.'

'When will that be?'

'Tomorrow night – early the next morning probably. I can hire a pilot and a plane in the Cap Gris district; I've done it before. There's a private airfield between Hythe and Ashford. I should be in London by one o'clock or three at the latest. I know where you're staying, the girl told me.'

'Taleniekov.'

'Yes?'

'Her name's Antonia.'

'I know that.'

'Let me speak to her.'

'Of course. Here she is.'

He found the name in the London directory: *R. Symonds, Bradbry Lane, Chelsea.* He memorized the number and placed the first call at 7.30 from a booth in Piccadilly

477

Circus. The woman who answered told him politely that Mr Symonds was on his way home from the office.

'He should be here any mo' now. Shall I tell him who called?'

'The name wouldn't mean anything. I'll call in a while, thank you.'

'He's got a marvellous memory. You're sure you don't care to leave your name?'

'I'm sure, thank you.'

'He's coming directly from the office.'

'Yes, I understand that.'

Scofield hung up, disturbed. He left the booth and walked down Piccadilly past Fortnum and Mason's to St James's Street and beyond. There was another booth at the entrance to Green Park; slightly more than ten minutes had passed. He wanted to hear the woman's voice again.

'Has your husband arrived?' he asked.

'He *just* called from the local, the Brace and Bit on Old Church Street. He's quite irritable. Must have had a *dreadful* day.'

Bray hung up. He knew the number of MI6-London; it was one a member of the fraternity kept in mind. He dialled.

'Mr Symonds, please. Priority.'

'Right away, sir.'

Roger Symonds was not on his way home, nor was he in a pub called the Brace and Bit. Was he playing a domestic game?

'Symonds here,' said the familiar English voice in the familiar casual tone Scofield remembered.

'Your wife just told me you were on your way home, but got detained at the Brace and Bit. Is that the best you could come up with?'

'I what? . . . Who's this?'

'An old friend.'

478

'Not much of a one, I'm afraid. I'm not married. My friends know that.'

Bray paused, then spoke urgently. 'Quickly. Give me a sterile number, or one on a scrambler. *Quickly!*'

'Who is this?'

'Two thousand pounds.'

It took Symonds less than a second to understand and adjust; he reeled off a number, repeated it once, then added. 'The cellars. Twenty-five storeys high.'

There was a click; the line went dead. Twenty-five storeys high to the cellars meant halving the figure, minus one. He was to call the number in exactly twelve minutes – within the one-minute span – when scrambling and jamming devices would be activated. He left the booth to find another as far away as time and rapid walking permitted. Telephone intercepts were potentially two-way traces; the booth at Green Park could be under observation in a matter of minutes.

He went up Old Bond Street into New until he reached Oxford Street, where he turned right and began running. At Wardour Street he slowed down, turned right again, and melted into the crowds of Soho.

Elapsed time: nine and a half minutes.

There was a booth at the corner of Shaftesbury Avenue; inside a callow young man wearing an electric-blue suit was screaming into the phone. Scofield waited by the door, looking at his watch.

Eleven minutes.

He could not take the chance. He took out a five-pound note and tapped on the glass. The young man turned; he saw the bill and held up his middle finger in a gesture that was not co-operative.

Bray opened the door, put his left hand on the electric-blue shoulder, tightened his grip, and as the offensive young man began screeching, pulled him out of the booth, tripping him with his left foot, dropping the fiver on top of him. It floated; the youth grabbed it and ran.

Eleven minutes, thirty seconds.

Scofield took several deep breaths, trying to slow the rapid pounding of his chest. Twelve minutes. He dialled.

'Don't go home,' said Bray the instant Symonds was on the line.

'Don't *you* stay in London!' was the reply. 'Grosvenor Square has an alert out for you.'

'You *know*? Washington called you in?'

'Hardly. They won't say a word about you. You're terminated personnel, an off-limits subject. We probed several weeks ago when we first got word.'

'Word from *where*?'

'Our sources in the Soviet. In KGB. They're after you, too, but then they always have been.'

'What did Washington say when you probed?'

'Played it down. Failure to report whereabouts, something like that. They're too embarrassed to put an official stamp on the nonsense. Are you authoring something? There's a lot of that over there . . .'

'How did you know about the alert?' interrupted Scofield. 'The one out for me now?'

'Oh, come now, we do keep tabs, you know. A number of those Grosvenor Square has on its payroll quite rightly have first loyalties to us.'

Bray paused briefly, bewildered. 'Roger, why are you telling me this? I can't believe two thousand pounds would make you do it.'

'That misappropriated sum has been sitting in a Chelsea bank drawing interest for you since the morning after you bailed me out.'

'Then why?'

Symonds cleared his throat, a proper Englishman facing the necessity of showing emotion. 'I have no idea what your quarrel is over there and I'm not sure I care to know –

you have such puritanical outbursts – but I was appalled to learn that our prime source in Washington confirmed that the State Department subscribes to the Soviet ploy. As I said, it's not only nonsense, I find it patently offensive.'

'A ploy? What ploy?'

'That you joined forces with the Serpent.'

'The "Serpent"?'

'It's what we call Vasili Taleniekov, a name I'm sure you recall. To repeat, I don't know what your trouble is, but I *do* know a goddamned lie, a macabre lie at that, when I hear one.' Symonds cleared his throat again. 'Some of us remember East Berlin. And I was here when you came back from Prague. How dare they . . . after what you've *done*? Churlish bastards!'

Scofield took a long, deep breath. 'Roger, don't go home.'

'Yes, you said that before.' Symonds was relieved they were back to practicality; it was in his voice. 'You say someone's there, claiming to be my wife?'

'Probably not inside, but nearby, with a clear view. They've tapped into your phone and the equipment's good. No echoes, no static.'

'*My* phone? They're trailing me? In *London*?'

'They're covering you; they're after me. They knew we were friends and thought I might try to reach you.'

'Goddamned *cheek*! That embassy will get a bolt that'll char the gold feathers off that fucking ridiculous eagle! They go too *far*!'

'It's not the Americans.'

'*Not* the? . . . Bray, what in God's name are you talking about?'

'That's just it. We have to talk. But it's got to be a very complicated route. Two networks are looking for me, and one of them has you under glass. They're good.'

'We'll see about that,' snapped Symonds, annoyed, challenged and curious. 'I daresay several vehicles, one or two decoys, and a healthy bit of official lying can do the trick. Where are you?'

'Soho. Wardour and Shaftesbury.'

'Good. Head over to Tottenham Court Road. In about twenty minutes, a grey Mini – rear licence plate askew – will come in from Oxford Street and stall at the kerb. The driver's black, a West Indian chap; he's your contact. Get in with him; the engine will make a remarkable recovery.'

'Thank you, Roger.'

'Not at all. But don't expect me to have the two thousand quid. The banks are closed, you know.'

Scofield got in the front seat of the Mini, the black driver looking at him closely, courteously, his right hand out of sight. The man had obviously been given a photograph to study. Bray removed the Irish hat.

'Thank you,' said the driver, his hand moving swiftly to his jacket pocket, then to the wheel. The engine caught instantly and they sped up Tottenham Court Road. 'My name is Israel. You are Brandon Scofield – obviously. Good to make your acquaintance.'

'Israel?' he asked.

'That's it, man,' replied the driver, smiling, lending a pronounced West Indian lilt to his voice. 'I don't think my parents had in mind the cohesiveness of minorities when they gave it to me, but they were avid readers of the Bible. Israel Isles.'

'It's a nice name.'

'My wife thinks they blew it, as you Americans say. She keeps telling me that if they had only used Ishmael instead, all my introductions would be memorable.'

' "My name is Ishmael" . . .' Bray laughed. 'It's close enough.'

'This banter covers a slight nervousness on my part, if I may say so,' said Isles.

'Why?'

'We studied a number of your accomplishments in training; it wasn't that long ago. I'm chauffeuring a man we'd all like to emulate.'

The trace of laughter vanished from Scofield's face. 'That's very flattering. I'm sure you will if you want to.' *And when you get to be my age, I hope you think it's been worth it.*

They drove south out of London on the Brighton road, branching west at Redhill and heading into the countryside. Israel Isles was sufficiently perceptive to curtail the banter. He apparently understood that he was driving either a very preoccupied or exhausted American. Bray was grateful for the silence; he had to reach a difficult decision. The risks were enormous no matter what he decided.

Yet part of that decision had already been forced upon him, which meant he had to tell Symonds that Washington wasn't the immediate issue. He could not permit Roger to vent his misplaced outrage on the American embassy; it was not the embassy that had placed the intercept on his telephone. It was the Matarese.

Yet to tell the whole truth meant involving Symonds, who would not remain silent. He would go to others and those others to their superiors. It was not the time to speak of conspiracy so massive and contradictory that it would be branded no more than the product of two terminated intelligence officers – both wanted for treason in their respective countries. The time *would* come, but it was not now. For the truth of the matter was that they did not possess a shred of hard evidence. Everything they knew to be true was so easily denied by powerful, faceless men of undoubted congeniality as the paranoid ramblings of lunatics and traitors. On the surface, the logic was with their enemies. Why would the leaders of mammoth corporations, conglomerates that depended on stability, finance chaos?

Chaos. Formless matter, clashing bodies in space . . .

'Another few minutes, we'll reach our first destination,' said Israel Isles.

'First destination?'

'Yes, our trip's in two stages. We change vehicles up ahead; this one is driven back to London – the driver black, his passenger white – and we proceed in another, quite different car. The next leg is less than a quarter of an hour. Mr Symonds may be a little late, however. He had to make four changes of vehicles in city garages.'

'I see,' said Scofield, relieved. The West Indian had just provided Bray with his answer. As the rendezvous with Symonds was in stages, so, too, would be the explanations *to* Symonds. He would tell him part of the truth, but nothing that would implicate the Foreign Secretary, David Waverly. However, Waverly had to be given information on a most confidential basis; decisions of foreign policy could be affected by the news of massive shifts of capital being manipulated secretly. *This* was the information Scofield had come across and was tracing: massive shifts of capital. And although all clandestine economic manoeuvres were subjects for intelligence scrutiny, these went beyond MI5 and 6, just as they superseded the interests of the FBI and the CIA.

In Washington, there were those who wanted to prevent him from disclosing that which he knew, but could not prove. The surest way of doing so was to discredit him, kill him, if it came to that. Symonds would understand. Men killed facilely for money; no one knew it better than intelligence officers. So often it was the spine of their . . . accomplishments.

Isles slowed the Mini down and pulled to the side of the road. He made a U-turn, pointing the car in the direction from which they came.

Within thirty seconds another, larger automobile approached; it had picked them up along the way and had followed at a discreet distance. Bray knew what was expected; he got out, as did the West Indian. The Bentley came to a stop. A white driver opened the rear door for a black companion. No one spoke as the exchange was made, both cars now driven by blacks.

'May I ask you a question?' said Israel Isles hesitantly.

'Sure.'

'I've gone through all the training, but I've never had to kill a man. I worry about that sometimes. What's it like?'

Scofield looked out the window at the shadows rushing past. *It's like walking through a door into a place you've never been before. I hope you do not have to go there, for it's filled with a thousand eyes – a few angry, more frightened, most pleading . . . all wondering. Why me now?* 'There's not very much of that,' said Bray. 'You never take a life unless it's absolutely necessary, knowing that if you have to, you're saving a lot more. That's the justification, the only one there should ever be. You put it out of your mind, lock it away behind a door somewhere in your head.'

'Yes, I think I understand. The justification is in the necessity. One has to accept that, doesn't one?'

'That's right. Necessity.' *Until you grow older and the door opens more and more frequently. Finally it will not close and you stand there, staring inside.*

They drove into the deserted parking area of a picnic site in the Guildford countryside. Beyond the post-and-rail fence were swings and slides and seesaws, all silhouetted in the bright moonlight.

A car was waiting for them, but Roger Symonds was not in it; he was expected momentarily. Two men had arrived early to make certain there was no one else in the picnic ground, no intercepts placed on phones considered sterile.

'Hello, Brandon,' said a short, stocky man in a bulky overcoat, extending his hand.

'Hi, how are you?' Scofield did not recall the agent's name, but remembered his face; he was one of the best men fielded by MI6. *Cons Op* had called him in – with British permission – when the Moscow–Paris–Cuba espionage ring was operating inside the Chamber of Deputies. Bray was impressed at seeing him now. Symonds was using a first team.

'It's been eight or ten years, hasn't it?'

'At least,' agreed Scofield. 'How've you been?'

'Still here. I'll be pensioned off before too long. Looking forward to that.'

'Enjoy it.'

The Englishman hesitated, then spoke with embarrassment. 'Never did see you after that awful business in East Berlin. Not that we were such friends, but you know what I mean. Delayed condolences, old chap. Rotten thing. Fucking animals, I say.'

'Thanks. It was a long time ago.'

'Never that long,' said the MI6 man. 'It was my source in Moscow that brought us that garbage about you and the Serpent. Beowulf and the Serpent! My God, how could those pricks in D.C. swallow such rot?'

'It's complicated.'

He saw the headlights first, then heard the engine. A London taxi drove into the picnic ground. The driver, however, was no London cabbie; it was Roger Symonds.

The middle-aged MI6 officer climbed out and for a second or two blinked and stretched, as if to get his bearings. Roger had not changed during the years since he and Bray had known each other. The Englishman was still given to an excess pound or two, and his thatch of rumpled brown hair was still unmanageable. There was an air of disorientation about the veteran operative that masked a first-rate analytical mind. He was not an easy man to fool – with part of the truth or none of it.

'Bray, how *are* you?' said Symonds, hand held out. 'For God's sake, don't answer that, we'll get to it. Let me tell you, those are *not* easy cars to drive. I feel as though I've just limped through the worst rugger match in Liverpool. I'll be far more generous with cabbies in the future.' Roger looked around, nodding to his men, then spotting the opening in the fence which led into the playground. 'Let's take a stroll. If you're a good lad, I may even give you a push or two in one of the swings.'

The Englishman listened in silence as Bray, sitting still on a swing, told his story of the massive shifting of funds. When Scofield had finished, Symonds walked behind him and shoved him between the shoulder blades.

'There's the push I promised you, although you don't deserve it. You haven't been a good lad.'

'Why not?'

'You're not telling me what you should.'

'I see. You don't understand why I'm asking you not to use my name with Waverly?'

'Oh, no, that's perfectly all right. He has to deal with Washington every day. Granting an *unofficial* meeting with a retired American intelligence officer is not something he'd care to have on the Foreign Office's record. I mean, we don't actually defect to one another, you know. I'll take that responsibility, if it's to be taken.'

'Then what's bothering you?'

'The people after you. Not Grosvenor Square, of course, but the others. You haven't been candid; you said they were good, but you didn't tell me *how* good. Or the depth of their resources.'

'What do you mean?'

'We pulled out your dossier and selected three names known to you, calling each, telling each that the man on the line was an intermediary from you, instructing each to go to a specific location. All three messages were intercepted; those called were followed.'

'Why does that surprise you? I told you as much.'

'What surprises me is that one of those names was known only to us. Not MI5, not Secret Service, not even the Admiralty. Only us.'

'Who was it?'

'Grimes.'

'Never heard of him,' said Bray.

'You only met him once. In Prague. Under the name of Brazuk.'

'KGB,' said Scofield, astonished. 'He defected in 'seventy-two. I gave him to you. He wouldn't have anything to do with us and there was no point in wasting him.'

'But only you knew that. You said nothing to your people and, frankly, we at Six took credit for the purchase.'

'You've got a leak, then.'

'Quite impossible,' replied Symonds. 'At least regarding the present circumstances as you've described them to me.'

'Why?'

'You say you ran across this global financial juggling act only a short while ago. Let's be generous and say several months, would you agree?'

'Yes.'

'And since then, those who want to silence you have been active against you, also correct?' Bray nodded. The MI6 man leaned forward, his hand on the chain above Scofield's head. 'From the day I took office two and a half years ago, Beowulf Agate's file has been in my private vault. It is removed only on dual signatures, one of which must be mine. It has not been removed, and it is the only file in England that contains any connection between you and the Grimes-Brazuk defection.'

'What are you trying to say?'

'There's only one other place where that information might be found.'

'Spell it out.'

'Moscow.' Symonds drew out the word softly.

Bray shook his head. 'That assumes Moscow knows Grimes' identity.'

'Entirely possible. Like a few you've purchased, Brazuk was a bust. We don't really want him, but we can't give him back. He's a chronic alcoholic, has been for years. His job at KGB was ornamental, a debt paid to a once-brave soldier. We suspect he blew his cover quite a while ago. Nobody cared, until you came along. Who are these people after you?'

'It seems I didn't do you any favours when I handed over Brazuk,' said Scofield, avoiding the MI6 man's eyes.

'You didn't know that and neither did we. Who are these people, Bray?'

'Men who have contacts in Moscow. Obviously. Just as we do.'

'Then I must ask you a question,' continued Symonds. 'One that would have been inconceivable several hours ago. Is it true what Washington thinks? Are you working with the Serpent?'

Scofield looked up at the Englishman. 'Yes.'

Calmly Symonds released the chain and rose to his full height. 'I think I could kill you for that,' he said. 'For God's sake, *why*?'

'If it's a question of either your killing me or my telling you, I don't have a choice, do I?'

'There's a middle ground. I take you in and turn you over to Grosvenor Square.'

'Don't do it, Roger. And don't ask me to tell you anything now. Later, yes. Not now.'

'Why should I agree?'

'Because you know me; I can't think of any other reason.'

Symonds turned away. Neither spoke for several moments. Finally, the Englishman turned again, facing Bray. 'Such a simple phrase. "You know me." Do I?'

'I wouldn't have reached you if I didn't think you did. I don't ask strangers to risk their lives for me. I meant what I said before. Don't go home. You're marked . . . just as I'm marked. If you covered yourself, you'll be all right. If they find out you met with me, you're dead.'

'I am at this moment logged in at an emergency meeting at the Admiralty. Phone calls were placed to my office and my flat demanding my presence.'

'Good. I expected as much.'

'Goddamn you, Scofield! It was always your gift. You pull a man in until he can't stand it. Yes, I *do* know you, and I'll do as you ask – for a little while. But not because of your melodramatics; they don't impress me. Something else does, however. I said I could kill you for working with Taleniekov. I think I could, but I suspect you kill yourself a little every time you look at him. That's reason enough for me.'

29

Bray walked down the steps of the private hotel into the morning sunlight and the crowds of shoppers in Knightsbridge. It was an area of London compatible with staying out of sight; from nine A.M. on the streets were jammed with traffic, the pavements teeming with customers anxious to part with pounds, marks, yen, dollars and riyals. It was a concrete version of an ancient bazaar, anchored by the imposing monument that was Harrods.

Scofield stopped at a news-stand, shifted his attaché case to his left hand, picked up *The Times* and went in to a small restaurant. He slipped into a chair, satisfied that it provided a clear view of the entrance, more satisfied still that the pay telephone on the wall was only feet away. It was a quarter to ten; he was to call Roger Symonds at precisely 10.15 on the sterile number that could not be tapped.

He ordered breakfast from the laconic Cockney waitress and unfolded the newspaper. He found what he was looking for in a single column on the upper left section of the front page.

Verachten Heiress Dead

Essen. Odile Verachten, daughter of Walther, granddaughter of Ansel Verachten, founder of the Verachten Works, was found dead in her Werden Strasse penthouse last evening, an apparent victim of a massive coronary stroke according to a family physician. For nearly a decade, Fräulein Verachten had assumed the managerial reins of the diversified companies under the guidance of her father, who has receded from active participation

491

during the past years. Both parents were in seclusion at their estate in Stadtwald, and were not available for comment. A private family burial will take place within the residential grounds. A corporate statement is expected shortly, but none from Walther Verachten who is reported to be seriously ill.

Odile Verachten was a dramatically attractive addition to the boardrooms of this city of coldly efficient executives. She was mercurial, and when younger, given to displays of exhibitionism often at odds with the behaviour of Essen's business leaders. But no one doubted her ability to run the vast Verachten Works . . .

Scofield's eyes quickly scanned the biographical hyperbole that was an obituary editor's way of describing a spoiled, headstrong bitch who undoubtedly slept around with the frequency if not the delicacy of a Soho whore.

There was a follow-up story directly beneath. Bray began reading and knew instantly, instinctively, that another fragment of the elusive truth was being revealed.

Verachten Death Concerns Trans-Comm

New York, N. Y. In a move that took Wall Street by surprise, it was learned today that a team of management consultants from Trans-Communications, Incorporated, was flying to Essen, Germany for conferences with executives of the Verachten Works. The untimely death of Fräulein Odile Verachten, 47, and the virtual seclusion of her father, Walther, aged 76, has left the Verachten companies without an authoritative voice at the top. What astonished supposedly well-informed sources here was the extent of Trans-Comm's holdings in Verachten. In the legal labyrinths of Essen, American investments are often beyond scrutiny, but rarely when those holdings exceed twenty per cent. Rumours persist that Trans-Comm's are in excess of fifty per cent, although denials labelling such figures as ridiculous have been issued by the Boston headquarters of the conglomerate . . .

The words sprang up from the page at Scofield, *the Boston headquarters* . . .

Were *two* fragments of that elusive truth being revealed? Joshua Appleton IV was the senator from Massachusetts, the Appleton family the most powerful political entity in the state. They were the Episcopal Kennedys, far more restrained in self-evocation, but every bit as influential on the national scene – which was intrinsic to the international financial scene.

Would a retrospective of the Appletons include connections – covert or otherwise – with Trans-Communications? It was something that would have to be learned.

The telephone on the wall behind him rang. It was eight minutes past ten; another seven and he would call Symonds at MI6 headquarters. He glanced at the phone, annoyed to see the waitress answer it. He stared at her lips. He hoped her conversation would not last long.

'Mister *Hagate*? Is there a Mister B. *Hagate* 'ere?' The question was shouted angrily by the irate waitress.

Bray froze. *B. Hagate 'ere?*

Agate, B.

Beowulf Agate.

Was Symonds playing some insane game of one-upmanship? Had the Englishman decided to prove the superior quality of British Intelligence's tracking techniques? Was the damn fool so egotistical he could not leave well enough alone?

God, what a fool!

Scofield rose as unobtrusively as possible, holding his attaché case. He went to the phone and spoke.

'What is it?'

'Good morning, Beowulf Agate,' said a male voice with vowels so full and consonants so sharp they could have been formed at Oxford's Balliol College. 'We trust you've rested since your arduous journey from Rome.'

'Who's this?'

'My name's irrelevant; you don't know me. We merely wanted you to understand. We found you; we'll always be able to find you. But it's all so tedious. We feel that it would be far better for everyone concerned if we sat down and thrashed out the differences between us. You may discover they're not so great after all.'

'I don't feel comfortable with people who've tried to kill me.'

'I must correct you. *Some* have tried to kill you, others have tried to save you.'

'For what? A session of chemical therapy? To find out what I've learned, what I've done?'

'What you've learned is meaningless, and you can't do anything. If your own people take you, you know what you can expect. There'll be no trial, no public hearing; you're far too dangerous to too many people. You've collaborated with the enemy, killed a young man your superiors believe was a fellow intelligence officer in Rock Creek Park, and fled the country. You're a traitor; you'll be executed at the first opportune moment. Can you doubt it after the events on Nebraska Avenue? *We* can execute you the instant you walk out of that restaurant. Or before you leave.'

Bray looked around, studying the faces at the tables, looking for the inevitable pair of eyes, a glance behind a folded newspaper, or above the rim of a coffee cup. There were several candidates; he could not be sure. And without question, there were unseen killers in the crowds outside. He was trapped; his watch read eleven minutes past ten. Another four and he could dial Symonds on the sterile line. But he was dealing with professionals. If he hung up and dialled was there a man now at one of these tables – innocuously raising a fork to his mouth or sipping from a cup – who would pull out a weapon powerful enough to blow him into the wall? Or were those inside merely hired guns, unwilling to make the sacrifice the Matarese demanded of its élite? He had to buy time and take the risk, watching the tables every second as he did so, preparing himself for that instant when escape came with sudden movement and the conceivable – unfortunate – sacrifice of innocent people.

'You want to meet, I want a guarantee I'll get out of here.'

'You've got it.'

'Your saying it isn't enough. Identify one of your employees in here.'

'Let's put it this way, Beowulf. We can hold you there, call the American embassy, and within blinking time they'd have you cornered. Even should you get past them, we'd be waiting on the outer circle, as it were.'

His watch read twelve past ten. *Three minutes.*

'Then obviously you're not that anxious to meet with me.' Scofield listened, his concentration total. He was almost certain the man on the line was a messenger; someone above wanted Beowulf Agate taken, not killed.

'I said we felt it would be better for everyone concerned . . .'

'Give me a face!' interrupted Bray. The voice *was* a messenger. 'Otherwise call the goddamned embassy. I'll take my chances. *Now.*'

'Very well,' came the reply, spoken rapidly. 'There's a man with rather sunken cheeks, wearing a grey overcoat . . .'

'I see him.' Bray did, five tables away.

'Leave the restaurant; he'll get up and follow you. He's your guarantee.'

Thirteen past ten. Two minutes.

'What guarantee does he have? How do I know you won't take him out with me?'

'Oh, come now, Scofield . . .'

'I'm glad to hear you've got another name for me. What's your name?'

'I told you, it's irrelevant.'

'Nothing's irrelevant.' Bray paused. 'I want to know your name.'

'Smith. Accept it.'

495

Ten-fourteen. One minute. Time to start.

'I'll have to think about it. I also want to finish my breakfast.' Abruptly, he hung up the phone, shifted his attaché case to his right hand and walked over to the plain-looking man five tables away.

The man stiffened as Scofield approached; his hand reached under his overcoat.

'The alert's off,' said Scofield, touching the concealed hand under the cloth of the coat. 'I was told to tell you that; you're to take me out of here. But first, I'm to make a telephone call. He gave me the number; I hope I can remember it.'

The hollow-cheeked killer remained immobile, speechless. Scofield walked back to the telephone on the wall.

Ten-fourteen and fifty-one seconds. Nine seconds to go. He frowned, as if trying to recall a number, picked up the phone, and dialled. Three seconds past 10.15 he heard the echoing sound that followed the interruption of the bell; the electronic devices were activated. He inserted his coin.

'We have to talk fast,' he said to Roger Symonds. 'They found me. I've got a problem.'

'Where are you? We'll help.'

Scofield told him. 'Just send in two sirens, regular police will do. Say it's an Irish incident, possible subjects inside. That's all I'll need.'

'I'm writing it down, they're on their way.'

'What about Waverly?'

'Tomorrow night. His house in Belgravia. I'm to escort you, of course.'

'Not before then?'

'*Before* then? Good God, man, the only reason it's so soon is that I managed an open-end memorandum from the Admiralty. From that same mythical conference I was logged into last night.' Bray was about to speak, but Symonds rushed on. 'Incidentally, you were right. An inquiry was made to see if I was there.'

'Were you covered?'

'The caller was told the conference could not be interrupted, that I would be given the message when it was over.'

'Did you return the call?'

'Yes. From the Admiralty's cellars an hour and ten minutes after I left you. I woke up some poor chap in Kensington. An intercept, of course.'

'Then if you got back there, they saw you leave? You didn't use my name with Waverly, did you?'

'I used a name, not yours. Unless your talk is extremely fruitful, I expect I'll take a lot of stick for that.'

An obvious fact struck Bray. Roger Symonds' strategy had been successful. The Matarese had him trapped inside the Knightsbridge restaurant, yet Waverly had granted him a confidential interview thirty-six hours away. Therefore, no connection had been made between the interview in Belgravia and Beowulf Agate.

'Roger, what time tomorrow night?'

'Eightish. I'm to ring him first. I'll pick you up around seven. Have you any idea where you'll be?'

Scofield avoided the question. 'I'll call you at this number at four-thirty. Is that convenient?'

'So far as I know. If I'm not here, leave an address two blocks north of where you'll be. I'll find you.'

'You'll bring the photographs of all those following your decoys yesterday?'

'They should be on my desk by noon.'

'Good. And one last thing. Think up a very good, very official reason why you can't bring me to Belgravia Square tomorrow night.'

'*What?*'

'That's what you'll tell Waverly when you call him just before our meeting. It's an intelligence decision; you'll pick him up personally and drive back to MI6.'

'*MI6?*'

'But you won't take him there; you'll bring him to the Connaught. I'll give you the room number at four-thirty. If you're not there, I'll leave a message. Subtract twenty-two from the number I give.'

'See here, Brandon, you're asking *too* much!'

'You don't know that. I may be asking to save his life. And yours.' In the distance, from somewhere outside, Bray could hear the piercing, two-note sound of a London siren; an instant later it was joined by a second. 'Your help's arrived,' said Scofield. 'Thanks.' He hung up and started back to the hollow-cheeked Matarese killer five tables away.

'Who were you talking to?' asked the man, his cold eyes nervous, his accent American. The sirens were drawing nearer; they were not lost on him.

'He didn't give me his name,' replied Bray. 'But he did give me instructions. We're to get out of here fast.'

'Why?'

'Something happened. The police spotted a rifle in one of your cars; it's being held. There's been a lot of IRA activity in the stores around here. Let's go!'

The man got out of his chair, nodding to his right. Across the crowded restaurant, Scofield saw a stern-faced, middle-aged woman get up, acknowledge the command by slipping the wide strap of a large purse over her shoulder, and start for the door of the restaurant.

Bray reached the cashier's cage, timing his movements, fumbling his money and his bill, watching the scene beyond the glass window. Two black police cars converged, screeching simultaneously to a stop at the kerb. A crowd of noisy, curious pedestrians gathered, then dispersed, curiosity replaced by fear as four helmeted London police jumped out of the vehicles and headed for the restaurant.

Bray judged the distance, then moved quickly. He reached the glass door and yanked it open several seconds before the police had it blocked. The hollow-cheeked man and the middle-aged woman were at his heels, at the last moment side-stepping around him to avoid confronting the police.

Scofield turned suddenly and lurched to his right, clutching his attaché case under his arm, grabbing his would-be escorts by the shoulders and pulling them down.

'These are the ones!' he shouted. 'Check them for guns! I heard them say they were going to bomb Scotch House!'

The police fell on the two Matarese, arms and hands and clubs thrashing the air. Bray dropped to his knees, releasing his double-grip and dived to his left out of the way. He scrambled to his feet, raced through the crowds to the corner and ran into the street, threading his way between the traffic. He kept up the frantic race for three blocks, stopping briefly, under canopies and at shop windows, to see if anyone followed him. None did, and two minutes later he slowed down and entered the enormous bronze-bordered portals of Harrods.

Once inside, he accelerated his pace as rapidly and as unobtrusively as possible, looking for a telephone. He had to reach Taleniekov at the flat in the rue du Bac before the Russian left for Cap Gris. He *had* to, for once Taleniekov reached England, he would head for London and a small hotel in Knightsbridge. If the KGB man did that he would be taken by the Matarese.

'Through the chemist's towards the south doorway,' said an imperturbable clerk. 'There's a bank of phones against the wall.'

The late-morning telephone traffic was light; the call went through without delay.

'I was leaving in a few minutes,' said Taleniekov, his voice oddly hesitant.

'Thank Christ you didn't. What's the matter with you?'
'Nothing. Why?'

'You sound strange. Where's Antonia? Why didn't she answer the phone?'

'She stepped out to the grocer's. She'll be back shortly. If I sounded strange, it's because I don't like answering this telephone.' The Russian's voice was normal now, his explanation logical. 'What is the matter with *you*? Why this unscheduled call?'

'I'll tell you when you get here, but forget Knightsbridge.'

'Where will you be?'

Scofield was about to mention the Connaught, when Taleniekov interrupted.

'On second thoughts, when I get to London I'll phone tower-central. You recall that exchange, don't you?'

Tower-central? Bray hadn't heard the name in years, but he remembered. It was a code name for a KGB drop on the Victoria Embankment, abandoned when Consular Operations discovered it some time back in the late 'sixties. The tourist boats that travelled up and down the Thames, that was it. 'I remember,' said Scofield, bewildered. 'I'll respond.'

'Then I'll be going . . .'

'Wait a minute,' interrupted Bray. 'Tell Antonia I'll call in a while.'

There was a brief silence before Taleniekov replied. 'Actually, she said she might take in the Louvre; it's so close by. I can get to the Cap Gris district in an hour or so. There's nothing – I repeat – nothing to worry about.' There was a click and the line to Paris went dead. The Russian had hung up.

There's nothing – I repeat – nothing to worry about. The words cracked with the explosive sounds of near-by thunder, his eyes blinded by bolts of lightning that carried the message into his brain. There *was* something to worry about and it concerned Antonia Gravet.

Actually, she said she might take in the Louvre . . . I can

get to the Cap Gris district in an hour or so . . . Nothing to
worry about.

Three disconnected statements, preceded by an interruption that prohibited disclosure of the contact point in
London. Scofield tried to analyse the sequence; if there
was meaning it was in the progression. The *Louvre* was
only blocks away from rue du Bac – across the Seine, but
near-by. The *Cap Gris district* could not be reached in an
hour or so; two and a half or three were more logical.
Nothing – I repeat – nothing to worry about; then why the
interruption? Why the necessity of a third contact point,
avoiding any mention of the second?

Sequence. Progression. Further *back*?

I do not like answering this telephone. Words spoken
firmly, almost angrily. That was *it*. Suddenly Bray understood and the relief he felt was like cool water sprayed over
a sweat-drenched body. Taleniekov had seen something
wrong – a face in the street, a chance meeting with a former
colleague, a car that remained too long on the rue du Bac
– any number of unsettling incidents or observations. The
Russian had decided to move Toni out of the Rive Gauche,
across the river into another flat. *She* would be settled
in an *hour or so* and he would not leave until she was;
that was why there was nothing to worry about. Still,
on the assumption that there could be substance to a
disturbing incident or observation, the KGB man had
operated with extreme caution – always caution, it was
their truest shield – and the telephone was an instrument
of revelation. Nothing revealing was to be said.

Sequence, progression . . . meaning. Or was it? The
Serpent had killed his wife. Was he finding comfort where
none existed? The Russian had been the first to suggest
eliminating the girl from the hills of Porto Vecchio – the
love that had come into his life at the most inopportune
time of his life. *Could* he? . . .

No! Things were different now! There was no Beowulf

Agate to stretch to the breaking point, because that breaking point guaranteed the death of the Serpent, the end of the hunt for the Matarese. The best of professionals did not kill unnecessarily; the results were always geometric.

Still, he wondered, as he picked up the phone in Harrods' south entranceway, what was necessity but a man convinced of the need? He put the question out of his mind; he had to find sanctuary.

London's staid Connaught Hotel not only possessed one of the best kitchens in London but was an ideal choice for quick concealment, as long as one stayed out of the lobby and tested the kitchen from room service. Quite simply, it was impossible to get a room at the Connaught unless a reservation was made weeks in advance. The elegant hotel on Carlos Place was one of the last bastions of the Empire, catering in large measure to those who mourned its passing and had the wealth to do so gracefully. There were enough to keep it perpetually full; the Connaught rarely had an available room.

Scofield knew this, and years ago had decided that occasions might arise when the Connaught's particular exclusivity could be useful. He had reached and cultivated a director of the financial group that owned the hotel and made his appeal. As all theatres have 'house seats', and most restaurants keep constantly 'reserved' tables for those exalted patrons who have to be accommodated, so do hotels retain empty rooms for like purposes. Bray was convincing; his work was on the side of the angels, the Tory side. A room would be at his disposal whenever he needed it.

'Room six-twenty-six,' were the director's first words when Scofield placed his second, confirming call. 'Just go right up in the lift as usual. You can sign the registration in your room – as usual.'

Bray thanked his accomplice, and turned his thoughts

to another problem, an irritating one. He could not return to the small hotel several blocks away, and the only clothes except those on his back were there. In a duffelbag on the unmade bed. There was nothing else of consequence; his money as well as several dozen useful letterheads, identification cards, passports and bank books, were all in his attaché case. But apart from the rumpled trousers, the cheap tweed jacket and the Irish hat, he didn't have a damn thing to wear. And clothes were not merely coverings for the body, they were intrinsic to the work and had to match the work; they were tools, consistently more effective than weapons and the spoken word. He left the bank of telephones and walked back into the aisles of Harrods. The selections would take an hour; that was fine. It would take his mind off Paris. And the inopportune love of his life.

It was shortly past midnight when Scofield left his room at the Connaught, dressed in a dark raincoat and a narrow-brimmed black hat. He took the service elevator to the basement of the hotel and emerged on the street through the employees' entrance. He found a taxi and told the driver to take him to Waterloo Bridge. He settled back in the seat and smoked a cigarette, trying to control his swelling sense of concern. He wondered if Taleniekov understood the change that had taken place, a change so unreasonable, so illogical that he was not sure how he would react were he the Russian. The core of his excellence, his longevity in his work, had always been his ability to think as the enemy thought; he was incapable of doing so now.

I'm not your enemy!

Taleniekov had shouted that unreasonable, illogical statement over the telephone in Washington. Perhaps – illogically – he was right. The Russian was no friend, but he was not *the* enemy. That enemy was the Matarese.

And crazily, *so* unreasonably, through the Matarese he had found Antonia Gravet. The love . . .

What had *happened*?

He forced the question out of his mind. He would learn soon enough, and what he learned would no doubt bring back the relief he had felt at Harrods, diminished by too much time on his hands and too little to do. The telephone call to Roger Symonds, made precisely at 4.30, had been routine. Roger was out of the office so he had given information to the security room operator. The unexplained number that was to be relayed was six-four-three . . . minus twenty-two . . . Room 621, Connaught.

The taxi swung out of Trafalgar Square, up the Strand, past Savoy Court, towards the entrance of Waterloo Bridge. Bray leaned forward; there was no point walking any farther than he had to. He would cut through side streets down to the Thames and the Victoria Embankment.

'This'll be fine,' he said to the driver, holding out payment, annoyed to see that his hand shook.

He went down the cobbled lane by the angling structure of dark stone that was the Savoy Hotel, and reached the bottom of the hill. Across the wide, well-lighted boulevard was the concrete walk and the high brick wall that fronted the River Thames. Moored permanently as a pub was a huge refurbished barge named *Caledonia*, closed by the 11.00 curfew imposed on all England's drinking halls, the few lights beyond the thick windows signifying the labours of clean-up crews removing the stains and odours of the day. A quarter of a mile south on the tree-lined Embankment were the sturdy, wide-beamed, full-decked river boats that ploughed the Thames most of the year round, ferrying tourists up to the Tower of London and back to Lambeth Bridge before returning to the waters of Cleopatra's Needle.

Years ago these boats were known as tower-central,

drops for Soviet couriers and KGB agents making contact with informers and deep-cover espionage personnel. Consular Operations had uncovered the drop; in time, the Russians knew it. Tower-central was taken out; a known drop was eliminated for some other that would take months to find.

Scofield cut through the garden paths of the park behind the Savoy; music from the ballroom floated down from above.

He reached a small band amphitheatre with its rows of slatted benches. A few couples were scattered around talking quietly. Bray looked for a single man, for he was within the vicinity of tower-central. The Russian would be somewhere in the area.

He was not. Scofield walked out of the amphitheatre into the widest path that led to the boulevard. He emerged on the pavement; the traffic in the street was constant, bright headlights flashing by in both directions, mottled by the winter mists that rolled off the water. It occurred to Bray that Taleniekov must have hired an automobile. He looked up and down the avenue to see if any were parked on either side; none was. Across the boulevard, in front of the Embankment wall, strollers walked casually in couples, threesomes and several larger groups; there was no man by himself. Scofield looked at his watch; it was five minutes to one. The Russian had said he might be as late as two or three o'clock in the morning. Bray swore at his impatience, at the anxiety in his chest whenever he thought about Paris. About Toni.

There was the sudden fire of a cigarette lighter, the flame steady, then extinguished, only to be relighted a second later. Diagonally across the wide avenue, to the right of the closed, chained gates of the pier that led to the tourist boats, a white-haired man was holding the flame under a blonde woman's cigarette; both leaned against the wall, looking at the water. Scofield studied the figure, what he could see of the face, and had to stop himself from breaking into a run. Taleniekov had arrived.

Bray turned right and walked until he was parallel with the Russian and the blonde decoy. He knew Taleniekov had seen him and wondered why the KGB man did not dismiss the woman, paying her whatever price they had agreed upon, and get her out of the way. It was foolish – conceivably dangerous – for a decoy to observe both parties at a contact point. Scofield waited at the kerb, seeing now that Taleniekov's head was fully turned, the Russian staring at him, his arm around the woman's waist. Bray gestured first to his left, then to his right, his meaning clear. Get her out! Walk south; we'll meet shortly.

Taleniekov did not move. What was the Soviet *doing*? It was no time for whores!

Whores? The whore that never was? The *courier's whore*? Oh, my *God*!

Scofield stepped off the kerb; an automobile horn bellowed, as a car swerved towards the centre of the road to avoid hitting him. Bray barely heard the sound, was barely aware of the sight; he could only stare at the woman beside Taleniekov.

The arm around the waist was no gesture of feigned affection, the Russian was holding her up. Taleniekov spoke in the woman's ear; she tried to spin around; her head fell back on her neck, her mouth open, a scream or a plea about to emerge, but nothing was heard.

The strained face was the face of his love. Under the blonde wig, it was *Toni*. All control left him; he raced across the wide avenue, speeding cars braking, spinning wheels, blowing horns. His thoughts converged like staccato shots of gunfire, one thought, one observation, more painful than all others.

Antonia looked more dead than alive.

30

'She's been *drugged*,' said Taleniekov.

'Why the hell did you bring her *here*?' asked Bray angrily, taking his face away from Antonia's. 'There are hundreds of places in France, dozens in Paris, where she'd be safe! Where she'd be cared for! You know them as well as *I* do!'

'If I could have been certain, I would have left her,' replied Vasili, his voice calm. 'Don't probe. I considered other alternatives.'

Bray understood, his brief silence an expression of gratitude. Taleniekov could easily have killed Toni, probably would have killed her had it not been for East Berlin. Which meant that the Russian also understood. 'A doctor?'

'Helpful in terms of time, but not essentially necessary.'

'What was the chemical?'

'Scopolamine.'

'When?'

'Early yesterday morning. Over eighteen hours.'

'*Eighteen* . . . ?' It was no time for explanations. 'Do you have a car?'

'I couldn't take the chance. A lone man with a woman who could not stand up under her own power; the trail would have been obvious. The pilot drove us up from Ashford.'

'Can you trust him?'

'No, but he stopped for petrol ten minutes outside of London and went inside to relieve himself. I added a quart of oil to his fuel tank; it should be taking effect on the road back to Ashford.'

'Find a taxi.' Scofield's look conveyed the compliment he would not say.

'We have much to discuss,' added Taleniekov, moving away from the wall.

'Then hurry,' said Bray.

Antonia's breathing was steady, the muscles of her face relaxed in sleep. When she awoke she would be nauseous, but it would pass with the day. Scofield pulled the covers over her shoulders, leaned down and kissed her on her pale white lips, and got up from the bed.

He walked out of the bedroom, leaving the door ajar. Should Toni stir he wanted to hear her; hysterics were a by-product of scopolamine. They had to be controlled; it was why Taleniekov could not risk leaving her alone, even for the few minutes it would have taken to lease a car.

'What happened?' he asked the Russian, who sat in a chair, a glass of whisky in his hand.

'This morning – yesterday morning,' said Taleniekov, correcting himself, his white-haired head angled back against the rim of the chair, his eyes closed; the man was clearly exhausted. 'They say you're dead, did you know that?'

'Yes. What's that got to do with it?'

'It's how I got her back.' The Russian opened his eyes and looked at Bray. 'There's very little about Beowulf Agate I don't know.'

'And?'

'I said I was you. There were several basic questions to answer; they were not difficult. I offered myself in exchange for her. They agreed.'

'Start from the beginning.'

'I wish I could, I wish I knew what it was. The Matarese, or someone within the Matarese, wants you alive. It's why certain people were told that you are not. They don't look

for the American, only the Russian. I wish I understood.'
Taleniekov drank.

'What *happened*?'

'They found her. Don't ask me how, I don't know. Perhaps Helsinki, perhaps you were picked up in Rome, perhaps anything or anyone, I don't know.'

'But they found her,' said Scofield, sitting down. 'Then what?'

'Early yesterday morning, four or five hours before you called, she went down to a bakery; it was only a few doors away. An hour later she had not returned. I knew then I had two choices. I could go out after her – but where to start, where to look? Or I could wait for someone to come to the flat. You see, *they* had no choice, I knew that. The telephone rang a number of times but I did not answer, knowing that each time I did not, it brought someone closer.'

'You answered my call,' interrupted Bray.

'That was later. By then we were negotiating.'

'Then?'

'Finally two men came. It was one of the more testing moments of my life not to kill them both, especially one. He had that small, ugly little mark on his chest. When I ripped his clothes off and saw it, I went nearly mad.'

'Why?'

'They killed in Leningrad. In Essen. Later you'll understand. It's part of what we must discuss.'

'Go on.' Scofield poured himself a drink.

'I'll tell it briefly, fill in the spaces yourself; you've been there. I kept the soldier and his hired gun bound and unconscious for over an hour. The phone rang and this time I answered, using the most pronounced American accent I could manage. You'd have thought the sky over Paris had fallen, so hysterical was the caller. "An impostor in London!" he squeaked. Something about a "gross error having been made by the embassy, the information they received completely erroneous".'

'I think you skipped something,' interrupted Bray again. 'I assume that was when you said you were me.'

'Let's say I answered in the affirmative when the hysterical question was posed. It was a temptation I could not resist, since I had heard less than forty-eight hours previously that you had been killed.' The Russian paused, then added, 'Two weeks ago in Washington.'

Scofield walked back to the chair, frowning. 'But the man on the phone knew I was alive, just as those here in London knew I was alive. So you were right. Only certain people inside the Matarese were told I was dead.'

'Does that tell you something?'

'The same thing it tells you. They make distinctions.'

'Exactly. When either of us ever wanted a subordinate to do nothing, we told him the problem was solved. For such people you're no longer alive, no longer hunted.'

'But why? I *am* hunted. They trapped me.' Bray sat down, revolving the glass in his hand.

'One question with two answers, I think,' said the Russian. 'Like any diverse organization, the Matarese is imperfect. Among its ranks are the undisciplined, the violence-prone, men who kill for the score alone or because of fanatic beliefs. These were the people who were told you were dead. If they did not hunt you, they would not kill you.'

'That's your first answer; what's the second? Why does someone want to keep me alive?'

'To make you a *consigliere* of the Matarese.'

'*What?*'

'Think about it. Consider what you'd bring to such an organization.'

Bray stared at the KGB man. 'No more than you would.'

'Oh, much more. There are no great shocks to come

510

out of Moscow, I accept that. But there are astonishing revelations to be found in Washington. You could provide them; you'd be an enormous asset. The sanctimonious are always far more vulnerable.'

'I accept that.'

'Before Odile Verachten was killed, she made an offer to me. It was not an offer she was entitled to make; they don't want the Russian. They want you. If they can't have you, they'll kill you, but someone's giving you the option.'

It would be far better for all concerned if we sat down and thrashed out the differences between us. You may discover they're not so great after all. Words from a faceless messenger.

'Let's get back to Paris,' said Bray. 'How did you get her?'

'It wasn't so difficult. The man on the phone was too anxious; he saw a generalship in his future, or his own execution. I discussed what might happen to the soldier with the ugly little mark on his chest; the fact that I knew about it was nearly enough in itself. I set up a series of moves, offering the soldier and Beowulf Agate for the girl. Beowulf was tired of running and was perfectly willing to listen to whatever anyone had to say. He – I – knew I was cornered, but professionalism demanded that he – you – extract certain guarantees. The girl had to go free. Were my reactions consistent with your well-known obstinacy?'

'Very plausible,' replied Scofield. 'Let's see if I can fill in a few spaces. You answered the questions: what was my mother's middle name? Or when did my father change jobs?'

'Nothing so ordinary,' broke in the Russian. ' "Who was your fourth kill? Where?" '

'Lisbon,' said Bray quietly. 'An American beyond salvage. Yes, you'd know that . . . Then your moves were made by a sequence of telephone calls to the flat – my call from London was the intrusion – and with each call you gave new instructions, any deviation and the exchange was cancelled. The exchange ground itself was in traffic, preferably one-way traffic, with one vehicle, one man and Antonia. Everything to take place within a time span of sixty to a hundred seconds.'

The Russian nodded. 'Noon on the Champs Élysées, south of the Arch. Vehicle and girl taken, man and soldier bound at the elbows, thrown out at the intersection of the Place de la Concorde, and a swift, if roundabout, drive out of Paris.'

Bray put the whisky down and walked to the hotel window overlooking Carlos Place. 'A little while ago you said you had two choices. To go out after her, or wait in the rue du Bac. It seems to me there was a third but you didn't take it. You could have got out of Paris yourself right away.'

Taleniekov closed his eyes. 'That was the one choice I didn't have. It was in her voice, in every reference she made to you. I thought I saw it in Corsica, that first night in the cave above Porto Vecchio when you looked at her. I thought then, how *insane*, how perfectly . . .' The Russian shook his head.

'Unreasonable?' asked Bray.

Taleniekov opened his eyes. 'Yes. Unreasonable . . . as in unnecessary, uncalled for.' The KGB man raised his glass and drank the remaining whisky in one swallow. 'The slate from East Berlin is as clean as it will ever be; there'll be no more cleansing.'

'None will be asked for. Or expected.'

'Good. I presume you've seen the newspapers.'

'Trans-Communications? Its holdings in Verachten?'

'Ownership would be more like it. I trust you noted the location of the corporate headquarters. Boston, Massachusetts. A city quite familiar to you, I think.'

'What's more to the point, it's the city – and state – of Joshua Appleton the Fourth, patrician and senator, whose grandfather was the guest of Guillaume de Matarese. It'll be interesting to see what – if any – his connections are to Trans-Comm.'

'Can you doubt they exist?'

'At this point I doubt everything,' said Scofield. 'Maybe I'll think differently after we've put together those facts you say we now have. Let's start with when we left Corsica.'

Taleniekov nodded. 'Rome came first. Tell me about Scozzi.'

Bray did, taking the time to explain the role Antonia had been forced to play in the Red Brigades.

'That's why she was in Corsica, then?' asked Vasili. 'Running from the Brigades?'

'Yes. Everything she told me about their financing spells Matarese . . .' Scofield clarified his theories, moving swiftly on to the events at Villa d'Este and the murder of Guillamo Scozzi, ordered by a man named Paravicini. 'It was the first time I heard that I was dead. They thought I was you . . . Now Leningrad. What happened there?'

Taleniekov breathed deeply, silently, before answering. 'They killed in Leningrad, in Essen,' he said, his voice barely audible. 'Oh, how they kill, these twentieth-century *fida'is*, these contemporary mutants of Hasan ibn as-Sabbāh! I should tell you, the soldier I pushed from the car in the Place de la Concorde had more than a blemish on his chest. His clothes were stained by a gunshot that left another mark. I told his associate it was for Leningrad, for Essen.'

The Russian told his story quietly, the depth of his feelings apparent when he spoke of Lodzia Kronescha, the scholar Mikovsky and Heinrich Kassel. Especially Lodzia; it was necessary for him to stop for a while and replenish the whisky in his glass. Scofield remained silent; there was nothing he could say. The Russian finished with the field at night in Stadtwald and the death of Odile Verachten.

'Prince Andrei Voroshin became Ansel Verachten, founder of the Verachten Works, next to Krupp the largest company in Germany, now one of the most sprawling in all Europe. The granddaughter was his chosen successor in the Matarese.'

'And Scozzi,' said Bray, 'joined Paravicini through a marriage of convenience. Blood-lines, a certain talent, and charm in exchange for a seat in the boardroom. But the chair was a prop; it's all it ever was. The count was expendable, killed because he made a mistake.'

'As was Odile Verachten. Also expendable.'

'And the name Scozzi-Paravicini is misleading. The control lies with Paravicini.'

'Add to that Trans-Communication's ownership of Verachten. So two descendants of the *padrone*'s guest list are accounted for, both a part of Matarese, yet neither is significant. What do we have?'

'What we suspected, what old Krupsky told you in Moscow. The Matarese was taken over, obviously in part, possibly in whole. Scozzi and Voroshin were useful for what they brought or what they knew or what they owned. They were tolerated – even made to feel important – as long as they were useful, eliminated the moment they were not.'

'But useful for what? That's the question!' Taleniekov banged his glass down in frustration. 'What does the Matarese want? They finance intimidation, and murder through huge corporate structures; they spread chaos, but *why*? This world is going mad with terror, bought and paid for by men who lose the most by it. Their investment is in total *disorder*! It makes no sense!'

Scofield heard the sound – the moan – and sprang out of the chair. He walked quickly to the bedroom door; Toni had changed her position, twisting to her left, the covers bunched around her shoulders. But she was still asleep; the cry had come from her unconscious. He went back to the chair and stood behind it.

'Total disorder,' he said softly. 'Chaos. The clashing of bodies in space. Creation.'

'What are you talking about?' asked Taleniekov.

'I'm not sure,' replied Scofield. 'I keep going back to the word "chaos" but I'm not sure why.'

'We're not sure of *anything*. We have four names – but two didn't amount to much – and they're dead. We see an alignment of companies who are the superstructure – the *essential superstructure* – behind terrorism everywhere, but we cannot prove the alignment and don't know why they're sponsoring it. Scozzi-Paravicini finances the Red Brigades, Verachten no doubt Baader-Meinhof. God only knows what Trans-Communications pays for – and these may be only a few of the many involved. We have *found* the Matarese, but still we do not see them! Whatever charges we levelled against such conglomerates would be called the ravings of madmen, or worse.'

'Much worse,' said Bray, remembering the voice over the restaurant's telephone. 'Traitors. We'd be shot.'

'Your words have the ring of prophecy. I don't like them.'

'Neither do I, but I like being executed less.'

'A profound statement. Also a *non sequitur*.'

'Not when coupled with what you just said. "We've found the Matarese, but still we don't see them," wasn't that it?'

'Yes.'

'Suppose we not only found one, but had him. In our hands.'

'A *hostage*?'

'That's right.'

'That's insane.'

'Why? You had the Verachten woman.'

'In a car. In a farmer's field. At night. I had no delusions of taking her into Essen and setting up a base of operations.'

Scofield sat down. 'The Red Brigades held Aldo Moro eight blocks away from a police headquarters in Rome. Although that's not exactly what I had in mind.'

Taleniekov leaned forward. 'Waverly?'

'Yes.'

'*How?* The American network is after you, the Matarese nearly trapped you; what did *you* have in mind? Dropping into the Foreign Office and proffering an invitation for tea?'

'Waverly's to be brought here – to this room – at eight o'clock tonight.'

The Russian whistled. 'May I ask how you managed it?'

Bray told him about MI6's Roger Symonds. 'He's doing it because he thinks whatever convinced me to work with you must be strong enough to get me an interview with Waverly.'

'They have a name for me. Did he tell you?'

'Yes. The Serpent.'

'I suppose I should be flattered, but I'm not. I find it ugly. Does Symonds have any idea that this meeting has a hostile basis? That you suspect Waverly of being something more than England's Foreign Secretary?'

'No; the reverse, in fact. When he objected, the last thing I said to him was that I might be trying to save Waverly's life.'

'Very good,' said Taleniekov. 'Very frightening. Assassination, like acts of terror, is a spreading commodity. They'll be alone then?'

'Yes, I made a point of it. A room at the Connaught; there'd be no reason for Roger to think anything's wrong. And we know the Matarese haven't made the connection between me and the man Waverly is supposedly meeting at the MI6 offices.'

'You're certain of that? It strikes me as the weakest part of the strategy. They've got you in London, they know you have the four names from Corsica. Suddenly, from nowhere, Waverly, the *consigliere*, is asked to meet secretly with a man at the office of a British intelligence agent known to have been a friend of Beowulf Agate. The equation seems obvious to me; why should it elude the Matarese?'

'A very specific reason. They don't think I ever made contact with Symonds.'

'They can't be sure you didn't.'

'The odds are against it. Roger's an experienced field man; he covered himself. He was logged in at the Admiralty and later returned a blind inquiry. I wasn't picked up in the streets and we used a sterile phone. We met an hour outside of London, two changes of vehicle for me, at least four for him. No one followed.'

'Impressive. Not conclusive.'

'It's the best I can do. Except for a final qualification.'

'Qualification?'

'Yes. There isn't going to be a meeting tonight. They'll never reach this room.'

'No *meeting*? Then what's the purpose of their coming here?'

'So we can grab Waverly downstairs before Symonds knows what's happened. Roger'll be driving; when he gets here, he won't go through the lobby, he'll use a side entrance, I'll find out which one. In the event – and I agree it's possible – that Waverly is followed, you'll be down in the street. You'll know it; you'll see them. Take them out. I'll be right inside that entrance.'

'Where they least expect you,' broke in the Russian.

'That's right. I'm counting on it. I can take Roger by

surprise, knock him out and force a pill down his throat. He won't wake up for hours.'

'It's not enough,' said Taleniekov, lowering his voice. 'You'll have to kill him. Sacrifices inevitably must be made. Churchill understood that with Coventry and the Ultra; this is no less, Scofield. British Intelligence will mount the most extensive manhunt in England's history. We've got to get Waverly out of the country. If the death of one man can buy us time – a day perhaps – I submit it's worth it.'

Bray looked at the Russian, studying him. 'You submit too goddamn much.'

'You know I'm right.'

Silence. Suddenly Scofield hurled his glass across the room. It shattered against the wall. 'God*damn* it!'

Taleniekov bolted forward, his right hand under his coat. 'What is it?'

'You're right and I *do* know it. He trusts me and I've got to kill him. It'll be days before the British will know where to start. Neither MI6 nor the Foreign Office know anything about the Connaught.'

The KGB man removed his hand, sliding it on to the arm of the chair. 'We need the time, Scofield. I don't think there's any other way.'

'If there is, I hope to God it comes to me.' Bray shook his head. 'I'm sick to death of necessity.' He looked over at the bedroom door. 'But then she told me that.'

'The rest is detail,' continued Taleniekov, rushing the moment. 'I'll have an automobile on the street outside the entrances. The moment I'm finished – if indeed, there's anything for me to do – I'll come inside and help you. It will be necessary, of course, to take the dead man along with Waverly. Remove him.'

'The dead man has no name,' said Scofield quietly. He got out of the chair and walked to the window. 'Has it occurred to you that the closer we get, the more like them we become?'

'What occurs to me,' said the Russian, 'is that your strategy is nothing short of extraordinary. Not only will we have a *consigliere* of the Matarese, but *what* a *consigliere*! The Foreign Secretary of England! Have you any idea what that means? We'll break that man wide open, and the world will listen. It will be *forced* to listen!' Taleniekov paused, then added softly, 'What you've done lives up to the stories of Beowulf Agate.'

'Bullshit,' said Bray. 'I hate that name.'

The moan was sudden, bursting into a prolonged sob, followed by a cry of pain, muffled, uncertain, desperate. Scofield raced into the bedroom. Toni was writhing on the bed, her hands clawing her face, her legs kicking viciously at imaginary demons that surrounded her. Bray sat down and pulled her hands from her face, gently, firmly, bending each finger so that the nails would not puncture her skin. He pinned her arms and held her, cradling her as he had cradled her in Rome. Her cries subsided, replaced once more by sobs; she shivered, her breathing erratic, slowly returning to normal as her rigid body went limp. The first hysterics brought about by the dissipation of scopolamine had passed. Scofield heard footsteps in the doorway; he angled his head to signify that he was listening.

'It will keep up until morning, you know,' said the KGB man. 'It leaves the body slowly, with a great deal of pain. As much from the images in the mind as anything else. There's nothing you can do. Just hold her.'

'I know. I will.'

There was a moment of silence; Bray could feel the Russian's eyes on him, on Antonia. 'I'll leave now,' Taleniekov said. 'I'll call you here at noon, come up later in the day. We can refine the details then, co-ordinate signals, that kind of thing.'

'Sure. That kind of thing. Where'll you go? You can stay here, if you like.'

'I think not. As in Paris, there are dozens of places here.

I know them as well as you do. Besides, I must find a car, study the streets. Nothing takes the place of preparation, does it?'

'No, it doesn't.'

'Good night. Take care of her.'

'I'll try.' Footsteps again; the Russian walked out of the room. Scofield spoke. 'Taleniekov.'

'Yes?'

'I'm sorry about Leningrad.'

'Yes.' Again there was silence; then the words were spoken quietly. 'Thank you.'

The outside door closed; he was alone with his love. He lowered her to the pillow and touched her face. So illogical, so unreasonable. *Why did I find you? Why did you find me? You should have left me where I was – deep in the earth. It isn't the time for either of us, can't you understand that? It's all so . . . uncalled for.*

It was as if his thoughts had been spoken out loud. Toni opened her eyes, the focus imperfect, the recognition slight, but she knew him. Her lips formed his name, the sound a whisper.

'Bray . . . ?'

'You'll be all right. They didn't hurt you. The pain you feel is from chemicals; it will pass, believe that.'

'You came back.'

'Yes.'

'Don't go away again, *please*. Not without me.'

'I won't.'

Her eyes suddenly widened, the stare glazed, her white teeth bared like a young animal's caught in a snare that was breaking its back. A heartbreaking whimper came from deep inside her.

She collapsed in his arms.

Tomorrow, my love, my only love. Tomorrow comes with the sunlight, everyone knows that. And then the pain will pass, I promise you. And I promise you something

else, my inopportune love so late in my life. Tomorrow,
today, tonight . . . I will take the man who will bring
this nightmare to a close. Taleniekov is right. We will
break him – as no man has ever been broken – and
the world will listen to us. When it does, my love, my
only adorable love, you and I are free. We will go far
away where the night brings sleep and love, not death,
not fear and loathing of the darkness. We will be free
because Beowulf Agate will be gone. He will disappear –
for he hasn't done much good. But he has one more thing
to do. Tonight.

Scofield touched Antonia's cheek. She held his hand
briefly, moving it to her lips, smiling, reassuring him with
her eyes.

'How's the head?' asked Bray.

'The ache is barely a numbness now,' she said. 'I'm
fine, really.'

Scofield released her hand and walked across the room
where Taleniekov was bent over a table, studying a road
map. Without having discussed it, both men were dressed
nearly alike for their work. Sweaters and trousers of dark
material, tightly strapped shoulder holsters with black
leather belts laterally across the chest. Their shoes were
also dark in colour, but light in weight, with thick rubber
soles that had been scraped with knives until they were
coarse.

Neither man had spoken with the other about the
topic of clothing; it would have been foolish. The only
subsequent remark was made by Vasili when he arrived
at the hotel room and was about to remove his loose-fitting
topcoat.

'I must commend your tailor,' he had observed.

Taleniekov now glanced up as Bray approached the
table. 'After Great Dunmow, we'll head east towards
Coggeshall on our way to Nayland. Incidentally, there's an

airfield capable of handling small jets south of Hadleigh. Such a field might be of value to us in a few days.'

'You may be right.'

'Also,' added the KGB man with obvious reluctance, 'this route passes the Blackwater River; the forests are dense in that area. It would be a . . . good place to drop off the package.'

'The dead man still hasn't got a name,' said Scofield. 'Give him his due. He's Roger Symonds, honourable man, and I hate this fucking world.'

'At the risk of appearing fatuous, may I submit – forgive me, suggest – that what you do tonight will benefit that sad world we both have abused too well for too long.'

'I'd just as soon you didn't submit or suggest anything.' Bray looked at his watch. 'He'll be calling soon. When he does, Toni will go down to the lobby and pay Mr Edmonton's bill – that's me. She'll come back up with a steward and take our bags and briefcase down to the car we've rented in Edmonton's name and drive directly to Colchester. She'll wait at a restaurant called Bonner's until 11.30. If there are any changes of plans or we need her, we'll reach her there. If she doesn't hear from us, she'll go on to Nayland, to the Double Crown Inn where she has a room reserved in the name of Vickery.'

Taleniekov pushed himself up from the table. 'My briefcase is not to be opened,' he said. 'It's tripped.'

'So's mine,' replied Scofield. 'Any more questions?'

The telephone rang; all three looked at it – a moment suspended in time, for the bell meant the time had come. Bray walked over to the desk, let the phone ring a second time, then picked it up.

Whatever words he might have expected, whatever greetings, information, instructions or revelations that might have come, nothing on this earth could have prepared him for what he heard. Symonds' voice was a cry from some inner space of torment, a pain of such extremity that it was beyond belief.

'They're all *dead*. It's a *massacre*! Waverly, his wife, children, three servants . . . *dead*. What in *hell have you done*?'

'Oh, my *God*!' Scofield's mind raced, thoughts swiftly translated into carefully selected words. 'Roger, listen to me. It's what I tried to *prevent*!' He cupped the phone, his eyes on Taleniekov. 'Waverly's dead, everyone in the house killed.'

'Method?' shouted the Russian. 'Marks on the bodies. Weapons. Get it all!'

Bray shook his head. 'We'll get it later.' He took his hand from the mouthpiece; Symonds was talking rapidly, close to hysterics.

'It's *horrible*. Oh, God, the most terrible thing! They've been slaughtered . . . like animals!'

'*Roger!* Get hold of yourself! Now listen to me. It's part of a pattern. Waverly knew about it. He knew too much; it's why he was killed. I couldn't reach him in time.'

'You couldn't? . . . For the love of God . . . why *didn't* you, *couldn't you* . . . *tell me*? He was the Foreign Secretary, England's *Foreign Secretary*! Have you any idea of the repercussions, the . . . oh, my *God*, a tragedy! *A catastrophe! Butchered!*' Symonds paused. When he spoke again it was obvious that the professional in him was struggling for control. 'I want you down in my office as soon as you can get there. Consider yourself under detention by the British government.'

'I can't do that. Don't ask me.'

'I'm not asking, Scofield! I'm giving you a direct order backed up by the highest authorities in England. You will *not* leave that hotel! By the time you reached the lift, all the current would be shut off, every staircase, every exit under armed guard.'

'All right, all right. I'll get to MI6,' lied Bray.

'You'll be *escorted*. Remain in your room.'

'Forget the room, Roger,' said Scofield, grasping for whatever words he could find that might fit the crisis. 'I've got to see you, but not at MI6.'

'I don't think you *heard* me!'

'Put guards on the doors, shut off the goddamned elevators, do anything you like, but I've got to see you *here*. I'm going to walk out of this room and go down to the bar, to the darkest booth I can find. Meet me there.'

'I *repeat* . . .'

'Repeat all you want to, but if you don't come over here and listen to me, there'll be other assassinations – *that's* what they are, Roger! *Assassinations*. And they won't stop at a Foreign Secretary, or a Secretary of State . . . or a President or a Prime Minister.'

'Oh, my . . . *God*!' whispered Symonds.

'It's what I couldn't tell you last night. It's the reason you looked for when we talked. But I won't put it on-record, I can't work in-sanction. And that should tell you enough. Get over here, Roger.' Bray closed his eyes, held his breath; it was now or it was not.

'I'll be there in ten minutes,' said Symonds, his voice cracking.

Scofield hung up the phone, looking first at Antonia, then Taleniekov. 'He's on his way.'

'He'll take you in!' exclaimed the Russian.

'I don't think so. He knows me well enough to know I won't go on-record if I say I won't. And he doesn't want the rest of it on his head.' Bray crossed to the chair where he had thrown his raincoat and travel bag. 'I'm sure of one thing. He'll meet me downstairs, and give me a chance. If he accepts, I'll be back in an hour. If he doesn't . . . I'll kill him.' Scofield unzipped his bag, reached into it and pulled out a sheathed, long-bladed hunting knife. It still had the Harrods' price tag on it. He looked at Toni; her eyes told him she understood. Both the necessity and his loathing of it.

Symonds sat across from Bray in the booth of the Connaught lounge. The subdued lighting could not conceal the pallor of the Englishman's face; he was a man forced to make decisions of such magnitude that the mere thought of them made him ill. Physically ill, mentally exhausted.

They had talked for nearly forty minutes. Scofield, as planned, had told him part of the truth – a great deal more of it than he cared to – but it was necessary. He was now about to make his final request of Roger, and both men knew it. Symonds felt the terrible weight of his decision; it was in his eyes. Bray felt the knife in his belt; his appalling decision to use it if necessary made it difficult for him to breathe.

'We don't know how extensive it is, or how many people in the various governments are involved, but we know it's being financed through large corporations,' Scofield explained. 'What happened in Belgrave Square tonight can be compared to what happened to Anthony Blackburn in New York, to the physicist Yurievich in Russia. We're closing in; we have names, covert alliances, knowledge that intelligence branches in Washington, Moscow and Bonn have been manipulated. But we have no proof; we'll get it, but we don't have it now. If you take me in, we'll never get it. The case against me is beyond salvage; I don't have to tell you what that means. I'll be executed at the first . . . opportune moment. For the wrong reason, by the wrong people, but the result will be the same. Give me *time*, Roger.'

'What will you give me?'

'What more do you want?'

'Those names, the alliances.'

'They're *meaningless* now. Worse than that, if they're recorded, they'll either go farther underground, cutting off all traces, or the killing, the terrorism, will accelerate. There'll be a series of bloodbaths . . . and you'll be dead.'

'That's my condition. The names, the alliances. Or you will not leave here.'

Bray stared at the man from MI6. 'Will you stop me, Roger? I mean here, now, at this moment, will you? *Can* you?'

'Perhaps not. But those two men over there will.' Symonds nodded to his left.

Scofield shifted his eyes. Across the room, at a table in the centre of the lounge, were two British agents, one of them the red-haired stocky man he had spoken with last night at the moonlit playground in Guildford. That same man now stared at him, no sympathy, only hostility in his look. 'You covered yourself,' said Scofield.

'Did you think I wouldn't? They're armed and have their instructions. The names, please.' Symonds took out a notebook and a ballpoint pen; he placed them in front of Bray. 'Don't write nonsense, I beg you. Be practical. If you and the Russian are killed, there's no one else. I may not be in a class with Beowulf Agate and the Serpent, but I'm not without certain talents.'

'How much time will you give me?'

'One week. Not a day more.'

Scofield picked up the pen, opened the small notebook and began to write.

4 April 1911
Porto Vecchio, Corsica
Scozzi
Voroshin
Waverly
Appleton

Current:
Guillamo Scozzi – Dead
Odile Verachten – Dead
John Waverly – Dead
Joshua Appleton – ?

Scozzi-*Paravicini*. Milan
Verachten Works. (Voroshin.) Essen
Trans-Communications. Boston.

Below the names and the companies, he then wrote
one word:
Matarese

Bray walked out of the elevator, his mind on air routes,
accessibilities and cover. Hours now took on the significance of days; there was so much to learn, so much to
find, and so little time to do it all.

They had thought it might end in London with the
breaking of David Waverly, *consigliere* of the Matarese,
Foreign Secretary of the United Kingdom. They should
have known better; the descendants were expendable.

Three were dead, three names removed from the guest
list of Guillaume de Matarese for the date of 4 April 1911.
Yet one was left. The golden politician of Boston, the man
few doubted would win the summer primaries and without
question the election in the fall. He would be President of
the United States, Joshua Appleton IV seemed truly to be
contemporary America's man-for-all-seasons. Many had
cried out during the tragic, violent 'sixties and 'seventies
that they could bind the country together; Appleton was
never so presumptuous as to make the statement, but
most of America thought he was perhaps the only man
who could.

But bind it for what? For whom? That was the most
frightening prospect of all. Was he the one descendant
not expendable? Chosen by the council, by the shepherd
boy, to do what the others could not do?

527

They would reach Appleton, thought Bray as he rounded the corner of the Connaught hallway towards his room, but not where Appleton expected to be reached – *if* he expected to be reached. They would not be drawn to Washington, where chance encounters with State, FBI and Company personnel were ten times greater than any other place in the hemisphere. There was no point in taking on two enemies simultaneously. Instead, they would go to Boston, to the conglomerate so aptly named Trans-Communications.

Somewhere, somehow, within the upper ranks of that vast company, they would find one man – one man with a blue circle on his chest or connections to Milan's Scozzi-Paravicini or Essen's Verachten, and that man would whisper an alarm sounding Joshua Appleton IV. They would trap him, take him in Boston. And when they were finished with him the secret of the Matarese would be exposed, told by a man whose impeccable credentials were matched only by his incredible deceit. It *had* to be Appleton; there was no one else. If they . . .

Scofield reached for the weapon in his holster. The door of his room twenty feet down the corridor was open. There were no circumstances imaginable that allowed it to be *conceivably* left open by choice! There had been an intruder – intruders.

He stopped, shook the paralysis from his mind, and ran to the side of the door, pivoting, pressing his back into the wall by the moulding. He lunged inside, crouching, levelling his gun in front of him, prepared to fire.

There was no one, no one at all. Nothing but silence and a very neat room. Too neat; the road map had been removed from the table, the glasses washed, returned to the silver tray on the bureau, the ashtrays wiped clean. There was no evidence that the room had been occupied. Then he saw it – them – and the paralysis returned.

On the floor by the table were his attaché case and travel

528

bag, positioned – neatly – beside each other, the way a steward or a bellboy might position them. And folded – neatly – over the travel bag was his dark blue raincoat. A guest was prepared for departure.

Two visitors had already departed. Antonia was gone, Taleniekov was gone.

The bedroom door was open, the bed fully made up, the bedside table devoid of the water pitcher and the ashtray which an hour ago had been filled with half-smoked cigarettes – testimony to an anxious, pain-stricken night and day.

Silence. Nothing.

His eyes were suddenly drawn to the one thing – again on the floor – that was not in keeping with the neatness of the room, and he felt sick. On the rug by the left side of the table was a circle of blood – a jagged circle, still moist, still glistening. And then he looked up. A small pane of glass had been blown out of the window.

'*Toni!*' The scream was his; it broke the silence, but he could not help himself. He could not think, he could not move.

The glass shattered; a second window pane blew out of its wooden frame and he heard the spinning whine of a bullet as it embedded itself in the wall behind him. He dropped to the floor.

The telephone rang, its jangling, erratic bell somehow proof of insanity! He crawled to the desk below the sight-line of the window.

'Toni? . . . *Toni!*' He was screaming, crying, yet he had not reached the desk, had not touched the phone.

He raised his hand and pulled the instrument to the floor beside him. He picked up the receiver and held it to his ear.

'We can always find you, Beowulf,' said the precise English voice on the other end of the line. 'I told you that when we spoke before.'

'What have you *done with her*!?' shouted Bray. 'Where *is she*?'

'Yes, we thought that might be your reaction. Rather strange coming from you, isn't it? You don't even inquire about the Serpent.'

'*Stop* it! Tell me!'

'I intend to. Incidentally, you had a grave lapse of judgement – again strange for one so experienced. We merely had to follow your friend Symonds from Belgravia. A quick perusal of the hotel register – as well as the time and the method of registering – gave us your room.'

'What have you *done* with her? . . . *Them?*'

'The Russian's wounded, but he may survive. At least sufficiently enough for our purposes.'

'The *girl!*'

'She's on her way to an airfield, as is the Serpent.'

'Where are you taking her?'

'We think you know. It was the last thing you wrote down before you named the Corsican. A city in the state of Massachusetts.'

'Oh, *God* . . . Symonds?'

'Dead, Beowulf. We have the notebook. It was in his car. For all intents and purposes, Roger Symonds, MI6, has disappeared. In view of his schedule, he may even be tied in with the terrorists who massacred the Foreign Secretary of England and his family.'

'You . . . *bastards*.'

'No. Merely professionals. I'd think you'd appreciate that. If you want the girl back you'll follow us. You see, there's someone who wants to meet with you.'

'Who?'

'Don't be a fool,' said the faceless messenger curtly.

'In Boston?'

'I'm afraid we can't help you get there, but we have every confidence in you. Register at the Ritz-Carlton

Hotel under the name of . . . Vickery. Yes, that's a good name, such a benign sound.'

'Boston,' said Bray, exhausted.

Again there was the sudden shattering of glass; a third window pane blew out of its frame.

'That shot,' said the voice on the phone, 'is a symbol of our good faith. We could have killed you with the first.'

31

He reached the coast of France, the same way he had left it four days ago: by motor launch at night. The trip to Paris took longer than anticipated; the drone he had expected to use wanted no part of him. The word was out, the price for his dead body too high, the punishment for helping Beowulf Agate too severe. The man owed Bray; he preferred to walk away.

Scofield found an off-duty *gendarme* in a bar in Boulogne-sur-Mer; the negotiations were swift. He needed a fast ride to Paris, to Orly Airport. To the *gendarme*, the payment was staggering; Bray reached Orly by daybreak. By 9.00, a Mr Edmonton was on the first Air Canada flight to Montreal. The plane left the ground and he turned his thoughts to Antonia.

They would use her to trap him, but there was no way they would permit her to stay alive once the trap had closed. Any more than they would let Taleniekov live once they had learned everything he knew. Even the Serpent could not withstand injections of scopolamine or sodium amytal; no man could block his memory or prohibit the flow of information once the gates of recall were chemically pried open.

These were the things he had to accept, and having accepted them, base his every move on their reality. He would not grow old with Antonia Gravet; there would be no years of peace. Once he understood this, there was nothing left but to try to reverse the conclusion, knowing that the chances of doing so were remote. Simply put, since there was absolutely nothing to lose, conversely there was no risk not worth taking, no strategy too outlandish or outrageous to consider.

The key was Joshua Appleton; that remained constant. Was it possible that the senator was such a consummate actor that he had been able to deceive so many so well for so long? Apparently it was so; one trained from birth to achieve a single goal, with unlimited money and talent available to him, could possibly conceal anything. But the gap that Scofield needed filling was found in the stories of Josh Appleton, Marine combat officer, Korea. They were well known, publicized by campaign managers, emphasized by the candidate's reluctance to discuss them, other than to praise the men who had served with him.

Captain Joshua Appleton had been decorated for bravery under fire on five separate occasions, but the medals were only symbols, the tributes of his men paeans of genuine devotion. Josh Appleton was an officer dedicated to the proposition that no soldier should take a risk he would not take himself; and no infantryman, regardless of how badly he was wounded or how seemingly hopeless the situation, was to be left to the enemy if there was any chance at all to get him back. With such tenets, he was not always the best of officers, but he was the best of men. He continuously exposed himself to the severest punishment to save a private's life, or draw fire away from a corporal's squad. He had been wounded twice dragging men out of the hills of Panmunjom, and nearly lost his life at Ch'osan when he had crawled through enemy lines to direct a helicopter rescue.

After the war, and he was home, Appleton had faced another struggle as dangerous as any he had experienced in Korea. A near fatal accident on the Massachusetts Turnpike. His car had swerved over the divider, crashing into an onrushing truck, the injuries sustained from head to legs so punishing the doctors at Massachusetts General had about given him up for dead. When the bulletins were issued about this decorated son of a prominent family, men came from all over the country. Mechanics, bus drivers, farmhands and clerks; the soldiers who had served under 'Captain Josh'.

For two days and nights they had kept vigil, the more demonstrative praying openly, others simply sitting with their thoughts or reminiscing quietly with their former comrades. And when the crisis had passed and Appleton was taken off the critical list, these quiet men went home. They had come because they had wanted to come; they had left not knowing whether they had made any difference, but hoping that they had. Captain Joshua Appleton IV, USMCR, was deserving of that hope.

This was the gap that Bray could neither fill nor understand. The captain who had risked his life so frequently, so openly for the sake of other men; how could those risks be reconciled with a man programmed since birth to become the President of the United States? How could repeated exposures to death be justified to the Matarese?

Somehow they had been, for there was no longer any doubt where Senator Joshua Appleton stood. The man who would be elected President of the United States before the year was over was inextricably tied to a conspiracy as dangerous as any in American history.

At Orly, Scofield picked up the Paris edition of the *Herald-Tribune* to see if the news of the Waverly massacre had broken; it had not. But there was something else, on the second page. It was another follow-up story concerning Trans-Communications' holdings in Verachten, including a partial list of the Boston conglomerate's board of directors. The third name on the roster was the senator from Massachusetts.

Joshua Appleton was not only a *consigliere* of the Matarese, he was the sole descendant of that guest list seventy years ago in Porto Vecchio to become a true inheritor.

'*Mesdames et messieurs, s'il vous plaît. À votre gauche, Les Îles de la Manche . . .*' The voice of the pilot droned from the aircraft's speaker. They were passing the Channel Islands; in six hours they would reach the coast of Nova Scotia, an hour later Montreal. And four hours after that, Bray would cross the US border south of Lacolle on the Richelieu River, into the waters of Lake Champlain.

In hours the final madness would begin. He would live or he would die. And if he could not live in peace with Toni, without the shadow of Beowulf Agate in front of him or behind him, he did not care to live any longer. He was filled with . . . emptiness. If the awful void could be erased, replaced with the simple delight of being with another human being, then whatever years he had left were most welcome.

If not, to hell with them.

Boston.

There's someone who wants to meet you.

Who? Why?

To make you a consigliere *of the Matarese . . . consider what you bring to such an organization.*

It was not hard to define. Taleniekov was right. Beowulf Agate knew where the bodies were, and how and why they no longer breathed. He could be invaluable.

They want you. If they can't have you, they'll kill you.

So be it; he would be no prize for the Matarese.

Bray closed his eyes; he needed sleep. There would be little in the days ahead.

The rain splattered against the windshield in continuous sheets, streaking to the right under the force of the wind that blew off the Atlantic over the coastal highway. Scofield had rented the car in Portland, Maine with a driver's licence and credit card he had never used before. Soon he would be in Boston but not in the way the Matarese expected. He would not race half-way across the world and announce his arrival by registering at the Ritz-Carlton as Vickery, only to wait for the Matarese's next move. A man in panic would, a man who felt the only way to save the life of someone he deeply loved would – but he was beyond panic, he had accepted total loss, therefore he could hold back and conceive of his own strategy. It was the fundamental advantage of a man who had lost hope; there was nothing not worth trying.

He would be in Boston, in his enemy's den, but his enemy would not know it. The Ritz-Carlton would receive two telegrams spaced a day apart. The first would arrive tomorrow requesting a suite for Mr B. A. Vickery of Montreal, arriving the following day. The second would be sent the next afternoon, stating that Mr Vickery had been delayed, his arrival now anticipated two days later. There would be no address for Vickery, only telegraph offices on Montreal's King and Market Streets, and no request for confirmations, the assumption here being that someone in Boston would make sure rooms were available.

Only the two telegrams, sent from Montreal; the Matarese had little choice but to believe he was still in Canada. What they could not know – suspect surely, but not be certain – was that he had used a drone to send them. He had. He had contacted a man, a felony-prone *séparatiste* he had known before, and met him at the airport, giving him the two handwritten messages on telegraph forms along with a sum of money and instructions when and from where to send them. Should the Matarese phone Montreal for immediate confirmation of origin, they would find the forms written in Bray's handwriting.

He had three days and one night to operate within Matarese territory, to learn everything he could about the conglomerate, Trans-Communications, and its hierarchy. To find another flaw, one significant enough to summon Senator Joshua Appleton IV, to Boston – on *his* terms. In panic.

So much to learn, so little time.

Scofield let his mind wander back to everyone he had ever known in Boston and Cambridge – both as student and professional. Among that crowd of fits and misfits there had to be someone who could help him.

He passed a road sign telling him he had left the town of Marblehead; he'd be in Boston in less than thirty minutes.

It was 5.35, the horns of impatient drivers blaring away on all sides as the taxi inched its way down Boylston Street's crowded shopping district. He had parked the rented car in the farthest reaches of the Prudential underground lot, available should he need it, but not subject to the vagaries of weather or vandalism. He was on his way to Cambridge; a name had come into focus. A man who had spent twenty-five years teaching corporate law at the Harvard School of Business. Bray had never met him; there was no way the Matarese could make him a target.

It was strange, thought Bray, as the cab clamoured over the ribs of the Longfellow Bridge, that both he and Taleniekov had been brought back – however briefly – to those places where it had begun for each of them. A lifetime ago . . . two students, one in Leningrad, one in Cambridge, Massachusetts, with a certain, not dissimilar talent for foreign languages.

He had begun a career in the State Department and been given such a fine title: Special Foreign Service Officer, Consular Operations. Neither the pay nor the grade was much, but the future was bright, productive . . . and, well, benevolent. Christ, the *irony*!

Had it happened that way with Taleniekov? Had the student from Leningrad pursued one course, veering into another, gradually, inexorably driven into waters he had not known were on any map? Until the pressures were so strong there was nothing left but to become the expert in order to survive? The questions were rhetorical; neither he nor the Russian would have become what they became unless the fundamentals had been there in the first place. Events shaped men, perhaps, but they did not remove alternatives of choice. It was not a pleasant thing to think about.

Was Taleniekov still alive? Or was he dead or dying somewhere in the city of Boston, Massachusetts?

Toni was alive; they'd keep her alive . . . for a while.

Don't think about them. Don't think about her now! There is no hope. Not really. Accept it, live with it. Then do the best you can . . .

The traffic congealed again at Harvard Square, the downpour causing havoc in the streets. People were crowded in storefronts, students in ponchos and jeans racing from kerb to kerb, slapping the hoods of cars, jumping over the flooded gutters, crouching under the awning of the huge newspaper stand . . .

The newspaper stand. *Newspapers From All Over The World* was the legend printed across the white sign above the canopy. Bray peered out the window, through the rain and the collection of bodies. One name, one man, dominated the observable headlines.

Waverly! David Waverly! England's Foreign Secretary!

'Let me off here,' he said to the driver, reaching for the soft travel bag and the hard-shelled briefcase at his feet.

He pushed his way through the crowd, grabbed two domestic papers off the row of twenty-odd different editions, left a dollar, and ran across the street at the first break in traffic. Half a block down Massachusetts Avenue was a German-style restaurant he vaguely remembered from his student days. The entrance was jammed; Scofield excused his way to the door, using his travel bag for interference, and went inside.

There was a line waiting for tables; he went to the bar, and ordered Scotch. The drink arrived; he unfolded the first newspaper. It was the Boston *Globe*; he started reading, his eyes racing over the words, picking out the salient points of the article. He finished and picked up the second paper; it was the Los Angeles *Times*, the story identical to the *Globe*'s wire service report, and almost surely the official version put out by Whitehall, which was what Bray wanted to know.

The massacre of David Waverly, his wife, children and servants in Belgrave Square was held to be the work of terrorists, most likely a splinter group of fanatical Palestinians. It was pointed out, however, that no group had as yet come forth to claim responsibility, and the P.L.O. vehemently denied participation. Messages of shock and condolence were being sent by political leaders across the world; parliaments and praesidiums, congresses and royal courts, all interrupted their businesses at hand to express their fury and grief.

Bray re-read both articles and the related stories in each paper, looking for Roger Symonds' name. It was not to be found; it would not come for days, if ever. The speculations were too wild, the possibilities too improbable. A senior officer of British Intelligence somehow connected to the slaughter of Britain's Foreign Secretary. The Foreign Office would put a clamp on Symonds' death for any number of reasons. It was no time to . . .

Scofield's thoughts were interrupted. In the dim light of the bar he had missed the insert; it was a late bulletin in the *Globe*.

LONDON, March 3 – An odd and brutal aspect of the Waverly killings was revealed by the police only hours ago. After receiving a gunshot in the head, David Waverly apparently received a grotesque *coup de grâce* in the form of a shotgun blast directly into his chest, literally removing the left side of his upper abdomen and rib cage. The medical examiner was at a loss to explain the method of killing, for the administering of such a death wound – considering the caliber and the proximity of the weapon – is considered extremely dangerous to the one firing the gun. The London police speculate that the weapon might have been a primitive short-barreled, hand-held shotgun once favored by roaming gangs of bandits in the Mediterranean. The 1934 *Encyclopedia of Weaponry* refers to the gun as the Lupo, the Italian word for 'wolf'.

The medical examiner in London might have trouble finding a reason for the 'method of killing', but Scofield did not. If England's Foreign Secretary had a jagged blue circle affixed to his chest in the form of a birthmark, it was gone.

And there was a message in the use of the Lupo. The Matarese wanted Beowulf Agate to understand clearly how far and how wide the Corsican fever had spread, into what rarefied circles of power it had reached.

He finished his drink, left his money on the bar with the two newspapers and looked around for a telephone. The name that had come into focus, the man he wanted to see, was Dr Theodore Goldman, a dean of the Harvard School of Business and a thorn in the side of the Justice Department. For he was an outspoken critic of the Anti-Trust Division, incessantly claiming that Justice prosecuted the minnows and let the sharks roam free. He was a middle-aged *enfant terrible* who enjoyed taking on the giants, for he was a giant himself, cloaking his genius behind a facade of good-humoured innocence that fooled no one.

If anyone could shed light on the conglomerate called Trans-Communications, it was Goldman.

Bray did not know the man, but he had met Goldman's son a year ago in The Hague – in circumstances that were potentially disastrous for a young pilot in the Air Force. Aaron Goldman had got drunk with the wrong people near the Groote Kerk, men known to be involved in a KGB infiltration of NATO. The son of a prominent American Jew was prime material for the Soviets.

An unknown intelligence officer had got the pilot away from the scene, slapped him into sobriety and told him to go back to his base. And after countless cups of coffee, Aaron Goldman had expressed his thanks.

'If you've got a kid who wants to go to Harvard, let me know, whoever you are. I'll talk to my dad, I swear it. What the hell's your name anyway?'

'Never mind,' Scofield had said. 'Just get out of here, and don't buy typing paper at the Co-op. It's cheaper down the block.'

'What the . . .'

'Get out of here.'

Bray saw the pay phone on the wall; he grabbed his luggage and walked over to it.

32

He picked up a small wet piece of newspaper on the rain-
soaked sidewalk and walked to the MBTA subway station
in Harvard Square. He went downstairs and checked his
soft leather suitcase in a locker. If it was stolen that would
tell him something, and there was nothing in it he could
not replace. He slid the wet scrap of paper carefully under
the far right corner of the bag. Later, if the fragile scrap
was curled, or the surface broken, that would tell him
something else: the bag had been searched and he was in
the Matarese sights.

Ten minutes later he rang the bell of Theodore Goldman's
house on Brattle Street. It was opened by a slender,
middle-aged woman, her face pleasant, her eyes curious.

'Mrs Goldman?'

'Yes?'

'I telephoned your husband a few minutes ago . . .'

'Oh, yes, of course,' she interrupted. 'Well, for heaven's
sake, get out of the rain! It's coming down like the forty-day
flood. Come in, come in. I'm Anne Goldman.'

She took his coat and hat; he held his attaché case.

'I apologize for disturbing you.'

'Don't be foolish. Aaron told us all about that night in
. . . The Hague. You know, I've never been able to figure
out where that place *is*. Why would a city be called *the*
anything?'

'It's confusing.'

'I gather our son was very confused *that* night; which is
a mother's way of saying he was plastered.' She gestured
towards a squared-off, double doorway so common to old
New England houses. 'Theo's on the telephone and trying

to mix his stinger at the same time; it's making him frantic. He hates the telephone and loves his evening stinger.'

Theodore Goldman was not much taller than his wife, but there was an expansiveness about him that made him appear much larger than he was. His intellect could not be concealed, so he took refuge in humour, putting guests – and, no doubt, associates – at ease.

They sat in three leather armchairs that faced the fire, the Goldmans with their stingers, Bray drinking Scotch. The rain outside was heavy, drumming on the windows. The recapping of their son's escapade in The Hague was over quickly, Scofield dismissing it as a minor night out on the town.

'With major consequences, I suspect,' said Goldman, 'if an unknown intelligence officer hadn't been in the vicinity.'

'Your son's a good pilot.'

'He'd better be; he's not much of a drinker.' Goldman sat back in his chair. 'But now, since we've met this unknown gentleman who's been kind enough to give us his name, what can we do for him?'

'To begin with, please don't tell anyone I came to see you.'

'That sounds ominous, Mr Vickery. I'm not sure I approve of Washington's tactics in these areas.'

'I'm no longer attached to the government; the request is personal. Frankly, the government doesn't approve of me any longer, because in my former capacity, I think I uncovered information Washington – especially the Department of Justice – doesn't want exposed. I believe it should be; that's as plain as I can put it.'

Goldman, the legal nemesis of the Justice Department, rose to the occasion. 'That's plain enough.'

'In all honesty, I used my brief meeting with your son as an excuse to talk to you. It's not admirable, but it's the truth.'

'I admire the truth. Why did you want to see me?'

Scofield put his glass down. 'There's a company here in Boston, at least the corporate headquarters are here. It's a conglomerate called Trans-Communications.'

'It certainly is.' Goldman chuckled. 'The Alabaster Bride of Boston. The Queen of Congress Street.'

'Now I don't understand,' said Bray.

'The Trans-Comm Tower,' explained Anne Goldman. 'It's a white stone building thirty or forty storeys high, with rows of tinted blue glass on every floor.'

'The ivory tower with a thousand eyes staring down at you,' added Goldman, still amused. 'Depending on the angle of the sun, some seem to be open, some closed, while others appear to be winking.'

'Winking? Closed?'

'*Eyes*,' pressed Anne, blinking her own. 'The horizontal lines of tinted glass are huge windows, rows and rows of large bluish circles.'

Scofield caught his breath. *Perro nostro circulo.* 'It sounds strange,' he said without emphasis.

'Actually, it's quite imposing,' replied Goldman. 'A bit *outré* for my taste, but I gather that's the point. There's a kind of outraged purity about it, a white shaft set down in the middle of the dark concrete jungle of a financial district.'

'That's interesting.' Bray could not help himself; he found an obscure analogy in Goldman's words. The white shaft became a beam of light; the jungle was chaos. A beam of light shooting through a dark void filled with clashing bodies in space. Light piercing chaos. *Chaos*.

'So much for the Alabaster Bride,' said the lawyer-professor. 'What did you want to know about Trans-Comm?'

'Everything you can tell me,' answered Scofield.

Goldman was mildly startled. 'Everything? . . . I'm not

sure I know that much. It's your classic multi-national conglomerate, I can tell you that. Extraordinarily diversified, brilliantly managed.'

'I read the other day that a lot of financial people were stunned by the extent of its holdings in Verachten.'

'Yes,' agreed Goldman, nodding his head in that exaggerated way a man does when he hears a foolish point being repeated. 'A lot of people *were* stunned, but I wasn't. Of course, Trans-Comm owns a great deal of Verachten. I daresay I could name four or five other countries where its holdings would stun these same people. The philosophy of a conglomerate is to buy as far and as wide as possible and diversify its markets. It both uses and refutes the Malthusian laws of economics. It creates aggressive competition within its own ranks, but does its best to remove all outside competitors. *That's* what multi-nationals are all about, and Trans-Comm's one of the most successful anywhere in the world.'

Bray watched the lawyer as he spoke. Goldman was a born teacher – infectious in delivery, his voice rising with enthusiasm. 'I understand what you're saying, but you lost me with one statement. You said you could name four or five other countries where Trans-Comm has heavy investments. How can you do that?'

'Not just me,' objected Goldman. 'Anybody can. All he has to do is read and use a little imagination. The laws, Mr Scofield. The laws of the host country.'

'The laws? Of a host country?'

'They're the only things that can't be avoided, the only protection buyers and sellers have. In the international financial community they take the place of armies. Every conglomerate must adhere to the laws of the country in which its divisions operate. Now, these same laws often ensure confidentiality; they're the frameworks within which the multi-nationals have to function – corrupting and altering them when they can, of course. And since they do, they must seek intermediaries to represent them. *Legally*. A Boston attorney practising before the Massachusetts bar would be of little value in Hong Kong. Or Essen.'

'What are you driving at?' Bray asked.

'You study the *law firms*.' Goldman leaned forward again. 'You match the firms and their locations with the general level of their clients and the services for which they're most recognized. When you find one that's known for negotiating stock purchases and exchanges, you look around to see what companies in the area might be ripe for invading.' The legal academician was enjoying himself. 'It's really quite simple,' he continued, 'and a hell of an amusing game to play. I've scared the be-jesus out of more than one corporate flunkie in those summer seminars by telling him where I thought his company's money men were heading. I've got a little index file – three by five cards – where I jot down my goodies.'

Scofield spoke; he had to know. 'What about Trans-Comm? Did you ever do a file card on it?'

'Oh, sure. That's what I meant about the other countries.'

'What are they?'

Goldman stood up in front of the fire, frowning in recollection. 'Let's start with the Verachten Works. Trans-Comm's overseas reports included sizable payments to the Gehmeinhoff-Salenger firm in Essen. Gehmeinhoff's a direct legal liaison to Verachten. And they're not interested in nickel-and-dime transactions; Trans-Comm had to be going after a big chunk of the complex. Although I admit, even I didn't think it was as much as the rumours indicate. Probably isn't.'

'What about the others?'

'Let's see . . . Japan. Kyoto. T-C uses the firm of Aikawa-Onmura-and-something. My guess would be Yakashubi Electronics.'

'That's pretty substantial, isn't it?'

'Panasonic can't compare.'

'What about Europe?'

'Well, we know about Verachten.' Goldman pursed his lips. 'Then, of course, there's Amsterdam; the law firm there is Hainaut and Sons, which leads me to think that Trans-Comm's bought into Netherlands Textiles, which is an umbrella for a score of companies ranging from Scandinavia to Lisbon. From here we can head over to Lyon . . .' The lawyer stopped and shook his head. 'No, that's probably tied in with Turin.'

'Turin?' Bray sat forward.

'Yes, they're so close together, the interests so compatible, there's no doubt prior ownership is buried in Turin.'

'Who in Turin?'

'The law firm's Palladino-E-LaTona, which can only mean one company – or companies. Scozzi-Paravicini.'

Scofield went rigid. 'They're a cartel, aren't they?'

'My God, yes. They – *it* – certainly is. Agnelli and Fiat get all the publicity, but Scozzi-Paravicini runs the Colosseum and all the lions. When you combine it with Verachten and Netherlands Textiles, throw in Yakashubi, add Singapore, and Perth, and a dozen other names in England, Spain, and South Africa I haven't mentioned, the Alabaster Bride of Boston has put together a global federation.'

'You sound as if you approve.'

'No, actually, I don't. I don't think anyone can, when so much economic power is so centralized. It's a corruption of the Malthusian law; the competition is fake. But I respect the reality of genius when its accomplishments are so obviously staggering. Trans-Communications was an idea born and developed in the mind of one man. Nicholas Guiderone.'

'I've heard of him. A modern-day Carnegie or Rockefeller, isn't he?'

'More. Much more. The Geneens, the Luces, the Bluhdorns, the wonderboys of Detroit and Wall Street, none of them can touch Guiderone. He's the last of the vanishing giants, a really benign monarch of industry and finance. He's been honoured by most of the major governments of the West, and not a few in the Eastern bloc, including Moscow.'

'Moscow?'

'Certainly,' said Goldman, nodding thanks to his wife, who was pouring a second stinger into his glass. 'No one's done more to open up East–West trade than Nicholas Guiderone. As a matter of fact I can't think of anyone who's done more for world trade in general. He's over eighty now, but I understand he's still filled with as much pee and vinegar as he was the day he walked out of Boston Latin.'

'He's from Boston?'

'Yes, a remarkable story. He came to this country as a boy. An immigrant boy of ten or eleven, without a mother, travelling with a barely literate father in the hold of a ship. I suppose you could call it the definitive story of the American dream.'

Involuntarily, Scofield gripped the arm of the chair. He could feel the pressure on his chest, the tightening in his throat. 'Where did that ship come from?'

'Italy,' said Goldman, sipping his drink. 'Southern part. Sicily, or one of the islands.'

Bray was almost afraid to ask the question. 'Would you by any chance know whether Nicholas Guiderone ever knew a member of the Appleton family?'

Goldman looked over the rim of his glass. 'I know it, and so does most everyone in Boston. Guiderone's father worked for the Appletons. For the senator's grandfather at Appleton Hall. It was old Appleton who spotted the boy's promise, gave him the backing, and persuaded the schools to take him. It wasn't so easy in those days, the early nineteen hundreds. The two-toilet Irish had barely got their second john, and there weren't too many of them. An Italian kid – excuse me, *Eye*talian – was nowhere. Gutter meat.'

Bray's words floated; he could hardly hear them himself.

'That was Joshua Appleton the second, wasn't it?'

'Yes.'

'He did all that for this . . . child.'

'Hell of a thing, wasn't it? And the Appletons had enough troubles then. They'd lost damn near everything in the market fluctuations. They were hanging on by the skin of their teeth. It was almost as if old Joshua had seen a message on some mystical wall.'

'What do you mean?'

'Guiderone paid everything back several thousand fold. Before Appleton was in his grave he saw his companies back on top, making money in areas he'd never dreamed of, the capital flowing out of the banks owned by the Italian kid he'd found in his carriage house.'

'Oh, my *God* . . .'

'I told you,' said Goldman. 'It's one hell of a story. It's all there to be read.'

'If you know where to look. And why.'

'I beg your pardon?'

'Guiderone . . .' Scofield felt as though he were walking through swirling circles of mist towards some eerie light. He put his head back and stared at the ceiling, at the dancing shadows thrown up by the fire. '*Guiderone*. It's a derivative of the Italian "*guida*". A guide.'

'Or shepherd,' said Goldman.

Bray snapped his head down, his eyes wide, riveted on the lawyer. 'What did you say?'

Goldman was puzzled. 'I didn't say it, he did. About seven or eight months ago at the UN.'

'The United Nations?'

'Yes. Guiderone was invited to address the General Assembly; the invitation was unanimous, incidentally. Didn't you hear it? It was broadcast all over the world. He even taped it in French and Italian for Radio-International.'

'I didn't hear it.'

'The UN's perennial problem. Nobody listens.'

'What did he say?'

'Pretty much what you just said. That his name had its roots in the word "*guida*", or guide. And that was the way he'd always thought of himself. As a simple shepherd, guiding his flocks, aware of the rocky slopes and uncrossable streams . . . that sort of thing. His plea was for international relationships based on the mutuality of material need, which he claimed would lead to the higher morality. It was a little strange philosophically, but it was damned effective. So effective, in fact, that there's a resolution on this session's agenda that'll make him a full-fledged member of the UN's Economic Council. That's not just a title, by the way. With his expertise and resources, there's not a government in the world which won't listen very hard when he talks. He'll be one damned powerful *amicus curiae*.'

'Did you hear him give that speech?'

'Sure,' laughed the lawyer. 'It was mandatory in Boston; you were cut off the *Globe*'s subscription list if you missed it. We saw the whole thing on Public Television.'

'What did he sound like?'

Goldman creased the flesh around his deep-set eyes and looked at his wife. 'Well, he's a very old man. Still vigorous, but nevertheless old. How would you describe him, darling?'

'Just as you do,' said Anne. 'An old man. Not large, but quite striking, with that look of a man who's so used to being listened to. I do remember one thing, though – about the voice. It was high-pitched and maybe a little breathless, but he spoke extremely clearly, every phrase very precise. You couldn't miss a word he said.'

Scofield closed his eyes and thought of a blind woman in the mountains above Corsica's Porto Vecchio, twisting the dials of a radio, and hearing *a voice crueller than the wind*.

He had found the shepherd boy.

33

He had found him!

Toni, I've found him! Stay alive! Don't let them destroy you. They won't kill your body. Instead, they'll try to kill your mind. Don't let them do it. They will go after your thoughts and the way you think. They will try to change you, alter the processes that make you what you are. They have no choice, my darling. A hostage must be programmed even after the trap is closed; professionals understand that. No extremity is beyond consideration. Find something within yourself – for my sake. You see, my dearest love, I've found something. I've found him. The shepherd boy! It is a weapon. I need time to use it. Stay alive. Keep your mind!

Taleniekov, the enemy I can't bring myself to hate any more. If you're dead there's nothing I can do but turn away, knowing that I'm alone. If you're alive, keep breathing. I promise nothing; there is no hope, not really. But we have something we never had before. We have him. We know who the shepherd boy is. The web is defined now and it circles the world. Scozzi-Paravicini, Verachten, Trans-Communications . . . and a hundred different companies between each one. All put together by the shepherd boy, all run from an alabaster tower that looks over the city with a thousand eyes . . . And yet there's something else. I know, I feel it! Something else that's in the middle of the web. We who've 'abused this world so well for so long' develop instincts, don't we? Mine is so strong I can taste it. It's out there. I just need time. Keep breathing . . . my friend.

I can't think about them any longer. I've got to put them out of my mind; they intrude, they interfere, they are barriers. They do not exist; she does not exist and I have lost her. We will not grow old together; there is no hope . . . Now, move. For Christ's sake, move!

He had left the Goldmans quickly, thanking them, bewildering them by his abrupt departure. He had asked only a few more questions – about the Appleton family – questions any knowledgeable person in Boston could answer. Having the information was all he needed; there was no point in staying longer. He walked now in the rain, smoking a cigarette, his thoughts on the missing fragment his instinct told him was a greater weapon than the shepherd boy, yet somehow part of the shepherd boy, intrinsic to the deceits of Nicholas Guiderone. What *was* it? Where was the false note he heard so clearly?

He knew one thing, however, and it was more than instinct. He had enough to panic Senator Joshua Appleton IV. He would telephone the senator in Washington and quietly recite a bill-of-particulars that began over seventy years ago, on the date of 4 April 1911, in the hills of Porto Vecchio. Did the senator have anything to say? Could he shed any light on an organization known as the Matarese which began its activities in the second decade of the century – at Sarajevo, perhaps – by selling political murder? An organization the Appleton family had never left, for it could be traced to a white skyscraper in Boston, a company honoured by the senator's presence on its board of directors. The age of Aquarius had turned into the age of conspiracy. A man on his march to the White House would have to panic, and in panic mistakes were made.

But panic could be controlled. The Matarese would mount the senator's defences swiftly, the presidency too great a prize to lose. And charges levelled by a traitor were no charges at all; they were merely words spoken by a man who had betrayed his country.

Instinct. Look at the man – the *man* – more closely.

Joshua Appleton was *not* as he was perceived to be

by the nation. The middle-aged paternal figure whose appeal ran across the spectrum. Then what about the day-to-day individual? Was that the smaller life, a dwarf with warts and blackheads and bloated appetites? Was it possible that the everyday man had weaknesses he'd find it infinitely more difficult to deny than a grand conspiracy levelled by a traitor? Was it conceivable – and the more Bray thought about it, the more logical it seemed – that the entire Korean experience had been a hoax? Had commanders been bought and medals paid for, a hundred men convinced by money to keep a vigil none gave a damn about? It would not have been the first time war had been used as a springboard for a celebrated civilian life. It was a natural, the perfect ploy, if the scenario could be executed with precision – and what scenario could not be with the resources controlled by the Matarese?

Look at the man. The *man*.

Goldman had brought the Appleton family up to date for Bray. The senator's official residence was a house in Concord where he and his family stayed only during the summer months. His father had died several years ago; Nicholas Guiderone had paid his last respects to the son of his mentor by purchasing the outsized Appleton Hall from the widow at a price far above the market, promising to keep the name in perpetuity. Old Mrs Appleton currently lived on Beacon Hill, in a brownstone on Louisburg Square.

The mother. What kind of a woman was she? In her middle seventies, Goldman had estimated. Could she tell him anything? Involuntarily perhaps a great deal. Mothers were much better sources of information than was generally believed, not for what they said, but for what they did not say, for subjects were changed abruptly.

It was twenty minutes past nine. Bray wondered if he could do it, reach Appleton's mother and talk with her. The house might be watched, but not on a priority basis.

A car parked in the Square with a view of the brownstone, one man, possibly two. If there were such men and he took them out, the Matarese would know he was in Boston; he was not ready for that. Still the mother might provide a short cut, a name, an incident, something he could trace quickly; there was so little time. Mr B. A. Vickery was expected at the Ritz-Carlton Hotel, but when he got there he had to bring leverage with him. At the optimum, he had to have his own hostage; he had to have Joshua Appleton IV.

There was no hope. There was nothing not worth trying. There was instinct.

The steep climb up Chestnut Street towards Louisburg Square was marked by progressively quieter blocks. It was as if one were leaving a profane world to enter a sacred one; garish neons were replaced by the muted flickering of gas lamps from another era, the cobblestone streets washed clean. He reached the Square, staying in the shadows of a brick building on the corner.

He took out a pair of small binoculars from his attaché case and raised them to his eyes. He focused the powerful Zeiss-Ikon lenses on each stationary car in the streets around the fenced-in park. It was the centre of Louisburg Square.

There was no one.

Bray put the binoculars back in his attaché case, left the shadows of the brick building and walked down the peaceful street towards the Appleton brownstone. The stately houses surrounding the small park with the wrought-iron fence and gate were quiet. The night air was bitterly cold now, the gas lamps flickering more rapidly with the intermittent gusts of winter wind; windows were closed, fires burning in the hearths of Louisburg Square. It *was* a different world, remote, almost isolated, certainly at peace with itself.

He climbed the white stone steps and rang the bell. The carriage lamps on either side of the door threw more light than he cared for.

He heard the sound of footsteps; a nurse opened the door and he knew instantly. The woman recognized him; it was in the short, involuntary gasp that escaped her lips, in the brief widening of her eyelids. It explained why no one was on the street: the guard was *inside* the house.

'Mrs Appleton, please?'

'I'm afraid she's retired.'

The nurse started to close the door rapidly. Scofield jammed his left foot into the base, his shoulder against the heavy black panel, and forced it open.

'I'm afraid you know who I am,' he said, stepping inside, dropping his attaché case.

The woman pivoted, her right hand plunging into the pocket of her uniform. Bray countered, pushing her farther into her own pivot, gripping her wrist, twisting it downward and away from her body. She screamed. Scofield yanked her to the floor, his knee crashing up into the base of her spine. With his left arm, he vised her neck from behind, forearm across her shoulder blades, and pulled up violently as she fell; ten more pounds of pressure and he would have broken her neck. But he did not want to do that. He wanted this woman alive; she collapsed to the floor unconscious.

He crouched in silence, removing the short-barrelled revolver from the nurse's pocket, waiting for sounds or signs of people. The scream must have been heard by anyone inside the house.

There was nothing – there was *something*, but it was so faint he could not channel a perception of what it was. He saw a telephone next to the staircase and crept over to pick it up. There was only the hum of a dial tone; no one was using the phone. Perhaps the woman had told the truth; it was entirely possible that Mrs Appleton had retired. He'd know shortly.

First, he had to know something else. He went back to the nurse, pulled her across the floor under the hallway light and ripped apart the front of her uniform. He tore the slip and brassiere beneath, pushed up her left breast, and studied the flesh.

There it was. The small, jagged blue circle as Taleniekov had described it. The birthmark that was no birthmark at all, but instead, the mark of the Matarese.

Suddenly, from above, there was the whirring sound of a motor, the vibration constant, bass-toned. Bray lunged across the unconscious body of the nurse, into the shadows of the stairs, and raised the revolver.

From around the curve of the first landing an old woman came into view. She was sitting in the ornate chair of an automatic lift, her frail hands holding the sculptured pole that shot up from the guard rail. She was encased in a high-collared dressing gown of dark grey, and her once-delicate face was ravaged, her voice strained.

'I imagine that's one way to leash the bitch-hound, or corner the wolf-in-season, but if your objective is sexual, young man, I question your taste.'

Mrs Joshua Appleton III was drunk. From the looks of her, she had been drunk for years.

'My only objective, Mrs Appleton, is to see *you*. This woman tried to stop me; this is her gun, not mine. I'm an experienced intelligence officer employed by the United States government and fully prepared to show you my identification. In light of what happened I am checking for concealed weapons. I would do the same in like circumstances anywhere, any time.' With those words, he had begun; and with an equanimity born of prolonged alcohol-saturation, the old woman accepted his presence.

Scofield carried the nurse into a small drawing room, bound her hands and feet in slipknots made from the torn nylon of her hose, saving the elastic waistband for

556

a gagging brace, pulled between her teeth, tied firmly to the back of her neck. He closed the door and returned to Mrs Appleton in the living room. She had poured herself a brandy; Bray looked at the odd-shaped glass and at the decanters that were placed on tables about the room. The glass was so thick that it could not be broken easily, and the crystal decanters were positioned so that a new drink was accessible every seven to ten feet in all directions. It was strange therapy for one so obviously an alcoholic.

'I'm afraid,' said Scofield, pausing at the door, 'that when your nurse regains consciousness I'm going to give her a lecture about the indiscriminate display of firearms. She has an odd way of protecting you, Mrs Appleton.'

'Very odd, young man.' The old woman raised her glass and cautiously sat down in an antimacassared armchair. 'But since she tried and failed so miserably, why don't you tell me what she was protecting me from? Why did you come to see me?'

'May I sit down?'

'By all means.'

Bray held her partially unfocused eyes. 'As I mentioned, I'm an intelligence officer attached to the Department of State . . .' He began his ploy, the words spoken with restraint and sympathy. 'A few days ago we received a report that implicates your son – through his father – to an organization in Europe known for years to be involved in international crime.'

'In *what*?' Mrs Appleton giggled. 'Really, you're very amusing.'

'Forgive me, but there's nothing amusing about it.'

'What are you talking about?'

Scofield described a group of men not unlike the Matarese council, watching the old woman closely for signs that she had made a connection. He was not even sure he had penetrated her clouded mind; he had to appeal to the mother, not the woman. 'The information from Europe was sent and received under the highest security classification. To the best of my knowledge, I'm the only one in Washington that's read it, and further, I'm convinced I can contain it. You see, Mrs Appleton, I think it's very important for this country that none of this touch the senator.'

'Young *man*,' interrupted the old woman. 'Nothing can touch the senator, don't you know that? My son will be the President of the United States. He'll be elected in the fall. Everybody says so. Everybody wants him.'

'Then I haven't been clear, Mrs Appleton. The report from Europe is devastating and I need information. Before your son ran for office, how closely did he work with his father in the Appleton business ventures? Did he travel frequently to Europe with your husband? Who were his closest friends here in Boston? That's terribly important. People that only you might know, men and women who came to see him at Appleton Hall.'

' "Appleton Hall . . . way up on Appleton Hill,"' broke in the old woman in a strained, whispered sing-song of no discernible tune. ' "With the grandest view of Boston . . . and ever will be still." Joshua the First wrote that over a hundred years ago. It's not very good, but they say he picked out the notes on a harpsichord. So like the Joshuas, a harpsichord. So like us all, really.'

'Mrs Appleton? After your son came back from the Korean War . . .'

'We *never* discuss that war!' For an instant the old woman's eyes became focused, hostile. Then the clouds returned. 'Of course, when my son is President they won't wheel me out like Rose or Miss Lillian. I'm kept for very special occasions.' She paused and laughed a soft, eerie laugh that was self-mocking. 'After very *special* sessions with the doctor.' She paused again and raised her left forefinger to her lips. 'You see, young man, sobriety isn't my strongest suit.'

Scofield watched her closely, saddened by what he saw. Beneath the ravaged face there had been a lovely face, the eyes once clear and alive, not floating in dead sockets as they were now. 'I'm sorry. It must be painful to know that.'

'On the contrary,' she replied whimsically. It was her turn to study him. 'Do you think you're clever?'

'I've never thought about it one way or the other.' *Instinct*. 'How long have you been . . . ill, Mrs Appleton?'

'As long as I care to remember and that is quite long enough, thank you.'

Bray looked again at the decanters. 'Has the senator been here recently?'

'Why do you ask?' She seemed amused. Or was she on guard?

'Nothing, really,' said Scofield casually; he could not alarm her. Not now. He was not sure why – or what – but something was happening. 'I indicated to the nurse that the senator might have sent me here, that he might be on his way himself.'

'Well, there you *are*!' cried the old woman, triumph in her strained, alcoholic voice. 'No wonder she tried to stop you!'

'Because of all these?' asked Bray quietly, gesturing at the decanters. 'Bottles filled – obviously every day – with booze. Perhaps your son might object.'

'Oh, don't be a damn fool! She tried to stop you because you *lied*.'

'Lied?'

'Of course! The senator and I meet only on special occasions – after those *very* special treatments – when I'm trotted out so his adoring public can see his adoring mother. My son has never been to this house and he would never come here. The last time we were alone was over eight years ago. Even at his father's funeral, although we stood together. We barely spoke.'

'May I ask why?'

'You may not. But I can tell you it has nothing to do with that gibberish – what I could make of it – you talked about.'

'Why did you say you never discussed the Korean War?'

'Don't presume, young man!' Mrs Appleton raised the glass to her lips; her hand trembled and the glass fell, brandy spilling on her gown. '*Damn!*' Scofield started out of his chair. 'Leave it alone,' she commanded.

'I'll pick it up,' he said, kneeling down in front of her. 'No point stumbling over it.'

'Then pick it up. And get me another, if you please.'

'Certainly.' He crossed to a near-by table and poured her a brandy in a fresh glass. 'You say you don't like to discuss the war in Korea . . .'

'I said,' interrupted the old woman, 'I *never* discussed it.'

'You're very fortunate. I mean just to be able to say it and let it go at that. Some of us aren't so lucky.' He remained in front of her, his shadow falling over her, the lie calculated. 'I can't. I was there. So was your son.'

The old woman drank several swallows without stopping, the way alcoholics do, needing the extra half ounce in their throats, abstractly convinced that it might not be there. She looked up at him, the brandy filling her head. 'Wars kill so much more than the bodies they take. Terrible things happen. Did they happen to you, young man?'

'They've happened to me.'

'Did they do those awful things to you?'

'What awful things, Mrs Appleton?'

'Starve you, beat you, bury you alive, your nostrils filled with dirt and mud, unable to breathe? Dying slowly, consciously, wide-awake and dying.'

The old woman was describing tortures documented by men held captive in North Korean camps. What was the relevance? 'No, those things didn't happen to me.'

'They happened to him, you know. The doctors told me. It's what made him change. Inside. Change so much. But we must never talk about it.'

'Talk about . . . ?' What was *she* talking about? 'You mean the senator?'

'Shhh!' The old woman drank the remainder of the brandy. 'We must never, *never* talk about it.'

'I see,' said Bray, but he did *not* see. Senator Joshua Appleton IV had never been held captive by the North Koreans. Captain Josh Appleton had *eluded* capture on numerous occasions, the very acts of doing so behind enemy lines a part of his commendations. Scofield remained in front of her chair and spoke again. 'But I can't say I ever noticed any great changes in him, other than getting older. Of course, I didn't know him that well twenty years ago, but to me he's still one of the finest men I've ever known.'

'*Inside!*' The old woman whispered harshly. 'It's all inside! He's a *mask* . . . and people adore him so.' Suddenly the tears were in her clouded eyes, and the words that followed a cry from deep within her memory. 'They *should* adore him! He was such a beautiful boy, such a beautiful young man. There was no one ever like my Josh, no one more loving, more filled with kindness! . . . Until they did those terrible things to him.' She wept. 'And I was such a dreadful person. I was his mother and I couldn't understand. I wanted my Joshua back! I wanted him back so badly!'

Bray knelt down and took the glass from her. 'What do you mean you wanted him back?'

'I couldn't understand. He was so cold, so distant. They'd taken the joy out of him. There was no *joy* in him! He came out of the hospital . . . and the pain had been too much and I *couldn't understand*. He looked at me and there was no joy, no love. Not inside!'

'The hospital? The accident after the war – just after the war?'

'He suffered so much . . . and I was drinking so much . . . so much. Every week he was in that awful war I drank more and more. I couldn't stand it! He was all I *had*. My husband was . . . in name only – as much my fault as his, I suppose. He was disgusted with me. But I loved my Josh so.' The old woman reached for the glass. He got to it first and poured her a drink. She looked at him through her tears, her floating eyes filled with the sadness of knowing what she was. 'I thank you very much,' she said with simple dignity.

'You're welcome,' he answered, feeling helpless, his mind pounding, but nevertheless helpless.

'In a way,' she whispered, gripping the glass tightly, 'I still have him but he doesn't know it. No one does.'

'How is that?'

'When I moved out of Appleton Hall . . . on Appleton Hill . . . I kept his room just the way it was, the way it had been. You see, he never came back, not really. Only for an hour one night to pick up some things. So I took a room here and made it his. It will always be his, but he doesn't know it.'

Bray knelt down in front of her again. 'Mrs Appleton, may I see that room? *Please*, may I see it?'

'Oh, no, that wouldn't be right,' she said. 'It's very private. It's his, and I'm the only one he lets in. He lives there still, you see. My beautiful Joshua.'

'I've got to see that room, Mrs Appleton. Where is it?' *Instinct*.

'Why do you have to see it?'

'I can help you. I can help your son. I know it.'

She squinted, studying him from some inner place. 'You're a kind man, aren't you? And you're not as young as I thought. Your face has lines, and there is grey at your temples. You have a strong mouth; did anyone ever tell you that?'

'No, I don't think anyone ever did. Please, Mrs Appleton, I *must* see that room. Allow me to.'

'It's nice that you ask. People rarely ask me for anything any more; they just tell me. Very well, help me to my lift, and we'll go upstairs. You understand, of course, we'll have to knock first. If he says you can't come in, you'll have to stay outside.'

Scofield guided her through the living room arch to the chair lift. He walked beside her up the staircase to the first-floor landing, where he helped her to her feet.

'This way,' she said, gesturing towards a narrow, darkened corridor. 'It's the last door on the right.'

They reached it, stood in front of it for a moment, and then the old woman rapped lightly on the wood. 'We'll know in a minute,' she continued, bending her head as if listening for a command from within. 'It's all right,' she said, smiling. 'He said you can come in, but you mustn't touch anything. He has everything arranged the way he likes it.' She opened the door, and flipped a switch on the wall. Three separate lamps went on; still the light was dim. Shadows were thrown across the floor and up on the walls.

The room was a young man's room, mementoes of an expensive youth on display everywhere. The banners above the bed and the desk were those of Andover and Princeton, the trophies on the shelves for such sports as sailing, skiing, tennis and lacrosse. The room had been preserved – eerily preserved – as if it had once belonged to a Renaissance prince. A microscope sat alongside a chemistry set, a volume of *Britannica* lay open, most of the page underlined, handwritten notes in the margins. On the bedside table were novels of Dos Passos and Koestler, beside them the typewritten title page of an essay authored by the celebrated inhabitant of that room. It was called: *The Pleasures and Responsibilities of Sailing in Deep Waters. Submitted by Joshua Appleton, Senior. Andover*

Academy. March 1945. Protruding from below the bed were three pairs of shoes: loafers, sneakers and black patent leathers worn with formal clothes. A life somehow covered in the display.

Bray winced in the dim light. He was in the tomb of a man very much alive, the artefacts of a life preserved, somehow meant to transport the dead safely on its journey through the darkness. It was a macabre experience when one thought of Joshua Appleton, the electric, mesmerizing senator from Massachusetts. Scofield glanced at the old woman. She was staring impassively at a cluster of photographs on the wall. Bray took a step forward and looked at them.

They were pictures of a younger Joshua Appleton and several friends – the same friends, apparently the crew of a sailboat – the occasion identified by the centre photograph. It showed a long banner being held by four men standing on the deck of a sloop. *Marblehead Regatta Championship – Summer 1949.*

Only the centre photograph and the three above it showed all four crew members. The three lower photographs were shots of only two of the four. Appleton and another young man, both stripped to the waist – slender, muscular, shaking hands above a tiller; smiling at the camera as they stood on either side of the mast, and sitting on the gunwhale, drinks held forward in a salute.

Scofield looked closely at the two men, then compared them to their associates. Appleton and his obviously closer friend had a strength about them absent in the other two, a sense of assurance, of conviction somehow. They were not alike except perhaps in height and breadth – athletic men comfortable in the company of each's peer – yet neither were they dissimilar. Both had sharp if distinctly different features – strong jaws, wide foreheads, large eyes and thatches of straight, dark hair – the kind of faces seen in scores of Ivy League yearbooks.

There was something disturbing about the photographs. Bray did not know what it was – but it was there. *Instinct.*

'They look as if they could be cousins,' he said.

'For years they acted as though they were *brothers*,' replied the old woman. 'In peace, they would be *partners*, in war, *soldiers* together! But he was a coward, he betrayed my son. My beautiful Joshua went to war alone and terrible things were done to him. He ran away to Europe, to the safety of a château in France and Switzerland. But justice is odd; he died in Gstaad, from injuries on a slope. To the best of my knowledge, my son has never mentioned his name since.'

'Since? . . . When was that?'

'Twenty-five years ago.'

'Who was he?'

She told him.

Scofield could not breathe; there was no air in the room, only shadows in a vacuum. He had found the shepherd boy, but instinct told him to look for something else, a fragment as awesome as anything he had learned. He had found it. The most devastating piece of the puzzle was in place. He needed only proof, even the semblance of proof, for the truth was so extraordinary.

He was in a tomb; the dead had journeyed in darkness for twenty-five years.

34

He guided the old woman to her bedroom, poured her a final brandy and left her. As he closed the door she was sitting on the bed chanting that unsingable tune. *Appleton Hall . . . way up on Appleton Hill.*

Notes picked out on a harpsichord over a hundred years ago. Notes lost, as she was lost without ever knowing why.

He returned to the dimly-lit room that was the resting place of memories and went to the cluster of photographs on the wall. He removed one and pulled the small picture hook out of the plaster, smoothing the wallpaper around the hole; it might delay discovery, certainly not prevent it. He turned off the lights, closed the door, and went downstairs to the front hall.

The guard-nurse was still unconscious; he left her where she was. There was nothing to be gained by moving her or killing her. He turned off every light, including the carriage lamps above the front steps, opened the door and slipped out into Louisburg Square. On the pavement, he turned right and began walking rapidly to the corner where he would turn right again, descending Beacon Hill into Charles Street to find a taxi. He had to pick up his luggage in the subway locker in Cambridge. The walk down the hill gave him time to think, time to remove the photograph from its glass frame, folding it carefully into his pocket – folding it very carefully so that neither face was damaged.

He needed a place to stay. A place to sit and fill up pages of paper with facts, conjectures and probabilities, his bill-of-particulars. In the morning, he had several things to do, among which were visits to the Massachusetts General Hospital and the Boston Public Library.

The room was no different from any other room in a very cheap hotel in a very large city. The bed sagged, and the single window looked out on a filthy stone wall not ten feet from the cracked panes of glass. The advantages, however, were the same as everywhere in such places; nobody asked questions. Cheap hotels had a place in this world, usually for those who did not care to join it. Loneliness was a basic human right, not to be tampered with lightly.

Scofield was safe; he could concentrate on his bill-of-particulars.

By 4.35 in the morning, he had filled seventeen pages. Facts, conjectures, probabilities. He had written the words carefully, legibly, so they could be clearly reproduced. There was no room for interpretation: the indictment was specific even where the motives were not. He was gathering his weapons, storing his bandoliers of ammunition; they were all he had. He fell back on the sagging bed and closed his eyes. Two or three hours' sleep would be enough.

He heard his own whisper float up to the cracked ceiling.

'Taleniekov . . . keep breathing. Toni, my love, my dearest love. Stay alive . . . keep your mind.'

The portly female clerk in the hospital's Department of Records and Billing seemed bewildered but she was not about to refuse Bray's request. It wasn't as if the medical information held there was that confidential, and a man who produced government identification certainly had to be given co-operation.

'Now, let me get this *cleah*,' she said in her Boston accent, reading the labels on the front of the cabinets. 'The senator wants the names of the doctors and the nurses who attended him during his stay here in 'fifty-three and 'fifty-four. From around November through March?'

'That's right. As I told you, next month's a sort of an anniversary for him. It'll be twenty-five years since he was given his "reprieve", as he calls it. Confidentially, he's sending each of them a small medallion in the shape of the medical shield with their names and his thanks inscribed on them.'

The clerk stopped. 'Isn't that just like him, though? To *remembah*? Most people go through an experience like that and just want to forget the whole thing. They figure they beat the reaper so the hell with everybody. Until next time, of course. But not him; he's so . . . well, concerned, if you know what I mean.'

'Yes, I do.'

'The *votahs* know it too, let me tell you. The Bay State's going to have its first President since J.F.K. And there won't be any of that religious nonsense about the Pope and the *cahdnells* running the White House, neither.'

'No, there won't,' agreed Bray. 'I'd like to stress again the confidential nature of my being here. The senator doesn't want any publicity about his little gesture . . .' Scofield paused and smiled at the woman. 'And as of now you're the only person in Boston who knows.'

'Oh, don't you worry about that. As we used to say when we were kids, my lips are sealed. And I'd really treasure a note from Senator Appleton, with his signature and everything, I mean.' The woman stopped and tapped a file cabinet. 'Here we are,' she said, opening the drawer. 'Now, remember, all that's here are the names of the doctors – surgeons, anaesthesiologists, consultants – listed by floor and Operation Room desks; the staff nurses assigned, and a schedule of the equipment used. There are no psychiatric or medical evaluations; they can only be obtained directly through the physician. But then you're not interested in any of that; you'd think I was *tahkin'* to one of those damned insurance sneaks.' She gave him the file. 'There's a table at the end of the aisle. When you're finished, just leave the folder on my desk.'

'That's OK,' said Bray, knowing better. 'I'll put it back; no sense bothering you. Thanks again.'

'Thank *you*.'

Scofield read through the pages rapidly to get a general impression. Medically, most of what he read was beyond his comprehension, but the conclusion was inescapable. Joshua Appleton had been more dead than alive when the ambulance had brought him to the hospital from the collision on the Turnpike. Lacerations, contusions, convulsions, fractures, along with severe head and neck wounds, painted the bloody picture of a mutilated human face and body. There were lists of drugs and serums used to prolong the life that was ebbing, detailed descriptions of the sophisticated machinery employed to stop deterioration. And ultimately, weeks later, the reversal began to take place. The incredibly more sophisticated machine that was the human body started to heal itself.

Bray wrote down the names of the doctors and the attending nurses listed in the floor and O.R. schedules. Two surgeons, one a skin-graft specialist, and a rotating team of eight nurses appeared consistently during the first weeks, then abruptly their names were no longer there, replaced by two different physicians and three private nurses, assigned to eight-hour shifts.

He had what he needed, a total of fifteen names, five primary, ten secondary. He would concentrate on the former, the last two physicians and the three nurses; the earlier names were removed from the time in question.

He replaced the folder and went back out to the clerk's desk. 'All done,' he said, then added as if the thought had just struck him. 'Say, you could do me – the senator – one more favour, if you would.'

'If I can, sure.'

'I've got the names here, but I need a little updating. After all, it was twenty-five years ago. Some of them may not be around any longer. It would help if I got some current addresses.'

'I can't help,' said the clerk, reaching for the phone on her desk. 'But I can send you upstairs. This is patient territory; they've got the personnel records. Lucky *bahstaads*, they're computerized.'

'I'm still very concerned about keeping this confidential.'

'Hey, don't you worry, you've got Peg Flannagan's word for it. My girl-friend runs that place.'

Scofield sat next to a bearded black college student in front of a computer keyboard. The young man had been assigned to help by Peg Flannagan's girl-friend. He was annoyed that his office-temp job had suddenly required him to put down his textbooks.

'I'm sorry to bother you,' said Bray, wanting a temporary friend.

'It's nothin', man,' answered the student, punching the keys. 'It's just that I got an exam tomorrow and any piss ant can run this barbarian hardware.'

'What's the exam?'

'Tertiary kinetics.'

Scofield looked at the student. 'Someone once used the word "tertiary" with me when I was in school around here. I didn't know what he meant.'

'You probably went to Harvard, man. That's turkey-time. I'm at Tech.'

Bray was glad the old school spirit was still alive in Cambridge. 'What have you got?' he asked, looking at the screen above the keyboard. The black had keyed in the name of the first doctor.

'I've got an omniscient tape, and you've got nothin'.'

'What do you mean?'

'The good doctor doesn't exist. Not as far as this

institution is concerned. He's never so much as dispensed an aspirin in this joint.'

'That's crazy. He was listed in the Appleton records.'

'Speak to the lord-of-the-*phi's*, man. I punched the letters and up comes *No Rec*.'

'I know something about these machines. They're easily programmed.'

The black nodded. 'Which means they're easily de-programmed. Rectified, as it were. Your doctor was *dee*-leted. Maybe he stole from Medicare.'

'Maybe. Let's try the next.'

The student keyed in the name. 'Well, we know what happened to this boy. *Ceb Hem*. He died right here on the third floor. Cerebral haemorrhage. Never even got a chance to get his tuition back.'

'What do you mean?'

'Med school, man. He was only thirty-two. Hell of a way to go at thirty-two.'

'Also unusual. What's the date?'

'21 March 1954.'

'Appleton was discharged on the thirtieth,' said Scofield as much to himself as to the student. 'These three names are nurses. Try them, please.'

Katherine Connally. Deceased 3–26–54.

Alice Bonelli. Deceased 3–26–54.

Janet Drummond. Deceased 3–26–54.

The student sat back, he was not a fool. 'Seems there was a real epidemic back then, wasn't there? March was a rough month, and the twenty-sixth was a *baad* day for three little girls in white.'

'Any cause of death?'

'Nothin' listed. Which only means they didn't die on the premises.'

'But all three on the same *day*? It's . . .'

'I dig,' said the young man. 'Crazy.' He held up his hand. 'Hey, there's an old cat who's been here for about

571

six thousand years. He runs the supply room on the first floor. He might remember something; let me get him on the horn.' The black wheeled his chair around and reached for a telephone on the counter. 'Get on line two,' he said to Bray, pointing to another phone on a near-by table.

'*Furst* floor supply,' was the voice in a loud Irish brogue.

'Hey, Methuselah, this is Amos – as in Amos and Andy.'

'You're a nutty boy-o, you are.'

'Hey, Jimmy, I got this honky friend on the horn here. He's looking for information that goes back to when you were the terror of the angels' dorm. As a matter of fact, it concerns three of them. Jimmy, you recall a time in the middle 'fifties when three nurses all died on the same day?'

'Three . . .' The breathing over the line was that of a man remembering. 'Oh, indeed I do. T'was a terrible thing. Little Katie Connally was one of 'em.'

'What happened?' asked Bray.

'They drowned, sir. All three of the girls drowned. They was in a boat and the damn thing pitched over, throwin' 'em into a bad sea.'

'In a boat? In *March*?'

'One of those crazy things, sir. You know how rich kids prowl around the nurses' dormitories. They figure the girls see naked bodies all the time, so maybe they wouldn't mind lookin' at theirs. Well, one night these punk-swells were throwin' a party at this fancy yacht club and asked the girls up. There was drinkin' and all kinds of nonsense, and some jackass got the bright idea to take out a boat. Damn fool thing, of course. As you say, it was in March.'

'It happened at night?'

'Yes, indeed, sir. The bodies didn't wash up for a week, I believe.'

'Was anyone else killed?'

'Of course not. It's never that way, is it? I mean, rich kids are always such good swimmers, aren't they now?'

'Where did it happen?' asked Scofield. 'Can you remember?'

'Sure, I can, sir. It was up the coast. Marblehead.'

Bray closed his eyes. 'Thank you,' he said quietly, replacing the phone.

'Thanks, Methuselah.' The student hung up, his eyes on Scofield. 'You got trouble, don't you?'

'I got trouble,' agreed Bray, walking back to the keyboard. 'I've also got ten more names. Two doctors and eight nurses. Can you run them through for me just as fast as you can?'

Of the eight nurses, exactly half were still alive. One had moved to San Francisco – address unknown; another lived with a daughter in Dallas, and the remaining two were in the St Agnes Retirement Home in Worcester. One of the doctors was still alive. The skin-graft specialist had died eighteen months ago at the age of seventy-three. The first surgeon, Nathaniel Crawford, had retired and was living in Quincy.

'May I use your phone?' asked Scofield. 'I'll pay whatever charges there are.'

'Last time I looked, none of these horns was in my name. Be my guest.'

Bray had written down the number on the screen; he went to the telephone and dialled.

'Crawford here.' The voice from Quincy was brusque but not discourteous.

'My name is Scofield, sir. We've never met and I'm not a physician, but I'm very interested in a case you were involved with a number of years ago at Massachusetts General. I'd like to discuss it briefly with you, if you wouldn't mind.'

'Who was the patient? I had a few thousand.'

'Senator Joshua Appleton, sir.'

There was a slight pause on the line; when Crawford spoke, his brusque voice took on an added tone of weariness. 'Those goddamned incidents have a way of following a man to his grave, don't they? Well, I haven't practised for over two years now, so whatever *you* say or *I* say, it won't make any goddamned difference . . . let's say I made a mistake.'

'Mistake?'

'I didn't make many; I was head of surgery for damn near twelve years. My summary's in the Appleton medical file; the only reasonable conclusion is that the X-rays got fouled up, or the scanning equipment gave us the wrong data.'

There was no summary from Nathaniel Crawford in the Appleton medical file.

'Are you referring to the fact that you were replaced as Appleton's surgeon?'

'Replaced, hell! Tommy Belford and I got our asses kicked four-square out of there by the family.'

'Belford? Is that Belford the skin-graft specialist?'

'A *surgeon*. A plastic surgeon and a goddamned artist. Tommy put the man's face back on like he was Almighty God himself. That whiz-kid they brought in messed up Tommy's work, in my opinion. Sorry about him, though. The kid hardly finished when his head blew.'

'Do you mean a cerebral haemorrhage, sir?'

'That's right. The Swiss was right there when it happened. He operated but it was too late.'

'When you say "the Swiss", do you mean the surgeon who replaced you?'

'You got it. The great *Herr Doktor* from Zurich. That *bahstaad* treated me like a retarded med. school drop-out.'

'Do you know what happened to him?'

'Went back to Switzerland, I guess. Never was interested in looking him up, myself.'

'Sir, you say you made a mistake. Or the X-rays did or the equipment. What kind of a mistake?'

'Simple; I gave up. We had run him on total support systems, and that's exactly what I figured they were. Total support; without them he wouldn't have lasted a day. And if he had, I thought it would be a waste; he'd live like a vegetable.'

'You saw no hope of recovery?'

Crawford lowered his voice, strength in his humility. 'I was a surgeon, I wasn't God. I was fallible. It was my opinion then that Appleton was not only beyond recovery, he was dying a little more with each minute . . . I was wrong.'

'Thank you for talking to me, sir.'

'As I said before, it can't make any difference now, and I don't mind. I had a hell of a lot of years with a knife in my hand; I didn't make many mistakes.'

'I'm sure you didn't, sir. Goodbye.' Scofield walked back to the keyboard; the black student was reading his textbook. 'X-rays . . . ?' said Bray softly.

'What?' The black looked up. 'What about X-rays?'

Bray sat down next to the young man. If he ever needed a temporary friend it was now; he hoped he had one. 'How well do you know the hospital staff?'

'It's a big place, man.'

'You knew enough to call Methuselah.'

'Well, I've been working here off and on for three years. I get around.'

'Is there a repository for X-rays going back a number of years?'

'Like maybe twenty-five?'

'Yes.'

'There is. It's no big deal.'

'Can you get me one?'

The student raised an eyebrow. 'That's another matter, isn't it?'

'I'm willing to pay. Generously.'

The black grimaced. 'Oh, man! It's not that I look

askance at bread, believe me. But I don't steal and I don't push and God knows I didn't inherit.'

'What I'm asking you to do is the most legitimate – even moral, if you like – thing I could ask anyone to do. I'm not a liar.'

The student looked into Bray's eyes. 'If you are, you're a damned convincing one. And you've got troubles. I've seen that. What do you want?'

'An X-ray of Joshua Appleton's mouth.'

'Mouth? His *mouth*?'

'His head injuries were extensive, dozens of pictures had to be taken. There had to be a lot of projected dental work. Can you do it?'

The young man nodded. 'I think so.'

'One more thing. I know it'll sound . . . outrageous to you, but take my word for it, nothing's outrageous. How much do you make a month here?'

'I average eighty, ninety a week. About three-fifty a month. It's not bad for a graduate student. Some of these interns make less. 'Course, they get room and board. Why?'

'Suppose I told you that I'd pay you ten thousand dollars to take a plane to Washington and bring me back another X-ray. Just an envelope with an X-ray in it.'

The black tugged at his short beard, his eyes on Scofield as though he were observing a lunatic. '*Suppose?* I'd say "feets, do your stuff!" Ten thousand *dollars*?'

'There'd be more time for those tertiary kinetics.'

'And there's nothin' illegal? It's straight – I mean really straight?'

'For it to be considered remotely illegal as far as you're concerned, you'd have to know far more than anyone would tell you. That's straight.'

'I'm just a messenger? I fly to Washington and bring back an envelope . . . with an X-ray in it?'

'Probably a number of small ones. That's all.'

576

'What are they of?'
'Joshua Appleton's mouth.'

It was 1.30 in the afternoon when Bray reached the library on Boylston Street. His new friend – Amos Lafollet – was taking the two P.M. shuttle to Washington and would return on the eight o'clock flight. Scofield would meet him at the airport.

Obtaining the X-rays had not been difficult; anyone who knew the bureaucratic ways of Washington could have got them. Bray made two calls, the first to the Congressional Liaison Office and the second to the dentist in question. The first call was made by a harried aide of a well-known Representative suffering from an abscessed tooth. Could Liaison please get this aide the name of Senator Appleton's dentist. The senator had mentioned the man's superior work to the congressman. Liaison gave out the dentist's name.

The call to the dentist was a routine spot check by the General Accounting Office, all bureaucratic form, no substance, forgotten tomorrow. GAO was collecting back-up evidence for dental work done on senators and some idiot on K Street had come up with X-rays. Would the receptionist please pull Appleton's and leave them at the front desk for a GAO messenger? They would be returned in twenty-four hours.

Washington operated at full speed; there simply was not enough time to do the work that had to be done and GAO spot checks were not legitimate work. They were irritants and complied with in irritation, but nevertheless obeyed. Appleton's X-rays would be left at the desk.

Scofield checked the library directory, took the elevator to the second floor, and walked down the hallway to the *Journalism Division – Current and Past Publications. Microfilm.*

He went to the counter at the far end of the room and spoke to the clerk behind it.

'March and April 1954, please. The *Globe* or the *Examiner*, whatever's available.'

He was given eight boxes of film, and assigned a cubicle. He found it, sat down and inserted the first roll of film.

By March of '54 the bulletins detailing the condition of Joshua Appleton – 'Captain Josh' – had been relegated to the back pages; he had been in the hospital over twenty weeks by then. But he was not ignored. The famous vigil was covered in detail. Bray wrote down the names of several of those interviewed; he would know by tomorrow whether there'd be any reason to get in touch with them.

21 March 1954
Young Doctor Dies of Cerebral Haemorrhage

The brief story was on page sixteen. No mention of the fact that the surgeon had attended Joshua Appleton.

26 March 1954
Three Mass. Gen'l Nurses
Killed in Freak Boating Accident

The story had made the lower left corner of the front page, but again, there was no mention of Joshua Appleton. Indeed, it would have been strange if there had been; the three were on a rotating twenty-four-hour schedule. If they were all in Marblehead that night, who was at the Appleton bedside?

10 April 1954
Bostonian Dies in Gstaad Skiing Tragedy

He had found it.

It was – naturally – on the front page, the headlines prominent, the copy written as much to evoke sympathy as to report the tragic death of a young man. Scofield studied the story, positive that he would come to certain lines.

He did.

> *Because of the victim's deep love of the Alps – and to spare family and friends further anguish – the family has announced that the burial will take place in Switzerland, in the village of Col du Pillon.*

Bray wondered who was in that coffin in Col du Pillon. Or was it merely empty?

He returned to the cheap hotel, gathered his things together and took a cab to the Prudential Center Parking Lot, Gate A. He drove the rented car out of Boston, along Jamaica Way into Brookline. He found Appleton Hill, driving past the gates of Appleton Hall, absorbing every detail he could within the short space of time.

The huge estate was spread like a fortress across the crest of the hill, a high stone wall surrounding the inner structure, tall roofs that gave the illusion of parapets seen above the distant wall. The roadway beyond the main gate wound up the hill around a huge brick carriage house, covered with ivy, housing no fewer than eight to ten complete apartments, five garages fronting an enormous concrete parking area below.

He drove around the hill. The ten-foot-high wrought-iron fence was continuous; every several hundred yards small lean-to shelters were built into the earth of the hill like miniature bunkers, and within a number of them he could see uniformed men sitting and standing, smoking cigarettes and on the telephone.

It was the seat of the Matarese, the home of the Shepherd Boy.

At 9.30 he drove out to Logan Airport. He had told Amos Lafollet to get off the plane and go directly to the dimly-lit bar across from the main news stand. The booths were so dark it was nearly impossible to see a face five feet in front of one, the only light a series of flashes from an enormous television screen on the wall.

Bray slid into the black plastic booth, adjusting his eyes to the lack of light. For an instant he thought of another booth in another dimly-lit room and another man. London, the Connaught Hotel, Roger Symonds. He pushed the memory from his mind; it was an obstacle. He could not handle obstacles right now.

He saw the student walk through the bar's entrance. Scofield stood up briefly; Amos saw him and came over. There was a manilla envelope in his hand and Bray felt a quick acceleration in his chest.

'I gather everything went all right,' he said.

'I had to sign for it.'

'You *what*?' Bray was sick; it was such a little thing, an obvious thing, and he had not thought of it.

'Take it easy. I wasn't brought up on 135th Street and Lennox Avenue for nothing.'

'What name did you use?' asked Scofield, his pulse receding.

'R. M. Nixon. The receptionist was real nice. She thanked me.'

'You'll go far, Amos.'

'I intend to.'

'I hope this'll help.' Bray handed his envelope across the table.

The student held it between his fingers. 'Hey, man, you know you don't really have to do this.'

'Of course, I do. We had an agreement.'

'I know that. But I've got an idea you've gone through a lot of sweat for a lot of people you don't know.'

'And a number that I know very well. The money's incidental. Use it.' Bray opened his attaché case and slipped the envelope inside – right above a file folder containing Joshua Appleton's X-ray from twenty-five years ago. 'Remember, you never knew my name and you never went to Washington. If you're *ever* asked, you merely ran some forgotten names through a computer for a man who never identified himself. *Please*. Remember that.'

'That's going to be tough.'

'Why?' Scofield was alarmed.

'How am I going to dedicate my first textbook to you?'

Bray smiled. 'You'll think of something. Goodbye,' he said, getting out of the booth. 'I've got an hour's drive and several more of sleep to catch up on.'

'Stay well, man.'

'Thanks, professor.'

Scofield stood in the dentist's waiting room on Main Street in Andover, Massachusetts. The name of the dentist had been supplied – happily, even enthusiastically – by the Nurse's Office of Andover Academy. Anything for Andover's illustrious – and generous – alumnus, and by extension the senator's aide, of course. Naturally, the dentist was not the same name who had tended Senator Appleton when he was a student; that practice had been taken over by a nephew a number of years ago, but there was no question that the present doctor would co-operate. The Nurse's Office would call him and let him know the senator's aide was on the way over.

Bray had counted on a psychology as old as the dentist's drill. Two young boys who were close friends and away at prep school might not see eye-to-eye on every issue, but they would share the same dentist.

Yes, both boys had gone to the very same man in Andover.

The harried dentist came out of the door that led to a storeroom, half-glasses perched on the edge of his nose. In his hand were two sheets of cardboard, small negatives embedded in each. X-rays of two Andover students taken over thirty years ago.

'Here you are, Mr Vickery,' said the dentist, holding out the X-rays. '*Damn*, will you look at the primitive way they used to mount these things! One of these days I've got to clean out that mess back there, but then you never know. Last year I had to identify an old patient of my uncle's who was burned to death in that fire over in Boxford.'

'Thank you very much,' said Scofield, accepting the X-ray sheets. 'By the way, sir, I know you're rushed but I wonder if you'd mind one more favour? I've got two newer sets here of both men and I've got to match them with the ones you're lending us. Of course, I can get someone to do it, but if you've got a minute.'

'Sure. Won't even take a minute. Let me have them.' Bray removed the two sets of X-rays from their envelopes; one stolen from the Massachusetts General Hospital, the other obtained in Washington. He had placed white tape over the names. He gave them to the dentist, who carried them to a lamp and held them in sequence against the glare of the light bulb above the shade. 'There you are,' he said, holding the matching X-rays separately in each hand.

Scofield put each set in a different envelope. 'Thanks again.'

'Any time.' The dentist walked rapidly back into his office. He was a man in a hurry.

Bray sat in the front seat of the car, his breathing erratic, perspiration on his forehead. He opened the envelopes and took out the X-ray sheets.

He pulled off the small strips of tape that covered the names.

He had been right. The awesome fragment was irrevocably in place, the proof in his hand.

The man who sat in the Senate, the man who unquestionably would be the next President of the United States, was not Joshua Appleton IV.

He was Julian Guiderone, son of the Shepherd Boy.

35

Scofield drove south-east to Salem. Delay was irrelevant now, previous schedules to be thrown away. He had everything to gain by moving as fast as he could, as long as every move was the right move, every decision the perceptive decision. He had his cannons and his nuclear bomb – his bill-of-particulars and the X-rays. It was a question now of mounting his weapons properly, *using* them, not only to blow the Matarese out of existence but first – above all, *first* – to find Antonia and force them to release her. And Taleniekov, if he was still alive.

Which meant he had to create a deception of his own. All deceptions were based on illusion, and the illusion he had to convey was that Beowulf Agate could be had, his cannons and his bomb defused, his assault stopped, the man himself destroyed. To do this he had to take the initial position of strength . . . the weakness to follow.

The hostage strategy would not wash any longer; he would not be able to get near Appleton. The Shepherd Boy would not permit it, the prize of the White House too great to place in jeopardy. Without the man there was no prize. So his position of strength lay in the X-rays. It was imperative he establish the fact that only a single set of X-rays existed, that duplicates were out of the question. Spectro-analysis would reveal any such duplicating process and Beowulf Agate was not a fool; he would expect an analysis to be made. He wanted the girl; he wanted the Russian; the X-rays could be had for them.

There would be a subtle omission in the mechanics of the exchange, a seeming weakness the enemy would pounce on; but it would be calculated, no weakness at all. The Matarese would be forced to go through with the exchange. A Corsican girl and a Soviet intelligence officer for X-rays that showed incontrovertibly that the man sitting in the Senate, on his way to the presidency, was not Joshua Appleton IV – legend of Korea, politician extraordinary – but instead, a man supposedly buried in 1954 in the Swiss village of Col du Pillon.

He drove down towards Salem harbour, drawn as he was always drawn towards the water, not precisely sure what he was looking for until he saw it: a shield-shaped sign on the lawn of a small hotel. *Efficiency Suites*. It made sense. Rooms with a refrigerator and cooking facilities. There'd be no stranger eating in restaurants; it was not the tourist season in Salem.

He parked the car in a lot covered with white gravel and bordered by a white picket fence, the grey water of the harbour across the way. He carried his attaché case and travel bag inside, registered under an innocuous name, and asked for a suite.

'Will payment be made by credit card, sir?' asked the young woman behind the counter.

'I beg your pardon?'

'You didn't check off the method of payment. If it's a credit card, our policy is to run the card through the machine.'

'I see. No, actually, I'm one of those strange people who use real money. One man's fight against plastic. Why don't I pay you for a week in advance? I doubt I'll stay any longer.' He gave her the money. 'I assume there's a grocery store near-by.'

'Yes, sir. Just up the street.'

'What about other stores? I've a number of things to get.'

'There's the Shopping Plaza about ten blocks west. I'm sure you'll find everything you need there.'

Bray hoped so; he was counting on it.

He was taken to his 'suite', which was in effect one large room with a pull-out bed and divider that concealed the smallest stove this side of a hot plate and a refrigerator. But the room looked out over the harbour; it was fine. He opened his attaché case, took out the photograph he had removed from the wall on Mrs Appleton's tomb for her son, and stared at it. Two young men, tall, muscular, neither to be mistaken for the other, but enough alike for an unknown surgeon somewhere in Switzerland to sculpt one into the other. A young American doctor paid to sign the medical authorization of discharge, then killed for security. A mother maintained as an alcoholic, kept at a distance, but paraded whenever it was convenient and fruitful to do so. Who knew a son better than his mother? Who in America would argue with, much less confront, Mrs Joshua Appleton III?

Scofield sat down and added a page to the seventeen in his bill-of-particulars. Doctors: *Nathaniel Crawford and Thomas Belford. A Swiss physician de-programmed from a computer; a young plastic surgeon dead suddenly of a cerebral haemorrhage. Three nurses drowned off Marblehead. Gstaad: a coffin in Col du Pillon; X-rays – one set from Boston, one set from Washington, two from Main Street, Andover, Massachusetts. Two different men merged into one, and the one was a lie. A fraud was about to become President of the United States.*

Bray finished writing, and walked to the window that looked out on the still, cold waters of Salem harbour. The dilemma was clearer than it had ever been: they had traced the Matarese from its roots in Corsica through a federation of multi-national corporations that encircled the globe; they knew it financed terror the world over, encouraged the chaos that resulted from assassinations and kidnappings, killing in the streets and aircraft blown out of the skies. They understood all this but they did not know why.

Why?

The reason would have to wait. Nothing mattered but the deception that was Senator Joshua Appleton IV. For once the son of the Shepherd Boy reached the presidency, the White House belonged to the Matarese.

What better residence for a *consigliere* . . .

Keep breathing, my old enemy.

Toni, my love. Stay alive. Keep your mind.

Scofield went back to his attaché case on the table, opened a side flap and took out a single-edge razor blade that was wedged down between the leather. He then took the two matted sheets of cardboard with the embedded X-ray slides of two Andover students thirty years ago and placed them on the table, one on top of the other. There were four rows of negatives, each with four slides, a total of sixteen on each card. Small red-bordered labels identifying the patients and the dates of the X-rays were affixed to the upper left-hand corners. He checked carefully to see that the borders of the cardboard sheets matched; they did. He pressed a manilla envelope down on the top sheet between the first and second rows of X-rays, took the razor blade and began to cut, slicing deeply so that the blade went through both sheets of X-rays. The top row fell clean, two strips of four X-ray negatives.

The names of the patients and dates of entry – typed on the small red-bordered labels over thirty-five years ago – were on the strips; the simplest chemical analysis would confirm their authenticity.

Bray doubted whether any such analysis would be made on the new labels he would purchase and stick on the remaining two sheets with twelve X-rays each; it would be a waste of time. The X-rays themselves would be compared with new X-rays of the man who called himself Joshua Appleton IV. Julian Guiderone. That was all the proof the Matarese would need.

He took the strips and the larger sheets of negatives, knelt down and carefully buffed the edges of the cuts across the rug. Within five minutes each of the edges was rubbed smooth, soiled just enough to match the age of the original borders.

He got up and put everything back in his attaché case. It was time to return to Andover, to put the plan in motion.

'Mr Vickery, is something wrong?' asked the dentist, coming out of his office, still harried, three afternoon patients reading magazines, glancing up in mild irritation.

'I'm afraid I forgot something. May I speak with you for a second?'

'Come on in here,' said the dentist, ushering Scofield into a small workroom, the shelves lined with impressions of teeth mounted on movable clamps. He lit a cigarette from a pack on the counter. 'I don't mind telling you it's been one hell of a day. What's the matter?'

'The laws, actually.' Bray smiled, opening his attaché case and taking out the two envelopes. 'HR Seven-Four-Eight-Five.'

'What the hell is that?'

'A new congressional regulation, part of the post-Watergate morality. Whenever a government employee borrows property from any source, for whatever purpose, a full description of said property must be accompanied by a signed authorization.'

'Oh, for Christ's sake.'

'I'm sorry, sir. The senator's a stickler for these things.' Scofield took the X-rays from the envelopes. 'If you'll re-examine these, call in your nurse and give her a description, she can type the authorization on your letterhead and I'll get out of here.'

'I suppose anything for the next President of the United States,' said the dentist, taking the shortened X-ray sheets and reaching for the telephone. 'Tell Appleton to lower my taxes.' He pressed the intercom button. 'Bring in your pad, please.'

'Do you mind?' Bray took out his cigarettes.

'Are you nuts? Carcinoma loves company.' The nurse came through the door, shorthand pad and pencil in hand. 'How do I start this?' asked the doctor, looking at Scofield.

' "To Whom It May Concern" is fine.'

'OK.' The dentist glanced at his nurse. 'We're keeping the government honest.' He snapped on a scanning lamp and held both X-ray sheets against the glass. ' "To Whom It May Concern. Mr" . . .' The doctor stopped, looking at Bray again. 'What's your first name?'

'B. A. will do.'

' "Mister B. A. Vickery of Senator Appleton's office in Washington, D.C. has requested and received from me two sets of X-rays dated 11 November 1943 for patients identified as Joshua Appleton and . . . Julian Guiderone." ' The dentist paused. 'Anything else?'

'A description, Doctor. That's what HR Seven-Four-Eight-Five calls for.'

The dentist sighed, the cigarette protruding from his lips. ' "Said identical sets include" . . . one, two, three, four across . . . "twelve negatives." ' The dentist stopped, squinting through his half-glasses. 'You know,' he interjected. 'My uncle wasn't only primitive, he was downright careless.'

'What do you mean?' asked Scofield, watching the dentist closely.

'The right and left bicuspids are missing in both of these. I was so rushed I didn't notice before.'

'They're the cards you gave me this morning.'

'I'm sure they are; there are the labels. I think I matched the upper and lower incisors. He held out the X-rays for Scofield and turned to the nurse. 'Put what I said into English and type it up, will you? I'll sign it outside.' He crushed out his cigarette and extended his hand. 'Nice to meet you, Mr Vickery. I've really got to get back in there.'

'Just one more thing, sir. Would you mind initialling these sheets and dating them?' Bray separated the X-rays and placed them on the counter.

'Not at all,' said the dentist.

Scofield drove back to Salem. A great deal was still to be clarified, new decisions to be made as events shaped them, but he had his overall plan; he had a place to begin. It was almost time for Mr B. A. Vickery to arrive at the Ritz-Carlton, but not yet.

He had stopped earlier at the Shopping Plaza in Salem where he had found small red-bordered labels almost identical to those used over thirty-five years ago, and a store selling typewriters where he had typed in the names and the dates, rubbing them lightly to give the labels an appearance of age. And while walking to his car he had looked briefly around at the shops, again seeing what he had hoped to see.

Copies Made While You Wait
Equipment Bought, Sold, Leased
Expert Service

It was conveniently two doors away from a liquor store, three from a supermarket. He would stop there now and have copies made of his bill-of-particulars, and afterwards pick up something to drink and eat. He would be in his room for a long time; he had phone calls to make. They would take five to seven hours to complete. They had to be routed on a very precise schedule through Lisbon.

Bray watched as the manager of the Plaza Duplicating Service extracted the collated sheets of his indictment from the levels of grey trays that protruded from the machine. He had chatted briefly with the balding man, remarking that he was doing a favour for a nephew; the young fellow was taking one of those creative writing courses at Emerson and had entered some sort of college competition.

'That kid's got some imagination,' said the manager, clipping the stacks of copies together.

'Oh, did you read it?'

'Just parts. You stand over that machine with nothing to do but make sure there's no jamming; you look. But when people come in with personal things – like letters and wills, you know what I mean – I always try to keep my eyes on the dials. Sometimes it's hard.'

Bray laughed. 'I told my nephew he'd better win or he'd be put in gaol.'

'Not any more. These kids today, they're great. They say anything. I know a lot of people don't like 'em for it, but I do.'

'I think I do, too.' Bray looked at the bill placed in front of him and took his money from his pocket. 'Say, you wouldn't by any chance have an Alpha Twelve machine here, would you?'

'Alpha *Twelve*? That's an eighty-thousand-dollar piece of equipment. I do a good business, but I'm not in that class.'

'I suppose I could find one in Boston.'

'That insurance company over on Lafayette Street has one; you can bet your life the home office paid for it. It's the only one I know of *north* of Boston, and I mean right up to Montreal.'

'An insurance company?'

'West Hartford Casualty. I trained the two girls who run the Alpha Twelve. Isn't that just like an insurance company? They buy a machine like that but they won't pay for a service contract. I'm probably a dollar and a half cheaper.'

Scofield leaned on the counter, a weary man confiding. 'Listen, I've been travelling for five days and I've got to get a report into the mails tonight. I need an Alpha Twelve. Now, I can drive into Boston and probably find one. But it's damn near four o'clock and I'd rather not do that. My company's a little crazy; it thinks my time is valuable and lets me have enough money to save it where I can. What do you say? Can you help me?' Bray removed a hundred-dollar bill from his clip.

'You work for one hell of a company.'

'That I do.'

'I'll make a call.'

It was 5.45 when Bray returned to the hotel on Salem harbour. The Alpha Twelve had performed the service he had needed, and he had found a stationery store where he had purchased a stapler, seven manilla envelopes, two rolls of packaging tape and a Park-Sherman scale that measured weight in ounces and grammes. A final stop had been at the Salem Post Office where he had bought fifty dollars' worth of stamps.

A porterhouse steak and a bottle of Scotch completed his shopping list. He spread his purchases on thc bed, removing some to the table, others to the Formica counter between the Lilliputian stove and refrigerator. He poured himself a drink and sat in the chair in front of the window overlooking the harbour. It was growing dark, the water barely seen except where it reflected the lights of the piers.

He drank the whisky in short swallows, letting the alcohol spread, suspending all thought. He had no more than ten minutes before the telephone calls would begin. His cannons were in place, his nuclear bomb in its rack. It was vital now that everything take place in sequence – always sequence – and that meant choosing the right words at the right time; there was no room for error. To do that, to

591

avoid error, his mind had to be free, loose, unencumbered – capable of listening closely, picking up nuances.

Toni . . . ?

No!

He closed his eyes. The gulls in the distance were foraging the waters for their last meal before darkness was complete. He listened to their screeches, the dissonance somehow comforting; there was a kind of energy in every struggle to survive. He hoped he would have it.

He dozed, awakening with a start. He looked at his watch, annoyed. It was six minutes past six; his ten minutes had stretched nearer to fifteen. It was time for the first telephone call, the one he considered least likely to bring results. It would not have to be routed through Lisbon, the chances of a tap so remote as to be practically non-existent. But practically was not totally, therefore his conversation would last no longer than twenty seconds, the minimum amount of time needed for even the most sophisticated tracing equipment to function.

The twenty-second limit was the one he had instructed the French woman to use weeks ago when she had placed calls for him all through the night to a suite of rooms at the hotel on Nebraska Avenue. Twenty seconds was not much time, but a great deal could be said without interruptions. More so in French.

He rose from the chair and went to his attaché case, taking out notes he had written to himself. Notes with names and telephone numbers. He walked over to the bedside telephone, pulled the armchair next to the phone, and sat down. He thought for a moment, composing a verbal shorthand French for what he wanted to say, doubting, however, that it would make any difference. Ambassador Robert Winthrop had disappeared over a month ago; there was no reason to think he had survived. Winthrop had raised the names of the Matarese with the wrong men – or man – in Washington.

He picked up the phone and dialled; three rings followed before an operator got on the line and asked for his room number. He gave it and more distant rings continued.

'Hello?'

'Listen! There's no time. Do you understand?'

'Yes. Go ahead.'

She knew him; she was with him. He spoke rapidly in French, his eyes on the sweep hand of his watch. 'Ambassador Robert Winthrop. Georgetown. Take two Company men with you, no explanations. If Winthrop's there ask to see him alone, but say nothing out loud. Give him a note with the words: "Beowulf wants to reach you". Let him advise in writing. The contact must be sterile. I'll call you back.'

Seventeen seconds.

'We *must* talk,' was the strong, quick reply. 'Call back.'

He hung up; she'd be safe. Not only was it unlikely that the Matarese had found her and tapped her, but even if they had, they would not kill her. There was nothing to gain, more to learn by keeping the intermediary alive, and too much of a mess killing the Company men with her. Besides, there were limits to his liability under the circumstances; he was sorry, but there were.

It was time for Lisbon. He had known since Rome that he would use Lisbon when the moment came. A series of telephone calls could be placed through Lisbon only once, for once those receiving the calls were listed in the overnight data banks, red cards would fly out of computers into alarm slots, the coded source traced through other computers in Langley, and no further calls permitted by that source, all transmissions terminated. Access to Lisbon was restricted to those who dealt solely with high-level defections, men in the field who in times of emergency had to go directly to their superiors in Washington who in turn were authorized to make immediate decisions. No more than twenty intelligence officers in the country had the codes for Lisbon, and no man in Washington ever refused a call from Lisbon. One never knew whether a general, or a nuclear physicist, or a ranking member of the praesidium or the KGB might be the prize.

It was also understood that any abuse of the Lisbon access would result in the severest consequences for the abuser. Bray was amused – grimly – at the concept; the abuse he was about to inflict was beyond anything conceived by the men who made the rules. He looked at the five names and titles he was about to call. The names in themselves were not that unusual; they could probably be found in any telephone book. Their positions, however, could not.

The Secretary of State
The Chairman of the National Security Council
The Director of the Central Intelligence Agency
The Chief Foreign Policy adviser to the President
The Chairman of the Joint Chiefs of Staff

The probability that one, possibly two of these men were *consiglieri* of the Matarese persuaded Bray not to try to send his indictment directly to the President. Taleniekov and he had believed that once the proof was in their hands the two leaders of both their countries could be reached and convinced. It was not true; Presidents and Premiers were too closely guarded, too protected; messages were filtered, words interpreted. The charges of 'traitors' would be dismissed; time not to be wasted on them. Others had to reach Presidents and Premiers. Men whose positions of trust and responsibility were beyond reproach; such men had to bring them the news, not traitors.

The majority if not all of those he was about to call were committed to the well-being of the nation; any one of them could get the ear of the President. It was all he asked for, and none would refuse a call from Lisbon. He picked up the telephone and dialled the overseas operator.

Twenty minutes later the operator called back. Lisbon

had, as always, cleared the traffic to Washington quickly; the Secretary of State was on the line.

'This is State One,' said the Secretary. 'Your codes are cleared, Lisbon. What is it?'

'Mr Secretary, within forty-eight hours you'll receive a manilla envelope in the mail; the name Agate will be printed in the upper left corner . . .'

'Agate? *Beowulf Agate?*'

'Please, listen to me, sir. Have the envelope brought directly to you unopened. Inside there's a detailed report describing a series of events which have taken place – and are taking place right now – that amount to a conspiracy to assume control of the government . . .'

'Conspiracy? Please be specific. Communist?'

'I don't think so.'

'You *must* be specific, Mr Scofield. You're a wanted man, and you're abusing the Lisbon connection! Self-seeking cries of alarm from you are not in your interest. Or in the interest of the country.'

'You'll find all the specifics you need in my report. Among them is proof – I repeat, *proof*, Mr Secretary – that there's been a deception in the Senate that goes back twenty years. It's of such magnitude that I'm not at all sure the country can absorb the shock. It may not even be in its interest to expose it.'

'Explain yourself!'

'The explanation's in the envelope. But not a recommendation. I haven't got any recommendations. That's your business. And the President's. Bring the information to him as soon as you get it.'

'I order you to report to me immediately!'

'I'll come out in forty-eight hours, if I'm alive. When I do I want two things: vindication for me and asylum for a Soviet intelligence officer – if he's alive.'

'Scofield, where *are you*?'

Bray hung up the phone.

595

He waited ten minutes and placed the second call to Lisbon. Thirty-five minutes later the Chairman of the National Security Council was on the line.

'Mr Chairman, within forty-eight hours you'll receive a manilla envelope in the mail; the name Agate will be printed in the upper left corner . . .'

It was exactly fourteen minutes past midnight when he completed the final call. Among the men he had reached were honourable men. Their voices would be heard by the President.

He had forty-eight hours. A lifetime.

It was time for a drink. Twice during the placement of calls he had looked at the bottle of Scotch, close to rationalizing the necessity of calming his anxieties, but both times rejected the method. Under pressure, he was the coldest man he knew; he might not always feel that way, but it was the way he functioned. He deserved a drink now; it would be a fitting salute to the call he was about to make to Senator Joshua Appleton IV, born Julian Guiderone, son of the Shepherd Boy.

The telephone rang, the shock of its sound causing Bray to grip the bottle in his hand, oblivious to the whisky he was pouring. Liquor spilled over the glass on to the counter. *It was impossible!* There was no way the calls to Lisbon could be traced so rapidly. The magnetic trunklines fluctuated hourly, insuring blind origins; the entire system would have to be shut down for a minimum of eight hours in order to trace a single call. Lisbon was an absolute; place a call through it and a man was safe, his location buried until it no longer mattered.

The phone rang again. Not to answer was not to know, the lack of knowledge infinitely more dangerous than any tracing. No matter what, he still had cards to play; or at least the conviction that those cards were playable. He would convey that. He lifted up the phone. 'Yes?'

'Room Two-twelve?'

'What is it?'

'The manager, sir. It's nothing really, but the outside operator has – quite naturally – kept our switchboard informed of your overseas telephone calls. We noticed that you've chosen not to use a credit card, but rather have billed the calls to your room. We thought you'd appreciate knowing that the charges are currently in excess of three hundred dollars.'

Scofield looked over at the depleted bottle of Scotch. Yankee scepticism would not change until the planet blew up; and then the New England bookkeepers would sue the universe.

'Why don't you come up personally and I'll give you the money for the calls. It'll be in cash.'

'Oh, not necessary, not necessary at all, sir. Actually, I'm not at the hotel, I'm at home.' There was the slightest, slightly embarrassed pause. 'In Beverly. We'll just attach . . .'

'Thank you for your concern,' interrupted Bray, hanging up and heading back to the counter and the bottle of Scotch.

Five minutes later he was ready, ice-like calm spreading through him as he sat down next to the telephone. The words would be there because the outrage was there; he did not have to think about them, they would come easily. What he had thought about was the sequence. Extortion, compromise, weakness, exchange. Someone within the Matarese wanted to talk with him, recruit him for the most logical reasons in the world; he'd give that man – whoever he was – the chance to do both. It was part of the exchange, prelude to escape. But the first step on the tightrope would not be made by Beowulf Agate; it would be made by the son of the Shepherd Boy.

He picked up the phone; thirty seconds later he heard the famous voice laced with the pronounced Boston accent that reminded so many so often of a young President cut down in Dallas.

'Hello? *Hello?*' The senator had been roused from his sleep; it was in the clearing of his throat. 'Who's there, for God's sake?'

'There is a grave in the Swiss village of Col du Pillon. If there's a body in the coffin below it's not the man whose name is on the stone.'

The gasp on the line was electrifying, the silence that followed a scream suspended in the grip of fear. 'Who . . . ?' The man was in shock, unable to form the question.

'There's no reason for you to say anything, Julian . . .'

'*Stop it!*' The scream was released.

'All right, no names. You know who I am – if you don't, the Shepherd Boy hasn't kept his son informed.'

'I won't *listen!*'

'Yes you will, Senator. Right now that phone is part of your hand; you won't let it go. You can't. So just listen. On 11 November 1943, you and a close friend of yours went to the same dentist on Main Street in Andover, Massachusetts. You had X-rays taken that day.' Scofield paused for precisely one second. 'I have them, Senator. Your office can confirm it in the morning. Your office also can confirm the fact that yesterday a messenger from the General Accounting Office picked up a set of more recent X-rays from your current dentist in Washington. And finally, if you're so inclined, your office might check the X-ray Depository of the Massachusetts General Hospital in Boston. They'll find that a single plate, frontal X-ray taken twenty-five years ago is missing from the Appleton file. As of an hour ago all are in my possession.'

There was a quiet, plaintive cry on the line, a moan without words.

'Keep listening, Senator,' continued Bray. 'You've got a chance. If the girl's alive you've got a chance, if she's not you don't. Regarding the Russian, if he's going to die,

I'll be the one who kills him. I think you know why. You see, accommodations can be made. What I know I don't *want* to know. What you do is no concern of mine, not any longer. What you want, you've already won, and men like me simply end up working for people like you, that's all that ever happens. Ultimately, there's not much difference between any of you. Anywhere.' Scofield paused again, the bait was glaring; would he take it?

He did, the whisper hoarse, the statement tentative. 'There are . . . people who want to talk with you.'

'I'll listen. But only after the girl is free, the Russian turned over to me.'

'The X-rays . . . ?' The words were rushed, cut off; a man was drowning.

'That's the exchange.'

'*How?*'

'We'll negotiate it. You've got to understand, Senator, the only thing that matters to me now is me. The girl and I, we just want to get away.'

'What . . . ?' Again the man was incapable of forming the question.

'Do I want?' completed Scofield. 'Proof that she's alive, that she can still walk.'

'I don't understand.'

'You don't know much about exchanges, either. A package that's immobile isn't any package at all; it voids the exchange. I want proof and I've got a very powerful pair of binoculars.'

'*Binoculars?*'

'Your people will understand. I want a telephone number and a sighting. Obviously, I'm in the Boston vicinity. I'll call you in the morning. At this number.'

'There's a debate on the Senate floor, a quorum . . .'

'You'll miss it,' said Bray, hanging up.

The first move had been made; telephones would be in use all night between Washington and Boston. Move and counter-move, thrust and parry, press and check; the negotiations had begun. He looked at the manilla envelopes on the table. Between calls he had sealed all of them, weighed and stamped them; they were ready to go.

Except one, and there was no reason to believe he would mail it, the tragedy found in the disappearance of the man and what he might have done. It was time to call his old friend from Paris back.

'Bray, thank God! We've been waiting for hours!'

'*We?*'

'Ambassador Winthrop.'

'He's *there*?'

'It's all right. It was handled extremely well. His man, Stanley, assured me that no one could possibly have followed them and for all purposes, the ambassador is in Alexandria.'

'Stanley's good!' Scofield felt like yelling to the skies in sheer relief, sheer *joy*.

Winthrop was alive. The flanks were covered, the Matarese destroyed. He was free to negotiate as he had never negotiated in his life before, and he was the best there was. 'Let me talk to Winthrop.'

'Brandon, I'm on the line. I'm afraid I took the phone from your friend quite rudely. Forgive me, my dear.'

'What *happened*? I tried calling you . . .'

'I was hurt – not seriously – but enough to require treatment. I went to a doctor I knew in Fredericksburg; he has a private clinic. It wouldn't do for the eldest of the so-called statesmen to show up at a Washington hospital with a bullet in his arm. I mean, can you imagine Harriman turning up in a Harlem emergency ward with a gunshot wound? . . . I couldn't involve you any further, Brandon.'

'*Jesus*. I should have considered that.'

'You had enough to consider. Where are you?'

'Outside of Boston. There's so much to tell you, but not

on the phone. It's all in the envelope, along with four strips of X-rays. I've got to get it to you right away, and you've got to get it to the President.'

'The Matarese?'

'More than either of us could ever imagine. I have the proof.'

'Take the first plane to Washington. I'll reach the President now and get you full protection, a military escort, if need be. The search will be called off.'

'I can't do that, sir.'

'Why *not*?' The ambassador was incredulous.

'There are . . . hostages involved. I need time. They'll be killed unless I negotiate.'

'Negotiate? You don't have to negotiate. If you have what you say you have, let the government do it.'

'It takes roughly one pound of pressure and less than a fifth of a second to pull a trigger,' said Scofield. 'I've got to negotiate . . . But you see, I *can* now. I'll stay in touch, pinpoint the exchange ground. You can cover me.'

'Those words again,' said Winthrop. 'They never leave your vocabulary, do they?'

'I've never been so grateful for them.'

'How much time?'

'It depends; it's delicate. Twenty-four, possibly thirty hours. It has to be less than forty-eight; that's the deadline.'

'Get the proof to me, Brandon. There's an attorney, his firm's in Boston but he lives in Waltham. He's a good friend. Do you have a car?'

'Yes. I can get to Waltham in about forty minutes.'

'Good. I'll call him; he'll be on the first plane to Washington in the morning. His name is Bergeron; you'll have to get his address from the phone book.'

'No problem.'

It was 1.45 A.M. when Bray rang the bell of the fieldstone house in Waltham. The door was opened by Paul Bergeron, dressed in a bathrobe, creases of concern on his ageing, intelligent face.

'I know I'm not to ask you your name, but would you care to come in? From what I gather, I'm sure you can use a drink.'

'Thanks just the same, but I still have work to do. Here's the envelope, and thanks again.'

'Another time, perhaps.' The attorney looked at the thick manilla envelope in his hand. 'You know, I feel the way Jim St Clair must have felt when he got that last call from Al Haig. Is this some kind of smoking-gun?'

'It's on fire, Mr Bergeron.'

'I called the airline an hour ago; I'm on the 7.55 to Washington. Winthrop will have this by ten in the morning.'

'Thanks. Good night.'

Scofield drove back towards Salem, scanning the roads instinctively for signs of anyone following him; there were none, nor did he expect to see any. He was also looking for an all-night supermarket. Their wares were rarely, if ever, restricted to foodstuffs.

He found one on the outskirts of Medford set back from the highway. He parked in front, walked inside, and saw what he was looking for in the second aisle. A display of inexpensive Big Ben alarm clocks. He bought ten of them.

It was 3.18 when he walked into his room. He took the alarm clocks from their boxes, lined them up on the table, and opened his attaché case, taking out a small leather case containing miniature hand tools. He would buy bell wire and the batteries first thing in the morning, the explosives later in the day. The charges might be a problem, but it was not insurmountable; he needed more show than power – and in all likelihood he would need nothing at all. The years, however, had taught him caution; an exchange was like the workings of a giant aircraft. Each system had a back-up system, each back-up an alternative.

He had six hours to prepare his alternatives. It was good he had something to do; sleep now was out of the question.

36

The shift from dawn to daybreak was barely discernible; winter rain was promised again. By 8.00 it had arrived. Bray stood, his hands on the window sill, looking out at the ocean, thinking about calmer, warmer seas, wondering if he and Toni would ever sail them. Yesterday there was no hope; today there was and he was primed to function as he had never functioned before. All that was Beowulf Agate would be seen and heard from this day. He had spent his life preparing for the few brief hours that would prolong it the only way that was acceptable to him. He would bring her out or he would die; that had not changed. The fact that he had effectively destroyed the Matarese was almost incidental now. That was a professional objective and he was the best . . . he and the Russian were the best.

He turned from the window and went to the table, surveying his work of the last few hours. It had taken less time than he had projected, so total was his concentration. Each clock was dismantled, every main wheel spring drilled at the spindle, new pinion screws inserted in the ratchet mechanisms, the miniature bolts balanced. Each was now prepared to accept the insertion of bell wires leading to battery terminals that would throw thirty seconds of sparks into exposed powder. These sparks would, in turn, burn and ignite explosives over a span of fifteen minutes. Each alarm had been set and reset a dozen times, infinitesimal grooves filed across the gears insuring sequence; all worked a dozen times in sequence. Professional tools, no particular significance attached to his knowing them. The designer was also a mechanic, the architect a builder, the critic a practitioner of the craft. It was essential.

Powder could be obtained at any gunsmith's with the purchase of shells. As for explosives, a simple visit to a demolition or excavation site, armed with the proper government identification, was all that it took for an on-the-spot inventory. The rest was a matter of having large pockets in a raincoat. He had done it all before; lay mentality was the same everywhere. Beware the man bearing a black plastic ID case and who spoke softly. He was dangerous. Co-operate; do not allow your name to get on a list.

He placed the clock mechanisms in a box given him by the supermarket clerk five hours ago, sealed the top and carried it downstairs, outside to his car. He opened the boot, wedged the box into the corner, closed the boot, and returned to the hotel lobby.

'I find that I'll be leaving shortly,' he said to the young man behind the counter of the front desk. 'I paid for a week, but my plans have changed.'

'You also had a lot of phone calls billed to your room, mister.'

'True,' agreed Scofield, wondering how many people in Salem were also aware of it. Did witches still burn in Salem? 'If you'd have the balance ready for me, I'll be down in about a half hour. Add these papers to my bill, please.' He took two newspapers from the stacks on the counter, the morning *Examiner* and a local weekly. He walked back up the staircase to his room.

He made instant coffee, carried the cup to the table, and sat down with the newspapers and the Salem telephone book. It was 8.25. Paul Bergeron had been in the air thirty minutes, weather at Logan Airport permitting. It was something he would check when he moved to the telephone.

He opened the *Examiner*, turning to the classified section. There were two openings for construction workers, the first in Newton, the second in Braintree. He wrote

605

down the addresses, hoping to find a third or a fourth nearer by.

He did. In the Salem weekly, there was a photograph taken five days ago showing Senator Joshua Appleton at a groundbreaking ceremony in Swampscott. It was a federal project co-ordinated with the state of Massachusetts, an enormous middle-income housing development being built on the rocky land north of Phillips Beach. The caption read, *Blasting and excavation to commence* . . .

The irony was splendid.

He opened the telephone book, and found a gunsmith in Salem; he had no reason to look further. He wrote down the address.

It was 8.37. Time to call the lie that went under the name of Joshua Appleton. He got up and went to the bed, deciding impulsively to phone Logan Airport first. He did, and the words he heard were the words he wanted to hear.

'Seven-fifty-five to Washington? That would be Eastern Flight Six-two. Let me check, sir . . . There was a twelve-minute delay, but the plane's airborne. No change in the E.T.A.'

Paul Bergeron was on his way to Washington and Robert Winthrop. There would be no delays now, no crisis-conferences, no hastily summoned meetings between ranking arrogant men trying to decide how and when to proceed. Winthrop would call the Oval Office; an immediate audience would be granted and the full might of government would be pitted against the Matarese. And tomorrow morning the senator would be picked up by Secret Service and taken directly to Walter Reed Hospital where he would be subjected to intensive examinations. A twenty-five-year fraud would be exposed, the son destroyed with the Shepherd Boy.

Bray lit a cigarette, sipped his coffee and picked up the phone. He was in full command; he would concentrate totally on his negotiations, on the exchange that would be meaningless to the Matarese.

The senator's voice was tense, exhaustion in his tight delivery. 'Nicholas Guiderone wants to see you.'

'The Shepherd Boy himself,' said Scofield. 'You know my conditions. Does he? Is he prepared to meet them?'

'Yes,' whispered the son. 'A telephone number he agrees to. He's not sure what you mean by a "sighting".'

'Then there's nothing further to talk about. I'll hang up.'

'*Wait!*'

'Why? It's a simple word; I told you I had binoculars. What else is there to say? He's refused. Goodbye, Senator.'

'No!' Appleton's breathing was audible. 'All right, all right. You'll be told a time and a location when you call the number I give you.'

'I'll be *what*? You're a dead man, Senator. If they want to sacrifice you, that's their business – and yours, I suppose, but not mine.'

'What the hell are you talking about? What's wrong?'

'It's unacceptable. I'm not *told* a time and a location, I tell *you* and you tell them. Specifically, I give you a location and a time *span*, Senator. Between three and five o'clock this afternoon, at the north windows of Appleton Hall, the ones looking out over Jamaica Pond. Have you got that? Appleton Hall.'

'That *is* the telephone number!'

'You don't say. Have the windows lighted, the woman in one room, the Russian in another. I want mobility, conversation; I want to see them walking, talking, reacting. Is that clear?'

'Yes. Walking . . . reacting.'

'And, Senator, tell your people not to bother looking for me. I won't have the X-rays on me; they'll be with someone else who's been told to send them if I'm not back at a specific bus stop by five-thirty.'

'A *bus* stop?'

'The north road below Appleton Hall is a public bus route. Those buses are always crowded and the long curve around Jamaica Pond makes them slow down. If the rain keeps up they'll be slower than usual, won't they? I'll have plenty of time to see what I want to see.'

'Will you *see* Nicholas *Guiderone*?' The question was rushed, on the edge of hysteria.

'If I'm satisfied,' said Scofield coldly. 'I'll call you from a phone booth around five-thirty.'

'He wants to talk with you *now*!'

'Mr Vickery doesn't talk to anyone until he checks with the Ritz-Carlton Hotel. I thought that was clear.'

'He's concerned you may have duplicates made; he's very concerned about that.'

'These are twenty-five- and thirty-six-year-old negatives. Any exposure to photographic light would show up on a spectrograph instantly. I won't get killed for that.'

'He insisted you reach him *now*! He says it's vital!'

'Everything's vital.'

'He says to tell you you're wrong. So very, *very* wrong.'

'If I'm satisfied this afternoon he'll have a chance to prove it later. And you'll have the presidency. Or will he?' Bray hung up and crushed out his cigarette. As he had thought, Appleton Hall was the most logical place for Guiderone to hold his hostages. He had tried *not* to think about it when he had driven around the massive estate – the nearness of Toni was an obstruction he could barely surmount – but instinctively he had known it. And because he knew it, his eyes had reacted like the rapid shutters of a dozen cameras clicking off a hundred images. The grounds had space; acres filled with dense trees and thick shrubbery and guards in lean-to shelters positioned around the hill. Such a fortress was a likely target for an invasion – indeed the possibility was obviously never far from Guiderone's mind – and Scofield intended to capitalize on that fear. He would mount an imaginary invasion, its roots in the sort of army the Shepherd Boy understood as well as anyone on earth.

He made a last call before leaving Salem; to Robert Winthrop in Washington. The ambassador might well be tied up for hours at the White House – his advice intrinsic to any decision made by the President – and Scofield wanted first line of protection. It was his only protection, really; imaginary invasions had no invaders.

'*Brandon?* I haven't slept all night.'

'Neither did a lot of other people, sir. Is this line sterile?'

'I had it electronically checked early this morning. What's happening? Did you see Bergeron?'

'He's on his way. Eastern Flight Six-two. He's got the envelope and will be in Washington by ten.'

'I'll send Stanley to meet him at the airport. I spoke to the President fifteen minutes ago. He's clearing his calendar and will see me at two o'clock this afternoon. I expect it will be a very long meeting. I'm sure he'll want to bring in others.'

'That's why I'm calling now; I thought as much. I've got the exchange ground. Have you a pencil?'

'Yes, go ahead.'

'It's a place called Appleton Hall in Brookline.'

'Appleton? *Senator* Appleton?'

'You'll understand when you get the envelope from Bergeron.'

'My *God*!'

'The estate's above Jamaica Pond, on a hill called Appleton Hill; it's well known. I'll set the meeting for eleven-thirty tonight; I'll time my arrival exactly. Tell whoever's in charge to start surrounding the hill at eleven-forty-five. Block off the roads a half-mile in all directions, using detour signs, and approach carefully. There are guards inside the fence every two or three hundred feet.

Station the command post on the dirt road across from the front gate; there's a large white house there, if I remember correctly. Take it and sever the telephone wires; it may belong to the Matarese.'

'Just a minute, Brandon,' interrupted Winthrop. 'I'm writing all this and my hands and eyes aren't what they once were.'

'I'm sorry, I'll slow down.'

'It's all right. "Sever telephone wires." Go on.'

'My strategy's right out of the book. They may expect it, but they can't stop it. I'll say my deadline's fifteen minutes past midnight. That's when I'm to go out the front door with the hostages to my car and strike two matches one after the other; they'll recognize the pattern. I'll tell them a drone is outside the gate with an envelope containing the X-rays.'

'Drone? *X-rays?*'

'The first is only a name for someone I hire. The second is the proof they expect me to deliver.'

'But you *can't* deliver it!'

'It wouldn't make any difference if I did. You'll have enough in the envelope Bergeron's bringing you.'

'Of course. What else?'

'When I strike the second match, tell the C.P. to give me corresponding signals.'

'Corresponding . . . ?'

'Strike two matches.'

'Of course. Sorry. Then?'

'Wait for me to drive down to the gate. I'll time everything as close to twelve-twenty as I can. As soon as the gate's opened, the troops move in. They'll be covered by diversionary static – tell them it's just that. Static.'

'What? I don't understand.'

'They will. I've got to leave now, Mr Ambassador. There's still a lot to do.'

'Brandon!'

'Yes, sir?'

'There's one thing you do *not* have to do.'

'What's that?'

'Worry about vindication. I promise you. You were always the best there was.'

'Thank you, sir. Thank you for everything. I just want to be free.'

The gunsmith on Salem's Hawthorne Boulevard was both amused and pleased that the stranger purchased two gross of *Ought-Four* shotgun shells during off-season. Tourists were damn fools anyway, but this one compounded the damn-foolery of paying good money not only for the shells, but for ten plastic display tubes that the manufacturers supplied for nothing. He spoke with one of those smooth, kinda' oily voices. Probably a New York lawyer who never had a gun in his hand. Damn fools.

The rain hammered down, forming pools in the mud as disgruntled crews of construction workers sat in cars waiting for a break in the weather so they could sign in; four hours meant a day's pay, but without signing in there was nothing.

Scofield approached the door of a pre-fabricated shack, stepping on a plank sinking into the mud in front of the rain-splashed window. Inside he could see the foreman sitting behind a desk talking into a telephone. Ten yards to the left was a concrete bunker, a heavy padlock on the steel door, the red-lettered sign stencilled across it explicit.

DANGER
AUTHORIZED PERSONNEL ONLY
SWAMPSCOTT DEV. CORP.

Bray rapped first on the window, distracting the man on

the phone inside the shack, then stepped off the plank and opened the door.

'Yeah, what is it?' yelled the foreman.

'I'll wait till you're finished,' said Scofield, closing the door. A sign on the table told the man's name. *A. Patelli*.

'That could be a while, pal! I got a thief on the phone. A fucking thief who says his fucking pansy drivers can't roll because it's wet out!'

'Don't make it too long, please.' Bray removed his ID case. He flipped it open, holding it in front of the man. 'You are Mr Patelli, aren't you?'

The foreman stared at the very official identification card.

'Yeah.' He turned back to the phone. 'I'll call you back, thief!' He got out of the chair. 'You government?'

'Yes.'

'What the hell's the matter *now*?'

'Something we don't think you're aware of, Mr Patelli. My unit's working with the Federal Bureau of Investigation . . .'

'The FBI?'

'That's right. You've had several shipments of explosive materials delivered to the site here.'

'Locked up tight and accounted for,' interrupted the foreman. 'Every fucking stick.'

'We don't think so. That's why I'm here.'

'*What?*'

'There was a bombing two days ago in New York, maybe you read about it. A bank in Wall Street. Oxidation raised several numbers on the serial imprint that blew with the detonating cap; we think it may be traced to one of your shipments.'

'That's fuckin'-a-nuts!'

'Why don't we check?'

The explosives inside the concrete bunker were not sticks, they were solid blocks roughly five inches long, three inches high and two thick, packaged in cartons of twenty-four.

'Prepare a statement of consignment, please,' said Scofield, studying the surface of a brick. 'We were right. These are the ones.'

'A statement of *what*?'

'I'm taking a carton for evidentiary analysis.'

'*Who*?'

'Look, Mr Patelli, your ass may be in a very tight sling. You signed for these shipments and I don't think you counted. I'd advise you to co-operate fully. Any indication of resistance could be misinterpreted; after all, it's your responsibility. Frankly, I don't think you're involved, but I'm only the field investigator. On the other hand, my word counts.'

'I'll sign any fucking thing you want. What do I write?'

At a hardware store, Bray bought ten dry-cell batteries, ten five-quart plastic containers, a roll of bell wire and a can of black spray-paint. He asked for a very large box to carry everything in through the rain.

He sat in the back seat of his rented car, placed the last of the clocks into its plastic container, pressing the explosive brick down beside the battery. He listened for the steady tick of the mechanism; it was there. Then he snapped the edges of the cover into place and sealed it with tape.

It was forty-two minutes past noon, the alarms set in sequence, the grooves in the gears locked by the teeth of the pinions, the sequence to begin in precisely eleven hours and twenty-six minutes.

As he had done with the previous nine, he sprayed the container with black paint. A great deal of it soiled the rear seat cushion; he would leave a hundred-dollar bill in the crease.

*　　*　　*

He inserted the coin in the pay phone; he was in West Roxbury, two minutes from the border of Brookline. He dialled, waited for the line to be answered and roared into the mouthpiece.

'Sanitation?'

'Yes, sir. What can we do for you?'

'Appleton Drive! Brookline! The sewer's packed up! It's all over my *goddamn* front lawn!'

'Where is that, sir?'

'I just told you. Appleton Drive and Beachnut Terrace! It's terrible.'

'We'll dispatch a truck right away, sir.'

'Please, hurry!'

The Sanitation Department van made its way haltingly up Beachnut Terrace towards the intersection of Appleton Drive, its driver obviously checking the sewer drains in the street. When he reached the corner, a man in a dark-blue raincoat flagged him down. It was impossible to go around the man; he moved back and forth in the middle of the street, waving his arms frantically. The driver opened his door and shouted through the rain.

'What's the *mattah*?'

It was the last thing he would say for several hours.

Within the Appleton Hall compound, a guard in a cedar lean-to picked up his wall telephone and told the operator on the switchboard to give him an outside line. He was calling the Sanitation Department in Brookline. One of their vans was on Appleton Drive, stopping every hundred feet or so.

'There are reports of a blockage in the vicinity of Beachnut and Appleton, sir. We have a truck checking it out.'

'Thank you,' said the guard, pushing a button that was

the intercom for all stations. He relayed the information and returned to his chair.

What kind of idiot would check out sewers for a living?

Scofield wore the black rain slicker with the stencilled white letters across the back. *Sanitation Dept. Brookline.* It was 3.05. The sighting had started: Antonia and Taleniekov standing behind windows on the other side of the estate; the concentration in Appleton Hall would be on the road below. He drove the sanitation van slowly up Appleton Drive, staying close to the kerb, stopping at every sewer drain in the street. As the road was long, there were roughly twenty to thirty such drains. At each stop he got out carrying a six-foot extension snake and whatever other tools he could find in the van that seemed to fit a hastily imagined problem. This was at every stop; at ten, however, he added one other item. A five-quart plastic container that had been sprayed black. Seven of them he was able to wedge between the spikes of the wrought-iron fence beyond the sightlines of the lean-to's, pushing them into the foliage with the snake. With three he used what was left of the bell wire and suspended them beneath the grates of the sewers.

At 4.22 he was finished and drove back to Beachnut Terrace, where he began the embarrassing process of reviving the sanitation employee in the rear of the van. There was no time to be solicitous; he removed the rain slicker and slapped the man into consciousness.

'What the hell *happened*?' The man was frightened, recoiling at the sight of Bray above him.

'I made a mistake,' said Scofield simply. 'You can accept that or not, but nothing's missing, no harm's been done, and there is no problem with the sewers.'

'You're crazy!'

Bray took out his money clip. 'I'm sure it appears that way, so I'd like to pay you for the use of your truck. No one has to know about it. Here's five hundred dollars.'

'Five . . . ?'

'For the past hour you've been checking the drains along Beachnut and Appleton, that's all anyone has to know. You were dispatched and did your job. That is, if you want the five hundred.'

'You're *crazy*!'

'I haven't got time to argue with you. Do you want the money or not?'

The man's eyes bulged. He took the money.

It did not matter whether they saw him now; it only mattered what he saw. His watch read 4.57, three minutes remained before the sighting was terminated. He drove, stopped the car directly below the midpoint of Appleton Hall, rolled down his window and raised the Zeiss-Ikon binoculars to his eyes. He focused through the rain on the lighted windows three hundred yards above.

The first figure to come into view was Taleniekov, but it was not the Taleniekov he had last seen in London. The Russian stood motionless behind the window, the side of his head encased in a bandage, a bulge beneath the open collar of his shirt further evidence of wounds wrapped tightly with heavy gauze. Standing beside the Soviet was a dark-haired muscular man, his hand hidden behind Taleniekov's back. Scofield had the distinct impression that without that man's hand, Taleniekov would collapse. But he was alive, his eyes staring straight ahead, blinking every other second or so; the Russian was telling him he *was* alive.

Bray moved the glasses to the right; his breathing stopped, the pounding in his chest like a rapidly accelerating drum in an echo chamber. It was almost more than he could bear; the rain blurred the lenses; he was going out of his mind.

There she *was*! Standing erect behind the window, her head held up, angled first to her left, then to her right, her eyes levelled, responding to voices. *Responding*.

And then Scofield saw what he dared not hope to see. Relief swept over him and he wanted to shout through the rain in sheer exuberance. There was fear in Antonia's eyes, to be sure, but there was also something else. *Anger*.

The eyes of his love were filled with anger, and there was nothing on earth that took its place! An angry mind was a mind intact.

He put the binoculars down, rolled up the windows and started the engine. He had several telephone calls and a final arrangement to make. When these were done, it was time for Mr B. A. Vickery to arrive at the Ritz Carlton Hotel.

'Were you satisfied?' The senator's voice was more controlled than it had been that morning. The anxiety was still there but it was farther below the surface.

'How badly is the Russian hurt?'

'He's lost blood; he's weak.'

'I could see that. Is he ambulatory?'

'Enough to put him into a car, if that's what you want to do.'

'It's what I want to do. Both he and the woman in my car with me at the exact moment I say. I'll drive the car down to the gate and, on my signal, the gate will be opened. That's when you get the X-rays and we get out.'

'I thought you wanted to kill him?'

'I want something else first. He has information that can make the rest of my life very pleasant, no matter who runs what.'

'I see.'

'I'm sure you do.'

'You said you'd meet with Nicholas Guiderone, listen to what he has to say.'

'I will. I'd be a liar if I didn't admit I had questions.'

'He'll answer everything. When will you see him?'

'He'll know when I check into the Ritz-Carlton. Tell him to call me there. And let's get one thing clear, Senator. A telephone call, no troops. The X-rays won't be in the hotel.'

'Where will they be?'

'That's my business.' Scofield hung up and left the phone booth. He'd place his next call from a booth in the centre of Boston, to check in with Robert Winthrop, as much as to get the ambassador's reaction to the material in the envelope as anything else. And to make sure his protection was being mounted. If there were hitches he wanted to know about them.

'It's Stanley, Mr Scofield.' As always, Winthrop's chauffeur spoke gruffly, not unpleasantly. 'The ambassador's still at the White House; he asked me to come back here and wait for any calls from you. He told me to tell you that everything you asked for is being taken care of. He said I should repeat the times. Eleven-thirty, eleven forty-five and twelve-fifteen.'

'That's what I wanted to hear. Thanks very much.' Bray opened the door of the drugstore telephone booth, and walked over to a counter that sold construction paper and felt markers in varying colours. He chose bright yellow paper and a dark-blue marker.

He went back outside to his car and, using his attaché case for a desk, wrote his message in large, clear letters on the yellow paper. Satisfied, he opened the case, removed the five sealed manilla envelopes, stamped and addressed to five of the nation's most powerful men, and placed them on the seat next to him. It was time to mail them. Then he took out a sixth envelope and inserted the yellow page; he sealed it with tape and wrote on the front.

FOR THE BOSTON POLICE

He drove slowly up Newbury Street looking for the address he had found in the telephone booth. It was on the left side, four doors from the corner, a large painted sign in the window.

Phoenix Messenger Service
24 Hour Delivery – Medical, Academic, Industrial

He parked in a space vacated by a taxi, got out and went

inside. A thin, prim-looking woman with an expression of serious efficiency rose from her desk and came to the counter.

'May I help you?'

'I hope so,' said Scofield, efficiency in his voice as he opened his identification. 'I'm with the BPD, attached to Inter-departmental Examinations.'

'The police? Good heavens . . .'

'Nothing to be concerned about. We're running an exercise, checking up on precinct response to outside emergencies. We want this envelope delivered to the station on Boylston tonight. Can you handle it?'

'We certainly can.'

'Fine. What's the charge?'

'Oh, I don't think that will be necessary, officer. We're all in this together.'

'I couldn't accept that, thank you. Besides we need the outside record. And your name, of course.'

'Of course. The charge for night deliveries is usually ten dollars.'

'If you'll let me have a receipt, please.' Scofield took the money from his pocket. 'And if you wouldn't mind, please specify that delivery is to be made between eleven and eleven-fifteen, that's very important to us. You will make sure of it, won't you?'

'I'll do better than that, officer. I'll deliver it myself. I'm on until midnight, so I'll just leave one of the boys in charge and go right over there myself. I really admire the sort of thing you're doing. Crime is simply astronomical these days; we've all got to pitch in, I say.'

'You're very kind, ma'am.'

'You know, there're a lot of very strange people around the apartment house where I live. *Very* strange.'

'What's the address? I'll have the patrol cars look a little more closely from here on.'

'Why *thank* you.'

'Thank *you*, ma'am.'

It was 9.20 when he walked into the lobby of the Ritz-Carlton. He had driven down to the piers and eaten a fish dinner, the time spent thinking about what he and Toni would do after the night was over. Where would they go? How could they live? Finances did not concern him; Winthrop had promised vindication and the calculating head of Consular Operations, the would-be executioner named Daniel Congdon, had been generous in pension and unrecorded benefits that would come his way as long as his silence was maintained. Beowulf Agate was about to disappear from this world; where would Bray Scofield go? As long as Antonia was with him, it did not matter.

'There's a message for you, Mr Vickery,' said the desk clerk, holding out a small envelope.

'Thank you,' said Scofield, wondering if beneath the man's white shirt there was a small blue circle inked into his flesh.

The message was only a telephone number. He crumpled it in his hand and dropped it on the counter.

'Is something wrong?' asked the clerk.

Bray smiled. 'Tell that son of a bitch I don't make calls to numbers. Only to names.'

He let the telephone ring three times before he picked it up. 'Yes?'

'You're an arrogant man, Beowulf.' The voice was high-pitched, crueller-than-the-wind. It was the Shepherd Boy, Nicholas Guiderone.

'I was right, then,' said Scofield. 'That man downstairs doesn't work full-time for the Ritz-Carlton. And when he showers, he can't wash off a small blue circle on his chest.'

621

'It's worn with enormous pride, sir. They are extraordinary men and women who have enlisted in our extraordinary cause.'

'Where do you find them? People who'll blow themselves away and bite into cyanide?'

'Quite simply, in our companies. Men have been willing to make the ultimate sacrifice for causes since the dawn of time. It does not always have to be on a battlefield, or in a wartime underground, or even in the world of international espionage. There are many causes; I don't have to tell you that.'

'Such as themselves? The *fida'is*, Guiderone? Hasan ibn as-Sabbāh's cadre of assassins?'

'You've studied the *padrone*, I see.'

'Very closely.'

'There are certain practical and philosophical similarities, I will not deny it. These men and women have everything they want on this earth, and when they leave it, their families – wives, children, husbands – will have more than they ever need. Isn't that the dream? With over five hundred companies, computers can select a handful of people willing and capable of entering into this arrangement. A simple extension of the dream, Mr Scofield.'

'Pretty damned extended.'

'Not really. Far more executives collapse from heart seizure than from violence. Read the daily obituaries. But I'm sure this is only one of many questions. May I send a car for you?'

'You may not.'

'There's no cause for hostility.'

'I'm not hostile, I'm cautious. Basically I'm a coward. I've set a schedule and I intend to stick with it. I'll get there at exactly eleven-thirty; you talk, I'll listen. At precisely twelve-fifteen, I'll walk out with the girl and the Russian. A signal will be given, we'll get into the car and drive to your main gate. That's when you'll get the X-rays and we get away. If there's the slightest deviation, the X-rays will disappear. They'll show up somewhere else.'

'We have a right to examine them,' protested Guiderone. 'For accuracy and spectro-analysis; we want to make sure no duplicates were made. We must have time for that.'

The Shepherd Boy bit; the omission of the examination was the weakness Guiderone quite naturally pounced upon. The huge electronic iron gate had to be opened and stay open. If it remained shut, all the troops and all the diversions that could be mounted, would not prevent a man firing a rifle into the car. Bray hesitated. 'Fair enough. Have equipment and a technician down at the gatehouse. Verification will take two or three minutes, but the gate has to remain open while it's being done.'

'Very well.'

'By the way,' added Scofield, 'I meant what I said to your son . . .'

'You mean Senator Appleton, I believe.'

'Believe it. You'll find the X-rays intact, no light-marks of duplication. I won't get killed for that.'

'I'm convinced. But I find a weakness in these arrangements.'

'A weakness . . . ?' Bray felt cold.

'Yes. Eleven-thirty to twelve-fifteen is only forty-five minutes. That's not much time for us to talk. For me to talk and you to listen.'

Scofield breathed again. 'If you're convincing, I'll know where to find you in the morning, won't I?'

Guiderone laughed softly in his eerily high-pitched voice. 'Of course. So simple. You're a logical man.'

'I try to be. Eleven-thirty, then.' Bray hung up.

He had *done* it! Every system had a back-up system, every back-up an alternative. The exchange was covered on all flanks.

*   *   *

It was 11.29 when he drove through the gates of Appleton Hall and entered the drive that curved up past the carriage house to the walled mansion on the crest of the hill. As he drove by the cavernous garage of the carriage house, he was surprised to see a number of limousines. Between ten and twelve uniformed chauffeurs were talking; they were men who knew each other. They had been here before together.

The wall surrounding the enormous main house was more for effect than protection; it was barely eight feet high, designed to look far higher from below. Joshua Appleton, the first, had erected an expensive plaything. One-third castle, one-third fortress, one-third functional estate with an incredible view of Boston. The lights of the city flickered in the distance; the rain had stopped, leaving a chilly translucent mist in the air.

Bray saw two men in the glare of his headlights; the one on the right signalled him to stop in front of a separation in the eight-foot-high wall. He did so; the path beyond the wall was bordered by two heavy chains suspended from thick iron posts, the door at the end set in an archway. All that was missing was a portcullis, deadly spikes to come crashing down with the severing of a rope.

Bray got out of the car and was immediately shoved over the hood, every pocket, every area of his body searched for weapons. Flanked by the guards, he was escorted to the door in the archway and admitted.

At first full glance, Scofield understood why Nicholas Guiderone had to possess the Appleton estate. The staircase, the tapestries, the chandeliers . . . the sheer magnificence of the great hall was breathtaking. The nearest thing to it Bray could imagine was the burned-out skeleton in Porto Vecchio that once had been the Villa Matarese.

'Come this way, please,' said the guard on his right, opening a door. 'You have three minutes with the guests.'

Antonia ran across the room into his arms, her tears

moistening his cheeks, the strength of her embrace desperate. 'My darling! You've come for us!'

'*Shhh . . .*' He held her. *Oh, God, he held her!* 'We haven't time,' he said softly. 'In a little while we're going to walk out of here. Everything's going to be all right. We're going to be free.'

'He wants to talk to you,' she whispered. 'Quickly.'

'What?' Scofield opened his eyes and looked beyond Toni. Across the room Taleniekov sat rigidly in an armchair. The Russian's face was pale, so pale it was like chalk, the left side of his head taped; his ear and half his cheek had been blown away. His neck and shoulder blade were also bandaged, encased in a T-squared metal brace; he could barely move them. Bray held Antonia's hand and approached. Taleniekov was dying. 'We're getting out of here,' said Scofield. 'We'll take you to a hospital. It'll be all right.'

The Russian shook his head slowly, painfully, deliberately.

'He can't talk, darling.' Toni touched Vasili's right cheek. 'He has no voice.'

'*Jesus!* What did they . . . ? Never mind, in forty-five minutes we're driving out of here.'

Again Taleniekov shook his head; the Russian was trying to tell him something.

'When the guards were helping him down the staircase, he had a convulsion,' said Antonia. 'It was terrible, they were pulled down with him and were furious. They kept hitting him – and he's in such pain.'

'They were pulled down . . . ?' asked Bray, wondering, looking at Taleniekov.

The Russian nodded, reaching under his shirt to the belt underneath. He pulled out a gun and shoved it across his legs towards Scofield.

'He fell all right,' whispered Bray, smiling, kneeling down and taking the weapon. 'You can't trust these

Commie bastards.' Then he shifted into Russian, putting his lips close to Taleniekov's right ear. 'Everything's clean. We've got men outside. I've set explosive charges all around the hill. They want the proof I've got; we'll get out.'

The KGB man once more shook his head. Then he stopped, his eyes wide, gesturing for Scofield to watch his lips.

The words were formed: *Pazhar . . . vsyegda pazhar.*

Bray translated into English. 'Fire, always fire?'

Taleniekov nodded, then formed other words, a barely audible whisper now emerging. '*Zazhiganiye . . . pazhar.*'

'Explosions? After the explosions, fire? Is that what you're saying?'

Again, Taleniekov nodded, his eyes staring, beseeching.

'You don't understand,' said Bray. 'We're covered.'

The Russian once more shook his head, now violently. Then he raised his hand, two fingers across his lips.

'A cigarette?' asked Scofield. Vasili nodded. Bray took the pack out of his pocket along with a book of matches. Taleniekov waved away the cigarettes and grabbed the matches.

The door opened; the guard spoke sharply. 'That's it. Mr Guiderone's waiting for you. They'll be here when you're finished.'

'They'd better be.' Scofield rose to his feet, hiding the gun in his belt beneath his raincoat. He gripped Antonia's hand and walked with her to the door. 'I'll be back in a while. No one's going to stop us.'

Nicholas Guiderone sat behind the desk in his library, his large head with the fringe of white hair supporting an old man's face, the pale skin taut, receding into the temples and stretched, sinking into the hollows that held his dark, shining eyes. There was a gnomelike quality about him; it was not hard to think of him as the Shepherd Boy.

'Would you care to reconsider your schedule, Mr Scofield?' asked Guiderone in his high, somewhat breathless voice, not looking at Bray, but instead studying papers. 'Forty minutes is really very little time, and I've got a great deal to tell you.'

'You can tell me some other time, perhaps. Tonight the schedule stands.'

'I see.' The old man looked up, now staring at Scofield. 'You think we've done terrible things, don't you?'

'I don't know what you've done.'

'Certainly you do. We've had nearly four full days with the Russian. His monologues were not voluntary, but with chemical assistance, the words were there. You've uncovered the pattern of huge companies linked across the world; you've perceived that through these companies we have funnelled sums of money to terrorist groups everywhere. Incidentally, you're quite right. I doubt there's an effective group of fanatics anywhere that has not benefited from us. You perceive all this but you can't understand why. It's at your fingertips, but it eludes you.'

'At my fingertips?'

'The words are yours. The Russian used them, but they were yours. Under chemical inducement, multi-lingual subjects speak the language of their sources . . . *Paralysis*, Mr Scofield. Governments must be paralysed. Nothing achieves this more rapidly or more completely than the rampant global chaos of what we call terrorism.'

'Chaos . . .' Bray whispered; *that* was the word he kept coming back to, never sure why. *Chaos*. Clashing bodies in space . . .

'Yes. Chaos!' repeated Guiderone, his startling dark eyes wide, two shining black stones reflecting the light of the desk lamp. 'When the chaos is complete, when civilian and military authorities are impotent, admitting they cannot destroy a thousand vanishing wolfpacks with tanks and warheads and tactical weapons, then men of reason will

627

move in. The period of violence will at last be over and this world can go about the business of living productively.'

'In a nuclear ash-heap?'

'There'll be no such consequences. We've tested the controls; we have men at them.'

'What the hell are you talking about?'

'Governments, Mr Scofield!' shouted Guiderone, his eyes on fire. 'Governments are obsolete! They can no longer be permitted to function as they have functioned throughout history. If they do, this planet will not see the next century. Governments as we have known them are no longer viable entities. They must be replaced.'

'By whom? With what?'

The old man softened his voice; it became hollow, hypnotic. 'By a new breed of philosopher-kings, if you like. Men who understand this world as it has truly emerged, who measure its potential in terms of resources, technology and productivity, who care not one whit about the colour of a man's skin, or the heritage of his ancestors, or what idols he may pray to. Who care only about his full productive potential as a human being. And his contribution to the market-place.'

'My God!' said Bray quietly. 'You're talking about conglomerates.'

'Does it offend you?'

'Not if I owned one.'

'Very good.' Guiderone broke into a jackal-like laugh; it disappeared instantly. 'But that's a limited point of view. There are those among us who thought you of all people would understand. You've seen the other futility; you've lived it.'

'By choice.'

'Very, very good. But that presumes there is no choice in our structure. Untrue. A man is free to develop his full potential; the greater his productivity, the greater his freedom and rewards.'

'Suppose he doesn't want to be productive? As you define it.'

'Then obviously there's a lesser reward for the lesser contribution.'

'Who *does* define it?'

'Trained units of management personnel, using all the technology developed in modern industry.'

'I guess it'd be a good idea to get to know them.'

'Don't waste time with sarcasm. Such teams operate daily all over the world. The international companies are not in business to lose money or forfeit profits. The system *works*. We prove it every day. The new society will function within a competitive, non-violent structure. Governments can no longer guarantee that; they're on nuclear collision courses everywhere. But the Chrysler Corporation does not make war on Volkswagen; no planes fill the skies to wipe out factories and whole towns centred on one or the other company. The new world will be committed to the market-place, to the developing of resources and technology that insure the productive survival of mankind. There's no other way. The multi-national community is proof; it is aggressive, highly competitive, but it is non-violent. It bears no arms.'

'Chaos,' said Bray, his eyes locked with the Shepherd Boy's. 'The clashing of bodies in space . . . destruction before the creation of order.'

'Yes, Mr Scofield. The period of violence before the permanent era of tranquillity. But governments and their leaders do not relinquish their responsibilities easily. Alternatives must be given men whose backs are to the wall.'

'Alternatives?'

'In Italy, we control nearly twenty per cent of the Parliament. In Bonn, twelve per cent of the *Bundestag*; in Japan, almost thirty-one per cent of the *Diet*. Could we have done this without the *Brigata Rossa* or Baader-Meinhof or the Red Army of Japan? We grow in authority every month.

With each act of terrorism we are closer to our objective: the total absence of violence.'

'That wasn't what Guillaume de Matarese had in mind seventy years ago.'

'It's much closer than you think. The *padrone* wanted to destroy the corrupters in governments, which all too frequently meant entire governments themselves. He gave us the structure, the methods – hired assassins to pit political factions against adversaries everywhere. He provided the initial fortune to put it all in motion; he showed us the way to chaos. All that remained was to put something in its place. We have found it. We'll save the world from itself. There can be no greater cause.'

'You're convincing,' said Scofield. 'I think we may have a basis for talking further.'

'I'm glad you think so,' answered Guiderone, his voice suddenly cold again. 'It's gratifying to know one is convincing; but much more interesting to watch the reactions of a liar.'

'Liar?'

'You could have been part of this!' Once more the old man shouted. 'After that night in Rock Creek Park, I myself convened the council. I told it to re-assess, re-evaluate! Beowulf Agate could be of incalculable value. The Russian was useless, but not *you*. The information you possessed could make a mockery of Washington's moral positions. I myself would have made you director of all security! On my instructions, we tried for weeks to reach you, bring you in, make you one of us. It is, of course, no longer possible. You're relentless in your *deceptions*! In short words, you cannot be trusted. You can *never* be trusted!'

Bray sat forward. The Shepherd Boy was a maniac; it was in the maniacal eyes set in the hollows of his pale, gaunt skull. He was a man capable of quiet, seemingly logical discourse, but irrationality ruled him. He was a bomb; a bomb had to be controlled. 'I wouldn't forget the purpose of my coming here, if I were you.'

'Your *purpose*? By all means it will be achieved. You want the woman? You want Taleniekov? They're yours! You'll be together, I assure you. You will be taken from this house and driven far away, never to be heard from again, no loss to anyone.'

'Let's deal, Guiderone. Don't make any foolish mistakes. You have a son who can be the next President of the United States – as long as he's Joshua Appleton. But he's not, and I have the X-rays to prove it.'

'The X-rays!' roared Guiderone. 'You *ass*!' He pressed a button on his desk console and spoke. 'Bring him in,' he said. 'Bring in our esteemed guest.' The Shepherd Boy sat back in his chair as the door behind Scofield opened.

Bray turned, mind and body suspended in pain at what he saw.

Seated in a wheelchair, his eyes glazed, his gentle face bruised, Robert Winthrop was brought through the door by his chauffeur of twenty years. Stanley smiled, his expression arrogant. Scofield sprang up; the chauffeur raised his hand from behind the wheelchair. In it was a gun.

'Years ago,' said Guiderone, 'a Marine combat sergeant was sentenced to spend the greater part of his life in prison. We found more productive work for a man of his skills. It was necessary that the benign elder statesman whom everyone in Washington sought out for comfort and advice be watched very thoroughly. We learned a great deal.'

Bray looked away from the battered Winthrop and stared at Stanley. 'Congratulations, you . . . *bastard*! What did you do? Pistol-whip him?'

'He didn't want to come,' Stanley said, his smile vanishing. 'He fell.'

Scofield started forward; the chauffeur raised the gun higher, aiming at Bray's head. 'I'm going to talk to him,' said Scofield, disregarding the weapon, kneeling at Winthrop's feet. Stanley glanced at the Shepherd Boy; Bray could see Guiderone nod consent. 'Mr Ambassador?'

'Brandon . . .' Winthrop's voice was weak, his tired eyes sad. 'I'm afraid I wasn't much help. They told the President I was ill. There are no soldiers outside, no command post, no one waiting for you to strike a match and drive to the gate. I failed you.'

'The envelope?'

'Bergeron thinks I have it; he knows Stanley, you see. He took the next plane back to Boston. I'm sorry, Brandon. I'm so very, very sorry. About so many things.' The old man glanced up at the ex-marine he had befriended for so many years, then back at Scofield. 'Do you know what they've done? My *God*, do you know what they've *done*?'

'They haven't done it yet,' said Bray quietly.

'Next January they'll have the White House! The administration will be *their* administration.'

'That won't happen.'

'It *will* happen!' shouted Guiderone in his high-pitched voice. 'And the world will be a better place. *Everywhere!* The period of violence will stop – a thousand years of productive tranquillity will take its place.'

'A *thousand years* . . . ?' Scofield got to his feet. 'Another maniac said that once. Is it going to be your own personal thousand-year Reich?'

'Parallels are meaningless, labels irrelevant! There's no connection.' The Shepherd Boy rose behind his desk, his eyes again on fire. 'In our world, nations can keep their leaders, people their identities. But governments will be controlled by the *companies*. *Everywhere*. The values of the market-place will link the peoples of the world!'

Bray caught the word and it revolted him. '*Identities? In your world there *are* no identities! We're numbers and symbols on computers! Circles and squares.'

'We must forget degrees of self for the continuity of peace.'

'Then we are *robots*!'

'But alive. Functioning!'

'How? Tell me *how*? "You, there! you're not a person any more; you're a *factor*. You're *X* or *Y* or *Z*, and whatever you do is measured and stored on wheels of tape by experts trained to evaluate *factors*. Go on *factor*! Be productive or the experts will take your loaf of bread away . . . or the shiny new car!"' Scofield paused in a fever. 'You're wrong, Guiderone. *So* wrong. Give me an imperfect place where I know who I am.'

'Find it in the next world, Beowulf Agate!' screamed the Shepherd Boy. 'You'll be there soon enough!'

Bray felt the weight in his belt under his raincoat – the gun supplied by the dying Taleniekov. The visitor to Appleton Hall had been searched thoroughly for weapons, none found, yet one provided by his old enemy. The decision to make a final gesture was clinical; there was no hope after all. But before he tried to kill and was killed, he would see Guiderone's face when he told him. 'You said before that I was a liar, but you have no idea how extensive my lies were. You think you have the X-rays, don't you?'

'We know we have them.'

'So do others.'

'Really?'

'Yes, really. Have you ever heard of an Alpha Twelve duplicating machine? It's one of the finest pieces of equipment ever designed. It's the only copier made that can take an X-ray negative and turn out a positive print. A print so defined it's acceptable as evidence in court of law. I separated the four top X-rays off both the master sheets from Andover, made copies, and sent them to five different men in Washington! You're finished, you're through! They'll see to it.'

'And this has gone on long enough.' Guiderone came

around his desk. 'We're in the middle of a conference and you've taken up enough time.'

'I think you'd better listen!'

'And I think you should walk over to that curtain, and pull the cord. You will see our conference room, but those inside will not see you . . . I'm sure I don't have to explain the technology. You've been so anxious to meet the Council of the Matarese, do so now. Not all are in attendance tonight, and not all are equal, but there's a fair gathering. Help yourself. Please.'

Bray crossed to the drapery, felt the cord, and pulled it downward. The curtains parted, showing a huge room with a long oval conference table around which were seated twenty-odd men. There were decanters of brandy in front of each place setting, along with pads, pencils and pitchers of water. The lighting came from crystal chandeliers, swelled by a yellowish glow from the far end of the room where a fire was blazing. It could have been the enormous dining hall of the Villa Matarese, described in such detail by a blind woman in the mountains above Porto Vecchio. Scofield nearly found himself looking for a balcony and a frightened girl of seventeen hiding in the shadows.

But his eyes were drawn to the forty-foot wall behind the table. Between two enormous tapestries linked at the top border, was a map of the world. A man with a pointer in his hand was addressing the others from a small platform; all eyes were on him.

The man was in the uniform of the United States Army. He was the Chairman of the Joint Chiefs of Staff.

'I see you recognize the general in front of the map.' The Shepherd Boy's voice once more lived up to the blind woman's words: crueller than the wind. 'His presence I believe explains the death of Anthony Blackburn. Perhaps I should introduce you to a few of the others, *in absentia* . . . In the centre of the table, directly below the platform is the Secretary of State, next to him the

Soviet ambassador. Across from the ambassador is the director of the Central Intelligence Agency; he seems to be having a side conversation with the Soviet Commissar for Planning and Development, Moscow. One man you might be interested in is missing. He didn't belong, you see, but he telephoned the CIA after receiving a very strange telephone call routed through Lisbon. The President's chief adviser on foreign affairs. He's had an accident; his mail is being intercepted, the last X-rays are no doubt in our hands by now . . . Need I go on?' Guiderone started to pull the cord, shutting out the window.

Scofield put up his hand; the curtain arced before closing. He was not looking at the men at the table; the message was clear. He was looking at a guard stationed at a small recessed door to the right of the fireplace. The man stood at attention, his eyes forward. In his hand was a .30 calibre, magazine-loaded sub-machine gun.

Taleniekov had known about these betrayals at the highest levels. He had heard the words spoken by others as they had inserted the needles that further drained his life away.

His enemy had tried to give him his last chance to live. *His last chance.* What were the words?

Pazhar . . . vsyegda pazhar! Zazhiganiye pazhar!

When the explosions begin, fire will follow.

He was not sure what his enemy meant, but he knew it was the path he had to follow. They were the best there were. One trusted the only professional on earth that was one's equal.

And that meant exercising the control his equal would demand. No false moves now. Stanley stood by Winthrop's wheelchair, his gun levelled at Bray. If somehow he could turn, twist, get the weapon from under his rain-coat . . . He looked down at Winthrop, his attention caught by the old man's eyes. Winthrop was trying to tell him something, just as Taleniekov had tried to tell him something. It was in the eyes; the old man kept

635

shifting them to his right. That was it! Stanley was *by* the wheelchair now, not *behind* it. In tiny, imperceptible movements, Winthrop was edging his chair around; he was going to go after Stanley's gun! His eyes were telling him that. They were also telling him to *keep talking*.

Scofield glanced unobtrusively at his watch. There were six minutes left before the sequence of explosions began. He needed three for preparation; that left three minutes to take out Stanley and bring in another. One-hundred-and-eighty seconds. *Keep talking!*

He turned to the monster at his side. 'Do you remember when you killed him? When you pulled the trigger that night at Villa Matarese?'

Guiderone stared at him. 'It was not a moment to be forgotten. It was my destiny. So the whore of Villa Matarese is alive.'

'Not any longer.'

'No? That was not in the pages you sent to Winthrop. She was killed then?'

'By the legend. *Perro nostro circulo*.'

The old man nodded. 'Words that long ago meant one thing, now something else entirely. They guard the grave still.'

'They still fear it. That grave's going to kill them all one of these days.'

'The warning of Guillaume de Matarese.' Guiderone started back to his desk.

Keep talking. Winthrop was pressing the wheels of the chair, each press an inch.

'Warning or prophecy?' asked Bray quickly.

'They're often interchangeable, aren't they?' said the old man over his shoulder.

'They called you the Shepherd Boy.'

Guiderone turned. 'Yes, I know. It was only partially true. As a child I took my turn herding the flocks, but the occasions diminished. The priests demanded it; they had other plans for me.'

'The priests?'

Winthrop moved again.

'I had astonished them. By the time I was seven years of age I knew and understood the catechism better than they did. By eight years I could read and write in Latin; before I was ten I could debate the most complex issues of theology and dogma. The priests saw me as the first Corsican to be sent to the Vatican, to achieve high office . . . perhaps the highest. I would bring great honour to their parishes. Those simple priests in the hills of Porto Vecchio perceived my genius before I did. They spoke to the *padrone*, petitioning him to sponsor my studies . . . Guillaume de Matarese did so in ways far beyond their comprehension.'

Forty seconds, Winthrop was within two feet of the gun. Keep talking!

'Matarese made his arrangements with Appleton then? Joshua Appleton the Second.'

'America's industrial expansion was extraordinary. It was the logical place for a gifted young man with a fortune at his disposal.'

'You were married? You had a son.'

'I bought a vessel, the most perfectly formed female through which to bear children. The design was always there.'

'Including the death of young Joshua Appleton?'

'An accident of war and destiny. The decision was a result of the Captain's own exploits, not part of the original design. It was, instead, an unparalleled opportunity to be seized upon. I think we've said enough.'

Now! Winthrop lunged out of the chair, his hands gripping Stanley's gun, pulling it to him, every ounce of his strength clawing at the weapon, refusing to let it go.

It fired, as Bray pulled out his own gun, aiming it at the chauffeur. Winthrop's body arched in the air, his throat blown away. Scofield squeezed the trigger once; it was all he needed. Stanley fell.

'Stay away from that desk!' yelled Bray.

'You were *searched*! It's not possible. Where . . . ?'

'From a better man than any computer of yours could ever find!' said Scofield, looking briefly in anguish at the dead Robert Winthrop. 'Just as he was.'

'You'll never get out.'

Bray sprang forward, grabbing Nicholas Guiderone by the throat, pushing him against the desk. 'You're going to do what I tell you to do or I'll blow your eyes out!' He shoved the pistol up into the hollow of Guiderone's right eye.

'Do *not* kill me!' commanded the overlord of the Matarese. 'The value of my life is too extraordinary! My work is not *finished*; it must be finished before I die!'

'You're everything in this world I hate, Shepherd Boy,' said Scofield, jamming the gun in sharp cracks into the old man's skull. 'I don't have to tell you the odds. Every second you go on living means you might get another. Do as I say. I'm going to press the button – the same button you pressed before. You're going to give the following order. Say it right or you won't ever say anything more. You tell whoever answers: "Send in the guard from the conference room, the one with the sub-machine gun." Have you got that?' He shoved Guiderone's head down over the console and pressed the button.

'Send the guard in from the conference room.' The words were rushed, but the fear was not audible. 'The one with the sub-machine gun.'

Scofield viced his left arm around Guiderone's neck, dragged him over to the curtains, and pulled them open. Through the glass, across the conference room, a man could be seen approaching the guard. The guard nodded, angled his weapon to the floor, and walked rapidly across the room towards the archway exit.

'*Perro nostro circulo*,' whispered Bray. He yanked up with all his strength, the vice around Guiderone's throat clamping shut, crushing bone and cartilage. There was a snap, an expulsion of breath. The old man's eyes protruded from their sockets, his neck broken. The Shepherd Boy was dead.

Scofield ran across the room to the door, pressing his back against the wall by the hinges. The door opened; he saw the angled weapon first, the figure of the guard a split second later. Bray kicked the door closed, both his hands surging forward towards the man's throat.

The harassed desk sergeant at the precinct on Boylston Street looked down at the thin, prim-looking woman whose mouth was pursed, eyes narrowed in disapproval. He held the envelope in his hands.

'*OK*, lady, you've delivered it and I've got it. OK? The phones are a little busy tonight, OK? I'll get to it soon's I can, OK?'

'Not "OK", Sergeant . . . Witkowski,' said the woman, reading the name on the desk sign. 'The citizens of Boston will not stand idly by while their rights are being abridged by criminal elements. We are rising up in justifiable outrage, and our cries have not gone unheeded. You are being watched, Sergeant! There are those who understand our distress and they are testing you. I'd advise you not to be so cavalier . . .'

'OK, *OK*.' The sergeant tore open the envelope, and pulled out a sheet of yellow paper. He unfolded it and read the words printed in large blue letters. 'Jesus Christ on a fuckin' *raft*!' he said quietly, his eyes suddenly widening in astonishment. He looked down at the disapproving woman as if he were seeing her for the first time. As he stared, he reached over to a button on the desk; he pressed it repeatedly.

'Sergeant, I strenuously object to your profanity . . .'

Above every visible door in the precinct house, red lights began flashing on and off; from deep within, the sound of an alarm bell echoed off the walls of unseen rooms and corridors. In seconds, doors began opening and helmeted men came out, hastily donned two-inch shields of canvas and steel strapped over their chests.

'*Grab her!*' shouted the sergeant. 'Pin her arms! Throw her into the bomb room!'

Seven police officers converged on the woman. A precinct lieutenant came running out of his office. 'What the hell is it, Sergeant?'

'Look at this!'

The lieutenant read the words on the yellow paper. 'Oh, my *God!*'

> *To the Fascist Pigs of Boston, Protectors*
> *of the Alabaster Bride.*
> *Death to the Economic Tyrants! Death to Appleton Hall!*
> *As Pigs Read This Our Bombs Will Do What*
> *Our Pleas Cannot. Our Suicide Brigades Are*
> *Positioned To Kill All Who Flee The Righteous*
> *Holocaust. Death To Appleton Hill!*
> *Signed:*
> *The Third World Army of Liberation and Justice*

The lieutenant issued his instructions. 'Guiderone's got guards all around that place; reach the house! Then call Brookline, tell them what's going on, and raise every patrol car we've got in the vicinity of Jamaica Way; send them over.' The officer paused, peering at the yellow page with the precise blue letters printed on it, then added harshly, '*Goddamn* it! Get Central Headquarters on the line. I want their best SWAT team dispatched to Appleton Hill.' He started back to his office, pausing again to look in disgust at the woman being propelled through a door, arms pulled, stretched away from her sides, prodded by men with padded shields and helmets. 'Third World Army of Liberation of Justice! Freaked-out bastards! *Book her*,' he roared.

Scofield dragged the guard's body across the room, concealing it behind Guiderone's desk. He raced over to the dead Shepherd Boy, and for the briefest of moments, just stared at the arrogant face. If it were possible to kill beyond killing, Bray would do so now. He pulled Guiderone to the far corner, throwing his body in a crumpled heap. He then stopped at Winthrop's corpse, wishing there was time to somehow say goodbye. There was not.

He grabbed the guard's sub-machine gun off the floor and ran over to the curtains. He pulled them open and looked at his watch. Fifty seconds to go until the explosions would begin. He checked the weapon in his hands; all clips were full. He looked through the window into the conference room, seeing what he had not seen before because the man had not been there before.

The senator had arrived. All eyes were now on him, the magnetic presence mesmerizing the entire room; the easy grace, the worn, still-handsome face giving each man his attention, if only for an instant – telling that man he was special. And each man was seduced by the raw power of power; this was the next President of the United States and he was one of *them*.

For the first time in all the years Scofield had seen that face, he saw what a destroyed, alcoholic mother saw: it was a mask. A brilliantly conceived, ingeniously programmed mask . . . and mind.

Twelve seconds.

There was a burst of static from a speaker on the desk. A voice erupted. 'Mr Guiderone, we must interrupt! We've had calls from the Boston and Brookline police! There are reports of an armed attack on Appleton Hall. Men calling themselves the Third World Army of Liberation

641

and Justice. We have no such organization on any list, sir. Our patrols are alerted. The police want everyone to stay . . .'

Two seconds.

The news had been relayed to the conference room. Men leaped up from chairs, gathering papers. Their own particular panic was breaking out: how could the presence of such men be explained? Who would explain it?

One second.

Bray heard the first explosion beyond the walls of Appleton Hall. It was in the distance, far down the hill, but unmistakable. The sound of rapid-fire weapons followed; men were shooting at the source of the first explosions.

Inside the conference room, the panic mounted. The *consiglieri* of the Matarese were rushing around, a single guard at the archway exit poised with his sub-machine gun levelled through the arch. Suddenly Scofield realized what the powerful men were doing: they were throwing papers and pads and maps into the fire at the end of the room.

It was his moment; the guard would be first, but merely the first.

Bray smashed the window with the barrel of his automatic weapon and opened fire. The guard span as the bullets caught him. His sub-machine gun was on rapid-repeat; the death-pressure of his trigger finger caused the gun to erupt wildly, the spray of ·30 calibre shells flying out of the ejector, the bullets fanning out in all directions, walls and chandeliers and men bursting, exploding, collapsing under their impacts. Screams of death and shrieks of horror filled the room.

Scofield knew his targets, his eye rehearsed over a lifetime of violence. He smashed the jagged fragments of glass and raised the weapon to his shoulder. He squeezed the trigger in rapidly defined, reasonably aimed sequences. One step – one death – at a time.

The bursts of gunfire exploded through the window frame. The general fell, the pointer in his hand lacerating his face as he collapsed. The Secretary of State cowered at the side of the table; Scofield blew his head off. The director of the Central Intelligence Agency raced his counterpart from the National Security Council towards the arch, leaping over bodies in their hysteria. Bray caught them both. The director's throat was a mass of blood; the NSC chairman raised his hands to a forehead that was no longer there.

Where was he? He of all men had to be found!

There he was!

The senator was crouched below the conference table in front of the roaring fire. Scofield took the aim of his life and squeezed the trigger. The spray of bullets exploded the wood, some *had* to penetrate. They did! The senator fell back, then rose to his feet. Bray fired another burst; the senator spun into the fireplace, then sprang back out, fire and blood covering his body. He raced blindly, forward, then to his left, grabbing the tapestry on the wall as he fell.

The tapestry caught fire; the senator in his collapse of death pulled it off the wall. The huge cloth arced down in flames over the conference table. The fire spread, flames leaping to every corner of the enormous room.

Fire!

After the explosions. *Fire!*

Taleniekov.

Scofield ran from the window. He had done what he had to do; it was the moment to do what he so desperately *wanted* to do. If it were possible; if there was any hope at *all*. He stopped in front of the door, checking the remaining ammunition; he had conserved it well. The third and fourth charges had detonated at the base of the hill. The fifth and sixth were timed to explode within seconds of each other.

The fifth came; he yanked the door back, lunging

through, weapon levelled. He heard the sixth explosion. Two guards at the cathedral-like entrance doors sprang from the outside path into view. Bray fired two bursts; the guards of the Matarese fell.

He raced to the door of the room that held Antonia and Taleniekov. It was locked.

'Stand way back! It's me!' He fired five rounds into the wood around the lock casing; it splintered. He kicked the heavy door open; it crashed back against the wall. He ran in.

Taleniekov was out of the chair kneeling by the couch at the far end of the room, Toni beside him. Both were working furiously, tearing pillows out of slipcovers. Tearing . . . *pillows*? What were they *doing*? Antonia looked up and shouted.

'Quickly! Help us.'

'What?' He raced over.

'*Pazhar!*' The Russian had to force the voice; it emerged now as a whispered roar.

Six pillows were free of their cases. Toni got to her feet, grabbing and throwing five of the pillows around the room.

'Now!' said Taleniekov, handing her the matches he had taken from Bray earlier. She ran to the farthest pillow, struck a match and held it to the soft fabric. It caught fire instantly. The Russian held out his hand for Scofield. 'Help me . . . get *up*!'

Bray pulled him off the floor; Taleniekov clutched the last pillow to his chest. The seventh explosion was heard in the distance; staccato gunfire followed, piercing the screams of hysteria from within the house.

'Come on!' yelled Scofield, putting his arm around the Russian's waist. He looked over at Toni; she had set fire to the fourth pillow. Flames and smoke were filling the room. 'Come *on*! We're getting out!'

'No!' whispered Taleniekov. 'You! She! Get me to

the *door*.' The Russian held the pillow and lurched forward.

The great hall of the house was dense with smoke, flames from the inner conference room surging beneath doors and through archways, as men raced up the staircase to windows, vantage points – high ground – to aim their weapons at invaders.

A guard spotted them; he raised his sub-machine gun.

Scofield fired first; the man arched backwards, blown off his feet.

'Listen to me!' gasped Taleniekov. 'Always *pazhar*! With you it is sequence, with me it is fire!' He held up the soft pillow. 'Light this! I will have the race of my life!'

'Don't be a fool.' Bray tried to take the pillow away; the Russian would not permit it.

'*Nyet!*' Taleniekov stared at Scofield; a final plea was in his eyes. 'If I could, I would not care to live like this. Neither would you. Do this for me, Beowulf. I would do it for you.'

Bray returned the Russian's look. 'We've worked together,' he said simply. 'I'm proud of that.'

'We were the best there were.' Taleniekov smiled and raised his hand to Scofield's cheek. 'Now, my friend. Do what I would do for you.'

Bray nodded and turned to Antonia; there were tears in her eyes. He took the book of matches from her hand, struck one and held it beneath the pillow.

The flames leapt up. The Russian spun in place, clutching the fire to his chest. And with the roar of a wounded animal suddenly set free from the jaws of a lethal trap, Taleniekov lunged, propelling himself into a limping run, careening off the walls and chairs, pressing the flaming pillow and himself into everything he touched – and everything he touched caught fire. Two guards raced down the staircase, seeing the three of them; before they or Scofield could fire, the Russian was on them, hurling the flames and himself at them, throwing the fire into their faces.

'*Skaryei!*' screamed Taleniekov. 'Run, Beowulf!' A burst of gunfire came upon the command, smothered by the flaming body of the Serpent; he fell, pulling both the Matarese guards with him down the staircase.

Bray grabbed Antonia by the arm and ran out to the stone path bordered by the lines of heavy, black chain. They raced through the opening in the wall into the concrete parking area; beams of floodlights shot down from the roof at Appleton Hall; men were at windows, weapons in their hands.

The eighth explosion came from below, at the base of the hill, the charge so filled with heat that the surrounding foliage burst into flames. Men at the windows smashed panes of glass and fired at the dancing light. Scofield saw that three of the other detonations had caused small brush fires. They were gifts he was grateful for; he and Taleniekov were both right. Sequence and fire, fire and sequence. Each was a diversion that could save one's life. There were no guarantees – ever – but there *was* hope.

The rented car was parked at the side of the wall about fifty yards to their right. It was in shadows, an isolated vehicle that was meant to stay there. Bray pulled Toni against the wall.

'The car over there. It's mine; it's our chance.'

'They'll shoot at us!'

'The odds are better than running. There are patrols up and down the hill. On foot, they'd cut us down.'

They raced along the wall. The ninth charge of dynamite lit up the sky at the north-west base of the hill. Automatic guns and single-shot weapons erupted. Suddenly, from within the growing fires of Appleton Hall, a massive explosion blew out a section of the front wall. Men fell from windows, fragments of stone and steel burst into the night as half the floodlights disappeared. Scofield understood. The seat of the Matarese had its arsenals; the fires had found one.

'Let's *go!*' he yelled, pushing Antonia towards the car. She threw herself inside as he ran around the back towards the driver's side.

The concrete exploded all around him; from somewhere on the remaining roof a man with a sub-machine gun had spotted them.

There *were* men; they had weapons and they were using them. The glass of the windshield shattered as a fusillade of bullets came from the open garage doors.

Antonia had rolled down the window; she now pushed the gun through the frame, held the trigger against its rim, and the explosions once again vibrated through the racing automobile. Bodies lurched as screams and the shattering of glass and the screeching ricochets of bullets filled the cavernous garage of the carriage house. The last clip of ammunition was exhausted as Scofield, his face cut from the windshield fragments, came to the final two hundred yards towards the gates of Appleton Hall. There were men below, armed men, uniformed men, but they were not soldiers of the Matarese. Bray thrust his hand down to the knob of the light switch and repeatedly pushed it in and pulled it out. The headlights flickered on and off – in sequence, *always* sequence. A sequence was a signal of a thousand possibilities; in this case it was survival.

The gates had been forced open; he slammed his foot on the brake. The automobile skidded to a stop, tyres screeching.

The police converged. Then more police; black-suited men in paramilitary gear, men trained for a specialized warfare, the battlegrounds defined by momentary bursts of armed fanaticism. Their commander approached the car.

'Take it *easy*,' he said to Bray. 'You're out. Who are you?'

'Vickery. B. A. Vickery. I had business with Nicholas

Guiderone. As you say . . . we got out! When that hell broke loose, I grabbed my wife and we hid in a closet. They smashed into the house, in teams, I think. Our car was outside. It was the only chance we had.'

'Now calmly, Mr Vickery, but quickly. What's happening up there?'

The tenth charge detonated from the other side of the hill, but its light was the flames that were spreading across the crest of the hill.

Appleton Hall was being consumed by fire, the explosions more frequent now as more arsenals were opened, more ignited. The Shepherd Boy was fulfilling his destiny. He had found his Villa Matarese, and like his *padrone* seventy years ago, his remains would perish in its skeleton.

'What's *happening*, Mr Vickery?'

'They're killers. They've killed everyone inside; they'll kill every one of you they can. You won't take them alive.'

'Then we'll take them *dead*,' said the commander, his voice filled with emotion. 'They've come over here now, they've *really* come over. Italy, Germany, Mexico . . . Lebanon, Israel, Buenos Aires. Whatever made us think we were immune? . . . Pull your car out of here, Mr Vickery. Head down the road about a quarter of a mile. There are ambulances down there. We'll get your statements later.'

'Yes, sir,' said Scofield, starting the engine.

They passed the ambulances at the base of Appleton Drive and turned left into the road for Boston. Soon they would cross the Longfellow Bridge into Cambridge. There was a locker on the MBTA subway platform in Harvard Square; in that locker was his attaché case.

They were free. The Serpent had died at Appleton Hall, but they were free, their freedom his gift.

Beowulf Agate had disappeared at last.

648

Epilogue

Men and women were taken into custody swiftly, quietly, no charges processed through the courts, for their crimes were beyond the sanity of the courts, beyond the tolerance of the nation. Of all nations. Each dealt with the Matarese in its own way. Where it could find them.

Heads of state across the world conferred by telephone, the normal interpreters replaced by ranking government personnel fluent in the necessary languages. The leaders readily professed astonishment and shock, tacitly acknowledging both the inadequacy and the infiltration of their intelligence communities. They tested one another with subtle shades of accusation, knowing the attempts were futile; they were not idiots. They probed for vulnerabilities; they all had them. And with every word, each hoped for the reaction the other wanted to hear. Finally – tacitly – the single conclusion was universal. It was the only one that made sense in these insane times.

Silence.

Each to be responsible for his own deception, none to implicate the others beyond the normal levels of suspicion and hostility. For to admit the massive global conspiracy was to admit the existence of the fundamental proposition: governments were obsolete.

None cared for the theory to be analysed or given wide exposure; the analysis was never deep enough, the alternative too attractive in its simplicity.

They were not idiots. They were afraid.

In Washington, rapid decisions were made secretly by a handful of men.

Senator Joshua Appleton IV died as he had come into being. Burned to death in an automobile accident on a dark highway at night. There was a state funeral, the casket mounted in splendour in the Rotunda, where another vigil took place. The words intoned were befitting a man everyone knew would have occupied the White House but for the tragedy that had cut him down . . . on a dark highway at night.

A government-owned Lockheed Tristar was sacrificed in the Colorado Mountains north of Poudre Canyon, a dual engine malfunction causing the aircraft to lose altitude while crossing that dangerous range. The pilot and crew were mourned, full pensions granted their families regardless of their length of service. But the true mourning was accompanied by a tragic lesson never to be forgotten. For it was revealed that on board the plane were three of the nation's most distinguished men, killed in the service of their country while on an inspection tour of military installations relating to counter-strike preparedness. The Chairman of the Joint Chiefs of Staff had requested his counterparts at the Central Intelligence Agency and the National Security Council to accompany him on the tour. Along with a message of presidential sorrow, an executive order was issued from the Oval Office. Never again were such high-ranking government personnel permitted to fly together in a single aircraft; the nation could not sustain such a grievous loss again.

As the weeks went by upper-echelon employees of the State Department as well as numerous reporters who covered its day-to-day operations were gradually aware of an oddity. The Secretary of State had not been in evidence for a very long time. There was a growing concern as schedules were altered, trips abandoned, conferences postponed or cancelled. Rumours spread throughout the capital, some quarters insisting the secretary was involved with prolonged, secret negotiations in Peking, while others claimed he was in Moscow, close to a breakthrough with SALT. Then the rumours took on less attractive colorations; something was wrong; an explanation was required.

The President gave it on a warm afternoon in spring. He went on radio and television from a medical retreat in Moorefield, West Virginia, the mountains of the Shenandoah behind him in the distance.

'In this year of tragedy, it is my burden to bring you further sorrow. I have just said goodbye to a dear friend. A great and courageous man who understood the delicate balance required in our negotiations with our adversaries, who would not permit those adversaries to learn of his rapidly ebbing life. That extraordinary life ended only hours ago, succumbing at last to the ravages of disease. I have today ordered the flags of the capital . . .'

And so it went. All over the world.

The President sat back in his chair as Under-Secretary Daniel Congdon walked into the Oval Office. The commander-in-chief did not like Congdon; there was a ferret-like quality about him, his overly-sincere eyes concealing a dreadful ambition. But the man did his job well and that was all that mattered. Especially now, especially this job.

'What's the resolution?'

'As expected, Mr President. Beowulf Agate rarely did the normal thing.'

'He didn't lead much of a normal life, did he? I mean you people didn't expect him to, did you?'

'No, sir. He was . . .'

'Tell me, Congdon,' interrupted the President. 'Did you really try to have him killed?'

'It was mandatory execution, sir. We considered him beyond salvage, working with the enemy, dangerous to our men everywhere. To a degree, I still believe that.'

'You'd better. He is. So that's why he insisted on

negotiating through you. I'd advise you – no, I *order* you – to push such mandatory actions out of your mind. Is that understood?'

'Yes, Mr President.'

'I hope so. Because if it isn't, I might have to issue a mandatory sentence of my own. Now that I know how it's done.'

'Understood, sir.'

'Good. The resolution?'

'Beyond the initial demand, Scofield wants nothing further to do with us.'

'But you know where he is.'

'Yes, sir. The Caribbean. However, we don't know where the documents are.'

'Don't bother to look for them; he's better than you. And leave him alone; never give him the slightest reason to think you have any interest in him. Because if you do, those documents will surface in a hundred different places at once. This government – this nation – cannot handle the repercussions. Not now. There are still too many questions, too many answers we don't have, too many men we can't find. Perhaps in a few years, but not now.'

'I accept that judgement, Mr President.'

'You damn well better. What did the resolution cost us and where is it buried?'

'One hundred and seventy-six thousand, four hundred and twelve dollars and eighteen cents. It was attached to a cost over-run for naval training equipment, the payment made by a CIA proprietary directly to the shipyard in Mystic, Connecticut.'

The President looked out the window at the White House lawn; the blossoms on the cherry trees were dying, curling up and withering away. 'He could have asked for the sky and we would have given it to him; he could have taken us for millions. Instead, all he wants is a boat and to be left alone.'

March 198—

The sixty-eight-foot charter yawl, *Serpent*, its mainsail luffing in the island breezes, glided into its slip, the woman jumping on to the pier, rope in hand. She looped it around the forward post, securing the bow. At the stern, the bearded skipper tied off the wheel, stepped up on the gunwhale and over to the dock, swinging the aft rope around the nearest post, pulling it taut, knotting it when all slack had vanished.

At midships, a pleasant-looking, middle-aged couple stepped cautiously on to the pier. It was obvious they had said their goodbyes, and those goodbyes had been just a little bit painful.

'Well, vacation's over,' said the man, sighing, holding his wife's arm. 'We'll be back next year, Captain Vickery. You're the best charter in the islands. And thank you again, Mrs Vickery. As always, the galley was terrific.'

The couple walked up the dock.

'I'll take down the sails and stow the gear while you check on the supplies, OK?' said Scofield.

'All right, darling. We've got ten days before the couple from New Orleans arrive.'

'Let's take a sail,' said the captain, smiling, jumping back on board the *Serpent*.

An hour and twenty minutes passed; the supplies were loaded, the weather bulletins logged and the coastal charts studied. The *Serpent* was ready for departure.

'Let's get a drink,' Bray said, taking Toni's hand, walking up the sandy path into the hot St Kitts' street. Across the way was a café, a shack with ancient wicker tables and chairs and a bar that had not changed in thirty years. It was a gathering place for charter boat skippers and their crews.

Antonia sat down, greeting several friends, laughing with her eyes and spontaneous voice; she was liked by the rough, capable runaways of the Caribbean. She was a lady and they knew it. Scofield watched her from the bar as he ordered their drinks, remembering another waterfront café in Corsica. It was only a few years ago – another lifetime, really – but she had not changed. There was still the easy grace, the sense of presence and gentle, open humour. She was liked because she was immensely likable; it was as simple as that.

He carried their drinks to the table and sat down. Antonia had reached over to an adjacent table, borrowing a week-old Barbados newspaper. An article had caught her attention.

'Darling, look at this,' she said, turning the paper and pushing it towards him, her index finger marking the column.

TRANS-COMMUNICATIONS' LEGAL BATTLES OVER CONGLOMERATE REORGANIZES

Wash., D.C. – *Combined Wire Services*: After several years of ownership litigation in the federal courts, the way has been cleared for the executors of the Nicholas Guiderone estate to press ahead with re-organization plans which include significant mergers with European companies. It will be recalled that following the terrorist assault on the Guiderone mansion in Brookline, Massachusetts, when Guiderone and others holding large blocks of Trans-Comm stock were massacred, the conglomerate's line of ownership was thrown into a legal maze. It has been no secret that the Justice Department has been supportive of the executors, as, indeed, has been the Department of State. The feeling has been that, while the multi-national corporation has continued functioning, its lack of expansion due to unclear leadership has caused American prestige to suffer in the international market-place.

The President, upon learning of the final legal resolutions, sent the following wire to the executors:

'It seems fitting to me that during the week that marks my first year in office, the obstructions have been removed and, once again, a great American institution is in a position to export and expand American knowhow and technology across the world, joining the other great companies to give us a better world. I congratulate you.'

Bray shoved the paper aside. 'The subtlety gets less and less, doesn't it?'

They tacked into the wind out of Basseterre, the coast of St Kitts receding behind them. Antonia pulled the jib taut, tied off the sheet and climbed back to the wheel. She sat beside Scofield, running her fingers over the short, clipped beard that was more grey than dark. 'Where are we going, darling?' she asked.

'I don't know,' said Bray, meaning it. 'With the wind for a while, if it's all right with you.'

'It's all right with me.' She leaned back, looking at his face, so pensive, so lost in thought. 'What's going to happen?'

'It's happened. The mergers have taken over the earth,' he answered, smiling. 'Guiderone was right; nobody can stop it. Maybe nobody should. Let them have their day in the sun. It doesn't make any difference what I think. They'll leave me alone – leave us alone. They're still afraid.'

'Of what?'

'Of people. Just people. Trim the jib, will you please? We're spilling too much. We can make better time.'

'To where?'

'Damned if I know. Only that I want to be there.'

The Icarus Agenda
Robert Ludlum

FIGHT OF THE BLOODY MESSIAH

In the Sultanate of Oman over two hundred hostages are being held at gunpoint. And the world watches helplessly as the madness begins. The spirit of the Mahdi is abroad, intent on complete financial and political domination.

Evan Kendrick, a quiet Congressman, is an unlikely hero. But in his past is a violence that he cannot forget.

On the other side of the world, five very eccentric, very rich people are meeting. They are the Inheritors of Inver Brass. Their aim – to utterly transform the world. They seek a new saviour, an innocent messiah. Evan Kendrick is to be their unwilling victim . . .

'A fast-paced thriller from a reliable master'   *Daily Mail*

ISBN: 0 586 06455 9